BATTLETECH:
HOUR OF THE WOLF

BY BLAINE LEE PARDOE

BATTLETECH: HOUR OF THE WOLF
By Blaine Lee Pardoe
Cover art by Marco Mazzoni
Cover design by David Kerber

©2021 The Topps Company, Inc. All Rights Reserved. *BattleTech* & *MechWarrior* are registered trademarks and/or trademarks of The Topps Company, Inc., in the United States and/or other countries. Catalyst Game Labs and the Catalyst Game Labs logo are trademarks of InMediaRes Productions LLC. No part of this work may be reproduced, stored in a retrieval system, or transmitted in any form or by any means, without the prior permission in writing of the Copyright Owner, nor be otherwise circulated in any form other than that in which it is published.

Printed in USA.

Published by Catalyst Game Labs,
an imprint of InMediaRes Productions, LLC
7108 S. Pheasant Ridge Drive • Spokane, WA 99224

To my grandson, Trenton Davis Hester: may all your hits be crits! I promised him that I would do what I could to "make *BattleTech* cool again."
To him, and all of the fans in this book: "You're welcome!"

To my mother, Rosalee Pardoe, who passed away during the writing of the last chapter of this book's first draft. I miss you more every day, Mom. While you never liked reading *BattleTech*, I think you would have liked this one.

ACKNOWLEDGMENTS

At a *BattleTech* writer's summit, we decided it would be best to expand some of the stories and scope, so parts of the original draft of this book ended up in *Divided We Fall*, *Rock of the Republic*, *Icons of War*, and *Children of Kerensky*. I highly recommend that you read those books before this novel. While not required, they will give you a more complete story. *Hour of the Wolf*, however, is intended to be a story all on its own.

This novel wraps up a storyline we started in 1989, one I was honored to be a part of all of the way through. To say this is a massive undertaking would be an understatement. As such, it was impossible to tackle alone. Fortunately, I had good warriors in my *keshik* fighting by my side.

Our rocking creative and editorial team spent two years hammering out the key elements of the new era and some of the events in this book. Special recognition goes to:

Brent Evans
John Helfers
Ray Arrastia
Philip A. Lee

Jason Schmetzer
Michael A. Stackpole
Loren Coleman
Randall N. Bills

The fans of *BattleTech* are part of what makes it great. The following fans of *BattleTech* volunteered their names to be in this book. A number were "volunteered" by the creative team as well, or simply honored because they rocked. The Kickstarter backers are marked with a "(KS)." They are all canon now! *Seyla!*

(KS) Robin Apel
(KS) William (Will) Arnold
(KS) Ian Butler—Brigadier Graham Badinov
(KS) Andreas Büttner—Druss Ward
(KS) Colby Cram
(KS) Dr. Randolph P. Checkers, Esq.
(KS) Craig Evans—Pharaoh
(KS) Kevin Markley
(KS) Eris Griffon

(KS) Raymond Guethler
(KS) Justin Hall
(KS) John Healy—Physician Hobgood
(KS) Spencer Huff—Khalus Pryde
(KS) Aleksey Kopysov—Kaor
(KS) Chris Kornfeld
(KS) Aaron Krull
(KS) Andrew Krull
(KS) Jason Mayberry for Kai Nihari
(KS) Brendan (Bren) Mayhugh

(KS) Jason Mischke—Stroud
(KS) Daniel Nichols—Janus
(KS) Matthias Pfaff—Amanda McKenna
(KS) Shawn Rains—Colton Mcleod
(KS) Marvin Sims—Marv Roshak
(KS) Aaron Tarr—Star Colonel Kalidessa Kerensky
(KS) Jakapan Thunpithayakul
(KS) Christopher Toh—Merlin Buhallin
(KS) John Traver—Jack Traver
(KS) Jathniel Velazquez—Jathniel Kerensky
(KS) John Watson
(KS) Michael Mahoney—Sorsha
(KS) Lyle Wojciechowski—Star Colonel Havi Bekker
David Abzug
David Baker
Agustin Sierio Barj
Matthew Behrens
Ted Burger
Billy J. Caldwell
Kim Chapman
John "Fratricide" Craig
Paco Cubillo
Amy Delaney
Benno deJong
Stephen Dukes
David DuJordan
Adolfo Fernandez
William Fife
Noran Ghall
Oliver Haake

Thomas Heath
James "Tanker" Herring
Dirk "Derek" Kobler
Jean-Jacques Labbé
Jeff Lamm
Chew Hwee Leong
Joshua Adam Lonbom
Brianne Elizabeth Lyons
Dean Manning
John McNary
Jared Micks
Ed Miller
Joe Mooney
Rolf Peter
Max Prohaska
Andrew Quay
Krzysztof Strato Raczyński
Keith Richmond
Jamie Rife
Andrew Roy
Sebastian Schröder
Rowland Seckinger III
Volkmar Seifert
David Skinner
Jeremy Spurlock
Travis Sumpter
Lonnie Tapscott
Paul Tomaszewski
Cory Vigdal
Josh Waltz
Powers Wartman
Ben Weingart
Shawn "Gorilla" Willett
Ludvig Yabar
Sharizal Zarie

INTRODUCTION

Excerpt from: Terra Fallen: *The Rise of the IlClan*, by Dr. Randolph P. Checkers, Esq. (The Institute of Inner Sphere War Studies, 3161)

"The road to Terra is a thousand points of light in the night sky."
—Nicholas Kerensky

To fully appreciate the events that unfolded on Terra in the spring of 3151, it is necessary to recap the entire journey of humankind into space.

Between 2690 and 2765, the Star League was the manifestation of humanity at its pinnacle. Each of the ruling lords of the Inner Sphere's Great Houses were united under a single interstellar government that brought peace and stability for generations. The ills of humankind were put to rest. Innovation and prosperity ushered in a golden age.

Then came Stefan Amaris, the Usurper, who assassinated the ruling Cameron family on 27 December 2766, and seized power through a bloody coup in the heart of the Star League, Terra. Our brightest period was snuffed out by its darkest villain. There is a bit of cosmic justice there.

Aleksandr Kerensky, Commanding General of the Star League Defense Force, fought a bloody and vicious twelve-year war to reclaim his beloved Star League from Amaris. When he did, he realized the House Lords were falling back into their old animosities and rivalries. Rather than see his army used or destroyed in that looming conflict, he gathered his forces and set out on an Exodus into the vastness of space on 5 November 2784.

Without the SLDF to keep the peace, the Star League dissolved, and the Great Houses declared war on one another. For centuries, the House Lords battled each other in the Succession Wars, each trying to establish themselves as the new First Lord of a Star League. None succeeded.

Meanwhile, Kerensky's SLDF fought their own civil war on planets far from the Inner Sphere. Under the general's son, Nicholas Kerensky, the Clans emerged near the beginning of the 29th century. Named for fierce animals and ideals, the Clans were forged in the fires of war. Successive generations of Clan warriors were genetically bred, and their technology surpassed that of the Inner Sphere.

The Clans knew they would eventually return to Terra. According to the Founder, the first Clan to capture Terra would become ilClan—the Clan above all Clans—and would lead the united Clans in reestablishing the Star League and ushering in a new golden age.

In 3049, the Clans returned to the Inner Sphere in a stunning invasion, conquering a large piece of it during their single-minded drive toward Terra. But the techno-religious cult ComStar stopped the invaders short of their objective by challenging the honorbound Clans to a proxy war for Terra on a single planet, winner take all. On the agricultural world of Tukayyid, ComStar's military forces defeated the Clans and forced a fifteen-year term of unsteady peace starting in May of 3052.

Stunned by the return of Kerensky's SLDF descendants, the Inner Sphere created its own "Star League," little more than a fragile alliance, which struck back at the distant Clan Homeworlds. In 3060 they eradicated one Clan, the Smoke Jaguars, almost entirely. For a time, the threat abated as the Clans struggled with their newfound vulnerability and proof that their centuries of genetic engineering and technological superiority had been overcome by those they deemed inferior. The Clans chafed at peace and, bitter over their failure to reach and conquer Terra, turned on each other.

Then came the Jihad, a holy war waged by the Word of Blake, a separatist faction of ComStar that sought to bring all of the universe under its authoritarian rule. The Inner Sphere burned, and entire planets were eradicated in nuclear, biological, and chemical attacks, types of warfare not seen in centuries. No realm was spared, and at times it seemed the guttering light of the Inner Sphere might be extinguished forever.

Then one man, Devlin Stone, united humankind, ended the Word of Blake's atrocities, and formed the Republic of the Sphere. Centered on Terra and patrolled by the Knights of the Republic, Stone beat swords into plowshares better than any man before him, and there was peace for the universe for the first time in years. Some Clans, such as the Snow Ravens and the Ghost Bears, settled in the Inner Sphere and Periphery, and integrated with struggling Inner Sphere governments. But Stone ultimately disappeared; secretly having himself cryogenically frozen, should he be needed in the future. Then again, that is the popular version of the story.

The hyperpulse-generator network, which maintained interstellar communications throughout the Inner Sphere, collapsed on 7 August 3132 due to sabotage by unknown forces, cutting off 80 percent of Inner Sphere worlds from each other. Messages that would have been transmitted in seconds had to be physically carried by JumpShip to their destinations, sometimes taking weeks or months.

The sudden lack of communication rekindled old fears and hatreds, fueling conflict more than ever as suspicions grew and rumors flew about who had perpetrated the Blackout and why. The Great House leaders, and their intelligence services, were suddenly blinded and instantly paranoid. Some leaders took advantage of the communication collapse to settle old grudges. As the Blackout dragged on for months, then years, rearming was inevitable.

Everyone saw the Republic of the Sphere as ripe for conquest or sought to settle centuries-old scores with their rivals. Old enmities flared among the Great Houses once more, and wars broke out, most feasting on the worlds of the Republic. Humankind had endured war so long that it was part of our culture, which made the Republic a natural target. Stone's dream of peace was consumed in the flames of war. Historians call it the Dark Age, a term both sorrowful and fitting, a testimony to how numb we had all become to war and the chaos it brings.

The Clans, specifically the Jade Falcons and Wolves, once more turned their attention to Terra, entertaining thoughts of becoming the ilClan and forging a new Star League. Whichever Clan conquered Terra first would rule over all of the Clans and the Inner Sphere for the first time in history.

As an eleventh-hour defense, the Republic erected a technological barrier, Fortress Republic, which made jumping into its dwindling space—and therefore close to Terra—impossible, as ships that attempted to jump bounced back to their point of origin, mangled and broken. Then Devlin Stone returned from cryogenic sleep after fifteen years, prepared to save what was left of his empire, but found that little remained of the once mighty realm he had created.

There was a certain inevitability about the approaching storm. By 3150, it was clear that the Clans were coming to Terra, relentless and bent on fulfilling their destiny. It seemed that the end of one age was upon humankind, and a new era was about to begin—though for the betterment of civilization or its destruction, none could say...

THE PRODIGAL CHILDREN RETURN

PROLOGUE

DOMINION INTELLIGENCE BRIEFING ROOM
ASGARD, RASALHAGUE
RASALHAGUE DOMINION
16 DECEMBER 3150

Khan Dalia Bekker listened as the head of Clan Ghost Bear's Watch, Star Colonel Havi Bekker, finished his summation on the recent movement of Clan Wolf forces.

Things are unfolding rapidly, Dalia thought, leaning forward in her tall-backed chair. Speed was always the foe of the famed Ghost Bear patience.

The Khan had called Havi Bekker into the intelligence briefing room to provide analysis based on some startling reports. The circular room had a white-and-black marble shelf around the perimeter to display the masterpieces of the Ghost Bears. The room's colorful artwork—all painted, sculpted, and woven by Clan warriors—offered Bekker little comfort this morning. Still, as her green eyes fell on the artwork, pride swelled in her chest. Only the Ghost Bears encouraged their warrior caste to explore the arts, and as her eyes swept each piece, perfectly displayed against the mahogany wall panels, she felt as if her whole caste was in the room with her.

Havi Bekker sat at the end of the long rectangular table, opposite of Dalia, in a maroon leather chair. Prince Hjalmer Miraborg, with his immaculate short hair and light complexion, sat to her right. SaKhan Roy Jorgensson sat on her left, almost a negative of Miraborg. His hair was reddish-brown and only rarely encountered a brush. His jaw always had three days' growth of red-tinged beard. Where Miraborg looked stately, Jorgensson always appeared as if he had just come from a battle.

Havi Bekker rarely displayed emotion. His face was ruddy, somewhat dark, with a small pink scar on his chin. It struck Khan Bekker as odd that Havi looked the part of a spymaster somehow, as if he had been bred for that role. *His face does not reveal secrets, or convey any sense of emotion.*

At Havi's conclusion, Dalia took a moment before hedging. "That intel is most intriguing."

Hjalmer glanced over at her, then back at Havi. "You are a master of understatement, Khan Bekker. If this information is true, Clan Wolf is mobilizing its entire *touman*."

Roy Jorgensson jumped in. "They have done this before, when they relocated from their former occupation zone to this 'Wolf Empire' Khan Ward forged."

Havi shifted uneasily in his chair. "With all due respect, saKhan, during that migration, we were unaware of their destination. This time, there is only one place they could take all of their front-line units, technicians, and equipment."

"Terra," Dalia said. The word hung in the air like the fading echo of a tolling bell.

"*Aff*," Havi replied. "And this mobilization seems thoroughly planned and coordinated. Clan Sea Fox is providing additional JumpShips to expedite the move. It is clear this plan has been in place for some time."

Dalia nodded. *I expect nothing less from Alaric Ward.*

"They are stripping all garrisons from their planets?" Prince Miraborg asked.

"Almost," said Havi. "The units left behind are *solahma* for the most part, and some ungraduated *sibkos*—but there are very few. They are leaving their civilian populations, but taking their technician caste. It appears they are going all-in on seizing Terra."

"Can they defeat the Republic of the Sphere?" saKhan Jorgensson asked.

"From our estimates, it would be a close match between their military forces," Havi admitted. "There is a distinct chance that the Wolves can prevail. Their constant military operations have forged their ranks into seasoned veterans. The Republic has only a few experienced units."

"Any signs of activity from the Jade Falcons?" Dalia asked.

Havi shifted again at the mention of the Falcons. "We are hindered with this accursed HPG Blackout, so there is a considerable delay in gathering and transmitting our intelligence data. That said, the Falcons have only shifted a few units closer to Terra—not the large-scale mobilization we are seeing from Clan Wolf."

"*Yet*," Dalia amended. "If the Wolves have figured out how to penetrate Fortress Republic, it is only a matter of time before Malvina Hazen obtains that knowledge. She will not sit idly by and allow Clan Wolf to be crowned the ilClan—not without a fight. It goes against her very nature."

"*Aff*," replied Havi solemnly. "That is our analysis of her as well. Her Mongol Doctrine all but requires the Jade Falcons become the ilClan. She will never accept another Clan taking the title."

For a long moment, no one spoke.

"So," Khan Bekker finally said. "Do we care what the Wolves are doing? Or, more appropriately, what should our response be?"

"Of course we do!" Prince Miraborg said. "Whoever wins will seek to re-form some kind of a Star League. We are Clan, and if another Clan becomes the ilClan, that carries implications for our people. It means a new order among the Clans, a distinct leader. If we do nothing, it makes us subservient to whomever takes Terra. That impacts us directly."

Dalia nodded. "The thought of me taking orders from Clan Wolf as the ilClan *does* make me cringe. Khan Ward took one of our best and brightest warriors from us in a Trial of Possession. It was an insult to our honor then, and I have not forgotten the loss of the WarBear. It told me a great deal about Alaric's character, and his casual attitude toward our people. As the leader of Clan Ghost Bear, I would chafe under his rule.

"But that is me personally. As Khan, my responsibility is greater than my own emotions. We are not entirely Clan any longer. *Aff*, we have the traditions and rites of the Clans, but our people have settled here in the Dominion. We have integrated with the people of Rasalhague. We still call ourselves Clan, but we are also something else: citizens of the Dominion. It is not like the old days, when we were all in the same camp, with the same shared view of the future. We are in a state of slow, progressive change."

"You are proposing we sit back and do nothing, *quineg*?" saKhan Jorgensson asked with a hint of anger in his voice.

Dalia shook her head. "*Neg*, Roy. I am merely pointing out that any action taken will generate some resistance from our people."

"So what *do* we do?" Miraborg asked.

Dalia organized her thoughts before speaking. "We have four possible courses of action. We could do nothing—simply let the Wolves, the Jade Falcons, and the Republic resolve this matter among themselves. Or, after the dust has settled from those battles, we could attempt to take Terra ourselves. We have long maintained Warden ways, so we could voice a desire to become the ilClan to protect the Inner Sphere. Or we could be cautionary and shift troops closer to Terra, so we can respond quickly to what is clearly a changing situation." Dalia leaned back in her seat. "*Or* we rush in and fight alongside the Republic of the Sphere, against our fellow Clans. That, however, would come at a price."

"We would sacrifice our mortal souls," Prince Miraborg said. "And some of our more traditionalist warriors might feel such an action is wrong. I am not saying we would face mutiny, but we will have some that might resist fighting against the end goal of Clan culture—the ilClanship."

"Exactly." Dalia nodded again. "We would be turning our back on centuries of Clan rites and *rede*, and siding with the Inner Sphere against our own people."

"A high price, but so is living under the heel of another Clan," saKhan Jorgensson replied.

"Hence the other choices at our disposal," said Dalia. "Doing nothing leaves our fate in the hands of others. Taking Terra ourselves—while tempting—would divide our people so greatly, it could jeopardize everything we have built here in the Dominion. I believe we should mobilize Alpha and Beta Galaxies and advance them to the Republic border. That puts us in a position to react to the changing situation on Terra."

"Agreed," Prince Miraborg replied. "A controlled response to a fluid situation."

"I concur," said Jorgensson. "What if Terra and the Republic fall? What then?"

Dalia's eyes narrowed. "It would depend on who takes it, would it not? Khan Ward took Ramiel Bekker, one of our *ristars*, from us. I have not forgotten that, but that single act does not warrant all-out war with Clan Wolf. Regardless of my personal feelings about Alaric Ward, the Wolves still have honor.

"The Jade Falcons, on the other hand, will slaughter billions if Malvina Hazen takes Terra. We will do what ghost bears in the wild do—wait, carefully stalk our prey, and only pounce when the opportunity is right."

CHAPTER 1

MCKENNA-CLASS BATTLESHIP SLS *MCKENNA'S PRIDE*
MERCURY ASSEMBLY POINT
REPUBLIC OF THE SPHERE
1 JANUARY 3151, 0840 HOURS (T-MINUS 9)

Star Admiral Haake Sukhanov watched the timer in the corner of the main viewscreen with a patience that impressed Wolf Khan Alaric Ward.

Over an hour ago, the Wolves' Task Force Ostend had made the first jump to Terra, targeting the nadir jump point's two massive defense stations. *We have no idea if they were remotely successful*, thought Alaric, impatience gnawing at him.

As the genetic offspring of Katherine Steiner-Davion, her brother Victor, and Vlad Ward, Alaric was surprised at his edginess. *Did Victor ever feel like this before a major operation? Did Khan Vlad Ward?* He pushed deep down any thoughts about his genemother and what she might have thought or said. *If Katherine were alive still, she would be whispering in my ear, telling me what to do, how to feel, what to expect.* In that moment, he acknowledged once more that killing her had been the right thing to do. *This is to be* my *victory, not hers.*

As if hearing Alaric's thoughts, Sukhanov turned to his Khan, a wicked grin on his narrow face. "If my estimates are right, the Republic Navy will be recovering their fighters and rearming them for our arrival. That process will give us time to assume our battle formation. Their rearming means many fighters will be waiting their turn in the launch bays, forcing the flight crews to rush out some fighters with low ammunition. All of this will give us time to get in position and strike. With your permission, my Khan, the time has come to get underway."

Alaric nodded, suppressing his own urge to smile. "You are go for Operation Nostos."

Alaric had won possession of Sukhanov—a former Snow Raven—as a bondsman during the funeral of Victor Steiner-Davion. Having a genius Snow Raven-turned-Wolf leading this attack would ensure Clan Wolf's naval victory. Sukhanov had developed new formations to protect the troop transports, devised plans for dealing with the jump-point defenses, and had given the Wolf navy a renewed and invigorated sense of purpose. Though he was the product of Clan Snow Raven's genetics program, Haake Sukhanov was every bit a Wolf, especially since he was now an *abtakha*, an officially adopted member of the Clan.

They had traveled a long road to get here. Sukhanov wasn't the only member of the team Alaric had built to safeguard victory. Every member had a role to play.

General Chance Vickers would implement the Wolf conquest of the Republic of the Sphere. Ramiel Bekker, an *abtakha* from Clan Ghost Bear, was a tactical genius who could counter whatever the Republic Armed Forces might throw at them. Wolf saKhan Garner Kerensky had recovered the ship they now piloted, the SLS *McKenna's Pride*—once the flagship of the Star League Defense Force. The *Pride* was every bit an icon for the Clans as it was for the Inner Sphere. *The enemy will see this ship and know what is about to befall them.*

Alaric had spent his entire life preparing for this moment: leading the Wolves to Terra to claim the ilClanship. Now, on the bridge of *McKenna's Pride*, he couldn't help but think of his genemother Katherine, telling him stories of his provenance when he was a child. Or of his ordeal as Anastasia Kerensky's prisoner, and how he had brought her into the fold. The loss he had suffered with the death of Verena—a loss that still staggered him sometimes, in his quieter moments. The memories of his short-lived victory on Tharkad, and his first meeting with Malvina Hazen tugged at him as well.

Fate whirled around Alaric Ward like a storm, devastatingly powerful and uncompromising. *I have already surpassed the Khans who came before me,* he mused. *Now I stand at the threshold of destiny. The great houses have long fought over the carcass of the Terran Hegemony in hopes of taking Terra. I will take it and usher in a new era, righting the wrongs of the past.*

Alaric treated the conquest of Terra like a game of chess where the stakes were life and death, not just for him, but everyone around him. He knew the rules and used them to his advantage at every turn. He had picked the right pieces, and thanks to his careful strategies, they were all in position to seize victory.

Sukhanov nodded to the communications officer, Star Commander Baker Rhyde. "Open a tactical channel to the fleet."

The Star Commander's fingers blurred over the controls. "Star Admiral, you are on."

"Khan Ward," he said. "The honor is yours."

Alaric nodded. "This is Khan Alaric Ward. Clan Wolf fleet, stand by for jump in sixty seconds on my mark...mark!" He paused, savoring the moment. "Remember your orders, the drills we have done, and your place in the formations. Do that, and we will be victorious. I will see you all in Terran space."

The timer ran down, until finally—*finally*—Alaric uttered the order.

"Clan Wolf—*jump!*"

ESSEX-CLASS DESTROYER RSS *ABUNDANTIA*
TERRAN SYSTEM
REPUBLIC OF THE SPHERE
1 JANUARY 3151 (T-MINUS 9)

The thin strip of red warning lights showing the ship was at general quarters made Admiral Jean-Jacques Labbé's white mustache shimmer as he took in the sensor-contact report. "Repeat," he said through gritted teeth. Wolf Clan ships had begun to flicker into Republic space, but… *There must be a mistake.*

Captain Dunlap floated over to the sensor station. "Confirmed, Admiral. A ping on a transponder that registers as the *McKenna's Pride.*"

Just the mention of that ship affected the bridge crew. Labbé could see it in their faces. Jaws hung open; one young officer looked over at him, her face's normally pink tone faded to white.

They are afraid. I need to calm them. "So they dusted off an antique," he scoffed. "That ship probably hasn't seen battle in ages. Give me the full picture."

Captain Dunlap glanced down, sweat gleaming on his brow. "Five additional Clan Wolf WarShips. I am picking up over a dozen assault DropShips. Multiple JumpShips debarking troop transports—well over two hundred and fifty at this point, and more arriving every few minutes or so. Sir, it appears that *all* of Clan Wolf is jumping in-system. They are out of range and are taking formation maneuvers. We are reading fighter launches as well. That formation is very compact. It'll be tough to get in there."

For the moment, Labbé ignored the naval formation and fought the urge to pound his armrest in frustration. *I have forces at the zenith jump point, and we are in the middle of fighter recovery and rearming. Damn that Wolf admiral!*

"Very well, then," he said, keeping his voice calm to avoid further worrying the crew. "Just like we planned, people. Comms to all ships: launch all fighters, regardless of their status. Attack Plan Alpha—go after those DropShips. Our remaining ships will target those WarShips. All vessels, converge on *Abundantia*. Helm, plot an intercept course and get us underway at battle speed, Wild Star formation. Comms, encrypt a message to Solitude: 'Clan Wolf navy in Terran system.' Send them vid-stream of the targets with their transponder tags."

The bridge crew was already snapping into action. Labbé braced himself against the push of acceleration as the ship began to maneuver.

SLS *MCKENNA'S PRIDE*
NADIR JUMP POINT

Sukhanov was in his natural element, commanding a task force. Alaric watched him bark out orders, deploying the fleet into the formation he had devised: "Comms to *Bloody Fang*: tighten up with the rest of the fleet—you are opening a gap."

Sukhanov headed to the sensor station next. Not realizing the admiral was behind him, the ready-alert officer called out: "Republic WarShips *Auspicium*,

Abundantia, Triumphus, Shield of the Republic, ten assault DropShips, and heavy fighter escort—all are forming up and moving to intercept. We have multiple squadron-size formations of aerospace fighters in the lead. It appears they are holding formation, providing combat air patrol for the larger WarShips."

Sukhanov nodded, confident despite the staggering numbers. "Noted and expected. Order Alpha and Bravo's fighters to deploy in front of the fleet on the far edges. Keep Charlie back to protect our DropShips."

Alaric nodded back. He knew the plan all too well. Sukhanov had deployed the Clan Wolf WarShips around the troop-carrying DropShips, but their formation was compact, leaving little room for maneuvering between the ships. It made fighter attacks on the DropShips subject to a brutal crossfire from multiple vessels. The Clan Wolf assault DropShips led the formation, forming a brutal gauntlet of fire there. The fighters in the fleet's Alpha and Bravo units were poised to funnel the Republic Navy fighters into the heart of the formation—where they wanted to go regardless.

Haake had long anticipated that the Republic would be building its defense around static bases, aerospace fighters, and assault DropShips. It made the most sense logistically. They would want to take out the ground forces and supplies on the troop-carrying DropShips. That irresistible bait would force them into the heart of his tight formation. There were reasons that this was not normally done. Gunnery in such tight quarters would make it tricky to avoid accidentally hitting friendly ships. Haake had trained the Wolf navy for this, and had been able to keep friendly fire to a minimum in simulation.

But we are no longer in a simulation.

The ready-alert officer called out, "Star Admiral, we are picking up some strange signals."

Sukhanov frowned. "What do you have?"

"Just inside the proximity of this jump point, we are picking up more JumpShips. All are powered down, completely cold on infrared, and have no active station-keeping thrusters."

Sukhanov floated closer to the viewing screens. "That is peculiar. Even shut down, we should still get *something*."

"If these magres readings are accurate, those JumpShips all seem to be *hollow*. It is as if their K-F drives are *missing*."

"Problem, Star Admiral?" Alaric asked.

"*Neg,* Khan Ward." Sukhanov turned to Alaric. "A mystery, but one I cannot focus on at present. It will be dicey enough here soon."

"As expected. We shall see if your plans are up to the test." Alaric focused on the white dot on the display tagged as terra.

On the bridge of the WarShip, Khan Ward was more of a spectator, and Haake understood that. Alaric was smart enough to let his commanders do their job, which was his responsibility. There was something in the way Alaric moved, fidgeting with the nearby handhold, that told him how uncomfortable his leader was.

Haake locked his gaze with Alaric. "I have this in hand, my Khan. I will get Clan Wolf to Terra."

Alaric nodded, and Haake swung back around, prepared to do battle.

OVERLORD-C-CLASS ASSAULT DROPSHIP CWS *WARD'S BANE*

"Distance to weapons range?" Star Captain Willett called from his raised center seat on the bridge.

"Twenty seconds, sir," the sensor officer replied.

"Gunnery, give me numbers and types."

"Twenty-four fighters, sir," Star Commander Mooney responded. "Most are *Schrack*s, with three *Simurgh*s and one *Chippewa*."

"Understood, Star Commander. All turrets are weapons free. Fire at will as they come in range. We lead the formation, so it is our job to bloody them before they get through. Per the Star Admiral's plans, we will execute a turn to port after we start engagement so we can bring full broadsides to bear. Helm, stand by."

A warning alarm blared. "Incoming fire," Mooney called out.

All around Star Captain Willett, the air filled with the sounds of battle: the humming metallic noise of the turrets turning, the high-pitched tones of weapons firing, more alarms shrieking while the crew called orders over it all.

The *Ward's Bane* quaked under a heavy rain of Gauss-rifle rounds. For now, Willett ignored the barrage. What mattered was the plan.

The DropShip's particle projection cannons throbbed as they fired. While Willett couldn't see the beams from his position, he knew some Republic fighter was paying a high price for their attack. Another rumble shook the bridge: missile impacts.

"Helm," said Willett, "bring us ninety degrees to port, pivot on our axis. Gunnery, tell your gunners we are repositioning so they avoid wasting shots."

"*Aff*, sir," Mooney called.

The *Ward's Bane* rattled again from another enemy salvo. "Damage control, sitrep," Willett barked.

"Starboard armor is taking a beating, Captain," Apel said from the engineering station off to Willett's right.

"Hang tough," Willett said. He could roll the ship if needed, to let the portside armor absorb the damage.

"Fighters converging," Mooney reported. "They are starting their strafing runs."

"Let me see it."

The viewscreens changed to show the wave of approaching fighters. There was a flash—no doubt a heavy PPC—and one fighter started spinning madly. The others bore in, seeming to fly straight at him.

Willett looked up. "Gunnery, ready your portside gunners. Tear those fighters apart."

"Already on it, Star Captain," Mooney replied.

The ship shuddered from another series of hits, and seconds later, Apel called, "Sir! We just took a hit near the reactor. Coolant housing damaged. Emergency bulkheads in place."

"Noted," Willett said through his teeth. Another deep vibration rattled the ship. *That cannot be good. I know every sound on my ship, and that one is foreign to me. Is that the keel under stress?* He ignored the thoughts of damage he did not know about yet.

"Port side engaged," reported Mooney.

Willett looked back to the viewscreen in time to see one of the *Schrack* fighters hurtling straight for them. *He is going to ram us!*

He shouted: "*All hands, brace for impa—*"

The Republic fighter collided with the *Ward's Bane*, jolting the entire ship. Willett was thrown into the armrest of his command seat as the bridge shook. Lights flickered and viewscreens sputtered. Distant rumbling broke through the noise of the alarms. Dull-yellow emergency lights flicked on.

As he caught his breath, Willett smelled ozone—the scent of electrical damage. "Damage control," he managed.

Apel checked his monitor. "We have a hull breach and internal damage. Starboard PPC turret destroyed." As he spoke, the sounds of the battle were returning, finally overtaking the rumbling. "Access to engineering is cut off, but we still have power."

"Star Captain," said Mooney. "Incoming Republic WarShip, accelerating rapidly. IFF tags it as the *Shield of the Republic*."

"That name demands validating," Willett replied. "All right then—Helm, bring us around on an axis roll of one-eight-zero. There is no point in letting our starboard side have all of the fun."

NADIR JUMP POINT

Star Commander Manning angled his *Jagatai* toward a lance of Republic fighters attempting to skirt the formation. "Ravager Two, follow me in."

Some aerospace pilots preferred fighting in space, some loved the thrill of aerial combat in the atmosphere, and others liked ground-support missions. Manning loved them all. What gave him the biggest thrill was pushing his *Jagatai* to the limit and beyond, much to the chagrin of his techs.

Serving in Bravo Trinary of the Howling Furies, in the Second Wolf Assault Cluster, Beta Galaxy, he got to do it all. The unit was a mix of OmniFighters, OmniMechs, tanks and Elementals, and they trained to work together in close formation under the red-headed firebrand Star Colonel Kalidessa Kerensky. Now the rest of his unit was loaded in DropShips, though. *This is my time...my chance to protect them.*

His OmniFighter was configured for long-range damage with a pair of extended-range PPCs, three large pulse lasers, and long-range missiles. While the rest of his Ravager Star chipped away at a Republic fighter group known as the White Witches Squadron, two of the big Republic *Simurghs* were making a run toward the heart of the Clan Wolf formation.

Vigdal, just off Manning's right wing, flew a *Jagatai* also configured for long-range engagement, but with a deadly punch if someone wanted to get close. "They seem in a bit of a hurry," he said as both fighters accelerated.

"*Aff.* We have to protect those DropShips," Manning replied.

Following the enemy fighters seemed easy, but the moment they arced low and he and Vigdal followed, Manning found himself and his Pointmate in a maelstrom of battle churning with missiles, lasers, and autocannon fire.

"*Blitzking surat*-spawn!" Vigdal cursed as he violently juked his *Jagatai* from side to side. "They do know we are on their side, *quiaff*?"

Manning felt the g-forces slosh his body to one side as he banked hard to avoid a stream of silent-but-deadly autocannon shells. "I hope so," he spat back through gritted teeth.

He ignored the fire all around him and concentrated on the first of the two *Simurgh*s. It was already badly damaged; black streaks along the wings showed where lasers had struck it.

"I have the leader," said Manning. He drifted his OmniFighter over so that the targeting reticle crossed the zigzagging enemy.

One of his pilots, Guethler, dove straight at one of the White Witches, weapons blazing. A beam of laser fire clipped his wing, and he began a violent spin.

"You okay, Ravager Three?" Manning radioed.

A strained voice replied in his headset, "Strong g's. Reaction thrusters..." Guethler stammered, fighting the forces, "...getting control. Do not worry about me... Take care of these *surats*."

Something hit Manning's port side; the fighter rocked, but his armor held. He ignored it. *I have to protect those DropShips. My Cluster is counting on me!*

The *Simurgh* fired a heavy Gauss slug in a silvery blur. It tore into the armored hull of a DropShip, ripping a gash open.

You will pay for that! Manning drifted his reticle back onto the *Simurgh* and opened up with his ER PPCs. The weapons flashed—and hit, searing off the starboard wing entirely and sending the fighter spinning madly off into space.

"Woohoo!" he called out. "Splash one Witch!"

"*Seyla*," Vigdal said, though his voice was strained, a sign of heightened concentration.

CWS *Jerome Winson*'s massive naval PPCs struck next, buckling the fighter in the middle. The *Simurgh*'s thrusters went black, and it careened end-over-end into the battle.

"Excellent shooting," Manning murmured. His body had never felt quite this energized. Every muscle was taut; his eyes drank in every detail. *I am in the Terran system, fighting to be the ilClan!* The dreams of tens of thousands of warriors before him were about to be fulfilled.

He swung hard to join Vigdal, whose target *Simurgh* was twitching wildly. Vigdal's short bursts made it clear he couldn't get a weapons lock on his target. "This bandit is all over the place," he said, firing and missing again.

Manning's entire universe focused on the *Simurgh* his Pointmate was pursuing. The White Witch was erratic, juking in every direction, pulling tight barrel rolls and wide banks. This was a foe worthy of him.

"Do a series of jukes to your starboard, tight stuff. I will move into position," he ordered. Manning maneuvered to get a shot, but rather than continue its run on the DropShips, the enemy craft angled sharply upward, heading for *McKenna's Pride*. As it made a pass across the hull, its rotary autocannons barely pockmarked the massive battleship. Only its heavy Gauss rifle had any effect, the slug carving a ten-meter gouge in the hull as it angled off.

Vigdal jerked his fighter to starboard, waiting until the *Pride* was clear. The Republic fighter misjudged the distance, opening up the gap so Vigdal had room to maneuver.

"Break hard to port, roll and fire!" Manning called out.

Vigdal unleashed a torrent of laser fire again and missed.

Manning's own senses saw the Republic fighter's next move, almost in slow motion. "Tallyho!" he called out so that Vigdal would break off. Manning's PPCs whined and his LRMs roared around him, mauling the white Republic fighter's tail. Bits and pieces of shredded armor filled the vacuum, and Vigdal's *Jagatai* flew right through the expanding cloud of metal fragments. Manning banked hard enough to hear the OmniFighter's metal frame protest with a low moan, but he avoided the debris.

What remained of the *Simurgh* banked away from the Wolf fleet, venting gas in its wake.

Vigdal's breathy voice came over the comms. "I am hit. One of our own turrets. Can you believe that, *quiaff*? I swear I will find that gunner..."

"Call it. How bad?"

"Bad enough. Slow leak in the cockpit. My flight suit has integrity for now, so I am still combat capable."

Manning felt a slight relief, but he also knew Vigdal—his Pointmate was pushing his safety. He had to order Vigdal out of the fight, and that weighed heavily on him. "Break off for the *Bloody Fang* and signal for recovery."

"*Neg!*" Vigdal snapped. "I will not, Star Commander. This is the most important fight of our lives. This is Terra!"

Manning grinned. *A true Wolf if there ever was one.* "I understand," he said. "Form up on my port side aft. We need to rejoin our Star."

Suddenly his own ship kicked from the rear. It was from a missile shot at extreme range, from a fighter barely on his scope. *I got sloppy—blast it!*

Damage indicators flickered red the instant before his power cut out. Manning's gray-and-white OmniFighter pitched forward, nose down. Heart pounding, he hit his emergency-power switch, and the displays flickered back on.

This is not good. I need to recover. Try as he might, his controls suddenly turned sluggish, unresponsive.

"Star Commander?" came Vigdal's static-filled voice. "How bad are you hit?"

The picture the alarms painted was not good. Manning's reactor had auto-scrambled, and despite his attempts to force an emergency restart, it remained a useless hunk of metal. The whole fighter continued to tip forward, and his stomach protested the change in orientation. "My reactor is gone and I am in an end-over-end spin. Vigdal—listen. Take command of the Star, regroup at Waypoint Bravo and continue the mission."

"*Aff,*" Vigdal replied. "I will signal for a recovery team."

Manning admired his Pointmate's devotion, but their victory depended on them following orders. "*Neg*, forget about me," he insisted. "Protect those DropShips!"

All he could do was watch the flickers and flashes of battle—and hope his Wolves could keep the Republic fighters away from the DropShips.

NORUFF-CLASS ASSAULT DROPSHIP CWS *WHITE LUPU*

Four Republic fighters—a *Chippewa*, a *Lucifer*, and a pair of *Simurgh*s—angled their attack run straight at the *White Lupu*. In the glow of red battle-station lights at the edges of the bridge, Star Captain Lonbom's eyes narrowed. *What they lack in tactics, they make up for in audacity.*

"Forward battery, I want targeting on that second *Simurgh* in the formation," he commanded, hands tightening on his armrests. "Concentrate your fire on that one, take it out. That will shake them up. Helm, as soon as we fire, bank us to port, bring the bow up, then yaw to starboard to bring our batteries to bear on the remaining fighters."

"They are at maximum range in five," the weapons officer called.

"Standing by to angle and yaw," replied the helm.

Clan Wolf has not fought a true naval battle in ages, thought Lonbom as he counted down. *And now our survival in this one depends on my actions.*

"Targets remain on vector," the operations officer called out.

"Forward battery—fire!" Lonbom barked.

The heavy autocannon fire made the *White Lupu* lose just enough forward momentum to make it noticeable. Lonbom slid forward against his shoulder restraints. On the forward viewscreen, he saw the *Simurgh*'s armor rip and peel off under a barrage of explosive shells. The Republic aerospace pilot tried to hold what was left of the craft on course, but fell back, banking off in a long arc. Big pieces of armor, blasted free of the fighter, continued on course. *They have had their fill. Now for the others.*

"Helm, execute port bank, eighty degrees. Yaw to bring forward batteries to bear on target."

The enemy fighters opened fire. Lonbom heard the distant metallic *pings* of incoming munitions, and saw the DropShip's damage indicator lights flash on. "Cease yaw at weapons officer's discretion."

White Lupu pitched and spun at the same time; Lonbom's officers leaned in their chairs to compensate. A noteputer someone had failed to secure spun in the air and hit the ceiling.

"Helm," said Star Commander Rolf from the weapons console, "halt yaw. We have a firing solution on the remaining fighters, Star Captain."

"I want that *Chippewa* and the other *Simurgh*," Lonbom said.

"Locked on, sir," Rolf replied.

"Fire!"

Eighty long-range missiles streaked into space. He could hear the *whoosh* as they cleared the turret, speeding off at their approaching foes. Most of the warheads exploded on the *Chippewa*. Some struck the *Simurgh*. The big *Chippewa*'s delta-wing armor was mangled, but its pilot continued on— accelerating straight at the *White Lupu*. The remaining *Simurgh* fired another fusillade with its rotary autocannnons, then tried to break off.

"The *Chippewa* is setting a collision course and accelerating," the operations officer called out.

Not today. "Helm, angle us down twenty degrees. Prepare for emergency burn if that craft survives. Plot a course that brings us back to the formation. I do not want a warning message from Star Admiral Sukhanov saying we have wandered off. Weapons, make sure that warrior does not get their chance. Destroy them."

Lonbom found himself smiling. This was not quite how he had envisioned the opening to the battle for Terra going, but he could not imagine being anywhere else.

SLS *MCKENNA'S PRIDE*

Star Admiral Sukhanov moved to the holotank on the bridge to get a three-dimensional view of the evolving battle. The big gray structure had a yellow holofloor tile and upright corner supports that projected the holographic images.

Khan Ward stood and watched, soaking in every burst of light or silent explosion. He had held back from asking inquires because Sukhanov had been so busy, but there seemed to be a momentary lull. "Sitrep?"

"The Republic navy is putting up a good fight," Haake said as his eyes darted from display to display around him. "They saw through our decoys jumping into the pirate point near Saturn. That means the admiral I am facing is no fool."

"They have had years to prepare," Alaric replied. "I would hope Devlin Stone would put a good officer in charge of his fleet."

"Indeed he has," Haake replied. "Fifteen of our DropShips have been damaged enough to be rendered combat ineffective. Only three are total losses. It is not as bad as it could have been, but it lies within range of our projections."

Each damaged DropShip hurt Alaric's invasion plan. *The crews may yet be alive, their BattleMechs and hardware recoverable, but we have dead, and there will be no reinforcements coming.* "WarShip losses?"

Haake shook his head. "None yet, but that may change shortly. I am about to break formation, per our plan. Every one of our WarShips has sustained damage, but we are all still in this fight. The same cannot be said of the Republic. Two of their assault DropShips are destroyed, the others have executed a wide arc out of our long-range weapons fire." He pointed to the holographic image and zoomed in, showing the ships attempting to evade.

"Thoughts?"

"This Republic admiral is holding them back. I am unsure why, unless they believe we need to hold this jump point, and they want to harass any incoming supplies and reinforcements." Haake pulled up a display in the holotank, which showed three windowed live-feeds of Republic WarShips. The big vessels that remained were badly battered, their hulls charred, pitted, and cratered. They had put up a vigorous fight, but so far the Wolves were holding their own. The tight formation Sukhanov had devised had crushed the Republic fleet.

"Now you move to finish this, *quiaff*?" Alaric asked.

"*Aff*, indeed I do, my Khan," Sukhanov said, his brilliant blue eyes ablaze with excitement.

He studied the images and zoomed out to see the rest of the Republic fleet. His eyes never left the holotank. "Their fighters inflicted some damage, but were decimated because we used our proximity against them. That increases the pressure on our enemy to take greater risks. Their admiral has been fighting conservatively. This will either change that or break them. Right now, my opposition is considering making a run against us with their battlewagons. They are wondering if we have suffered enough damage to possibly shatter our formation."

The image of the Republic fleet showed drive flares increasing. The sight made Sukhanov and Alaric trade grins.

"Star Admiral, enemy WarShips are accelerating," the ready-alert officer called. "They are tightening their arc to try punching through us."

"Acknowledged," Sukhanov said, eminently calm. "Star Commander Baker Rhyde, send the following message to the fleet: 'Railroad.' Send it twice and get confirmation."

"*Aff*, Star Admiral," the comms officer responded. A few heartbeats later, he said, "All ships have confirmed."

"They will follow us," Sukhanov replied. "All hands, brace for maneuvers. Helm, tight angle, starboard, thirty-five degrees. Once we have made the turn, I want acceleration and a roll to bring our batteries to optimum firing positions as we pass the enemy fleet."

In the holotank, Alaric felt the ship pitch around him to the point where he had to tighten his grip on one of the handrails to keep upright as *McKenna's Pride* began its turn.

Sukhanov seemed immune to the maneuvers, he was so transfixed by the holotank images. "Place the *Victoria Ward* and our assault DropShips on patrol duty. Have *Bloody Fang* break formation and align so that we both make a pass on opposite sides of the Republic battle line. Ready the *Jian*-class cutters for their run."

"*Aff*, sir." Star Commander Rhyde relayed the orders in a crisp voice.

Sukhanov nodded, then turned to Alaric. "Respectfully, sir, I recommend you retire to the vault. It is the safest place aboard the ship. We will be at close range, and we cannot risk a hit to the bridge taking out both of us."

Alaric agreed. "You are in command, Star Admiral."

The path to the vault took him floating down two decks. Outside the vault hovered an Elemental honor guard. From a far-off section of the *McKenna's Pride*, a low rumble reached his ears—another hit from a Republic ship.

Alaric gestured to the door. "I would like a few minutes in the vault alone."

"Of course, my Khan," the senior guard said, stepping aside as Alaric entered. The door closed behind him and sealed shut.

Here, in the heart of *McKenna's Pride*, lay the one person who could understand Alaric's situation, the true burden of what he carried.

General Aleksandr Kerensky.

Looking at the glass coffin, Alaric saw his own reflection—his long hair, chiseled chin, the brilliant blue eyes. He had seen those eyes before, in an image of Victor Steiner-Davion—one of his genefathers.

Looking past his own image, Alaric was still struck by the great general's old age and lack of hair. Old age was a rarity in the warrior caste. The Great Father lay with his arms crossed over his chest. His uniform was pristine, and his medals—harkening back to the Star League centuries ago—had not lost their luster. There was a look of calm and nobility about the man.

Alaric leaned over the glass top of the casket and touched it. "The last time you came to Terra," he said, "you led an army. You came to liberate humankind from a madman, the Usurper. In some respects, I am doing the same. Clan Jade Falcon is coming soon, and leading it is a Khan that rivals the Usurper of your time." *How does one compare villains?*

"I come to establish a new era, one where your children, your very blood, will reignite the Star League. If you could speak, you might caution me—tell me that bringing war to our beloved Terra should not be done lightly. You were an agent of the gods of war, but fought for peace."

He floated down the length of the coffin. "I have read your works and studied your life, as have all of your Trueborn children. You believed warriors have a responsibility to a greater cause: the protection of those who cannot protect themselves. When you saw that peace could not prevail, you left the Inner Sphere. I respect that choice."

Alaric paused, turning back to the general. "The time has come for your offspring to return and reclaim what you left behind, as you knew they would. Malvina Hazen's Jade Falcons come, and they come with a vengeance. She seeks to remake the Inner Sphere, as do I, but her image of it is an empire built on ash and corpses. She would destroy any that oppose her. Fear will be how she maintains control—fear and terror. If the Jade Falcons prevail in the coming conflict, then humankind will suffer in their bloody talons. I will not let that come to pass. I will wage war to protect the innocent, as you did. They will be protected under my rule when the Wolves become the ilClan. When I am done, the Inner Sphere will be remade. I will not repeat the mistakes that led to the Star League's downfall."

It was a promise to General Kerensky—and to himself.

"We are men of destiny," Alaric said, ignoring another series of distant *booms* echoing through the ship. "My Star League—*neg, our* Star League—will usher in a new golden age for humanity. I will see you returned to your rightful place. I swear it."

RSS *ABUNDANTIA*

"They are doing *what*?" Admiral Labbé asked in astonishment.

Captain Dunlap leaned forward to get a better view of the main screen. "Four of the Wolf WarShips are coming right at us."

Impossible. "They wouldn't leave their DropShips exposed like that."

"Our fighters did damage," said Dunlap, "but most are reporting depleted ammunition, and some squadrons are simply gone. We are the only threat to those DropShips. When we turned toward them, they turned toward us."

Labbé's stomach clenched. *They are baiting us—and I have no choice but to bite.* "Then we need to make it count." He pulled up a holodisplay of his ships. "Have *Triumphus* adjust course to be first in the battle line. Divert *Gladius Terrae* outward, so that *Dire Wolf* passes between it and our lines." His assault DropShips were in the vanguard, paying a high price for attempting to penetrate the Wolves' tight formation as his other WarShips moved in to face Clan Wolf almost head-on. *The time has come put our testicles on the table.*

"Message from *Shield of the Republic,* Admiral," the comms officer called. "Two Wolf cutters, class unknown, have dropped Elementals on their hull."

"They have ships that can do that?"

"Apparently, sir."

Labbé balled his fists in anger, saying nothing. He looked out and saw one of his lead ships open up on the CWS *Rogue*. One shot went wide of her forward hull, but another caused a yellowish-crimson blast on the Clan Wolf ship. A massive hole remained where a magazine of naval autocannon rounds had exploded. Wisps of venting oxygen mixed with the blasted bits of blown hull armor and superstructure. *Yes!*

Before Labbé could respond, a flash appeared on the holodisplay, small but brilliant. "What was that?" he asked.

The ready-alert officer answered. "That was *Glory of the Republic,* sir. It just came under the guns of *McKenna's Pride*."

So much for the Pride *being an antique…a relic.* "We will mourn our dead later," Labbé said through clenched teeth. "Right now, we must stay focused. Bring us in close to those DropShips. If we can get past them, we can savage their fleet and end this invasion before it starts."

ESSEX-CLASS DESTROYER RSS *SHIELD OF THE REPUBLIC*

Star Commander Parac Shaw felt the fast-moving Wolf cutter CWS *Durandal* bump and skid across the armored hull of the *Shield of the Republic,* rising slightly just a few meters over the target ship. The bay depressurized, and Parac saw the big doors open. His warriors were right where they wanted to be—on the hull of the enemy vessel, cruising along its surface some five to ten meters up.

"Mag locks on," Parac barked as he used his tongue to trigger the magnetic boot plates that would allow him and the other twenty-four Elementals in his Star to walk on the ship's hull.

"*On!*" his Star responded, almost in unison.

"Star Commander," Jac spoke up, several warriors down. "We are moving awfully fast."

Parac Shaw grinned. "No one ever claimed it would be easy. If it was, they would not have sent us."

Star Admiral Sukhanov had devised this plan. The cutters were stripped-down light DropShips that used magnetic grapples to attach to the hull of the target vessel. The *Durandal* came down hard again, this time skidding to a stop as it fired its reverse thrusters. On the hull, the DropShip lay below the firing arc of the WarShip's turrets, though the journey down had been harrowing, tossing the Elementals about hard, despite their restraining straps.

As Parac stepped out of the bay, he could see the vastness of space around him and the flashes of explosions in the distance. Dizziness caught him, a common experience when making a spaceborne assault like this. Parac turned his attention back to the hull of the vessel.

This was not his first time to Terra. He had accompanied the Clan Wolf delegation to Victor Steiner-Davion's funeral in 3135. At the time, he had been an honor guard who had the distinction of teaching a young Alaric then-Wolf, how to fight in zero-g. That he had been privileged to teach the Khan was a matter of pride for the massive warrior. Years had passed, and Parac now fought in Beta Galaxy, Second Wolf Assault Cluster.

I never dreamed we would come back in this manner. Alaric brought us to Terra, and now I will bring him glory!

"Bane Star, you know the drill! Plant your charges. Primary targets are airlocks, weapons bays, and turrets. Make sure they are secure!" He stepped off the ship and could hear and feel the metallic *clunk* of his magnetic boots on the hull. "Alpha Point, on me!"

Walking took a great deal of effort due to forcing their footpads off the hull with each step. Trudging as quickly as possible, he and the four Elementals of his Point closed on the nearest target, one of the massive naval autocannon turrets. When he reached the turret, it spun, elevated, and fired silently at a target—a fellow Wolf. The sight angered him, making his assignment even more urgent.

Reaching down to his side, Parac took out one of the small shaped charges and slapped it on the turret as it began to track another target. "Set one," he called out, hitting the red arming stud on the bowl-shaped charge. Three others of his Point followed suit.

Kobler called out, "I set one on an airlock off to your right."

Parac turned and saw his comrade's orange-streaked ebony armor. "Get clear," he said, and the Elementals thudded along the hull nearly thirty meters from the turret. "Detonate in three...two...one... Detonate." He used a deliberate pattern of eye blinks to signal the blast code for his planted charge.

The ship quaked for a moment under his feet, enough for him to bend down slightly, lowering his center of gravity in hopes it would keep him on the hull. The explosion had been silent in the vacuum of space, but the results were clear. The turret shot forth a momentary funnel of flames, then debris exploded out from where it had been. Where Kobler had set his charge, the airlock vented atmosphere into space for several seconds—along with the bodies of three Republic crew, spinning out of control.

"Advance to the next targets," Parac said, eyeing a Barracuda missile tube off to his right. "Move it people! The fleet is counting on us!" As he spoke, he spotted a Republic aerospace fighter, an old *Lucifer*, swing around and strafe the hull—no doubt targeting the rest of his Elementals.

They are desperate, but that is no match for our determination! "Bane Star, incoming fighters! Double-time it!"

SLS *MCKENNA'S PRIDE*

"Targeting *Abundantia*," the tactical officer called.

Sukhanov nodded. "The moment you get a firing solution, let loose with Killer Whales. Empty the magazines. I want that ship to break off," he said through gritted teeth. His head was slick with sweat that stung his brilliant blue eyes, but he ignored it. *This is the fight I have lived my entire life for.*

"We have target lock," announced the fire-control officer. "Autocannons and missiles, sir."

"Fire at will," said Sukhanov.

The Winchester-Boeing naval autocannons spewed their deadly barrage into the Republic WarShip with a thunderous rumble, echoed by the higher-pitched rush of the AR-10 capital-missile launchers firing Killer Whale warheads. The ship shuddered from the force of it.

The ready-alert officer spun toward him. "Incoming missiles!"

"All hands, brace for incoming fire!" Sukhanov called, grabbing for a handhold.

Abundantia's wave of Barracuda missiles hit *McKenna's Pride* hard, each explosion making the old ship groan in protest. The ship shook violently, but Haake did not, making him slam his left shoulder into the bulkhead near the holotank. For a moment, he lost his physical orientation on the bridge, but quickly regained it, thanks to a nearby handhold.

"Keep firing," he urged as he pulled up the damage display. Yellow indicators flickered down the length of the digital cutaway of the *Pride*'s hull, but none of the shots had punched through their armor.

Checking his fleet, he saw *Abundantia* was caught between *Pride* and *Dire Wolf*. *Dire Wolf* was between *Abundantia* and *Triumphus*, blazing away with both broadsides. Even as the *Pride* still fired on *Abundantia*, the Republic ship was starting to move out of range.

"Tactical," said Sukhanov, "new target—that next ship in the line, *Auspicium*. Comms, let *Rogue* know *Abundantia* is their primary."

The officers confirmed his orders and furiously barked out their own. Sukhanov felt their massive naval autocannons thunder once more as

Auspicium came into range. One shot missed, but another tore into the hull near the bridge. Sparks flickered in the jagged crater; gas sprayed out as the vessel began a slow roll along its keel, angling out of the line of battle. The *Auspicium*'s naval lasers and cannon tried to fire back, but at their angle, most of the shots went wide, missing the *Pride* entirely.

Nice try, thought Sukhanov—just as *Auspicium* began to turn sharply back toward *Pride*. Her drive plumes flared brilliantly astern.

"Helm, evasive maneuvers!" he called. "*Auspicium* is attempting to ram us!"

McKenna's Pride turned, shoving Sukhanov shoulder-first into the upright holotank support again. He shook off the pain and studied the holoimage. A lifetime of training in naval combat allowed him to do the math, and he realized the Republic ship may actually hit them. It would be only a glancing impact, but it would devastate both vessels.

For a millisecond, he actually admired the Republic captain for their daring.

"Adjust thrusters!" he barked. "Forward hull down as much as we can push it!"

The *McKenna's Pride* dipped nose-down. Its naval autocannons roared once more, ripping at *Auspicium*'s bow and sending bits of blasted armor careening into space. *This is going to be close...*

Sukhanov saw a flicker—another Wolf vessel—suddenly move into his tactical space. It was *White Lupu* at nearly full acceleration, its forward battery flashing as it charged at *Auspicium*.

To the Republic's credit, *Auspicium* did not hesitate or veer off, but continued arrowing toward the *McKenna's Pride*—until it collided with the *White Lupu* in a horrific mix of mass, momentum, and chaos.

The hit had not been dead-on, but at that speed, it devastated both ships. *White Lupu* broke into a spin, showing that the impact had torn through its hull. The forward turret was adrift, spinning on its own. The running lights flickered for a moment, then went off.

The *Auspicium* looked as if someone had taken a big bite out of its long hull. Oxygen vented into space, and shattered pieces of superstructure dangled from the massive gash, held on by cables or piping that had refused to yield. Large pieces of the hull twisted off from the impact, drifting into the blackness. The bulk of the vessel started to spin, probably from a misfired maneuvering thruster, gaining speed with each twist.

Sukhanov stared, transfixed, until a voice behind him spoke, "What ship is that?"

Khan Ward had returned to the bridge.

Sukhanov snapped back to attention. "The *White Lupu*. Gunnery, get us a lock on the next Republic ship."

"Sir, the Republic forces are breaking formation and angling away at zero-seven-five degrees on a solar orbital approach. Do you wish us to order pursuit?"

Sukhanov pondered that, then turned to Alaric. "We have crippled their forces here," he said. "They are likely going for the zenith jump point or diverting for a burn to the Titan Shipyards. We can finish them off."

"Are they a threat?"

Sukhanov studied the holoimage for a moment. "They pose no threat to our landing on Terra. If they do retreat to the Titan Shipyards, they may be able to effect repairs there, but by then, we will already be in Terra's orbit."

"So we shall," Alaric said. "Let them reach the zenith jump point. It will give Malvina something to deal with. Proceed on to Terra."

Sukhanov nodded, then turned to the bridge crew. "Initiate recovery operations."

CWS *WHITE LUPU*

Star Captain Lonbom struggled into his emergency evac suit. His dislocated shoulder made it difficult, sending lightning bolts of pain through his battered body. Thick smoke curled through the dark bridge; the only illumination came from small, yellow emergency lights. Life support was failing, but he was thankful he had any at all. His eyes ached from the pressure change due to the hull leaks, even after his suit's helmet seal hissed and returned him to normal air pressure. Despite the splatter of blood inside his emergency helmet, he watched Star Commander Rolf get into his own suit and manage a thumbs-up.

Lonbom's ship was dead, and his actions had likely cost him most of his crew.

Despite the pain, he smiled. *It was worth it.*

The *White Lupu* had already been on a high-speed burn to reach the line of battle when Lonbom saw the *Auspicium* turn to ram the *McKenna's Pride*. It had taken every ounce of Rolf's conning skill to adjust the ship's angle to ram the Republic vessel first. The collision showed no favorites, savaging the *White Lupu* and the *Auspicium* indiscriminately. The impact had been so hard Lonbom was sure he had cracked a rib when tossed into the side of his seat.

At that speed, we were only going to get a few shots anyway—and we were already burning up what was left of our engines. He remembered the smiles of ferocious joy on the faces of the bridge crew when he ordered them to ram the enemy. "They will not take out our flagship and our Khan!" he had roared. "Not on my watch!"

His crew had made him proud.

Rolf headed over to Lonbom, pushing a floating, damaged panel out of the way. Drops of blood from his head injury floated inside his helmet. "Orders, Star Captain?"

"We have done our duty and earned our glory," Lonbom said, looking around the shattered remains of the bridge. "All hands, abandon ship."

RSS *ABUNDANTIA*

A haze from burned wire insulation hung in the air of the bridge as Admiral Labbé's flagship peeled away from the Wolf fleet. He had given the fallback order to save what was left of his own task force.

Even if I had broken through to their DropShips, he thought, *they have firepower and a barely scratched WarShip. I would have only been ordering the senseless deaths of my crew.* But as much as he tried to console himself, it did not help. A part of him wished he had died in the fight. *That would be better than telling the Exarch what happened.*

He had watched the Wolf DropShip collide with *Auspicium* and had fought down the urge to vomit. The Republic ship now spun wildly out of control, bleeding air, dead in space. As he watched, he suppressed the temptation to extract revenge. *I could still order the fleet to wheel about and make a death-dive on those ships. We are bound to get a few of them before they destroy us.*

Then, as if the Wolves could read his mind, their ragged line of battle made the long turn back to protect their ships.

My orders are to preserve the fleet. We may yet need it before this is over.

"Comms," he called, "signal all Republic vessels to rendezvous at Fort Grec at the zenith jump point. I want damage-control teams to commence repairs immediately. Launch our recovery craft. There are a lot of lifeboats out there we need to retrieve."

For a moment, he surveyed his exhausted bridge crew. Nothing he could say would make this any easier. And there was nothing to do except keep them focused on their duties. *We will fight another day...I swear it.*

CHAPTER 2

On the situation room's holodisplay screen, Admiral Labbé's face looked sunken, almost pale. Even his white mustache seemed to droop. His projection illuminated the faces of the Republic's military leadership around the long table, casting them all in the pallor of his failure.

Solitude lay deep under Geneva. A black, oval holographic table filled the majority of the massive room's space. The light-gray ferrocrete walls were adorned with the banners of the RAF's storied brigades: the Hastati Sentinels, Principes Guards, Triarii Protectors, Stone's Brigade… One blank spot showed where a banner had been taken down—the star-and-shield sigil of Stone's Shadows, the Fidelis, was absent. The harsh white lights surrounding the edges of the room made the bare spot on the wall stand out even more.

Seated around the table with Exarch Devlin Stone were Paladin Damien Redburn, former Exarch; Paladin Janella Lakewood, Stone's head of intelligence; Tara Campbell, the Countess and legate of Northwind, and commander of the Highlanders mercenary battalion; Paladin Jonah Levin, former Exarch; Tucker Harwell, an ex-ComStar adept serving as Stone's aide; and several young staff officers. All eyes focused on the holographic image of Admiral Labbé hanging in the space before them, but many glanced at Stone to watch his reaction.

Devlin Stone said nothing as the admiral spoke. He sat in his chair, his cheeks sagging more than usual. His mix of gray and white hair had a cowlick that stood up near the back of his head, one of the few things that defied him. He looked decent for 108 years old, though he had spent fifteen of those years in cryogenic sleep. The stasis had taken a toll on him, though no one dared to say it other than Tucker Harwell. Determination—that was what kept him going…a gritty drive to preserve the Republic he had built.

"*Auspicium* is nearly a complete loss," said Labbé, "and *Triumphus* is gone. We are only getting signals from survivors calling for help. *Shield of the Republic* is under tow. We are doubtful it can be salvaged, but we may be able to scrap it for parts. Of our assault DropShips, four can maneuver under their own power."

Stone shook his head as if to ward off the words, and changed the subject. "*McKenna's Pride*. Our intelligence left that out of our reports." He glanced over at Knight-Errant Edie Miller, a military-intelligence specialist who reported to Paladin Lakewood. Her usually pale face reddened at his question, and she unconsciously brushed her short, black bangs out of her face. *Good*, he thought. *You should be nervous. An iconic battleship shows up out of nowhere, and we don't even get an inkling that it's in play until it's already destroying our forces?*

"No, Exarch," said Labbé. "My apologies for the failure. Our latest intel said the *Pride* was with the Homeworld Clans, but there has been no contact with the Clan Homeworlds in almost a century. No one has seen *McKenna's Pride* in the Inner Sphere since Kerensky's Exodus, almost four centuries ago. That is likely why Ward brought it."

"What do you mean?" Lakewood asked from her seat at the large oval table.

"Our profile on Alaric shows an obsession with symbols and images," said Miller. "And that ship represents the pinnacle of the Star League. If our reports are right, General Kerensky himself is entombed aboard the *Pride*. Alaric is using the ship to remind us that he is the legitimate heir to the Star League."

"Our citizens will not accept him in that capacity," Lakewood scoffed. "They are loyal to the Republic."

Stone let some of his frustration with Miller wane before weighing in. "People are subject to change. Lady Miller is right. Symbols count, and Alaric knows how to use them effectively. It is like that stunt he pulled on Tharkad, declaring himself the rightful Archon of the Lyran Commonwealth. It doesn't have to sway everyone—just some of them." *Damnation, he is smart. He's thought this through carefully.*

"Forget the ship," Stone said, shaking his head. "It's water under the bridge. Admiral, how long until you can repair what is left of our fleet?"

"Our sensors show the Wolves are diverting DropShips and the *Bloody Fang* on a trajectory toward Titan," Labbé said. "I've alerted the shipyards there, but without Titan, our fleet can only do minimal repairs at Fort Grec. We still hold Mars, but Mars does not have heavy repair facilities. It is mostly a garrison force and some DropShips." He looked dejected. Broken. "Exarch, I still have forces at the zenith jump point. I propose combining these and making a run in pursuit of the Wolves. We can burn in fast and catch up to them, hit them hard with what we have left."

Stone asked the question everyone in the room was wondering: "Can you win?"

Labbé sighed. "It is questionable at this point. We bloodied Clan Wolf, sir. They did not escape this fight without some losses. However, we failed to take out a significant number of their DropShips, and the ones we did cripple, they have in tow. If I go in with everything, including the DropShips at Mars, we might just get lucky and hamstring them. They have hundreds of DropShips in their formation, not to mention aerospace fighters."

"But would it cost us the fleet?"

Labbé nodded, unable to say the words.

"What is the alternative?" Lakewood asked.

The admiral shifted. "I can divert to the zenith jump point, join our forces there, and wait for the right opportunity to strike. The two defense stations there can help us with some of our repairs. Clan Wolf did not leave any of their vessels at the nadir jump point."

"How will they protect their supply lines?" Jonah Levin asked.

Labbé shrugged. "Based on the number of DropShips, they may not intend to maintain a supply line. They may have brought everything with them."

"Can we still inflict some damage to them before they enter orbit?" Stone pressed.

Labbé nodded, his beefy jowls bouncing slightly. "We have our small orbital stations over Terra and a number of aerospace squadrons. It's not enough to stop the Wolves, but they won't make planetfall unscathed."

Stone slowly rose to his feet, using his arms to push himself up. "I'm not prepared to bet our entire navy on a strategy that requires luck. We will need those ships when we have beaten back the invaders...to retake the worlds of the Republic. Besides, the Jade Falcons and the Capellans are still out there, still a threat."

Stone paused, then nodded reluctantly. "We will go with your recommendation, Jean-Jacques. You have served the Republic well today." Before Labbé could reply, Stone shut off the display. He looked over at Janella Lakewood and Damien Redburn, frustration evident on Damien's face. The former Exarch was in his mid-sixties, but still sported red hair streaked with gray.

"It's a tough call," Redburn said. "I fought Clan Wolf in the Remnant for years. You are allowing them the chance to get closer to their prize...to *us*."

"The Republic is more than just Terra," Stone said firmly. "When this is over, we will rebuild."

"Very well," Damien said. "Your orders, Exarch?"

"Send out the JumpShip *Gaul* to find Julian Davion. It carries a verigraphed message for him." Stone allowed himself a smirk. *Julian owes us, and House Davion will pay its debts.*

Tara Campbell spoke up. "Exarch, you cannot seriously expect Julian to come rescue us." She and her Highlanders had just come from Northwind, where they had tangled with a Capellan invasion force for control of the planet's functioning HPG. She wore a dress kilt and a pristine tan uniform top, and her wiry, slender frame and spiky blond hair made her look more like a model than a MechWarrior. Not only did she command the Highlanders, a storied mercenary battalion that could trace its origins back to the Star League and Scotland, she was the Countess of Northwind. When she spoke, everyone paid attention.

"The Federated Suns is the Republic's greatest ally," Stone said. "Julian will come."

Campbell shook her head. "Sir, with all due respect, the Federated Suns has a knife at its throat. Julian is in no condition to come to our aid. Even our own Ghost Knights have told you that House Davion is on the verge of collapse."

Stone waved his hand in the air. "Your concerns are noted. Trust me, the Federated Suns will not let the Clans take Terra. You need faith." Years of experience fighting the Jihad alongside House Davion gave Stone confidence. "Send out the JumpShip. Julian will come."

His eyes swept over every person in the room. "In nine days, the Wolves will arrive. When they reach orbit, we will see what kind of fight they intend to wage. Perhaps we can get Ward to bid away some of his force to even the odds." *I knew you would come, Alaric, but you will find that coming to Terra and conquering it are two very different things.*

After a few more minutes of conversation, the meeting broke up, with everyone getting various assignments—everyone except Tucker Harwell. Stone lowered himself back to his seat and looked across the black table at the young man who had thawed and revived him. Harwell wore an expression Stone knew well, that exasperated look that said he was going to challenge Stone.

Harwell waited until the door closed and they were alone. "You don't seem too worried, Devlin. Why?"

"I am served by good people, smart people, including you."

"No, I know you. You're hiding something."

Stoen frowned. *Surely I'm not* that *easy to read.* "You know our military strategy—you've sat in on the meetings for years."

Tucker nodded. "Of course!" he said sarcastically. "You've raised new units, you've built these redoubts—these 'Stalingrads' you're so proud of. You want the enemy to fight a war of attrition, one where you wear them down and then pounce on them with your armies. I've seen these defenses, and they are impressive, but then again, I have no practical military experience."

"It can work," Stone said. "Yes, if we throw everything at Clan Wolf when they land, we might very well win. But that is fighting the way the Clans prefer to fight, one big combat trial. They have fought on hundreds of worlds and seen us do that time and time again, and are more than prepared for such a contest. But I refuse to play their game and risk losing it all. The system of redoubts will slant the odds to our favor. Everything the Clans do is built around fast and decisive engagements. I will not give them that. We will be tempted to throw everything we have at them, but if we do that, we play to their strength. They prefer that kind of fight."

Tucker's eyes narrowed, and he ran his hand through his hair to cover the bald spot on the back of his head, a reminder of the Blessed Order holding him captive. The secret ComStar sect had installed a cybernetic interface there against his will and forced him to work on repairing the malfunctioning HPG on Wyatt. Stone could read his young aide's face, and knew he wasn't convinced.

"You're too confident, even for your ego," Tucker said. "There's something else in play here. What is it?"

Stone didn't have to tell him anything: he was Devlin Stone, founder of the Republic! But a part of him could not resist. *He needs to hear what I have planned, to see that I am still every bit the great man I was in my youth.* In that moment, he gave into his hubris. "Very well. You know our military strategy. What I have planned is more bold...it is political."

"Truth be told, I am *glad* that Clan Wolf is here. It is surely better than the Jade Falcons showing up. The Wolves will come, and we will engage them in a series of trials for Terra. If we win, Clan Wolf will be here to help us fight the Jade Falcons when they eventually arrive. We will still have a functioning military, as will they. That is how the Clans fight, to minimize losses. I intend to use their misguided sense of honor to bleed Alaric and the Wolves and bring them to heel."

For a moment, Tucker Harwell said nothing. "And what if we lose?"

Stone flashed a grin. "Even if we lose, the RAF will be here. Alaric will *have* to leverage us when Malvina Hazen arrives. We will fight alongside Clan Wolf to ensure the Jade Falcons do not take Terra. We will wage a war to destroy her and this crazy-ass doctrine of hers. The Falcons are the real threat, Tucker. Even you know that."

"If Alaric wins, it means the Wolves will be the ilClan."

"Yes, and we will be there at his side. He will owe the Republic. We will be at the heart of his new Star League, a perfect place for me to ensure the soul of our people is preserved. Alaric is a conqueror, not a ruler; it is in his genes. He will need me, need the Republic. How else will he administer what he has conquered?"

Tucker chuckled, which annoyed Stone. "You make it sound so easy. Things may not play out the way you think."

"You lack faith and vision, boy. Look at the big picture. Ultimately, we end up with the Falcons destroyed, and the Wolves spent and wasted in the effort. The Republic will prevail. Terra will hold. The Wolves coming is the best thing that could have happened because it allows *us* to control this war. When it is all over, we can regroup and fight to retake back the worlds the Houses have taken from us. The Republic will be resurgent.

"*That* is why I am glad Clan Wolf is here, that we will face them first. It is perfect, exactly what I wanted."

"You haven't told any of your advisors about this, have you?" Harwell asked.

Stone could tell he already knew the answer. "No. They need to focus on the military campaign. This would be a bothersome distraction."

Harwell shook his head. "All of this assumes that the Clans will dance to your tune, Devlin. There are a lot of ifs in play here."

Stone leaned back in his chair, his lower back aching more than usual. "I know the Clans better than most men. Don't forget, they fought with me against the Word of Blake in the Jihad. They will remain true to their nature. They never cooperate with each other. They always fall back on honorable combat trials—it is who they are. You should have a little more confidence. You've seen what I am capable of."

Harwell shook his head again. "I know that some of your plans fail miserably. When they do, people die, worlds fall, things go to shit. You're betting the fate of the Inner Sphere on your intuition, and the price of your gut feelings will be paid in blood."

CHAPTER 3

Alaric hovered in the Combat Information Center, arms crossed as he watched the holographic footage of the last orbital defense station explode. The squat, ball-like station was no match for the Wolf fleet's firepower, though that did not mean they were ineffective. Unlike the massive bases at the jump point, these were smaller, lightly manned, and built around a hard-hitting capital-ship weapon. The stations had concentrated their fire, and succeeded in damaging a dozen DropShips with naval PPC, autocannon, and laser fire. Four DropShips had been deemed complete losses, unrepairable, though some of their contents and crews were being recovered. The Wolf WarShips, however, were more than enough to destroy the lightly armored stations.

The image flickered away from the destroyed station to Terra itself. The Republic had thrown four squadrons of aerospace fighters into the battle, but Haake had kept his formation tight, allowing numerous overlapping fields of fire. All of the Wolf ships had suffered some sort of damage from their runs, but the cost to the Republic, in terms of pilots and fighters, was high. By the time the fighters broke off from the thirty-minute engagement, only a single battered RAF squadron managed to retreat to Terra.

Alaric said nothing for a moment, savoring the holographic globe of Terra before him. Across the table, floating above her seat, was General Chance Vickers, her black hair cropped back, her gaze almost as intense as his own.

Across from her was SaKhan Garner Kerensky, who was also regarding the target world with hooded gray eyes. Despite his inoffensive appearance—head slightly balding, his almost pale skin shimmering under the glow of humanity's birthplace—his demeanor was pure predator, salivating for the kill.

Next to him was Ramiel Bekker, Alaric's former bondsman, known affectionately as the WarBear. Big and burly, with a heavy black beard and curly black hair, he eyed Terra with almost the same gleam as Garner. Ramiel commanded Alaric's rapid response unit, the Tactical Response Cluster. The way he stirred, floating above his seat, he seemed to be chafing for battle.

Star Admiral Haake Sukhanov drifted at the far end of the table. "That was the last defense station over our area of operation. We left some over areas where we do not have immediate ops planned—we can deal with them later, or leave them for any...*visitors*. The stations are not very maneuverable, so we are clear to commence landing operations at your discretion, Khan Ward."

Alaric thought about where he was, the very room where General Aleksandr Kerensky had overseen liberating Terra from the Usurper. *It is only fitting that my next orders come from this room.* "Commence our combat assault as soon as we are aboard our DropShips."

Garner, always gruff, crossed his arms defiantly. "Australia..." he said, letting the word hang in the air. "Who would have thought it would begin there?"

Chance Vickers, Alaric's second-in-command, weighed in quickly. "It offers us a chance to ensure we have the initiative in the upcoming fight. It is *exactly* what we need. First, it can be secured. If the Republic opts to fight us there, they will have to shuttle their forces in. We will quickly establish air superiority, and once we hold the continent, it will be easy to defend, and it provides us with a launching point to southern Asia. Second, Melbourne and Perth have armor and munitions facilities. We will need those for repairing battle damage and rearming. Third, the Republic won't expect it. Thanks to the intel from the Custos, we know they have based their defenses on a series of redoubts, the largest one being in Geneva. They anticipate we will go for that first and foremost."

The rest of the Wolf strategy was just as bold. Alaric had not come to crush the Republic Armed Forces—he had come to conquer Terra. From Australia, his forces would ferry to South Asia, where they would break into two broad fronts. One force, under Chance, would drive west, through the Middle East, toward Europe. Alaric and Garner would drive north into China, with Garner heading off across Russia's plains and Alaric crossing into North America. It was a broad-front war, not the traditional fight the Clans waged. All along the way, the Wolves would secure useful industries and plants that manufactured the things he needed to keep his *touman* operating.

The linchpin to Alaric's strategy was giving Malvina Hazen of the Jade Falcons the means to come to Terra through the Fortress Republic barrier. It was a calculated risk, but he believed the Wolves and Jade Falcons would ultimately vie for the right to be called the ilClan. Bringing in Malvina meant the Republic would have two Clans to contend with. The Jade Falcons were the most feared; their Mongol Doctrine was brutally efficient, using terror and violence to compel compliance. Faced with two enemies, Devlin Stone would have to throw most of his effort against the Jade Falcons.

And in the end, we will face them.

Alaric rose from his seat, his blue eyes sweeping his command staff. "You all know your assignments. I will see you on Terra."

COMMAND POST SOLITUDE
GENEVA, TERRA
REPUBLIC OF THE SPHERE
10 JANUARY 3151, 0930 HOURS (T-DAY)

The members of the RAF High Command looked at the orbital drop projections on the holodisplay.

"Australia..." Stone muttered as he tried to process it.

Former Exarch Damien Redburn glanced at the man who had forged the Republic of the Sphere and saw Alaric's move had surprised him. *He was so sure the Wolves would come at us here, in Geneva.*

Devlin Stone was far from infallible. Most of the command staff refused to see it, but Redburn did not cling to the illusion that Stone was anything more than human. Damien had been outside Fortress Republic for years, defending the Republic Remnant, a sliver of planets still loyal to the Republic of the Sphere, fighting off Clan Wolf and all other invaders. That was, until Stone had hauled him back to Terra against his will.

Their relationship had remained icy ever since. Damien had kept his frustration with Stone somewhat in check, and Stone had publicly welcomed him back as a trusted advisor. Damien had then buried himself in duty, helping form and train several new units, making sure the redoubts were prepared and the few in-service Castle Brian fortresses scattered across Terra were appropriately staffed and supplied. Still, as he watched the ill-concealed astonishment on Stone's face while the tiny dots of holographic light showed the Wolves' descent from orbit, he found himself both amused and secretly delighted. *For all your planning, Devlin, Alaric has already surprised you. Maybe now Jonah and the others will see that you are not a god among men.*

"Alert Redoubt Sydney," Stone finally uttered. "Also, we will need to scramble an aerospace fighter response—hit those DropShips on the way down. We need to see what their secondary targets are."

"We have two squadrons in Sydney, and three more can be deployed from New Guinea," Janella Lakewood said. "I can call them up immediately...if that is what we believe best."

There was a hesitancy in her voice though, and Damien understood why. *Battle is often about the math...and she is seeing what I do.*

Damien studied the dots of light showing the incoming Wolves, squinting slightly to see them better. "You'd be sending them to their doom," he said. "Look at the sheer number of DropShips. This isn't just a small portion of the Wolves. He's landing *all* of his DropShips. What's the count, Lady Miller?"

The Knight-Errant's eyes darted down at her noteputer. "We show...over four hundred DropShips on landing vectors." As she spoke, her face noticeably paled in the situation room's light.

Stone seemed unshaken by the numbers. "There are no secondary targets, not yet."

"Exarch," Lakewood said. "Sending those fighters against that number of ships would be suicide. I recommend holding them back for the defense of Redoubt Sydney."

Stone nodded. "We will need reinforcements there—and fast."

Damien rose to his feet. "I will take in my Redburn Guards."

Stone held up a hand and shook his head. "No, Damien, I need you here."

"I wasn't asking permission," Redburn said, his face suddenly hot. "I'm taking them in."

Jonah Levin spoke up. "Now may not be the time." He gestured to the seat Damien had just vacated.

Redburn was terse with Stone, but he held Levin in utter contempt. Jonah had been the one who had come to Callison and dragged Redburn back to Terra after convincing the Fidelis to turn on him. *If Jonah is against me going, that only makes it more appealing.* It was hard, but Redburn suppressed a smile. "I'm going. We can be on the move in less than an hour. The Guards are a rapid-deployment force, and have been on alert since the Wolves arrived in-system. They are built for this. I'm taking them in."

There would be words...debate...concerns—he had no time for any of it. *They have been fighting a war in simulation, from this room. I was out in the Remnant for years, fighting* this *enemy.* "This isn't the time for half measures, Devlin. Let me go and kick Alaric in the balls."

There was a long pause, then Stone gave a single curt nod. "No grandstanding," he said. "Hit him hard. I don't need a martyr, I need you at my side. Remember, this is a long game. The redoubts will whittle them down."

The words were kind, though Damien questioned their sincerity. "I have no intention of dying in Australia. I know the Wolves' tactics and have squared off against some of their commanders. That makes me the best person for this job. You don't beat Clan Wolf by playing fair, you beat them methodically. It also sends a message to our troops on that continent that their leadership is behind them. We have to hit the Wolves hard, over and over, and my unit is designed for that. I will contact you once we've deployed."

By the time he reached the door, Damien was beaming with joy—less about his mission than defying the desires of Devlin Stone.

CHAPTER 4

OVERLORD-C-CLASS DROPSHIP *RAGING WOLF*
ON APPROACH OVER AUSTRALIA
TERRA
REPUBLIC OF THE SPHERE
10 JANUARY 3151, 0952 HOURS (T-DAY)

Alaric checked the straps across his coolant vest for the third time. His *Savage Wolf* BattleMech was ready. *He* was ready. *All that remains is to convince the Republic that they do not stand a chance.* His enemies had spent years to prepare for his coming to Terra. *But I have spent a lifetime.*

The *Raging Wolf* rumbled as it burned through the atmosphere. The low quaking was oddly reassuring.

His neurohelmet earpiece chirped. "Khan Ward, incoming priority communication for you."

"From whom?" he asked.

"Exarch Devlin Stone."

Alaric grinned. *So, he has finally emerged.* "Put him through."

"Khan Ward," came a deep voice—old and defiant. "I have been waiting for you to contact us. I am surprised you have not yet offered a *batchall* for Terra. I presume one is forthcoming."

"Devlin Stone. I was surprised to learn you are still alive—welcome back to the realm of the living. As it turns out..." Alaric paused, savoring it. "A *batchall* was not necessary for Terra. I presumed you would defend it with all you have, and I intend to come at it with all *I* have. If I were to bid, it would be Clan Wolf. My *entire* Clan."

"Better you than the Jade Falcons, I suppose." Stone sounded strangely relaxed, as if things were progressing as *he* had planned.

"Your feelings on who you face are of no consequence," Alaric said. "The heirs to Aleksandr Kerensky have come home. We are more than enough to defeat your crumbling little Republic."

"I was fighting decades before you were poured out of your iron womb, son," Stone said firmly. "I have fought the worst of mankind and defeated them. I built an empire on their ashes."

"Empires rise and fall. I will found an era. You have faced the worst of mankind, you say? Now you face the best: Clan Wolf."

Stone paused before responding. "There is no need for us to wage war all over Terra and put innocent civilians at risk. Instead, I offer you a series of trials—much like what ilKhan Ulric Kerensky waged at Tukayyid. My best units against yours."

Alaric laughed. "An amusing offer, Exarch, but a meaningless one. I am not Ulric Kerensky. Nor are you Anastasius Focht, I suspect. I have not battled my way here just to put the ilClanship at risk." His smile faded quickly. "I will not play games for what I want. Nicholas Kerensky said whichever Clan *conquers* Terra would be the ilClan, and that is exactly what I intend to do. My people will take what they desire, and when it is all over, the entire Inner Sphere will know of your defeat. Prepare for war, old man."

The hesitation told him Stone had been ill-prepared for his response—but the Exarch tried. "We will beat you, Khan Ward. We will tear into you, and you will lose everything. The Republic will emerge from this fight triumphant, and take back what was stolen from us."

Alaric nodded. "Excellent. All Wolves love a challenge in battle, and you have promised that. But know this: it is *I* who will do the taking now. I will take your spirit from you and crush it under my BattleMech. And I will start with Australia."

With those words, he cut off the transmission.

Eight long minutes later, the *Raging Wolf* landed. The 'Mech bay ramp dropped, and daylight flooded in on Alaric. Instantly, his cockpit's armored ferroglass tinted against the blazing sunlight.

Terra.

His entire life had led to this moment. Even before he was born, Katherine Steiner-Davion manipulating his genes...it had all been for this instant, to stand on Terra with his entire Clan at his side. The trials and tribulations of the Grand Crusade that began over a century earlier would be erased with this victory.

This moment...this is destiny.

The DropShip was surrounded by low, undulating hills and weeds—beige against a blue sky. Dust still settled from the landing of the ships, powdering the brush and sparse foliage. Despite the landscape's bleakness, he found himself swelling with pride.

"Wolves," Alaric commanded, "*deploy!*"

But looking out at the other DropShips, he saw no Clan Wolf 'Mechs debarking. He double-checked his communications channel and broadcast again. "Wolves, deploy!"

But instead of action, he only saw lowered, empty ramps.

"*Neg*, my Khan," Chance Vickers said. "You alone have the honor of being the first Wolf on Terra to complete our crusade. No one will join you until you stand on the sacred soil."

Alaric's heart swelled with pride; he clenched his jaw against the tide of emotion.

He guided his 'Mech down the ramp onto Terra. The moment he touched the ground, the tactical channel came alive with whoops and cheers. Wolf Clan BattleMechs, Elementals, tanks, and conventional infantry poured out of the DropShips, churning up the dusty soil.

Nicholas, your people have come home.

EAST OF PERTH, AUSTRALIA
TERRA
REPUBLIC OF THE SPHERE
10 JANUARY 3151, 1244 HOURS (T-DAY)

First blood for Alaric came when a battalion of assault 'Mechs emerged from cover east of Perth, an hour and a half after landing. His pickets signaled their drive, and he could not resist moving his *Savage Wolf* to engage.

He saw the orange and tan dust they kicked up in the distance before his sensors picked up their reactor signatures. The ground was broken, uneven, with deep, dry gullies and scrub brush. Long, sloping hills gave a deceptive look of openness, but Alaric knew better. The hills gave cover for the Republic forces to maneuver.

The enemy finally broke into the open and it was hard not to contain a sense of glee, something he rarely felt. When he zoomed in his cockpit view, he saw the aggressors' 'Mechs were all painted gray, with three bright-red stripes on their shoulders. The battlecomputer had no record of this unit, which was no surprise. *Fifteen years behind their precious Fortress Republic, they were bound to have raised new regiments.*

The enemy charged straight at Beta Galaxy's line—rushing forward, weapons blazing and flashing, piercing the dust on the wind. One, a *Doloire*, sent a Gauss-rifle round at him at extreme range. The slug slammed into his 'Mech's left shin and embedded there. He felt the *Savage Wolf* lurch, but maintained his gait.

"This one is mine," he declared on the tactical channel. Honor still bound the Wolves, and none would dare challenge his right. He closed the distance, bringing his extended-range large lasers to bear. One missed, but one hit, burning a glowing crimson scar on the upper body of the Republic 'Mech.

The Republic MechWarrior's next Gauss-rifle round missed, but their large pulse laser stitched a series of black marks up the right side of Alaric's torso. The *Doloire* burst into a sprint, weaving side to side as it tried to close the gap between them.

Alaric grinned. He was more than willing to bring his foe in closer. Near the approaching enemy, a Republic *Marauder IIC* blazed away at a newly designed *Thresher Mk II*, two of its PPCs searing off most of the *Thresher*'s upper-body armor, sending a hot splatter of melted metal into the air like fireworks.

Another Wolf warrior, in a new *Stormwolf,* moved so fast that a hail of missiles targeting it left a trail of explosions in the wake of the dust it kicked up.

Bringing his targeting reticle onto the *Doloire,* Alaric unleashed eighteen advanced tactical missiles. Their thin, white contrails snaked and twisted in the air as they rained down on the *Doloire* and tore into its right side and arm, sending armor bits flying.

As he fired his ER large lasers, an explosion rocked him hard—not from incoming missile fire, but from a bomb that had gone off near him. Shrapnel from the explosion scarred his 'Mech. His tactical display showed four enemy bombers breaking off—with his own aerospace elements swooping in to engage them.

His attention snapped back to the *Doloire,* and the millisecond he heard the metallic *snap* and *thunk* of the missile rack completing its reload, he unleashed another wave of ATMs. Their roar on both sides of his cockpit gave him a sense of confidence...a rush of adrenaline. His missiles filled the air between him and his target, and blasted massive craters into the armor of the Republic BattleMech.

For a moment, the *Doloire* stopped its run, skidding in the sandy soil. Beside it lumbered one of the Republic's *Ares* superheavies, a three-legged BattleMech that resembled a *King Crab* on steroids. It laid down a wave of long- and short-range missiles at a pair of fast-moving *Kit Fox*es that survived only on their speed alone, their fire nicking and marring the legs of the 135-ton monstrosity.

"Chance," Alaric said over his command channel. General Vickers was deployed several kilometers away with Epsilon Galaxy. He did not have to say anything more; he knew she would be analyzing the situation.

Her voice was crisp and to the point, "They shuttled this reinforced regiment in via DropShip just a few minutes ago. Orbital recon shows that the force in front of you is a blocker. A larger force is moving along the right flank, six Stars' worth of enemy approaching."

As if to confirm that, a roar of exploding artillery rumbled like thunder off to Alaric's right. Chance's voice remained calm, steady, in control—as always. "Their aerospace made a bombing run and is circling back for strafing. Our CAP is intercepting."

Alaric had spent a lifetime in war, preparing for this fight. He knew a trap when he saw one and, based on Chance's comments, this had all of the earmarks. "Beta Galaxy, this is Wolf Prime," he said calmly as he kept his targeting reticle on his foe. "Swing left—then retrograde. Lay down suppression fire on the force in front of us."

I will not be lured into a defeat so soon after landing. He let loose again with his ER large lasers and missiles, and stopped his charge, slowly backstepping as his barrage found their target.

Captain Jack Traver of the Redburn Guards watched a wave of advanced tactical missiles engulf Major Alice Simpson's *Doloire* in devastating explosions.

Stabbing crimson laser beams slashed at her as well, wreathing her BattleMech in smoke and carnage.

Former Exarch Redburn had ordered Jack's unit to get the Wolves' attention and hold it. Based on the incoming brilliant bursts of lasers and missiles, Jack knew he had succeeded. They had been masterfully deployed, just as they had trained to do.

It was an honor to fight in the Redburn Guards. Damien Redburn had been fighting the Wolves outside of the Fortress walls for years. There had been rumors of him disregarding orders in the Remnant, but Devlin Stone himself had said those tales were enemy propaganda. Jack ignored the rumors. What mattered to him was the man, and Redburn was a seasoned combat veteran, which counted a great deal.

Jack had been born in North America and had passed many rigorous qualification tests for piloting the massive superheavies. One did not merely get assigned to the Redburn Guards. Hundreds tested for the chance each year, and Redburn himself personally supervised these tests. They had been grueling, physically and mentally. Redburn wanted MechWarriors who were not just good at their roles, but in peak physical condition. Jack was so dedicated that he had shaved his red hair so that his neurohelmet leads made better contact with his temples. His skin was pinkish, and he sunburned after only a few minutes, especially with a lack of hair. He hated being bald at the age of twenty-three, but the three crimson stripes on the hull of his *Ares* made it all worthwhile.

Traver had no personal qualms with Clan Wolf, other than that they'd had the gall to invade Terra. Most of the talk in the Guards was not about the Wolves as much as the Jade Falcons. Most believed Malvina Hazen would take no prisoners. She saw the people of the Republic as little more than targets in a shooting gallery, and she was holding the rifle.

Jack would fight the Wolves—but he would fight the Jade Falcons to the death without question. The Falcons' threat had been his primary reason for enlisting in the RAF, having watched the holovid docudramas that told stories of their atrocities. *I will fight anyone coming at the Republic, but I want to fight the Jade Falcons.*

He was in his first real battle now, and though drenched with sweat, his whole body tingled with excitement. All of his senses were amped up, as if he were outside on the hull of the hulking OmniMech. The massive 'Mech was a part of him like it had never been before. He felt every vibration, every footfall. He had been worried he might freeze or panic when exposed to real combat, but that wasn't the case. In fact, he felt exhilarated like he had never been before in his life.

Jack loved it.

From the pilot seat of his *Ares* superheavy OmniMech, he called "Major!" into his neurohelmet's microphone, a warning that came far too late. Several missiles dug deep into the armor of Major Simpson's *Doloire*, making it quake as he advanced beside her.

An azure beam of PPC fire from a BattleMech model he did not recognize nudged the lumbering *Ares* hard. The damage scarred Jack's left torso so much that his center of gravity shifted, and he struggled to compensate. The 'Mech, a 65-tonner, was not in his warbook, and it moved like the manmade lightning bolt it had lanced into him. As it skirted to his flank, he again turned to the major's *Doloire* just in time to see it fall. Even in his 135-ton 'Mech, he felt the tremor of the nearby impact.

"Jack, my gyro is in pieces," Major Simpson said in a strained voice. "I need you to take command."

"Roger that," he said grimly as another PPC hit his right leg. This time the firing 'Mech was a Clan Wolf *Loki* nestled in one of the twisting dry gulches that contorted through the desertlike terrain.

His gunner, Corporal Tina "Cheetah" Charms, unleashed the left arm's pair of extended-range PPCs and followed it with ten long-range missiles. The *Loki*'s position in the gully gave it some protection. One PPC's brilliant blue-white blast hit the ground in front of the enemy 'Mech, throwing dirt and rocks into the air as the other charged-particle beam lashed its right side. Half of the missiles missed, but the rest blasted bits of armor from the *Loki*'s upper body.

"Good shooting, Cheetah," he said through gritted teeth.

Her curt voice came back from the seat below and in front of him. "Move us sixty meters due west, keep firing profile with the lead Wolf units." Jack had gotten used to her tone. While he was the pilot and technically the commander of the *Ares*, he knew their success came from coordinating their actions.

His engineer, Staff Sergeant Mia Fowler, called from her seat in the cockpit behind him. "We just lost A-Pod number three, leg one. Goddamn *Ullers*! Cheetah, can you take one out, please?"

Jack moved the massive 'Mech on the path Cheetah had requested, and pulled up the tactical display. The Wolf advance had stopped...in fact, aside from the lead elements, the enemy was starting to pull back. *That isn't part of the plan.*

He hit the command comm channel. "Sir Redburn," he said as the blinding flash of another PPC blast narrowly missed the cockpit by only a few meters. "This is Captain Traver. Looks like the Wolves are onto us. They are pulling back—" His voice was cut off as a wave of long-range missiles rained down on his *Ares*, rocking the OmniMech hard. "We're under heavy suppression fire. Major Simpson is down, I've got command in the center."

While he waited for a reply, the hissing roar of short- and long-range missiles poured out of his 'Mech. Off to his left, he saw an *Uller* collapse under a cascade of exploding warheads. As it rose, its limp right leg dragged as it tried to put distance between it and the firepower Cheetah could pour into it.

"Confirmed, Captain Traver. They are reforming a new line of battle. We can't spring the same trap twice. Order your battalion to fall back to Phase Line Zulu. We'll have to hit them again tomorrow."

Cheetah managed one final PPC shot into the limping *Uller*, and blew its leg off. The Wolf 'Mech crashed to the ground in a plume of sand and smoke.

The thought of retreating ate at Jack, but he had his orders. *At least we let them know this is not going to be a cakewalk.* He trudged his *Ares* back toward where the major had gone down.

"What are you doing?" Cheetah shouted. "The enemy is the other way!"

"Orders," he replied grimly. "The Wolves figured out what we were up to."

"Ugh!" his gunner grunted. "Hell of a way to start a war."

"You're telling me," he replied, angling the big OmniMech out of range of the Wolf 'Mechs.

CHAPTER 5

For the past two days, the BattleMechs of the Redburn Guards had thrown themselves at Alaric's forces. Each time, the Wolves beat them back. The Guards' attacks were well coordinated and hard hitting, and they usually faded away before the Wolves could bring the brunt of their numbers and firepower to bear. The Guards had made Perth their base, and defended it with a ferocity that impressed Alaric.

Impressed, but not unnerved.

His battle against Redburn was not the only fight on the continent. Sydney was the heart of a fortified redoubt, with rings of defenses, turrets, and prepared positions, in addition to the subterranean tunnel system of a decommissioned Castle Brian complex. When saKhan Garner Kerensky had gotten bogged down there, Alaric had sent in the WarBear—Galaxy Commander Ramiel Bekker.

Bekker's tactical genius was the reason Alaric had wrested him from the Ghost Bears to begin with. Aloof, arrogant, and almost always right, Bekker had become a true Wolf.

Here in Sydney, he used aerospace forces to blast a corridor through the minefields and defensive positions. This tactic let Garner force the defender, a mercenary regiment of Hansen's Roughriders, out of their positions.

Epsilon Galaxy had caught the Roughriders in the open, flanking them. The Roughriders tried to fall back, only to find that the Forty-First Wolf Guard Battle Cluster had moved into Sydney in their absence. The mercenaries then pivoted to make a break for Melbourne, taking the fighting all along the coast—and it was still going, though it appeared to be winding down.

Not so with the Redburn Guards Alaric faced. The Republic's losses had been over 60 percent, but still they kept coming. *Lesser units would have crumbled or surrendered by this point*, he thought. Alaric admired their determination, but it was clear they were near a breaking point.

"Khan Ward, we are picking up the Redburn Guards again," came the voice of Star Commander Iain Sender of the Wolf's Fury Cluster. It was a new unit that had already proved its merit in the battle for Perth. The Cluster was poised at the farthest tip of the Wolf line on a low ridge covered with debris from previous clashes. "They are coming directly toward your position."

"Understood," Alaric said. "Wolf's Fury, execute a fighting retreat on the left flank. Silver Keshik, Bent-Bow formation with me in the center. Nineteenth Wolf Striker Cluster, feign falling back after the initial contact. Retrograde to the right, swing into their rear. This fight ends with this assault."

A cloud of dust and a low rumble in the ground announced the coming battle a few moments later. Alaric angled himself into position with the rest of the Wolf formation. His 'Mech had lost some armor, but hasty field repairs had gotten him back in the fight. A particularly aggressive *Kheper* from the Redburn Guards had cost him half of his ATM ammunition; he hoped he'd have enough left for today.

The instant the Redburn Guards rose over the crest of a long ridgeline, the Wolves filled the air with laser and missile fire. A *Lament* staggered out drunkenly, firing its medium lasers at three Silver Keshik warriors. The Republic 'Mech triggered a vicious response; PPCs from three different angles seared the *Lament* simultaneously. It wavered, but responded with its own PPCs, bathing a *Warwolf* in brilliant blue light and sending armor rocketing into the air. The *Lament* struggled and started a slow backward walk down the ridge.

Alaric did not fire immediately. He was looking for the right target. *These are the Redburn Guards, so the former Exarch must be with them.*

Then he saw it—a hulking *Atlas III*. This one had been badly burned and blasted; its patchwork armor did not cover all of its holes. Its skull-like head was painted flaming crimson, matching the triple stripes on each shoulder.

That is him. Spurlock Conners of the Wolf Watch had tagged this *Atlas III* as Damien Redburn's.

Alaric swung his targeting reticle to target the 'Mech and fired his pair of extended-range large lasers. The shots struck the torso and left-arm armor, the crimson beams slicing and melting away the 'Mech's protective skin.

"Wolves, slow advance," he commanded. "Maintain our flanks."

Another Wolf warrior launched a salvo of long-range missiles into the *Atlas III*, enveloping it in a cloud of explosions, smoke, and hot shrapnel.

"*Neg*," Alaric said over the tactical channel. "This one is mine!"

The attacker broke off. Through the dissipating cloud of smoke, and despite the explosion of a 'Mech right beside it, the *Atlas III* moved forward, each footfall rocking the ground. Slowly, it turned toward Alaric.

The instant he gained missile lock, he sent eighteen advanced tactical missiles streaking toward the red-skulled 'Mech. The high-explosive warheads blasted vicious holes into the legs and torso of the *Atlas III*, but did not topple it.

It returned fire with a wave of twenty long-range missiles. Its rotary autocannon bombarded Alaric with shells as he darted to the left, his *Savage Wolf* rocking, and he fought to keep it upright. The autocannon shells stitched a diagonal scar just below his canopy.

As the heat rose in his cockpit, he heard the gurgle of his coolant vest combatting the excess heat. He narrowed his eyes, focusing, bringing the targeting reticle onto the *Atlas III*'s right arm, right above the rotary autocannon. His red beams stabbed at the Republic BattleMech just as a Republic SM1 passed it, flames lapping from the rear of the hovertank. Nearly 300 meters behind it, he saw a hulking three-legged *Ares* raining fire down on a *Dominator* slowly being whittled apart with missile fire.

Alaric heard the metallic *clunk* of his ATMs completing their loading cycle. Angling hard left, he swung around to reach his target's flank.

The enemy 'Mech hesitated. Following Alaric would mean exposing his rear to the advancing Wolf line. It was only a moment's pause, but that was all it took.

Alaric fired his ATMs. One missed, flying into the side of the ridge. The others plowed into the *Atlas III*'s legs and side. Flames sprouted up to the cockpit canopy, blackening the crimson skull as the 'Mech reeled. The *Atlas III* fell forward and skidded into the sandy soil, digging a long trench as it went. Alaric could hear its armor plates grinding.

He toggled an open channel. "Damien Redburn, this is Khan Alaric Ward. You have fought bravely, but this battle is over. Your Guards are spent, your supplies are under my control. You cannot win this fight. You are simply too stubborn to acknowledge it."

The *Atlas III* struggled to right itself and rose on its mangled left knee. "This isn't over until you leave Terra," a ragged voice—Damien Redburn's— said from the battered assault 'Mech. "The Republic will prevail!" His right arm snapped up, and its rotary autocannon tore into Alaric's torso to accentuate his point.

Suddenly, three Simian battle-armor suits sprang into Alaric's field of vision, firing their recoilless rifles as they rose into the air on jump jets. The shells exploded on his right arm and leg. Cursing, he swerved out of their flight path. Blitzking *battle armor!*

He brought his secondary targeting reticle onto the lead Simian suit and fired his small pulse lasers. The emerald-green burst caught the battlesuit's squat legs, searing off the armor as it superheated. The Simian lost thrust and dropped some fifteen meters into the hillside, landing with a sickening *whump*. Its comrades angled away, fearful of the same treatment.

The *Atlas III* was back on its feet. Alaric turned to face it just as he heard the missile-lock tone. Six Streak short-range missiles struck his *Savage Wolf*, one exploding against his cockpit ferroglass and leaving a blackened mark. Two of the *Atlas III*'s medium X-pulse lasers riddled him with green bursts of energy; one furrowed deep into his left arm, leaving a smoking black hole where it had penetrated. The hits tossed him hard against his restraints, and he concentrated, straining to keep his balance. *Redburn is stubborn, a worthy foe.*

As Alaric dodged left, he saw two of Redburn's armor plates had been blasted off the right leg, still smoking in the sagebrush. He brought his targeting reticle over that vulnerable spot and fired his ER large lasers. The brilliant red beams seared the air in an unbroken streak, seeming to join the two BattleMechs for a moment.

Then the knee actuator on the *Atlas III* exploded in a spray of lubricant, coolant, and the black goo of melted myomer.

Redburn tried to compensate, and lurched backward as Alaric fired his right-hand rack of ATMs, riddling both legs in the process. It was too much for the former Exarch. The *Atlas III* fell again, this time on its right side. The cacophonous grating of crushed armor plating was almost painful to hear, but Alaric wasn't done. He fired his second rack of ATMs, which hit Redburn's rotary autocannon, blasting the barrels into useless scrap.

The *Atlas III* flinched, as if attempting to stand once more. Leaning backward, it angled away from Alaric. Then the ejection seat fired. Redburn blasted clear of the Wolf front line, west toward Perth. Alaric saw his parachute deploy as his opponent landed several hundred meters behind where the *Atlas III* fell over in a crumpled heap. A fast-moving Republic hovercraft set out in pursuit of where the seat had landed, no doubt executing a recovery.

Alaric checked his tactical display. The Redburn Guards were falling back. He had let them retreat before, giving his force breathing room, but not this time.

"Nineteenth Wolf Striker Cluster, full pursuit. Chase them to the sea."

JOONDALUP, AUSTRALIA
TERRA
0838 HOURS

"Talk to me, Mia," Jack Traver called from the pilot seat of what remained of the once mighty *Ares*. Two days of fights with Clan Wolf had left the superheavy OmniMech a battered and blackened shadow of its former self. Traver and his crew had been living in their cockpits, and Mia had executed several engineering miracles to keep them in the fight this long.

"Number three leg is toast," came the sergeant's ragged voice from deep within the massive 'Mech. "Left arm's seized up too. I have the PPC capacitors charged up, but you'll have to aim manually, and it'll be your last shot with them. We lost the power coupling."

"Any *good* news?"

"The engine's roasting me down here, the gyro sputters, and we've lost most of our weapons," her exasperated voice came back. "When we blew out our LRM ammo, it hosed up most of the controls on the left side."

"Give me pilot control for a minute," Cheetah said from the gunner's seat. "Let me get off one more shot."

"You got it, Corporal," Jack said, lifting his hands off the joystick and the throttle.

Cheetah listed the hulking 'Mech hard to one side, almost toppling it over. Jack's hands shot down to the joystick to compensate, but she caught it first.

She fired; the *snap-crack* of the ER PPCs shot forth with a pair of charged-particle beams that flashed like lightning strikes. In the distance, Jack saw only one find its mark on a Carnivore tank. The other went wide. *We got in one final lick at least.*

A wave of Arrow IV missiles rained down a heartbeat later as he grappled with the controls, fighting gravity, the damaged gyro, and the concussion waves. He lost that fight, and the *Ares* plowed into a small building as it careened over, crushing the café there into rubble.

Smoke from a fried circuit board filled the air as he disconnected his neurohelmet. "Mia?" Jack called, half-worried she might be trapped somewhere in the bowels of the big 'Mech.

Her ragged voice came back. "Well, that's not gonna buff out."

"Can we get her up?"

"No, sir. We just lost the number one leg. And even if you could somehow stand us up, our weapon systems are toast."

Jack slammed his hands on the joysticks in frustration. *I've lost my first BattleMech in combat. Damn it!* He regained his composure quickly. "All right, abandon ship. The Wolves are closing in."

He hit the cockpit-hatch release, and the canopy yawned open. The steamy cockpit air rose out, and he felt the cooler air chill the sweat that drenched him.

Cheetah crawled out of the lower cockpit seat, and he helped her up as Mia emerged from the rear, where she had been working.

"We gave as good as we got," Cheetah said.

Jack nodded as they climbed down into the rubble of the café. *But is that good enough?*

JOONDALUP, AUSTRALIA
TERRA
1605 HOURS

At the foot of his *Savage Wolf*, Alaric surveyed the battlefield—a fallen city the Redburn Guards had used to make their last stand.

Broken BattleMechs lay about, many still smoking, ripples of heat rising from the once-proud war machines. Cratered buildings marked where the enemy had tried to take cover. The Southern Hemisphere's summer air was acrid with ruin, the low light of the setting sun bringing the flicker of the remaining scattered streetlights. It all told a story of a vicious battle to the end.

Only a dozen Republic MechWarriors and tank crews had surrendered. The military casualties were, in Alaric's mind, wasteful. *The battle had been lost earlier. Redburn was bleeding me.* Had this been a normal combat trial, it never would have been fought in a city where civilian casualties could have occurred. He saw the long progression of vehicles heading out of Perth as the locals fled. *Redburn* chose *to fight in the city. He* forced *me to hit him here. These losses are on his head, not mine.*

Technicians made field repairs on his 'Mech's armor as General Chance Vickers walked over from her own *Savage Wolf*, parked next to his. Her MechWarrior togs were soaked in sweat. Her short black hair was slicked back.

"Any sign of Redburn?" Alaric asked.

"*Neg*. The prisoners indicated he was put on a high-speed hovercraft and evacuated with the last of their wounded."

"We will face him again," Alaric said flatly. "What of Garner?"

"The Roughriders surrendered to him. They caught us all a bit off guard. It appears the Republic hired them to train new regiments about the time we conquered the Remnant worlds. But they are ours now, thanks to Garner and Ramiel. It gives us some operational and easily repairable BattleMechs...which is more than I can say for these Redburn Guards." She nodded at two burned 'Mechs nearby, a gutted *Doloire* and *BattleMaster*, kneeling and leaning on each other like an improvised grave marker.

Alaric did not like surprises, and the Roughriders' presence had surprised him. *Devlin Stone is proving a worthy adversary.* "If Damien Redburn thought their tenacity would break my will to fight, he made a costly mistake."

Vickers smirked. "We still have some units mopping up. One Roughriders company broke off before their surrender and went rogue. Another day or so, and Australia is ours completely, my Khan."

"Excellent. Any other issues?"

"One. Per our plans, Star Colonel Damon Ward was establishing a repair garrison post east of Perth, but a guerrilla force, led by a Knight named Justin "Cloud" Hall, attacked. They blew up two ammunition haulers and a coolant truck. The damage they inflicted was minimal."

"Where is their base of operations?"

"Atitjere, allegedly."

"We prepared for this." Alaric looked out over the quiet battlefield. "We must send a message—one the people of Terra can understand. We will not tolerate support of terror tactics or insurrection. I want them to see the difference between Clan Wolf and what Malvina Hazen is bound to do once she arrives."

THE SHADES
UPPER COERT, RIGIL KENTARUS
JADE FALCON OCCUPATION ZONE
13 JANUARY 3151

Malvina Hazen stood with her arms crossed, her black, bionic right arm warm against her skin just below the sleeve of her T-shirt. "Our test jump shows that Clan Wolf sent us accurate information. They have foolishly given us the means to take Terra from the Republic, and from them."

"Do we go now, before the rest of our Clan arrives?" Galaxy Commander Stephanie Chistu asked. "Or do we wait for the other Galaxies to arrive before jumping in?"

Malvina eyed her with contempt. Alaric had sent Chistu—not Malvina—the information on how to penetrate Fortress Republic. *Is this part of what you and Khan Ward have conspired—to create this dilemma for me?* She wished she had something to prove Chistu's betrayal. *She met with Alaric before all of this. She* must *be in league with him.*

But all Malvina had was suspicion.

"We are Jade Falcon," she said firmly. "We go now. We sent Birthright orders for our people to come, and they will. We had a number of our front-line units poised near the edge of Fortress Republic already, waiting for this moment. We must move swiftly, like our namesake. We cannot risk Clan Wolf taking Terra before we even depart. Each day we linger here is a day the Wolves creep closer to victory, a victory *we* have earned. I wish we had time on our side, but we do not."

"We know nothing of Terra's defenses, Chingis Khan," Galaxy Commander Jane Thastus said from the huddle of officers in the strategic operations room. "We are going in blind." Her use of the title *Chingis Khan*, ruler of the universe, was deliberate. Malvina had long adopted the title, and Stephanie Chistu did what she could to avoid using it.

"We have our WarShips," Malvina said with a dismissive gesture of her bionic arm. "Alaric will have left some Republic naval forces in-system for us to deal with. Our navy will crush them, and we will burn to Terra. Our raptors will rain down on the Republic. There will be nothing they can do to stop us."

The gathered officers called out "*Aff!*" Even Chistu.

Alaric, you will pay for your arrogance, Malvina thought. *You should have never given me the keys to the kingdom. If you think I have forgotten your stunt on Tharkad, leaving my Jade Falcons to suffer the Lyrans' counterattack, then you are wrong. I will take Terra from you and break you before you die at my feet.*

SOUTH CHINA SEA, APPROACHING SINGAPORE
TERRA
13 JANUARY 3151, 2052 HOURS

Damien Redburn looked up and saw Captain Jack Traver standing over him. Redburn's arm was in cast, his head bandaged, his head and ribs ached every time the evacuation hovercraft broke a wave crest. He had scraped his chin on a rock upon his ejection seat landing, but it looked worse than it felt. The aches, the throbbing joints, it was more than age. *Men my age are rarely in a 'Mech cockpit, let alone leading counterattacks.*

"You wanted to see me, sir?" Traver asked.

"Your crew get out with you?" Redburn said, pulling himself up on the makeshift bed. Just the slight movement added to his discomfort.

"Yes, sir. Are you okay?"

Redburn saw concern on the young man's face, and he smiled momentarily while shifting to a sitting position, fighting each ache with determination and forced movement. "The doctors told me I shouldn't be ejecting at my age. Imagine that. You don't need a PhD to know that."

"It's probably good advice, sir." It was Captain Traver's turn to smile. He lost his balance momentarily as the hovercraft bucked another wave. Damien didn't feel the effects as much. Sitting up helped.

"I've ignored a lot better advice over the years," Redburn replied, then shifted subjects. "Word is you did a hell of a job back there, Captain," he said with a hint of pride in his voice.

Jack ran a hand over his shaved head. "I lost my 'Mech, but we took out three of the Wolf 'Mechs and three tanks before we dropped. Their new 'Mechs are fast, *very* fast."

The hovercraft rocked again, making Traver wobble and Redburn wince. "Khan Ward is full of surprises. We need good fighters. I'm bumping you up to major."

Traver's face blushed. "T-Thank you, sir," he stammered.

"Don't act surprised. You hung in there, buying us time to get our folks out. Myself included."

"I just assumed...I mean...the Guards are gone. We lost all of our equipment and a lot of good people."

Redburn nodded. "The Republic will prevail. We did our job, hitting Alaric Ward's Beta Galaxy. He's got to know by now that this isn't going to be a stroll in the park." With those words, Damien Redburn allowed himself a thin smile. The battle had given him what he needed since the affair on Callison: focus, purpose, and confidence. *The next time we meet I will take you down, Alaric Ward. I swear it!*

COMMAND POST SOLITUDE
GENEVA
TERRA
15 JANUARY 3151, 1010 HOURS (T+5)

Devlin Stone watched former Exarch Damien Redburn slowly take his seat at the situation-room table. Redburn's head was bandaged, as was a scrape across his chin. Age was beginning to show in his movements. His fingers had a slight quake to them. Stone hoped it was just the medication, but a part of him knew it was not. *Time is catching up with me as well, old friend. That hibernation process may have given me fifteen years, but it took some years from me as well.*

"This message came in this morning," Lakewood said, indicating the holotable display—BattleMechs firing on a city. Flames leaped into the sky, and rolling black smoke churned in the air. Snaking lines of refugees clogged the roads in the distance. No structures were left intact. "Alaric broadcast it in the clear, and the media ran with it before we could censor it."

Stone watched in speechless anger. It was everything he had always feared about the Clans, everything he had come to expect. *They are predators coming to level our cities. Kill our people.* He felt sick.

Alaric Ward's face appeared in the holocamera footage. *"I am Khan Alaric Ward of Clan Wolf. We have taken Australia, and are coming for what remains of the Republic on this world."* It wasn't a boast—merely the truth. *"But before we do, we must turn our attention to Atitjere."*

He gestured to the city under attack behind him. *"An hour ago, I ordered the civilians of Atitjere to evacuate. They provided assistance to a band of guerrilla fighters who attacked one of our repair bases. My Clan will not tolerate that kind of terrorism. In response, we are leveling the city entirely."*

Bastards, Stone fumed, his hands clenching into white-knuckled fists. *You miserable bastards!* "He is a four-star sonofabitch for broadcasting this!" he spat through gritted teeth.

Ward continued, *"Any community that supports or provides comfort to these partisans will find their homes, businesses, and livelihoods likewise destroyed. We follow the path of honor as laid out by Nicholas Kerensky and do not kill innocents, but we will not allow a handful of deluded rebels to threaten our operations. So look to Atitjere, and consider your actions carefully."*

The Wolf Khan stepped out of frame as the final stages of destruction began.

Lakewood shut off the holodisplay. "A powerful message," she said as the image faded away.

"It sure as hell is," snapped Brigadier General Andrew Turner, commander of Stone's Brigade. "We're counting on guerrilla operations as part of our long-term strategy. We should recall Ghost Knight Cloud, if we can find him."

Stone fought to rein in his fury. *Ghosts operate in the shadows. He is behind enemy lines—if alive at all.* "If we mount more guerrilla operations, all it will do is cost innocent people their homes, businesses, and livelihoods. The population now knows this. We need to shift away from that plan of attack. The use of such forces is no longer in the Republic's interest."

"Why Australia?" Lakewood asked. "For planetary assaults, Clans always target key cities and strategic military targets. Alaric only deployed in Australia. There's not even a 'Mech production facility there."

"He is unpredictable," Stone said through a clenched jaw. "And he doesn't need a 'Mech facility. There's an armor operation in Melbourne and munitions plants in Perth. Alaric looks to be playing a long game rather than a lightning-quick victory. We never anticipated he would land his entire force in one location, and the Glen Valley Castle Brian has been decommissioned for decades. It doesn't matter anyway—he won't remain there long. Given that he has opted for a beachhead in this invasion, it only makes sense that he will launch his next wave of attacks in Southeast Asia. We need to prepare for his next move as best we can."

"We could land troops there, shuttle them in," suggested General Turner. "Maybe even move troops into Glen Valley, and strike at him from there. Keep him bottled up in Australia."

"We've been over this before, General," Stone said. "The Castles Brian are a waste of resources when fighting an invading Clan force. The Wolves need visible targets, not hidden ones that will anger them into taking drastic measures we cannot afford to repel."

Redburn nodded his bandaged head slowly. "Stone is right. And shuttling in troops would just be sending them into a meat grinder. Alaric has tight lines of command and control, with his entire Clan at his disposal. We would be the ones that would be stretched. He took the aerospace fields in New Guinea yesterday. We throw everything we have in the region at him there, and he will devour us like the beast his Clan is named for. Trust me, I know."

"We have a strategy," Stone said. "It's always tempting to stray from it, but now is not the time. Our redoubts will whittle his invasion force down far more effectively than mass troops movements or staffing any of the mothballed Castles Brian can. So we stick to the plan. We need to let him come out, spread his forces thin. Then we can take him out—one command at a time."

We just have to do it before he does the same to us...

CHAPTER 6

SHEUNG FA SHAN
NORTH OF HONG KONG
TERRA
REPUBLIC OF THE SPHERE
20 JANUARY 3151, 0905 HOURS (T+10)

The journey to Hong Kong had encountered marginal resistance until Alaric reached the city.

Clan Wolf's massive fleet of DropShips had shuttled the forces into Vietnam, where the Wolf forces split in two. Chance had left with three Galaxies in-tow, heading west. Alaric and Garner Kerensky drove east, toward Hong Kong. Vietnam had seen Republic militias attempting to snipe at his supply lines along the coast with some degree of success. Pursuing the Republic troops had proved time consuming, and led to a number of small ambushes that inflicted an unacceptable number of casualties. Alaric then shuttled a large force from Delta Galaxy into the militia's rear, enough to rout them from the jungles they used for cover. All of which took time, which he did not like.

Alaric found himself oddly admiring Devlin Stone's calm. Any lesser commander would have thrown their entire military might at Alaric's Wolves, forcing a massive and decisive confrontation. The Clans salivated over such battles. They were quick, and the Clans, with their technological advantages, could often control these engagements.

But Stone was not playing that game. *He is sticking to his defenses around the redoubts, using them to slow us, whittle us down by attrition. I, too, have studied the Battle of Tukayyid, Exarch. What can be built by man can be dismantled by man.*

Sydney was the first redoubt his Clan had dealt with on Terra. The defensive belts were well planned, and had inflicted some damage. Each belt had to be dismantled under fire, carefully and meticulously. Some were simply destroyed. His aerospace fighters bombed corridors through minefields and strafed each pillbox Alaric's ground forces spotted. The Republic's own aerospace fighters often contested the ground-support attacks, proving to be worthy foes.

Alaric crested the hills overlooking Hong Kong as Wolf artillery rained down on the Republic's 102nd Armored Regiment, the Horde. A Star of his aerospace fighters bombed the Tsing Tsuen Bridge, cutting off the Republic forces trying to fall back to Tsing Yi Island. *Now their only way out is to the northeast*, he thought. *Through their own minefields.*

The Horde had used Hong Kong's redoubt and urban environment to their advantage. Battles in cities tended to be costly and dragged out, and the Republic's defenses were formidable. Turrets disguised as building HVAC systems or Dumpsters, organized vibramine fields—all had taken a toll on the Wolves, despite Alaric's efforts.

Until, at the suggestion of Ramiel Bekker, he had used aerospace fighters and artillery to blow corridors into the fortified city. Now his Wolves had the defenders hemmed into a small area in the Kwai Chung neighborhood.

It is time to end this.

Alaric activated his command channel. "WarBear, this is Wolf Prime. Analysis?"

Ramiel Bekker's calm voice filled his neurohelmet's speakers. "The Horde is mostly armor—a lot of DI Schmitts, hoverbikes, and JES missile carriers supporting a smaller number of BattleMechs. I recommend sending the Silver Keshik's jump-capable 'Mechs from the southeast—it will keep the Horde retreating to the northeast. Our northern forces should be able to cut off their path of retreat, then mop them up."

"Thank you." Alaric heard the distant rumble of artillery explosions wreaking havoc below. Plumes of white and gray smoke rose from the city as the Horde tried to weather the incoming barrages.

Alaric issued the Silver Keshik orders to engage, then added, "Hit them hard—hit them fast. Make them regret their attempt to fight here."

KWAI CHUNG, HONG KONG
1111 HOURS

Alaric steered his *Savage Wolf* around the corner of the tall building slowly, cautiously. His command Star flanked him on the streets to his right and left, but he held the center. Most of Beta Galaxy had extended into the Kwai Chung neighborhoods and the rising hills around the city, slowly flushing the defenders out of the redoubt.

The Republic defenders were fierce—a few minutes before, he had been raked with portable SRMs from an infantry platoon in a hardened building that, on the surface, looked like a grocery store. He had devastated the storefront, but there was no way to know for sure if he had killed his attackers or they had simply fallen back. As a result, such uncertainty made for slow going.

Alaric wanted this battle; he wanted to take on a redoubt himself. It was one thing to read a report, look at battleROM footage, but it was another to face his enemy. He wanted to see firsthand how the Republic had prepared; he wanted to soak in the details, mentally process the defenses, and find ways to break them. That was one of the reasons he had insisted on going in with Beta Galaxy at the front lines.

"Khan Ward," MechWarrior Sorsha signaled from her *Timber Wolf* the next street over. "I am picking up a reactor signature, moving from right to left, crossing you in two."

"Confirmed," he said, detecting it himself.

He slowly rounded the corner and saw his prey several blocks up—a hulking *Uraeus*. The 75-ton Republic 'Mech was pockmarked with blackened craters from missile hits. A nasty black laser scar ran across its front. It didn't notice Alaric approach; it was firing its Ultra-class autocannon at another target.

Sorsha emerged from her side street at the same moment. Faced with two foes, the *Uraeus'* MechWarrior unleashed its autocannon at Alaric. The exploding rounds tore into his *Savage Wolf*'s right side.

Clan honor demanded that he deal with this foe, no matter how much Sorsha desired the role. Alaric did not shirk from honor, he embraced it.

His own 'Mech had mangled armor plates on the legs, but his weapons were fully intact. Raising his ER large lasers, he aimed his targeting reticle over the upper body of the *Uraeus*. The millisecond he heard the weapons-lock tone, he hit the trigger.

Crimson beams sliced the *Uraeus* in the left arm and torso. The pilot jerked the 'Mech away, leaving a hot, glowing scar that melted the surrounding armor. Its turret-mounted Bombast laser swung toward Alaric and fired, hitting the mangled armor on his left leg with a brilliant red flash.

He felt the armor evaporate under the hit as he backpedaled around the corner. He smiled grimly. The *Uraeus* pilot was proving to be an admirable opponent.

And according to his sensors, the enemy 'Mech was turning toward him. *That is right—follow me*. Alaric nudged his 'Mech back into the *Uraeus'* line of sight, just enough to get the pilot's attention, then pulled back. Sorsha moved in closer, ready to engage if he fell, but knowing not to interfere. The enemy 'Mech loosed a salvo of laser, autocannon, and missile fire into the building and the air where Alaric had been. Dust and broken glass rained onto his *Savage Wolf*.

Now!

He sprang out from behind the building in the aftermath of those wasted shots. Full weapons lock sounded; he hit his thumb and finger triggers at the same time.

Alaric's alpha strike unleashed all of his weapons. Crimson beams from his large lasers raked across the *Uraeus'* upper body; hot splatters of metal pelted down on the ferrocrete road. Most of his ATMs found their marks, ripping away the last chunks of armor and digging deep into the body of the Republic war machine. One small pulse laser struck a building behind his target, but the other hit the cockpit. Its emerald bursts left more blackened scars around the canopy.

His reward was a soaring temperature in the cockpit, making it a searing sauna in a matter of seconds. He ignored the heat as he saw the *Uraeus* stagger back, then topple over, plowing into a restaurant and an apartment building. Flames erupted in the rubble where the BattleMech fell. His sensors told him at least one of his missiles had hit the enemy's fusion reactor.

"I yield," the fallen Republic warrior said over the open channel. "Hold your fire."

"Power down," Alaric commanded, "and you will be my prisoner. Do anything else, and you will die."

"Agreed," she said.

Alaric popped the faceplate of his neurohelmet, brushed sweat from his brow, and checked his sensors. The *Uraeus* was indeed shutting down, and his tactical display told him the bigger story unfolding around him.

The remnants of the Horde were breaking off from the Silver Keshik, heading northeast in a full rout. His *keshik* would pursue for several kilometers, whittling away at them, but his orders had been clear. They would leave survivors.

A part of Alaric was relieved. He had faced the defenses of the Republic and beaten them. For him, it was akin to beating their creator, Devlin Stone. The redoubts could be taken, not through a rush of battle, but with care and planning. This confirmed that ultimate victory over the Republic was possible, one defeated redoubt at a time.

A woman emerged from the wreckage of the fallen *Uraeus*. She was dark skinned, wet with sweat, and her near-black eyes glowed with rage. It was slow going with her neurohelmet in hand, climbing down the ruins of her once-proud BattleMech. When at last she found solid ground, she stood straight, glaring up at Alaric's 'Mech. "I am Brigadier General Leong of the 102nd."

The commander of the redoubt...how fortunate that I was the one that took her down. "I am Khan Alaric Ward," he announced through his external speakers "You will remove your sidearm and march west with your hands up. Your troops have fought well, General. I commend you."

"Khan Ward?" Her brows rose. "At least I did not fall to some grunt just out of his crèche. You may have won the day. Hong Kong is yours, but my troops who managed to get away will fight you again."

"Perhaps," Alaric replied with a confident smirk. "Then again, they might not. Now proceed to our lines for processing."

NORTHWEST OF CHITTAGONG

General Chance Vickers' *Savage Wolf* was painted exactly like Khan Ward's—a tactic that would cause confusion about Alaric's true location. It had been Spurlock Conner's idea, one she embraced. Republic troops would be looking for him, and having more than one BattleMech on more than one front that matched his would sow confusion in their enemies. It was one of the things she admired about Alaric, his use of the unorthodox. *We rarely employ such deception as a people... He is changing our game.* For her it was an honor.

The grand strategy called for Chance to lead a force west, along the Andaman Sea and the Bay of Bengal, sweeping on a wide front. The Bangalore redoubt was hers to take. Once secured, she would drive farther west, through the Middle East and the North African coast, and up into Italy. Alaric and Garner Kerensky would go north together, then split—with Garner driving west through Russia and Alaric securing parts of North America.

Time was a factor as well. Their plan for Nostos required that Clan Wolf secure certain geographies before the arrival of the Jade Falcons. For years, Chance had buried herself in the logistics and numbers associated with the plan. Alaric had assured Chance and the other leaders that Malvina would not attack Clan Wolf until the Republic of the Sphere surrendered. Holding a significant portion of Terra would control where the Jade Falcons could land, and what enemies they would face.

The reason for a second front was relatively simple. If Clan Wolf only operated in one region, it might allow the Republic to concentrate its forces. Splitting forces, dividing them before the enemy, forced the RAF to spread out. There were risks...namely that Stone might concentrate on one front and try to take it out piecemeal. But by maintaining the initiative and forcing the Republic to fight defensively, in several areas at once, Alaric hoped to mitigate such a risk.

There was another important aspect about a broad front, something Chance suspected, but Alaric rarely spoke of. He took Nicholas Kerensky's words literally. The Clan that conquered Terra was to be the ilClan. Alaric did not want just strategic targets, he wanted to *conquer* the whole of Terra. To do that meant seizing and holding ground.

The broad-front strategy also ensured good lines of transportation and supply. While the Wolves did have local air superiority, the Republic had proven most tenacious by targeting DropShips ferrying troops and supplies. The wider the front, the more exposed enemy incursions became—at least, that was the plan. The Republic, as it turned out, had its own plan. They had been deploying ground units for hit-and-run attacks along the coast, using enough force to go beyond a mere annoyance.

Now, to address such a threat, Chance climbed down the leg of her BattleMech to meet Galaxy Commander Niels Carns and Star Colonel Damon Ward of Epsilon Galaxy. As she arrived at the green camouflaged portable command dome, they saluted her, which still felt strange, but she returned the gestures. These two warriors had been her superiors until Alaric had promoted her to general and appointed her as his aide-de-camp with a field command.

Carns' tense expression told Vickers he was still coming to grips with being passed over for the position. Damon was far more supportive, since he was part of the small circle of Wolves who had known about Operation Nostos well before it had begun.

"They hit us again?" Vickers asked.

"*Aff*," Carns replied. "It is these accursed Tigers. Same pattern as before. They riddle us with inferno rounds, shoot at us long enough to inflict casualties, then run and hide before we can concentrate and pursue."

The Thai Tigers were a unit commissioned during the years Terra had enjoyed Fortress Republic's protection. From what Vickers could tell, the RAF had seeded the unit with veterans who knew how to engage and frustrate Clan warriors. *They believe they can control this engagement, and that is their mistake.*

"What are our losses this time?" she asked.

Carns grimaced. "Four BattleMechs, and nearly an entire Star of Wraith battle armor."

Vickers started to walk, forcing the two to follow her. She wanted to make sure Carns and Damon both understood who was leading this front. "The enemy seeks to slow us down," she said. "Bleed us with a thousand pinpricks."

"Let me take Epsilon and hunt them down," Galaxy Commander Carns said.

It is time to use our force as intended: as an army. "Neg, Galaxy Commander. This goes beyond a single commander going off on their own. We must coordinate our actions."

"General?" Carns asked.

She brushed the door flaps of the command dome aside and headed straight for the holotable. Carns and Damon gathered across from her as she activated the display.

"We are strung out along the coastal highway," she said, indicating the three-dimensional image of the region now lit up before them. "They are using the jungle for cover, hitting us as we move. So we will surround them, using our DropShips to maneuver. Gamma Galaxy will shuttle to the rear, Epsilon to the southeast, and Sigma here—to Raozan. All three Galaxies will converge on the Tigers."

Carns frowned. "With all due respect, General, the Thai Tigers struck at *my* Galaxy. They are my enemy to defeat. Honor demands it."

Alaric trusted me to act in his stead, and I must do so now. Chance squared her shoulders and met her subordinate's gaze. "They attacked the *Wolves*, Galaxy Commander, not just your Galaxy. You are fighting alongside your entire Clan now. Act like it. If we allow ourselves to get bogged down with every potential slight to our honor, we will not meet our timetable. These Tigers are slowing us down, and their raids must come to an end. If you want to redeem your honor, you can start by contributing to this battle plan."

She could see he was suppressing his frustration, but Carns reined in his pride...at least for the moment. "As you wish, General Vickers," he seethed.

Vickers nodded. "When we have them penned in, I want you and Epsilon there for the kill."

THE KARNAPHULI RIVER VALLEY
SOUTHEAST ASIA
TERRA
21 JANUARY 3151 (T+11)

An hour before daybreak, the Thai Tigers collided with Gamma Galaxy, the Wolf Hussars. As they fought, Chance launched her plan of attack. She led Epsilon

Galaxy, her old command, into the jungle, and ordered Sigma to close in from Raozan.

Meanwhile, Gamma turned the Tigers back, herding them into the Karnaphuli River valley—right in between Epsilon on one side of the river and Gamma Galaxy on the other.

For the first thirty minutes, the plan progressed as expected. Her role was to direct operations, with her Command Star held in reserve. It was a role she reveled in. When a Star's worth of Tigers attempted to break to the east, she had directed aerospace strafing runs to force them back into the trap. When Gamma stumbled into a minefield, she redirected their path of attack. *Never before have I had such power in my hands... Never has it seemed so right.*

Vickers maneuvered her *Savage Wolf* over the crest of the ridge overlooking the thick foliage of the valley. The area was alive with flashes of PPC fire, columns of smoke, and several brilliant beams of errant laser fire.

"General," Galaxy Commander Niels Carns said over the command channel. "We have a problem." There was something in the way he pronounced her rank, a tiny lilt in his voice, which rang of disrespect in her ears.

"Proceed."

"The Republic has mounted a strong counterattack in the center. We are holding the flanks, but the center is coming toward your position."

We have two Galaxies engaged...meaning these Tigers are better than we thought or have reinforcements we are unaware of. "Very well, we will move in to shore up the center."

Chance did what any Trueborn Clan warrior would do: she charged down the ridge to join the fray. Her sensors picked up enemy BattleMechs and tanks, but the jungle growth was so thick, she had line of sight on none of them.

As she advanced, she reached a clearing alongside a *Stormcrow* with MechWarrior Burger in the pilot's seat. On the far side of the clearing was a *Banshee* painted like a massive tiger, with a few smoldering hits in its armor. Ten suits of Kopis battle armor, all painted in the same brilliant tiger-stripe camouflage, surrounded the 'Mech and blazed away at the *Stormcrow*. The *Banshee* stalked Burger as well; one of its shots missed and destroyed a massive tree in a blast of splinters.

As Chance entered the clearing, the Tigers stared at her 'Mech for just a moment, reassessing the situation.

Then the Kopis troops sprang at both Wolves, filling the air with laser fire while the *Banshee* fired its pair of extended-range particle projection cannons.

"The Kopises are mine!" Burger cried over the tactical channel.

Vickers did not respond; she did not have time to. The *Banshee*'s brilliant white-and-blue flash enveloped her *Savage Wolf*, and she quickly reeled around. Damage displays showed hits high on her 'Mech's torso—the first damage she had taken in the campaign so far. *You will pay for that*, she thought as she aimed her targeting reticle at the *Banshee*. A Gauss-rifle round from the Tiger 'Mech streaked past her shoulder-mounted missile rack.

She heard the weapons-lock tone and fired her ATMs, then her ER large lasers. The lasers seared smoking streaks into the *Banshee*'s right arm; the warheads riddled its upper body, rocking it back.

Vickers angled back into the brush as the *Banshee* followed; behind it, she saw the Kopises rushing Burger, whose lasers vaporized one of the suits as they sprinted across the open ground. His challenge lay in facing an enemy 'Mech and the battle armor at the same time. Where Clan warriors fought foes with honor, usually in one-on-one duels, the Republic was not burdened with such thinking. Working together, the 'Mech and battle armor might wear him down and defeat him.

Vickers ignored the rising heat in her cockpit and fired her small lasers as her missiles reloaded. One laser missed entirely, firing off into the jungle; the others left pockmarks along the *Banshee*'s right arm.

It retaliated with its PPCs and Gauss rifle. The Gauss slug tore into her 'Mech's left leg below the knee actuator, knocking her back slightly—enough to avoid both PPC shots. The beams passed by so close the discharging particles seared a layer of paint off her armor.

Vickers fired again, first with her lasers, then the ATMs. Though everything hit this time, blasting gaping holes in the *Banshee*'s arm and leg, a wave of short-range missiles fired back at her and exploded across her arms and lower torso.

She accelerated around to the right, maneuvering to flank her foe as the enemy 'Mech made a slow turn, seemingly unafraid of her. It outmassed her, and it was ignoring Burger's *Stormcrow*. *They know how we fight and are using our honorable methods against us.* As she let the heat vent for a few precious seconds, she saw Burger still engaged with three of the Kopis armored suits, his lasers hitting jungle foliage more often than they hit fast-moving infantry.

The rest of her command Star had moved out to her far left, engaging a knot of Tigers 'Mechs and battle armor attempting to break through. *I need help—honor be damned.* She swung her targeting reticle around to the nearest pair of Kopis and fired her ATMs. The missiles were far more effective against the battle-armored troopers than Burger's lasers. The explosions caught them by surprise, sending limbs and bits of the armor spraying into the air.

Burger came on the tactical channel. "General, those were my enemies to defeat!"

"My apologies, MechWarrior. If you join me in defeating this 'Mech, the kill is yours."

"Bargained well and done!" Burger unloaded a salvo at the *Banshee* in response.

Chance stepped back, having yielded the honor to her fellow Wolf. Burger went to work, using his crimson laser beams like butcher knives to cut up the enemy as he swung around it in a deadly dance of death. It took only a few minutes for his shots to detonate the *Banshee*'s Gauss rifle. With that, the Republic 'Mech fell hard and plowed deep into the soft soil of the river valley. For a moment, Vickers and Burger stood nearby with weapons trained on the *Banshee*, making sure it stayed down.

"Your honor is intact, as is mine, *quiaff*?" Vickers said.

"*Aff*, General," said Burger, weary but pleased.

"Good. Let us see if we can find more of these Tigers before Galaxy Commander Carns destroys them all."

LUOHU
NORTH OF HONG KONG

Galaxy Commander Ramiel Bekker stepped into the mobile headquarters and stood before his Khan. The mobile HQ was a long, enclosed semitrailer, like an armored recreational vehicle, its roof covered with antennas and satellite-relay dishes. Its exterior was gray digital-urban camouflage, trying its hardest to not attract attention to itself.

"News from the western front," he announced. "General Vickers reports that the Thai Tigers are no longer operational. Only a reinforced company of them remained when they surrendered. Our forces have recovered a significant stockpile of munitions as well. The general has continued her advance along the coast, and will be in India tomorrow."

"Excellent." Alaric's trust in her had paid off. "Send the general my compliments."

"*Aff.*" Bekker inclined his head. "Meanwhile, almost an entire battalion of the Horde has broken out and is heading west."

Alaric nodded. "I trust that you and the TRC are up to the task of destroying them, *quiaff?*"

The WarBear grinned broadly. "It would be an honor."

Ramiel had enjoyed advising Alaric, but had been chafing for an opportunity to get into the fight himself. Alaric understood that feeling all too well. *Fighting on Terra—this is a battle every Clan warrior has dreamed of.*

"Then it is your honor to win."

The nearby communications officer called out. "Priority message from Star Admiral Sukhanov for Khan Ward."

Alaric moved over to the comms station. "What is it?"

"Jade Falcon WarShips have arrived at the zenith jump point. They are engaging the Republic bases and fleet there."

Alaric turned back to Bekker and smiled. "Malvina is coming."

COMMAND POST SOLITUDE
GENEVA

Devlin Stone turned to his intelligence chief. "Lady Miller, any word from Julian Davion?"

"No, sir," she replied. "The *Gaul* has not returned, and we are unable to receive any messages from outside the Fortress walls."

Countess Tara Campbell shifted in her seat enough to get Stone's attention, her brows high. *She isn't saying "I told you so," but she wants to.*

"He will come," Stone assured his Paladins. *He has to.* "Where are the Wolves?"

Lakewood pulled up a map of Terra. Australia was shown in shocking red, as was all of Southeast Asia, through Hong Kong and into the north. "Clan Wolf has taken most of southern China and is advancing north, toward Beijing.

We have some militia in the way of his drive, but not nearly enough. The Thai Tigers...well..."

"How bad?" asked Stone.

Campbell pulled up the report on her noteputer. "General Ratanapol surrendered early this morning. They fought right up to the end, Exarch."

His chest constricted at the news. "Tara, where is Alaric himself?"

"That's the thing," Campbell replied. "We have sightings of him on multiple fronts. Beta Galaxy is in China; it makes the most sense for him to be there. Still, we can't be sure. They use DropShips to shuttle themselves around, and it makes our intel somewhat unreliable."

Stone grimaced. *He's keeping us guessing.* "What of Anastasia Kerensky?"

Miller shook her head. "Nothing. Garner Kerensky has been spotted—but there's no sign of Anastasia. I have teams searching for her."

Stone did not like that. "Our intel said Garner Kerensky had disappeared and Anastasia was saKhan of the Wolves. Now Garner is back, and there's no sign of Anastasia. She is one of the best MechWarriors of her generation. It bothers me deeply that we haven't seen her yet."

Anastasia Kerensky's mysterious absence on the field of battle disturbed Stone more than he let on. For years, she had commanded several elite mercenary units, and had proven herself to be one of the best tactical fighters in the Inner Sphere. She had fought against the Republic, the Jade Falcons, the Wolves, and if reports were correct, she was the only person who had defeated Alaric Ward in single combat—having taken him prisoner for some time. *She is a dangerous element to ignore...making it worth the resources to locate her.*

Miller nodded. "If she is here on Terra, she is lying low for some reason."

No doubt she will appear at the most inconvenient time for us. "And this strategy of Ward's, conquering vast areas of territory? It isn't very Clan-like."

"No, it isn't," Campbell agreed. "He's using local air superiority and DropShips to move his troops at will. We have been hammering him with our aerospace elements, but the number of DropShips he uses provides him ample firepower. He suffered some losses in Hong Kong, but eventually cracked that nut. The speed of his advance is staggering. We are moving more troops into eastern Russia as a counterattack force, should he decide to turn west or north. We already have some troops in India."

"Is it time to reconsider our strategy of bleeding the Wolves on the redoubts?" Damien Redburn asked. "Because Janella and I have a potential modification."

Stone grimaced, but nodded. "Let's hear it."

Lakewood gestured to the map. "I suggest moving the Fourteenth Hastati Sentinels to China under the command of Tyrina Drummond. We will go right for the jugular: Beta Galaxy, Alaric's personal command. The Fourteenth Hastati is one of our best units. Let's see how he deals with that. We intended to have forces mount counterattacks outside the redoubts, but so far they've only had marginal success. The Fourteenth is tough, and Tyrina will maul Beta Galaxy if given a chance."

Stone nodded. "It is still our strategy to use the redoubts, but let's shake things up for Alaric. Deploy the Fourteenth."

Miller glanced at her noteputer, and Devlin saw her face fall. "Exarch, we have a flash message from Admiral Labbé."

Stone nodded. "Show me."

The Admiral's face appeared on the holodisplay, replacing the map. His white mustache drooped, and he seemed pale, like he had been after the battle with Clan Wolf at the nadir jump point. Worry and concern showed in every wrinkle.

"Exarch, we have multiple WarShips and JumpShips emerging at the zenith jump point. We are currently engaging the entire Jade Falcon navy."

CHAPTER 7

**CAMERON-CLASS BATTLECRUISER CJF *TURKINA'S PRIDE*
ZENITH JUMP POINT
REPUBLIC OF THE SPHERE
21 JANUARY 3151, 1723 HOURS (T+11)**

Chingis Khan Malvina Hazen seethed at the images she saw in the holotank. Her Jade Falcon task force had emerged at the jump point between two stationary defense bases. On top of that, a nearby squadron of Republic Navy vessels had just started firing a maelstrom of shots into her fleet.

Alaric left this for us, she thought. *I hope he suffered when he jumped into the system.*

"Helm!" called Star Admiral Sharizal Binetti, turning from the holotank beside Malvina. "Bring us about! Port batteries, stand by for new firing solutions. Comms, tell *Red Talon* to engage emergency thrust to get out of range of that station."

Turkina's Pride began its turn, forcing Malvina toward the bulkhead. She grasped a handhold with her bionic hand, ignoring the stress in her shoulder. The ship quaked a few seconds later under incoming fire.

The tactical officer looked over from his post. "Star Admiral, port batteries have firing solutions on the closest station."

"Fire at will," Binetti commanded grimly.

There was a thundering sound from the *Cameron*-class battlecruiser's autocannon turrets and a humming purr as the heavy naval PPCs discharged. Malvina's gaze darted to the viewscreen, and she watched the shots tear into the saucer-like station, peeling off armor plating and propelling debris into the darkness of space.

"Incoming fire from *Abundantia*," Judith, the ready-alert officer, called. "And missiles incoming from the station."

"All hands, brace for impact," Binetti commanded. *Turkina's Pride* emitted a low rumbling noise as missiles erupted along the hull. "Helm, give me a slow starboard arc around that station. Put that station between us and *Abundantia*, then kill our speed so we can saturate it."

Again, Malvina felt the ship lurch, pushing her body under the g-forces of the maneuver. When Alaric had provided Stephanie Chistu with the means to penetrate Fortress Republic, he had designated the zenith jump point for her Clan's destination. The Republic had prepared it with two large saucer-like defense stations, which her forces had jumped right on top of. Adding to that, Alaric had not destroyed all of the Republic WarShips. *I hope he suffered under the same firepower at his jump point.*

Alaric had granted her *safcon* to Terra, but there were conditions. First, she would not come at his Wolves until the Republic had been dealt with. Second, Alaric had claimed the nadir jump point for his Clan, and had told Malvina that Mars and the zenith jump point were hers to deal with. She was tempted to violate these terms, especially after the humiliation Alaric had bestowed on her at Tharkad, leaving her to clean up his mess. Still, Malvina held to her honor. *This is no ordinary battle, this is for everything—the ilClanship. My victory needs to be clean, as honorable as possible.*

"*Red Talon* has lost its engines," the comms officer barked.

Binetti moved in the holotank like a predator, zooming in on the image, narrowing her eyes, wetting her lips. "Acknowledged. Order *Jade Tornado* to get in point-blank range to provide coverage. Signal *Jade Talon* to concentrate fire on the second base."

"Incoming fire," the ready-alert officer announced.

Everyone on the bridge grabbed something to steady themselves as a wave of missiles detonated along the hull.

"Damage report," said Binetti.

"Portside naval laser turrets are unresponsive," said the damage-control officer. Another rumble shook the ship. "And our forward AR-10s are offline."

Muscles strained along Binetti's cheek. "I am through with this shit," she spat. "Helm, keel roll. Bring the starboard batteries around, and tighten our arc fifteen degrees."

The sensors officer, Roberta, turned to them, her face redder than it had been minutes earlier, prior to the jump to Terra. "Star Admiral, Republic fighters are maneuvering for our DropShips."

"Send in the Soaring Falcons Cluster. Signal *Jade Aerie* and *Blue Talon* to break off from the Republic vessels and make a hot burn for the DropShips to provide cover."

Another hit sounded—louder, closer. Malvina did not flinch. *I will not die out here. Fate will not deny me the ilKhanship.*

On the viewscreen, a fast-moving Jade Falcon assault DropShip erupted in a brilliant flash. Massive chunks of the ship continued on their original trajectory, still burning. Sharizal pounded her fist on the upright support on the holotank.

The closest defense station continued to belch missiles into the Jade Falcon vessels swarming around it. The base itself looked crumpled and mangled thanks to all the incoming fire. Tiny explosions flickered along its hull. It was a wonder it could still fight back.

The tactical officer called out, "Starboard batteries in position."

"Tear that base apart," Binetti growled.

The entire hull rumbled and throbbed as the ship's massive firepower unloaded on the base. The impacts devastated the saucer-like station's hull. The outer edge crumbled and melted, and the maneuvering thrusters could not correct the station's slow roll. Still, the base released a steady barrage of missiles. Another Jade Falcon assault DropShip careened away from its pass on the station. Malvina could see gases from holes in the hull streaming in the ship's wake.

The Republic is putting up a fight, she thought. *It will make their defeat something to savor.*

RSS *ABUNDANTIA*

Admiral Labbé grinned as *Abundantia*'s missiles tore holes into a Jade Falcon DropShip—holes big enough to disgorge the ship's cargo of BattleMechs and vehicles into space.

"Helm," he said, "wide sweep to port. Bring us in line to get another pass at *Jade Talon*."

"Aye aye, Admiral."

As the ship came about, Labbé allowed himself a thin smile. The arrival of Clan Jade Falcon—almost on top of Forts Grec and Abernathy—had been a surprise, but only for a moment. *A target is a target, and these invaders are targets just like the Wolves.*

What was left of his aerospace fighters had dived in on the Jade Falcon DropShips and scored numerous hits. Now Jade Falcon fighters swarmed the battle en masse, but the damage was already done.

The ready-alert officer called out, "We have two incoming Falcon WarShips, Admiral—*Blue Talon* and *Jade Aerie*. *Aegis* and *Black Lion*-classes. They are approaching the DropShips likely to provide cover fire."

We are in no shape to face two WarShips like that. "Helm, adjust course and cross the *T* with *Jade Talon*. Comms, tell *Fire of the Republic* to disengage from the DropShips and follow us in line."

Admiral Labbé's eyes darted to the screen that showed Fort Grec. A barrage of naval autocannon fire silently blasted the station's squat-round hull. The station's lights flickered off, on, then off again, plunging it into darkness. As another weapon hit it, a flash from a naval PPC, it began to drift. *Damnation and hellfire!*

"Are we in range of the *Jade Talon* yet?" he asked the weapons officer.

"Coming into extreme range in ten seconds," said Captain Dunlap, who hovered near the gunnery station.

"Hit them with a full broadside," Labbé barked.

The big ship rolled around him, and the admiral grabbed a handhold to maintain his orientation as the weapons batteries were brought into alignment. The *Abundantia* roared from its naval autocannon fire, followed a few moments later with the humming of the big naval lasers. The sensor officer splashed up the image of the target vessel for the entire bridge crew to see.

From his raised seat on the bridge, Admiral Labbé could see the holes torn in the *Jade Talon*'s hull. Gas and several bodies spewed out into space as *Abundantia* made its pass. The Falcon WarShip's drive plumes flickered, then went out altogether.

A cheer rose from the bridge crew, and Labbé smiled grimly. *Welcome to Terra, you green bastards.*

"Admiral," called the comms officer, "message from Fort Abernathy. Commodore Chapman on a secured channel."

"Put him through," said Labbé.

The viewscreen flickered and Commodore Kim Chapman appeared. The bridge behind him was filled with smoke and crew members scrambling to get into emergency evac suits. His lean face was barely visible through the fogged-up faceplate on the emergency suit helmet.

"Admiral," said Chapman, "Fort Grec is gone. The Falcons are blowing up their lifeboats." His voice trembled with shock and frustration.

Labbé sat back, his momentary smile gone. *It is senseless slaughter...I should have expected no less from Malvina Hazen.*

Chapman continued, unconcerned with struggling into an evac suit of his own. "We are manually transferring missiles to the two launchers we have left. Our engineering section has been breached, and personnel there are unresponsive. We need to evacuate, but if we do, we are signing our death sentence."

Labbé nodded. "Helm, emergency course change. Bring us alongside Fort Abernathy. Order our retrieval units to stand by to pick up survivors."

Chapman's shoulders sagged with relief. "Thank you, Admiral."

"Can you hold out until we get there?"

"Do I have a choice?"

Labbé smiled grimly. "Get your people ready."

CJF *TURKINA'S PRIDE*

"Star Admiral, message from *Jade Talon*," the comms officer called out.

"To the tank," Binetti said.

Star Captain Krzysztof Von Jankmon appeared on the display. He was wearing his emergency suit and floating on a dark, empty bridge. "Star Admiral," he said, his crackling voice breathy through his helmet microphone. "We are adrift without power. Our reactor is blown, and a surge fried our primary power systems and backups."

Malvina watched Binetti carefully from her place in the holotank. *This is our first fleet action in decades. Does Sharizal have the blood of the Jade Falcon in her veins?*

She hated the space battle. Not out of fear, but out of a feeling of uselessness. Like all Jade Falcons, she had been trained in naval strategy and tactics at an early age, but her area of specialization was ground operations. For most of this fight, she could do nothing—it was as if she did not matter, and that galled her to no end. Trust in others, even loyal members of her Clan, did not come easy, and in a naval battle, her fate was less her own, and more in the hands of warriors like Binetti. *The sooner we make landfall, the faster I can do what I do best.*

"Understood," Binetti replied. "Any chance of salvage?"

"Doubtful. If the blast hit where I think it did, our K-F drive has been damaged."

Malvina floated in beside the Star Admiral. "The Republic is breaking off, *quiaff*?"

"*Aff*, Chingis Khan," Binetti said, studying the tactical display. "It appears they are heading off on the same vector, likely to a rendezvous or other waypoint."

"Pursue them," Malvina ordered.

Binetti hesitated only a moment. "My Khan, we have secured the jump point. The route to Terra and Mars is open. If we turn from our course to pursue that handful of broken ships, it will delay our landing on Terra by days—"

The crew around them held their breath.

Malvina eyed her with a bit of contempt—and also a hint of respect for daring to speak up. *She is right to point this out. The real fight is on Terra.*

"Very well, Star Admiral," she said through her teeth. "Proceed to Terra. But if those surviving Republic ships intervene in any way, I will hold you personally responsible." It was not a threat—it was validation of fact.

Binetti's sigh of relief was quick and quiet, but Malvina noticed it all the same. "*Aff*, Chingis Khan."

It was time to head to Terra. *Stone, Ward, Kerensky...we are coming for you all.*

COMMAND POST SOLITUDE
GENEVA
TERRA
21 JANUARY 3151, 1757 HOURS (T+11)

Devlin Stone sat with Tucker Harwell in the otherwise empty conference room as word came in via holodisplay. "How big is the remaining Jade Falcon task force?" he asked Admiral Labbé, glowing on the display in the dim room.

"Not as large as Clan Wolf's," Labbé replied. "We took out one of their WarShips, three of their assault DropShips, and badly damaged or destroyed more than a dozen of their troop-carrying DropShips. They have most in tow, which means they can salvage some of their cargo and any survivors."

"You still have a functional fleet?"

Labbé grimaced. "'Functional' may be a strong word. I adhered to your operational orders, salvaging what I could for future operations. I have the surviving ships rallying at Waypoint Trafalgar to resupply and repair. We are all low on missiles and naval autocannon rounds. The *Abundantia* is missing half of its weapons systems. At best, I have five ships—if we can do field repairs on *Shield of the Republic* and get *Triumphus* to operate under its own power. We have enough for one more good fight, if it's a short one. Give me the word, Exarch, and I will face them one more time."

Stone shook his head. "Not yet. We need to assess the situation before I commit your task force. I will be in touch." He turned off the communication console.

"Was *this* part of your plans?" Tucker asked as the admiral's holographic image flickered away.

"No," Stone replied. *Not yet, at least. I have contingencies in place that you cannot fathom.* "We knew the Jade Falcons would eventually find a way through the Fortress Wall. Just not this soon."

"We're already in the middle of an invasion," Harwell said, a note of panic in his voice. "Now *Malvina Hazen* is burning in toward us. Against one Clan, we stood a good chance. Against two..."

Devlin forced a smile. "Have some faith, Tucker. This is not the end. This was just our first round with the Jade Falcons, and we bloodied them. Our day is coming. The farther Clan Wolf pushes, the thinner their lines get—making them vulnerable. Each redoubt eats away at their strength. The time is coming when we will launch counterattacks that send the Wolves scrambling back to Australia, and eventually, to their defeat."

CHAPTER 8

CLAN WOLF FIELD HQ
LUOYANG, CHINA
TERRA
27 JANUARY 3151 (T+17)

The last five days had been a whirlwind for Clan Wolf.

Having secured Hong Kong, Alaric rested his forces for a day of repairs and refit, then began driving north, into the mountainous regions of central China. It had been slow going, with each highway Alaric tried to use carefully staged for an ambush. BattleMechs could be repaired or replaced—and he had brought plenty—but every death of a warrior hurt Clan Wolf.

On the western front, Chance Vickers had encircled the Bangalore redoubt and was tightening the noose on its defenders. Progress was slow, and the Republic had surprised her with a massive aerospace strike, designed to break off her assault. The Wolves had been bombed and strafed until she had brought in her own aerospace forces, massed for the first time since the battles for Australia. From the footage she had relayed to Alaric, the dogfights over India had been spectacular, and in the end, the Republic, despite inflicting losses, had pulled back.

No doubt they refuse to commit everything because of Malvina Hazen's presence in the system, Alaric thought. *She has not even landed yet, but is already proving useful.*

He had had no communication with the Jade Falcon Khan yet, nor did he expect to. From what Star Admiral Sukhanov had told him, the Falcons were progressing to Terra on a standard burn, and Malvina had sent an attack force to Mars, a little gift Alaric had left for her to deal with.

There was an odd satisfaction with the arrival of Clan Jade Falcon. Alaric had counted on Malvina to be unable to resist coming—but there had always been a chance she would refuse his invitation. Some of his officers thought her erratic, but Alaric knew she possessed excellent military acumen. *Having her here means all of the key players are at the proverbial table.* That he had been the impetus of her coming gave him a feeling of control. *If I had not invited her, she would have found a way here on her own, and that would have introduced a random factor into an already dangerous situation.*

Three days into the Wolves' northern drive through China, the Republic had launched a counterstrike with the Fourteenth Hastati Sentinels, led by Paladin Tyrina Drummond. These were some of the best troops of the Republic, and it showed in their ferocity. The engagements with them had been some of the most vicious fighting he had witnessed since the battles against the Redburn Guards.

The Fourteenth had hit Beta and Tau Galaxies twice in two days. Tau's Galaxy Commander, Victoria Conners, had been badly wounded in one onslaught, though she insisted on returning to duty before the medtechs would clear her. In both attacks, the Fourteenth had fought with tenacity—then fell back to the west. It was such a deliberate maneuver, and Alaric refused to take the bait, ordering his warriors not to pursue. *I will not play the Republic's game*, he thought. *Instead, they will play mine.*

Galaxy Commander Ramiel Bekker entered the mobile HQ and strode toward Alaric and the holodisplay. "Your instincts were right, my Khan. Our aerial recon tells us there is a reason Paladin Drummond's troops are trying to pull you west."

He toggled the map. The highway running east and west to Zhengzhou flickered to life on the display, showing a series of red dots concentrated to the west. "From the looks of it," said Bekker, "they rushed some of their elite units forward along this highway, which is who we have been facing. More than half of their forces are still coming up along the road. She wants to feign falling back to lure us toward the bulk of her forces."

Alaric frowned at the map. "How long until they reach us if we just stay in position?"

"We give it five days."

And when they arrive, Paladin Tyrina Drummond will have more elite troops and her other forces to throw at us. "We need to hit them first," he said. "If we can deprive the Fourteenth of these fresh troops, they will be vulnerable. We can use DropShips to send a Cluster to deal with them."

Bekker nodded, but couldn't hide his growing frown.

Alaric cocked an eyebrow. "You disagree, *quiaff*?"

"*Aff.* These Hastati Sentinels are unlike the Republic units we have faced before. They are experienced warriors under a proven, battle-hardened field commander, a Paladin from Devlin Stone's inner circle. They will see our DropShips coming. I would."

Alaric raised his other eyebrow. "I trust you have a solution."

"I do." Bekker gestured to the map, where a river ran parallel to the highway. "The locals dammed the Yellow River some time ago. The depth makes it almost impossible to detect reactor signatures. We can use it like a hidden highway to move along their flank."

That is quite a solution. Alaric zoomed in on the display. "We will need to convince Tyrina Drummond that we are still here, not moving to flank her."

"My thoughts exactly. We need a diversion, something that will keep her attention focused here, while the bulk of Beta and elements of Tau move for a flanking maneuver out of the river. An officer commanding such a force will need to convince the enemy that they are much more numerous than they are. This will require...audacity."

That word triggered an immediate choice in his mind. Alaric activated the communications link. "Send me Star Colonel Kalidessa Kerensky." The mention of her name made Ramiel Bekker flash a broad smile.

Kalidessa's reputation for tenacity and daring arrived before she did. Three minutes later, a tall, pale woman with slicked-back fiery-red hair entered. Her sweaty, coolant-stained T-shirt was emblazoned a Clan Wolf logo, with the wolf's jaw open and snarling—the insignia of the Second Wolf Assault Cluster, which she had nicknamed the Howling Furies just prior to the invasion. It was clear she had just come from working on her 'Mech. The aroma of sweat and lubricant came with her like an invisible fog. "You asked to see me, my Khan?"

"Star Colonel," Alaric said, beckoning her closer for a better view of the map. "Commander Bekker and I have a mission for your Cluster—and a Cluster from Tau, temporarily under your command."

Kalidessa smiled. "I am ready, as always."

"I need you to attack the Fourteenth Hastati Sentinels." Alaric indicated them on the map. "It is a risky mission, but you are more than capable."

"I will destroy them," she said proudly.

"*Neg*," Bekker said. "Just hold their attention. I want them to think they are facing the entirety of Beta and Tau Galaxies."

"What is my support?"

"No support."

Kalidessa winced at that.

"You are a diversion," Alaric continued. "You are to convince them and their commander that they are facing an entire Galaxy of force while we move on their flank."

Kalidessa paused. "Have I done you a disservice or disappointed you, my Khan?"

"*Neg*. Why do you ask?"

"The enemy has hit us three times in the last few days. The Hastati Sentinels are elite fighters. Sending me up against them, alone, could be interpreted as a suicide mission. My Howling Furies are up to it, but we had hoped to see this war to the end."

Alaric appreciated her bluntness. "On the contrary, Kalidessa. I am assigning you this mission because you are good, *very* good. If anyone can convince Paladin Drummond's troops that they are facing a Galaxy or more, it is you. There are few I would trust with this task. I want you to hit them, bloody them, and fall back, over and over again. Do not get lured into a trap. Drummond will try to goad you into moving west—do not do it. Keep their attention above all else. And one more thing," he said with a smile. "If it will put your mind at ease, I am counting on your survival."

"Understood," Kalidessa replied, smiling back. "When do we move out?"

"Tomorrow. I will send you timetables and your planned axis of attack. You are dismissed, Star Colonel."

"My Khan. Commander." She nodded to Alaric and Ramiel, then did an about-face and left the mobile HQ.

Alaric powered down the map. "Let us get to work."

LUOYANG
CHINA
TERRA
29 JANUARY 3151 (T+19)

For two days Kalidessa Kerensky and her Howling Furies, along with the additional attached units, had fought battles against the Fourteenth Hastati Sentinels. The engagements had a pattern, though she doubted the RAF forces saw it. Painted like a different Wolf Clan unit each time, her warriors would attack, usually riddling the Fourteenth's front line. When Drummond's troops tried to lure Kalidessa's in by falling back, she would use the opportunity to break off. Then it was back to the field-repair station to be rearmed, repaired, and painted like a different Cluster. *At this point, my 'Mech probably has enough coats of paint to qualify as additional armor.*

The cost, however, had been high. The Hastati Sentinels were much better than the other Republic forces the Wolves had faced thus far. Paladin Drummond used them masterfully. She didn't just want to lure the Howling Furies in, she wanted to outright destroy them. Kalidessa's attack force had lost several 'Mechs and tanks already. While replacements were available, the constant hit-and-run strikes were beginning to take a toll on the Wolf warriors. Few were sleeping, and between engagements, most looked like zombies— their faces devoid of expression, a stagger in their walk. *I hope we are buying enough time for the Khan and the WarBear...*

The morning assault had shifted its axis of attack. Rather than use the road network to travel through the rocky terrain, the Second Wolf Assault Cluster was pushing across the rugged ground in a wide arc, hoping to catch Drummond's force off guard. Along with the hasty paint jobs, Kalidessa hoped it would further the illusion of different units being employed in the fight.

Her gray and brown *Dire Wolf* fired its Gauss rifle and all three large pulse lasers at a massive, four-legged Republic *Lich* drone. The slug hit the *Lich* in the right foreleg, furrowing deep into the armor and leaving a hole with glowing-yellow edges. When the enemy 'Mech flinched back, it avoided one of Kalidessa's pulse lasers—but the other two left gray smoking holes in both forelegs.

The *Lich* rallied, firing its light Gauss rifles. One shot went wide; the other plowed into her 'Mech's torso, denting the armor plating. Kalidessa growled in frustration.

She advanced and swung into a low copse of trees, keeping her reticle on the *Lich*. Just beyond it, she saw Druss Ward's *Timber Wolf* unleash a devastating salvo of missiles into what was left of a light-gray Republic *Peacemaker*, engulfing the 'Mech in explosions and toppling it.

The *Lich* suddenly jerked and fell back to the west.

Not this time. Kalidessa unloaded her pulse lasers again, hitting the 'Mech's rear in a tight pattern to disintegrate the armor. The drone paused mid-stride, noticing the damage—and she fired a Gauss round right into the weakened spot.

The *Lich* hit the ground.

She sighed. *There is little honor in killing a drone. No one pleading for their life. No bondsmen to claim.*

"They are falling back again," Druss called out. "Permission to pursue."

"*Neg.* Return to the depot so the techs can throw on new paint. The next time we hit them, I want them to think we are a different unit. You have your orders—comply."

Their time is coming, even if it is not at my hand.

YELLOW RIVER
CHINA
TERRA
3 FEBRUARY 3151 (T+24)

In the murky brown water, Khan Ward had to maneuver his *Savage Wolf* more with his sensors than his eyes and intuition. Even running with infrared didn't help under water. The attack force in the river stirred the silt, making visual and sensor sighting difficult.

Beta Galaxy and elements of Tau were nearly in position, moving carefully against the current as they came alongside the highway. Somewhere nearby, columns of the Fourteenth Hastati Sentinels were moving east, to where Paladin Drummond and her lead elements were slugging it out against Kalidessa Kerensky's force.

Conventional-infantry scouts on the far bank of the river watched and waited for the Fourteenth's arrival. They would be strung out, exposed.

"Echo-Wolf Squad," said the Tau Galaxy Squad Commander on the far bank. "Enemy force is almost in position. One minute."

Alaric switched to the tactical channel. "Wolf Prime to strike forces. We do this by the numbers. Everyone select a separate target. We need to hit them hard as our vehicles advance up the highway. Do this right, and we will avenge Galaxy Commander Victoria Conners." He knew his last words would stoke fire in the hearts of the Tau warriors, as Conners had died in a different attack after her initial injuries several days ago.

The comm channel crackled. It was the Tau Galaxy Squad Commander: "Enemy force is in position."

Alaric gave the order: "Wolves—*attack!*"

He emerged from the river and charged up the embankment. Muddy water poured off his cockpit canopy as his tracking system plotted all of the enemy targets. There they were—lined up along the edge of the river, turning in surprise as the Wolves surged from the water.

He locked onto a Republic *Peacekeeper*. The missile-lock tone sounded, and he let loose his large lasers and advanced tactical missiles. Eighteen ATMs bore in on the *Peacekeeper's* right leg and side, throwing chunks of armor skyward. Alaric steered his 'Mech back down the embankment so the cool river could help vent his heat.

The *Peacekeeper* reeled under the attack, as did most of the Republic force along the highway. The *Jackalope* beside it lost an arm, which hit the *Peacekeeper's* legs, nearly tripping it. Staggering, it fired its large laser and heavy PPC at Alaric. The laser slashed across his 'Mech, but the PPC discharge hit the river, lighting up the water around him in a sheet of blue light.

The *Peacekeeper* pilot fired their jump jets, leaping off the bank and descending toward the river. Alaric followed and switched his comms to a tactical channel. "Star Colonel Kerensky—your time has come. Marshal your forces and head to our position."

"With pleasure, my Khan," Kalidessa replied.

Just before the *Peacekeeper* touched down, Alaric fired his large lasers and another salvo of ATMs. The Republic BattleMech raised its right arm to fire its heavy PPC and plasma rifle, and managed a shot just before Alaric's weapons blasted the arm backward, ripping it off. Hot yellow plasma seared his 'Mech, and wisps of steam rose from around his submerged legs from the heat he was generating.

The damage and loss of mass unbalanced the *Peacekeeper*. It toppled, falling onto its left arm. Alaric's next salvo riddled its damaged flank; two missiles punched through the armor and tore into the internal mechanisms. The air rippled as heat spilled from the fusion reactor. His next laser shots stabbed into the back of the enemy 'Mech's head, furrowing deep. The *Peacekeeper* seized up, then dropped and lay still.

Alaric turned away. *That pilot died a warrior's death.*

Down the line, Wolves were tearing the Fourteenth apart. The enemy forces still on the highway were starting to fall back eastward, apparently to link up with the part of Drummond's force that faced Kalidessa Kerensky.

"This is Wolf Prime to all forces," said Alaric. "Advance out of the riverbed and pursue, and let us show these Hastati the definition of retribution."

OVERLORD-C-CLASS DROPSHIP *CLAW OF THE FALCON*
ON APPROACH TO TERRA
3 FEBRUARY 3151 (T+24)

Malvina Hazen was satisfied that the fighting she had encountered in the Terran system so far was worthy of her Jade Falcons. *Of course Alaric left defenses for us to deal with.* She respected that; she would have done the same thing.

At the moment, her people were fighting on Mars, battling with the Republic defenders there. It was not the battle she wanted. *Fighting on Mars is isolated, no chance to exploit victory.* Still, it could not be ignored. Mars had a garrison, aerospace fighters, and a dozen DropShips at its disposal. From its orbital path, it was well situated to strike at any forces burning in from the zenith jump point—and the Jade Falcons would be coming in as they mobilized from the occupation zone. Having a Republic garrison along her supply route presented a risk her strategic planning could not ignore.

The communications system in her *Shrike*'s cockpit chirped. "Message from the Exarch for you," the communications officer said, strained.

"Excellent," said Malvina. "Put Exarch Levin through."

The image on the holodisplay flickered, then she saw a very old man. His wrinkles were disgusting to her, a mark of a warrior far past his prime. To her welcome surprise, this was not Jonah Levin, but Devlin Stone. Stone had disappeared over a decade ago, presumed dead. *Now it appears I have the honor of crushing one of the greatest military minds of the last era.* It made the conquest of Terra all that more appealing.

"Khan Hazen," Stone said.

"*Chingis* Khan," Malvina corrected. "It is a title worthy of the ilClan— though you may not need to know it long, since I will see you and your Republic of the Sphere dead and buried once we land."

"Khan Ward and Clan Wolf have already landed," said Stone, ignoring her correction. "Weeks ago. But you are here, however late, to contest their claim to the ilClanship."

Malvina tried not to bristle. "In due time. If it is your hope that my Falcons face Clan Wolf when we land, perish that thought. We will deal with your Republic first. Once we have gutted you, *then* I will address the Wolves and any claims they might make. That is a matter for *Trueborn* warriors, not decrepit relics such as you."

She was pleased to see that the old man appeared shaken by her reply. "Your reputation precedes you, Malvina Hazen. We will fight you, no quarter asked or given. You will not do here what you did on Wotan and Blackjack."

"I expect nothing less," she said. "Prepare to experience what the Inner Sphere will face under my rule."

She cut off the transmission without waiting for a response. "Comm," she barked, "contact Khan Ward."

It took three minutes to establish the link with Alaric. His neurohelmet framed his face; clearly he was broadcasting from his BattleMech. "Khan Hazen."

"Chingis Khan is my title," she replied, almost daring him to challenge it.

"That title has no meaning to the Clans," said Alaric. "But you may call yourself whatever title you wish. I bid you welcome to Terra. I will have my logistics officer send you our areas of operation so you can avoid landing on territory Clan Wolf has already claimed in battle."

Malvina's smile at his words was devoid of humor or warmth. "We will land where we wish."

Alaric frowned. "My message to Galaxy Commander Chistu stated that we invited you here with the understanding that you came to fight the Republic of the Sphere first. If you violate that understanding, you will sacrifice your honor and pay dearly for such a betrayal. Many Clan warriors would refuse to follow anyone who would trample on honor so carelessly."

Malvina glowered back at him. "Do not worry about the honor of Clan Jade Falcon, Khan Ward, it is not your concern. If it puts you at ease, I have not come this far to fight you...yet. Send us your positions, and we will honor the territory you have taken. But once we crush the Republic, we will rend your Wolves completely and utterly. I have not forgotten your attempt to manipulate me at Tharkad. Soon you will bow before me and call me Chingis Khan. You will know defeat at the hands of the superior Clan, and watch my Jade Falcons eradicate every trace of the Wolves that ever existed." She spoke not with fiery bravado, but the casual certainty of someone reading a to-do list. "I will take your life. And I will build an empire on the dust of the Inner Sphere."

"Brave words, Malvina Hazen," said Alaric, unmoved. "But words do not win wars. You speak of empires? I have already built one. I do not waste time with empires. I will build a *dynasty*, one that will last centuries."

"You can try, pup," she countered. "I cannot wait to see your face when you have lost everything...including your dreams of a so-called Wolf dynasty."

And she cut off the communications channel.

SUBURBS OF ZHENGZHOU
CHINA
TERRA
4 FEBRUARY 3151 (T+25)

Constant strikes against the Fourteenth Hastati Sentinels had whittled Star Colonel Kalidessa Kerensky's force down by a third. When Khan Ward's attack force hit the enemy's flank along the river, she could have just dug in and awaited the linkup with her Khan as he drove toward them. Given how weary and battle-worn her unit was, it would have been the safe move.

But Kalidessa Kerensky did not play things safe.

She ordered her unit to strike out—not as a diversion, but to complete the linkup. It led them to the suburbs of Zhengzhou, a city along the Yellow River. The battle was winding down, sputtering into a string of individual fights rather than a cohesive onslaught, a sign that the Fourteenth Hastati were finally nearing their end.

From the driver's seat of his massive Carnivore assault tank, Warrior Hawkins maneuvered through the field of battle that ran through the city. His maroon-and-yellow-streaked 80-ton tank, *Fratricide*, had already engaged several enemy vehicles, destroying a JES Missile Carrier and finishing off an *Awesome* that had blasted away a lot of *Fratricide*'s frontal and left-side armor. *We will need another refit after this,* he thought, *but we still have plenty of protection.*

Their Star was part of the Second Wolf Assault Cluster of the Howling Furies of Beta Galaxy. A mixed-forces Star, they served Star Colonel Kerensky and had weathered some of the more brutal fighting. Hawkins respected the Star Colonel's tenacity, if not her desire to constantly throw his Star at the Hastati. *If all of the Republic units fight like this, it will take a long time to seize Terra. Does she keep sending us in because she honors us, or because she wants us dead?*

Hawkins was proud of what he and his gunner, DuJordan, had contributed to this fight. Hawkins was getting old, due for posting to a *solahma* unit in a year or two. The fight for Terra might very well be his last campaign, so achieving glory in the name of the Clan was important to him.

He picked up a signal from his far left, on a rise overlooking the suburb...a perfect vantage point. The transponder identified it as the 'Mech Khan Ward piloted.

"Heads up—the Khan is watching us." In Hawkins' mind, Alaric was a genius, pure and simple. No other Khan had taken their warriors to Terra itself. *If not for him, we would not be here, fighting for our birthright.*

"Do not do anything foolish," his gunner chided. "*You* may be old enough to afford the embarrassment, but I am not."

Movement caught Hawkins' eye. A massive, four-legged Republic *Trebaruna* was rising into the air on its jump jets—coming straight at a battered Wolf *Firestorm*. The *Firestorm* managed to fire its pair of medium lasers just before the *Trebaruna* came down hard, trampling the Wolf 'Mech under its right legs. Sparks poured from the crushed cockpit; there was no chance the warrior within had survived.

The *Trebaruna* paused for a half a second, clearly detecting both Khan Ward's 'Mech in the distance and Hawkins' tank. It then headed off on an attack vector toward Khan Ward.

Hawkins saw the approach and mentally calculated his intercept point, surging *Fratricide* forward to put it between his Khan and the charging Republic 'Mech. "Target the front of that *Trebaruna*," he said. "Weapons free."

"Locking on," DuJordan said—then fired his twin Gauss rifles.

The tank lurched backward with the force of the shot, the slugs flashing silver just before they furrowed deep into the *Trebaruna*'s body, peeling back its armor. The 'Mech turned slowly, until it lined up on them—then froze in recognition that it would have to deal with them before reaching Khan Ward.

"Well," Hawkins said, "we got its attention."

The *Trebaruna* broke into a run, heading right toward them, firing its Gauss rifle and light PPCs. Hawkins felt *Fratricide* shudder around him as the blasts tore into his front armor. He gunned the engine into full reverse. One of the Gauss rifle holes in their armor left a smoking trail Hawkins could see out the front viewport.

"Keep some distance between us, would you?" DuJordan said from the turret behind him.

"What do you *think* I am doing?" Hawkins grumbled, turning to his rear camera displays. "Do not tell me how to drive our tank."

"*Someone* should," DuJordan replied.

Hawkins swung *Fratricide* around the rubble of a small outdoor restaurant. *The last thing we need is to get hung up on debris.*

DuJordan fired his dual Gauss rifles again; both shots plowed into the front legs of the oncoming *Trebaruna*. One round peeled back a sheet of armor that rubbed against the 'Mech's torso as it ran, finally ripping off entirely. The other hit left a crater just below the right foreleg's knee. But the *Trebaruna* was still closing; it filled more and more of Hawkins' forward viewscreen as he maneuvered through the battle.

DuJordan fired a volley of ER medium lasers. One missed, but the other struck with a brilliant red beam, leaving a hot, jagged scar across the *Trebaruna*'s torso.

There was a flash as the enemy 'Mech fired its trio of light PPCs, almost blinding Hawkins with dots of white and blue light. He shook his head, hoping to clear the afterimage.

The tank plowed into the corner of a small two-story building, throwing him against his safety harness. Debris rained down as he cursed.

"What did we hit?" DuJordan asked as Hawkins refocused.

"Nothing important," he replied as a Gauss-rifle slug rammed into *Fratricide*, pushing it backward a little faster. His front-right tread assembly started to smoke as they roared through the rubble of the building.

"Try off to the right," DuJordan sniped from the turret. "You *completely* missed hitting a building there. Perhaps we can swing back around and you can drive through it on the second pass."

"You are not helping," Hawkins said through gritted teeth. He twisted and turned the Carnivore through the streets, hoping to break up line of sight and fire.

"That *surat* is almost on us," DuJordan warned. "It will be harder to target up close, and I am running low on ammunition."

"I understand. Do your duty—and do not miss."

Hawkins angled the rear of the tank around. DuJordan fired again with the Gauss rifles and medium lasers. One rifle slug hit the *Trebaruna* in its left knee so hard the actuator locked up. The BattleMech spilled forward onto the roadway, grinding its armor into the torn-up pavement. The lasers raked its legs and body, their bright red beams melting hot gashes along what armor remained. Dust kicked up from the road, littered with the debris of other blasted structures.

"If you are not too busy hitting things, I would like a clear field of fire," DuJordan said. "Take us back to them while they are down. I will use my last rounds on them."

"*Neg*," Hawkins said, lining *Fratricide* up with the fallen BattleMech. He saw on the tactical display that Khan Ward was still nearby. "Prepare for ramming speed."

"*Aff.*"

Hawkins jammed the shift and throttle forward as far as they could go; the surge tossed him hard back into his seat. *Fratricide*'s fusion reactor throbbed as the tank lurched straight at the downed *Trebaruna*.

The 'Mech struggled to rise—and fired its trio of light PPCs again. Hawkins couldn't swerve in time; two of the shots tore off *Fratricide*'s remaining front armor.

"I cannot get a clean shot with the big guns," DuJordan growled. "And we have no front armor left." He let loose with the rest of the Carnivore's armaments. Yellow tracers from the heavy machine guns splattered the cockpit and body, while a medium laser seared open another red-hot hole. "Of all the things you have hit today, by the Great Father, make this one count!"

The Republic warrior got the *Trebaruna* almost standing, the damaged leg locked in position. Sparks flew from one of the holes where a laser beam had bored into the 'Mech's internals. But by then it was too late.

Hawkins braced himself in his seat. "Hang on!" he bellowed as the tank roared forward.

Fratricide plowed right into the *Trebaruna*'s legs, driving up them like a ramp. The quad-treaded tank roared upward onto the semi-prone BattleMech, grinding what armor remained as it churned ahead, angling toward the torso.

Hawkins was thrown forward, biting through his lower lip and banging his head on the communications console hard enough to crack his helmet. Metallic grinding filled his ears, and the scent of ozone mixed with the iron taste of his own blood. *Fratricide* rose up, its treads crawling over and tearing into the *Trebaruna*. His head pounding, Hawkins reversed, hearing more metallic shrieks of protest as the assault tank struggled to get free, then jerked loose.

Fratricide backed up through billowing black smoke. Hawkins was surprised to see that their left tread had crushed the cockpit canopy of the prone BattleMech. A red smear of blood splattered what ferroglass remained. Ripples of heat rose from a hole on the BattleMech, a sign that its reactor was damaged. His own damage display showed *Fratricide* was badly mangled, but at least partially operational. *Star Colonel Kalidessa Kerensky definitely cannot fault us for not being aggressive enough this time out.*

"DuJordan," he managed with a strained voice, "you are okay, *quiaff*?"

"*Aff*," the gunner groaned. "Please tell me you are not backing up to ram them again."

"*Neg*," Hawkins replied. "I believe our enemy is dead."

"Good," DuJordan said. "Two BattleMech kills in one day... We have honored our Clan."

Hawkins checked his tactical readout and saw the fighting in the vicinity had died down—which was a relief, given *Fratricide*'s battered condition.

Just then, Khan Ward's distinctive gray-and-red 'Mech appeared, looming over the fallen *Trebaruna*. The side hatch opened, and the Wolf Khan appeared.

Hawkins popped his top hatch and rose, the smoke and cool air stinging his nostrils. He wiped blood from his mouth. What few sounds of battle from the suburb seemed far in the distance and dwindling.

"Wolf warriors," the Khan called out. "What are your names?"

"Hawkins and DuJordan," Hawkins said just as DuJordan popped the turret hatch, knocking away a piece of torn armor and sending it rattling down the side of the Carnivore.

"Hawkins and DuJordan," Alaric Ward repeated. "You have done a great service today. I saw what happened. That BattleMech outmassed you. And its pilot was Tyrina Drummond, a Paladin of the Republic. Your choice of attack was remarkable. I have never seen a tank take down a foe then ram it for the kill quite like that."

Remarkable—Khan Ward called our *attack remarkable!* Hawkins did not hide his surprise, but still kept his voice calm as he replied, "We did our duty, my Khan."

"You did more than that," the Khan said. "With Drummond's death, what remains of these Hastati Sentinels is going to crumble. You have brought glory to Clan Wolf, and for that, I will see you honored in *The Remembrance.*"

Hawkins felt his face flush. "Thank you, my Khan." The words were stifled, choked in his throat. "All we ask is that *Fratricide* here be fixed so we may fight another day."

"It will be done," the Khan said. "Tonight, you will join me for dinner while our equipment is repaired."

"We are honored, my Khan," DuJordan said.

"*Neg.*" The Khan smiled as he climbed back into his 'Mech. "The honor is mine."

CHAPTER 9

Alaric Ward paced around the holographic map in his mobile HQ, half listening to Devlin Stone's voice on the comms while planning his next moves. The defeat of Paladin Drummond's forces now left him with several options in the Nostos plans, and he wanted to choose them carefully. While he respected Stone to a degree, he found the old man's interruption less than productive. *He wants something, and his desires are of little concern to me.*

The fighting had stopped altogether two hours ago with the encirclement of what was left of the Fourteenth Hastati, and he had allowed Kalidessa Kerensky to accept their surrender. Her Second Wolf Assault Cluster had been critical to the victory, and Alaric wanted her to savor the moment. Few things felt as good as the crushing defeat of an honorable foe, and the Fourteenth Hastati Sentinels had been such an enemy. When the ranking officer surrendered, Star Colonel Kerensky had taken his sword as *isorla*, and was now wearing it as a badge of her victory.

"I understand Lady Drummond was killed," Stone said solemnly, "and the remnants of the Fourteenth Sentinels have surrendered."

"*Aff* on both counts. I saw her fall. She fought and died with honor—a warrior's fate. One cannot ask for more than that."

Stone did not answer for a long moment. Alaric thought he might have switched off the comm until the Exarch said, "I am sure you know Malvina Hazen has entered the system. She will be landing at any moment."

"*Aff.*"

Stone was speaking as a diplomat now—measured and even. "Hazen is ruthless. Her reputation for brutality is well documented. She is a war criminal. On top of that, she pursues the same thing you do: the right to call yourself ilClan. That makes her a mutual enemy. It puts us on the same side."

Alaric paused his pacing to cautiously agree. "Malvina is...driven." It was one of the few positive words he could summon to describe his fellow Khan.

"However, her arrival creates an opportunity for *both* of our people," Stone continued, "What I propose is simple: an immediate ceasefire between our forces. We can work together to deal with the Jade Falcon threat. It is in our mutual interest to unite against them. I have heard you are a reasonable man. I am confident that neither of us wants to see the Jade Falcons become the ilClan."

Alaric suppressed the urge to laugh. "I do not think you fully appreciate the situation, Exarch. There will be no ceasefire. I will deal with Malvina Hazen after she *and* I crush your Republic."

"But...the Falcons have long been enemies of the Wolves," Stone said, horror creeping into his voice. "Surely it makes sense to deal with them first. We should unite our forces, Alaric, while we still can."

"*Neg*, it does not make sense. This is not a situation you can influence. Who do you think gave Malvina the secret to penetrating your Fortress Republic? I *invited* the Jade Falcons to Terra. They are here at *my* behest."

When he finally replied, Stone's voice was faint with shock. "You...you *invited* her? Why would you do that? The Falcons are your sworn enemies. Eventually, she will come for you."

"*Aff*, I did invite her. And *aff*, Malvina will come for my Wolves. But it will be on my terms, *after* the demise of the Republic you cherish so dearly."

"This is madness!" Stone snapped. "You have doomed us all. You must listen to me, Khan Ward—"

"The Inner Sphere governments and Great Houses can no longer tell my people what to do—much less assume that I would betray another Clan, even the Jade Falcons. You have no say in the destruction of a Clan; only the Clans themselves have that right. *I* will deal with the Jade Falcons when the time comes, and I will do it *without* your assistance."

"Don't be a fool, Alaric." Stone was nearly pleading. "We can negotiate. Work together—"

Alaric paused and crossed his arms. He smiled, a rare expression of emotion. *This is how it is meant to be, the Inner Sphere groveling before the might of the Clans. Stone still believes he can manipulate us, twist our* rede *and honor to his advantage. Only now does that withered old man realize the inevitable fate of his Republic.*

"I have not come to Terra to negotiate," he said. "I have come to conquer, and that is what I will do. I will fulfill the ambition of Nicholas Kerensky, and unite the Clans in a way that none could have imagined. Whether you stand in our way is up to you."

He shut off the comm and returned to studying his maps, chuckling over his foe's angst. As he looked at the holomap, he decided this was the perfect time to split his force between himself and saKhan Garner Kerensky. Such a split would further frustrate Stone, especially with the Jade Falcons landing. Alaric would drive north, then cross the Bering Strait via DropShip, then sweep south into the west coast of North America. Garner, per the Nostos plans, would take a force and head west, across Russia.

Alaric mulled over where the Jade Falcons would strike. There was little doubt in his mind. *She will go for what she thinks is the prize, Stone's jugular.*

CJF DROPSHIP *CLAW OF THE FALCON*
NANCY, FRANCE
TERRA
4 FEBRUARY 3151, 1032 HOURS (T+25)

The dull green Jade Falcon DropShips descended quickly, forming a wide landing zone around the city of Nancy.

Even from inside her BattleMech, *Black Rose,* Malvina Hazen felt the *thud* as the footpads of *Claw of the Falcon* landed. The drop ramp hissed and descended, and fresh evening air poured into the ship. She moved *Black Rose* slowly down the ramp.

Terra! In the twilight, it looked very much like Skye to her.

Other *thuds* sounded as nearby DropShips opened their ramps and their BattleMechs emerged, eager to survey the land.

The sight nearly choked her with fury. She jabbed her comm to the open channel. "*Jade Falcons, hold!* This is your Chingis Khan. No one may touch the soil of this world before I do!"

The Falcons all stopped.

Satisfied, Malvina moved her *Shrike* down the ramp so that all Falcons in the LZ could see her. As she stepped onto the earth, *Black Rose*'s footpads sank slightly into the grassy field.

She spun at the waist, surveying her initial landing force. *This is where humankind began. This is the same ground Aleksandr Kerensky walked. It is where the Star League began and where it will be rekindled under my leadership.* She had trod on dozens of planets in her life, spilled blood on all of them, conquered many, but none of those mattered in that moment. Terra—this was sacred soil.

Her plan was simple. After landing in France, she would secure a strong drop zone, since her forces would be arriving at irregular intervals. She would leave one Galaxy to hold that ground, while her initial four Galaxies would go for the true prize—Geneva, Devlin Stone's capital. Taking that would break the will of the Republic. If she was fortunate and could move fast enough, she could grab Stone himself. *Alaric can take the rest of the planet for all I care. The strategic objective that matters most is Geneva.* Once she had conquered that city, she would pluck other prime objectives from the remaining fruit on the Republic's withering vine.

I am already master of this world...it is simply unaware of that reality.

"Jade Falcons—deploy. Join me on this, the end of our Grand Crusade. Execute Birthright, Ground Phase. Let us show the Republic and the Wolves how true warriors fight."

COMMAND POST SOLITUDE
GENEVA
TERRA
4 FEBRUARY 3151, 1102 HOURS (T+25)

Stone rested his elbows on the table, his hands propping up the sides of his pale face, accented by dark hollows under his eyes, as Lakewood spoke. "They came down in Nancy, France, five Galaxies of force. She has sent one Galaxy west, toward Redoubt Normandy. The rest are moving fast toward Geneva, no doubt to encircle us."

Tucker Harwell watched Stone, who said nothing at first. "Geneva is one of the most fortified cities in the Inner Sphere," Stone finally said. "We planned for an all-out assault by a Clan here, and Malvina is delivering it to us."

The bravado commonly heard in his voice had faded after his conversation with Khan Ward. Tucker understood all too well. *He says this is still going according to plan, but his plan has turned to utter shit.*

"Exarch," Jonah Levin spoke cautiously. "We had anticipated fighting one Clan. We now have two facing us at once."

"Your point being?"

"We may need to rethink our strategy," Levin replied.

Stone lowered his hands and shook his head. "This is a surprise, that I'll grant you, but the redoubts will work. Tyrina Drummond dealt a nasty blow to Alaric's Beta Galaxy, and that was with just one regiment. The key is attrition, and the redoubts will ensure that. Combine that with some precise counterattacks, and we can break the backs of these invaders."

Damien Redburn shifted in his seat as if it was suddenly uncomfortable. Tucker liked him. Levin and Lakewood always acquiesced to Stone, bowing to his experience and confidence. Redburn, however, was a man after Tucker's own heart, and seemed to enjoy challenging the older man. "Devlin, we may need to consider more drastic tactics."

Stone surveyed him carefully. "If you are thinking of WMDs, the answer is no. I will not do what the Master did during the Jihad. We would just be inviting the Clans to do the same."

"No, I'm not suggesting that," Redburn said. "But sticking to our strategy against one Clan when we face two isn't the solution. We may need to fight dirty before this is over. I have an idea I'm putting together just for this kind of contingency."

Stone reluctantly nodded. "I'm open to any suggestions at this point. In the meantime, let's get word out to the civilians left in the city that this is their last chance to evacuate."

With those words, the command staff rose and filtered out of the room. A minute later, it was just Tucker and Stone behind the closed door.

Stone raised his head and gazed wearily at his aide. "Don't start, Tucker."

"Exarch, your plan has gone straight to hell. You hoped to play Clan Wolf against the Jade Falcons, but Alaric *invited* them here. You need to accept the reality that we are in a situation we may not be able to overcome."

Stone's face sagged more than usual today. The exhaustion in his eyes was becoming more common. "I don't understand. The Clans *never* work together. They don't share with each other...*especially* the Wolves and Jade Falcons. It should be impossible."

"Well, they *are* working together now," Harwell said, driving the point home. "Alaric clearly isn't going to dance to your tune. Malvina isn't either. The rest of the staff may not ask the hard questions, but I do because I know what you've been planning behind the scenes. I also know you. You always have a plan or two in play, some sort of scheme. If there ever was a time to activate it, it's now. What is your secret plan to save Terra now?"

Store looked at him, but the fire was fading from his eyes. He ran a trembling hand over his sunken cheeks. "I have a Ghost Knight out there. We may be able to get word to her."

"To do what?"

"Tucker," Stone replied, slowly gathering his remaining strength. "There are *other* Clans...and they may not be at all comfortable at the thought of the Wolves or Jade Falcons taking the prize."

INTERLUDE

Captain-General Nikol Halas-Hughes Marik tugged at the right sleeve of her uniform, hoping to make it feel comfortable. It was to no avail. No matter what the tailors did, she felt ill at ease wearing it, both physically and emotionally. Its gray color with purple lapels and cuffs felt too masculine for her taste. It did make her strawberry blond hair appear blonder, which was its only saving grace. Her fair complexion and penetrating blue-gray eyes made for good press images for the public, but she hated the uniform of the office.

She was never supposed to be Captain-General, but fate always played a role in her realm and its leaders. Nikol had been fifth in line for the position, but her mother had trained her in politics regardless. Being so far removed from the seat of power, Nikol had pursued a military career, and was successful as the commander of the Eagle's Talons. She had waged war to reunite the Free Worlds League and to keep it together. Her mother had married Thaddeus Marik, giving her that family name and the twisted history that went with it. Thaddeus' death at the hands of Alaric Wolf, the assassination of her mother and her eldest brother, and the disinterest, disgrace, and disinheritance of her remaining siblings had thrust her into the Captain-Generalcy. She had never wanted the position, but had slowly come to realize her mother had been grooming her for it all along.

That did not make the role any less distasteful to her.

Nikol was glad to be alone in her office—a rarity. One of the challenges of the Free Worlds League was that someone was always standing in the wings, prepared to offer their opinion or voice on any matter. She cherished time alone without the voices, the political opinions, the sycophants, the potential allies, or the would-be successors constantly filling her ears and her head.

Someone knocked on the door, and it opened at her word to the guard on the other side. In stepped General William Arnold of the Free Worlds Guards.

He clicked his heels and saluted as her aide, Adamina Stewart, closed the door to leave them alone.

"At ease, William," Nikol said, gesturing to a seat opposite her desk. The middle-aged man with black hair was always perfect in his movement. Her eyes caught the streaks of gray in his sideburns, and she admired the fact that he didn't try to cover them up like some officers.

"Captain-General," he said. "I have begun the work necessary to mobilize the Guards."

"For what purpose?" she said, stunned.

"To aid the Republic on Terra, of course," he said gruffly.

"I gave no such order," she said flatly.

General Arnold drew a long breath in, and a bit of pink appeared on his lean cheeks. "Begging your pardon, Your Grace, I presumed we would be mobilizing to help the Republic of the Sphere. I saw the intelligence reports. The Wolves have all but disappeared from their Empire—at least their warrior and technician castes. There is little speculation as to where they have gone. The reports also said the Jade Falcons are on the move toward Terra, and Ghost Bears are positioning forces at the border of Fortress Republic. Your orders were to develop options—so I assumed you were going to send us in to fend off the Clans. I was good friends with your stepfather, Thaddeus. Alaric Ward killed him in battle. Shouldn't we be shoring up the Republic?"

She knew Arnold well. He was not one to carve out a position of power for himself: he served the realm before his personal needs. "I wanted options, not action—not yet."

"If I may…" he began. Nikol nodded for him to continue. "The nations of the Inner Sphere have been fiddling around with the Clans for a century. ComStar bought us all fifteen years of blunting their drive to Terra. Now the Clans are about to *take* Terra. I'm not sure that sitting on the sidelines is in our realm's best interest."

She appreciated that he skipped over mentioning the Jihad. House Marik's role in that horrific war was not something officers talked about. At the same time, she loathed the sports metaphor. "I am not prepared to lay down the lives of our people for a nation that has done nothing for the Free Worlds League."

Devlin Stone's dream of peace had started falling apart the moment he had disappeared in 3130. Shortly after he left, the HPG network collapsed, large parts of ComStar were sold off to the Sea Foxes, and the Republic became the largest target on the map. Every Great House had used the Blackout to take back worlds seized by the Republic. Stone had beaten swords into plowshares, and everyone coveted the worlds of his realm, which left the Republic ripe for conquest. The Capellans were also driving on Terra themselves, no doubt hoping to do what centuries of fighting had never permitted—a House Lord seizing the homeworld of humankind.

We were so desperate to get back to conquering planets that we armed mining and forestry 'Mechs in those first few years. Jonah Levin is a good man, but it takes more than a good man to beat the Wolves and Falcons.

"Captain-General, the Republic fights our enemies."

"We have a nonaggression pact with Clan Wolf," she reminded him. "And we have never fought Clan Jade Falcon."

"Nonaggression pact..." General Arnold grumbled. "Fine, if you don't want to go save the Republic, there are plenty of other targets. They hold a number of former League worlds. Let me assemble a task force. I can pull in the Oriente Hussars and a number of Marik Militia regiments. The Wolf Empire worlds are barren of defenses. In just a few weeks we can retake what Stone's peace stole from us."

Nikol appreciated the zeal in his voice, misdirected though it was. "General, I respect you, but consider this. The Republic has been dying for years now. Terra is a powerful symbol, that I will grant you, but it is one planet. Even if the Clans seize it, that alone does not re-form a new Star League. They will have to wage war to unify the Inner Sphere to do that. Sending some of our troops to help Exarch Levin is short-sighted. While we might help save Terra and prop up what is left of the Republic, would that leave us any better off? Sooner or later, House Liao or someone else will simply finish the Republic off."

"Then you think the rumors that Devlin Stone has returned are false?"

Nikol and the FWL's intelligence department had disregarded the rumors that Stone had somehow miraculously returned to save the Republic. "I find that hard to believe. What would he be now, over a hundred years old? And he was a master of war, so if he *was* truly back, surely his little empire never would have crumbled like it has." Nikol wondered how Stone would've fared against the likes of Malvina Hazen and Alaric Ward. *These are not the Clans Stone knew.*

"I still feel action is called for. I hate sitting and waiting."

"I understand. But consider this. Former Archon Melissa Steiner of the Lyran Commonwealth betrayed Clan Wolf, holding their civilians hostage. She stabbed them in the back. Ultimately, she paid for her arrogance with her life and nearly her realm when both Clans Jade Falcon and Wolf hit her capital world."

"Your point being?"

"Antagonizing the Clans comes with a high price tag."

"So, we just sit and do nothing?" General Arnold said in a dejected tone.

"Of course not!" Nikol fired back. "If Clan Wolf is destroyed trying to take Terra, we need to be prepared to move in and claim the worlds they seized from the Marik-Stewart Commonwealth during their relocation to the Wolf Empire. We can also pay back the Lyrans for their last little war with us, too. Such actions would have no repercussions, and I would be comfortable with the risks versus the rewards." *Others are free to cross Clan Wolf if they desire. I will not plunge my people into a conflict that will make me the next Melissa Steiner. If they are wiped out, then we can look at liberating the planets that were League worlds long ago.*

"I will assemble the general staff and make plans immediately," Arnold said, rising to his full height, towering over her. He saluted, and Nikol nodded, dismissing him.

As the door closed to her office, Nikol walked over to the small liquor cabinet, where she poured herself some whiskey, neat. The bottles were almost empty, and she thought for a moment about her mother—a woman with a certain fondness for alcohol. *Perhaps intoxication was a virtue for my ancestors. It would explain a great many things.*

General Arnold's aggressive stance had given her some unease. It was far too easy to start a war, and some people were looking to do so at any moment. She wished she knew what was happening on Terra. Terra itself was a symbol for many. It represented not only the birthplace of humans, but the seat of the Star League. What it represented to House Marik was less about the planet and more about who held it. If a Clan were to seize it, they could potentially unite all of the Clans under a single banner. *The Star League could be reborn. If it is, what would our role be? Vassal to some Clan overlord? Would we be as we were in the original Star League, treated as equals among the other House Lords, or would the ilKhan have a different, more oppressive view?*

As she settled back into her large, red-leather chair, she activated a holomap of her realm and what was left of the Republic of the Sphere. She had seen Alaric Ward on Terra at Victor Steiner-Davion's funeral in 3135. Then, he had been a young Clan officer, aloof, arrogant, and awkward. She had not given him the time of day, and he had not noticed her. *We have both come far since then.* Nikol lifted her glass in a silent toast to the Wolf Khan.

If the Republic wins, will they come to take back the worlds they lost? If the Wolves win, will they reshape the Inner Sphere? If the Jade Falcons win... She shuddered, and knocked back a healthy slug of whiskey.

My people have not faced Hazen's Falcons—nor do I wish them to. The massive SAFE file on Malvina told a chilling story. Some went so far as to say she was mad, but Nikol believed differently. *One does not rise to power on madness alone, but power can make one mad.* Caleb Davion came to mind, and that gave her a chill. *No, Malvina is smart. She knows how to focus her people. And if she unites all of the Clans under her, none will ever call her mad again.*

Nikol took another swallow of her drink. *History is being made. The last massive turning point was the Jihad. The Free Worlds League took the wrong side, and we paid a price for our decision in blood and years. We are still suffering from the results of backing the wrong horse. Rash actions offer great results, but also come with great risks.*

She leaned back in her chair. "This time," she said to herself, "the Free Worlds League is going to sit back and prepare for a coming storm, rather than opening the door and inviting it in."

ORCIM SALT FLATS
SHAULA
JADE FALCON OCCUPATION ZONE
4 FEBRUARY 3151 (T+25)

Star Colonel David Thompson's *Thunder Stallion* thudded out onto the dried lakebed in pursuit of the last Jade Falcon still fighting, a *Lynx C*. The antiquated BattleMech's best years were decades ago, its armor a patchwork of repairs, its faded green paint showing signs of long wear. Yet the Falcon warrior pressed forward at Thompson, despite being outgunned and outmatched, despite their Starmate's *Naja* lying behind them, billowing smoke from the gaping hole blown through its torso.

Thompson angled his four-legged 'Mech slightly, mostly to reduce their closure rate. The *Lynx*'s large pulse laser tore at his right foreleg, leaving a string of burn holes that failed to penetrate the armor. He responded with a wave of sixty long-range missiles that arced in the air between them and savaged the already-damaged *Lynx* almost everywhere, including a pair that slammed into the cockpit. Only three missiles missed, exploding on the dry lakebed floor, kicking up clouds of salt and sand.

The Jade Falcon warrior was good, but the sudden loss of so much armor made their 'Mech's center of gravity shift. The *Lynx* staggered, fighting for balance, somehow managing to stay upright. While it did, Thompson closed on it, and at maximum range unleashed his autocannon at the same time the *Lynx*'s PPC fired.

The *Thunder Stallion* roared around him as the big gun sent a stream of shells into the Jade Falcon 'Mech, tearing off its right arm entirely, leaving strands of myomer dangling. Its PPC strike ate at what was left of his right-side armor, sending hot gobbets of molten metal hissing into the sands of the flats. His damage display flickered to crimson on that side, but Thompson ignored it. He could taste the victory at hand, despite the damage.

The loss of armor was too much for the Jade Falcon warrior. The *Lynx C* toppled, plowing into the dry lakebed, kicking up sand as it skidded on its front armor and left bits of protection in its wake.

The Star Colonel vented his excess heat as he closed the distance, keeping his targeting reticle on the Jade Falcon. The *Lynx* tried to rise, but without the arm, it was a struggle. It had gotten to its knees when Thompson heard the metallic *snap* of his missiles finishing their reload cycle. He loosed another salvo at the kneeling BattleMech. For a moment it disappeared in the explosions, the dust, smoke, and shrapnel. As a low breeze cut across the salt flats, he saw the mangled remains of the old BattleMech, only bits of its green armor still visible.

"*Seyla*," he declared over the close-range communications channel. "You cannot win. Stand down."

"It would be merciful if you killed me," a weary voice replied.

"I will not," said Star Colonel David Thompson, commander of the Hell's Horses Watch. "I have questions for you.

Thirty minutes later, Khan Gottfried Amirault joined Thompson. While the Watch commander was covered in dust that clung to his sweat, Khan Amirault stood tall, his bronzed skin shimmering in the heat of Shaula's sun. He was bald, save for a long ponytail at the back of his head.

Seated before them on the arm of the wrecked *Lynx C* was Janus, the warrior who had fought to the bitter end. Thompson stroked his brown goatee and glared at the warrior with scornful brown eyes. Janus seemed as ancient as his BattleMech, easily in his fifties, far past prime for a Clan warrior—*solahma*. He wore a weathered patch of the Falcon Fusiliers, no doubt one of the units he had fought with over the years. His unconscious comrade, whom Thompson had also defeated, had been transported to a hospital. Janus sat on the arm of his fallen *Lynx*, grinning, his white hair shimmering in the orange glow of the afternoon sun.

"Where is the garrison of this world?" Amirault asked sternly.

"I am under no compulsion to tell you. I am too old to be your bondsman, and you did not see fit to kill me in battle." Janus paused, rubbing the bruise on his shoulder and wincing. "But I will answer your question. Not out of any sense of honor, but for the enjoyment it will give me." His smile showed an arrogant cockiness. "We *are* the garrison, Bethany and I. We are all that remains of the forces that once held this world."

"Where are the others?"

"Off to Terra," Janus said, smiling more broadly.

"So, Khan Hazen has found the means to penetrate Fortress Republic, *quiaff*?" Khan Amirault asked in his deep, entrancing voice.

Janus nodded. "We were deemed too old, undeserving of completing the Grand Crusade. It was better to fill our space on the DropShip with munitions. A bit shortsighted, if my opinion mattered, which clearly it does not."

Thompson turned to Khan Amirault, putting his back to Janus. His Khan's gaze narrowed and his jaw clenched as he digested this information. "And your reports on Clan Wolf say they have mobilized their entire *touman* as well."

The Star Colonel nodded. "The lack of HPGs took weeks to get the message from my operatives, but *aff*, both Clans are heading for Terra. This leaves us with useful intelligence and decisions to make," he added, hoping to curb some of the anger he saw in his Khan's face. "The Jade Falcon Occupation Zone is ripe for the taking. If Malvina Hazen moves on Terra, all Falcon planets will likely be garrisoned like this. We could take them all."

Amirault rubbed his hand over the top of his bald head, taking a wave of sweat and dust with it. "I do not want the occupation zone. I want the ilClanship."

"That leaves us with Stampede," Thompson said.

Operation Stampede called for the mobilization of all of Clan Hell's Horses and driving toward Terra. In order to secure the necessary logistics chain, a string of Jade Falcon worlds would have to be claimed along the Rasalhague Dominion border. The Horses would follow the advance of the Jade Falcons and swing on Terra.

Amirault nodded. "The timing and logistics involved are challenging. We can have two Galaxies mobilized to start the drive. The rest will have to follow as quickly as possible."

"My Khan," Thompson said carefully. "Even if we start today, by the time we reach the Fortress barrier, we lack the means to penetrate it. And given that both the Falcons and Wolves are likely either on Terra or en route, the matter of who would be ilClan may already be settled."

"Unacceptable!" Amirault spat.

"If I may," the Star Colonel continued, "this should be seen as a great opportunity. We could send our best two Galaxies along the path planned for Stampede. Other forces could take advantage of this moment, and swing through the Jade Falcon Occupation Zone."

Amirault pondered the concept for a moment. "We would still have forces poised near Terra to take advantage of any changes there. If the Wolves win, they will not care that we have taken Jade Falcon worlds. Whoever wins the struggle on Terra, they will be weak. Either way, our two forward Galaxies will be well poised for a Trial of Refusal of whoever claims to be ilClan, while we consume what the Jade Falcons have left behind."

"Either way," Thompson said, "Clan Hell's Horses emerges stronger."

Amirault shook his head. "I loathe this. The Wolves and Jade Falcons have much to answer for, going to Terra and not letting us join in that struggle."

Thompson nodded. "It is both arrogance and folly on their parts. For the time being, it will cost Malvina Hazen the most. Namely, the worlds we will take from her."

"Good," Amirault said with a sneer. "She took our Mongol Doctrine from us and twisted it into an abomination. Our Clan is tainted by every life she takes in its name." He paused, his expression hardening into a scowl, then continued. "Whoever wins on Terra will face a reckoning—and it will come under the hooves of our BattleMechs and the flames of our weapons."

CHAPTER 10

Devlin Stone hated the cane. He had started using it a few days ago, simply for assistance, but was already finding that he leaned on it more every day. His body was struggling to keep pace with his mind, the result of a cryogenic process that was far from perfect. *I just need a few more months, just enough to defeat these invaders and get things set on the right path for the rebirth of the Republic.*

The Wrecking Ball forward command post was built into the side of a mountain, amid large warehouses, pillboxes, and turrets. Nestled in the Caucasus Mountains, it was a mini-redoubt in and of itself. His lead forces had been south of here when they were hit by Clan Wolf's western thrust. A mix of Stone's Revenants, the Ninety-First Republic Militia, and a battalion of the Third Principes Guards, they had given as good as they had gotten for two days before being forced to fall back to Wrecking Ball. Heavy damage had been done to both units, despite the propaganda released to the citizens about a 'stunning Republic victory.' The Ninety-First would likely be disbanded discreetly, as their command structure had been gutted. The other two units would take weeks to repair and refit.

Despite the pain, Stone rose to his full height and looked at the three officers before him, two female, one male. "Your actions against Clan Wolf were outstanding, each of you. Your fighting withdrawal in the face of overwhelming odds bought us precious time, and kicked the Wolves in the teeth."

All three officers beamed. Stone understood their reaction: he was giving them a great honor...and after all, they stood before the man that had ended the Jihad...him.

He took the Exarch's sword in his left hand and tried to ignore its dull weight and the quaking in his grip. The officers dropped to one knee before him, and with a wavering hand, he touched the sword on each shoulder. "In the name of the Republic, I knight you, both in recognition of what you have done, and what you will have to do in the coming fight." He glanced up at the teleprompter to get their names and honor each of them, one at a time.

As he finished, Tucker Harwell moved to his side and took the sword of office from him. "Arise, Knights of the Republic!" Stone said, and the small gathering in the conference room applauded. Leaning on the cane, he took a moment to shake their hands, comforted by the thought that he was boosting morale.

The new Knights-Errant left, basking in the glow of their elevation, shaking hands with Jonah Levin on their way out. Stone waited for the door to close before taking a seat. Wrecking Ball was not the Solitude command post; it was far more spartan. No banners on the walls, only dull-gray painted ferrocrete. The rectangular table was military grade, not nice wood, just plastic and steel. Stone settled into the chair, having spent his physical strength with the ceremony, and drew a long, deep breath as Levin and Lakewood sat beside him. Tucker Harwell skirted around the table to the far end, where he could look Stone in the eye.

"How goes the staging for the counterattack?" Stone asked Janella.

"We have assembled a fairly sizable task force under Sir Paco 'Danger' Cubillo. The Tenth and Sixteenth Principes Guards form the core of our assault force. We have amassed a significant number of superheavies in those units. The Thirteenth Hastati Sentinels are in the mix, and we have cobbled together an ad hoc battalion of survivors from other units Clan Wolf has routed."

Stone nodded, and did what he could to hold back his long-delayed pleasure at the new situation. The time for the counterattack had come when the Wolves had refused to pursue and destroy the 130th Armor Brigade of the Thirteenth Hastati Sentinels after they fell back into the Caucasuses. They had tried, but the narrow mountain roads were perfect for Republic ambushes. The Wolf commander—a general by the name of Chance Vickers, from what they had gathered—had left behind a reinforced Cluster to cork the bottle in the mountains. Intelligence indicated they were *solahma*, older warriors past their peak, with second-line equipment.

The Jade Falcons had been far from idle as well. Malvina's forces had struck to encircle Geneva and had very nearly done so, if not for a gallant action by Stone's Lament, which blunted their eastern thrust, at least for the time being. Her forces drove west into the perimeter of Redoubt Normandy, only to be hit by fast-striking attacks from the Northwind Highlanders, who refused to commit to the large-scale confrontation the Falcons desired. More Jade Falcon JumpShips had materialized at the zenith jump point, disgorging their DropShips. Unlike Alaric, Hazen was not coming in all at once. *Which gives us a chance to deliver a real blow to the Wolves, perhaps get Alaric to see the wisdom of fighting Hazen instead of us.*

Jonah shifted in his seat. "If we wait a day or two, we can add in the Old Guard."

Stone slammed his fist on the table. "*No!* They are my last reserves. We only send in the Old Guard if we have to. This isn't their time."

This was the second time Levin had tried to insist on their use, and the second time Stone had refused. *When the Old Guard take the field, it will be a message to our enemies that their doom is upon them. I need to hold them for the perfect moment...and this is not it.* "Besides, we are more than a match for that Cluster south of us. When we hit them with this much force, it will kill their offensive. They will have to yield ground, and that gives us the initiative for the first time in weeks."

The plan was bold. Operation Four Horsemen was to smash though the Wolves' blocking force and drive south into Iran. Once the task force reached the Persian Gulf, the Wolves' western offensive, which was just starting to reach Greece, would be cut off entirely. While the cut-off Wolves could resupply via DropShip, it would be a slow process, further hindered by a surge of Republic aerospace forces.

Janella had argued to have the task force drive west, into the rear of the Wolves under General Vickers. Stone opted to go east instead, into the territory where the Wolves were weakest and most spread out. They would move to the now-abandoned redoubt in Bangalore and even potentially drive into China. The task force would be isolated, but it would pressure the Wolves' offenses to stop and turn back to deal with the threat in their rear, allowing the Republic to counterattack in other areas. Moreover, it would give the occupied civilian populations hope in the Republic. A much-needed morale boost.

Stone was proud of his decision; it was something he had done before, during the Jihad a generation earlier, with great success. *Alaric and this Vickers woman will never see this coming...*

OUTSIDE OF ZANJAN, IRAN
TERRA
9 FEBRUARY 3151, 0841 HOURS (T+30)

Major Jack Traver enjoyed piloting the replacement *Ares* superheavy OmniMech almost as much as he had their original ride. This model was outfittted in the Hades configuration, augmenting the standard loadout with medium-range missiles, an Ultra-class autocannon, and a TSEMP, a tight stream electromagnetic pulse cannon. His gunner, Cheetah, loved the TSEMP, able to fry enemy electronics at range, and Jack knew he would hate being on the receiving end of such a weapon.

Jack and his crew had hoped that the Redburn Guard would be rebuilt, but the unit had been retired. They were merged with other surviving 'Mechs and tanks, a hodgepodge of paint colors and unit designations. Jack commanded Plunder Company, a designation that prompted him to order their equipment painted black, with a white skull-and-crossbones on the front of each unit. That had helped with unit cohesion by at least giving them a sense of identity.

They had hit some light Clan Wolf defenses, but the Wolf commander had done something that few in the Republic had ever seen: she had fallen back after inflicting some losses to the Thirteenth Hastati.

As he drove the *Ares* forward, Jack looked out and saw a trio of other superheavies, including a red-and-blue *Poseidon* from Saber Company, lumbering along the broken ground and scrub brush. *With all of these slow superheavies working together, the Wolves are trading ground and time for a chance to hit us on ground of their choosing.*

His long-range sensors suddenly started showing dots of crimson, enemy forces at the end of their range. "This is Plunder Actual. Looks like we have company, due southwest. I am picking up ten—no, make that fifteen Wolf BattleMechs and supporting vehicles."

"Permission to engage," came the voice of Lieutenant Colton Mcleod, from his *Highlander*, some hundred meters in front of him.

"Stand by," Jack replied as he switched to the command channel. "General Cariveau, this is Plunder. We have targets, bearing two-zero-five—Trinary in strength."

"Copy that, Plunder," replied Brigadier General Malik Cariveau's almost courtly English accent. "Recon has targets painted in the front and to the east. It looks like the Wolves plan on trying to envelop us."

"Permission to attack."

"By all means," the general replied. "I will inform Sir Cubillo. Plunder has the west, lads, we have the rest."

Jack grinned and switched to Plunder Company's channel. "All right folks, we do this right and we give these bastards some payback. I want a tight Delta formation with me as the point. Overlap your fields of fire. Keep the big boys together, let the kids have their fun on the edges." He paused for a moment as a rush of energy flooded his body. "Engage!"

Angling the *Ares* to the west, Jack felt the machine surge with power. He tapped his internal comm system. "We are going in. Cheetah, I want overwhelming firepower on targets, everything we have. Pick a target and hit it until it's down and smoking. Mia, we're going to push the power limits, so watch the relays and be ready to manually trip them if you have to." His crew nervously acknowledged as he did what he could to rush forward.

Plunder Company's lighter 'Mechs swung around the Wolf force. His warbook on the battlecomputer began picking up targets for 'Mechs he had never fought before, either in simulation or real life: a pair of *Woodsman*s, a *Coyotl*, an *Orion C*. Older stuff, not front-line hardware. A grin rose on Jack's face. *They are outclassed!*

A pair of Wolf Hawk Moth II VTOLs roared toward him, their ER large lasers stabbing at his *Ares*. One Hawk Moth missed entirely and broke off due to waves of LRMs that skewed its aim. The other's attack hit dead on, searing a black hole just above the cockpit canopy. It broke off as well, diving and weaving as missile contrails twisted in after it.

A *Woodsman* rushed forward, past the light Republic 'Mechs, heading straight for him.

"We've got our first customer, Cheetah," Jack said as he tagged the target. "Make them pay for it."

"Bringing the rain," she muttered as weapons-lock tones filled his ears.

The *Woodsman* and *Ares* unleashed their salvos at the same time. Crimson beams of laser light stabbed through the space between the 'Mechs, and most hit the hulking superheavy. Jack's own 'Mech roared in response, as if he had been thrust into an angry thunderstorm. Forty medium-range missiles tore into the left side of the tan-and-green *Woodsman*, throwing armor fragments everywhere in the light brush and sands. It reeled as the Ultra autocannon blasted its legs with a barrage of shells. Long- and short-range missiles rained in a heartbeat later, explosions shredding bits of armor.

The last sound was a high-pitched *wing!* as the TSEMP fired. While there was no visible beam, he watched the *Woodsman*, a mere shell of its former self, stop mid-stride and fall face forward. The MechWarrior didn't even try to use the 'Mech's arms to break the fall. The *Woodsman* hit the side of a sandstone formation, pulverizing the stone and grinding away even more armor.

"Damn fine shot, Cheetah," Jack said as a wave of heat rose around him.

Suddenly, a Gauss-rifle round slammed into his right leg, blasting through and taking armor plates with it. He turned the *Ares* to face the new foe, an older-model *Black Knight*, one sporting an arm-mounted Gauss rifle. A squad of battle-armored infantry suddenly burst from cover, raining short-range missiles at the legs of his 'Mech at point-blank range.

Retreat...I bet that's something new for Clan Wolf. Jack savored it as Cheetah locked onto the *Black Knight*.

1056 HOURS

Jack and his crew stood atop the massive *Ares*, its cockpit canopy open. He enjoyed the warm breeze; at least it felt better than the stifling humidity of the cockpit.

As he surveyed the battlefield, all he saw was debris—bits and pieces of military hardware and the smoking remains of destroyed BattleMechs. The air reeked of burned metal, fried myomer, melted plastic, and expended ammunition. He savored it for a long moment.

The fight had been brutal. The unit they faced was old men and women, warriors who wanted only two things, a final chance at glory and death in combat. *Solahma* was what the general had called them. "Fanatics" was the word Jack thought of. They had been willing to fight to the very last, and that had been costly for the Republic strike force. The *solahma* had hit the Thirteenth Hastati harder than Plunder Company, though he had lost three 'Mechs on the battlefield. The Wolves had torn into the Hastati Sentinels pretty badly, but by the end of the contest, the entire *solahma* Cluster had been taken down, wiped off the map as a unit.

Word from General Cariveau said the Sixteenth Principes Guards had skirted the fight, instead driving to the Persian Gulf. "We've split the Wolves in half, by God!" the general had proclaimed. The media had said that the Wolf force that had fallen back in Georgia had been a victory, in that the Republic defenders had avoided destruction. No one had entirely bought that piece of propaganda. This though, this was different.

Mia carefully walked up alongside him, her coveralls damp with sweat and grease. He turned to her and saw a smudge of green lubricant on her lean face. "You smell that, Sergeant?" he asked with a wry grin.

"Sir?" She looked around for some damage she may have missed. "What do you mean?'

"That," Jack said, pointing to the field littered with the wreckage of battle. "That is the smell of victory."

FIELD COMMAND POST DROPKICK
THESSALONIKI, GREECE
TERRA
10 FEBRUARY 3151 (T+31)

General Chance Vickers stared at the holomap image and clenched her teeth in anger and frustration. The Republic had blasted through a Cluster of her *solahma* forces in Iran. The strike force had massed their superheavy BattleMechs for the first time since the invasion, and it had proved effective— much to her chagrin. The Republic's thrust south had also cut her land-transport lines for supplies.

She had hoped they would drive west, toward her at the front. It made sense, cut off the enemy force and attempt to destroy it piecemeal. But Devlin Stone had refused to play that classic move. Instead, he had sent the force driving eastward, toward Pakistan and Afghanistan, according to the orbital view provided by Haake Sukhanov. There were a few *solahma* units operating in the rear, mostly to protect the supply lines in case of insurgent activities, but they were no match for the size of the force the Republic had rammed through her front. She had relocated the units in the Republic's path, saving them for a later fight...for her own solution to the problem.

Galaxy Commander Niels Carns of Epsilon Galaxy, her former unit, entered the portable command dome. His field jumpsuit was pristine, clearly a new change of uniform. Unlike many in her command, he was clean-shaven, his wavy brown hair perfectly styled. "You sent for me, General?"

"We have a situation," she said.

"I am aware. The Republic broke out of the Caucasuses and effectively sliced us in half." There was something in his voice, a bit of happiness.

"I received word you are loading your Galaxy onto DropShips," she replied.

"Someone has to deal with this threat. My Galaxy was refitting, but I will go and crush this assault." She knew this bravado in his voice from when she had served under him.

"You will not."

Her words hung in the air for a moment.

"I am a Clan Wolf warrior," Carns said, "a *Galaxy Commander*. I will go where I am needed the most. That is the way of our people." The smugness, the arrogance, it was all there.

"*Neg*. You will go back to your assignment."

"I cannot sit back and do nothing when our conquest is at risk. Khan Ward will understand once I have smashed this counterattack."

"I outrank you. This is for me to address, not you. I have plans for Epsilon. Order your troops out of their DropShips, *now*."

"I propose we settle this in a Circle of Equals," he said puffing his chest out slightly.

Chance stood before him and said nothing for a moment, curbing her own rage. "This is exactly the kind of thinking that has prevented the Clans from taking Terra," she said in a low voice. "I need you to clear your head, Galaxy Commander. The Republic has hit us in our rear. What do you think they will do here, where we are right now? What would *you* do?"

For a moment, he said nothing. Then, "I would wait until we reacted to the threat, then hit us here, where we will have made ourselves vulnerable."

"Exactly. Loading up your troops and running off to fight them is playing right into their hands," Chance replied. "You want to fight? Fine. I am rotating you to the front, and we will hit them before they hit us."

"What will you do about that force in our rear?"

"*I* will resolve it."

Carns, grumbling, left the portable command dome as Star Colonel Damon Ward entered, grinning. "I imagine that was rough."

"How you can be his aide is beyond me," Chance said. Damon had been her CO years earlier, when Alaric had been taken prisoner by Anastasia Kerensky. Chance had tried to mount a rescue operation without Damon's authorization, and rather than punish her when he discovered the reason behind her plan, he had opted to join Alaric's command team for planning the invasion of Terra. Alaric had placed him in charge of assembling Clan Wolf's massive army of technicians for the campaign.

"Did you have to stick a gun to his head?" Damon asked with an even wider grin, hearkening back to his own confrontation with her.

"It was tempting," she confessed.

"You and I—two of his subordinates at one point—were brought in on the planning for this invasion. Not him, people under him. He is taking that personally, an insult, so he feels he has something to prove."

"Will he come around?"

Damon shook his head. "*Neg*. I have tried to talk to him on the matter, but he will not listen."

Chance nodded. "Very well. I appreciate your support at least."

"Tell me what I can do."

"Leave me. I need to speak with the Khan...alone. In the meantime, get your people ready to move out. I plan on renewing our offensive."

Damon cocked his eyebrow, then left her. As soon as the cover flap closed, she activated her communications system. A minute later, the holoimage of Alaric Ward appeared before her.

"I received your earlier message," Alaric said. "Haake sent me the images from orbit. Stone's strategy is commendable. It is a good strike at a weak area. We did not expect him capable of massing that much force without our detection, and the choice of his strike location is well planned. You know the Republic is going to come for you there, now that they have cut your lines."

Most people would have taken his words as calm, but Chance knew Alaric. He was worried, and rightfully so. Counterattacks were expected, but the scale and location of this one was surprising.

"I do. That is why I am going on the offensive—a spoiling attack, hit them before they can hit us again. Getting supplies by DropShip will be slower, but I am not going to dig in and let them fight on their terms. That still leaves me with a problem in my rear area. I do not want them reoccupying the Bangalore redoubt or moving farther into our rear."

Alaric nodded. "That still leaves the enemy that split our forces and is driving into our rear. Not exactly a desirable situation, Chance. What do you need from me?"

"I need the WarBear," she replied. "He may want some additional warriors, but this is what the TRC was designed for."

"Agreed. Ramiel will contact you and make the necessary arrangements. Between the two of you, I trust this counterattack can be dealt with."

With those words, Alaric's face disappeared, leaving Chance very much alone, yet oddly more comfortable.

LIAONING
CHINA
10 FEBRUARY 3151 (T+31)

Star Colonel Kalidessa Kerensky assembled the Second Wolf Assault Cluster just after 0300 in the warehouse they had commandeered for use as a hangar and barracks. No one was happy about being rolled out of their cots, but they knew enough not to grumble. She had when Ramiel Bekker had awakened her, however. When she heard the reason why, she had stopped her griping and listened.

Since the fighting in Central China, Beta Galaxy had been moving north. While the Republic did strike out with a local militia unit, the Mongolian Cavaliers, it had done little to slow Beta's advance. Their CO had gotten drawn in and surrounded, opting to make a last stand on a forested hilltop. It had taken two days, but the Cavaliers, what was left of them, finally surrendered.

"Attention," Kalidessa said to her assembled warriors. "The Republic of the Sphere has launched a counterattack, a big one, in the Middle East. The TRC is being deployed, and the WarBear has asked us to join them." Mentioning Ramiel Bekker would help. His training of Wolf warriors and his creation of the Tactical Response Cluster had earned him respect within the warrior caste.

"Star Colonel," Star Commander Manning spoke from the middle of the group. "What did we do to draw the sticky end of the stick?" There were a few chuckles.

Kalidessa Kerensky was not amused, however, and it showed as her eyes narrowed and her voice frosted over. "Laugh it up, Manning. The Republic has surged its aerospace support over their counterattack forces. You want to know why us? I will tell you what the WarBear told me twenty minutes ago. He said this counterattack puts our invasion at risk. He said he needed a unit that would go into the fight and not stop until the job was done. He needed warriors brave enough and stupid enough to take the mission." She paused. "Those warriors were unavailable, so he woke me up and asked for us."

A roar of laughter came from her Howling Furies. Kalidessa allowed herself the barest hint of a grin. *Good. This may be the last time we get a good laugh together, given what we are up against.*

"When do we go, Star Colonel?" DuJordan asked from the back row.

"We are set for immediate departure," she replied, with murmurs increasing among her Cluster.

Parac Shaw, standing in front of his Star of Elementals, spoke next, his deep voice booming in the room. "What is the force size, Star Colonel?"

"I do not have exact numbers, but recon estimates between three and four regiments." Someone whistled from the back of the room—Hawkins, no doubt. "Look, this will not be easy. They have a lot of their superheavies out there, which they have never massed before. We have to prevent them from getting back into one of their redoubts. If they do, it will take days to dig them out again. I, for one, hate to retake the same piece of property twice." Those words brought nods of agreement.

"All right, then. Get your butts in gear. Drop prep is in thirty. All I want to see is assholes and elbows, warriors!"

The group scrambled instantly at her orders.

CHAPTER 11

KIRTHAR NATIONAL PARK
PAKISTAN
TERRA
14 FEBRUARY 3151, 0716 HOURS (T+35)

This was the battle Galaxy Commander Ramiel Bekker had been planning for since he had become a bondsman of Alaric Ward. The Tactical Response Cluster was nearly a Galaxy in size and had been designed as a "firefighting unit" within Clan Wolf, used for plugging holes in the line or waging counterattacks where needed. Moreover, Ramiel had drilled the unit on dealing with the superheavies the Republic was expected to deploy.

The question as to where to deploy had been driven by the path of the counterattack, swinging through Pakistan towards the India redoubt. Bekker, along with Star Colonel Kalidessa Kerensky, had chosen the Kirthar National Park for several reasons. It was rough, broken ground, with sparse plant life clinging to rocks and boulders. The areas with brush were small, but provided cover for infantry or battle armor. The long, undulating hills were deceptively steep, and the low mountains offered obscured fields of fire. Deep ravines and nearly nonexistent roads gave Ramiel a battlefield where he could use the rolling contours of ground for defensive positions and limit deception from the enemy.

The Republic commander, a Knight named Paco "Danger" Cubillo, was no fool. No doubt his aerial recon flights had detected the DropShips that had shuttled the TRC into place. He had also ignored the *solahma* Clusters Chance had drawn to the north, likely not seeing them as a threat. Ramiel had put these warriors under his command and had them ready to deploy. *Odds are Cubillo senses a trap...which makes this far more interesting.*

Ramiel arranged his forces on a long, bowed arc running north to south. The bend in the bow pointed eastward—the direction the Republic forces were advancing. He would bend that arc back in the center and give up ground, once the fighting started. *Warriors are always naturally drawn to where the shooting is. They will come there, and once they have advanced their superheavies far enough, I will bring in the northern and southern wings.*

Ramiel's face was set like stone in the cockpit of his *Stormwolf* B, awaiting the inevitable confrontation. *This battle stands to define me...one way or another.*

All it required was for the RAF forces to play along.

10,000 METERS OVER KIRTHAR NATIONAL PARK
PAKISTAN
TERRA
0736 HOURS

Star Commander Manning of Ravager Star rose above the cloud formation in his *Jagatai*. The Republic had been able to maintain local air superiority at the start of their counterattack, which had helped them during their drive out of the Caucasuses. As the Wolves had fallen back, they had destroyed the airstrips they controlled, leaving the advancing Republic aerospace very little to work with. Now though, the Wolf fighters had to fly longer distances, so their ability to respond to threats from distant airfields was limited. Their CAP was in place, but could not be maintained indefinitely.

"Got them, sir," Vigdal called on the tactical channel. "To the south, three Stars' worth of fighters, lights and mediums. I show a mix of *Poignard*s, *Sagittarii*s, *Schrack*s, a *Seydlitz*, and a *Tomahawk*."

"Tallyho on the lead *Poignard*," Jeremy called out with a hint of excitement.

"Hold fire," Manning said. "Track them for now, keep in the clouds. We have four minutes to showtime. The last thing I need is for Star Colonel Kerensky to chew me out over you *surats* jumping the gun."

KIRTHAR NATIONAL PARK
PAKISTAN
TERRA
0739 HOURS

The Carnivore tank *Fratricide* was mostly concealed behind a rocky outcropping. The two-warrior crew had put every bit of scrub brush they could on top of the vehicle to help conceal it. Hawkins did most of the concealment effort, but DuJordan said there was little point in it. "Once we open up, all of that stuff just becomes kindling anyway."

Hawkins had followed Star Colonel Kerensky's orders regardless. Anyone in the Second Wolf Assault Cluster knew the price of not following her orders. Besides, it had helped pass the time.

"All I am saying is that she is very quick to volunteer our unit," DuJordan said as Hawkins crawled back inside the tank. "This is a long campaign. I would hate for us to be taken out early in the fighting. Losing us would be a waste of precious resources."

"How do you know she volunteered us for this operation? Perhaps Khan Ward chose us."

"He would not do that," DuJordan said. "Khan Ward likes us."

"I agree," Hawkins replied. "Maybe you should take it up with her?"

"Never mind," his gunner replied.

"You are afraid of her."

"*Aff*. So are you. We all are."

Hawkins was going to reply, but his sensors started painting targets...a lot of them. "We are not alone. I have targets coming in. Plotting tracks. Relay the readings to the rest of the Cluster."

Using the controls on his viewscreen, he zoomed in on the closest target, an *Ares* superheavy. He had seen a destroyed one in China, but never one on the move, slowly thudding along the sand and rock of the wildlife park. It kicked up a dust storm that obscured other BattleMechs in the row. "Are you seeing this?"

"*Aff*," DuJordan said. "Message has gone out. She wants us to hold fire for her word."

Hawkins watched the lumbering war machine move diagonally across his field of fire, creeping closer with each step. *I hope she gives that word soon...*

11,000 METERS OVER KIRTHAR NATIONAL PARK
PAKISTAN
TERRA
0740 HOURS

"You are a go, Star Commander," Star Colonel Kalidessa Kerensky said crisply. "Take the Ravagers in."

Star Commander Manning grinned. "All right, Ravagers, call your targets. We are weapons free."

A chorus of "*Tallyhos*" rang out in his neurohelmet as his Star dove after the Republic fighters. Almost instantly the Republic aerospace elements broke formation and climbed to where Manning and his Star were diving in at them.

His *Jagatai* felt like an extension of his body as he arced in on the farthest target, a Republic *Sagittarii* painted in a blotched camouflage pattern of grays and whites. The pilot was good, weaving as tightly as the boxy aerospace fighter could. Its snub-nose PPC flashed, unleashing a beam that narrowly missed his starboard wing.

Manning did not weave; instead he focused, boring in on the target, checking his tactical display as the rest of the Star engaged. He launched his long-range missiles and fired the pair of extended-range PPCs simultaneously as the *Sagittarii* reached the apex of one of its weaves. Both PPCs slammed into the forward fuselage, blasting off chunks of armor and sending secondary arcs of discharged particles dancing down the airframe. A moment later, two-thirds of Manning's missiles exploded along the target's wings, leaving smoky gray streaks in the sky behind the Republic fighter. The missiles that missed rained down on the Pakistani desert below.

"Splash one *Seydlitz*!" Guethler, piloting Ravager Three, called out.

"Always gunning for the easy kills," Vigdal remarked.

Manning ignored the chatter. The pilot he pursued juked hard to the right, and Manning followed, his trio of large pulse lasers filling the air with emerald green bursts. Two missed, but one hit the tail of the aerofighter, blasting the vertical stabilizer into scrap metal. The *Sagittarii* went into a death spin, corkscrewing toward the ground as Manning turned to find his next target.

Ramiel Bekker looked at the tactical display as the center of his formation drifted back, just as planned. The Republic had been brilliant in massing the firepower of their superheavies, but they sacrificed mobility. A gap was opening between the faster, lighter forces of the Republic and their hulking cousins.

From his 'Mech's concealed position in the rolling hills, he felt a surge of satisfaction. He didn't just want to defeat Cubillo; he was glad to be there. He wanted a taste of combat. *This is my fight,* he thought. *My own piece of our victory.*

"Recon Stalker Two to WarBear," said a voice in his neurohelmet. "They are ten kilometers north of your position, now heading east."

"Roger, Stalker Two," Bekker replied. He switched to the tactical channel. "Wolves, our enemy approaches. Remember your training. Stick to your units and to the plans, and we will take them down."

He shifted in the new console seat of his pristine *Stormwolf* B and checked his readings. The *Stormwolf*, though manufactured by the Sea Foxes for Clan Wolf, was his design, and it was built for speed and firepower. His was adorned with a splotched pattern of grays and greens and a flamboyant red paint around the cockpit—the camouflage of the TRC.

"We stand ready," came the voice of Kalidessa Kerensky.

"Designate targets," he commanded, and the enemy triangles of light on the display pulsated as his teams locked on. Bekker chose an *Ares* as his Star's target. He waited, letting the enemy move into a relatively flat area north of his position—until at last, the moment came. "Wolves, this is WarBear. *Engage!*"

His strike team consisted of his *Stormwolf*, a *Thresher Mk II*, and a *Kit Fox*. "WarBear has the ball," he said. "Follow me." He led them around a large hill and started up another low ridge, where they finally caught sight of their foe.

There were seven superheavies, a number of lances of small hovercraft, a swarm of hoverbikes, and battle armor. The *Ares* they targeted was ponderously slow and bristled with weapons. Explosions went off in their midst as the other members of the TRC pounced on their targets.

Bekker darted forward down the ridge, firing his ER PPC and plasma cannon at one of the Ares' legs. The hits blasted at the thick armor plating there—little more than pinpricks to the huge BattleMech. An *Amarok*, also a new Wolf model, joined in the fray, unleashing its rotary autocannon, whose purr filled the air and its yellow tracers looked like laser beams.

The *Ares* turned toward him and fired its long-range missiles. Only half found their mark; minor explosions left pitted and mauled armor in their wake. It made Bekker smile. First blood in a new BattleMech was something to be remembered, and the circumstances of this fight made it even more notable.

MechWarrior McNary, in his fleet-footed *Kit Fox*, moved to flank the *Ares*, drawing its lasers and short-range missiles. McNary fired a barrage of LB-X autocannon rounds that left blackened marks on another thick leg of the *Ares*.

Bekker saw Fife's *Thresher Mk II* close in as well, almost a blur from how fast it ran. It did not fire, but stole the *Ares'* attention. Honor demanded that the *Ares* fire first, which it did, raking the *Thresher* with small-laser fire. The bright red beams stood out against the low purple-gray clouds rolling in in the distance, leaving black burn marks all over. But Fife's PPC blasted the same leg that Bekker had hit, turning a big black circle of armor into a rain of melted splatter that set some of the brush ablaze.

Movement caught Bekker's eye; Star Captain Agustin Tutuola and his Star of Black Wolf battle armor moved along a hill line, weaving in and out of deep gorges as they moved in against the swarm of hoverbikes. Three of the Republic craft disappeared in a barrage of fire, and the others scattered.

Good, all three of us are engaged. Superheavy 'Mechs were intimidating, but Bekker was confident that light, fast BattleMechs working in trios could take one down. Even as the *Ares* turned to deal with Fife and McNary, it exposed its flank and rear, and Bekker shot it with an alpha strike of his plasma cannon, ER PPC, and paired ER medium lasers. The searing blasts rocked the *Ares* hard, sending glowing, fist-sized chunks of armor into the sandy soil below.

The *Ares* let loose everything it had at the *Kit Fox*. Many of the short- and long-range missiles missed, spraying dirt into the air, but enough struck the *Kit Fox* to shake McNary. As the smoke and dust rolled clear, Bekker saw the gutted shell of the *Kit Fox*, its canopy blown in and a lit furnace roaring out of it. In the skies far beyond it, he saw a pair of smoke streaks stabbing downward, aerospace fighters plunging to their demise. *Kalidessa's people are good. Let us hope those are Republic fighters.*

Fife avenged his battered Starmate; his PPC and short-range missiles riddled one of the damaged *Ares'* legs. The 'Mech ignored the hits and turned to concentrate on Bekker instead. It fired and missed with one medium laser, but hit with the small ones and a wave of short-range missiles. Bekker's 'Mech jerked as armor melted off, but he kept his balance and used his speed to make follow-up hits impossible. His new 'Mech moved fluidly, despite the damage it had sustained, as he headed for the larger BattleMech's rear. *That is right, keep your attention on me.*

Fife's lightning-fast *Thresher Mk II* took advantage of Bekker's flanking maneuver by blasting away at the legs of the *Ares*. Flames from Fife's inferno rounds roared up the hulking 'Mech, and ripples of heat rose as wave after wave of missiles soared in. Bekker fired his own ER PPC at the *Ares* and hit one of the battered and flaming legs, melting a black hole in the armor.

Missiles rained down on him, but his *Stormwolf's* laser anti-missile system turned most of them into raining bits of harmless shrapnel. Fife continued to pump fire at the legs of the *Ares*—which was clearly overwhelmed.

It swayed and fought for balance with one unresponsive leg. The *Ares* toppled over—hard. The impact and sick, metallic grinding of twisting armor reached Bekker even through his sealed cockpit.

Fife did not relent; he took advantage of the prone enemy, saturating the big target with everything he had. The *Ares* fired back at the *Thresher Mk II* and knocked Fife to the ground—leaving his right leg still standing upright. A pair of hoverbikes spun around him, peppering his 'Mech with shots until he turned on them. One evaporated in a PPC blast, and the other sped off.

Bekker fired his plasma cannon at the *Ares*' middle cockpit canopy, where the pilot sat. Between his cannon and Fife's PPC hits, which sent arcs of blue electrical discharge dancing over the fallen foe, the indicators soon showed that the *Ares* had powered down.

Bekker turned to the battlefield. A brutish Republic *Poseidon* was toppling in a haze of heat, smoke, and dust. His TRC was hitting two other superheavies, and the other massive 'Mechs were starting to fall back. All around him, the ground was littered with armor, hot shrapnel, and the remains of the support units that had tried to protect the superheavies.

Ramiel switched to the tactical channel. "Kalidessa, it is time for Slingshot."

"Agreed," she replied.

A moment later, a *Sassanid*-class DropShip roared over the battlefield toward the Republic line.

Bekker grinned.

0748 HOURS

Star Commander Parac Shaw bounded out of the open DropShip doors and descended toward the rearmost *Ares*. His Bane Star and the TRC's Silver Streak Star had split targets, striking at a total of four of the hulking 'Mechs. Using his eye controls, he feathered his leg jets to control his descent, and landed hard on the superheavy 'Mech's green-and-brown hull. His knees ached as he stabbed his suit's clawed hand between two armor plates and held on.

Kobler had landed just above the cockpit and fired his small laser right at the canopy. Parac climbed and clawed his way there and joined him, the heat from their lasers rippling the air around them. The rest of his Star was on the arms and outer edges of the 'Mech's flattened torso, firing with their lasers and machine guns. Beneath him, the *Ares* continued to shoot at Wolf 'Mechs, a testimony to the skill of its crew. He caught a glimpse of Stroud, who hung on with his clawed arm under the *Ares*' right arm, swinging madly as the huge OmniMech gyrated.

The MechWarrior tried to shake them off, but the 'Mech's bulk and slow speed only resulted in a low-speed turn. Parac adjusted his aim and hit the canopy's hinge until it seared through. At the same moment, Kobler blasted the upper canopy's armored ferroglass, which popped inward with a *clunk*.

Parac plunged his clawed arm into the melting hole that Kobler had blown and grappled with the MechWarrior. He pulled hard, but the restraining straps held firm, and the BattleMech rocked beneath him as the warrior struggled. The second pull likely broke some of the MechWarrior's bones, but they failed to pull free. *Come on!*

His third pull wrenched the MechWarrior, a large woman, from her seat. Her shoulder was dislocated, blood soaked her chest where his battle claw had dug into her, and she was unconscious in his grip. The *Ares* stopped moving, stopped firing, and seized up. He was prepared for it to collapse, but it remained upright.

Parac tossed her out across the 'Mech's flattened hull, and her limp body skidded and rolled, leaving a crimson smear on the armor. "Bane Star, new target—the one to the west," he said, pointing his laser off into the distance.

0812 HOURS

DuJordan fired another volley from *Fratricide*'s Gauss rifles at the *Poseidon* in his sights. Both slugs slammed into the already-mauled right leg, leaving hot, smoking holes where they cratered the armor. A Wolf *Dominator* blazed away at the same damaged leg with its ER PPC, the brilliant burst of azure energy hit between the Gauss rifle craters, connecting them with a searing scar.

The *Poseidon* lost balance as its pilot attempted to reposition the leg, and fell forward, cascading into a rock formation that was pulverized under the weight of the falling 'Mech. Bits of armor flew in every direction.

"It figures," Hawkins said as he drove *Fratricide* forward. "We do all the hard work, and someone else gets credit for the kill."

0829 HOURS

Star Colonel Kalidessa Kerensky eyed one of the last of the superheavies from the cockpit of her *Dire Wolf*, angling in for the kill. Her ER large lasers blazed away, their scarlet beams slicing at the thick hide of the three-legged beast. Splatters of melted armor rained down as she closed the gap.

The *Ares* launched medium-range missiles into her, making the *Dire Wolf* quake. Amber and red warning light flickered on her damage display, but nothing alarmed her. The fighting had already taken a lot out of the *Ares*, and she was here to finish the work of other brave warriors.

The bulk of the Republic forces were falling back, albeit stubbornly, but this *Ares* refused to do so. It advanced, no doubt in hopes of buying its comrades time. Kalidessa respected that; it showed honor. *It will be a shame to kill such warriors.*

She let loose with four medium pulse lasers, the brilliant emerald bursts stitching the legs of the *Ares*. The superheavy fired SRMs at her in response, half of which found their mark.

Then her targeting computer flickered for a moment, and went blank—then began a reboot cycle.

Stravag! *An EMP attack!*

Sweat rolled down her forehead and stung her eyes as she shifted to manual targeting. She blasted away with her Ultra autocannons, missing with one. Using the first one as a guide, she adjusted her torso and arm so that the second shot hit the *Ares'* mangled lower body. The explosions blew away big pieces of the already twisted armor there, and some exploded deep in the torso.

The *Ares* wobbled a few steps as her targeting system flickered back online. It fired at her with another wave of MRMs, which destroyed her long-range missile launcher. She had run out of ammunition early in the battle, so the loss was negligible.

As her lasers hummed with energy, she fired the large ones again. This time, rather than leaving scars, the weapons bore straight in, like a crimson lance wielded by a charging knight. The holes glowed orange and smoked from the heat as the *Ares* wavered, its gait suddenly uneasy.

The superheavy came down on its knees, hard, straining the armor so much that three plates popped off. The metal groaned enough for Kalidessa to hear it in her cockpit. Yet the gunner continued to fire, blazing their medium and small lasers at her with futile effort. While the small crimson beams found their mark, slashing at her thick leg armor, the mediums went wild—one exploding a rock near her. *They fight, despite being down... Such determination is to be recognized.*

She jogged up near the *Ares* and unleashed her Ultra autocannons at nearly point-blank range. Both salvos gutted what little armor remained on the forward hull, exploding deep within the OmniMech's guts. For a moment, it quaked, not from the explosions, but from something mechanical dying within.

Slowly, agonizingly, it fell over on its side toward her, the cockpit only scant meters away. With one barrage, she could finish the crew off.

Kalidessa Kerensky held her fire.

Major Traver's head throbbed, and his body protested every movement as his *Ares* fell over. Metallic bones crunched upon impact, and his vison tunneled for a moment. The gyro ground to a halt, and the engine billowed heat into the cockpit, its insulation housing destroyed. There would be no recovery.

Looking upward out of his cockeyed cockpit, he saw the *Dire Wolf* he had been fighting. The logo on it, a wolf baying into the air, was strangely visible to him in that moment. Ejection was suicide at this angle, and his OmniMech was ruined, rendered into worthless scrap. *Go on. If you're going to kill us, get it over with...*

His headset hissed as the Wolf warrior broadcast on a tightbeam to him. "*Ares* crew—you fought with honor. I am Star Colonel Kalidessa Kerensky of the Second Wolf Assault Cluster, and I offer you a rare honor. I claim you as bondsmen of Clan Wolf. That, or you will become prisoners of war until we crush the Republic and the Jade Falcons. The choice is yours."

"Don't do it!" Cheetah said. "I'd rather be in a POW camp than a prize of some Wolf."

Traver said nothing for a moment. Then he hit his comm button. "Star Colonel, this is Major Jack Traver. We cannot fight against the Republic. But like you, I have no desire to see the Jade Falcons win. I will agree to your bondsman terms as long as we get a chance to defend Terra against the Jade Falcons... and them alone."

There was a pause, and he wondered for a moment if he had overplayed his hand. Then came the stern voice over the comm system again.

"Well bargained and done, Jack."

0903 HOURS

Bekker stood atop a fallen *Poseidon* and surveyed the now-quiet battlefield. Pillars of black smoke rolled up from destroyed 'Mechs and vehicles, drifting in the light breeze. The cold winter air was refreshing after the near-sauna of his cockpit.

There had been a handful of survivors. Bekker had brought MedTechs in to tend to them. McNary joined him on the hull, his own jumpsuit torn, a bloody cut on his leg staining the green material dark maroon.

"Did you find him?" Bekker asked.

"*Neg*, Galaxy Commander," McNary said. "We found Cubillo's 'Mech, a *Hera* configuration, but not his body. There was a lot of blood in the cockpit. We do not believe he could have gotten far."

"Do not count on that," Bekker replied. "Extend our patrols. If he is out there, I want him." He eyed McNary's bloodied leg. "And see a MedTech for that."

"It will be done," McNary said. He saluted, then carefully clambered back down.

Bekker activated his personal communications unit. "Send word to General Vickers. Tell her the TRC sends their regards." He grinned. "Then tell her that Sir Cubillo's counterattack has been utterly destroyed."

CHAPTER 12

Alaric watched from the rocky hill looking to the west as his Beta Galaxy drove into the mercenaries in front of him, smashing their center.

What should have been a routine mission had been complicated from the start. His seemingly easy trip across the Bering Straits had ended with his DropShip getting shot down by a lucky Republic air-ambush. He had nearly drowned in the icy waters just off the North American shore, managing to get out in a *Skinwalker*, eventually wading onto land. For some, the incident would have been a warning that their life could end with a stray shot or a freak accident in battle—but Alaric did not harbor such fears. *Taking Terra is my destiny. It was what I was conceived to do.*

The fighting in Alaska had also been much more arduous than expected. Once across the Bering Strait, Alaric and his Beta Galaxy had collided with two foes. First was the bitter cold of an Alaskan winter. The deep snows had made advances slow and ponderous. While it helped with BattleMech heat, it took a toll on equipment and personnel.

Second was the resistance. Two battalions of Hansen's Roughriders awaited him there, and another mercenary unit, the Gray Gunny Lancers, had literally leaped into the fray to sow chaos in the fight. The mercenaries had proven to be worthy foes; they'd mangled a Cluster of his best troops, no small feat.

But now he had them falling back. From his hilltop, he surveyed the carnage stretching out on the snow-covered plains. The Roughriders shifted, trying to blunt the Wolf drive in the center. They were clearly fighting a holding action. In the distance, he saw the drive plumes of DropShips approaching from the west.

"Spurlock," he said over his command channel. "They are bringing in Dropships, *quiaff*?"

"*Aff*, my Khan, they are," his Watch commander replied. "They are on a trajectory some fifteen kilometers due west of your position."

Why? The Roughriders still had a viable fighting force on the ground, as did the Lancers. "Where did the ships come from?"

"South of us, some four thousand kilometers," Spurlock Conners replied.

Alaric stared. It made no sense. His was the only Clan force in North America. While the mercenaries had taken some losses, they were not behaving like other Republic units. *I expected them to take a stand, wear us down further. I could order pursuit, but once our forces get in the range of those DropShip turrets, the odds will shift in their favor. Perhaps the Republic is facing a graver threat elsewhere—the Falcons?*

As much as he wished to destroy the force, Alaric held back. "This is Wolf Prime to all Wolves—disengage. If they wish to leave, let them."

Two hours later, Alaric entered his mobile HQ and tossed his neurohelmet on an empty seat. The warmth of the vehicle was welcome, and he handed his winter jacket to a duty officer. *It will be good to start south and get out of this frigid weather.*

He had received word that Chance was reaching out to him, and the mobile HQ was the best place to warm up and have secure communications. A staff officer provided him a hot cup of coffee that he cradled and sipped for strength as he moved in front of the holotable. Chance's holographic face hovered in the air before him.

"My Khan," she said, bowing her head for a moment. "I am pleased to report that the WarBear was successful. The Republic counterattack has been crushed. The enemy has suffered nearly seventy percent casualties, with some of their lighter BattleMechs and vehicles fleeing to the north, toward Russia."

Alaric expected nothing less. Stone had stunned him with the counterattack, and it had been a success, albeit a short-lived one. "Excellent. And your situation?"

"I correctly assumed the Republic was preparing to attack us, so we struck first. I ordered Epsilon dropped in the Republic's rear, twenty kilometers behind their front lines while I thrust at them from the front. They put up a vicious fight, but are retreating at this moment. I am letting them do so. That gives us some time to restore our supply situation."

Alaric nodded. "Excellent. Alpha and Theta Galaxies are under Garner's command and heading west through Russia. I am proceeding on to the south to Strategic Objective One."

"Very good. The TRC is with us right now, refitting. The Second Wolf Assault Cluster will be returning to you tomorrow." She paused. "I appreciate the assistance in rectifying this matter."

"Think nothing of it," Alaric said. "Your victory is our victory."

"What news of the Falcons?"

Alaric manipulated the holomap of Terra, updated with the Watch's field reports, zooming in on the mountainous region the Falcons were currently attacking. "They have been forced into a slow siege of Geneva, and Malvina has swept south in France as well. The Northwind Highlanders have been harassing her out of northwestern France with a remarkable degree of success. Malvina landed a Galaxy in North Africa this morning, so we do not know their degree of success yet, short of seizing Alexandria."

"I need a day or two for refit and rest," Chance said.

"Take it. Your personnel will need it in the battles to come."

The image cut off, and Alaric stared into the empty space before him. Nursing his cup of coffee, he studied the holographic map. The red of Clan Wolf was slowly consuming the yellow of the Republic. The Jade Falcon green covered small areas, but that would change. *We were ready for the drive on Terra, already mobilized. Malvina was less so. Her forces will come in slowly. When they strike, they will disrupt matters—not just for the Republic, but for us as well.*

ANNEMASSE, GENEVA
TERRA
15 FEBRUARY 3151, 1420 HOURS

Star Captain Marv Roshak, of Gamma Galaxy's Jade Falcon Guards, angled his *Night Gyr* around the narrow Avenue Émile Zola near the monorail line, catching a Republic *Lament* before it could duck back under cover behind the library. He unleashed his twin ER particle projection cannons and Ultra-autocannon simultaneously at his foe. The flash of the PPCs in the early morning light caught the right arm of the *Lament*, blasting it off in a shower of sparks and smoke. The autocannon rounds tore into the corner of the library as the Republic MechWarrior finally got to cover.

Smoke rolled over Geneva from a hundred different fires throughout the city. A late snow had fallen the night before, mixing with the ash. The rumble of artillery made the ground tremble under his OmniMech. The low clouds, purple and white, were streaked every so often by aerospace fighters, their flashing lasers making the overcast sky flicker. Several times a day, a massive explosion or two—directed orbital bombardments from Jade Falcon WarShips—targeted those strongholds that could not be taken by conventional means.

Roshak passed some houses that seemed completely undamaged, however, as if the savage battle had missed them entirely. Their colorful shutters were closed, as if merely weathering a storm. As he glanced out over the city to the west, he struggled with the contrasts. At one time, Geneva might have been quaint, almost charming. *Look at what the Republic has made us do to it.*

He trotted forward to angle for a shot, but a laser tagged him from the roof of the library. The emerald pulses of energy struck his right side, causing him to face the new threat: a pop-up turret activated by his presence.

Another one! Blitzking *Republic!* Roshak moved his targeting reticle onto it and fired his trio of medium pulse lasers. Two found their mark as the turret fired again, its pulses hitting his torso armor with a *pop-hiss* sound. The turret exploded, throwing sparks in the air. For a second, he felt a wave of pleasure.

It was cut short by a heavy PPC blast from the *Lament*, which had doubled back on him. The shot struck his right leg, tearing through the remaining armor. A warning light flashed red for his knee actuator. He tried to step forward, but the actuator was locked, no doubt fused into a single piece by the charged-particle blast.

The *Lament* did not wait for a counterstrike. But instead of following up on its attack, it fell back to cover.

MechWarrior Mathews came up alongside him, piloting a blackened *Hel*, one that had suffered earlier under an artillery barrage. "Star Captain, Jaylee is down. Her OmniMech lost both legs to a vibramine. Also, Pharaoh's *Mad Dog* has lost both arms."

Roshak kept his reticle aimed at the corner of the library. "My right leg is hindered. We need to fall back," he said bitterly. "I will contact the Galaxy Commander and tell her our status." He dreading sending the message. Galaxy Commander Jane Thastus was a just commander, but she echoed the Chingis Khan's demands far too often.

"She will be displeased we did not advance farther," Mathews said.

"She can *be* displeased," Roshak fired back.

This campaign was not what he had imagined. The Jade Falcons were built for swift lightning strikes, and victory had always come quickly for them. They were supposed to have taken Geneva in two days, three at most. Now it had become a siege. Every street, every building seemed to be fighting for the Republic. RAF snipers had even gotten behind the lines and were targeting Jade Falcon warriors. *Terra is proving itself worthy of fighting the Clans.* That was the only thought that gave him solace.

The Jade Falcon Guards had been reconstituted only a year before. The fight for Terra was their baptism by fire, and so far it had been a hellish grind. Roshak had led his Trinary around the south of Geneva, but they and the rest of Gamma Galaxy had become bogged down in the Annemasse suburb east of the city. Stone's Liberators had sortied against them six times so far, only to fall back each time before the Guards could mass against them. All the while, Galaxy Commander Thastus said Khan Hazen demanded results.

Results? *Neg.* The Republic seemed intent on keeping Geneva.

"Let us fall back to Phase Line Bravo," Roshak said, reining in his frustration. "We can refit there and try again this afternoon." Silently, he wondered if the victory the Chingis Khan demanded would cost the life of every Jade Falcon warrior.

COMMAND POST SOLITUDE
1623 HOURS

Tucker Harwell watched Stone absorb the news of his counterattack as Miller and Lakewood presented the information. The Exarch's shoulders slumped a bit with each piece of bad news. The conference table seemed bigger to Tucker whenever the news was bad, and today it was bad again.

For the past few days, after the Republic counterattack had cut the Wolf lines, it seemed the Devlin Stone of old had returned. *Now everything's gone to hell again.* The Wolves had launched their own counterattack, and the Republic forces had been routed. When Miller and Lakewood finished, Stone sighed heavily and seemed unable to summon enough energy to respond.

"What will the people think?" Damien Redburn asked. The question sucked the life out of the room for a moment.

Stone turned to his friend, his face stiffening with resolve. "They will think what we tell them to think. We will say we secured a great victory for the Republic, and our forces are redeploying to crush the invaders. That is the story the media will feed them. The citizens want victories and heroes, and we must give them that." He spoke with such confidence that Tucker was sure he believed it. But Tucker Harwell's grim, pragmatic mind knew the truth.

Stone is giving them all a lie.

Redburn wasn't buying his response. "Devlin, we cannot sustain this fighting for much longer. We have refugee cities springing up everywhere from our evacuations and people fleeing the advancing armies. People are starving. Alaric is in North America, and his Wolf armies are in Greece and driving across Russia. Malvina is literally right on top of us." He jabbed his index finger skyward. "Our strategy of relying on the redoubts will not win this war any more than spewing propaganda to the people will."

"What do you suggest?" Lakewood asked. Tucker was sure she did it to spare Redburn from Stone's rebuttal.

"We should mass our armies against the Jade Falcons, take them out, and sue for peace with Alaric," Redburn said. "That, or we should cut the heads off both snakes."

Stone shook his head. "Now isn't the time for us to change strategy. Trust me, the redoubts are wearing our enemies down. The Jade Falcons are struggling to take Geneva and suffering grave losses. Alaric has seized ground, but his Wolves have to be nearing exhaustion. You have to give this time, Damien."

"Why did you extract the Roughriders and Lancers?" Redburn pressed. "We had Alaric's force in the open. There was a real chance to take him out."

Stone waved his hand. "A chance is not a guarantee. Besides, they were needed elsewhere," was all he offered.

Tucker's suspicion rose. When Devlin Stone said little, it usually meant he was hiding something.

Redburn stood and walked to the door of the conference room. He paused there, his angry gaze sweeping everyone in the room, including Tucker. "The RAF is not a plaything. These decisions are costing *lives*. Everyone here is too timid to say it, but they agree with me, Devlin. We need to alter our strategy. And you will come to that realization too, soon. For all our sakes, I just hope it's not too late." With that, Redburn stalked out.

Tucker watched the room descend into a murmur of several conversations. Leaning back in his chair, he considered Redburn's words. *He is right, they are all intimidated by Stone to one extent or another. Stone's ego is so big he doesn't want to admit he's played this wrong—he* never *expected to be fighting two*

Clans at once. We crippled the Wolves for a few days, but they recovered far faster than anyone anticipated. Malvina will whittle us down until she has all our heads on pikes.

Just how much time do we have left?

CHAPTER 13

COURT OF THE STAR LEAGUE
UNITY CITY, PUGET SOUND
NORTH AMERICA
TERRA
19 FEBRUARY 3151, 0905 HOURS (T+40)

Khan Alaric Ward walked slowly across the grounds, savoring each footfall. He sighed as he looked around at the site and drank in every detail. *This is history... and it is mine alone to take in.*

He stood in what had been the Court of the Star League long ago. Gone was the once-stunning architecture, blasted into ruins over the centuries. Bits of walls poked up from where the rubble had been cleared. Markings on the ground showed where the great Court had stood. Historical plaques marked various rooms and chambers, including the High Council chamber, where Stefan Amaris had killed First Lord Richard Cameron and plunged the Star League into chaos and war centuries ago, and the spot where the bodies of House Cameron's members had been unceremoniously buried. The rooms were long gone, now just markers and bits of stone beneath a brilliant blue sky.

His jumpsuit did nothing to stop the cold winter breeze. The sunshine offered some warmth—rare, this time of year—but he paid it no heed. His security detail hovered nearby, weapons at the ready, though the site had been cleared prior to his arrival.

It had taken much to reach this place. *Sacred ground.*

He was here now. That was what mattered.

To the side of the ruins stood a tourist stand, now abandoned with the arrival of the Wolf Clan. Alaric beckoned for one of his warriors. "Assemble some *solahma* troops," he said, then nodded at the tourist booth. "Have them remove that structure. This is not a place to sell books and trinkets—it is our home." *Our destiny.*

The warrior acknowledged the order and departed.

Only the Republic would cheapen such sacred ground like this.

General Vickers had originally questioned this part of the invasion plan, but Alaric assured her that securing this site was necessary. Symbols were important for people, especially the Clans. Taking control of the Court of the Star League now would give him legitimacy when the fighting was over. *Every person in the Inner Sphere knows this was the seat of power for the Star League. They know its history.*

I will rebuild this palace when I re-form the Star League. It will once more be a beacon of hope and prosperity for humankind. Standing here, where people like the Great Father had walked, only confirmed to Alaric that he had made the right decision in taking possession of the site. Now he just had to keep it from forces who would stop him—like the Jade Falcons.

Malvina Hazen was fighting in Europe, and having a hard time of it, according to Spurlock Conners' Watch reports. She was squeezing Geneva, the capital of the Republic and a symbol of its strength. "If Malvina wants the rotting corpse of the Republic," he had told Spurlock, "she can fight for every bloody meter of it." For Alaric, taking Geneva would be prohibitively costly; he had known that before landing. And even if it fell, that would not be the end of the Republic. Their armed forces would fight on. *Malvina fights for the jewel in a crown. I fight for the crown itself.*

But Malvina was struggling in Geneva partly because her forces were arriving piecemeal. She had hit hard on her initial landing, but the city had held, and now it was costing her. Where the Wolves had massed their entire Clan for the assault on Terra, the Jade Falcons had initially come with five Galaxies. The rest of their troops were trickling in, arriving every few days.

The Northwind Highlanders still clung to Paris and western France, entrenching there in the Normandy redoubt. The arrival of the Jade Falcons had prompted a stronger resistance effort from Devlin Stone's troops—drawing forces away from the Wolves. Malvina's reputation was a weapon in and of itself. It sowed fear and hatred in her enemies, and it unified most of the Jade Falcons in a way they had not been in generations. Her Mongol Doctrine gave her victories, and those victories kept her people loyal.

Alaric turned around slowly, still appreciating the ruins of the Court of the Star League as he pondered the war so far. *We need to rest and use a few days to refit. Our wounded need healing, and our BattleMechs demand repair. There is no better place to do that than here.* He knew the Wolves who visited this site would find it as spiritual as he did. *It will remind them what we are fighting for—what will come when the dust settles.*

His perscomm chirped at his wrist, and he activated it. "Wolf Prime, go."

"Priority message from Star Admiral Sukhanov, encrypted text only," said the communications officer.

"Read it."

"The message says 'Reunion.'"

Alaric smiled. "Message confirmed." *On schedule...perfect.* "Designate them for landing near my current position. Pass on the message to General Vickers as well."

One key element to the Malvina issue was in-system. Another was still unheard from, but he was sure it would be on time.

He lowered his wrist and stared at a thick growth of pines that marked the perimeter of the old Court. *The Falcons' brutality will play to our advantage. I hope Malvina enjoys whatever is left of Geneva.*

GENEVA
1411 HOURS

The orbital bombardment roared down from the heavens, enveloping a block of the city in death and destruction. A massive, superheated wall of dust and debris rushed out from the epicenter to envelop *Black Rose*, Malvina's *Shrike*, blocking her vision until the cloud of dust rolled by. *That will teach you to fire on my Command Star.*

As her view of the blasted area cleared, she saw the remains of a few structures still jutting upward, more rubble than anything. Fires raged through the ruins, giving off smoke, but no more enemy fire. Bits of ash billowed in the light wind as the snow melted off.

This is the price of the Republic's arrogance in resisting my Jade Falcons.

"Star Colonel Mehta," she said, "take your Thirteenth Dragoons in and seize that block in the name of your Clan."

"It shall be done, Chingis Khan!" Mehta replied. His forces surged into the burning ruins and charged over fallen walls and mounds of brick littered with burning bits of houses and the debris of human life—

An explosion engulfed a *Fire Falcon*, ripping its left leg off and peeling the remaining armor upward. The 'Mech fell hard on its side, unmoving. *Vibramines!*

"*Blitzking surats*!" Malvina cursed, then toggled the comm channel again. "Move into the blown-up ruins. Avoid using the streets where possible."

Star Colonel Mehta acknowledged her orders again—far too late for the MechWarrior piloting the *Fire Falcon*.

Inferno rounds launched from some of the taller structures rained down on the Thirteenth Falcon Dragoons, washing Mehta's BattleMechs in roaring flames as lasers stabbed from the next block.

That has to be Paladin Ergen and his Tenth Hastati Sentinels, or Stone's Liberators. At least they have proven worthy enemies to kill. I will take this city if I have to blast it apart one block at a time.

"Eighth Falcon Velites," Malvina barked, "advance with the Dragoons and provide suppression fire on those buildings to the north."

A squad of Republic Kage battle armor rose on jump jets and spat machine-gun fire on the burning Falcon war machines. Before the Falcons could fight back, the Kages dropped behind a building in the next block.

Fury blazed through the Jade Falcon Khan. "Find that battle armor and *kill them all*!" She turned *Black Rose*, ready to join the fight herself.

FOUR BLOCKS NORTH

Lieutenant Colonel Chris Kornfeld had never been this close to one of the Jade Falcon orbital bombardments before. Even from six blocks away, he felt the deafening roar inside his *Lament*'s cockpit, and the dust from destroyed buildings cast a fog that was almost impenetrable on the streets. Visibility was zero for a few moments, and he had to rely entirely on his sensors—a nerve-wracking proposition.

A Jade Falcon *Eyrie* jumped through the dust, landing right in front of his 'Mech, swirling the dust as it landed and clearing it enough for both MechWarriors to see each other in the smoke and fine gray particles that had been a block of Geneva before the orbital blast.

There was no time to think. Kornfeld swung his weapons to bear and hit every firing stud on his joystick. The *Eyrie*'s pilot must have done the same, as its ATMs destroyed Kornfeld's already-damaged left-shoulder actuator in an explosion that showered hot shrapnel against his cockpit canopy. Through the smoke and dust, the lieutenant colonel hit the enemy cockpit with his medium lasers, killing the Jade Falcon MechWarrior and toppling the *Eyrie* into a street strewn with bricks and rubble. The 35-ton 'Mech lay there while Kornfeld leaned his *Lament* over it for a few moments, looking for any sign of movement.

I need to get patched up again. I'm no good without being able to aim my left PPC. He slowly limped his battered 'Mech around the corner. Resting there, almost entirely buried in bricks, was a Hetzer wheeled tank. Moving around the block again, he saw a crew hoisting a pallet of autocannon rounds onto the roof of a stately house, which already had a hole in its front facade.

Chris caught himself breathing hard, and paused for a moment, taking several deep breaths to calm down. He snaked down a narrow alley where he had to turn the *Lament* sideways in two places to get through, then came to a large red-brick structure. Heading to a false wall on the building, he paused to make sure the sentries identified him. Once the entry signal was given, he passed through the holographic projector and started down the ramp to one of the Republic's hidden sortie points spread all over Geneva. Guards with SRM launchers and infantry-portable PPCs lowered their weapons when they saw his Republic 'Mech.

Most of Geneva was this way now, and had been for a while. Chris had been fighting the Falcon Guards in Annemasse earlier, and was glad he wasn't still. It had cost his BattleMech an arm, and he'd nearly lost his life. The Falcon Guards had been vicious. Every time he thought he had knocked them down, they somehow managed to scrape together an operational 'Mech.

His *Lament* had also been refitted and repaired since then. The mottled gray-and-white camouflage pattern existed only in a few spots; the rest were primer gray replacement armor plates.

He had been on Terra only a few months before Clan Wolf arrived. War had been coming, one world at a time, since the HPG network had gone down. All had seemed lost until Devlin Stone had returned. Kornfeld's former unit, the First Battalion of the Fourteenth Principes Guards, had been deployed on Outreach, but Capellan Confederation troops had mauled them in 3149, and precious few members of his battalion had managed to escape. Once he and the other survivors reached Terra, they had been assigned to RAF units where needed, in anticipation of the coming invasion. Like many citizens of the Republic, he had always wanted to see Terra, but not like this, being destroyed one block at a time.

As he backed into repair bay, he got the signal from the repair officer to power down. The crews were exhausted and filthy, but he was too. He climbed down and told them about the PPC actuator. He looked up and saw some of the damage from the fight: seared scars from lasers, nasty autocannon craters that had torn up myomer bundles. *I was a lot worse off than I thought.*

One of his junior officers, Lieutenant Chad Hollings, came over with a cup of coffee. "You look like shit, sir."

Kornfeld just took the cup and sipped. Somehow, despite all the chaos on the street, the Republic still had good coffee. He savored it for a moment. "I lost Dutch and Kramer," he said slowly. They had gone down early in the fighting, two hours ago. "Dutch punched out. Any word on him?"

Hollings shook his head. "Damn! I was only two blocks from their patrol path. What happened?"

Kornfeld took another life-affirming drink. "Orbital bombardment. Goddamn Falcons."

"Where's our navy?"

"I don't know. Stone must be holding them for the right moment. He knows what he is doing." The words came out with a marked lack of enthusiasm.

"I hope you're right," Hollings said. "Word is Stone's Liberators have been pulled to Geisendorf for repair and refit."

"They earned it. I heard about what they did to the Falcons in the monorail yards in Sécheron. Hell of a fight. That last bombardment was only a few blocks from here. These techs need to patch us up and evac to one of the other bunkers." Kornfeld slammed back the last of the coffee. "Go and tell the yard commander this position is not tenable for much longer. A day, maybe less."

Hollings nodded and took off.

Kornfeld tossed his cup in the trash receptacle and walked to the ersatz restroom the techs had cobbled together. He went to wash his hands and splash water on his face, anything to stay awake. The cold water on his grimy skin and two days' worth of beard felt amazing.

When he looked down, he was stunned to see his hands quaking uncontrollably. They had never done that before. He ignored it and splashed more water on his face. Looking into the stainless-steel mirror the techs had mounted on the wall, he didn't recognize his own face at first. There were bags under his hazel eyes, and around them his skin was dark, as though bruised. His sallow cheeks were sunken from too many sorties and too little sleep. *I've lost weight.*

He leaned closer to the mirror and tried to brush his sweat-slicked brown hair into a semblance of style, but it refused to cooperate. *This is taking a toll on me, on all of us. I can only pray that the Exarch has a plan where the Republic survives all of this...*

1801 HOURS

Malvina studied the portable holodisplay in the relative safety of her temporary command dome. Her forces had seized eight more blocks of southern Geneva that day, but the victory had been costly. She was feeding her troops into a meat grinder. Galaxy Commander Clarence Pryde's Rho Galaxy were inbound from France, but the fighting there was taking a toll on his troops too. The Republic forces refused to surrender; instead, when overwhelmed, they fell back and fought to the last warrior.

Still, she was confident in her plan. *When Geneva falls, it will cripple their war effort. It will be proof that the Republic is doomed. That is why they fight so hard for it.* She had anticipated that the RAF would dig in, entrench, make her bleed for every meter.

Outside Geneva, her forces were still coming in-system. The Republic navy had sortied several times to target incoming DropShips, even managing to take a few out. She had dispatched most of her naval forces in response to escort each convoy from the jump point to Terra's orbit.

On-planet, the Northwind Highlanders and several other units, including a recently arrived battalion of Hansen's Roughriders, still held Paris and a string of fortifications known as Redoubt Normandy. She had landed one Galaxy in North Africa, which was fighting the kind of war she enjoyed: fast and swift, swinging into the Sinai, pinning down a stubborn Republic garrison there. Stephanie Chistu had driven into Germany with stunning success. Malvina was deliberately denying her a role in the capture of Geneva, and that made her indulge in a smile. *When this is over, there will be no great honor, no glory for her.* In central Africa, Malvina had ordered a Cluster dropped onto a Republic fighter base, where her warriors wiped out the defenders and secured the base that had been harassing her forces in the northern part of the continent. *Everything will change when Geneva falls.*

Her commander of the Watch, Star Colonel Abzug Helmer, entered the command dome with his noteputer in hand. Behind him, two officers led a shackled Republic officer inside. The prisoner's face was bruised, his breaths labored; he had clearly been beaten and tortured. Malvina lifted a brow.

"Chingis Khan," Helmer said, bowing his head. "This is Sir Ludvig Yabar, Knight of the Republic and leader of the 110th Assault Regiment. He has been fighting Galaxy Commander Chistu's forces at Frankfurt. He was...reluctant... to provide us with much information, but we persuaded him to be more forthcoming."

"And?" Malvina waited.

"The Republic is bringing two more assault regiments to Geneva. The Northwind Highlanders are being reinforced by mercenary troops shuttled in from South America. And Devlin Stone is still here in the city, directing the defenses, along with Paladin Janella Lakewood."

Malvina eyed Yabar with contempt. "Do you know anything else of value?"

Yabar coughed, drooling blood. "I know the Republic will crush your Jade Falcons. Stone knows of your war crimes. He won't let you do that here on Terra. He will make you pay."

"Good," she said. "If he knows my past, then he knows I am the future the Inner Sphere will face. I will take down the House Lords, then create a new foundation for my reign."

"The Republic will prevail!" Yabar spat.

"It is sad that you believe that." She pulled out her sidearm and shot Yabar in the head.

Blood and gray matter burst all over the two guards. They did not even flinch. Instead, they hastily dragged Yabar's body away, trailing a streak of crimson on the ground.

Malvina saw Cynthy recoil and curl up in her seat. *Still timid when I show you my true power, little one.* She offered her pet a reassuring smile.

"Anything else?" she asked Helmer.

Helmer betrayed no emotion at the murder of the Knight—demonstrating some intelligence on his part—though he did eye the sidearm still in Malvina's hand. "No, my Khan."

"What of Anastasia Kerensky?" she asked. "She is supposed to be one of the best warriors in the Inner Sphere, but you have not found her yet."

"We have obtained a great deal of intel from prisoners of war—but the Wolves remain elusive. We have found no sign of her, nor has the Republic."

Malvina's face darkened at the update. "What happened to her? She took Garner Kerensky's place as saKhan. Now Garner is back, and she has vanished. Is she still alive, or did she die in some combat trial?"

"Unknown," Helmer replied. "I have made it a priority to find out, but so far, we do not know."

Malvina took a slow step closer. "One of the best warriors, an ally of our enemy, is missing. And *still* you have nothing?" Another step. "You are supposed to be my intelligence officer, yet you continue to fail at this one simple request."

"Chingis Khan—"

Malvina raised her sidearm and fired. Helmer flinched away, but not quickly enough. The bullet tore off his lower jaw and punched into the wall of the command dome. He dropped to his knees, hands helplessly cupping the shattered remains of his lower face. Crimson poured through his fingers as he moaned. The rush of blood steamed in the icy winter air.

Holstering her sidearm, Malvina turned away. "Get to the medical tent, Star Colonel. Next time, I will take your head off. We cannot afford any more surprises. The next time you open your mouth, you will only speak to me about your progress in finding that Kerensky witch!"

She motioned for Cynthy to follow her. The pair of them left the tent as Helmer struggled to get to his feet and slipped on his own blood, his boots crunching on bits of his shattered teeth.

CHAPTER 14

THE BANKS OF THE VOLGA RIVER
NIZHNY NOVGOROD, RUSSIA
TERRA
21 FEBRUARY 3151 (T+42)

SaKhan Garner Kerensky feathered the jump jets of his *Blood Reaper*, bringing it down in a two-meter-deep snowbank on the flank of the Wolf line of battle. He missed his *Timber Wolf*, since his technicians had insisted on giving it a full refit, but the *Blood Reaper* was a fine replacement, as replacements went. The Wolf Clan prided itself on its second-line BattleMechs for a reason.

Alpha and Iota Galaxies had been operating under his direct command since he and Khan Ward had split their forces more than two weeks ago, and Garner reveled in his new responsibility. He had slogged halfway across Russia before finding a point of resistance worthy of him.

The Republic's Volga River redoubt was garrisoned by the Thirty-Second Republic Militia, known as the Iron Boots—a combined-arms regiment. The snow-covered ground brimmed with minefields and obstacles designed to slow his warriors down while the Iron Boots struck at them.

Their initial attacks had done considerable damage to the Golden Keshik, Alpha Galaxy's elite leadership Cluster, and since then, the Boots had been fighting in a slow withdrawal, luring him deeper into the redoubt. Spurlock Conners of the Watch soon found out the reason for the baiting maneuver. The Boots were being reinforced by another unit: First Battalion of Hansen's Roughriders. Iota Galaxy had shifted to blunt the Roughriders' first attacks, while Garner had concentrated on the Iron Boots.

For Garner, this was a rarity. Not since the fighting in central China had the Republic sortied an attack force in his combat sector. More importantly, this was *his* battle. Alaric had cut him loose, sending him west to link up with General Vickers. Even in Australia, Garner had felt Alaric's presence on the other side of the continent. But this fight was his and his alone. *Aff*, Alaric was on his way, but Garner hoped the fighting would be over by the time he arrived. *I will finally show him what I am capable of.* This snow-covered ground was a place where he could earn honor for himself, not in support of Alaric or anyone else. A victory here would define him in the fight for Terra.

Garner understood his role in the war for Terra, and his relationship with his Khan was solid. He had always had reservations about the young Wolf Khan; Garner had not forgotten that Alaric had given his position to Anastasia Kerensky while he had recovered the *McKenna's Pride*. Garner knew he represented the previous generation of warriors in the eyes of Khan Ward—but Alaric had been true to his word so far.

And the Wolf Khan had brought new thinking to his Clan, from forming the Wolf Empire to building a command team for invading Terra that pointedly included a former Ghost Bear and a Snow Raven *ristar*. Garner may have represented the old ways of Wolf thinking, but it had taken Alaric's ideas and leadership for the Clan to make it to Terra. It was Alaric who had brought them this close to conquering Terra.

But today—today was *his* battle to win.

A transmission from Star Colonel Tracy Carns of the Fourth Wolf Guards broke into his thoughts. "We have BattleMechs across the Volga," she said. "They are at our perimeter marker and moving this way. Three of their superheavies, fully supported."

"Numbers?" Garner asked, checking his tactical display. The enemy's images floated at the far end of the screen, slowly advancing toward his position.

"All of them," Carns replied. "The Thirty-Second has come in force."

Garner switched to his command channel. "Iota Prime, this is Alpha Prime. I have a full Republic regiment heading this way. Watch your front. They are likely to coordinate their assault with the Roughriders."

"*Aff*, you are correct. We have enemy BattleMechs on the outer markers," Star Colonel Malcolm Vickers replied.

"Good hunting then," Garner replied. "Ninth Wolf Battle Cluster, fall back."

"SaKhan," came the booming voice Star Colonel Tutuola of the Ninth. "Respectfully submitted, you will need us in this fight."

"*Aff*," Garner agreed. "I *do* need you, Henry. I simply need you someplace else." He quickly snapped out orders, putting the Golden Keshik at the extreme right, with the bulk of Alpha Galaxy in a diamond formation on the left and center. The Ninth Wolf Battle Cluster had its own mission, a hail-mary maneuver around the edge of the battlefield to seize the bridge over the Volga in the rear of the Republic forces.

Once the orders were acknowledged and his forces were moving into position, he tightened his restraint straps. "Alpha Galaxy—prepare to move on my mark." He drew a long breath. "Wolves—howl! Advance!"

Garner rushed to the next hill and saw an *Ares* and a *Poseidon* opening fire on his warriors. Missiles and lasers filled the air between the onrushing armies.

"Follow our doctrine on those superheavies," he barked. "Pull in their support forces, eradicate them...then worry about the large ones."

The *Ares* and *Poseidon* had learned to adapt to the Wolves' previous anti-superheavy tactics, however. This time they stayed within each other's fields of fire, and nearly a dozen hoverbikes, a Star's worth of Pegasus hovertanks, and a Star of light and medium BattleMechs supported the superheavies.

Alpha held true to its orders and unleashed a mass of fire on the support forces. A flaming Pegasus exploded while the others scattered between the superheavies. A Republic *Nyx* darted right and left, blasting away with lasers and short-range missiles at a *Stormwolf* C on the front of the Wolves' battle line. The Wolf 'Mech's anti-missile lasers whittled the missile assault into nothing, but it lost precious armor from the lasers. The *Stormwolf* C pilot engaged their supercharger and took off after the *Nyx*, tearing into it with large and medium lasers, melting off leg armor. Clods of sod and snow flew behind it as it ran.

Nearby, a Republic *Jackalope* charged right at the Wolf lines and fired its jump jets while raining advanced tactical missiles downward to sow chaos in the formation. It disappeared amid waves of long- and short-range missiles.

The Pegasuses rallied, tearing apart a Wolf *Mad Dog* in a devastating salvo of short-range missiles. A pair of lightning-fast *Dominator*s raced into the hovertanks' formation, blasting them with PPC fire at point-blank range. The bright bursts were so close together that it was almost blinding, as if the gods of old were hurling lightning bolts down on the Republic forces.

Republic infantry in battle armor rushed past the superheavies, firing SRMs and support PPCs. Machine guns blazed at the Wolves, chattering against the approaching wall of BattleMechs with little effect other than to earn Garner's respect for the infantry's courage.

A daring Wolf *Pack Hunter II* tried to flank the *Ares*, only to find itself caught in the full force of the *Poseidon*'s massive armament. As Garner rushed forward, the *Pack Hunter II* emerged from a billowing cloud of smoke—both arms missing, its armor shredded.

An artillery barrage rained down in front of him, catching a Point of Gray Wolf battle armor in concussive blasts and searing-hot shrapnel. Three of the suits were knocked to the ground; two were badly mauled, but all managed to rise and continue forward.

Garner skirted around the field of fire and locked onto the *Poseidon*. His ER PPCs flashed, their azure beams searing the 'Mech's armor with two devastating burn marks. The brutish superheavy shrugged off the attacks even as a Wolf Balac VTOL fired a wave of ATMs into its upper hull.

The *Poseidon* loosed its medium- and long-range missiles in response. Many of the medium-range missiles missed Garner, but the long-range salvo slammed into his *Blood Reaper*'s right side, the explosions tearing at him as he ran. He shook it off and riposted with his own ATMs. The tactical missiles bore in on the *Poseidon* and hit its left leg. A normal 'Mech would have shown significant damage, but on the 125-ton superheavy, the exploded warheads left mere scratches on the thick armor.

An *Amarok* sprinted before the *Poseidon* and raked it with a purr of rotary-autocannon fire. Bekker had designed the 'Mech for use against the Jade Falcons, but it was being rotated in as a replacement for BattleMechs lost in combat. Garner flanked the superheavy to the right, firing his ATMs and PPCs. The shots tore into the *Poseidon*'s curved body, tearing open holes and sending a splatter of melted armor into the air.

It wavered—but unleashed a full barrage of missiles and lasers at Garner. The MRMs mostly missed, but everything else hit hard, ripping into his legs and lower torso, knocking him off-balance. As he started to fall backward, he hit his jump jets for just a moment. The resulting burst pushed his 'Mech back onto its feet, and Garner allowed himself a chuckle. He had never been able to pull off such a maneuver before.

A Wolf Carnivore tank fired at the *Poseidon* with its dual Gauss rifles. The silver flashes hit the superheavy's advancing left leg hard enough to knock it askew. Its pilot tried to regain balance, but the 'Mech fell back hard onto the snowy, frozen ground. The Wolf Balac swooped in on the fallen giant, shooting its lasers and ATMs before a wave of LRMs from the nearby *Ares* drove it off.

The heat in Garner's cockpit rose as he clambered back to his feet. The *Ares* locked onto him and fired its medium lasers and missiles. One warhead hit square against his canopy, but he was too busy moving to blink. The other blasts mangled his *Blood Reaper*'s legs and arms, but he leaned forward, into the concussions, to keep moving.

"Alpha Prime," a ragged voice said through a hiss of static—discharges from nearby PPC fire. "This is Star Captain Quay Vickers of the Fifth Wolf Battle Cluster. Star Colonel Krystal Vickers is dead. Request permission to fall back and regroup."

Garner zoomed out on the tactical display. The Fifth was the end of the line connecting to Iota Galaxy. *They are attempting to split our forces, finish us off piecemeal.* "Neg. Hold firm."

"We need reinforcement," Quay insisted.

"And you shall have it," another voice said on the command channel. "We are closing on your position now. You heard Alpha Prime: hold, or we risk being split."

"Who is this?" Quay asked.

"This is Wolf Prime," Khan Ward said. "Beta Galaxy is on the field. Let us teach these Republic troops a lesson they will not soon forget." In that moment, Garner picked up the faint signals of the DropShips of Beta Galaxy to the east.

A mix of emotions hit him at the sound of Alaric's voice. He had planned to finish the battle before Khan Ward rendezvoused with him. Garner had expected to be celebrating victory by now—but the Republic had not complied. Another laser beam hit his *Blood Reaper* as he broke into a run. The second emotion tore at him as well, one that tugged at his Clan heart—victory. One thing all warriors wanted—over honor, over pride—was the defeat of an enemy. If Alaric was on the field, the odds shifted to the Clan's advantage, a good thing no matter how one looked at it.

The battle raged for another hour as twilight set in. Garner's orders to the Ninth Wolf Battle Cluster had paid off. They had skirted the battle, running north and moving along the Volga River, and destroyed the bridge the Iron Boots had crossed. That left the Thirty-Second Republic Militia trapped on the Wolves' side of the river.

The Republic lines had folded, collapsing into the rear of Hansen's Roughriders. The Roughriders had given a much better showing, but in the end, less than a battalion of them managed to ford the Volga and fall back in full retreat. Only one battered company survived and surrendered to tell the tale. Iota Galaxy was so impressed that they made the Roughrider survivors bondsmen.

It was late when Garner finally arrived at Khan Ward's mobile HQ, which had just been unloaded from its DropShip. Alaric greeted him with a firm handshake and the offer of a seat. The coffee was good and hot, and dinner was brought in for the pair. Garner was grateful; Russian winters were everything history had taught him. He did not know what he was eating—it did not matter. Exhaustion loomed over him like a shadow, ready to overtake him at any time.

"You arrived just at the right moment," he told the Khan.

"We wanted to debark out of line of sight," said Alaric. "That, and I wanted to see where the Republic committed their attack. My presence, however, was unnecessary. You had this victory in hand, Garner. All I did was expedite it."

"I appreciate the support. We could have beaten them without you, but our losses would have been unacceptable."

"I am not so sure of that," Alaric said, leaning back in his seat. "Your move to take out the bridges was well executed. This victory is yours, not mine. Relish it."

"Thank you, my Khan," Garner said, basking in his success for a moment as he cradled the hot mug of coffee.

"The fighting in North America took slightly longer than we expected," Alaric conceded. "We faced another battalion of Roughriders, along with the Gray Gunny Lancers. They fought well, and with honor." He frowned before continuing. "For some reason, the Republic pulled them out before we could definitively conclude the fight."

"You secured the objective, *quiaff*?"

Alaric grinned and nodded. "The Court is once more in the hands of the descendants of the true Star League."

Garner relished those words, offering his own rare smile in return. *I cannot wait to see it for myself.* "What is the word from General Vickers?"

"Progress in Greece has been slow, but we have secured that ground and moved into Italy. She has stopped for a day or so for rest and refit."

"What of the Jade Falcons?"

"They hold northeastern France as far south as Geneva. Stone is brilliantly pummeling them there, but Malvina wants that city. She is no fool. Geneva is politically important, if not militarily. If she captures Devlin Stone, it will be a blow to the Republic's morale, one they may not recover from. If she takes the city, it tells the citizens of the Republic that their end is near. And more Jade Falcon units are arriving almost every other day. She has most of the city surrounded at this point. I anticipate her opening another front any time now, since Europe has become such a sticking point for her. Falcon doctrine calls for sweeping moves, not meat grinders."

Garner understood Malvina's focus on Geneva. It was a common strategy for the Clans to strike at the key strategic and political objectives. Common... until Alaric Ward had come along. "It is a shame that the honor of Geneva's fall will go to the Jade Falcons."

"A costly shame," Alaric countered. "No doubt it will elevate her surviving warriors' morale considerably. But enough of our emerald friends. How fares your force in the last few days?"

"We have had some resistance from Siberian partisans," Garner conceded. "They have no cities we can destroy, so our usual threats have fallen on deaf ears. I had to dispatch several *solahma* Stars to protect our rear."

"Their resistance will be moot once we crush the Republic," Alaric said. "We have received confirmation: Reunion and Amalgamation. Reunion is already on the ground in North America. Amalgamation will be joining them in a few days' time." He smiled again.

Garner should have been surprised, but he was well-acquainted with Alaric's acumen at accomplishing the seemingly impossible. "Both? Remarkable." He eyed the Khan over the rim of his mug. "I guess this means Anastasia and I will need to square off for my title, then."

"*Neg*," Alaric said. "Anastasia has a role to fulfill. I told her I would leave the fate of Malvina Hazen to her. She knows that. She hates being forced to wait for the opportunity, but knows her duty."

"Regardless, she may desire my title once more," Garner said. Anastasia had temporarily been the Wolf saKhan while Garner had gone to recover the *McKenna's Pride. I know her ambition. She will want to oust me.*

"We will not bog down our advance with Trials of Position. You are my saKhan, Garner Kerensky, until this campaign ends." Alaric put his hand on Garner's shoulder, one of the rare times he had done so.

Garner's face warmed. "I know we do not always see eye-to-eye, Khan Ward, but as you have seen, I will fight for you, and die for you, if I must. We stand here on Terra because of you. We *will* be the ilClan." His voice wavered with the last few words.

Alaric slowly nodded at his words. "That is why I brought you here—all of you. You all believe in the destiny of Clan Wolf as much as I do. That is why we are unstoppable."

He rose to his feet. "Come, there is much to be done between then and now," Alaric said. "We must plan for our link-up with General Vickers' force and our drive into Europe."

COMMAND POST SOLITUDE
GENEVA

The Solitude command post was deep under Geneva, but not so deep that it muffled the constant rumble of the war being waged above.

The worst was the orbital bombardments. They were actually strong enough to send a fine dust shivering down from the ceiling. It served as a reminder to Devlin Stone that the war had reached the Republic's front doorstep, and the Jade Falcons were pounding to get in. Each time a tremor shook the command post, it made the conference room seem smaller. The wall banners of storied units—some of which no longer existed—were now dusted with a powdery film.

He still had ways out—long, hidden tunnels that could take everyone far beyond the Jade Falcon lines. Some had suggested that Stone depart, that he was too important to risk falling into Malvina Hazen's hands. So far, he had resisted. His place was here, he insisted. With his people.

"What is the word from General Herring's regiment?" he asked, though the 122nd Republic Militia Regiment had ceased to be a "regiment" long ago, thanks to the orbital bombardments. It was a ghost of its former self. Stone had seen the casualty reports and some of the footage. The 122nd had been fighting a series of holding actions, a block or two at a time. Their infantry used a department building's windows to rain down hundreds of short-range missiles onto the Falcons, only to have the building destroyed moments later—blasted by artillery fire.

Lakewood checked her noteputer. "They are on the north edge of the Ansermet neighborhood, holding on by their fingernails. They are doing what they can, but their losses are over seventy percent. I will need to pull them out and shift in some of our reserves."

"We are running out of reserves," Brigadier General Turner said. "We have equipment, but it is hard to replace the dead. I still have Stone's Liberators in a bunker in Geisendorf. They have been in the fight already, but they are ready for action again. Give me the word, Exarch, and I will put them in."

"Thank you, General Turner," Stone said. "I was thinking of the Liberators as well."

"That will give General Herring some much-needed breathing room," Lakewood said. "Switching them out under fire will be difficult, but otherwise, we risk the 122nd simply evaporating soon."

"Then make it happen," Stone said. "What of the Roughriders in North America?"

Miller spoke up. "Per your orders, sir, they are redeploying near Detroit and Toronto."

Damien Redburn stirred in his seat. His head bore scars from the fighting in Australia, and a clump of his hair was missing entirely. "There is an alternative, Exarch," he said. "My Nighthawk plan can still be deployed. We've salvaged enough 'Mechs to pull this off, and have units readied in London. Give the word, and we can deliver a sword thrust the Clans cannot parry."

Stone sighed. Nighthawk kept coming up in conversation. It was meant to be a last resort, but now Redburn mentioned it daily. *Is this the time for such rash action?* "No, Damien," he finally said. "Not yet. I appreciate your counsel on the matter, but once we go down that path, we are no better than Malvina Hazen."

Redburn leaned back in his seat, his lips compressed to a thin line. "As you wish. But our options are steadily dwindling."

"Any word from Julian Davion?" Stone asked.

Blank stares came in response. At last Tucker Harwell said flatly, "None, Exarch." The *I-told-you-so* lurked in his tone like an invisible slap.

"We just have to buy a little more time," Stone insisted. "The Federated Suns will not let the Clans become united under an ilClan. They know what that means. Julian will come. We helped him, he will repay the gesture. Julian will not fail us."

CLAN WOLF REAR AREAS
NIZHNY NOVGOROD, RUSSIA

In a recently captured warehouse, a Wolf senior technician stood before three battle-ravaged OmniMechs. Several of the 'Mechs' arms and legs lay spread out. All were superheavies, *Ares* class, but none could even stand on their own. They leaned, listed, and in one case lay in a jumbled heap. Above them, heavy gantry-crane hooks hung low on massive cables. Once the pride of the Republic, these great OmniMechs were now simply casualties of war.

For Jack Traver and his crew, it was a sickening sight. Their *Ares* had been blasted out from under them during the great counteroffensive. Now, as Clan Wolf bondsmen, they looked at what had been their pride and joy. Jack wondered if humiliation was part of the bondsman process.

To her credit, Star Colonel Kalidessa Kerensky did not seem to be that kind of person. She had spent time with them, explaining that, as bondsmen, they were to prove their worth to Clan Wolf. If they did so, she would honor her promise to give them a chance to fight the Jade Falcons. Jack had accepted that promise at face value, unlike Cheetah, who saw them aiding an enemy of the Republic.

The senior technician faced them squarely. "I am Senior Technician Morrow. Star Colonel Kalidessa Kerensky has a task for you. You crewed an OmniMech like these, so we need you to help us rebuild them."

Staff Sergeant Mia Fowler, ever defiant, balled her fists and planted them on her hips. "You can't figure it out for yourself?"

Morrow frowned. "We are more than able to repair such machines, but it is not a priority. Our technicians are working around the clock to keep our warriors in the battle. The Star Colonel feels that such OmniMechs might prove useful, and since we will not waste precious technical resources on them, the task falls to you as bondsmen."

Cheetah stepped forward, next to Mia. "You are asking us to help you when you are at war with the Republic."

Morrow nodded. "*Aff.* You are a bondsman. If you refuse this task, the Star Colonel will send you to a POW camp. It means nothing to me where you spend the rest of this war. But know this, Clan Wolf has conquered Australia, Asia, the Middle East, southern Europe, and Russia. The Republic you served faces two Clans. Its flame is flickering in the wind. If you do not wish to do this task, simply say so and I will arrange your transfer. But accept this task and do it well, and you may yet get a chance to fight the true enemy of the Inner Sphere, Malvina Hazen and her Jade Falcons."

For a moment, none of the trio spoke.

Jack finally shattered the silence. "We will do it."

"Excellent," Morrow replied. "Tools and parts are available upon request. I will be monitoring your progress. It is our hope that out of these three 'Mechs, we have enough to repair at least two." With that, he walked way.

As soon as he left, Mia turned to Jack. "We should be planning our escape, sir."

Jack shook his head. "We're in the middle of Russia, behind enemy lines. Where exactly do you envision us going?" *Where is safety on Terra at this point?*

Cheetah weighed in as well. "I can't believe you want us to help them, sir."

Jack held up his hands. "You both need to think this through. Maybe the Republic will win, and if that's the case, we'll be freed. But right now, if my choice is assisting the Wolves or the Jade Falcons, I will always side against the Falcons."

"You sound as if you don't think the Republic can win," Mia snapped.

Jack was silent for a long moment. "Right now...I don't know. From everything I've heard, the Wolves aren't fighting like Clans usually do. They are here to conquer, and they are not stopping for anything. We've already had our 'Mech blown out from under us twice. I'm as patriotic as the next Terran, Sergeant, but I'm also pragmatic. We cannot help the Republic any further, not from here. If we're in a POW camp, we are doing nothing but sitting by and letting our fate spin in the wind. If Clan Wolf believes it is going up against the Jade Falcons, then I say we help them. I, for one, prefer to do something as opposed to nothing. And if we get these 'Mechs ready to be used against the Jade Falcons, well, that is fighting the good fight in my book."

Mia sagged at his words; her shoulders slumped, she ran a hand through her short hair. "It just feels so...*dirty*...doing this for them after they tried to kill us."

"I know, Mia...I feel the same way," Jack replied. "But for now, this is our best way forward." He looked at the pieces of the three *Ares* 'Mechs. "Let's get started."

CHAPTER 15

SOUTH OF KRAKÓW, POLAND
TERRA
1 MARCH 3151, 0650 HOURS (T+50)

The trio of gray-and-green Republic Marksman M1 battle tanks swerved in front of the Wolf line of battle, firing at Star Colonel Kalidessa Kerensky's *Tundra Wolf 4*. Her *Dire Wolf* had suffered enough damage to require an overhaul, so she had taken the *Tundra Wolf 4* as a temporary replacement. Some Wolves saw piloting anything other than an OmniMech as a step down, but she did not. The firepower and speed of the *Tundra Wolf 4* was seductive to her.

The Republic had sent the Eighth Republic Guard, The Killing Machines, south of Kraków to slam into the Wolves' southern flank. Alaric had sent her Second Wolf Assault Cluster to deal with them, and the Eighth had proven themselves more than capable adversaries. Rather than rush in, they had broken into three battlegroups, each one capable of delivering a devastating hit. One had been crushed, but the other two were still elusive, falling back before Kalidessa could concentrate her forces.

They had also selected a battlefield that gave neither side an advantage. The rolling hills, wet from a cold rain, reduced the 'Mechs to careful maneuvers with limited line of sight. The wooded areas provided only light cover, as no leaves had blossomed on their branches. The cold helped BattleMechs deal with overheating, but Kalidessa still wished they were fighting someplace warmer than Kraków in March.

The Marksmans' Gauss rifles spit rounds into the legs and lower body of the 75-ton Wolf BattleMech, sending a sickening amount of armor flailing into the air. Kalidessa struggled hard, completely off-balance, spinning up the gyro to peak pitch to keep her 'Mech upright.

"*Blitzking surat*s!" she spat. "No honor at all."

MechWarrior Powers landed his *Pack Hunter II* right in front of the lead Republic tank, which clipped his leg, marring the paint and crumpling one armor plate. "He hit me," he said, blasting his medium lasers at the passing craft. "That makes him my target."

"Honor is given," Kalidessa said, blasting one of the other Marksman tanks with her pair of large pulse lasers. Emerald bursts of energy shredded the side of the turret, sending bits of hot armor ricocheting and hissing in the small puddles on the wet Polish countryside.

"And taken," Powers replied. He launched his shoulder-mounted extended-range PPC at his target. The bright, flashing beam slammed into the side of the vehicle as it made a long, slow arc to get another pass, its turret turning on him as he moved.

Another BattleMech entered the field—a *Savage Wolf* in light gray with maroon trim—pitted from autocannon and machine-gun hits on its left side. Kalidessa's IFF transponder only identified it as a Clan Wolf BattleMech. *Khan Ward! It must be—it is his colors.* She was surprised to see him in this area of the battlefield. As the *Savage Wolf* came down the hillside, one of the Marksman tanks blasted at it. One silvery slug wrenched the 'Mech around from the impact.

Kalidessa could not believe her fortune—she was finally fighting alongside Khan Ward! She focused on his own Marksman, firing her large pulse lasers. The air filled with energy beams that seared into the side of the tank, and she followed up with a wave of ATMs. Most of the missiles plowed in on top of the damage already done. *Good—feel that pain.*

Kalidessa fired her ER medium lasers, the emerald beams searing into the tank. Bits of tread spiraled into the air as her shots left red-hot scars on the side of the hull. The Marksman fired back with a wave of medium- and short-range missiles. Kalidessa turned her 'Mech hard at the last moment. Most of the MRMs missed, but the short-range missiles tore into her *Tundra Wolf*'s thick armored hide.

Off to her side, Powers leaped into the air and blasted away with his PPC, hitting the rear right side of the tank and spraying the air with hot globs of molten armor.

An identical wave of missiles showered Kalidessa's 'Mech, most of them hitting. Her right-leg damage indicator degraded from amber to red as the missiles devoured armor plating. She almost fell from the onslaught, barely able to keep her balance.

Breaking into a faster run, she got the rear of the slower-moving Marksman in her sights. Kalidessa unleashed the ruby bursts from her large pulse lasers and the *Tundra Wolf*'s antipersonnel Gauss rifles. The lasers ate a string of hot holes through the tank's armor plating, compromising it in several spots. The Gauss rifles' stream of deadly hyperaccelerated flechettes punched through the thinner rear armor and into the engine shielding. The heat inside her 'Mech rose until she heard the gurgle of her coolant vest churn faster.

Powers jumped again, and his laser and PPC fire rained down on the top of his target tank, tearing into the turret and hull. It fired back with its Gauss rifle mid-flight. The silvery slug tore off his 'Mech's left leg at the knee, sending the limb plummeting to the frozen sod. It was clear to Kalidessa from the way he wavered that Powers was struggling to compensate, but he landed on his one good leg and somehow managed to stay upright long enough to squeeze off another shot. Despite the heat risk, he fired his PPC again, this time hitting the Marksman's turret. The MRM rack and missiles in the tank's loader went off, blasting a hole in the side of the turret. The tank stopped dead in its tracks, and its turret barrel lowered. It was either surrendering or had suffered worse damage than met the eye.

Kalidessa's targeted Marksman continued rotating in place to protect its rear, but she broke into a full sprint and fired two of her extended-range large lasers. Both crimson beams found their mark, burrowing deep into the tank. There was a flash as the fusion reactor breached and shut down. Dorsal hatches popped open on the hull, and the crew bailed out as smoke churned skyward from the open hatches. Two of the tankers got free, but one collapsed back into the fire now rising from the hatch.

Kalidessa turned to see how her Khan was faring. His BattleMech stood next to another Marksman tank, one footpad on its upper hull, flames roaring from the top of the turret. The scene was so perfectly posed it reminded Kalidessa of an image from one of the Inner Sphere MechWarrior holovids.

"Khan Ward," she said on the tactical channel. "It is an honor to fight alongside you."

"*Neg*," a woman's voice responded. "And the honor is mine. This is General Vickers. I am looking for Khan Ward."

At that moment, Kalidessa saw a long line of BattleMechs, all painted with the snarling-wolf emblem of Delta Galaxy, starting to come down the hill to join the general. Two battle forces of the Wolf Clan were reconnecting. The fronts were now connected.

"I am not sure where the Khan is, General," Kalidessa said. "I assume he is somewhere to the north of this position. Would you like an escort?"

RSS *ABUNDANTIA*
INBOUND TO TERRA
1 MARCH 3151, 0955 HOURS (T+50)

Terra loomed larger by the moment as the last vestiges of the Republic of the Sphere's navy approached. Admiral Jean-Jacques Labbé steered the fleet toward the Jade Falcon WarShips in geosynchronous orbit over Geneva.

His battered fleet had performed some miraculous repairs, but were not entirely up to fighting trim. They had harassed incoming Jade Falcon DropShips that entered the system with some degree of success, blasting several into worthless metal. The Falcons had taken to using WarShips to escort their inbound vessels, which had forced Labbé to stop such attacks. Devlin Stone had made it clear that he wanted to save his precious WarShips.

Until now.

Word had come from the Exarch seven days earlier: "You must put an end to the Jade Falcon orbital bombardments."

Labbé was filled with icy resolve. "This will cost you your navy, Exarch."

Devlin Stone had rubbed his temples and said simply, "I am well aware of what I am asking. Geneva can hold only if these bombardments end."

And that was that.

Labbé had joined the Republic Navy with high hopes of a long career. Now that dream was coming to an end. There were not many scenarios he could concoct where he would come through the fight alive. The Jade Falcon fleet, though injured at the zenith jump point, was larger than his. He had managed to get the *Shield of the Republic* and the *Triumphus* somewhat repaired, though he couldn't replace the crew each ship had lost. The *Redemption* had fared well in the strikes against the Jade Falcon convoys, but this would be its first major WarShip action. The crew of the *Ciaravella* was more than ready for a fight, and the other five assault DropShips were still stinging from the first skirmish with the invading Clans at the jump points. Crude patches on their hulls did a poor job of hiding all the scorch marks from the earlier battle.

Labbé opened a comm channel to his fleet and shifted in his raised captain's seat. He thought of his family for a moment, doubting he would see them again. He pulled out an old photo he carried of his wife and son and studied it one more time before sliding it back into his chest pocket. *I will miss you, Francine and Klaus.* There was a steely resolve though; he hoped they would remember him as a hero of the Republic.

"Ships of the Republic Navy," he began. "The Exarch has called us to his aid and the aid of all our people on Terra. We will answer that call. He has ordered us to stop the Jade Falcons at all costs.

"The enemy is vicious and heartless. Their orbital bombardments are killing tens of thousands of civilians. They outnumber us. They are genetically bred for battle. But we have something they do not. We have the spirit of the Republic in us! We are answering the call of Devlin Stone, the greatest leader the Republic has ever had, and the call of the Republic itself at its greatest time of need. We will shatter the enemy. We will drive straight at them on a high arc. Any ship that takes major damage, you are hereby ordered to turn your vessel on the Jade Falcons and ram them. Let none of their vessels come through this fight intact.

"We do this—our duty—and the Exarch will defeat them on the ground. The flag of the Republic will return to the places stolen from us. We will be remembered as the sword driven straight through the Jade Falcons' heart."

He shut off the channel to the fleet and opened a new one to the *Abundantia* crew. "All hands—general quarters. Secure all stations for collision. Gunnery, we are weapons hot and free. Let's make these bastards pay for what they have done."

EAST OF KRAKÓW, POLAND
TERRA
1103 HOURS

Outside the mobile HQ, the late-winter winds howled, an occassional chilly draft even penetrating the heated air within. Despite this, General Chance Vickers was drinking a cold can of Fizzblitz as if it were the sweet nectar of life.

Alaric, sitting across from her, sipped black coffee out of a chipped mug. *She never did develop a taste for coffee.*

"I will be heading for Italy in the morning," she said. "I need to extend our front into northern Italy and southern France in the next week, or we will fall behind our timetable. Some of the Republic's counterattacks have put us several days behind, especially in southern Italy, where they use the mountainous terrain to their advantage."

"Your progress has been remarkable, despite the time lost with that counterattack," Alaric said. "Any word from Task Force Zebra?"

"None since they arrived in Antarctica. The facilities there contain much more than Terra's HPG array. We found—well..." Chance put down her soda. "A complex of sorts. From what our scientists can tell, it is some sort of highly advanced targeting system, somehow linked to the HPG array. Very large, with the largest power capacitors we have ever seen. Given the satellite relays and transmission capabilities, we believe the complex may be the key to Fortress Republic."

"What of the defenders there?"

"Less than a Cluster, according to Spurlock's estimate. They may have a number of forces hidden in the complex. But so far, nothing but silence."

Alaric considered this. Chance's smile said she recognized that look. "We give them another forty-eight hours," he said at last. "If there is no response, we will send in our people. If that base has anything to do with Fortress Republic, we need to take control."

She nodded. "Agreed."

Alaric sipped his coffee. "I saw your reports on the POW situation."

"An odd situation. Since the Jade Falcons landed, a number of Republic units have surrendered to us—usually only after a short fight. Frankly, I am thankful for the replacement equipment, but it is tying up a large number of *solahma* units to guard the prisoners—more than we had anticipated."

Alaric nodded. "It is fear that makes them surrender. The Jade Falcons do not take prisoners. We do."

"I propose we turn this to our advantage." Vickers leaned back, taking her soda with her. "Some of these units can be made bondsmen. They have a stake in this, too, especially in fighting the Jade Falcons."

"Agreed—but we must be very selective. They will likely always see themselves as freebirths that fought and lost to us. Task some of our seasoned warriors to sort through them. We want the best of the Republic, not their cowards."

Vickers nodded just as the comm system activated. "Khan Ward," came the voice of communications officer. "Incoming priority message from Star Admiral Sukhanov."

Their gazes met.

"Put him through," Alaric replied.

CJF *TURKINA'S PRIDE*
IN ORBIT OVER GENEVA
TERRA
2 MARCH 3151, 1320 HOURS (T+51)

Star Admiral Sharizal Binetti clutched her command seat as two Killer Whale missiles detonated on the outer hull. The bridge lights flickered before remaining on. The scent of ozone from a damaged console somewhere on the bridge stung her nostrils. "Damage report!"

Star Captain Krzysztof Von Jankmon mopped sweat from his brow with a handkerchief smeared crimson with his own blood. "Starboard lateral damage along the keel," he reported. "We have no operational naval autocannons on the starboard side. We also lost our Barracuda missile launcher. Engineering reports the hull is compromised from the *Dolabra*'s ramming attack. It is not showing any signs of engine power, and is adrift off of our starboard bow. We are stabilizing orbit."

"Fleet status," Binetti ordered.

The tactical command officer pored over the data. "We have lost three assault DropShips, five more are on-station and showing amber on the boards in terms of combat operations. Three remain. *White Aerie* avoided a ramming attempt and is operational. *Blue Talon* was rammed, but is reporting battle-ready. *Jade Tornado* is still fully operational."

"What of the Republic fleet?" Binetti asked the tactical officer.

"Star Admiral, the Republic feet has been eliminated, but..." There was a pause, a long and awkward one. And there was no cheering.

"What is it?" Binetti demanded.

"Star Admiral, I—"

"Out with it!"

"The Clan Wolf fleet is bearing down on us—led by—*McKenna's Pride*." The officer looked back at Binetti, pale.

"Impossible," Binetti scoffed. She pushed over to the tactical station. "That ship was left behind in the home worlds."

But the scopes confirmed the tactical officer's words. Neg! *It is true!*

"Maintain general quarters," Binetti ordered. "I want weapons held for now. We are not fighting the Wolves just yet. Comm, patch me through to the Chingis Khan *now*."

1521 HOURS

"Haake, are you in position?" Alaric asked on the naval command channel from his mobile headquarters.

"*Aff,*" Sukhanov replied. "We are positioned one hundred and fifty meters from the Jade Falcon ships, blocking their ability to fire, per your orders. Weapons are hot and locked."

When they had discussed this contingency, Haake had explained that *McKenna's Pride* had to be that close, otherwise the Jade Falcons could fire above or below it. At that range, it was impossible for them to fire on Terra without hitting the *Pride*. Other Wolf WarShips were taking similar positions against their Jade Falcon counterparts.

"If you are fired upon, I expect you to destroy them," Alaric said.

"Khan Ward, if they so much as break wind, I intend to unleash hell."

Alaric opened an unsecured channel that broadcast directly to the Jade Falcons. "This is Khan Ward of Clan Wolf. I have ordered my ships to impede your orbital bombardment of Terra. Khan Hazen, if you wish to fire, you will have to do so through my WarShips. And we will return fire."

"What are you doing, Alaric?" Malvina Hazen demanded. "You are interfering with Jade Falcon military operations. You have no right to do so. If you believe I will not destroy your ships, you are mistaken. I do not take orders from anyone—especially Clan Wolf."

"I am not *ordering* you to do anything," Alaric countered. "Your unmitigated destruction and the killing of innocents is against the tenets of our people. We are Clan, and it is time the Jade Falcons begin acting as such again. I am simply helping you return to the honorable way to defeat the Republic, Khan Hazen."

"My title is *Chingis Khan*," she said through gritted teeth. "Do not lecture me on how to wage war. If I want to order my ships to fire on these bellycrawling Republic forces, I will do so at my discretion. You granted us operational freedom, and now you are violating that."

"Chingis Khan," Alaric replied, fighting a smile. *She is so easily provoked.* "I am not violating our conditions. No Wolf ship has fired on yours. You are the one threatening to violate those conditions."

"You have no idea who are you up against."

"Nor do you. Verify the ID of the ship that is blocking your flagship. It is the *McKenna's Pride*."

"So I have been told. I do not know where you found that relic or managed to hide it from our sensors, but if you think parking an antique between my ships and Terra will stop me, you are sadly mistaken."

"That 'antique' was the flagship of General Aleksandr Kerensky. His mortal remains are still aboard. If you fire on us, you will destroy the genetic remains of the Great Father himself. You will no longer have the moral authority to call yourself a Clan."

"You cannot bully me with threats."

"I am broadcasting in the clear," Alaric said. "Everyone can hear me—your forces on Terra and your ships in orbit. If you give the order to bombard Terra and thus fire into my ships, destroying our people's only sacred relic, and violating our agreement..." He paused, just long enough to cut her off before she could start speaking again. "I am willing to bet my own life that many of your officers will *not* obey that order. There is still honor within the Jade Falcons. Not all will commit such sacrilege simply to feed your bloodlust. If you want to strike the Republic, continue to do so on the ground. Raining fire from orbit is beneath the glorious history of the Jade Falcons and the Clans. Your warriors on the ground should be more than a match for the Republic—let them do their duty."

Alaric heard silence in reply. Long, nerve-gnawing silence. *Malvina may be issuing the orders against our fleet right now,* he thought. *Sukhanov will devastate her ships, but we will lose many good warriors in the process.* He waited, letting patience guide him. Chance had delayed her departure when word of the space battle had started, and she looked over at him with similar resolve. He appreciated her support in this moment.

A *hiss* and *snap* came over the speakers. "I would not ask my warriors to do something I would not do myself," Malvina said. "And we gain nothing from destroying your WarShips. Even that artifact, the *McKenna's Pride*. Jade Falcons loathe waste, and firing on your Wolves would be a waste of ammunition. We will settle this on the ground.

"But know this, Alaric Ward. You have challenged my honor in front of my Clan. This is a slight I do not take lightly. Before this is over, you will bow before me. You will see the triumph in my eyes before I kill you. You will bleed out at my feet knowing I have defeated you and consumed your Wolves."

The channel went dead. Alaric shut off his microphone.

"You took an incredible risk," Chance said.

"I did not. All Jade Falcons could hear what I said, as did the Republic. I knew if she gave the orders, some would not follow them. Those who did would be forever stained in the eyes of honorable Falcons. And if none did, others would question her ability to lead the Falcons. Malvina could not afford to risk that a single warrior might not do her bidding. She was destined to submit."

"And the Republic?"

"Its conquest is inevitable, and as more of Stone's troops realize this, they will see us as a safer alternative to the Jade Falcons. We stopped the hail of fire from the stars, saving lives, but Malvina will still raze their cities and kill her prisoners."

"Brilliant," Vickers said. "You have changed the moral context of this war."

Alaric nodded. "Malvina will never understand. This was never about bombardment. *Aff*, I manufactured this confrontation, and I did it to save them as a Clan. I will have need for the Falcons, should they survive what is coming."

JADE FALCON FORWARD COMMAND POST
GENEVA
TERRA

In the silence that followed Alaric's transmission, Galaxy Commander Merlin Buhallin spoke first. "Why would he take such a risk?"

Malvina glared at him. "He seeks to undermine me," she said through clenched teeth. "Alaric believes this little stunt of his will divide our people."

"We are all with you, Chingis Khan," Buhallin said firmly. "This Wolf does not understand us. We are here, above Terra, because of you and what you believe."

For a moment, his words were enough to soothe Malvina's fury. "Somehow he has obtained the *McKenna's Pride*," she said at last. "Either he violated the Council's edict against going to the Homeworlds, or he is somehow in league with one of the Clans there. The other Clans will not stand for this—certainly not the Ghost Bears. When this ends, they will side with me. They will agree that the destruction of Clan Wolf is necessary and just. Alaric has certified his own death by bringing in that ship."

"As you say, Chingis Khan," Buhallin replied, bowing his head in both fear and respect.

Malvina flashed a grin. *When this is over, all that will remain of the Wolves will be ashes and graves.* Tau Galaxy would be arriving within twenty-four hours, and she had slated them for landing in Japan. While it was likely a redoubt, she would crush it, giving her Falcons a much-needed victory.

Galaxy Commander Stephanie Chistu had secured most of Germany. While the operation was successful, Malvina would not credit her for it openly. Her disdain for Chistu ran deep. *I will send her someplace else, somewhere where her victories will not be noticed.*

The fighting in Africa was progressing well, but the Normandy redoubt still held firm, and the sallies from there were becoming more than an annoyance. Once Geneva fell, she could turn her full attention to France. She savored the impending defeat of the Northwind Highlanders there.

But first, Geneva would fall, and when it did, it would crush the spirit of the Republic, especially if she captured and killed Devlin Stone. *I will surge our forces into the city, crush the remaining pockets of resistance.*

Once the Republic was gone—she could turn her attention to the final retribution, the destruction of Clan Wolf.

CHAPTER 16

This was a moment of glory for the Chingis Khan and for all of Clan Jade Falcon. Geneva was a sea of debris and rubble, but it was the Jade Falcons' doing. Much of the city amounted to little more than piles of broken stonework and masonry. Entire neighborhoods were engulfed in flames, left to burn themselves out. Some structures still stood, but all showed signs of battle. The majority were little more than gutted shells of their former selves. The air was uncommonly warm for the time of year, and the air reeked of ash, dust, and rotting flesh.

Malvina Hazen took it all in.

Alaric had forced her hand with Geneva, removing orbital bombardment from her holster. She had surged her forces, throwing in the newly arrived Omega Galaxy, fresh and ready for a fight, and elements of Zeta Galaxy, which had been in France. She finally had enough troops to do the job correctly and crush the last of the Republic defenders.

The battle had been brutal, vicious, building-to-building. Her artillery and aerospace fighters had bombed and blasted resistance points, then her battle armor, tanks, and BattleMechs had moved in. The Republic had fought hard, earning her respect. If they had not resisted so fervently, if they had simply surrendered, there would have been no glory in the fight. Only death.

She had taken far more losses than anticipated, but the capital of the Republic of the Sphere was in her hands. *Alaric conquers territory, I take strategic targets*—meaningful *targets. It is the Way of the Clans.*

Some Republic forces had still managed to escape, since several of her commanders had failed to effectively blockade the city. What was left of Stone's Liberators and Stone's Lament, led by former Exarch Jonah Levin, had fled through Lake Geneva's deep, icy waters and scattered outside of the Jade Falcon lines in the north. Malvina's scouts reported some of them were heading toward Paris, which frustrated her. A handful of her commanders would have to be taught the price of failure.

The Jade Falcons had not yet found the Republic's command bunker, though Malvina had construction 'Mechs working hard to uncover it. There was no sign of Devlin Stone or the Paladins who led the Republic. Despite her efforts, she had to acknowledge that they may have escaped. *If Stone somehow survived, the fight continues.*

Now, more than 100 survivors—the last defenders of the Republic's capital—were gathered on a section of the Rue de la Servette that was littered with chunks of blown-up buildings. They were a shattered people; she could see it in their faces while looking them over.

They all knelt, and most bowed their filthy heads, exhausted. Their uniformed were stained with blood, ripped and torn, marked with ash. MechWarriors from the Falcon Guards loomed over the prisoners, sidearms at the ready. *They fought well, more than I had anticipated the Republic capable of, but we are unstoppable. We are Jade Falcon.*

Malvina ordered the holovid cameras brought in. She was going to send a message to all of Terra.

While waiting for her communications team to set up the cameras, she assembled her officers. SaKhan Ryan Pryde's right forearm was bandaged from a shot to his cockpit that had nearly cost him his life. Next to him was Galaxy Commander Fred Buhallin, whose Epsilon Galaxy had been instrumental in the final assault. He required assistance to walk, thanks to his injuries. Both looked at her with complete devotion in their eyes.

Jade Falcons always follow strength, Malvina thought. *As long as I hand them glorious victories like this, they are devoutly steadfast in support of my reign.*

Missing from the ranks of officers to bask in the glory was Delta Galaxy's Stephanie Chistu. Chistu had fought well in the landings in France and her thrust into western Germany, but Malvina did not fully trust her. After all, Chistu had met with Khan Ward before the invasion and had received from Khan Ward the secrets to penetrating Fortress Republic.

The Jade Falcon Khan's other problem with Chistu was that she was exceedingly good at her job, giving the Jade Falcons victories despite the challenges Malvina sent her to tackle. Malvina had sent Chistu's Galaxy off to wage war in South America. *If you seek to consort with my enemy, you will not be allowed to bask in the warmth that victory brings.* Much to Malvina's consternation, Chistu was struggling against a Republic force outside of São Paulo, a battle group known as the Amazonians. *Sooner or later she will fail, and when she does, I will bring the hammer down on her.*

As the communications officer signaled, Malvina saw the green lights on the holovid cameras come on. She stepped in front of the prisoners, with burning Geneva framing her background.

"People of Terra, I am Chingis Khan Malvina Hazen. My Jade Falcons came here to bring about an end to the fallacy known as the Republic of the Sphere, to conquer Terra and be named ilClan. What you see behind me is what remains of Geneva, the heart of your once-precious Republic." She gestured to the ruins of the city as the cameras panned. *Let them see what happens when I come to wage war.*

"Look at the 'gem' of your Republic," she continued. "Geneva is no more. It will be erased from history, as will all references to your failed Republic. Your statues and memorials will be pulverized. In time, you will not even speak the name of the former regime. I have led Clan Jade Falcon to a complete victory here, on the home soil of all life, the birthplace of humankind.

"Clan Wolf paints themselves as benevolent benefactors even as they consume your lands in conquest. My Jade Falcons do not bother with such artifice. Know this: those who seek to resist us will face the same fate as Geneva. We offer no quarter. What you see here will be repeated on New Avalon, Luthien, Sian, and any other world that stands against us. We are Jade Falcon. We seize what we want and crush our enemies utterly—without remorse.

"To the Republic Armed Forces and Exarch Devlin Stone, if you still live, I send you this simple message: you cannot win. My people have been raised from conception to defeat you. We are the products of centuries of genetic engineering to make us the most formidable warriors ever born. Our technology is superior to yours, as is our drive to complete your destruction. If you fight, if you resist, if you shed the blood of Trueborn warriors, you will suffer the same fate as this city and its defenders." Malvina gestured to the men and women kneeling behind her. Some shed tears. *You are truly and utterly defeated. But you will not have to suffer much longer.*

She nodded to Star Captain Marv Roshak of the Falcon Guards. He raised his hand, and the guards lifted their rifles. As he dropped his hand, shots rang out. The air filled with red haze of splattered blood.

The green light on the cameras went out. Malvina beamed. She had led the Jade Falcons to one of their greatest victories, surpassing everything done during the Great Crusade.

ROSENHEIM
GERMANY
TERRA
4 MARCH 3151 (T+53)

Alaric watched the broadcast live from his rebuilt 'Mech's cockpit. Outside, the rolling hillsides were just starting to show a hint of green as the grass began to bloom. The only thing that marred the landscape was the smoldering wreckage of the fight that had just concluded there, the smoking hulks of hovercraft and the cratered areas of the grassy hillsides. Beautiful Bavarian church spires marked the city square in the distance. Alaric had paused his Wolves here because the Jade Falcons controlled western Germany.

He knew what Malvina was going to do with the prisoners long before she gave the order. Even so, watching it filled him with sadness. *She is sullying all of the Clans with her actions. Only time will erase this stain on their honor.*

Alaric had made plans for the Jade Falcons after his Wolves defeated them. He saw a distinct role for them in his Star League, but now he questioned it. *Is there anything redeemable left in them? Any fragments of their honor remaining? They have tossed aside Nicholas Kerensky's pledge to protect the weak—opting for slaughter instead.*

There *was* Galaxy Commander Stephanie Chistu. She had been sent to South America, no doubt a slight orchestrated by Malvina. Engaging with Chistu personally had been a deliberate move on his part. Alaric respected her silent resistance of the Mongol Doctrine. *Her victory in São Paulo was good, but is she smart enough to survive what Malvina may toss at her?*

He maneuvered his *Savage Wolf* along the rolling hills as Beta and Zeta Galaxies finished mopping up the First Bavarian Bravados—a Republic unit of battle armor and fast-moving hovercraft. Earlier, the Bravados had slid right through Beta's front lines, causing quite a bit of chaos before their individual units were isolated and defeated.

Alaric's command channel chirped; it was Chance Vickers. "General," he said.

"My Khan. You saw the broadcast, *quiaff*?"

"*Aff*. Not unanticipated, sadly."

"I concur. The damage Hazen's Galaxies suffered in Geneva will take considerable time to recoup from."

Alaric nodded. "What of their Tau Galaxy? It dropped two days ago in Japan, but we have not detected the kinds of signal traffic we should have from an invasion force of that size."

"Very strange," Vickers agreed. "I spoke with Spurlock, and he has no information either. We bypassed the Japan redoubt deliberately because the Custos' intel told us it would be hazardous to take. Still, it is odd that we are not picking up anything from them. No doubt they are facing vicious resistance."

Alaric surmised that Malvina's subordinates in Japan would be averse to pulling in additional units if matters got out of hand. *They fear her as much as the civilians of the Republic.*

"I did get word from Task Force Zebra," Vickers added. "It has been quite a struggle in Antarctica. The Republic threw the Eleventh Triarii Protectors at us with a vicious counterattack, but our forces triumphed and seized the strange facility there intact."

"Good. If it does control Fortress Republic, tell them to keep it operational. The last thing we need is an uninvited force arriving before we deal with the Republic or the Jade Falcons." Alaric knew control of the shield system preventing ships from jumping to the Terran system was vital. *The last thing I need is for another Clan or some House Lord deciding to come in and change this fight.*

"Agreed, and so ordered. I wanted you to know that the Republic garrison we were fighting in Verona immediately signaled their desire to surrender when they saw Malvina's broadcast. The garrison commander said he would rather fight alongside Clan Wolf against the Jade Falcons. Malvina is playing into our hands."

Alaric grinned. "Take only the best of their best as bondsmen, but they are not to be deployed against Republic troops. Hold them in reserve for now."

"*Aff*," Vickers said. "I received word that Amalgamation landed days ago in Puget Sound, next to Reunion. Word is that Amalgamation is asking for immediate deployment."

"*Neg*," Alaric said. "If she has an issue, tell her to contact me directly. For now, she is to hold position."

"She will not like it."

"I know. She knows the plan—she is simply chafing to fight. Amalgamation and Reunion are critical in our plans—especially after what we have just seen."

The days of the Republic are dwindling, Alaric thought, *which means we will soon shift from fighting them to fighting the Jade Falcons. And after today, we have seen just how far Malvina is willing to go to achieve victory.*

COLLEX-BOSSY, NORTH OF GENEVA
TERRA
6 MARCH 3151 (T+55)

Lieutenant Colonel Chris Kornfeld had drawn point for leading the last defenders of Geneva out of the tunnel system and into the farmlands north of the city. The evacuation orders had come a while ago, and the efforts to sneak the survivors out was both dangerous and slow. The Jade Falcons had taken Geneva, though pockets of defenders would emerge for days, if not longer, determined to make the Falcons pay for what they had done to their once-beautiful city. As he looked back from the cockpit of his battered *Lament*, he saw the smoke plumes rising as entire neighborhoods burned. Kornfeld held back his tears with surprising ease. It was hard for him to muster deep emotions after all the fighting he'd been through. He was numb to death and destruction, and that thought bothered him deeply.

Malvina Hazen had finally taken the prize, though she had won a blasted and charred scene of devastation. Kornfeld had mourned upon hearing word that Geneva had fallen. *It had been such a magnificent city, now it is only a memory.* He had connected with the survivors of Stone's Lament and a number of other units, most skeletal remains of their former glory, and had used the secret series of tunnels to get away, blowing them up as they went to prevent pursuit. Only Stone's Liberators came through the experience somewhat operational, though reduced to half their usual number. Now that they were in relatively open fields, he felt strangely exposed. His raw nerves had him looking in every direction.

An *Atlas III* moved up beside him. It bore some marks of battle, but much less damage than the other BattleMechs and tanks of the surviving ad hoc battalion he had been leading out. Having such a large 'Mech next to him should have seemed reassuring, but given Kornfeld's mental state, he felt it would merely draw more fire.

"Excellent work, Colonel," the voice said on the tightbeam transmission from the *Atlas III*. "This is where we part company, I'm afraid."

He knew that voice, having heard it before, in speeches and watching holovids. "Exarch Levin?"

"Yes," the voice said wearily.

"I thought you would have gotten out with Exarch Stone," Kornfeld finally replied.

"Stone has special plans for me," Levin replied. "Now that we have come up behind Jade Falcon lines, you and the other survivors are to drive north. There are DropShips waiting at Pontarlier. We are sending a company of the Liberators to Paris, and the rest of you are off for much-needed rest. Those ships will take you to safety."

Safety? Where on Terra is safe now?

Kornfeld fumbled for words. "You won't be coming with us, sir?"

"No. Like I said, I still have a mission to fulfill, something long-term. I wanted to stay and fight, but...well, we don't all get what we want." There was a sadness in Levin's voice. "I will be going on foot from this point. Have one of the Dispossessed take my 'Mech—I will clear the security codes. God knows you need it more than I do."

"Understood," Kornfeld lied. "Good luck, Exarch."

"And to you. God save the Republic," Levin replied as he started his power-down cycle.

The exhausted Kornfeld looked out at the survivors he had led out of the city. *Did the Exarch get out? And if he did, where would he go, now that Geneva has fallen?*

COMMAND POST STEADFAST
SANDHURST, ENGLAND
TERRA
6 MARCH 3151 (T+55)

Exarch Devlin Stone was exhausted, even beyond his age. It was a constant reminder of the toll the hibernation process had taken on his body.

The transit from Geneva to England had been rushed, and he and his command staff had nearly fallen prey to a Jade Falcon patrol on their way out. Steadfast—the administrative areas of a decommissioned Castle Brian complex beneath Sandhurst—did not feel like Solitude. Though larger, Steadfast had been abandoned until recently, and gone were the banners that hung on the walls and the nice conference table. Gray concrete walls and a spartan table that lacked any style spoke to the mothballed nature of the facility. Viewscreens on the walls showed images from around the globe, each one showing battles raging.

Janella Lakewood's usually pristine gray uniform was smudged, a bit of grease on one sleeve from a tunnel wall she had brushed against during their flight from Geneva. Tucker Harwell looked paler than usual, his lank, black hair longer now that he had been unable to get it trimmed. Only Damien Redburn seemed to have any energy or drive. As Devlin watched him, he remembered the fury Redburn had shown after his recall from the Remnant. *Damien always did have a reserve of strength.* Stone, in his current shape, couldn't help but envy his former protégé.

The Steadfast team had greeted their arrival with news—and then footage—of Malvina Hazen's broadcast. Stone had wept silently as he watched. He planned on sending a broadcast of his own as soon as possible, telling the citizens of Terra that he and the Republic were still very much alive. It would have to wait until the redness faded from his tired eyes. *They need to see the Devlin Stone of old, not the frail man I've become. Malvina's actions will rally many to our defense now that they have seen her brutality firsthand.*

"What is the word on the Liberators?" he asked Lakewood.

"Nothing. They were to operate under communications silence, lest they attract the Jade Falcons' attention. We assume Jonah got out. Some of the Liberators have been transferred to reinforce the garrisons in Paris, per your orders. The rest will go to North America."

"The odds may be against them, but I hope and pray they got out."

Lakewood glanced uncomfortably at the others.

Stone noticed. "What is it?"

"We've finally gotten word that Shimmer was able to extract Raul Ortega from Juba—some good news at last."

Stone stared at her. "But?"

"But the Jade Falcons have taken the Sinai Peninsula. And in South Africa, the Falcons have proven themselves to be very fast, even through normally rugged terrain. We had two regiments worth of local militia there, the Lions and the Pride of Zululand. They were routed and led the Jade Falcons on a weeklong chase that ended with their destruction a few hours ago. Hazen's Delta Galaxy has almost secured Brazil. Malvina has them doing mop up. Estimates show they will need refit time as well."

If the Wolves win, our surviving forces can help him take down Malvina. Right now, having Alaric achieve victory is more in our favor than a loss to both Clans. "We have the Eleventh Hastati in Panama," Stone said, almost a question.

"I anticipate that the Falcons will target them soon. I've sent word to Kristoff Erbe to prepare for an assault. Redoubt Panama is small, but its defenses are concentrated. It will be a tough nut to crack. And sir...our facility in Antarctica has fallen to Clan Wolf. Our counterattack force there failed to retake the complex, and has been forced to retreat."

Tucker Harwell made a frustrated noise and shook his head.

Stone resisted doing the same. *They now have the keys to Fortress Republic! But Julian and others already have the means to come through. The Federated Suns will not let us suffer under Falcon rule.* "Have they disabled the Wall?"

"No, sir. Fortress Republic protocols are still active."

"Then it is because Alaric wills it," Stone said. "He doesn't want anyone else coming to Terra and disrupting his plans. Perhaps we could send another force and take the facility back. Shut the whole thing down."

Lakewood shook her head. "We do not have the resources to spare. Unless you wish me to strip all the units from North America and bring them into play."

There she goes again, suggesting we mass forces, play the game the Clans want us to play. "No, Janella," Stone said. "I know the situation looks dire. But the last transmission we got from Japan indicated that the Falcons have lost there. We scored a decisive blow against them, costing them an entire Galaxy. See, the redoubts do work, and each day the Clans are growing weaker, their supplies are stretched further. You have to trust the overall strategy."

The fighting in Japan had been brutal and vicious. The entire main island of Honshu acted as a redoubt, and the local citizens insisted on being part of the defense force, giving it one of the largest standing armies. Tau Galaxy had landed everywhere on Honshu at once, thinking it would shatter the Republic defenders. Instead they dropped into minefields and on well-prepared defensive positions. There was no hint that the Jade Falcon commander had called for assistance, instead fighting to the brutal end. It was a victory, but not one the Republic could build from. *Our defenders there were devastated as well. We took out one Galaxy—but we can't afford to trade losses like this— not forever.*

Damien Redburn said, "My Nighthawk force is ready to strike, Exarch. I know you have reservations, but with the fall of Geneva, we cannot afford to wait any longer."

The words weighed heavily on Stone.

This used to be simple, he thought. Last time he faced such odds, the Word of Blake was entirely ruthless. They were practically a faceless enemy, a foe beyond redemption. Not so with the Clans. *The Jade Falcons are every bit as brutal as the Word of Blake, perhaps more so, and if they alone were the target of this plan, I would have sanctioned it sooner. But the Wolves are involved, too. If I launch Nighthawk, I risk infuriating them all.*

He had toyed with simply launching the operation against the Jade Falcons, but knew if it failed, it would only make things worse. If anything, the operation would push them to commit more war crimes, more acts of atrocity in retaliation. *If we do this, we are committing the cardinal rule of warfare— utilizing a strategy on an enemy that invites the same strategy in return. Hell, it's against the Ares Conventions, as if they still mattered.*

"If Nighthawk is successful," Redburn pressed, "the Clans will be stunned and confused, and we can use that confusion to counterattack." That was the one appealing part of his plan. Stone had always hoped that the Jade Falcons and Wolves would go at each other at some point, preferably with the Republic siding with the Wolves, if need be.

Stone understood the argument. It was seductive. *If this fails—if the truth comes out—we will lose the moral high ground in this war.*

"Our attack has to be coordinated against both Clans," Lakewood said. "As it stands, that won't be easy. The Northwind Highlanders are dug in tight in Redoubt Normandy. Our best bet is to launch a counterattack to pinch the Wolves in northern Italy—split their forces there. We can assemble what few survivors we have from northern France and Holland for a drive at the Jade Falcons in Switzerland, before they begin a new offensive from Geneva."

Will it be enough? What is the price of not trying? Will future historians look back at me and say, "He could have saved the Republic if he had only done this?" Stone hated that his options were so limited. But with Julian still missing...

He looked at Redburn and felt the exhaustion nearly overtake him as he spoke. "Nighthawk is authorized. We will send in your team, Damien. Hopefully our enemies will slaughter each other in the chaos."

NORTH OF SÃO PAULO
BRAZIL
TERRA
6 MARCH 3151 (T+55)

In the privacy of her portable command dome, Galaxy Commander Stephanie Chistu watched the footage from Geneva again, forcing herself to witness every image of the slaughter. It made her stomach knot in ways no battle ever had. *Malvina is every bit the monster I believed she was. If our Clan does not win and become ilClan, we all will face retribution for acts such as these.*

Malvina's demonstration of the Mongol Doctrine was being broadcast around the world. *She has made things so much worse for us. Our enemies will come at us with everything they have.*

The Chingis Khan had sent Chistu a message that her presence in Geneva was neither expected nor required. It had been intended as an insult; Chistu knew her Khan far too well. *She thinks I am somehow conspiring with Alaric Ward. She knows I do not subscribe to her twisted beliefs. Being here distances me from her actions—and prevents me from speaking out against them.* She had artfully dodged that debate for years. *Were I in Geneva, I could not have prevented this atrocity. Malvina would have done it just to spite me. But I could have been the voice of the Jade Falcons' conscience. I could have reminded the warriors there that we are better than this, that such acts do more damage to our Clan than good. Malvina would have drowned out my words, but I would have at least spoken them.*

An escort arrived, flanking Brigadier General Elisabete Guerra. Chistu shut off the holovid image. The Republic general's MechWarrior jumpsuit, camouflaged with a tiger-stripe pattern of white, black, and gray, was patchy with perspiration. She, like Chistu, still stank of sweat from the recent battle. Chistu herself had taken down Guerra's *Osprey* in the battle two hours ago, at the edge of the rainforest sanctuary.

"General Guerra," she said

Guerra was in no mood for formality. She brushed back her sweat-soaked black hair with one hand to reveal more of her bronzed complexion. "I take it you're going to tell me my troops are to be executed."

She has seen the footage.

Chistu had been ordered to not accept surrender from the enemy—the Chingis Khan had been quite explicit. At the same time, she knew how to contort a direct order to work to her advantage. *I will not walk the path that Malvina has paved for our Clan.*

"*Neg*, General," she said. "Your Amazonians fought with honor. Destroying them would be wasteful."

General Guerra's brows went up in surprise.

"At the same time," Chistu added, "I have been ordered not to accept my enemies' surrender."

"It appears we are at an impasse," Guerra said warily.

"Here is what we will do," said Chistu. "I cannot accept your surrender, but neither can I leave you as a functioning combat force. My official report will record that your unit abandoned their combat gear and vehicles. You faded into the countryside, ceasing to be any threat to my Clan. You and your officers, however, will remain as bondsmen—proof of your unit's defeat and dissolution. It ensures your former command will not re-form. I trust this is acceptable?"

Guerra eyed Stephanie carefully.

Chistu waited. *I cannot blame her suspicion, given what she has seen.*

At last, Guerra said, "Very well. I have no desire to be your bondsman, but if it will save the rest of my command, I agree. If you will allow it, I need to order my surviving troops to abandon what little equipment we still possess."

"Excellent," Chistu said. She pulled out a small cord and held it out for Guerra to see. "This is a bondcord. It links us, it binds you to the Clan, and in your case, it saves your people. It marks you as property of the Jade Falcons."

Guerra eyed the bondcord as if it were a heavy iron shackle. "Given what your Khan did earlier today, I do this with reluctance. I do not wish to be associated with your people in any way."

"I understand," Chistu replied. "But not all Jade Falcons follow the Mongol Doctrine like Malvina Hazen does. What you do today saves your people's lives. Otherwise, I would be forced to follow the Chingis Khan's orders." She stepped forward and looped the cord around Guerra's wrist. "You will find that I am not Malvina Hazen."

Guerra watched her tie the cord. "I am betting my life on that."

INTERLUDE

Khan Mori Hawker of Clan Sea Fox smiled. "So, the Jade Falcons have moved on Terra as well. Perfect."

SaKhan Petr Kalasa nodded. "Malvina Hazen would not have just let Clan Wolf seize Terra."

Still grinning, Hawker leaned back in his seat—more out of habit, given he was in microgravity. "We provided transports for Clan Wolf, we manufactured their new BattleMechs, and we sold them munitions. That fight will be a bloody—and profitable—one."

Kalasa looked less convinced. "The Jade Falcons may not be pleased that we sold weapons to the Wolves. Malvina carries a grudge to the ends of the galaxy and beyond. Is there a chance this can come back on us?"

Hawker shrugged. "There is always a chance. Think of it this way: Clans Wolf and Jade Falcon are going to battle for Terra, but first they must crush Stone's Republic. Now you have three armies on Terra vying for control, all fighting with everything they have. Whoever emerges from this fight will be weak. They will have lost warriors and, more importantly, equipment. Even if they wished to fight us, they need us to rebuild first. No Inner Sphere House will resupply them...they will all be too afraid of the Clans uniting under the ilClan. That leaves them one ready source for supplies and equipment."

"Us," Kalasa replied.

"*Aff*," Hawker said with pride. "Malvina may be angry with us, but if she wins, she will still need us." His eyes went to the far end of the stateroom where they were meeting. The large viewport showed the blackness of space, spattered with glimmering spots of starlight. *Each of them is opportunity. Each one has risks, but potential.*

"And if Clan Wolf is victorious, they are in our debt already, and they will need arms and equipment."

"Exactly," Hawker agreed, looking away from the vastness of space.

"So we will support whatever Clan wins Terra, *quiaff*?"

"Of course. It would be against tradition and our *rede* to do anything else. Whoever takes Terra will be the ilClan, and our people will be part of that bright future."

Khan Hawker paused for a moment, savoring the news. "Don't forget the words of our *Remembrance*, Petr: 'Peace is good for business. War is better.' Either way, Clan Sea Fox prevails in whatever path the ilKhan decides to lead our people."

CHAPTER 17

Alaric maneuvered his 'Mech along Zeta Galaxy's front lines. The last of the Republic's defenders of the Stuttgart redoubt—a militia unit known as the First Kriegsmaschine—emerged from their bunkers with their hands in the air.

The battle had been short and fierce. The Kriegsmaschine had sent two lances' worth of Scapha hovertanks to harass while their Kinnol, Demon, and DI Schmitt tanks had torn into Zeta's Galaxy's ranks. Republic Padilla artillery vehicles had rained down tight barrages while a lance-sized unit of their Taranis battle armor had overwhelmed two of Zeta's BattleMechs.

The warriors of Zeta appeared to fall back, but it was a ruse Ramiel Bekker exploited immediately. He and the TRC had redeployed alongside Beta Galaxy. Star Captain Agustin Tutuola led a Star of Black Wolf battle armor to the rear of the Kriegsmaschine, taking out their artillery, while the rest of Zeta Galaxy advanced on the flanks. The Republic forces, caught in a semicircle of fire, withered, then tried to flee to their bunkers. Most did not make it. Those who did surrendered ten minutes later.

The assault against the redoubt had been precise and well coordinated. Alaric had not been in the fighting, but had overseen the operation. As the battle ended, the Wolf Khan was searching for Bekker to congratulate him when he saw the approaching DropShip. It was an odd sight for a secured area, a ship on a low approach. Other Clan Wolf BattleMechs around him stopped as well, their pilots clearly wondering the same thing he was.

The craft, an older *Broadsword*-class vessel, gave off no transponder signal and dove in low, just over the treetops. Alaric noted that the flight path seemed to be heading right toward him.

This is not right.

Battle-honed instincts kicked in. Alaric juked his 'Mech to the right and broke into a sprint as the green *Broadsword* dove toward where he had been. Its turrets opened fire, a PPC flash tearing into his *Savage Wolf's* left leg and searing away armor there.

As death rained down on him, MechWarrior Sorsha from his Command Star sprang her *Timber Wolf* between him and the DropShip. Flashes and explosions devoured her OmniMech and blew it into thousands of bits, saving his life.

Even through the remains of her destroyed Omni, three medium pulse lasers scored his upper torso while the rest of the *Broadsword*'s shots poured in around him, charring the ground, throwing up hot clumps of sod. The DropShip disgorged a Star of BattleMechs as he moved, all of which went straight after him, ignoring the other stunned members of Zeta Galaxy and his Command Star.

"Wolves, we are under assault!" he barked as the lead BattleMech—a *Jade Hawk* in shades of bright green—opened fire. Its short-range missiles struck his cockpit and upper torso, sending fracture cracks chasing along his lower canopy. He returned fire as the small lasers from the *Jade Hawk* scoured his arms. One of his large lasers missed; the other ate into his attacker's frontal armor.

Alaric ran, swinging his *Savage Wolf* around to put some distance between himself and the new 'Mechs, but a *Marauder IIC* hit him with all three of its PPCs. Damage warnings flared yellow, seemingly everywhere, as he struggled to keep his 'Mech upright.

"Zeta, protect your Khan!" Bekker's voice roared over the tactical channel.

Fire erupted from every direction as Zeta Galaxy rallied and tried to move in.

Malvina, is this your revenge for what I did with the McKenna's Pride *over Geneva?*

Alaric battered the *Marauder IIC* with a wave of ATMs, most striking its birdlike legs. Heat rose in the cockpit; he ignored it as another attacker, a *Shadow Cat II*, launched a wall of long-range missiles at him. The warheads detonated all over his BattleMech, rattling him, as the *Jade Hawk* tore into him again with short-range missiles from his left flank. It was a furious grand melee—wild, uncontrolled, and deadly.

Alaric struggled with the loss of armor, the change in balance, and the heat. Another pair of PPC hits from the *Marauder IIC* sent static discharges dancing across his canopy.

It was too much for the 'Mech. Alaric's *Savage Wolf* fell hard on his left side, slamming through a decorative earthen berm that lined a roadway. Damage warning lights flared crimson everywhere on his display.

His cockpit faced the *Marauder IIC* closing in on him; its oblong, boxy arms took aim. The air flashed with bright-white charged particles as Alaric tried to rock his 'Mech back upright.

Two of the PPCs hit, one tearing into the body of his BattleMech, breaching the cockpit. A searing arc of electrical discharge burned his right arm and filled the cockpit with the smell of cooking meat. His world went red as he reeled from the damage. A rush of cooler air told him there was nothing left between his open cockpit and the approaching enemy. For the first time in the battle for Terra, he felt alone and trapped, his options dwindling.

It cannot end this way!

The pain made his vision tunnel as he rocked his 'Mech to its side and regained his center of gravity. He rose just as the *Jade Hawk* landed off to his left. The *Marauder IIC* in front of him leveled its PPC barrels for one more salvo.

Alaric's breathing was ragged as he struggled to raise his arm-mounted weapons pods, leveling them at the gray-green *Marauder IIC*.

Just as the enemy fired, a *Stormwolf* B with a red-painted cockpit darted in front of him. *Ramiel!* A brilliant burst of white and blue flared up like a sunrise, silhouetting the *Stormwolf* for a moment. Then it fell backward—toward Alaric, who was filled with a wave of pride.

He took the shot to save me.

Three Zeta Galaxy BattleMechs soaked the *Marauder IIC* in fire, and it twisted and fell at the feet of the *Stormwolf*'s charred remains.

But the *Jade Hawk* was still closing in. As Alaric rose, it unleashed a withering salvo of missiles and lasers at point-blank range. The left side of his cockpit blew inward, and he heard the distinctive *crack* of bone breaking. Part of his communications console had crushed his already-burned arm. Sparks rained down on him from the console.

The pain dizzied him. His vision narrowed and there was a roaring in his ears. His eyes rolled back as he tried to keep his BattleMech upright—but it plummeted. He did not feel it hit the ground, but heard the crunching around him as if a distant echo.

It cannot end this way! This cannot be my destiny!

But the pain and blood loss won out, and darkness consumed him.

Former Exarch Damien Redburn watched Alaric Ward's *Savage Wolf* collapse under a wave of missiles from his recently commandeered *Jade Hawk*. He smiled. For the first time in a long time, he broadly grinned. *I did it! I killed the Khan of the Wolves!*

His victory was short-lived as a *Tundra Wolf* charged his left flank. It knocked his *Jade Hawk* hard, toppling him into the ground. Most of the flight fins jutting up behind his 'Mech crumpled, now worthless. He rolled the captured Jade Falcon 'Mech over on its side and bent his knees to stand. A wave of missiles poured into his rear armor, shredding it

For Redburn, he had not felt this alive in years. His gyro pitched as one missile exploded near it. The damage made the 'Mech fight him as he struggled for balance.

Redburn managed to get the *Jade Hawk* standing as a trio of lasers seared armor off his right leg. He saw he was surrounded by Clan Wolf BattleMechs, all at point-blank range, all with their weapons trained on him. He heard a massive explosion behind him, no doubt the DropShip that had brought his team in. It didn't matter—all of the sacrifice had been worth it.

He started to squeeze his joystick triggers when all of the Wolves fired at him. The overwhelming onslaught consumed him, but in that last millisecond, Redburn found solace.

I saved the Republic!

LAMOURA WILDLIFE PARK
FRANCE
TERRA
7 MARCH 3151, 1011 HOURS (T+56)

The Chingis Khan wheeled *Black Rose* around as lasers and missiles riddled her from three sides. Damage warning indicators screamed for attention, but Malvina ignored them.

The enemy *Warwolf* had planted two Gauss rounds into her *Shrike* so far, and combined with the damage from a *Sun Cobra* and an ancient *Timber Wolf*, she was feeling the pressure. Her 'Mech was running hot, taking damage, and had lost half of its weapons in the first minute of combat. Four other Jade Falcon warriors moved in to protect her, but succumbed to devastating salvos of missiles and lasers, killing their advance in a deadly barrage of fire.

These were not Wolf warriors, despite their Wolf BattleMechs. It was obvious from the way they moved and fought.

Malvina knew she was outmatched. "Raptor Keshik, your Chingis Khan needs you *now*!" she barked, firing her pair of extended-range medium lasers into the *Timber Wolf*, reducing its left missile rack into a melted box of worthless metal. The Jade Falcons were nearby, but struggling under the faux-Wolf attacks. It was clear that part of the attacking force was there to isolate her from support, then kill her.

Blasts came from every direction and angle. Malvina moved with the fluidity of a prize fighter, firing her jump jets, landing, twisting, and blasting away at the *Sun Cobra*. The *Timber Wolf* aimed and she spun, giving the pilot her only good armor. The particle cannon bathed *Black Rose* in sparks and arcs of blue discharging particles while her cockpit roared from the heat below. Sweat stung at her eyes. *Engine hit*—stravag*! I have to even these odds.*

She charged the *Warwolf*, and in three running strides her green BattleMech became a blur. They collided in a shriek of overstressed metal. She raised her right arm and plowed the clawed hand straight into the enemy cockpit, plunging right through the ferroglass canopy to pulverize the warrior inside.

Malvina smiled as she took her fist back.

Another barrage, a wave of long-range missiles, tore into her left torso and riddled her internal structure. The gyro pitched hard as she struggled to maintain balance. She clenched her jaw and swung around to face the attacker.

Malvina saw only a silver blur from the Gauss round that slammed into *Black Rose* where the 'Mech's head rested on the battered torso. Something hit her arm hard, and she could not breathe. For long seconds she struggled to get air, but finally her lungs cooperated, albeit with a ripple of pain.

Nausea rolled through her as her BattleMech fell, as she saw the *Sun Cobra* drop under a wave of autocannon and missile blasts. Malvina struggled to pop the faceplate off her neurohelmet to catch her breath, but only gasped in the scents of coolant, smoke, and searing-hot air. Every breath was labored. She could not see; something blocked her view. As she tried to move, only a wave of pain told her she was still alive.

This cannot be happening, she thought. *My Jade Falcons are destined to rule…*

Then the darkness closed in and pulled her under.

TURIN, ITALY
TERRA
7 MARCH 3151, 1310 HOURS (T+56)

When Chance Vickers awoke, she gasped for air and jerked upright in her cot.

Two medtechs hovered over her. "General, please relax. You are in a field hospital."

Vickers gripped her head as pain flared across her face and beneath her right collarbone. She was dotted with bandages. *How did I get here?*

The last thing she remembered was a brilliant-green *Jade Hawk* sending a wall of short-range missiles into her 'Mech. The cockpit had blown in—and then she woke up here.

The Jade Falcons betrayed us. The Khan has to know about this. My troops…we need to brace ourselves. I need to know what is going on. She ignored the pain and glanced at the medtechs. "Who has command?"

"Damon Ward, I think," one of them said.

"Get him." She fought back a wave of nausea.

One medtech left. The other tried to help her. "General, you took some shrapnel in your chest and have a concussion. You need to rest."

"*Neg.*" She swung her feet to the ground.

Star Colonel Damon Ward rushed into the room in time to help her stand. "Sitrep," she commanded as she struggled for balance.

"It was a headhunter attack aimed at our command structure," Damon said. "General, I don't think—"

Vickers sent him a glare that would have vaporized an iceberg.

Damon kept his face carefully neutral. "They hit us three hours ago. We believe the attackers were Republic forces disguised to look like Jade Falcons. The situation is very confusing."

"I need to speak to Khan Ward immediately," she said, sitting up slowly in the hospital cot. She then rose painfully and took a wobbly step with the Star Colonel's aid.

"He is down…he—he may be dead."

"SaKhan Kerensky, then."

"Dead. The headhunters hit him, too."

"*Stravag!*" she said through gritted teeth. *That only leaves me.* The realization felt like dead weight heaped on her battered body. "Anything else?"

"Spurlock Connors indicated the Jade Falcons may have been struck as well. The details, such as we have, are elusive and confusing. The Falcons launched an attack on us in Europe. Apparently, they believe we were behind the attack on their leadership. At the same time, the Republic has mounted a massive counteroffensive here in Italy. They are taking full advantage of the situation, which points to them being behind it."

It made sense. *Cripple the command structure and then attack. Alaric...you have to be alive. Fulfilling Clan Wolf's destiny cannot fall to me alone.* Anguish, frustration, pain, and rage swelled up within her all at once—but she forced it under control until she'd honed it into cool resolve. *Lesser warriors like Niels Carns have tried to sidestep me, challenge my authority. Alaric once asked me to be his DeChavilier. Neg. I am General Chance Vickers. This was what I was forged to do, to lead the Wolves in Alaric's stead!* Every hint of uncertainty in her life evaporated in that moment. *This is my time, my moment!*

"Get me to the HQ," she said. "I am assuming command of all Clan Wolf forces until we sort this out. I need to speak to all Galaxy Commanders immediately. I need a map of where this Republic counteroffensive is taking place and where the Jade Falcons are striking us. *Now.*"

Damon led her to the domed field HQ. When she entered the room, the assembled warriors all stopped and stared at her, stunned, then saluted and broke into applause. Their smiles gave her strength.

"Glad to see you, General," said Star Commander Jathniel Kerensky, the communications officer. "Awaiting your orders."

She gripped the man's shoulder. "Jath, patch me through to all Galaxy Commanders, priority one. I want them on a secured channel immediately."

The Star Commander went to work.

Vickers turned back to Damon, who had activated the holotable to display the new RAF offensive. Someone brought a chair; she gratefully sat and leaned closer to the display.

The map appeared, and her trained eyes instantly saw what was happening. Republic forces were driving north to the Alps and had almost split the Clan Wolf forces in half. *Divide and conquer.* Her eyes danced over the troop dispositions as her stomach pitched. *They hit us hard and timed it perfectly. Now we must turn their counterattack back on them. They will pay for what they have done.*

"The Republic is counting on us being disorganized and confused," she told Damon. "Perhaps they believe we will turn on the Jade Falcons. We can use that against them." One by one, the individual unit identifiers for the Republic units were displaying as they became known. *It may be time to try something else,* she thought. *Something drastic. Would Khan Ward agree?*

She knew he would. Alaric had already reached out to the Falcons once— to Stephanie Chistu, specifically. Presented with the circumstances Vickers now faced...perhaps he would again.

Jathniel Kerensky spoke up. "General, I have the Galaxy Commanders of Alpha, Beta, Delta, Epsilon, Iota, and Rho on a secured channel."

"Very well." Vickers drew herself up and took a deep breath. *This will either be my finest hour, or my greatest failure. It* will *be the former!* "Clan Wolf commanders, this is General Chance Vickers. An emergency situation has arisen. Effective immediately, I am assuming direct control over all Clan Wolf forces..."

CHAPTER 18

Devlin Stone studied his battle map and was dismayed at n0t seeing more movement of his Republic forces. Brigadier General Turner, commander of Stone's Brigade, hovered at his side, taking the place of Janella Lakewood physically, if not emotionally. Her and Damien Redburn's absence made the Castle Brian's conference room seem even larger, emptier. Edie Miller, Janella's intelligence expert, stood where Redburn would have sat, and fed in live data from the battlefield. Tucker Harwell sat at the far end of the table, watching, biting his lower lip. Part of Stone felt lonely without his most trusted advisors.

He had hoped to see the thrust generate the same success as with the counterattack in the Middle East. Yes, his forces were driving hard, but were not penetrating as deeply as he wanted. *The Falcon and Wolf command structures should still be confused, in disarray. We should be crushing them...*

Janella Lakewood was leading the counterattack on the Jade Falcons. She had shoved them hard on the French front, gaining thirty kilometers of ground so far, though her progress was slowing. The remains of Stone's Lament had launched a strike under her leadership out of Paris, crushing a Falcon Cluster before they had been driven back to the city limits. *She is one of my best fighters,* thought Stone, *yet even she is getting bogged down. If she cannot break the Falcons, who can?*

Meanwhile, it looked like the Republic had nearly split the Wolf lines in northern Italy. As with such operations, he was getting bits and pieces from the front, having to assemble the full picture as the data came in.

Whatever the case, for the second time since the invaders had landed, the Republic was on the strategic offensive. Stone knew he should have rejoiced, but there was a foreboding sense of dread. *What I did to achieve this was wrong, but if it is successful, I will ensure that the history books don't tell that part of the story. As long as I am the victor, these actions will always be seen as justified.*

"Any word from Damien?" Stone asked again.

Tucker Harwell shook his head. "None, sir. And no word from any of his forces."

General Turner spoke up. "Redburn always assumed it was a one-way ticket, Exarch."

Stone felt the words drain life from his already tired body. "A part of me held out hope that he might somehow pull off a miracle and survive." *After all we went through, that whole incident in the Remnant—Damien proved to be the most loyal son of the Republic.*

"He changed the game, Exarch," Turner said gently. "From initial reports, we have hit and taken down all of our targets."

Good, thought Stone. *If we haven't killed them, they will come at us with everything they have.* "Then perhaps this operation has bought us more time... time for Julian and the Federated Suns to arrive."

Tucker Harwell cast him a stern, outright defiant glance. He had stopped trying to tell Stone that Julian was not coming. Stone had an alternative though—a long-shot, but one he hoped would work. *If House Davion isn't here yet, perhaps the Ghost Bears can be enticed...*

WEST OF STUTTGART
GERMANY
TERRA

It had been a strange day for Star Commander Manning. Rumor had it that Khan Ward had been killed by Clan Jade Falcon—but as soon as they began circulating, those rumors were denied. Right after that, the Jade Falcons had attacked the Wolves' position. It was said saKhan Garner Kerensky was leading the Wolves, but rampant rumors also claimed he was dead as well.

Star Colonel Kalidessa Kerensky had ordered her warriors to stop worrying about such rumors: "General Vickers is in command for the time being, and that is all that matters. Now do your *blitzking* jobs!"

Manning could not focus on the rumors, though. He had a role to perform.

He brought his trusted *Jagatai* OmniFighter into a steep dive, locking onto an advancing Jade Falcon *Shrike*. His eyes narrowed as he focused on the targeting reticle. The weapons lock hum purred in his ears, confirming what his senses told him.

The second he reached optimum range, he triggered his extended-range PPCs and a trio of large pulse lasers. One laser missed, scorching holes in the grass, but the others found their mark. The PPCs melted away three of the upright wing-like projections on the Falcon 'Mech, and the emerald bursts of laser light burned holes all over the upper torso.

The *Shrike* slowed its charge, tipping back to see the airborne threat. It was perfectly timed for Manning to fire his long-range missiles and bank away. He lost sight of the missiles, but his sensors told him they hit with devastating force.

"Ravager Two, what is your status?" he asked as a spray of long-range missiles snaked into his own flight path. A half dozen found his *Jagatai*, rattling him in the middle of his banking maneuver.

"Ravager One," Vigdal signaled back, "I am out of ordnance. I took three PPC hits as well. I am diverting to the airfield at Günzburg."

"This is Ravager Three," Guethler reported in. "Out of formation but working my way back."

Manning swung his *Jagatai* into a barrel roll as several lasers stabbed up at him. One struck his starboard vertical stabilizer. Craning his head, he saw the damage: a long black scar had melted into the control surface.

Blitzking *Falcons!*

"Roger that," he said, angling his fighter into a steep climb and turn. "These Jade Falcons are persistent. I want that *Shrike*."

JADE FALCON DELTA GALAXY FIELD HQ
NORTH OF SÃO PAULO
BRAZIL
TERRA

Stephanie Chistu sat in her portable command dome, trying to make sense of what she was hearing from other commands. Both Jade Falcon Khans were down or dead, and Clan Wolf had been blamed. The Galaxy Commanders had taken matters in their own hands by striking at the Wolves, and at the same time the Republic had launched its own counterattack on both Clans. *This all feels contrived, as if we are being manipulated. I have met Alaric Ward. I find it hard to believe he would have sent headhunters after Malvina.*

But what if the Chingis Khan was dead? That gave Chistu hope. *If Malvina is dead, her Mongol Doctrine may wither on the vine. The Jade Falcons can return to being honorable in our actions instead of brutal.* She secretly hoped the reports were all true.

She felt like she was in the dark, separated from the events in Europe. Then came the message a few minutes ago, from an unexpected source. *It is time to start removing the chaos and focus on the real enemy.*

She lifted the microphone near her mouth so her words would be crisp and clear. "Galaxy Commander Mehta, I have received word from Wolf General Chance Vickers." Her next words tasted bitter: "The Republic of the Sphere was behind the attack on our Khans. The Wolves were attacked as we were, by Republic troops posing as our Clan. You are to break off your attack on Clan Wolf immediately. They are not our enemy."

Mehta's voice came back with a crackle of static coming from the battle. "*Stravag*! But I saw footage of one of the 'Mechs used in that attack. It bore Clan Wolf Zeta Galaxy markings."

"It was a ruse," Chistu said grimly. "The Republic is trying to goad us into fighting each other. Break off your attack and fall back to Phase Line Tango."

"What if the Wolves are deceiving you?"

"If I am wrong, I will help you kill them all."

"I assume it is permissible to attack the Republic, *quiaff*?"

"*Aff*, of course. Make them pay for what they have done."

BERGAMO, ITALY
TERRA

"Incoming priority message, General," Star Commander Jathniel Kerensky transmitted. "It is the Watch Commander."

Chance heard the voice in her neurohelmet as she maneuvered her replacement *Blood Reaper* into the long line of Wolf 'Mechs forming up to blunt the Republic assault. "Put Spurlock through, Jath," she said, surveying the steep and rocky ground to the south, where they would advance. Several kilometers away, the Republic forces were surging north, toward the Alps behind her. *Here is where we will blunt their counterattack.*

"General. I wanted you to know first. Khan Ward is alive...wounded, but alive. Ramiel..." Spurlock Conners' voice hesitated in a way Chance had never heard before from the usually emotionless Watch leader. "The WarBear died saving Khan Ward's life."

A mix of emotions hit Chance all at once. Relief that Alaric lived. Sorrow at the loss of Ramiel. Tears welled up in the corners of her eyes. "What of Garner?"

"I have confirmation that saKhan Kerensky was killed as well. He died valiantly, or so I am told."

Chance paused. *Alaric lives—and that is hope.* "Thank you, Star Colonel."

She maneuvered into position as the Republic forces came into view to the south. She switched to her broadband channel so that all could hear. "Clan Wolf, your Khan lives! And today we fight against those that tried to kill him. Make Alaric Ward proud!"

A roar of Wolves cheering filled the airwaves. A small group howled like baying wolves—*no doubt Kalidessa Kerensky's Cluster.*

General Chance Vickers charged forward, wading into the line of advancing Republic BattleMechs with a fury she did not know she possessed. All around her, the Clan Wolf line of battle rushed forward, firing. The air came alive with lasers, PPCs, autocannon fire, explosions, and missiles contrails.

Vickers opened fire on a Republic *Griffin* with her twin ER PPCs. The shots tore off its left leg mid-sprint and sent the 'Mech tumbling onto the rocky hillside in the distance. She did not wait to see if it moved; instead she unleashed her heavy medium lasers and ATMs, shredding the *Griffin*'s back until oily black smoke rolled out of the holes she made.

It was the fourth such enemy she had destroyed so far, but as with every kill she'd made, she found no peace.

All she wanted was another target. She pushed past the pain of her wounds to discover new strength, new vigor, and new power. Around her, she caught glimpses of her fellow warriors, fighting with the same ferocious strength.

Shells tore into her *Blood Reaper* from the left, and she reeled about to see a Republic *Legionnaire* rushing straight at her. Its nose-like rotary autocannon blazed as it ran, the exploding rounds riddling her 'Mech's torso and canopy with fine cracks. *You should have fallen back*, she thought as she aimed her ER PPCs and fired, tearing off the left arm of the charging *Legionnaire*.

It swayed from the loss of mass, but did not break stride, and kept firing, targeting her torso and cockpit. Its rotary autocannon barrels glowed, and the stream of tracer rounds seemed to connect the two 'Mechs. Vickers fired her heavy medium lasers, which melted glowing scars on the *Legionnaire*, then juked her 'Mech hard to the right.

The *Legionnaire* was intent on a kill, firing another sustained salvo at her as it closed the distance. The shells hit below her cockpit, but then walked right up to where they had cracked the armored ferroglass before.

"Freebirth..." Vickers twisted her 'Mech's waist, but it was too late. The shells shattered her cockpit in a series of concussive blasts, and the hot rain of shrapnel tore into her body, throwing her back into her command seat. Her vision blurred, but only in one eye; the other saw nothing. Opening her mouth to call for help, she tasted a flood of copper.

Neg, I cannot let Alaric down... I cannot fail. Not now...not when we are so close...

Star Colonel Kalidessa Kerensky saw General Vickers' *Blood Reaper* drop.

Instincts honed over a lifetime of training took over. She aimed her repaired *Dire Wolf*'s four extended-range large lasers at the Republic BattleMech and fired. The crimson beams sliced into the *Legionnaire*'s damaged side, spraying melted armor everywhere. Still the Republic 'Mech remained standing. Kalidessa saw it move over the fallen *Blood Reaper* and angle down its nose-mounted rotary autocannon right at Chance Vickers' cockpit.

To Kalidessa it seemed as if her weapons fired themselves, it happened so fast. Lasers and missiles slammed into the *Legionnaire*'s cockpit and autocannon, the bright red beam searing off the front ends of the barrels, leaving them smoking and glowing. Just as the *Legionnaire* started to fall, the cockpit canopy popped, and an ejection seat blasted into the air.

Kalidessa ignored the ejecting warrior, as there were greater concerns. "This is Howling Fury Actual," she broadcast. "General Vickers is down. Medtechs to my signal. All Wolf forces, form up on my position to offer protection. Protect your general!"

Lady Crystal Livingston Synd, Knight-Errant of the Republic, had only ejected from a BattleMech a few times, but she was certain she'd never get used to it.

Her seat landed hard enough to knock the wind out of her. She was only a hundred meters from her downed *Legionnaire*. Quickly, she hit the release on the restraining straps to roll out of her ejection seat. Her ears still rung from the blast, and the explosions of battle seemed far away, mostly because her ears had popped during the ejection. As they popped again, she realized the battle was moving south, past her. Glancing back, she saw her fallen *Legionnaire* beside the *Blood Reaper* she had taken down.

Bits of dirt from a nearby explosion rained down on her. She scrambled for cover behind the fallen ejection seat, realizing just how exposed she was. The Wolves drove forward like a wave, moving right past her, wading into what was left of the RAF forces.

Synd had seen brutal fights before—hell, she had been trapped for years outside Fortress Republic—but nothing quite like this. *This is far worse than the battles in the Remnant, when we clung to a few worlds outside the Fortress, keeping the enemies at bay. Here the Wolves are driving right through our lines of battle.*

Clan Wolf forces quickly isolated the rest of her task force, then took them down. The Republic forces near the rear of their lines saw what was coming and made a mad dash south, hoping to escape. The faster 'Mechs of Clan Wolf pursued, running and gunning the whole way.

Synd's body ached. She shivered as the smoke-tinged air mixed with drying sweat. She removed her coolant vest, then glanced around the seat. With the Wolves rushing through the Republic's line of battle, there was little chance of getting away. *I am behind enemy lines. This is probably the end for me.*

Medical teams had arrived at the downed *Blood Reaper* and were now extracting the MechWarrior within. *They must have been a Galaxy Commander or Star Colonel, given the 'Mechs standing guard.* That gave Synd a moment of satisfaction. *Hopefully I dealt them a blow, since our attempt to break their lines died here.*

One of the Wolf infantry caught sight of her and gestured to their companions. In seconds, a squad approached her, their weapons drawn and aimed. "Drop your weapon," one of them commanded.

Synd had forgotten her sidearm and slowly unholstered it, tossing it on the grass.

Three of the Wolves moved in and zip-tied her arms. They handled her roughly; she could feel their anger oozing off them. "Take it easy."

"You had better hope the general lives," one of them said, twisting her arms behind her back as he pushed her forward.

Synd ignored the pain and suppressed a smile. *General? Well, that almost makes it worthwhile.*

CHAPTER 19

The crowd of gathered Falcon warriors filled the cobblestone courtyard in the center of the small town of Oyonnax. Shade from the taller buildings cast cold shadows on parts of the large courtyard, while the weak spring sun melted the remaining frost into thin wisps of mid-morning steam.

Despite her pronounced limp, Malvina Hazen managed to project defiance in her stride. Her bionic arm hung at her side, damaged in the attack that had nearly killed her. Medtechs had set her two broken ribs, but her chest still stung with each breath. *It is important that everyone see me quite alive, still able to fight.*

SaKhan Ryan Pryde couldn't give the same reassurance, as he still lay recovering in a field hospital. He had survived only by a twist of fate, though for how much longer, no one knew.

The assassins had attacked wearing the colors of Clan Wolf, but Malvina would never attribute that kind of fighting to Khan Ward. *He is ruthless, but not so brazen.* Her theory had been confirmed when Chistu radioed with a message from a Clan Wolf general, Chance Vickers. Vickers—herself a target of the attacks—had warned Chistu of the Republic's strategy. Chistu was then able to pull the Jade Falcons back from retaliatory attacks against the Wolves.

It grated on Malvina that the Wolves had not contacted her directly. What made it even more galling was that they chose Chistu—someone who did not follow the Mongol Doctrine. *She is in league with Clan Wolf even now, not just Alaric, but also that General of his. When I have proof of her betrayal, she will burn, as will Alaric.*

To Malvina, her survival only confirmed that it was her destiny to rule the Clans.

The holovid cameras were poised at the edge of the open space in the center of the courtyard. She turned to face them, squaring her shoulders. "I am Chingis Khan Malvina Hazen. Two days ago, your high and mighty Republic of the Sphere attempted to assassinate me. They struck like cowardly bandits, masking themselves as Clan Wolf. They failed. This dishonorable attempt on my life has stained the vaunted Republic."

She turned, gesturing to the captured Republic Knight nearby. The cameras followed eagerly.

The Knight, on his knees, still wore his combat jumpsuit, his hands bound behind him and his mouth covered with tape. His forehead was badly bruised and swollen, and several cuts marked his face. He struggled as Malvina drew close, as if he might slip his bonds and get free to finish the work he had begun.

"This is one of your Knights-Errant, Jodi Mazzanoble. He was the sole survivor of the assassination attempt. He brought no honor to the Republic, but lived long enough to show how contemptible the leaders of the Republic are. Citizens of this failed Republic, look upon him with shame. This is your government. This is who you fight for. Cowards and murderers. They come like thieves in the night rather than fighting with honor. If you continue to prop up the Republic, his fate is yours to share."

She tore the tape off the man's mouth.

"You bitch!" Mazzanoble spat.

Ignoring the insult, Malvina spun her captive around and kissed him on the lips.

Mazzanoble surprised her, though: at the last moment, he clenched his jaw and bit Malvina's lower lip. She recoiled under the surprised pain, broke free, and backhanded him hard. Blood from the wound drizzled on her uniform jacket, and she wiped her lip with her sleeve.

Her knife was already in Malvina's hand, and she sliced it across the Knight's throat from ear to ear. Blood poured forth in a shocking jet. Mazzanoble gurgled in fury before his eyes rolled back and he crumpled unceremoniously to the ground.

Her moment had been shaken by his last act of defiance, but Malvina pressed on as if it hadn't happened. She faced the camera and pointing her bloodied blade at it as her lip continued to drip. "Know this, Devlin Stone: you have attacked Kerensky's Clans without honor. I am coming for you, old man. Your death will not be as quick as this Knight's. You will *beg* for death while the Republic watches!"

The camera turned off. She relaxed somewhat, though she ached all over. One of her warriors handed her a bandage, and she used it for a minute to stem the blood from her lip. Then she motioned for Star Colonel Abzug Helmer to join her. He arrived, his artificial jaw an off-white color from the rest of his darker skin.

"Star Colonel," she said, handing her bloody knife to a nearby guard, "where is Devlin Stone?"

Helmer was still learning to speak with his synthetic lip, which slurred his words somewhat. He spoke slowly. "Our latest intelligence placed him in England—somewhere south of London."

"And the Wolves. How have they fared with these assassins?"

"We are confident that their saKhan, Garner Kerensky, is badly wounded, if not dead. Alaric Ward was downed, but we do not know if he survived. We are awaiting further news from the operatives we placed in the Wolf camp. They are posing as Republic soldiers who surrendered."

"What of Chance Vickers? The general who contacted Chistu?"

"She led a counterattack against the Republic's attempt to split her forces in Italy. One of my sources says she is near death as a result."

"Good," Malvina said. "And what of Anastasia Kerensky? The Wolves have never been weaker. If Alaric is down and she is alive, there is no way she will not surface and take command for herself."

"Nothing, Chingis Khan," Helmer said, unblinking, clearly determined not to show his fear despite what his lack of intel on Anastasia had earned him last time. "This supports the theory that she is no longer with Clan Wolf."

"But you do not know, *quiaff*?"

"*Aff*," he replied.

"Keep looking." Malvina turned away. "And find out the fate of Alaric Ward."

STUTTGART, GERMANY
TERRA
9 MARCH 3151, 1507 HOURS (T+58)

Alaric Ward's eyes opened, and then immediately narrowed against the light that hovered above his hospital cot.

What happened? He remembered the pain. The sickening smell of burning meat that came from his own arm. Ramiel's *Stormwolf* jumping in front of the enemy and taking the brunt of the attack that might have killed him.

He coughed, and his throat ached. *If I can feel pain, I am still alive.*

A physician whose name badge read hobgood hovered over him. "Khan Ward," she said, "you are in a field hospital outside Stuttgart. Please do not move just yet."

He caught a whiff of disinfectant hanging in the air, confirming what he was told. "How long?" His voice cracked as he spoke.

"Two days."

Two days! What have I missed?

"Situation," he managed to say.

"You suffered a compound fracture of your left arm. We have knit the bones back together and reinforced them with titanium rods, but it needs to be kept immobilized. And your arm was badly burned. We have wrapped it in synthskin."

"Not me," Alaric croaked, grateful that his wounds were not worse. "Our Clan."

Hobgood nodded. "I will bring you one of your officers."

In what seemed like no time at all, Galaxy Commander Tyler Cooper loomed in Alaric's field of vision. "My Khan, it pleases me to see you awake." The lanky aerospace pilot took a chair at the side of the bed.

"Sitrep," Alaric said, resisting the urge to sit up. Hobgood had impressed on him the importance of keeping still.

"It was a headhunter attack," said Cooper. "They also hit General Vickers, saKhan Kerensky, and the Falcon Khans. At the same time, the Republic launched an attack aimed at splitting our *touman*, driving north to the Alps."

Alaric cleared his throat, ready to ask about his officers, but a labored coughing fit overtook him. Cooper picked up a cup of water from the small table nearby and helped Alaric drink some. The cold water made his throat ache for a second, but it felt better, and his voice came easier. "Thank you, Galaxy Commander. Continue."

Cooper nodded, setting the water aside. "General Vickers was wounded, but organized the counterattack against the Republic. She was badly injured in the fighting. I only just received word that she lost her left eye and suffered other injuries. They have fitted her with a bionic replacement, but it will take some time for the tissue to heal around it. For now, she is hospitalized."

Chance lives. "Whatever she needs, she is to receive, understood? What of Garner?"

Cooper bowed his head. "I regret to inform you that the saKhan was killed in the Republic's attack. He and his killer struck each other with simultaneous cockpit hits. Your attacker, Damien Redburn, was also killed quickly."

"Damien Redburn led the attack?"

"*Aff*," Cooper replied. "He piloted the BattleMech that downed yours. Garner fought bravely and valiantly. He died with great honor."

Garner and I did not always see eye to eye. He represented the old ways of the Wolves. Yet I am sorry to lose him. Alaric fumed at the Republic's audacity. "Have we driven the Republic back?"

Cooper managed a smile. "Yes, my Khan. General Vickers rallied our forces and routed the Republic counterattack in Italy. And she stopped the Jade Falcons who attacked us because they thought we had attacked their Khans. She contacted one of their Galaxy Commanders, Stephanie Chistu, and informed her of the Republic's ruse."

Alaric wanted to smile back, but conserved his strength. *Chance must live to see the results of her efforts.* "What of the Jade Falcons? Did the Republic's attack on them succeed?"

"We just saw a broadcast that Malvina Hazen was wounded in the ambush, yet still lives."

Of course she does. She is far too angry and hateful to simply die. I almost pity the Republic. "Galaxy Commander, I need you to inform all commands that I am alive and well. And I will want to talk to Ramiel Bekker immediately."

Cooper's face fell. "I will inform all of your commanders, but...Khan Ward, the WarBear...it was Bekker who saved your life...with his own."

Alaric again saw the crimson *Stormwolf* bathed in hellish blue-white fire. *That was Ramiel?*

"The physicians tried their best," Cooper said carefully, "but his injuries were too severe."

Alaric felt a wave of nausea rise within. For a long moment, he could not speak. Then he said, "Take me to him."

"My Khan—"

"Take me to him *now*," Alaric repeated. He painstakingly sat up in bed and swung his feet to the ground. He battled a rush of vertigo as Galaxy Commander Cooper helped him to his feet. His own pain did not matter. *I have lost the WarBear.*

Hobgood lent Cooper a hand, and together the duo steered their Khan through the infirmary. Alaric felt the eyes of his fellow injured Wolves on him, and that gave him strength, helped him to stand up straighter.

Hobgood and Cooper took him down the corridor of hospital beds to a small closed-off area of the hospital. A dozen bodies lay on gurneys, covered in white sheets. Alaric was led to the third one in the row.

"Leave us," he said.

When they were gone, he gripped the side of the gurney with his uninjured arm, depending on it to keep him upright. With his left hand, he peeled back the sheet.

Ramiel Bekker was barely recognizable. The PPC shot that had killed him had incinerated his face, burning it right down to the charred bone. There was that stench again, the odor of cooked meat, that turned Alaric's stomach once more. Still, he did not cover up his former bondsman.

"You saved my life, Ramiel...a debt I do not know how to repay. You were conceived a Ghost Bear, but in the end you proved yourself to be one of the greatest Wolves who ever lived." Alaric paused, fighting back the stinging in his eyes. "The Ghost Bears will also know of your deeds," he promised. "You have proven yourself the best of both of our Clans."

For long moments, he said nothing, simply staring at the burned remains of his comrade. At last, Alaric covered Ramiel up. "Your loss will not be in vain," he vowed quietly.

COMMAND POST STEADFAST
SANDHURST, ENGLAND
TERRA
9 MARCH 3151, 1611 HOURS (T+58)

"Message for you, Exarch," the communications tech said. "Voice only. It is on a secured Wolf Clan channel, but is coming in unencrypted."

Stone was sitting in his usual spot at the mostly vacant facility. He looked over at Tucker Harwell, who only offered a shrug. "Put it through," Stone said. *Perhaps it is good news...*

"This is Khan Alaric Ward," came a firm voice. "Is this Devlin Stone?"

...or not. "It is." Stone rose from his seat slowly, propping himself up with his hands on the table.

"Your attempt to kill me has failed."

Stone lowered his head, at once furious and frustrated. *So I lost Damien for nothing.* "I wasn't left with a lot of options, Khan Ward. We are both fighters, you and I. I would do almost anything to save the Republic, just as I am sure you would do almost anything to save your Clan. I hate that you forced me to take such actions."

"*Neg*," came the cold voice of the Wolf Khan. "You have always flaunted that your Republic is morally superior, but when faced with defeat, your true colors emerged. You are no better than Periphery scum."

"*You* invaded *my* world, Khan Ward."

"*Aff*, I did. You are mistaken, however. Terra was never 'your world.' It belongs to the heirs of Aleksandr Kerensky. And regardless, I did not throw off my honor by liberating this planet. I have dealt with you honorably up to this point. I am no longer bound to that. Just like your friend, Damien Redburn, you will not see the next era of the Inner Sphere."

Stone reined in his anger before it got the better of him. *Damien is dead, I can't change that. Sacrifices must be made to win a chess match...and this gambit always was a long shot.* Stone had assumed Redburn was dead by now, but hearing Alaric confirm it so coldly...

"Look, son," Stone said, "you know I am not your true enemy. You need to worry about the Jade Falcons. Focusing on revenge, coming at the Republic, that only weakens you for the fight we both know is coming. The Republic could be your greatest ally against them."

"*Ally*? After what you just did?" Somehow, Alaric's tone dipped several more degrees. "You still do not understand. I may not approve of Malvina's methods, but she is still Trueborn Clan. She is my people, as are all Jade Falcons. I will not fight my own people while you still live."

"They are not at all like you—"

"But you attacked them just the same. You have sealed the fate of the Republic. Prepare to reap what you have sown." The message cut out.

Stone lowered himself to his seat.

"Did you honestly believe that would work?" Tucker asked with an incredulous frown from the opposite end of the conference table.

"Watch your tone, boy," Stone warned.

"You just tried to *kill* him, and now you ask if he will *ally* with you?"

"You know so little of war, Tucker. Every POW I ever captured was someone firing a gun at me a minute earlier. In time, many of them became my allies as well. It is the nature of war, something I understand. Besides, I was planting a seed, nothing more. Alaric is smart. He heard my words and will consider them. I know how to manipulate the Clans. I was doing it before you were born, and I'll be doing it when this whole 'ilClan' nonsense is over."

CHAPTER 20

FORÊT DE SÉNART
PARIS, FRANCE
TERRA
11 MARCH 3151, 1106 HOURS (T+60)

Clan Wolf Khan Alaric Ward had never felt so alone.

The loss of Ramiel Bekker and Garner Kerensky, Chance Vickers' injury—all of it angered him still. He had anticipated casualties of war. Death was always near for a warrior, from their training in a *sibko* to their first time in a 'Mech to their first time on the battlefield. What disturbed him was the loss of critical members of his command staff. He had lost people close to him before, but this hit him strangely hard. Somehow, it felt personal. It brought out a darker, grimmer mood. His arm, occasionally throbbing with sharp pain in its cast, was a reminder of just how close the Republic had come to killing him as well.

He had seen Chance in her hospital bed via a live communications feed as she began her slow recovery. She had said little, but managed to give him a thumbs-up. Shrapnel had destroyed her left eye and punctured her lung and her small intestine. While the prognosis was good, it did little to boost Alaric's spirits. *I feel as if I am working with one hand tied behind my back.*

The attack had taken his most trusted advisors on the ground. It was tempting to bring Haake Sukhanov down from orbit to fill one of those roles, but Alaric needed him where he was, ensuring that no outside forces made a dash for Terra.

To take over Bekker's Tactical Response Cluster, Alaric chose Star Captain Agustin Tutuola of the 279th, his expert on battle armor tactics. Tutuola accepted the role with the kind of vigor Alaric had hoped for. *He has great shoes to fill.*

Physician Hobgood had insisted that Alaric remain in bed for his own well-being, but he could not—not when fighting the Republic was bringing the Wolves and Jade Falcons in close proximity. His place was in the field.

Thus, he had suited up and moved out, despite the cast on his arm. Star Colonel Spurlock Conners accompanied him in a *Stormwolf*. *He is as worried about me as Hobgood.* Still, Alaric appreciated the support.

Now he gritted his teeth against the pain in his arm as he steered his temporary BattleMech, a *Tomahawk II,* onto a hilltop overlooking the Forêt de Sénart. The dense forest park was south of Paris, situated beside the Seine River.

RAF forces were down there. Paladin Janella Lakewood had abandoned Paris in hopes of sparing it Geneva's fate. Her troops had waged a fighting retreat into the forest as the Wolves came from the east, pulverizing any pockets of RAF defenders. The forest would provide excellent cover—perhaps even allow Lakewood's troops to cross the Seine and get away.

Lakewood did not know that the Jade Falcons waited on the other side.

Both Clans wanted to make sure the Republic paid the price for the attacks on their leaders.

"This is Khan Ward," he spoke on the command channel. "Delta Galaxy, form up on my position to the rear of Beta Galaxy. Move in your artillery and shell that forest—box and cage barrage patterns. Get their attention and keep it. Sigma Galaxy, swing to the south, come up along the river, hit them from the rear and prevent them from effecting a crossing. Zeta and Alpha will swing wide of the Republic position and hit from the north."

Confirmations came back quick and sharp. The Wolves wanted blood. They had not lost their discipline, but they had plenty of fury to sate in the woods below.

"We execute in thirty minutes," Alaric told them. "The Jade Falcons are operating on the far side of the river. No Wolf units are authorized to fire on the Jade Falcons unless they fire on us first. We are not here to fight them...yet. If fired upon, return fire only for protection, and break off if possible."

1318 HOURS

Warrior Hawkins accelerated *Fratricide* through the forested park of Forêt De Sénart and drove up over a steep rise so fast that his Carnivore seemed to fly. His stomach pitched as the tank came down, its treads digging into the soft, thawed soil.

"I am picking up targets ahead," DuJordan said. "An enemy *Tundra Wolf...*?"

"*Isorla,*" Hawkins replied. "It must be."

"Whoever it is has company. A Demon tank on the flank."

"Closing," Hawkins said, gunning the tank forward. *Fratricide* roared around them and he found it oddly reassuring.

"Friendlies in the fire zone. Delta Galaxy *Warhammer IIC,*" DuJordan called out. "Stay on course. I am traversing to target."

"Do not tell me how to drive," Hawkins said through gritted teeth as he angled the tank to avoid hitting a dense cluster of old-growth pines. As he did so, he found a large open glade, and across it, a kilometer and a half away was the Republic *Tundra Wolf*. It was red and gold in color, almost matching *Fratricide*'s paint scheme. In white, on the upper torso, the name andrea was stenciled. There were ugly rents and blast marks on the armor as the 'Mech moved. For the moment, it did not seem to sense the Carnivore's presence.

Breaking through the tree line opposite in the glen was a *Warhammer IIC*, painted in muted browns and greens, smoke trailing from its burned left shoulder and side.

"Locked," DuJordan said.

"They are already engaged," Hawkins said. "The honor is to the *Warhammer*."

"We can change that," DuJordan said wryly. "Get into the enemy's field of vision."

Hawkins understood. Clan rules of engagement were delicate matters, but if the *Tundra Wolf*'s fire hit them, they would be able to fight it as well. Otherwise the honor of destroying it went to the *Warhammer IIC*. "Remember, you asked me to do this," he said, angling the Carnivore so it would be under the *Tundra Wolf*'s guns.

Plumes of launched advanced tactical missiles seemed to head straight at Hawkins' driver's seat. Instead, he turned *Fratricide* to put the tank's thicker frontal armor to bear, and the missiles blasted the turret and right-side armor instead.

"Make that MechWarrior pay for their mistake."

DuJordan obliged.

The pair of Gauss rifles propelled their silvery slugs at hypersonic speeds into the *Tundra Wolf*'s upper body, making the hulking BattleMech list backward from the kinetic impacts. Before Hawkins could savor the moment, the Demon wheeled tank surged into the open space, firing at the *Warhammer IIC* with its medium pulse lasers. The brilliant green bursts tore into the 'Mech's legs, leaving smoking holes in their wake.

The Wolf MechWarrior in the *Warhammer IIC* unleashed both of its extended-range particle projection cannons and its five medium pulse lasers at the new threat. Hawkins watched the Demon try to turn and get out of the glen, only to be bathed in fire. The PPCs strikes blew off its front-left wheel, sending it spinning wildly in the air. The Demon bit into the soft black sod and nearly flipped as the lasers furrowed its thinner side armor. There was a *whomph* sound as the short-range missile magazine cooked off inside. Every hatch blew out at once, with a pillar of flames shooting skyward. Hawkins winced; being burned alive in their fighting compartment was every tanker's worst fear.

The *Tundra Wolf* turned back to the *Warhammer IIC* and fired long-range missiles and a large laser at the Wolf 'Mech as Hawkins slowed his speed to give DuJordan a clean shot. The MechWarrior in the *Tundra Wolf* had impressive aim as the missiles impacted every part of the BattleMech and the laser seared off the last bits of armor on the left side.

The capacitors for *Fratricide*'s Gauss rifles hummed as DuJordan fired again. One round tore off of the *Tundra Wolf*'s right arm; the other hit the left leg, which was already damaged. The impact was so hard that the knee buckled backward, the actuator reduced to scrap metal.

At the same moment, the *Warhammer IIC* fired its PPCs. One shot missed, torching the pines behind the Republic 'Mech. The other hit the damaged center torso, just below the cockpit. That shot burned deep and hot, causing a quaking motion as the *Tundra Wolf*, already overwhelmed with damage, began to fall.

The Republic MechWarrior ejected from their collapsing 'Mech, rising high above the glen, easy to spot against the brilliant blue skies. The parachute deployed, and the ejection seat drifted back down. Hawkins drove *Fratricide* over to where the pilot had landed, and the *Warhammer IIC* thudded over as well. A tall woman rose from the fallen seat and removed her now-useless coolant vest. Hawkins checked his sensors and saw no other enemies in the area. Off to his right, a secondary rumble shook the flaming remains of the Demon.

Both Hawkins and DuJordan popped their top hatches and stood as the *Warhammer IIC* pilot spoke over his external speakers. "I am Star Commander Weingart of Delta Galaxy, and I claim this victory. I was already engaged with this MechWarrior when you interfered."

"She fired on us," DuJordan called back. "The honor of the kill is ours."

Weingart said nothing for a moment. "I will grant you the kill, but I claim the MechWarrior and 'Mech as *isorla*."

Hawkins looked at DuJordan, who nodded. "Well bargained and done," he replied.

From the external speaker, Weingart's voice boomed: "Janella Lakewood, Paladin of the Republic, you are my prisoner."

"A Paladin?" DuJordan said, his bright blue eyes beaming.

Hawkins grinned broadly. "That is two for us!"

HALL OF MIRRORS
PALACE OF VERSAILLES
VERSAILLES, FRANCE
TERRA
13 MARCH 3151 (T+62)

Alaric had visited the restored Palace of Versailles the last time he was on Terra, years ago. He had used his invitation to the funeral of Victor Steiner-Davion to visit every important landmark he could on the planet—not out of a sense of history, but to study them first-hand for these battles. Then, as now, he found the palace gaudy and extravagant, especially the brilliant crystal chandeliers, but Malvina Hazen had chosen the site for their meeting.

Spurlock Conners wore his dress uniform for the first time since the start of the campaign. Alaric could tell his Watch commander appreciated the history of the moment—meeting the infamous Malvina Hazen in such a storied chamber. Alaric's own uniform felt uncomfortable after weeks in jumpsuits and MechWarrior togs. It had been hard to get his sleeve to fit over the cast, but he had managed.

The Jade Falcon escorts led them to the Hall of Mirrors. Standing before an ornate table was Malvina Hazen, Stephanie Chistu, and a Galaxy Commander Alaric did not recognize.

He noted their uniforms. Malvina and the unknown Galaxy Commander wore black Falcon uniforms; Chistu favored the more traditional green. *The black uniform is a mark of the Mongol Doctrine. Malvina had to have known that throughout history, only the darkest of warriors donned black as their uniform.*

The escorts left, and the two parties regarded each other.

"Khan Ward," Malvina said at length.

"Thank you for the invitation to meet, Chingis Khan Hazen," Alaric replied. *She expects me to be disrespectful, so I will confuse her by being gracious. This is not the time to goad her...not yet.* "May I present Star Colonel Spurlock Conners of the Wolf Watch."

Conners stood at attention and bowed his head politely.

"Charmed," Malvina replied, clearly anything but. "No doubt you brought your spymaster to size me up. What happened to this Wolf General of yours, Chance Vickers?"

She knows of Chance's condition... She is trying to provoke me. "General Vickers is mending well," Alaric said. "I will pass on your concern for her."

"Indeed." Malvina frowned, but indicated the others. "I believe you already know Galaxy Commander Chistu."

"*Aff*, we have spoken," Alaric replied. "It pleases me to see you again, Galaxy Commander."

Chistu inclined her head, but said nothing.

She is here by order, not by choice, he thought. *Malvina brought her hoping to provoke a response from either of us. She will get none from me.*

Malvina gestured to the other Galaxy Commander, a tall woman. "This is Galaxy Commander Jane Thastus. She is my acting saKhan until Ryan Pryde recovers from his injuries."

Thastus' light brown hair was uncommonly long for a MechWarrior. Her face was drawn, not quite gaunt, but close to it. The Galaxy Commander gave a formal, rigid bow, which Alaric and Spurlock returned.

Malvina gestured to the seats, and everyone sat. "Khan Ward, I understand you captured the Republic Paladin commanding the operations against us both."

"*Aff*," said Alaric. He had met with Lakewood and found her depressed, her spirit shattered. She had not just been beaten. She had been *utterly* defeated. *She has seen the doom coming down on her Republic, and knows it cannot be stopped.* "Lady Lakewood surrendered to us, as did what was left of her command."

"She had no choice but to surrender to you," Malvina replied. "My Falcons had chased her across France."

"As did my Wolves," Alaric said casually.

Malvina smiled thinly. "You and I both know the end of the Republic is looming. Before now, we could run our operations without a great risk of running into each other. I thought we should meet to avoid any unnecessary... complications. I propose we coordinate our activities going forward."

Alaric nodded. "I think that is wise."

"Then let us begin."

Alaric leaned forward on his good arm. "Most of central Europe belongs to our Clans, save for northwest France, where the Northwind Highlanders have dug in."

"The Highlanders are relics," said Malvina. "Painful reminders of the fall of the Star League. My Jade Falcons have no desire to wade into their rings of defenses simply to erase them. If you want them, they are yours. Though I do owe Tara Campbell for killing my *sibkin* Aleks. I would very much like to stand on top of her dead body before this is over."

"I cannot speak to that," Alaric replied. "That is between you and her, though from what I have heard, she is a formidable warrior."

He wasn't surprised that Malvina did not want to take on the Highlanders. Under Countess Tara Campbell, the Highlanders were entrenched into the deeply fortified Normandy redoubt. Mines, bunkers, and field-gun emplacements dotted the terrain. Wolf aerospace fighters had surveyed the region and found it to be belts upon belts of defenses overlapping each other. Going after the Highlanders would bleed several Galaxies—no doubt Malvina's intention. *She wants us to be weakened by fighting them, and we will certainly take losses. But I have a plan to minimize those losses.*

"Very well," said Alaric. "We will also take the British Islands, if that is agreeable."

"Enjoy them. Ireland and Scotland are devoid of meaningful defenses as far as I am aware. Only southern England has garrison forces. The best remaining Republic troops on Terra are in the Americas. I intend to strike Central America and move in to the Southwest. That is where we will find honor and glory."

Alaric drummed his fingers. "You should be aware that we have taken control of the equipment behind Fortress Republic in the Antarctic."

One of Malvina's brows rose. "That I did not know. I will need to discuss this with my commander of the Watch. I trust you have kept the barrier up, *quiaff*?" Based on Malvina's tone, Alaric felt a millisecond of pity for her Watch commander.

"*Aff*. It serves neither of us to invite outside interference."

"Good. This keeps matters between our two Clans—as it has always been."

Alaric agreed, though silently. "In terms of your operations in North America," he said, "you should know that my Wolves hold Puget Sound and the Court of the Star League. That garrison will remain in place. Once we have dealt with the remaining Republic forces in Europe, I too will move to the east coast of North America."

Malvina nodded once. "That is acceptable. If you wish to hold the rubble that is the old home of the Star League, I do not care. By the time you shift to the rest of the Americas, the fate of the Republic will be clear to all—even to that antique, Devlin Stone."

"The Exarch is a proud man, if not arrogant," Alaric said. "He carved out a tiny empire and returned in time to watch it fall. And when the Republic does fall, its remains will be the Clans' for the taking." He cast a quick glance at Chistu, whose jaw had clenched at his words. *She wishes to speak, but Malvina has ordered her not to. Her presence here is supposed to be for my benefit. Malvina believes there is more to our relationship than there is.*

"The fate of your Wolves will be sealed in battle," Malvina boasted. "And your arrogance toward my people will be repaid in blood."

"I have never taunted or insulted the Jade Falcons. Only you, Chingis Khan, and that doctrine you follow."

Her face reddened, which gave Alaric a second of satisfaction. "Your maneuver with my fleet has not been forgotten, Khan Ward," she said grimly. "You will pay for that once my Jade Falcons have crushed the Republic."

"I look forward to the attempt. All we did was remind you of the honor that forms the core of Clan spirit."

Malvina ignored the jab. "I am, however, curious how Clan Wolf came to possess the *McKenna's Pride.*"

"I am sure you are," Alaric said. "Once *both* of our Clans crush the Republic, we will face each other. In the meantime, I suggest that we come up with some protocols for communicating our forces' positions. I have no desire to shed Jade Falcon blood before the Republic is defeated."

"Perhaps our subordinates can work out those protocols," Malvina offered, glancing at the others. "I would have a word with you alone, Khan Ward."

He nodded. Chistu, Thastus, and Conners left the room, leaving the two Clan leaders alone.

Malvina waited until the door closed behind them. "I imagine you are surprised to see your ally here with me today."

"Stephanie Chistu is no ally of mine. I merely wanted to establish a contact with your Clan that I could trust. You are reading far too much into our relationship."

The Jade Falcon Khan's eyes flashed. "*Neg*, I am not. You gave her the secrets of penetrating Fortress Republic. When you were attacked by assassins, your subordinate warned us by contacting Chistu. Your relationship with her is inappropriate. I do not know what you promised her, but she will never go along with it."

Alaric leaned back in his chair. "No promises were made, or even implied."

"Yet you and your people have communicated with her rather than me," Malvina snapped.

"I will communicate with whomever I choose," Alaric said, his voice a warning. "It is my prerogative as a Khan, as it is yours."

Malvina rose from her seat slowly, like a snake ready to strike. "What if I bring her in here and shoot her dead?" Her hand drifted to her holster.

Alaric shrugged, leaning back in his seat. "If you wish to sacrifice one of your best field commanders, it would not bother me. In fact, I encourage it. I can provide a list of other warriors I would like to see killed, if you would like to take them out, too. You will just make it that much easier for my Wolves to defeat your Jade Falcons."

Her hand dropped from the sidearm, though Alaric knew she had been serious—which was disturbing on its own. "Tell me, Alaric, what has become of Anastasia Kerensky? What did you do with her?"

He smiled. "I am surprised your Watch has not found out, since it is not a secret. I gave Anastasia an assignment and sent her away with a handful of warriors. We have not spoken in some time." It was the truth.

"Her Steel Wolves meddling on Skye contributed to the death of my *sibkin*, Aleks. And she is said to be the greatest warrior of our time. I was looking forward to tasting her blood on my lips and seeing her lifeless body at my feet. How sad that you would deny me that by sending her away."

"We each lead our Clan in our own way."

"*Aff,*" Malvina said. "But in the end, there will only be one victor, Alaric. I have known that since we faced each other on Tharkad. I cannot wait to see the look on your face as you bend the knee before me, knowing that *you* invited us here. That *you* brought about your own downfall. Your anguish will keep me warm when I am ilKhan."

"You present an interesting scenario," Alaric countered. "It is also possible that you will die long before that moment, and that you will see my Wolves swarm over your Jade Falcons, consuming them in their jaws. Words do not win battles, Malvina, nor do derisions or slander. You are here because I recognize the greatness of your warriors, and wish to see them rise above what you have turned them into. I will have need of them in the future I will usher in. You seek only slaughter and death. I offer salvation and order."

He rose, bowing his head, and then headed for the doors. "Until we meet again, Chingis Khan."

Her silence followed him out.

CHAPTER 21

Alaric was comforted to hear Chance Vickers's voice on their private, secured channel, weary though she sounded. She was radioing in from the field command post south of London, where her hospital bed had been moved. "Are you certain this is the right course of action?"

"*Aff*," Alaric said, standing on a hill overlooking the flowing, grass-covered countryside. He was piloting a replacement *Savage Wolf* until his own could be repaired. "We are in position on ground of my choosing, refitted and rested. These are the last Republic holdouts in this part of the world. To get them here, one must simply stoke the fires that burn in their blood."

"Tara Campbell may not take the bait," Chance cautioned.

"She will," Alaric replied. "I have studied her dossier. Even if she refuses the challenge, the Highlanders cannot. It is in their nature. She can help a great deal when the fighting is over. She is battling for a lost cause, but does not realize that yet. We will show her the reality she faces. Then, we will give her purpose."

"Good hunting, my Khan."

"Rest up, old friend." Alaric toggled to an open unsecured channel, one the Highlander leader and her people were bound to pick up. "Countess Tara Campbell of the Northwind Highlanders, this is Khan Alaric Ward of Clan Wolf. Come in."

The response took just minutes. "Khan Ward, this is Campbell. I take it you are issuing one of your *batchalls?* We are more than ready for you here in Normandy."

"*Neg*, Countess, I have contacted you so that you can come and challenge me and my Wolves."

"And why would we abandon our prepared defenses to come at you? If you want to fight us, you know where we are."

"My Silver Keshik and two of my best Clusters stand on your Highlanders' ancestral homeland in southern Scotland, near Dumfries. It is under Wolf control now. We trod on it with our BattleMechs and fly our banners in your beloved Scottish skies." Alaric paused, letting is words sink in. "Come battle us. If Clan Wolf wins this fight, then you order your Highlanders to stand down. If you win this fight, however, we will honorably withdraw and leave Scotland in your capable hands. So, if you want Scotland...then come and take it."

1549 HOURS

The hills of Dumfries were tall, steep, and grass covered, with few trees or structures. The shallow lands below them easily blocked line of sight. It was a bright clear day, the dark blue skies making the spring grasses appear even more brilliant. The town of Dumfries itself was ancient, with a stone church and a number of quaint structures dating back centuries. Alaric had no intention of fighting in the town. He had come to wage war in the rolling hills.

Alaric had arrayed his Wolves carefully, placing the Nineteenth Wolf Striker Cluster to the north as a reserve. He assumed the Highlanders would land to the south, but they deployed on a long line. As such, he had tasked Kalidessa Kerensky's Howling Furies to drive out to the far flanks, sweeping around to cut off the Highlanders' retreat path to their DropShips. If all went as planned, he would quickly have them surrounded.

Tara Campbell had other ideas.

Rather than fight in formations, the Highlanders drove seemingly pell-mell into the Wolves. If it were any other unit, he would assume it was a glaring mistake. The Northwind Highlanders were not some green unit; they maneuvered like only a true elite force could. The result was that his Silver Keshik and the Second Wolf Assault Cluster had fragmented, their formations in some degree of disarray in the Highlanders' mad charge through their positions. This was not one big battle, but dozens of small, ruthless ones. The Highlanders had not brought just BattleMechs and tanks, they had come with a vengeance, for the Wolves were desecrating their ancestral homelands.

Exactly as he had hoped. *Fighting them here is infinitely better than in their redoubt.*

As a Highlanders *Shadow Hawk* collapsed under a salvo of his ATMs, Alaric surveyed the fighting around him. The right barrel arm of a *Black Watch* lay at his feet, still smoking. Flames roared from the crashed remains of the Hawk Moth II gunship shredded by a Wolf Aesir. Smoke rolled from a nearby Winston tank's hatches. Smoke from destroyed vehicles and fallen BattleMechs laid a strange, still haze over the ground. Formations were broken, battered, and scattered.

There was no battle line, which Tara Campbell had apparently planned. Alaric had ordered his own forces to fall back, trying to keep a semblance of order, but the Highlanders had not made it easy. They moved in close, at point-blank range, swirling around the Wolves, but ultimately, the Wolf warriors hit them and hit hard.

Alaric looked about and saw something rare in a battle: he was truly alone.

His *Savage Wolf* had been separated from the Silver Keshik, who were tasked with finding Countess Campbell on the battlefield. She seemed to be everywhere, her *BattleMaster* rushing in to help any beleaguered Highlanders. Alaric admired that about her. Some unit commanders were not hands-on warriors. Campbell was obviously not of that cloth.

Out of the smoke, a green-and-tan *BattleMaster* emerged. Its armor was blasted in several areas, especially its right arm and side. It loomed like a monstrous giant from another era.

Alaric broke into a quick trot, swinging his targeting reticle as he went. Two more 'Mechs—a battered *Highlander* painted in the tartan of the Fusiliers, and a dull gray *Black Watch*—appeared at his sides.

"*Alaric Ward!*" Campbell shouted over the open channel. Her *BattleMaster's* Gauss rifle started to track him.

Alaric did not wait for a perfect weapons lock; he loosed a volley of ATMs at Campbell, scoring several hits on her 'Mech's already-battered frame. Smoke trailed from the holes his missiles had torn in her armor.

Shrugging off mangled armor pieces, she fired her Gauss rifle. The metallic blur of the slug slammed into Alaric's left leg, obliterating the untouched armor there and rocking his 'Mech to one side.

From his side, still tracking him, the *Black Watch* rained medium-range missiles in his direction. Half of them tore into his 'Mech's left arm. Swinging about quickly, he avoided a hastily aimed Gauss rifle round from the *Highlander*, only for its LRMs to shred his right side. Alaric swung his reticle over the battered *Highlander* and raked it with laser fire. Its right arm tore off at the elbow.

The Wolf Khan grinned. He swung in a tight pivot, and closed range with the *BattleMaster* as it launched short-range missiles into his lower body, cratering armor there. When he swiveled his torso at the waist to keep his weapons trained on Campbell, he heard the noise of grinding metal. Armor was binding somewhere below his cockpit.

His large lasers blazed, their brilliant red beams stabbing like a knight's lance, and burned a pair of scars across the remaining armor on Campbell's torso. Three of the *BattleMaster's* medium lasers melted away parts of Alaric's left arm and side, and one hot glob of metal hit his canopy, searing a black spot in his field of vision. The heat from the hit made his skin feel as if it were sunburned.

Campbell's Gauss rifle flashed, missing him by several meters. The instant he heard the *clunk-snap* of his ATMs reloading, Alaric sent another wave of missiles into the countess. Most found their mark, plastering the front of her 'Mech, one of them slamming dead center into her canopy.

Campbell's lasers and missiles roared back, and Alaric felt his 'Mech's right arm drop, his targeting reticle flashing yellow in warning. Damage indicators showed that his shoulder actuator had failed; the slumping arm threw off his balance and he knew he would miss the ER large laser mounted there.

The *Black Watch* fired a Gauss rifle slug that hit his left knee—and tore off the leg, sending him reeling. Alaric's *Savage Wolf* dropped semi-prone onto its destroyed left knee, metal protesting audibly as he went down. He had to fight this out to the end.

Firing the left-arm laser, he scored another hit on Campbell's rushing *BattleMaster*. The damage inflicted to her hip slowed her stride, and her 'Mech took on a limp.

A shrill tone indicated his short-range lasers were in range, and Alaric fired them all. The heat in his cockpit went into the red zone, but he ignored it as the brilliant green beams sent pulses of laser energy into Campbell's 'Mech. Two of the lasers stitched holes up her right arm, and then a blast of sparks burst near the elbow actuator. His sensors told him the arm was out of commission—taking the Gauss rifle with it.

In a valiant effort, Alaric pivoted his 'Mech's waist to its full extent and blasted at the *Black Watch* with his ER large lasers. Both shots hit the upper torso, and the 'Mech toppled backward in mid-stride.

A wave of long-range missiles washed over Alaric as he struggled to keep upright. Campbell smelled blood and rushed him, slamming her battered 'Mech into him. He was already halfway down, on one destroyed knee, but her charge completed the fall.

Alaric was thrown forward against his emergency restraints. His left arm—already in pain from the headhunting attempt—throbbed as he throttled back and twisted his torso; the armor between the two BattleMechs groaned and squealed, but Alaric toppled over, into the soft Scottish hillside.

Looking up, wincing in pain, he saw two 'Mechs towering over him: the *BattleMaster* and the *Highlander*.

"Surrender, Alaric," said Campbell.

I will not be taken this way. He punched in a three-digit code, a signal to the Nineteenth Wolf Striker Cluster with their go-orders. *She has the upper hand, but not for long.*

Alaric chuckled—and sent a recovery signal out on a Wolf-only channel. *The clock is now ticking.* "I do not surrender," he replied on the open channel.

"We have you," Campbell said. "I beat you."

"You and two others. But I think you have misread the situation."

"You will order your Wolves to stand down, or I will kill you," she growled.

"You assume you have the upper hand," Alaric said. He was cradling his wounded arm against his chest now, gritting his teeth against the pain. Hobgood would not be pleased at the stress he had put it under, even with Clan medical bone-knitting tech. "I have already sent out a signal. The balance of my initial bid is now coming from the north, sweeping the flanks. Your perimeter forces should be picking them up any moment, and they will be on us in a matter of minutes." He paused. Every second that passed moved the advantage more to him.

"My Wolves will annihilate your Highlanders to get me back. I am the Khan who brought them to Terra. I have done what no other Khan ever has. I am a god to my Wolves. They all worship me, and that worship has been earned in blood. If you attempt to take me prisoner, you gain nothing but the destruction of the one thing you cherish: your Highlanders. You will never leave your homeland.

Instead, you will be buried here. Kill me and you will perish. With my WarShips in orbit, you cannot flee."

"No," Campbell said, though she sounded uncertain. "I beat you. I can end this now."

"If you martyr me, Tara Campbell, you will only give my Wolves reason to fight on and fight harder. They will become the very thing you fear. They will behave like Jade Falcons to avenge my death. So go ahead—just know that Northwind itself will burn until nothing remains. Your heritage, your history, all will be gone."

"Dinnae listen to this cur," came a woman's voice on the channel, thick with Scottish brogue—presumably from the *Highlander*.

"Check your path to your DropShips. You will find one of my best units between here and there. You have nowhere to flee."

For a moment she said nothing, no doubt having her forces check to see if his words were true. For his part, Alaric hoped Kalidessa Kerensky had fulfilled her mission. Each passing minute brought the Nineteenth closer into position, sweeping around the Highlanders, trapping them.

"You are still my hostage," Campbell barked.

Alaric laughed, not a deep rolling laugh, but a chuckle. It was faked, but he forced it with full bravado. "By now your pickets are detecting the OmniMechs and tanks of the Nineteenth Wolf Striker Cluster moving on our flanks. In a matter of seconds, we will all be surrounded."

"They won't move in if I threaten to kill you," Campbell said, a deep tone in her voice.

"Oh, they will. The Wolves do not take kindly to threats. If you do not believe me, ask the dead Archon of the Lyran Commonwealth, it cost Melissa Steiner dearly to try and blackmail my people. Malvina Hazen has leveled all manner of threats at me, to no effect. If the most homicidal leader in the Inner Sphere has used them, do you think your dwindling force will have more sway? I think not."

She said nothing again for another half-minute, clearly verifying Alaric's claims. In the distance, he heard the rumble of explosions as the Nineteenth began to engage. He did not wait for her to respond. *I need to be gracious as a leader, offer her a means out of this situation that allows her to save honor.*

"You know I am right," Alaric said, ignoring the weapons pointed at him and looking into Campbell's cockpit instead. "There is only one scenario where you come out of this with your beloved Highlanders alive."

"And what is that?"

"You will become *my* bondsman. Do that, and we will both order a ceasefire. The Highlanders will be spared the wrath of my Clan, and you will join me as part of Clan Wolf. They are free to return to Northwind once we have settled the ilClanship, but they will not fight Clan Wolf on Terra any further."

"No, Countess!" a man's voice cut in, likely from the downed *Black Watch*. "Kill that Wolf! We can handle them!"

"You have proven yourself to me today, Tara Campbell," Alaric pressed. "You did what others only dream of: you bested me in battle." The concession was more for her benefit, given it had taken three Highlanders concentrating their attacks to finally take him down. Still, he delivered the words with pure conviction and respect. "The leader of a pack tends to their own, and you must save your people. Do this, and you have my word that your Highlanders will be spared. Kill me, and my people will exterminate yours, and then go on to take Terra."

"We will find a way, Countess," the woman pleaded from the *Highlander*. "You canna' do this."

"This is not subject to negotiation," Alaric said. "And the clock is ticking."

There was a long moment of silence—then Campbell lowered her weapons. "Damn you, Ward. To save my people...I agree."

"All Wolf forces, this is Wolf Prime," he transmitted on an open channel. "Cease fire. Break off from the Highlanders. We have struck an accord. Say again, cease fire."

Campbell sent a similar message, though one ringing in deep sadness.

As Alaric popped his cockpit hatch, a Star of Wolves from the Silver Keshik approached, no doubt responding to his transmission. He held up his right hand to wave them off, and they stopped. Slowly he climbed out the cockpit and walked to the *BattleMaster* looming over him.

Campbell climbed down the rungs on the side of her 'Mech and stood before his fallen *Savage Wolf*. Her shoulders slumped, bitter with defeat.

"You made the right choice," Alaric said. He reached out and took her right wrist, then secured a length of cord around it.

Tears shone in her eyes, but she kept her chin up, her jaw clenched. "I wish I was dead and did not have to bear this humiliation."

"I will not grant you *bondsref*, Tara Wolf," Alaric said. "You see me as a monster. I am not. In fact, with the Republic crumbling, Clan Wolf is your best chance—your *only* chance—to stop Malvina Hazen. You have saved your homeworld and your precious Highlanders. For what it is worth, I respect you, as will your new Clan."

"Just promise me one thing, Alaric," Tara said. "Promise me you *will* stop the Jade Falcons. Crush them completely."

"That has always been my plan."

She nodded, a glimmer of relief in her gaze. "Good."

**OLD GUARD HQ
INDIANAPOLIS
TERRA
16 MARCH 3151 (T+65)**

The Republic's Old Guard was an homage to Napoleon's Old Guard—at least, that was how Stone had envisioned them. They had begun with the formation of the Republic, a unit of elite veterans, and were now the last untapped reserve of the Republic's armed forces. The best of the best. Each warrior had extensive combat experience. All were in peak physical condition. While only a regiment, they were a highly trained killing machine.

Jonah Levin had kept them in hidden reserve on Terra—the final line of defense. Their BattleMechs were new, pristine. They wore special uniforms, with a gold braid draped across their chests. Other units were to salute when the Old Guard passed in front of them. Their BattleMechs were flat black, with shimmering azure lightning bolts etched down and across them like a raging thunderstorm. Three bars of gold striped their right arms, and emblazoned on the upper-right torso of every BattleMech was the Old Guard's insignia, a shield painted with three vertical stripes, blue, white, and red.

Stone had held them back until now. There was only one target worthy of such a storied unit: Clan Jade Falcon.

Tucker Harwell pushed Stone's wheelchair into the Old Guard's secret base outside of Indianapolis in North America. It was a vast underground warehouse, the walls lined with BattleMechs and tanks. Gantries hung overhead, and a small army of technicians made sure each 'Mech was in pristine fighting order. It was not a controlled mess like many 'Mech bays; this was clean, organized, and orderly. Buried deep under the commercial aerospace port outside the city, the base had an array of access tunnels.

Since the evacuation of Geneva, Stone's body had begun to falter even more. He had ignored the pains and strains until he couldn't. The effects of his cryogenic hibernation were finally catching up to him. *I need to hold on a bit longer...to see the Republic rebuilt, or at least influence what is to come.*

His body wasn't all he was struggling with. He faced the grim realization that he was running out of troops. Those that remained were either garrisons, ill-equipped to take on the Clan war machines, or ad hoc battalions cobbled together from the survivors of shattered commands. *My strategy was to let the redoubts to wear down my enemies, then hit them hard. We are running out of space to do that. The time for the Old Guard contingency is now.*

The elite regiment's soldiers stood at attention before Stone in the middle of the vast 'Mech bay, in immaculate, crisp uniforms. Looking into their faces, Stone saw people who represented the very best of the Republic of the Sphere. Pride swelled in his chest as Harwell wheeled him past them all and stopped the chair in front of the podium.

Stone summoned a surge of strength to stand, grasping the podium to help him stay upright. Tucker moved to assist him, but Stone shook his head.

"I came here personally," he said to the assembled troops, "because I owed it to you all. You are my beloved Old Guard. You are the most elite forces of our Republic. Your predecessors gave birth to the Republic. You are beyond elite.

"We have always used your unit as the final contingency. That is the nature of the Old Guard, held back to the end, but when sent in, always emerging victorious. Well, my dear friends and comrades, the time has come for you to go into this fight. I need you to face down the Jade Falcons. And not just *any* Jade Falcons. Malvina Hazen is a war criminal of the worst possible kind. You have all seen the footage of what she does with prisoners. If she takes Terra and becomes the ilKhan, she will enslave the survivors under the banner of Clan Jade Falcon. This isn't just a fight for the Republic...it's a fight for your families and friends. Your wives, husbands, children, brothers, sisters, mothers, and fathers. For each other."

He paused and coughed several times, his ribs aching. Tucker started to move closer to him, but Stone waved him off.

"The Falcons are coming," he said once he wrestled his composure under control again. "I need the Old Guard to deliver a crushing blow to save our beloved Republic. You are our last line of defense. I am counting on you. The Republic is counting on you. The Inner Sphere and all of humanity is counting on you.

"You are not strong enough to take down all of the Jade Falcons, but you do not have to. Your mission is strategic. I need you to attack the Falcon's Raptor Keshik, their Khan's honor guard. In doing so, you have *one* objective and one alone—*kill Malvina Hazen.* Cut the head off the snake, or in this case, the bird. If she dies, so does her Mongol Doctrine. Kill her, and we can still turn this fight around."

Brigadier General Graham Badinov, the commanding officer of the Old Guard, stepped forward and saluted. "Exarch, the Old Guard will not fail you."

Stone returned the salute, and Tucker assisted him back into the chair.

"Sir," Tucker said, "a message came in from Lady Miller. She has been speaking to Lieutenant Colonel Cadha Jaffray of the Northwind Highlanders." He wheeled Stone off to one of the offices that dotted the far wall of the underground complex.

"What was the message? What has happened?" *Perhaps they have taken down Alaric!*

Harwell leaned in close. "It appears the Highlanders hold the ground in Scotland, and Clan Wolf has left the battlefield."

"Ah, so we won!" Stone said, smiling broadly. "I knew Tara Campbell wouldn't let me down. Never cross a Highlander."

"Well—" Harwell hesitated. "Not quite. She apparently brokered a deal that left the Highlanders alive in exchange for her. She is now a bondsman of Alaric Ward."

Stone's joy evaporated. *Bondsman? Tara? My Highlanders... How could she do that?*

"I *knew* something like this would happen once they got their blood up," he said. "Well, we beat them, that's the main point. We will order the Highlanders to redeploy to North America. Once they're refit, we can throw them at Hazen and her bloody damned Falcons. We will tell the citizens of the Highlanders' 'great victory.' It will play well in the media."

Harwell stopped the chair and leaned in. "Exarch, the Highlanders...they are standing down. Jaffray is asking to leave Terra as soon as the Fortress is down."

Stone sagged. He could deny their request, force them into the fight again—but he would not. "Damn Alaric Ward to hell!" he snapped. "Get me back to the command post. Maybe I can talk some sense into them."

A part of him knew that attempt was destined to fail. Tara had sacrificed herself to save her Highlanders, and not even he could persuade them turn against her will.

CHAPTER 22

Malvina's drive through Mexico and along the West Coast had slowed near the Los Angeles redoubt. Rather than rush in an assault, she had ordered her artillery to shell the fortifications for several days, followed up by fighter bombardment. It had taken precious time, but Malvina had learned the strength of the redoubts in Europe, and would not make the same mistake twice. The constant shelling and bombing forced the Republic troops out to engage her. Their battalion of the Fourteenth Triarii Protectors had plowed into her Vau Galaxy, and for a short time, forced part of Vau back to the mountains.

That was when Malvina led the Raptor Keshik in, catching the Fourteenth between her two forces. After two days of losses, the Republic troops tried a final breakout, only to be destroyed. A handful tried to surrender at the end, but Malvina ordered them killed to the last warrior. *One minute they are trying to kill me, and the next they demand I take them prisoner?* Neg. *This is better than dealing with any potential revenge or outbursts as they face the dishonor of their defeat.*

Just as the slaughter finished, Malvina received word that the Republic was sending in a new force—the Old Guard.

She had smirked upon hearing the news. *Stone is throwing* solahma *warriors at us. Truly a sign of desperation.*

But this was clearly no ordinary *solahma* regiment.

The Republic *Black Hawk* that led the charge at her came down on a plume of blue-orange jump-jet flames, unloading its Streak short-range missiles into *Black Rose*. The Chingis Khan sprang to the right on her own jump jets, and turned her extended-range PPCs on the ebony-streaked blue 'Mech, shredding armor on its left arm. She could see the exposed and partially severed myomer muscles just shy of the actuator.

The *Black Hawk* broke into a sprint, swinging around her while keeping its weapons locked. Its Series 7K extended-range large lasers speared her with deadly crimson beams. Both hit her lower legs, and her damage indicators there flickered yellow. As she landed, Malvina pivoted, firing her own extended-range medium lasers at the *Black Hawk*, burning deep into the stout body of the 'Mech.

The Old Guard pilot did not waver despite the damage. They fired Streak SRMs, which exploded against Malvina's right side, rumbling the chassis and setting off blaring damage indicators. *This fight needs to end.*

She ignited her jump jets, and her 95-ton *Shrike* roared upward, toward the *Black Hawk*. She dropped down hard, and her massive, claw-like footpads tore into its right side and arm with such force that the arm ripped away entirely. Her landing was off, and she staggered away, fighting gravity for balance as the *Black Hawk* fell backward.

Its remaining arm and legs convulsed as the MechWarrior kicked and punched to roll over and right themself. Malvina finally stopped her sideways stagger and reoriented her 'Mech. Carefully aiming her PPCs, she blasted the cockpit of the Republic 'Mech, punching through the torso and the armored cockpit's ferroglass. The *Black Hawk* went limp.

She smiled at her victory, then turned to the wall of BattleMechs that were rushing at her. They were a half a kilometer out, but the sandstorm they kicked up in their wake bespoke their numbers. Jade Falcons moved in front of the rushing wedge of Republic 'Mechs only to be blown to pieces. One *Dire Wolf* took out an Old Guard *Malice*, only to be hit by four other Republic 'Mechs. The *Dire Wolf* crumpled at the knees, fell prone, then was overwhelmed, kicked a half-dozen times, then trampled under the onslaught of charging 'Mechs.

In that moment, the truth hit her. *They are coming for* me.

Dozens of long-range and Arrow IV missiles arced from the obsidian wall of BattleMechs charging at her, and they rained down on her in a wave of destruction. Explosions engulfed *Black Rose* as she feathered her jump jets in an effort to fall back, away from the blasts. In the end, that last maneuver probably saved her life. The concussive force of the artillery coupled with over four dozen exploding missiles left her *Shrike* blackened, pockmarked, and near destruction.

"Jade Falcons," a voice said over the command channel. "The Chingis Khan needs you now!" It sounded like Galaxy Commander Jane Thastus' voice.

Sweat ran down Malvina's face as she fired everything she had at the rushing wall of 'Mechs heading for her. Memories of the assassination attempt at Lac de Lamoura came rushing forward along with a feeling of helplessness and possible death, but she suppressed those thoughts, replacing them with a single echo:

I am Jade Falcon!

In his brilliant-green *Night Gyr*, Star Colonel Marv Roshak rushed his Falcon Guards into the ever-narrowing space between the Chingis Khan and the charging Old Guard. Star Colonel Rachel Loudon, the Falcon Guards' commanding officer, had perished in the fighting in Geneva, ambushed by a trio of Stone's Lament 'Mechs on the last day of fighting, and Galaxy Commander

Jane Thastus had given Roshak command. At the time, he had wondered if she had promoted him because he was one of the Falcon Guards' few surviving senior officers, or if she indeed saw greatness in him, as she had claimed.

Now we will find out which is right.

"Fan out, and form a ring around the Chingis Khan," he commanded as the Falcon Guards deployed to his sides while he took the center of the line.

He targeted the lead Republic BattleMech, a *Jackalope*, and fired his Ultra autocannon and paired ER PPCs as his target sent a wave of ATMs streaking past him, no doubt aiming for Malvina Hazen. The crackling PPCs shots both hit the right leg of the *Jackalope* and sent the fast-moving light BattleMech into a stumble as Roshak's autocannon shells tore into its thinly armored back, furrowing deep into the fusion reactor. The stampede of rushing Old Guard crushed the fallen *Jackalope*, heedless of its destruction.

Ignoring the rise of temperature in his cockpit, Roshak triggered his trio of medium pulse lasers at a shimmering black *Malice* that thundered toward him. Pharaoh moved to his side, his replacement *Mad Dog* firing at the same target. Forty long-range missiles arrowed into the charging *Malice*, which seemed oblivious to the armor it had lost. The Republic BattleMech's LB-X autocannons roared, not at either Marv or Pharaoh, but at a target past them. At Malvina Hazen's battered *Black Rose*.

The wall of Old Guard 'Mechs neared with each heartbeat. Roshak fired again with his PPCs and struck the *Malice*'s left side. One large chunk of armor flew into the legs of a Republic *Thunder Fox* hard enough to throw off its gait as it rushed forward. The *Malice* slowed, moving to flank. The noose was now closed around the Falcon Guards, with Malvina in the middle, and it began to constrict.

Malvina felt the staccato rumble of autocannon rounds riddle her *Shrike*'s right side. Several shells bit deep into the body of her 'Mech and exploded. As her gyro indicator flashed crimson, a wave of nausea hit her—extreme vertigo. The neural feedback made her head feel as if it would burst. She threw up, forcing her to pop open the faceplate on her neurohelmet, then she lost balance. Vomit spilled out onto the sidewall of her cockpit as the dizziness made her eyes flicker. Red warning lights told her of the damage, but she did not need them. The grinding of the crushed armor as *Black Rose* fell told her how bad the damage was.

I will not die, not here, not now. Then she gave in to the darkness.

The Old Guard kept coming, and Star Colonel Roshak felt his ring of Falcon Guards shrink more each time a 'Mech fell. They were surrounded, and there was nowhere to retreat as the Republic forces desperately attempted to pour more fire into the Chingis Khan's downed *Shrike*. Sweat rolled down his face, some droplets clinging to his faceplate. Still he kept firing, kept cursing out orders, kept fighting.

"I am out of missiles!" Pharaoh called out. "They refuse to break off."

"Keep firing," Roshak urged. "Punch them, kick them if you have to." His own damage display blinked amber and red warning lights, but he ignored them. He had learned in his *sibko* that standing still was the worst thing a warrior could do. Mobility was part of the Clan doctrine of battle. *But we do not have that option. We must stay here and protect the Khan.* He twisted his torso side-to-side, peppering multiple attackers.

The *Malice* that charged him had been taken down right in front of him. A squat *Revenant* drone, with spindly legs like a spider, climbed on top of it, its medium lasers firing at him at the range of only a few meters. Its machine guns blazed away at a target past him, no doubt Khan Hazen's *Shrike*.

Brilliant emerald bursts filled his vision. The lasers melted away precious armor, but Roshak did not waver. On almost pure instinct he triggered his ER PPCs and speared through the *Revenant*, gutting its engine. There was a momentary hot flash as the fusion reactor flared, and it collapsed atop the fallen *Malice*, billowing smoke.

Star Captain Jaylee went down under a withering hurricane of missile and artillery fire. A dense fog of smoke from fallen BattleMechs and exploding ordnance filled the air around the circle where Roshak still fought; spent shrapnel rattled his canopy.

"Falcon Guards, retrograde five meters. Rife, take Jaylee's spot on the line." He stepped back methodically as a Republic *Kheper* climbed on top of the two destroyed 'Mechs in front of him. It was already badly damaged, having had to wade into the furious war-storm the Falcon Guards were unleashing.

The *Kheper's* multi-missile launcher sent a spread of short-range missiles at him, half of which flew past him. Its pulse laser started to track him as his Ultra autocannon and pulse lasers tore into the new target. The black and lightning-bolt paint scheme disappeared under a savage barrage, with the *Kheper* twisting left at the waist. One of Roshak's shots must have hit the Gauss rifle, because an internal explosion tore off the arm of the Old Guard 'Mech. The limb struck a *Lich* next to him, which stood on a fallen Republic *Atlas III* that two of the Falcon Guards had taken down, cutting it off at its knees.

The *Kheper* reeled from the damage, but turned to face him. Roshak brought his targeting reticle on the 'Mech's already mangled and melted right leg, and triggered one of his ER PPCs. The flash-blast hit the hip, gouging through it, splattering melting armor onto a crippled Republic *Osprey* in the smoky haze. The MechWarrior attempted to remain upright, but their 'Mech collapsed to the side and fell on the remains of the *Lich* and *Atlas III*.

His cockpit felt like a sauna, but he ignored it all. Falcon Guard Ashford fell off to his far left, leaving another gap.

"Falcon Guards, retrograde," he said through gritted teeth. A lightning-fast glance at his tactical display showed that he could not fall back any farther without being on top of the Chingis Khan herself.

Blitzking *hell!*

He took two steps back as a pair of Streak missiles slammed into his left leg, fragmenting the last bits of armor there. "No more falling back," he called out. "Falcon Guards, we fight to the end here!"

1420 HOURS

Malvina emerged from the haze of unconsciousness to the smell of her own vomit and a taste of copper in her mouth where she bit her lip on the scar Jodi Mazzanoble's bite had left. The cut itself stung with bile. Her ears rang, and the front of her head was in agony.

The damage screen of *Black Rose* showed it had been badly battered and blasted...yet she lived. Outside there were only distant sounds of battle, seeming to fade away.

She could not stand her BattleMech upright, due to the destroyed leg actuators. Reaching over, she hit the side hatch release, and the grinding sound of the hatch opening made her head throb even more. After removing her restraining straps, she tossed off her neurohelmet and coolant vest and slowly climbed out the hatch.

All around her stood a circle of green-and-gray Jade Falcon BattleMechs—most bearing the markings of a diving jade falcon holding a katana...the Falcon Guards. They surrounded her fallen *Shrike*, one of them standing on its crushed right foot. The smell of burned insulation and metal, the smoke of destroyed BattleMechs, and of the carnage of war stung her nostrils. She climbed out and up onto the smashed upper torso of her crumpled BattleMech.

There was a tall smoking ring of death and destruction around her Falcon Guards: a heap of fallen Republic 'Mechs and at least one tank. In some areas, the mound of blasted 'Mechs was two or three high. They were heaped on each other, many almost impossible to identify. The defeated 'Mechs radiated outward from where she stood, a field of death and destruction.

A MechWarrior came up to her, his MechWarrior togs damp with sweat. He had short blond hair and a brutish face that was the trademark of the Roshak Bloodname. "Chingis Khan, are you all right?"

"Sitrep," she said.

"We held our ground to protect you. The enemy kept coming, but they broke a few minutes ago. I will call you a medic."

The vaunted Old Guard has been routed? That gave her new strength.

She shook her head, and it hurt to do so. The throbbing in her brow protested. "You are with the Falcon Guards, *quiaff*?"

"*Aff*, I am their commander, Star Colonel Marv Roshak," he said with a hint of pride that was well earned.

She put her bionic hand on his shoulder and squeezed it. "You did well, Marv Roshak," she said, surveying the wreckage of the battle that encircled her. "Everyone always talks about Aidan Pryde when they speak of the Falcon Guards."

She paused and drew a deep breath, her headache beginning to fade. "To hell with Aidan Pryde! This day is what the Falcon Guards will be remembered for!"

COMMAND POST ROUGE
DETROIT, NORTH AMERICA
TERRA
24 MARCH 3151(T+73)
THREE HOURS LATER...

Alongside Devlin Stone, Tucker Harwell listened to the grisly details of Brigadier General Badinov's report. After the loss of Tara Campbell and the Northwind Highlanders, Stone had evacuated Command Post Steadfast, fearing the Wolves would come for him next. Against Alaric's determined warriors, the disused Castle Brian complex would be more of a liability than an asset.

Command Post Rouge was buried deep under the Rouge River basin south of Detroit. Unlike the previous command posts, this one lacked any creature comforts. It was never intended to be used as the last bastion of the Republic's military leadership.

The command center was small, with only enough seating for six, perhaps seven. The dingy gray walls lacked the datafeed screens Tucker had become used to. The holotable was old military gear—sturdy, but dinged and battered. Stone had insisted on taking the message from General Badinov alone, but Tucker had invited himself into the room with no protest from the Exarch. The air was musty, not horribly, but enough to remind him of how deep they were under the river.

What grasp the Republic held on Terra was dwindling down to North America. The Wolves had left Scotland and Europe, striking at a garrison in Iceland, then hitting the east coast of North America at Nova Scotia. They had shuttled across the St. Lawrence River, and according to Stone, appeared to be preparing for another offensive—likely driving on Toronto then onto Detroit. *Coming right at us.*

The Jade Falcons had been bogged down in Panama and on the West Coast, the redoubts doing what Stone had always claimed they would do. But they, like the Wolves, had learned lessons about dealing with such defenses. Rather than surround them, the Falcons had laid short sieges, blasting avenues through the redoubts, right into their center. The corridors were bombed and had artillery rain on them to the point that the minefields were neutralized along with most of the turrets. Using these corridors, the Falcons had assaulted both Redoubts Los Angeles and Panama from within their defensive rings, and were able to force the defenders to either flee or attempt to surrender. The word "attempt" was critical to Tucker because Malvina had openly broadcast the executions of her prisoners public. *She is killing our morale as much as she is killing our troops.*

Stone had sent the Old Guard in with high hopes. But the briefing sucked more life out of the old man. *It's almost like he's aging right in front of me.*

The commander of the Old Guard looked to be late fifties, and tears streaked down his cheeks in the holodisplay above the table. "We took her down, sir. She may be dead; we don't know for sure. Those Falcon Guards, they just would not give ground. We launched six assaults, and still they kept fighting. They are like the goddamn Black Watch. I have never seen anything like it."

Tucker shook his head outside the general's field of vision. *May be dead? No. We haven't had that kind of luck. Even if we did take her out, her Clan would want revenge. Stone refuses to see it.*

"They haven't pursued you?" Stone asked.

"Not yet, Exarch. We made what repairs we could and have rearmed from our mobile reserves. I propose falling back to Gunnison, Colorado. The Castle Brian nearby isn't in active use, but we can rest and repair there until we decide our next course of action."

Stone nodded. "Proceed."

"Sir," the general said, "I understand that I have ordered the Guard into retreat. I have stained their reputation and my own. I will resign my commission once the troops are on good ground and in fighting order."

Stone waved his hand. "That is unacceptable, General—I need you in the cockpit of a BattleMech. Hazen hasn't let a single unit leave a battlefield yet, so that says something. We should call it what it is: a remarkable victory."

"Yes, sir." Badinov saluted, then the image disappeared.

There was a rap at the door, and Edie Miller entered. With the loss of Janella Lakewood, the role of intelligence advisor fell to her. *We've lost so many. Lakewood, Redburn, Levin...our circle of friends is dwindling.*

Miller had dark circles under her eyes. Her usually well-kempt hair was greasy, uncombed. Tucker watched her, and felt sorry for the burden that had fallen to her.

"We need to draw back whatever forces we have and concentrate them in the Midwest of North America," Stone said. "We have a lot of militia, some survivors of Hansen's Roughriders, the bits of the Lament that are refitted, what is left of the Triarii Protectors, all of them. We can sort out the organizational issues as they come in. We may be able to use the Ohio River Valley as a good ground for defense."

He's ordering around units that are a shadow of their former selves. Tucker finally mustered himself to speak up.

"Exarch," he began carefully. "Your Old Guard was the best of the best, and the Jade Falcons repulsed them. You've tried killing the enemy leaders more than once. We have lost Europe and Asia to the Wolves, Africa and South America to the Jade Falcons. Your armies are stretched to the breaking point."

"What is your point?"

"The redoubts have done an admirable job," Tucker said, only half-believing it. "And we have inflicted great losses on both of our enemies. But maybe the time has come for us to surrender, to consider saving the lives of the rest of your troops."

"Give up the Republic?"

"To save lives instead of sacrificing them in fighting a hopeless cause? Yes!"

"Tucker—the Clans are as exhausted as we are, perhaps more. They never wage campaigns that last this long. Their logistics are strained. Hell, Malvina still has troops arriving at the jump point—that's how thin their supply line is. They are close to breaking, I can *feel* it." There was a red tinge of anger in the old man's usually pale skin as he spoke. "We need to hold out for one, maybe two battles. You will see. Every day we hold on opens the door for victory."

Harwell recoiled in his seat. "Exarch—if you are holding out hope that some House Lord will swoop in to save us, they aren't coming. Even if they did, the Clans hold the jump points in-system and Fortress Republic is still operating. We are *alone* here. End this now, while we still can."

Stone went silent for a moment, gathering his resolve. "As long as I live and breathe, so does the Republic. We will bleed the Clans, then drive them off-world." He slammed his fist on the table, ending the discussion.

Tucker closed his eyes for a moment. *He clings to his hopes and schemes, but it is the blood of others that keeps the Republic alive.* "I am not a military commander. I am not the great Devlin Stone. I have watched us win a handful of fantastic victories, but mostly I have watched you send tens of thousands of people to die in your name. At some point, Devlin, you need to shelve your ego and do what is right for the Republic, not hold onto some damn delusion that you can make it all better. It is *over.* No one else will say it to you, but I will. Your continuing to fight will not change the outcome. Open surrender talks, stop the damned shooting. Do your job, Exarch, and save your people!"

Stone was quiet for a long moment. "You have lost faith, if you ever had it. I *am* saving them, Tucker. The only way to save them is to defeat these invaders. I beat the Word of Blake, I will beat the Clans. You know me, I always have a card or two up my sleeve. You will see."

Tucker stormed out of the room, bumping into Miller on the way out. *That's what I'm afraid of Devlin...that I will be there at the end, and be forced to witness what you have wrought.*

INTERLUDE

DAVION SUMMER PALACE
ARGYLE
CRUCIS MARCH
THE FEDERATED SUNS
27 MARCH 3151 (T+76)

Julian Davion hunched over the desk and stared at the verigraphed message for the hundredth time.

Devlin Stone was calling in his favor.

Stone had loaned him troops and equipment several years ago. The aid of the Republic had helped Julian win battles, recover worlds, and stave off utter defeat. *Now he wants me to return the favor. And rightfully so. I gave him my word.*

The message was designed to tug at his heartstrings. *"The Federated Suns has always been the most loyal and trustworthy friend of the Republic,"* said Stone's holoimage. Across from Davion, Erik Sandoval-Groell, the Prince's Champion, watched just as intently. *"Now, First Prince, for the sake of all humankind, for the fate of the Inner Sphere, the Republic needs your help. If you do not answer this call, Terra may fall. If it does, the Clans will unite under an ilClan, and the entire Inner Sphere will burn."*

Julian rarely felt the anxiety of his position as much as he had with the arrival of this message the day before. It had taken a long time for the Republic courier to find him and deliver Stone's desperate plea. At any other time, he would have not hesitated to send help.

But things were different now. Draconis Combine forces occupied New Avalon. The Capellan Confederation held a number of Federated Suns worlds and still presented a threat, held at bay with a promise Julian had made. Mere words. While not known publicly, the Federated Suns was teetering on collapse. The economy was in turmoil. People had begun to lose faith in the realm. Julian had plans for reversing the losses, but they were going to come at a great price.

"Heavy is the head that wears the crown," said Erik.

"It isn't funny," Julian snapped. "The honor of our nation is at stake. Hell, the fate of the Inner Sphere may be in play."

The Prince's Champion stared at him, eyebrows raised. "You're actually considering this, aren't you?"

"If it wasn't for the help we received from the Republic, we may have lost the realm years ago."

"The situation is different now. You have a responsibility to your people."

"But what if the Jade Falcons take Terra?"

"That is not our immediate problem, and you know it."

"You do not understand the more strategic picture," Julian countered.

Erik leaned back in his leather seat and smiled. "I always find it amusing when you think I, the Prince's Champion, do not comprehend military or political strategy."

"That isn't what I meant."

"Then tell me what you meant."

"This isn't just about paying back Stone for military assistance," Julian said, frustrated. "The Clans invaded a century ago with one goal: the conquest of Terra. ComStar stopped them, but the Clans pushed the limits of that truce to the edge and beyond. Now you have Hell's Horses, the Sea Foxes, the Raven Alliance, the Rasalhague Dominion...all Clan-based nations carved out of the Inner Sphere. They take and take and take, and we lose more each time we fight them.

"Whichever Clan takes Terra could unite them all under one banner. We barely held off the Clans when they were operating alone, but imagine what they would be like if they ever acted in unison. Erik, I was on Tharkad when the Wolves and Jade Falcons took the planet. I have met Alaric Ward. I have seen these Clans in battle. They are ferocious. If they unite, we could be doomed."

Julian leaned forward, resting his elbows on the desk. "I gave my word to Devlin Stone. He has called in his marker on the Federated Suns. If I don't go to his aid, what kind of leader would I be? Who could trust me or my realm to keep our word?"

Erik sighed. "I am quite aware of the threat the Clans pose—alone *and* united. But the only way to be prepared to face them is to *have* a realm. We stand on the edge of utter extinction, and *you know it*. The Draconis Combine stands on New Avalon, for Christ's sake! You are the First Prince of the Federated Suns. Your first loyalty is to your people. And your people need you and your armies *right here, right now*. And—come on. 'Your word?' You didn't hesitate to break your word after you struck a bargain with Danai Liao-Centrella. But *now* you're worried about *optics*? I don't care how it looks, nor do the people of the Federated Suns. The safety of the realm takes precedence, and right now, we're on the ropes."

Bringing up Danai Liao-Centrella stung deep. Julian sat back, his jaw clenched. "That was a low blow."

"I am doing my job, Your Highness. All I ask is that you do yours."

Julian rubbed his temples, and after a moment, he conceded. "You may be right. Perhaps we could send a token force. I could ask the Dawn Guards for volunteers."

Erik shook his head. "For what, to ease your guilt with their blood? Let's say you send a few companies, a battalion—what happens to them? For all we know, the Republic may have already fallen. You ask for those volunteers, and you are asking them to give up their lives for a lost cause. Stone's Republic is over. It has been ever since the Blackout began. *But*—" He spread his hands. "If you give *me* those troops, *I* will use them against our enemies. *I* will kill Dracs, *I* will take back land, *I* will help our citizens." He studied his friend. "If you send those troops to Stone, you are turning your back on your own people."

For a long moment, Julian said nothing. Frustration and guilt welled up within him. *I am betraying my word, but Erik is right, damn it. I cannot try to save Terra when my own people suffer under enemy occupation on so many worlds.*

"You're right, of course," he said at last.

The Prince's Champion bowed his head. "If you need any more blunt advice, you know where to find me."

"I do, and I will," Julian said. "There are many dark days still ahead of us both."

He pulled out a pen, for a typed response would not suffice for something so personal.

Dear Exarch Stone, he began, *It is with a heavy heart that I respond to you...*

Each word he wrote seemed to take a piece of his soul.

OFFICE OF THE KHAN
ASGARD, RASALHAGUE
RASALHAGUE DOMINION
29 MARCH 3151 (T+78)

As she sat in her immaculate office, trimmed in five different kinds of exotic wood, Khan Dalia Bekker's face showed a rare expression: puzzlement. The formulas on the small noteputer screen were a blur of numbers and mathematic symbols, indecipherable to her cool gaze.

After several minutes of scrolling through it, she laid the device on the table between her and her Watch Commander. "I take it this is supposed to mean something to me?"

"It arrived this morning, addressed to you," said Star Colonel Havi Bekker. "A courier dropped it off—we...do not know who. They managed to avoid our surveillance imaging. At first, we did not know what to make of it. I took it to several of our senior techs. My Khan, it provides us with the means to penetrate Fortress Republic."

Dalia's brows rose. "One of Stone's fabled Ghost Knights delivered it, perhaps?"

"That is our current theory," Havi replied.

They are aptly named, then. "And it will work?"

"Our techs think so."

Dalia looked back down at the noteputer. *Devlin Stone has handed us the keys to Terra in hopes that we will come and save him.* That thought gave her a strange sense of strength. *All I have to do is give the order, and I can charge* to Terra. The Wolves and Jade Falcons have to be weakened by now. My Ghost Bears would be fresh, with pristine equipment. The ilClanship could be mine. Stone would not have smuggled this out to me unless the Republic was on the verge of collapse.

"Havi," she said, "who else knows of this?"

"You, me, and three of our techs," he replied.

Dalia nodded. "Keep it that way," she commanded. "Dismissed."

As he left, Dalia's mind raced with possibilities. We have always been true to the Warden ideal. What better way to ensure the protection of humanity than to take Terra ourselves? Roy would push for that. Many in our touman might as well. In one fell swoop, we could be the ilClan.

She steepled her hands. There might never be a greater chance. All I would have to do is to rush in. Hell's Horses would come at us; they will never bend their knee to an ilClan, regardless of who takes Terra. Even as I sit here, they have crossed the Jade Falcon border and struck Suk II, Domain, and Orkney, trying to establish a bridge between their occupation zone and Terra. The Snow Ravens may challenge us. I doubt the Sea Foxes would contest our taking Terra, but that is not the same as falling in line under Ghost Bear rule.

There were also the House Lords to consider. They do not think in terms of Wardens and Crusaders. They only see us as Clan, and they would come at any Clan who takes Terra, just to rip apart what is left of the Republic. While a Great House seizing Terra might negate the Wolves and Jade Falcons, it would start other wars. Those thoughts suggested caution, not fear.

Her warriors were never ones to shirk from battle. By the same token, they had rushed off to fight on such scant intelligence before, during the Jihad. We attacked the Word of Blake under the presumption that they were the spawn of the Not-Named Clan. Many Ghost Bear warriors fought and died, yet nary a drop of the Not-Named Clan's blood was ever found for all of their efforts. In the back of her mind, she wondered if her predecessors had been manipulated by Stone during the Jihad. Stone was either as ignorant as we were, misled by intelligence...or used us to do his bidding.

Shaking her head, Dalia sat back and asked herself the same question she asked every day: What is the best way to serve the people of the Dominion? That thought consumed her for several minutes.

She leaned back and looked at the painting on the wall, an abstract and colorful piece showing a Ghost Bear Clawing ritual. One of the Great Works produced by a warrior generations ago. In times like this, the blues and whites of the snow field in the painting gave her strength, focus, and inner calm.

Stone does not truly want my Ghost Bears on Terra. He simply wants us more than he wants the Wolves and the Falcons. But I will not shed my warriors' blood without cause.

Devlin Stone...you are on your own.

CHAPTER 23

Star Colonel Khalus Pryde piloted his hulking *Jupiter* BattleMech near a winding road overlooking a rugged river valley, maneuvering through the dense pines as if they were not there. The snapping of the limbs and trees around him did not cheer him at all. He wished the DropShip pilots had brought them in closer; no doubt this grueling march was the influence of the Chingis Khan.

He did not cherish the assignment Malvina had given his First Falcon Jaegers. The Old Guard had been routed more than a week ago, and despite harassment by aerospace fighters, they had been falling back toward a Republic base west of Cheyenne Mountain. Star Colonel Pryde's Cluster had landed on Terra only a week ago, one of the last units to drop, and Khan Hazen had specifically given him the task of making sure that the Old Guard did not reach their base.

To some, it would have seemed an honor for the Khan to pick him out for such a duty. Khalus knew the truth. Malvina wanted him dead or dishonored. This was not the first time she had sent him on a mission where failure was almost guaranteed. She had underbid him on Temperton to humiliate him for not meeting her timetable, and she was doing it again now with this mission. The Chingis Khan knew he did not fully endorse her Mongol Doctrine, so she had assigned him missions where he could either fail or die. So far though, he had denied her that pleasure.

His first clue came with the replacement warriors he got. Most commanders received *sibko* graduates—young, fresh warriors hoping to prove themselves. Instead he got older warriors, transfers from other units. In reviewing their codexes and talking to them, he found they all shared one thing: a disdain for Malvina's Mongol Doctrine. *She is lumping us together. No doubt she does not want us under Galaxy Commander Chistu's command, where she fears we might all conspire to oppose her rule.*

Khalus' second clue was that he had been sent in with a lone Trinary to face what remained of the elite Old Guard regiment, which had been badly bloodied in the fighting with the Falcon Guard. Looking at the orbital intelligence, he knew his forces were outnumbered almost three to one. *She sent us on a suicide mission. If we die, there will be fewer voices of the resistance to her blasted doctrine.*

In preparing for the attack, Khalus knew he might be well served to try replicating the victory of the Falcon Guards: dig in near Cheyenne Mountain, make the Old Guard hit him, fight a strong defense. Khan Hazen had even suggested it. *A last stand, that is what she plans for me. As such, I will not play her game.*

Rather than attempt to fight defensively, he intended to go on the offense.

Pausing his *Jupiter* in a small clearing, he studied his tactical sensors. The Republic forces would be coming down the road in a matter of minutes. He intended to rush them, get in the middle of their formation. The road, cut into the side of a mountain, was narrow, with the mountainside to the left, and to the right, a sheer drop-off that went down the mountainside nearly a kilometer onto jagged rocks below. If he could get his Trinary in the center of the Republic formation on the narrow roadway, he could gut them from the inside out. *The confusion and tight quarters will work to our advantage.*

"Savage Star, form up on me," Khalus said. "We will rush them head on. Pillage Star, come in behind us, and jump up and over. Get in the middle of them and fire both ways. Rend Star, you are our fire support. We will call out targets, and you will saturate them with LRMs."

A chorus of "*affs*" responded as he checked the sensors. *They should be coming any minute.* "All right then, Jaegers, let us finish what our *trothkin* began. Charge!"

He came through the brush and up onto the road. The lead Old Guard 'Mech, a battered *BattleMaster*, seemed to freeze in place, momentarily stunned to see an enemy in front of it. Khalus did not hesitate to fire thirty long-range missiles from the racks on either side of his cockpit. They roared out, and he followed the salvos with his paired ER PPCs. Missiles enveloped the *BattleMaster* in explosions. One PPC shot missed Khalus' target, instead hitting a black *Lament* off to the side, and the other shot slammed into the ebony *BattleMaster*'s cockpit. The Old Guardsman managed to fire a return shot from its PPC as it fell off the cliff, the beam furrowing the ferrocrete road in front of Khalus' 'Mech.

That is one.

Pillage Star rose on plumes of orange and blue jump jets and roared over him, raining fire down as they dropped. The Old Guard, now realizing the threat, did not cower. They rushed forward instead, right at Khalus and Savage Star. Missiles from Rend Star arced high over his head and arrowed down on the Old Guard by the dozens.

One of the Guard opened a wide-beam channel and howled, a guttural roar the likes of which Khalus had never heard before. In response, he let loose all four of his Ultra autocannons at the rushing wall of 'Mechs. The roar of his guns nearly drowned out the Old Guard's war cry. Empty shell casings clattered on the roadway as the First Falcon Jaegers fired everything they had.

1207 HOURS

The narrow highway was littered with shattered BattleMechs, random 'Mech limbs, smoking craters, and hot bits of shrapnel.

Khalus Pryde's breath was ragged as Thomas' *Jade Hawk* savagely kicked and punched the last Republic BattleMech still standing. The Old Guard had been surprised only two dozen kilometers from the safety of their bolt-hole. They had tried to form a defensive position on the road, hugging the mountainside, but it had been to no avail. They did not break, but instead kept coming, kept dying.

Khalus' own losses had been bad. Savage Star had two surviving warriors, but no functional BattleMechs. His own Star was reduced to him and Thomas. Only Rend Star had come through the fight with no lost personnel, though all of their 'Mechs were battered and beaten. *My warriors have paid the price for the Chingis Khan's hatred of me.*

The Old Guard had fought on after their 'Mechs fell. Some had climbed out with their sidearms drawn, firing at the Falcons' cockpits. Others had charged his force, throwing bits of broken ferrocrete or swinging whatever pieces of wreckage they could lay their hands on. Many of his MechWarriors loathed the Mongol Doctrine and understood why these pilots fought on—they knew death awaited if they surrendered. But Khalus' warriors killed them one by one, giving each one an honorable death in battle. *We do this not for Malvina, but for the honor of all the Clans.*

From down the road, Khalus was surprised to see a lone person stagger out of the smoke and debris down the road. Under his arm, the MechWarrior cradled a black neurohelmet that matched the Old Guard's black-and-lightning-bolt colors. The age of the Guardsman surprised Khalus. He had a gray goatee and long gray hair, wet with perspiration. As he staggered forward, he dropped the neurohelmet onto the roadway, stopping in front of Khalus' battered and charred *Jupiter.*

Solahma...they are all solahma *warriors.*

Khalus activated his external speaker. "The fight is over."

The man looked behind him and at the blasted litter of BattleMechs all around. "I am the last then," he yelled.

"*Aff.*"

"I take it you will not take me prisoner?" he called out.

Khalus wanted to, even though the man was old. Such spirit should be honored. There had been rumors of some Jade Falcons taking bondsmen, but he knew Malvina Hazen. *If I claimed him as a bondsman, she would kill him just to get to me.* "My Khan has insisted we take no prisoners."

The *solahma* nodded. "Then we both know what comes next." His hand fell to the pistol in the holster at his side.

He means to fight! He did not want to kill the warrior, but at the same time he admired his bravado in facing certain death.

Before Khalus could speak, the man drew his sidearm and fired. The slugs struck the cockpit canopy ineffectively. "For the Republic!" he screamed. "For Devlin Stone!"

The *Eyrie*, piloted by Julie, opened fire with one of her micro pulse lasers. The man's body superheated instantly with the laser hit and vanished into a crimson mist.

Such a waste. This is what we have become…not warriors, but murderers. Khalus' only satisfaction was that he had not been killed in the battle, which he knew would further frustrate Malvina Hazen.

SCOTTSBURG, NORTH AMERICA
3 APRIL 3151 (T+83)

The skies were gray and the rain came in sheets, hitting Lieutenant Colonel Chris Kornfeld's battered *Lament*. The wind gusted, and he could see each wave of intense rain batter his canopy. It was a shame. The day before he had seen the rolling hills north of Scottsburg and knew how lush and green they were. Now, as the thunder rumbled slowly overhead, he saw only the churned-up sod where BattleMechs had walked. He reached for a hip flask to take a drink and noticed how his hand quivered.

He had come a long way from the fall of Geneva. The group of survivors that made it out had gone to Paris, where they had launched a good counterattack on the Jade Falcons, only to be driven back. When Paladin Lakewood had fallen, Kornfeld had made it out with the last survivors aboard DropShips that had flown to Toledo, Ohio.

The unit he had served with was no longer a command. There were BattleMechs and tanks from Stone's Lament, a lance from Stone's Liberators, and the rest were salvaged from a half-dozen shattered, nonexistent units. Some of Hansen's Roughriders and other mercenary units filled out the line of battle. They were spread out across three hills, a line of battle designed to be perpendicular to the approaching Jade Falcon force. Brigadier General Turner himself had joined them; he was far too old and out of shape to successfully pilot a 'Mech in combat, but he did regardless.

The Jade Falcons were coming—and coming fast. Kornfeld knocked back a healthy slug of whiskey, recapped the flask, and slid it into the side compartment on his command console. The liquor burned as he swallowed it, but that did not bother him at all. He liked the feeling of warmth rising in his chest…it reminded him he was still alive.

"All right boys and girls," came the voice of General Turner into his neurohelmet. "They will be on us shortly. Remember your training. Keep tight fields of fire. I don't have to tell you how important this battle is. We are the last combat group operating in the area. If we go down, there's nothing to prevent the Jade Falcons from rolling north. We are the last line of defense for the Republic of the Sphere."

As the general spoke, Kornfeld looked to his right and left. *This is it? We are the end of the line? We are a hodgepodge of units. What chance do we have?*

"The Exarch is counting on you. Do your duty, fight like demons, save the Republic," the general said.

Chris shook his head. *We fought them in Geneva. We fought them in Paris. They just keep coming. Now there is nowhere else to retreat.*

In the haze of the gray rain, his sensors lit up on the tactical display. Scarlet dots flashed, far too many of them. A part of him wanted to turn and run, but he knew he had no place to go. His jaw set, and he gripped his joystick tight.

"Have at 'em!" General Turner shouted, rushing forward in an wobbly-looking *Atlas III*, its stride unsteady as it moved forward.

A chorus of men and woman yelled as lightning flashed and thunder boomed. Kornfeld was shocked to realize he was one of them.

He sprinted his *Lament* forward, singling out a *Mad Dog* through the sheets of torrential rain. His heavy PPCs added manmade lightning to nature's as he fired. One shot missed, the other slammed into the leg of the charging Jade Falcon. It paused for a moment, then leveled its pair of Gauss rifles and fired.

In the darkness of the storm, Chris never saw the slugs launch. He only felt the torso of his *Lament* under him crumple, and he staggered backward, fighting for balance. Red damage indictors screamed at him, but he ignored them as he struggled to keep the 'Mech upright. *I've lost my frontal armor—my reactor's been hit.*

He leaned forward, his balance returning slowly. He fired his ER medium lasers, and their crimson beams stabbed past a charging Republic *Nyx* and a *Malice* that was on fire, no doubt from inferno rounds. Two beams found their target, searing away armor on the *Mad Dog.*

Everything happened in a blur of seconds that would forever be jumbled and confusing in his mind. The Jade Falcon fired, and Kornfeld's world erupted. A vague sensation of falling blurred with a sharp pain in his right leg as the *Lament* toppled over. Searing heat filled his cockpit, and his vision blurred...for how long, he could not tell. Time seemed to stop, and everything went dark.

As he slowly regained consciousness, Chris struggled with his orientation. The *Lament* had come down on its right side. His damage indicators showed that one shot had gone straight through his fusion reactor core. *How did I survive that? Was it luck?* One thing was for sure, the *Lament* was dead—this time there would be no repairing the damage. *I didn't even get to take down one of the bastards.*

Outside the rain had slackened, making him wonder how long he had been out. Through his now-cracked canopy he saw figures walking in the downpour. His eyes struggled to focus. MechWarriors. Yes, he saw the neurohelmets in their hands. One was the portly General Turner, his leg showing horrible purple bruising. When lightning flashed overhead, he could see the cut on the old man's head, the rain washing the blood down his puffed-out, white-haired chest. He was one of eight Republic MechWarriors out there.

In front of them a man, a Jade Falcon warrior, was yelling at them. *Wish I could hear what he's saying.*

Kornfeld started to move, but a jolt of pain seared through his leg. Looking down, he saw a slender shard of metal from the floor sticking up through his thigh. The moment he saw it the pain ratcheted up a hundred times more.

His quaking hands went down to remove the piece, then he heard staccato gunfire outside. Glancing up, he saw the bodies of the Republic's last line of defense drop to the ground. Lightning flashed, and the roar of thunder ushered in another wall of rain.

He stopped moving. *If they see me, they'll kill me too. I am a witness. No, I'm a* target.

Kornfeld lay in his 'Mech, suspended on his side, for well over three hours, unmoving, almost afraid to breathe, until he was sure the Jade Falcons had moved on. He removed the metal shard and did what he could with his medkit to bandage the wound. His leg barely supported him as he carefully opened the hatch and climbed out.

The rain had slowed to a drizzle. Lying before him were the wet bodies of his comrades. Anguish and anger came over him, and he fell to his knees. Looking around, he saw the blasted remains of a tank, turned on its side, and an arm of a 'Mech lying some thirty meters away, its fingers pointing skyward. There were others in the distance, the wreckage of abandoned 'Mechs. The downed Jade Falcon 'Mechs were gone, likely taken by salvage teams. The Republic BattleMechs and tanks that were of use had vanished as well. What remained was the worthless debris. *I am part of those remnants.*

Looking at the executed MechWarriors, he cried, his knees sinking into the mud. The rain washed over him, but could not clear the images from his memory. *Was it worth it, fighting on for so long? They rolled right through us. Someone has to be held accountable for this. Someone has to be responsible.*

"The Exarch is counting on you," Turner had told them.

Screw the Exarch.

It was in that moment that Lieutenant Colonel Chris Kornfeld, the veteran of a half dozen battlefields on Terra, came to hate Devlin Stone.

NORTH OF TORONTO, NORTH AMERICA
TERRA
4 APRIL 3151 (T+84)

From his position on a rocky knoll, Alaric Ward looked out at the smoke rolling from the field of battle. It was thicker than usual because of the pines ignited in the fighting. It didn't hide occasional glimpses of his Clan's 'Mechs moving among the defeated enemy.

Star Colonel Spurlock Conners approached him. "My Khan."

"Who was this unit, again?"

"The lead unit was the Callison Rangers. They came to Terra with Damien Redburn from the Remnant. But the rest of the unit—there were elements of the Fifth Fides Defenders and at least two other militia units."

"Scraps and leftovers," Alaric replied. "Bits and pieces of different units. They never could have worked as one." *And they never stood a chance against us.* "Tell me, what do Malvina's forces face now?"

Conners pulled up his noteputer. "They met a combined force of Republic troops outside of Louisville. Stone's Lament, Stone's Liberators, Hansen's Roughriders, the Gray Gunny Lancers, a mix of the Fides Defenders and the last of the Hastati Sentinels."

"How did the battle fare?" Alaric asked.

"It was a fast fight. The Falcons suffered some fairly significant losses, namely in Vau and Omega Galaxies. The surviving Republic forces scattered in three different directions with the Falcons in pursuit. Very few managed to escape."

Alaric nodded as his gaze swept the field. *Gray Gunny Lancers...Hansen's Roughriders. Those merc units were fighting me on the West Coast, but were pulled away.* For a fleeting moment he wondered why, but let it go. All that mattered was that the Republic forces had been defeated. "They are throwing the best units they have left at the Jade Falcons then, *quiaff*?"

"*Aff*, that they are. You might say it is almost all that they have left."

"Excellent. We will move into Toronto and take out the militia there. That will give us some time to rest Beta and Lambda Galaxies. Any word on our patient?" He had asked Conners to keep an eye on Chance Vickers.

"Her physician wants her out of the hospital by tomorrow at the latest."

Alaric smiled. "She is fully recovered, then?"

"*Neg*. They are simply done trying to keep her there. She has been through four nurses so far. We both know Chance. She is patient, but only to a point."

Alaric nodded, pleased. *Good. With her return, I will have my right arm back...just in time to end the Republic once and for all.*

COMMAND POST ROUGE
DETROIT, NORTH AMERICA
TERRA
12 APRIL 3151 (T+92)

Devlin Stone stared at the holographic map, convinced the image was sucking the very life out of him. The Old Guard had died almost within sight of sanctuary in Colorado. No signal had come from them once the fighting started, so he could only assume the worst. All of Stone's Brigade, the Hastati, the Principes, the Fides—gone.

He had sent Jonah Levin out at the fall of Geneva, but had heard nothing from him. Tara Campbell was in Alaric's hands. Janella Lakewood was a Wolf prisoner, captured south of Paris. Damien Redburn, his dear friend, had given his life to cripple the Clan leadership. Stone's world was shrinking smaller and smaller by the day. Only Tucker Harwell, Ghost Knight Shimmer, Edie Miller, and Colonel Volkmar Seifert, a local garrison commander, remained of the once mighty RAF High Command. *The Inner Sphere once feared and respected us, and now we are all that is left.*

Shimmer, his trusted Ghost Knight, had recently returned with the message from Julian Davion. The Federated Suns had betrayed him. *After what*

I did to help him and the Federated Suns in their hour of need, he refused to come to our aid! Stone had quietly given up hope of Julian's arrival, but the message confirmed it. Stone kept the handwritten note in his pocket, pulling it out from time to time to reread it. He held faint hope that the Ghost Bears might come, but even if they were already en route, it was too late to save his beloved Republic. Reality gnawed at Devlin Stone, eating him from the inside out. *Everything I had planned...gone up in smoke.*

Shimmer stalked around the table like a caged lioness. "Exarch, we still have options."

He braced himself. Yesterday, she had argued in favor of nuclear weapons, which he immediately dismissed. It had devolved into a heated argument, but he had stood firm. *I will* not *destroy Terra to save it. I will not be the Word of Blake.*

But Shimmer wasn't thinking of a nuclear option this time. "We can send the word out to what is left of the RAF," she said. "We can fade back and wage a guerrilla war against the Clan invaders. It will take time, but it *will* work."

She still has heart, which makes this more difficult. "No. Alaric has already proven he has no tolerance for guerrilla warfare, while Hazen would just massacre civilians and burn our cities to the ground in response. All that would do is cost more innocent lives and livelihoods."

"Exarch," Tucker Harwell spoke up from his seat at the far end of the map. "Whether or not we use guerrilla tactics to fight back, any further resistance will only cost more lives. Neither Clan will tolerate that. That is why we didn't fully reactivate any of the Castles Brian." He gestured to map, where the sea of green and red patches surrounded the dwindling Republic positions on the map. "In a matter of days, if not hours, we will be under assault here. There is nowhere else for us to go. We are out of hiding holes."

"We will fight to the last man, then," Shimmer snapped. Her caped hood opened slightly, and Stone caught a glimpse of her scarred face and the glint in her eyes. She had been beautiful at one time, that was evident. *Everyone thought she was dead, yet she survived. And after all she has been through, she deserves something better than live the rest of her life as a hunted guerrilla fighter.*

"To what end?" Harwell asked.

Colonel Volkmar Seifert shook his grizzled head. He commanded the River Rats, a group of last-minute militia volunteers who had been persuaded to take up arms in defense of Detroit. His salt-and-pepper beard covered a rugged expression of determination, crafted in every wrinkle on his face. "We will fight if that is the order, Exarch," he said. "I have a reinforced battalion of armor with heavy infantry support and a company of BattleMechs, but realistically, we won't last an hour against a single Clan Galaxy." He pointed to the map. "And six of 'em are closing in on us from the south and the east. If you tell me to fight, I will. My father fought at your side, and I won't let him down—or you—by pulling back just because the odds are stacked against us. Remnants of broken units are making their way here, and we're readying our equipment and ammunition as we speak. Just give the word."

"What about the Lament?" Stone asked hopefully. They had been in the fighting at Louisville, and he wondered how many of them had survived. *They have always been the spine of the RAF.*

Miller spoke up. "In Toledo, what's left of them. They're on their way here." Her voice was soft, exhausted. She knew defeat was nigh. "But we are talking two battle-damaged lances of 'Mechs and a scattering of support troops, Exarch."

Stone ran a hand down his haggard face. *So the Lament is beaten as well? How many more must die to drive these bastards off-planet?*

Colonel Seifert leaned toward Stone. "We have a lot of troops left that would welcome the chance to slowly bleed these Clans to death. Give me the word, and we'll go in."

Miller nodded. "I am ready to assume my duties in the field. There is no more intelligence to gather. I would rather face my fate out there."

Stone needed more time—time he did not have. The walls were closing in. The time for a last stand was over. It had already happened on a half-dozen battlefields across Terra, and the Republic had lost on every one. *My Old Guard, my Lament... What has become of my army?* "What if...I were to surrender, but only to Clan Wolf?"

Tucker Harwell shook his head. "I understand your thinking, Exarch. Hazen won't honor it. She will continue to kill our soldiers."

Stone glowered at the younger man. There were times when he appreciated Harwell's perspective, but this was not one of them. "I have to try," he said wearily. "This is beyond the Republic. It is about the fate of the Inner Sphere. Alaric must be willing to listen to reason."

"If you surrender, that means there *is* no Republic anymore," Tucker countered. "It is over. All of it. Sure, we have some scattered units that didn't fall yet—but the Capellans are out there, waiting for the Wall to go down, and the other House Lords will make grabs for whatever scraps are left."

I don't need you to remind me, Tucker. "The Republic isn't dead as long as we believe in it." Stone struggled to pull himself upright and shut off the holomap. He swept the room, looking into the eyes of each and every one of the handful of survivors who advised him.

"All of you have done a remarkable job against incredible odds. People will remember what you did, the sacrifices of those who died before us. Each of you symbolize the reason I founded the Republic, a belief in something better.

"The truth is, I'm tired, and so are you. And if we continue to fight, it will only result in our deaths. Against one Clan, we would have won—I know it. Against two...well...it simply wasn't in the cards. Don't blame yourselves for this. The fault is my own."

"No, Exarch!" Miller said, sobbing. "We failed you. We should have prepared better. We should have fought harder. The blame lies on our shoulders." There were nods of agreement from all except Tucker Harwell.

It was exactly what Stone wanted to hear. *They have to accept responsibility for some of this.* His accepting the blame had been an act of grace on his part... but it wasn't entirely sincere. *I did my part, but did everyone else?* He allowed himself a paper-thin smile as he shook his head once, playing one more time to his audience.

"The blame is for the historians to sort out. Given our current situation, and the odds against us, I see no sense in continuing this fight. I will surrender to Clan Wolf. If that does not work...then I will surrender to both Khans. It is the only way to stem the bleeding."

He paused for dramatic effect. As he looked over, Tucker Harwell was the only person in the room not consumed with a wave of emotion. Instead, he was scowling. Stone sighed internally. *He blames me for the deaths when in reality, the fault lies with the invaders.*

"The struggles for Terra are not over when we stand down," Stone said. "These Clans will tear each other apart to be the ilClan. You all need to return home and do what you can to help your families and friends. I will do what I can to prevent the loss of more innocent lives.

"You have all served the Republic with honor and distinction. Let us put an end to this, and pray that peace prevails." With those words, Stone's energy left him. He sagged down into his chair at the end of holotable.

"Lady Miller, get me a clear channel and contact Khan Ward. Tell him I wish to discuss the terms of our surrender."

MISSISSAUGA, NORTH AMERICA
TERRA

Alaric moved to the communications station at the far end of the mobile HQ. "You have confirmed the source of the transmission?"

"*Aff,*" Jathniel Kerensky replied.

"Put me through."

"Khan Ward," came the voice of Devlin Stone, crackling slightly over the connection. "It is clear that further hostilities between my Republic and your Clan would only result in a senseless loss of life. I propose an immediate ceasefire between us, to be followed with the Republic's formal surrender to Clan Wolf."

He is truly beaten, yet even in defeat he hopes to dictate terms. Such arrogance. For far too long, the Inner Sphere had tried to tell his people what to do, how to act, and where to live. *That era is over.*

"Devlin Stone," Alaric replied, "I agree that further loss of life is undesirable. And while I will accept your surrender, Clan Jade Falcon must be a part of such an agreement."

"Khan Ward, I would prefer to surrender to you. Clan Jade Falcon has slaughtered any who surrender to them. I have no desire to let Malvina Hazen hold up my severed head as proof of her victory. I will not surrender to a joint Clan force unless you can promise me you'll keep the Falcons from killing every last one of my people. There's no point in giving up if we will be lined up against the wall and shot."

Like Stone, Alaric did not wish to see Malvina senselessly massacre others simply because she felt slighted. *And if only I accept the Republic's surrender, it will drive her mad. While that would be enjoyable, it will cost more lives. I must try to rein her in to protect the Republic survivors.* "Very well. You have my word."

There was a long pause. Finally, Stone said, "Damn you all to hell, Khan Ward. I agree to your terms. I will send you the coordinates for our meeting."

"Well bargained and done." Alaric glanced at the comms officer and slashed his hand across his throat. The officer shut off the transmission.

There were fewer than six warriors in the mobile HQ, and all of them stopped what they were doing to watch him.

"Contact the Chingis Khan of the Falcons," Alaric ordered.

It was tempting to send the message through Galaxy Commander Chistu, but this was far too important. Jathniel Kerensky began to transmit on a Clan channel.

"This is Chingis Khan Malvina Hazen," said Malvina over the speakers.

"This is Khan Ward. Devlin Stone asked for a ceasefire. He has agreed to surrender to us."

"Surrender? Why would I wish for his surrender? I can take what I desire by force."

"*Aff*, you can, but it is no longer necessary. Stone is willing to surrender to both of our Clans. We are victorious."

"I'm surprised he did not surrender only to you."

"He tried. I told him I would not accept his surrender alone. The Jade Falcons have won a portion of this victory, and we Wolves acknowledge that. So either you can share the victory, or I will be forced to accept the Republic's surrender to the Wolves alone. If that happens, we take all the glory, and Stone gets what he wants: a wedge driven between our Clans."

Silence came down the line, but it didn't go dead. She was listening.

"The choice is yours," said Alaric. "Though I should warn you that, should you accept, you must leave the Republic survivors alive. No more demonstrations, publicly broadcast or otherwise."

Malvina made a noise of disgust, but took another moment to consider. At last she said, "This victory never would have happened without my Falcons— and we will be there to relish the defeat of the Republic. I will inform Devlin Stone myself that we will also accept his surrender."

Alaric smiled. "Then I look forward to seeing you soon."

CHAPTER 24

BELLE ISLE, THE DETROIT RIVER
TERRA
14 APRIL 3151 (V-T DAY)

The gray skies brought a light mist of rain drizzling down on the city park in the middle of the Detroit River. It pattered on Alaric and his command staff as they disembarked from their DropShip.

Chance Vickers walked at his side. Her uniform hung loose on her body, as she had lost weight during the campaign and her hospitalization. Her new bionic eye was a little jarring to look at, but her presence gave him solace. Star Colonel Spurlock Conners followed them, as did Star Admiral Haake Sukhanov.

There were gaps in their ranks. Garner Kerensky was not there to savor the victory. Ramiel Bekker's absence was acute, and Alaric still felt the loss of the WarBear. *We have paid a high price to stand here today.*

Tara Wolf, wearing a dull gray jumpsuit, marched one step behind the rest of Alaric's delegation. Her spiked platinum-blond hair sagged in the misting rain. She had said little since becoming his bondsman. Alaric had brought her here as a symbol for Stone—living proof that any further fighting was fruitless—in case he attempted to bargain for terms. He also wanted Tara at his side to witness Malvina Hazen's reaction upon seeing her as a Wolf bondsman.

Malvina came a few minutes after the Wolves' arrival, along with a handful of her Galaxy Commanders. Alaric spotted Stephanie Chistu, who had been shunted to the rear of their ranks. He knew he had put her in an awkward position, but he also had a feeling she was not entirely bothered by being shunned by her Clan's leadership. *She represents what the Jade Falcons have forgotten: the honorable path.*

Behind the Jade Falcon officers trailed a young woman wearing a plain, olive-drab jumpsuit. Her sullen eyes darted around, and her blond hair looked unwashed. This had to be Cynthy, Malvina's adopted daughter and pet. It was hard not to feel sad for the girl. *The Watch's report was right—she is likely being abused.* The sight reminded Alaric what Malvina was capable of. *What has happened to this girl will happen to all of the Inner Sphere—and worse—if Malvina becomes the ilKhan.*

The two Clan delegations approached each other, surveying their opposites warily, but Alaric ignored them and marched up to Malvina, extending his hand. "Congratulations to you and your officers," he said. "This is a great day for the Children of Kerensky."

Malvina returned the gesture with her bionic hand, a firm grip that squeezed Alaric's bones together. It was painful, but he showed no reaction.

"On this matter, we can agree." She glanced over at Tara Wolf. "*You*," she said with a scowl. "You killed my *sibkin*, Aleks."

"I did," Tara said, glaring back at the Jade Falcon Khan. "I put a hatchet straight through his cockpit." Alaric did his best not to grin at that response.

"I should kill you here and now," Malvina said, reaching for her laser pistol in its holster.

"You will not," Alaric said. "She is my bondsman. Killing her would violate our agreement."

His words worked. Malvina's hand drifted away from her pistol. "If you wish to keep her as your bondsman, so be it. There will be plenty of time to kill her once I have crushed your Wolves," she said snidely. "I heard you had a fondness for collecting bondsmen. She must help fill the hole left by the death of your WarBear."

Again, Alaric refused to give her the satisfaction of a reaction. "I could say the same," he said, leaning to the left and locking his eyes on Cynthy. "Is that why you have brought her? I assume *she* is your bondsman."

Malvina's jaw clenched, but before she could reply, Alaric moved on. "I have long felt that the Inner Sphere has used our *rede* against us—turned our honor into a knife at our own throats. We both came here and did what generations of Clansmen dream of: we conquered Terra. The Inner Sphere has twisted our honor and *rede* against us at every turn. They played off the very things that made us great and turned them into weapons that held us back from this—" He gestured with his hand around the scene. "Terra, the ultimate goal of Clan civilization. No longer will the Inner Sphere nations use our own ways against us." He spoke loud enough so that all of the officers gathered could hear. *I want the Jade Falcons to know that I am not like their leader—that I see this as the start of a new era.*

"*Aff,*" Malvina replied. "Today marks the end of a failed experiment. Beating swords into plowshares—bah! The Republic offered peace. We are *warriors.* Peace is death to us."

The approaching motorcade caught everyone's attention. Alaric and the others watched five limousines cross the long, ornate bridge that connected the island to the city of Detroit. The Republic's delegation parked a short distance away from the gathering of Clans. Several security troopers emerged from the limousines with their assault weapons at the ready. Several RAF officers and a handful other nonmilitary personnel emerged as well.

Some of the security detail helped Devlin Stone into a wheelchair. The Exarch's hands shook as he took his seat. This was the man who had led the Republic to its doom...a *solahma* near death. One of the security guards wheeled Stone toward Alaric and Malvina, the officers and other personnel trailing them.

"Khan Ward," Stone said, extending his hand.

Alaric looked at it with indifference and did not shake it.

Stone reached out to Malvina instead. "Khan Hazen, then?"

Malvina eyed the proffered hand, her mouth turning downward in disgust. "It is *Chingis* Khan," she corrected. "And I do not shake hands with *freebirth* scum like you. Especially a leader who sacrificed his honor to send assassins to kill me."

"True, but it pales in comparison to ordering your own battleship to crash into the capitol city of your own people." Before a shocked Malvina could reply, Stone continued, "For the record, I only sent the headhunters after both of you as a last resort. I thought it was an underhanded way to fight, that it would lead to problems between us. But you left me no choice—my back was up against the wall. I had to secure victory through any possible means I had available. We are all fighters here—we all know victory is all that matters. I am sorry, if that means anything."

"It does not," Alaric said. Words could not bring back Garner Kerensky or Ramiel Bekker. "Words do not heal wounds."

Malvina did not even bother to reply, but just glowered at Stone with the fury of a thousand suns.

The Exarch looked over at Tara Wolf, who stood with the other Clan Wolf officers. "Tara, it is good to see you are well."

Tara's jaw clenched. Though her eyes shone with tears, she let none of them fall. "Exarch." She showed Stone her right wrist, which was encircled by a bondcord. The sight of it made Stone's gray face go even grayer.

"You are here to surrender, *quiaff*?" Alaric said.

Stone grimaced. "I am. I take it you have some document that you want me to sign?"

Malvina just laughed.

As Stone fumed, Alaric said, "We are Clan, Devlin Stone. Paper means nothing to us. It is meaningless to put something in writing when politicians will ignore it to suit their whims. We are warriors."

Malvina nodded. "We honor our word," she said. "If you or your followers do not, you will be exterminated."

Alaric looked down on the man in the wheelchair. "We will have our Loremasters copy our agreement to send to the other Inner Sphere leaders... when the time is right. State your terms, and we will tell you whether we accept them."

"Very well, then," Stone said, clearly frustrated with Malvina's scorn. But he drew himself up in his wheelchair. "I propose the immediate surrender of all remaining Republic Armed Forces on Terra. We will lay down our arms. Our personnel will be immediately decommissioned and paroled—free to return to their homes, leaving their weapons and equipment behind for you to deal with."

Alaric glanced at Malvina, whose face was rigid, emotionless. A gust of wind stirred her ice-blond hair.

"*Neg*," Alaric said. "It is not enough for my Wolves."

Malvina smirked in agreement.

"What else could I possibly give you?" Stone asked. "You...you have taken *everything*."

"Not quite everything," Alaric replied. "This, here and now, is the end of the Republic, *period*. Not just on Terra, but every world where a Republic of the Sphere flag is raised. I do not want your decommissioned officers trying to retake Terra after we have shed blood for it. You will surrender it *all*, Devlin Stone. The Republic of the Sphere is no more—now, and forever."

Stone sputtered, "Surely—"

"In this instance," said Malvina, "I agree with Khan Ward. There is no place for the Republic in the future."

Her biting words made the old man's shoulders sag. Stone looked about—at his advisors, at the Belle Island park—as if anything could help him. Finally, he said, "I...I agree. My Republic is no more. I have enough blood on my hands. As do you." He glared at Malvina, who ignored him.

"Bargained well and done," Alaric said.

"*Aff*," said Malvina. "Until we all shall fall."

"I would like to say a few words to my people," Stone said, bordering on hopeful. "Send them a broadcast, inform them of our terms, tell them how all of this came to pass. They will need context. I want to assure them this is the right thing to do. Perhaps lay the foundation for a smooth transition."

Alaric scoffed. "With exceptions, your troops fought with honor, but you tried to assassinate us using deceitful false-flag operations instead of attacking us openly and honorably. You will have no grand speech. No chance to spin your failure into success. You may tell the people that the Republic is no more, and to lay down their arms. We will handle any transition that is to come. Nothing more, nothing less."

Malvina nodded.

"And what of me?" Stone asked wearily. "Am I to be a bondsman or a prisoner of war?"

Alaric waved his hand dismissively. "*Neg*. Bondsmen are warriors. They add value to a Clan. You are a feeble old man—a shadow of your former self. I have no need of you. If Malvina wishes, she can take you prisoner. Beyond that, you can go do whatever former Exarchs of a conquered nation do."

Malvina sneered. "He is nothing but a bad memory now. A pitiful reminder of his failed experiment. The victor of our combat trial can deal with him as they see fit."

Alaric understood exactly what Malvina meant. If the Jade Falcons won, Stone would be executed—publicly, viciously.

Stone tried valiantly to recover. "You may find, Khan Ward, that I have a lot to offer. I know a great deal about the House Lords and their governance. I could be a useful asset."

With the eyes of all the Falcon and Wolf officers fixed on him, Alaric shook his head. "I have no need for your outdated expertise. I look to the future—where you have no role. What matters is that from this point forward, no matter what follows, Terra is under new leadership. We have achieved what no House Lord was able to during the Succession Wars. As such, do not press the courtesy we have extended to you thus far."

Stone ducked his head. "Then...there is nothing left to discuss."

"*Aff*," Alaric agreed. "There is not."

Stone signaled to the attaché steering his wheelchair. Together, he and his entourage headed back to their limousines.

"When this is all over, my first act as ilKhan will be to cut out that man's heart and hold it in my hand while he dies at my feet," Malvina said.

Alaric watched them depart in silence. Only when they were driving away did he finally speak, "General."

Chance was at his side in an instant. "My Khan."

"Detach a squad," he instructed. "Make sure the message he sends is appropriate."

She nodded and fell back toward the DropShip.

As Stone's motorcade rumbled back over the bridge to the mainland, Alaric turned to Malvina. "All that remains is our unfinished business."

She offered a thin smile. "As it should be—Jade Falcon against Wolf. I presume you want a series of combat trials, *quiaff*? I suggest best three out of five."

Alaric took a single step closer to her, all emotion erased from his face. "You are mistaken, Malvina—like Stone before you. I am not Ulric Kerensky. I will not fight a series of trials where fate hangs on multiple battles. *Neg*. We settle this once and for all. One fight, one Trial, with the victor as ilClan, now and forever."

Malvina's grin turned into a death's head grimace. "Very well. When should we meet?"

Alaric knew she had at least one fresh Galaxy, but the others had suffered losses throughout the campaign. Her Tau Galaxy had landed in Japan and been utterly crushed, obliterated from the Falcon *touman*. *We have been careful to rest and refit our forces—and thanks to Ramiel, we brought in a contingent of brand-new BattleMechs designed specifically to counter the Jade Falcons' tactical doctrine. We are ready.*

"I propose two days from now," he said. "We can arrange for a ceremony to mark such a momentous event. I suggest that one of your staff work with General Vickers on those arrangements. We can finalize things there, before our *toumans*."

"So much the better," said Malvina. "Strike fast, while our blood is hot. Well bargained and done." She took a step closer and lowered her voice to a hiss, "One more thing, Alaric. I have not forgotten the insults we have traded—and how you interfered with my orbital strikes on Geneva. These slights cannot be ignored. So know this: there will be *no* Wolves left once I win. I will remake Terra in my own image, as a monument to the Jade Falcons. Every last icon of Clan Wolf will be destroyed. You and your ilk will become yet another Not-Named Clan."

Alaric said nothing as he turned to face his officers and gestured them to move out. He had heard enough. There was nothing to gain arguing with Malvina.

Besides, he believed every word she had said.

INTERLUDE

MAGELLAN-CLASS JUMPSHIP CELESTIAL WIND
ZENITH JUMP POINT
KEID
CAPELLAN CONFEDERATION
14 APRIL 3151 (V-T DAY)

Chancellor Daoshen Liao watched the nearby JumpShip *Zhanmadao* from the bridge of his own vessel as the countdown continued. "Three...two...one."

Zhanmadao, an older *Merchant*-class vessel, had been equipped with special sensors and programmed for automation. It shimmered for a moment, as any ship did at the moment it jumped. The Chancellor of the Capellan Confederation watched, half holding his breath. His pristine jumpsuit bore the insignia of his rank on the collar and a simple green patch bearing the upthrust-sword sigil of House Liao sigil on his sleeve.

We have done much to reach this point. Our armies have crushed the Republic of the Sphere forces between Sian and here. We are at the doorstep to Terra itself. All we must do is figure out the right way to knock, to overcome this accursed Fortress barrier...

The Confederation had waged a vicious war with the crumbling Republic, liberating worlds Stone had seized from Daoshen's realm many decades ago. This campaign of Capellan vengeance had restored balance to the universe, and now all that remained was for him to achieve what no House Lord had ever done: conquer Terra.

As Daoshen's mind cleared, he saw the *Zhanmadao* contort, twisting... The ship turned itself inside out. In the silence of space, there was no sound, but the Chancellor imagined what it must look like inside the mangled, unrecognizable wreckage that remained.

The loss of the ship—that stung deeply. JumpShips were a rare commodity, difficult to build. *We can ill afford more disasters such as this.*

"Another failure," said the head of the Ministry of Resources, Dr. Bren Mayhugh. He ducked his head. "My deepest apologies, Celestial Wisdom. We believed we had found a way around the problem."

The twisted hulk of the ruined JumpShip started to spin, propelled by venting gases. Daoshen frowned at the image. "So the Fortress remains around Terra?"

"It appears so, Your Eminence," Mayhugh said, cringing. "We theorized that the barrier is tied to the emergence wave of a JumpShip—the K-F event caused by the hyperspace jump. We believed the modifications we made to the jump drive would circumvent it. But...I have failed you again, Chancellor. I stand ready to face whatever punishment you deem appropriate." He bowed low, awaiting his fate.

"Not today, Minister," Daoshen said. "Killing you would not put House Liao any closer to Terra. However, I will not tolerate future failures. JumpShips are far too rare to use for such costly experiments." He steepled his fingers in front of him. "According to Maskirovka intel, the Wolves and Jade Falcons have already found a way through this barrier. Yet we are still stymied by this technology. Why?"

"We do not know how the Clans have done this, but we will find out, Chancellor. You have my word. We will recover the sensors we installed on the *Zhanmadao*, and those may give us some of the answers we seek—or at least confirm whether our theories are correct."

Daoshen nodded a dismissal, and the scientist hurried to leave his chambers. *I stand with a task force ready to strike Terra, yet I am delayed by something I cannot see, bypass, or control. If the intelligence reports from the Maskirovka are correct, the Ghost Bears are mobilizing their forces, as are the Lyrans. Armies are beginning to assemble. I stand at the threshold of taking Terra for the honor of House Liao. My MechWarriors are already in place, yet I cannot penetrate this barrier!*

In addition to its robust military-industrial output, Terra was of great political value as the heart of the Inner Sphere. Through four Succession Wars and a Clan invasion, the birthworld of humankind had been the target of every House and Clan, as well as every nonaligned faction, such as the Word of Blake. What it represented to House Liao was something much more—a potent symbol of power. If he could take Terra, it would change Sphere-wide perceptions of the Capellan Confederation. *It will cement our true position with the other House rulers. No longer would we be seen as the realm Hanse Davion tromped over in the Fourth Succession War.*

So bitter was the rivalry that Maximilian Liao, Chancellor of the Confederation until 3036, had kept a dinner plate from the wedding of Melissa Steiner to Hanse Davion, with the name SIAN on it, signifying Hanse's intent to conquer the Confederation's capital as a "gift" to his new bride. The resulting war had cost House Liao half of their realm. Maximilian had kept the dinner plate in his office, displayed so he could see it from his desk. For Daoshen, the plate was a reminder that the wheels of fate could shift rapidly, a cautionary tale of just how perilous the fortunes of his realm truly were.

The on-again, off-again fighting with the Federated Suns had yielded the Confederation many rewards. Worlds long taken from his people were now under House Liao's divine rule once more. It was not just about citizens; it was about industry. Even now, factories were producing new weapons of war that equipped his units with new might. *Julian Davion believes he has a truce with us, but only a fool trusts a Davion.* The Draconis Combine stood on New Avalon...for now. His daughter, Danai Centrella-Liao, had brokered the recent ceasefire with Julian Davion. *When the time is right, we will break that vow, just as Julian broke his word with us before. We will not wait for him to break his word a second time.*

Jumping into the Terran system, with no intel on the events unfolding there, was a great risk. But it would be worth it if he succeeded. *Fate smiles on the swift.* The Wolves and Jade Falcons would destroy the Republic; nothing could stop that now. And the Clans' long-standing rivalry would leave one survivor, a so-called ilClan, weakened by combat.

With a decisive strike, I can seize Terra. My task force can crush this idea of an ilClan once and for all. We will be seen as the saviors of humankind— and the jewel in the Celestial Crown will be Terra itself. In one swift stroke, he would be handing future Capellan generations a dynasty that would include the homeworld of humanity.

Watching the twisted wreckage of the JumpShip spinning lifeless in space, Daoshen allowed himself a thin smile at the thought of Terra under his control. *Once I have it, I will consolidate my holdings. With a second wind, my Confederation will seize a wedge of worlds between Terra and New Avalon, cutting off the Draconis Combine's forces in the Federated Suns. Then we will constrict, tighten the knot. The Federated Suns is ours to take and hold. Despite the debacle on Northwind, the Combine may still believe we are carving it up together—but that mistake shall be their undoing.*

OFFICE OF THE COORDINATOR
IMPERIAL PALACE
IMPERIAL CITY, LUTHIEN
DRACONIS COMBINE
14 APRIL 3151 (V-T DAY)

Coordinator Yori Kurita called for her secretary. The young man, Kai Nihari, entered her plush office, head bowed. She could see the pale scar on his scalp, the one he had gotten during a failed assassination attempt on her months ago, one that had never made the press. Having a Draconis Elite Strike Team operative as her personal secretary had many advantages.

"Coordinator, I am prepared to serve."

"A brush and ink, please."

Nihari returned thirty seconds later, again bowing as he held out the instruments for her. She nodded and he left, closing the large mahogany inlaid doors behind him.

Some messages deserved to be written by hand, and this was one of them. *Gunji-no-Kanrei* Matsuhari Toranaga stood on formality, so he would respect it. She knew the man for what he was, a power-hungry military leader that thought she was still under his control. Yori understood that acts of defiance against such a man would bring grave risks. She held the title of Coordinator, but the *gunji-no-kanrei* believed he pulled her strings. *I am not so ignorant that*

I do not understand what my fate will be if I start showing my independence openly.

At that same time, she was a Kurita, a legitimate heir to the throne of the Draconis Combine. The burdens of that office often required a delicate balancing act between duty, honor, family, and the needs of the Combine.

After preparing her *sumi* ink, she dipped and blotted the ancient *fude* brush and began writing in neat and concise Japanese characters:

Honorable Gunji-no-Kanrei *Toranaga:*

The word honorable took some effort to write, but was required for formality. Dipping her brush in the ink, she continued:

It is my hope that this message finds you well. While our forces stand on New Avalon due to your excellent leadership, matters have been brought to my attention that require your input.

She chose each word and sentence carefully, a mix of respect but clarification of her role. *With him, I cannot push for action. I need to ask for his insights. I must ask for input, not give commands. If he is wise, input is all he will give me.*

Our foes appear to be mobilizing. The Internal Security Force indicates that Clans Jade Falcon and Wolf have all but disappeared from their worlds, and are presumably driving toward Terra. The latest report I have received indicates that the Rasalhague Dominion has moved several front-line Galaxies to their border with the Republic of the Sphere.

I want him to know that I am monitoring the ISF's intelligence reports. He may wonder whether I am seeing different information than he does. Such nervousness can be useful with such an egotistical man.

The larger matter was that one of the Clans would seize Terra and proclaim itself the ilClan. She had been tempted to put that in her note, but stayed her hand. *I do not need to reveal that I understand the implications of the Clans unifying under the leadership of an ilClan. By omitting it, he may assume I am too naive to have considered it.* Keeping him in the dark as to the depth of her knowledge was more useful than exposing it at this time. The thoughts of those implications worried her more than anything else, though. *What if an ilClan does unite all the Clan forces in the Inner Sphere? We struggled against individual Clans. United, they could prove unstoppable.*

At the same time, our ally, the Capellan Confederation, is presently within one jump of Terra. Our old enemy, the Lyran Commonwealth, is mobilizing as well, primarily along the Jade Falcon Occupation Zone.

She paused for a moment and thought of Archon Trillian Steiner's predecessor, Melissa, and the grave mistakes she made. *She tried to hold the lower castes of Clan Wolf hostage during their migration to the Wolf Empire. One does not put a Clan on a leash and not expect to be bitten. Now Trillian Steiner will have to deal with the ramifications of Melissa's acts. Such is the burden of being a House Lord.*

Regardless, it appears we may be facing the end of the Republic of the Sphere. Its collapse could prove a curse or a boon, depending on how we approach it. There is a chance, however remote, that the Republic may yet survive, which presents challenges as well. As always, I value your insight on matters such as this.

The Draconis Combine would shed no tears at the disappearance of the Republic of the Sphere. Since the collapse of the HPG network, it seemed it was only a matter of time before the realm died.

I am most curious as to your thoughts on what our response should be to such actions taking place by our allies and foes alike. Do you recommend troop movements? Should we curtail our operations in the Federated Suns until the situation on Terra has stabilized? What contingencies do you have for dealing with these activities?

Yori stopped and reread the paragraph again. It was always safer to ask questions instead of making demands of Toranaga. *I would like to know what he has in motion. By asking, he is pressured to tell me.*

I have also learned from several sources that elements of Wolf's Dragoons have disappeared. ISF indicates that a Clan Wolf representative visited them on Parma before their mysterious departure. Are they on an authorized DCMS mission? If so, can you provide me with the details of that operation? Again, I am understandably curious. It raises my concerns regarding the extension of their contract.

The Dragoons ranked the among most elite mercenary units in the Inner Sphere. While the media had not picked up on it, Gamma Regiment and parts of Alpha and Beta had abandoned their posts and taken off for parts unknown. Her own subtle inquiries had not produced answers. *The Dragoons are, as always, a closed book to our eyes. I assume he is in the dark as well, but I want him to admit it. ISF has told me he mismanaged the Dragoons, that they are unhappy with their combat assignments. He initially used them to achieve great victories, but then sidelined them, denying them the honor that came with those wins. I do not want to lose them because of one man's ego.*

It appears we have much to consider. Perhaps a face-to-face briefing is in order?

She did not like sitting down with him, for she could read the contempt on his face at times. Still, the line served purpose. It showed that he would brief her, remind him that his position was subservient to hers without being blatant. *Such subtleties are required with such a man...one who sees himself as the ruler of the realm I am responsible for.*

I thank you for your devotion and long service to the Dragon. As such, I look forward to your prompt replies to these inquiries.

—Yori Kurita, Coordinator of the Draconis Combine,
Duchess of Luthien, Unifier of Worlds

The full formal title was a courtly courtesy in most cases. In the case of *Gunji-no-Kanrei* Toranaga, it was also a less-than-subtle reminder of her position.

She glanced down at the line "It appears we have much to consider." Hai, Gunji-no-Kanrei, *we certainly do...*

THE ILCLAN

CHAPTER 25

Galaxy Commander Stephanie Chistu had come early to the ceremony, wanting to drink it all in. She peeked out for a few moments from backstage to survey the entire scene. *This is history. It is rare that one knows when a historic moment is happening right in front of them.* She wanted to savor this feeling.

The amphitheater was a large bowl of hillsides surrounding a large stage. The grass was just beginning to come in, enough green to add a sense of brilliance to the setting. Warriors of both Clan Jade Falcon and Clan Wolf covered the grounds. Most were adorned in their formal ceremonial leathers—the Wolves, black and crimson, the Jade Falcons mostly black with dark green trim. The Bloodnamed warriors wore their ceremonial masks, each one carved with unique likenesses of jade falcons and wolves.

The two groups initially gravitated to their own people as they had filtered in; Wolves to the right of the stage, the Jade Falcons to the left. The gap between them disappeared as the two groups came in contact. Several small groups from both sides spoke with each other in idle conversation, and Chistu watched them interact. To an outsider, it would seem odd, for these warriors would be facing each other in battle soon. For the Clans, it was normal. Combat trials were personal at times, but at their core they represented a test of arms, an opportunity to determine a course of action. Aff, *there has been bad blood between our people for centuries, but in recent times, most of it stems from Malvina's rhetoric, not true hate.*

Chistu's jade falcon mask was hot, her cheeks sweaty, but she did not care as she turned away from the gathering of the two Clans. She milled about backstage with the other Galaxy Commanders, most of whom did not want to talk to her, given her contentious relationship with the Chingis Khan. Malvina's use of fear was not just against her enemies, but against her own people, and that did not bother the other Galaxy Commanders in the least. Chistu was unphased by their cold shoulders. *Their unwillingness to speak out says more about them than it does about me.*

The Wolf Galaxy Commanders were backstage as well. She could not read their faces because of the masks, but knew they were sizing up their competition. *Generations of breeding have led to this, a moment when we will face off for the ultimate prize—the ilClanship.* There was no real tension, but the glimpses she caught of their eyes through the holes in their masks were that of hunters—narrow, focused, drinking in every detail. In that moment, it struck her that over the next few days, many of the people she was with backstage at that amphitheater were going to die.

The Wolf Loremaster, Aberdeen Mehta, wore a wolfskin cape and a more ornate mask than the others, though her fair skin poked through at her neck and hands. She stood next to the Jade Falcon Loremaster, Andwar Icaza. The ebony Elemental, dressed in a flowing black cape with green lining, towered over Mehta as the two conferred. In the past, the Falcons' ceremonial cape had been all green, but Malvina's Mongol Doctrine had affected even the wardrobe of her Clan.

Malvina's entrance to the backstage area caught everyone's attention. She walked with bold strides, her long, straight, silvery-white hair trailing behind her as she strolled to her Galaxy Commanders and took her place next to saKhan Ryan Pryde. The saKhan appeared gaunt and weak, from what little Chistu could see under his mask. *After the injuries he suffered, he is lucky to still be alive.*

Malvina's ceremonial leathers were all black, like her standard Mongol uniform. She did not wear a mask; instead she sported a broad, arrogant grin. On her left sleeve, starting at the wrist and going to the shoulder, tiny hashmarks of yellow thread were stitched in groups of five—four vertical marks crossed by one diagonal. There were hundreds of these marks in total, if not more, each one a tally of Malvina's kills, both on and off the battlefield.

Alaric followed her onto the stage, careful and deliberate as he walked. His black-and-red leathers were more subdued, and his long hair flowed down over his shoulders. He stood beside Malvina, and together they spoke briefly with the Loremasters.

"The time has come," Loremaster Andwar Icaza said in his deep voice to all gathered on stage behind the lowered curtain. "Wolves to the right, Falcons to the left."

Stephanie formed in a line next to her peers on the stage, and Malvina and Alaric moved to the front of their lines. There had been little rehearsal, but everyone seemed to know their parts.

The curtains opened, and the audience of warriors quieted, their conversations instantly silenced. They stood at attention, moving swiftly into pristine formations as if they were assembling for an inspection. Chistu could feel the many eyes on them. *They all sense it too, this moment.*

Loremaster Aberdeen Mehta moved beside her counterpart in the middle of the stage. "*Seyla*, warriors of Clans Wolf and Jade Falcon...defeaters of the Republic of the Sphere."

"*SEYLA!*" the vast audience responded, hundreds of voices in unison.

"We stand here today on the sacred ground of Terra, the birthplace of humankind," Mehta continued, her voice amplified through the sound system. "Both of our Clans have accomplished what no other Clan has. We came and conquered Terra. We removed the blight that was the Republic of the Sphere once and for all. The descendants of Nicholas Kerensky stand on the world that was promised to them." She paused and turned to Andwar Icaza.

His voice was louder, deeper, more penetrating. "We all know what the Founder said in *The Remembrance*, speaking of the purpose behind our Grand Crusade to Terra. It only seems fitting to read it today:

On Terra's firm soil, ready to rebuild
The Star League with their hearts and hands.
But who shall lead? Upon whose shoulders
Will the burden lie? The answer is the test;
The test is the journey. Whichever Clan
Carves its way through the barbarians
To reach that fabled cradle of us all
Shall be the vehicle of the League's rebirth. Upon
The Star League throne shall sit that Clan's
Wisest Khan. So should it be—So shall it be.

The Loremasters bowed their heads for a moment, and in unison said, *"Thus speaks Nicholas Kerensky, father of us all."*

"*SEYLA!*" the crowd responded.

Aberdeen Mehta spoke again, "Nicholas Kerensky proclaimed that whichever Clan conquered Terra would become the ilClan, the Clan above all Clans, and that its senior Khan would become ilKhan for life, with the right to appoint their successor from the ilClan. In his wisdom, the Founder intended the invasion of the Inner Sphere to be a test to determine from which Clan the First Lords of a resurrected Star League would descend.

"Two Clans have fulfilled that ultimate test, and they stand here today. What follows will determine the fate of our people, and all in the Inner Sphere."

The two Loremasters turned to their respective Khans, gesturing their arms in sweeping motions for them to take center stage. The Loremasters stood behind them for a moment. Both Khans extended their right hands, about a half meter apart from each other. The Loremasters then wrapped Alaric and Malvina's hands with a single gray sash, one that bore the mark of the Star League.

Alaric spoke first in a firm tone. "As my Wolves landed on Terra first, I claim the right of being the Hunted for this Trial."

Malvina nodded curtly. "I so acknowledge, and claim the right of the Hunter for this Trial."

Up to that point, Stephanie had wondered if Malvina would grandstand in some way, but she did not. *Even the Chingis Khan understands the gravity of this ceremony.*

"What would you defend with, Alaric Ward, Khan of the Wolves?"

"I bid all of my forces currently on Terra. No assault DropShips or WarShips. This will be fought on the ground—warrior to warrior."

"All forces on-planet then," Malvina agreed. "I bid my entire Clan, Clan Jade Falcon."

Chistu's body tensed. *We are going all-in. This is not just a trial—it will be a Reaving.*

"As the Hunted," Alaric continued, "we have the right to choose the venue for this trial. We will fight in the northern part of North America, where there are few cities—mostly forested terrain and lakes. I propose the forests between the cities of Ottawa and Winnipeg. My Wolves will make Ottawa their base."

Malvina nodded again. "And my Jade Falcons will headquarter in Winnipeg."

Alaric nodded slowly in response. "We deploy after this ceremony then, and commence at 0700 local time, if that is agreeable?"

"It is. The victor shall be the ilClan, for now and all time."

"*Aff*," Alaric said. "For now and all time."

Loremaster Icaza stepped forward and drew his dress sword from its scabbard. He cut the sash between them, letting it fall to the stage floor. "So this shall stand, until we all fall."

The gathering of the two Clans repeated the phrase in unison, as if it were a prayer. Alaric and Malvina bowed politely to each other and walked off stage, then the Loremasters did the same. The two rows of Galaxy Commanders stepped forward, each shaking hands with the others as they passed. The grips were all hard, deliberately so.

As the two Clans began to depart, Stephanie saw one Wolf leader remove her mask. She recognized the woman from the intelligence briefings—the black hair, the new bionic eye.

"General Vickers," Chistu said to the taller woman.

"Galaxy Commander Chistu."

"I want to thank you," Chistu said. "Reaching out to me saved lives that would have been needlessly lost on both sides."

Chance nodded, her face relaxing a little. "I only did what was necessary."

"If I may, General," Chistu began. "Why did you reach out to me specifically? We have never met. You could have contacted any other Jade Falcon, including the commander leading operations against your Wolves."

A thin smile rose to Chance's lips. "I contacted you because I asked myself a simple question… What would Alaric do?"

Chistu was at a loss for words, but Chance finished their conversation. "I hope we do not face each other across the field of battle before this is over. You are a rare bird indeed." With that, she walked away, leaving Chistu with more questions than answers.

UNION-C-CLASS DROPSHIP *WAVERIDER*
OAKLAND SPACEPORT, MICHIGAN
TERRA
16 APRIL 16 3151 (T+95)

Jack, formerly Jack Traver, watched the crews secure the last of the two *Ares* 'Mechs they had repaired. It has been painted maroon at the Star Colonel's insistence, complete with jagged bright-yellow bolts, almost like lightning, but not ending in a tip like a lightning bolt. Mia was still arguing with the DropShip techs as they adjusted the deployment straps over the massive 'Mech.

The last few weeks had been some of the hardest of Jack's life. It wasn't the physical work of repairing the two superheavies, though that had been strenuous, even with the help of the Clan Wolf technician caste. No, it was the unsettling realization that he was now *part* of Clan Wolf.

Being a prisoner of war would have been easy, as there were no expectations. Instead, He, Mia, and Cheetah had been talked down to by many of the warriors. They hurled the slur "freebirth" at Jack and his team at every turn, which he found amusing. *Of course I am a freebirth. I was born like nature intended.* He would never consider the word a curse, no matter how often he heard it or how derogatorily it was spoken.

Star Colonel Kalidessa Kerensky, his bondholder, had been instructive, teaching them about the history of Clan Wolf in what little spare time she had. Frankly, he found it interesting but unimportant. *They expect us to embrace who they are, to set aside a lifetime of our culture, but they are almost like aliens to us.* Such thoughts came with frustration. More than once he had told Cheetah and Mia to hold their tongues. "We need to be careful here. This isn't the RAF. These people see us as below them. They won't put up with some snide-ass off-the-cuff comment."

The worst of their ordeal had come when the Wolves had broadcast Devlin Stone's surrender message. The words were etched in Jack's mind, washed with the tears the three of them had shed: *"To all citizens of the Republic of the Sphere. As of this time, I have ordered the immediate surrender of the Republic Armed Forces to Clans Jade Falcon and Wolf. I do this freely, with deep sorrow and sadness. The great struggle we waged to save not just ourselves, but the Inner Sphere, is over. Further fighting would only result in a senseless loss of life. Our cause was just, but we faced overwhelming, insurmountable odds. I ask that all of you, as citizens of our realm, adhere to this peace. I bid you all the best of luck."*

Upon hearing the message, Jack and his crew had found a closed-off workroom where they could be alone. Cheetah had sat hunched over, rocking in her seat and crying uncontrollably. Mia tried to hide her tears by turning against the wall and refusing to make eye contact. Jack understood their feelings, and he felt the same, but only for a moment. Then he got mad.

A 'senseless loss of life'? Good men and women that he knew, that he considered his friends, were dead. *If we were going to surrender, why not do it weeks ago?* Stone spoke like a paternal figure, but that only stirred up Jack's own stormy relationship with his father. *How many of us lost everything because Stone chose to fight right up to the end?* Until that broadcast, Jack had always held the Exarch on high in his heart and mind. *He had to have known we couldn't win, but instead of surrendering, he sent us to die in his name with a promise of victory.* The thought left him shaken and chilled to the bone.

Now the next battle was about to commence, coming with the dawn. He would be facing the Jade Falcons, and from what little he had gathered, it would be a fight to the end.

When the 'Mech loading was complete, Jack turned to see Star Colonel Kerensky standing behind him. Mia and Cheetah joined him, facing their bondholder.

"I had promised you a chance to fight the Jade Falcons," Kalidessa said. "That time is upon us. You three have shown spirit and have honored your vows.

"Khan Ward has sent word that those that we deem worthy of fighting may be made *abtakha*, formally adopted into our warrior caste. The former citizens of the Republic realize what an abomination Malvina is. I believe each of you has the heart of the Wolf."

She grasped Jack's wrist and pulled it in front of her, then produced a combat knife and cut his bondcord. Reaching out to Cheetah, then Mia, she did the same. The severed cords fell on the deck at their feet.

"Besides," she said with a wry smile. "We are short-handed, and I can ill afford to put three of my MechWarriors in a single BattleMech. But you three have piloted, fought in, and repaired these 'Mechs together. Are you ready to command one in battle again, as part of my command?"

Jack looked at her for a moment. "They say Malvina's crazy—a bloodthirsty serial killer with a BattleMech. If the Falcons win, we will all die."

"That sums it up well," Kalidessa replied.

"Then I say we fight," Jack said. He turned to his crew, who both nodded.

"Very well. Welcome, MechWarriors, to the Second Wolf Assault Cluster—the Howling Furies. I have only two rules. One, when you fight, you go all out... hold nothing back."

Jack nodded. "Agreed. And the other?"

"Never play a game of chance with DuJordan or Hawkins. They cheat."

Jack blinked in surprise at that. He was unaccustomed to her having a sense of humor. In fact, the three of them had debated whether she even understood the concept of jokes. He glanced at Cheetah and Mia, who both grinned. *Guess I lost that bet.*

Before he could respond, Kalidessa saluted them as the DropShip engines whined during their preflight procedures. "I will see you in the staging area," she yelled over the noise. "We have a busy day ahead of us."

CHAPTER 26

WOLF CLAN HEADQUARTERS
OTTAWA, NORTH AMERICA
TERRA
16 APRIL 3151 (T+95)

General Chance Vickers was still struggling to adjust to her new eye. It was better, in some ways, than her organic right eye. Replacing both almost would have been easier to cope with, as trying to adjust between two different focuses gave her headaches and dizziness. The doctors had told her it would improve with time, and the medications helped, but the throbbing in her temples remained.

To her, such injuries were simply part of being a warrior. She felt lucky to be alive. *If I had died, I would miss all of this...the trial to determine who will be the ilClan.* She smiled, and the top of her cheek grazed the metallic mount of her new eye—another reminder of its existence.

She headed into the makeshift command post—a commandeered RAF bunker—to meet the other commanders. The room was dimly lit with a dull yellow light—its old-tech holotable swapped out with a portable Clan-built one. The air was musty, and she noticed peeling bits of khaki paint on the walls. Through the missing flakes of paint, she could make out an unexpected image: a downward thrust sword, the symbol of the Word of Blake. *This is indeed an old facility.* It was a late-night meeting, and despite the reinforced ferrocrete, she could hear the roar of DropShips deploying the last of the Clan's forces nearby.

As Khan Ward entered the room, she realized just how glad she was to be part of Clan Wolf. Alaric had always been a few moves ahead of his foes, right up to the headhunting mission that had nearly cost him his life. He had engineered the Clan's move from their occupation zone to the new Wolf Empire, fending off both other Clans and Great Houses along the way. He had taken Tharkad, the capital of the Lyran Commonwealth. And now, he had engineered the demise of the Republic of the Sphere.

All that remains is to end Clan Jade Falcon.

Tara Wolf, clearly torn between discomfort and humiliation, followed Alaric. Chance had seen that expression before—on Ramiel Bekker. When Alaric had taken him as a bondsman, the haughty Ghost Bear warrior had chafed in his new position for weeks. *Over time, he became one of the best of us. Will Tara ever reach that point?*

The surviving Galaxy Commanders and Star Colonels Spurlock Conners and Agustin Tutuola joined them, filling the now-cramped space. As the reinforced blast door closed, Alaric surveyed the room, making eye contact with everyone.

"I will keep this brief," he said. "Tomorrow, we will face the greatest battle in the history of our Clan. Malvina Hazen calls herself the Chingis Khan, the 'ruler of the universe.' You have heard her say that she intends not only to win, but to wipe out every Wolf. If she defeats us, she will eradicate us, and erase the history of our people so that we never existed."

Vickers glanced at her fellow officers. Even struggling with her two different eyes, she could tell that everyone in the room, including herself, was hanging onto their Khan's words.

"We are in the fight of our lives," said Alaric, "but so are the Jade Falcons. We should expect no quarter and give none." He turned to the head of his Watch. "Spurlock, you have studied Malvina. What can we expect?"

The Star Colonel straightened to attention. "The Jade Falcons will want us to commit our entire force. They always strive for a swift victory. Malvina will attempt to draw us in close and fast, make us commit everything we have. Many of their BattleMechs are equipped for close-quarters combat and are jump capable. We have always favored speed and maneuverability, and the Falcons are prepared for that with their current generation of BattleMechs.

"Some of the Jade Falcon Galaxies have been on the ground almost as long as us, but a few are relatively fresh—especially Kappa. For review, I have sent you full dossiers of the current state of their units.

"Malvina will launch human-wave attacks with her *solahma* forces." Spurlock pulled up a list of the relevant Jade Falcon forces he had identified. "In some recovered footage from the Republic, we saw that she designated some *solahma* teams to hunt and kill any MechWarriors who eject." A video appeared over the holotable, showing Jade Falcon infantry executing a Republic MechWarrior in a blur of gunshots and crimson mist. "She is not above sacrificing her own troops to kill ours. There is no moral line she will not cross. Where we will fall back to honor, she harbors the old-school Falcon philosophy of 'Strength is Honor.'

"Most of her officers follow her because she brings them victories. But they are not mindless automatons. Each is cunning in their own right. They are just as hungry for victory as Malvina, even if it comes at a high price. Remember, she crashed one of her own WarShips into a planet just to make a point." Conners paused. "Dismissing Malvina as a mere sociopath only causes us to underestimate her. She is a brilliant battlefield tactician. She fights to win, regardless of the cost. Do not underestimate her or her command staff."

Alaric nodded, then turned to Chance. "General Vickers is our acting saKhan. You have all had an opportunity to work with her, and I want you to know that she speaks for me. Consider her words to be my own. General, please present our plan."

Chance moved to the holomap and pulled up the vast, forested region between the Clans' bases. Bordered by Lake Superior to the south, it was an area of dense pine growth, marshes, and steep rolling hills. "The strategy I have devised is to deny the Jade Falcons the fight they want. Malvina will try to draw us in, get us to follow her. Get your field commanders to understand that and resist the temptation. If the Falcons are retreating, it is for a reason. Do not be fooled by this." She spoke with a confidence and calm she had never imagined having before. This was her moment, and she held it tight, embracing it.

"Traditional Clan Wolf doctrine is to rush in with everything, fast and quick. We are not going to do that. Both of our Clans have been fighting for weeks, and the Jade Falcons will want to end this battle swiftly. Our job is to drag this out, to deny the Falcons the quick fight they desire. Thanks to Star Colonel Damon Ward," she said, nodding at her former CO, "we have a ready pool of replacement hardware and enough techs and spare parts to repair just about anything we reclaim from the battlefield. The Jade Falcons *have* to fight fast and furious because they are likely stretched thin after their losses sustained in battling the Republic. Some of her warriors are fresh though, since they arrived near the end of the campaign.

"So our goal is to prosecute a *prolonged* encounter, over several days and nights. This will push the Falcons' resources past their limit. My models show that a longer engagement should give us an edge. Do this, and we will be on the path toward victory."

Chance adjusted the holotable to show a glowing yellow line running north and south on the map. "This is Phase Line Charlie. We will advance no farther west than this phase line. Make sure your subordinates know this. No matter what the Falcons do to entice you, do not pursue them past that demarcation."

The gathered officers leaned over the table, studying and nodding as Chance's briefing continued.

"We have several spec-ops missions on deck designed to further strain the Falcons' capacity as well as hurt their command-and-control facilities. I will be going over specific assignments in the morning." She glanced at Alaric. "Anything else, my Khan?"

Alaric paused to look at them all. "The Jade Falcons will try to get your blood up. They want you to overreact, to fall victim to their way of fighting. Do not give in. They want a large-scale engagement. Deny them this. Frustrate them at every turn. We *will* defeat them, but only if you do your duty and have faith in our strategy."

"We would follow you into hell if you ordered it, my Khan," said the hulking form of Agustin Tutuola of the TRC. There were nods of agreement around the holotable.

"Let us hope it does not come to that," Alaric said. "We do not need to visit hell, but we must send the Falcons there. Dismissed."

The assembly broke apart, with only Spurlock, Tara, and Chance remaining behind with the Khan. Alaric spoke for a few moments with Spurlock, then turned to Chance. "So, my old friend," he began with an uncustomary smile. "Are you ready for what is to come?"

"I am," Chance replied with solid conviction. "And you?"

Alaric braced his hands on the holotable. "I will not sleep much tonight," he admitted. "Then again, I am confident Malvina will not rest much either."

"We made it sound simple," Chance replied. "We both know it will not be."

"You have to defeat her," Tara said.

Alaric turned to his bondsman. "*We* have to defeat her," he corrected. "You are a bondsman of Clan Wolf now. Your fate is mine, and mine is yours."

"I am sorry," Tara said, not sounding as if she were. "Of course, I meant 'we.' I read the Republic's file on her and fought her Falcons in France. If she isn't stopped here, she will lay waste to the Inner Sphere."

"*Is not*," Alaric corrected. "If she *is not* stopped here. Contractions are unbecoming of a warrior like yourself."

Tara's face reddened. "I am bloody damn trying!"

"I know," Alaric said. "And you will be hard pressed to try again tomorrow. You will be accompanying me on the field."

"What?" Tara frowned. "I am just a bondsman."

"*Aff*. And I am your bondholder, and I order you to be there with me."

Puzzled, she shook her head. "I do not understand," she said, careful to avoid the contraction this time.

"You bested me in battle, Tara Wolf, though it took several of your Highlanders to take me down. Regardless, I have seen you fight, and I want you there. As I said in the meeting, this is as much your fight as it is ours."

Chance leaned in on their conversation. "I have known Alaric my entire life. We were *sibkin*, he and I. In battle, he has only seen defeat three times. First at the hands of Anastasia Kerensky; second, when the Republic's assassins attacked him; and third, when you defeated him. Anyone who can defeat Alaric honorably in battle has my respect."

"I—I am unsure how I feel about fighting for Clan Wolf," Tara said. "I feel as if I am betraying my people." Vickers could hear the strain in her voice, the tearing of her emotions and loyalty.

Alaric must have heard it too. "I understand your reservations," he said. "I was a bondsman myself at one point. I also know that you will do what is right when the time comes."

"Just like that?" Tara asked. "You just trust me to do the right thing?"

"*Aff*, I do. It is our way. I am not asking you to shed what you were to become a Wolf. I am asking you to find a way to integrate the two." Alaric turned to the door and inclined his head toward Chance. "Coming?"

"I would like a minute alone with Tara, if that is acceptable," she said. He nodded and left the room.

Once Alaric had gone, Chance studied Tara's face, trying to get a read on her. "You have trust issues with Alaric."

"Damned right I do! He forced me into this...relationship." Tara shook her wrist with the bondcord at Vickers. "It was the only way to save my people. What I did, I did under duress. Now he simply expects me to *be* a Wolf."

"That is the Way of the Clans."

"That is *your* way. It is not how *I* was raised. We Highlanders have deep roots."

"Which was how Alaric drew you to Scotland, to fight on his terms." *What she sees as strengths are also weaknesses.*

"I am here against my will."

Chance shook her head. "You are looking at this incorrectly. Alaric did what he did out of *respect* to you and your people, to preserve them and their history rather than being forced to annihilate them entirely. He is acknowledging your skill in taking him down. Being Alaric's bondman is a high honor among the Wolves. We have seen how he has elevated those who came before you." *Like Ramiel Bekker.* Chance pushed the thought aside. Alaric wasn't the only one feeling the WarBear's loss.

"And one more thing. Alaric understands the importance of symbolism. I believe he has you here because the Northwind Highlanders have such strong ties to both the Star League and the Inner Sphere. This fight against the Jade Falcons, it is not just about Clan Wolf. It is about saving mankind from what Malvina may unleash. Consider this: you may be here because you are destined to be here, as a representative of the Inner Sphere, to bear witness to these historic events."

"Ah, got it." Tara eyed Chance with open suspicion. "This is the part where we talk woman to woman, and you assure me that Alaric's intentions are wholesome."

"*Neg*," Chance replied flatly. "I am not here to bond with you. I am here to make sure you understand the consequences should you ever seek to betray Alaric in any way."

Tara sputtered, "Are you—are you threatening me?"

"*Aff*, in a manner of speaking. You are a Spherer, which means you are likely contemplating how to escape or turn this situation to your advantage. I do not blame you for this; it is your nature. But you may be considering betraying Alaric. I do not know, but I *do* care. I cannot be at his side in the coming fight, but you will be. He prefers to lead from the front, and you will likely be the only bondsman to accompany him. Let me assure you of one thing, Tara *Wolf*— if he falls in this fight and you are to blame, there is no place your beloved Highlanders can go to escape my vengeance. Do you understand?"

For a long moment, Tara said nothing, just studied Chance's face. At last she said, "I do. But this is not easy for me. Being a part of a Clan, actually helping Clan Wolf become the ilClan...it is something I never contemplated. From childhood we were told you were a high-tech invading horde, that all you respected was 'might makes right.' The ways of the Clans are alien to me."

"Choosing you as a bondsman tells me Alaric has something in mind for you. Maybe he seeks to bring about some healing with the Republic after all of this is settled. Maybe he has some other plan. I do not know, or need to know. I exist to execute his vision and bring Clan Wolf this final victory. I have always known that I would have this role at his side."

"Destiny," Tara suggested.

"*Aff*. I could have resisted, but there is something about him, something majestic...historic...inevitable." Chance turned to go, then said over her shoulder, "You need to see that in him, Tara. Once you do, your place in our Clan will be clear to all—even you."

CLAN JADE FALCON HEADQUARTERS
WINNIPEG, NORTH AMERICA
TERRA

Malvina's headquarters was a string of three portable command domes painted in mottled-green digital camouflage. Her Galaxy Commanders and key personnel huddled around her, cramped for space, each warrior waiting to hear every word she spoke.

This is my moment, the one I have dedicated my life to. Here is where the Jade Falcons will be defined forever. Here is where the Inner Sphere will be remade.

"In a few hours, we finish the Grand Crusade with the destruction of Clan Wolf. I have studied Alaric Ward. He envisions himself a master of war. Deception, misdirection, the unorthodox...these are the trademarks of his strategies. Rarely does he simply throw his forces into a slugfest with his enemies. Alaric loves to think he is the smartest person on the battlefield. He thinks himself cunning. It will be his downfall."

"Alaric will come at our flanks. Delta Galaxy will protect our northern flank." She glanced at Stephanie Chistu. "Your mission is to blunt any drive there. Omega, Rho, and Zeta will protect the southern flank, should he drive there. The rest of our forces will deliver a gut-punch into the center of his lines, and pressure him to commit everything he has. With his flanking attacks held in check, we will have him in position for total defeat. We will break the Wolf center, swing both north and south, then finish them off."

"I have tasked a contingent of aerospace fighters to locate and strike Alaric's command post at the start of operations. That should temporarily blind him to our deployments. We may even get lucky and kill him, but that is not their primary mission. By the time he realizes we have crushed his flanking maneuvers, we will have him." She savored every word she spoke. *I know you, Alaric, and I will use that knowledge to defeat you.*

"Chingis Khan," Stephanie Chistu spoke up. "You have positioned three Galaxies to the south, but only my Delta to the north. If he comes at us in force, we may be woefully undermanned to stop the Wolves."

It is dawning on you...is it not? "You are saying that Delta is unable to fulfill its mission, that your warriors are not equal to the task, *quineg?*"

Chistu saw the verbal trap and sidestepped it. "*Neg.* I am merely saying it may be difficult for us to hold if Alaric flanks with a large-enough force."

The redness in Chistu's cheeks told Malvina that she realized she was being sent into a situation where she would possibly lose. *Perhaps if you had used those tactical nukes on Coventry as you were ordered, or if you had adopted my beliefs, you would not find yourself in such a predicament.*

Malvina's eyes swept the rest of her Galaxy Commanders. "Any of you who are unable to fulfill your operations, say so now, and you will be relieved of command."

Nervously, sternly, all of them remained silent.

Finally, Jane Thastus of Gamma said, "We will do our duty and more, Chingis Khan."

"Good. If you all do your jobs, then with the dawn, we will see the end of our only rival, Clan Wolf. Every future generation of Jade Falcons is looking down on you. All you have to do is give them victory."

CHAPTER 27

WEST OF OTTAWA, NORTH AMERICA
TERRA
17 APRIL 3151
(T+97, DAY 1 OF THE ILCLAN TRIAL)

Alaric stood in his cramped mobile HQ along with his command staff and his Galaxy Commanders.

Today was different. Gone were the field jumpsuits from yesterday; instead, everyone wore MechWarrior togs, Elemental body stockings, or flight suits. Overhead, Alaric heard the rumble of their combat air patrol covering Clan Wolf's positions. The command tent hummed with tension.

Alaric savored every moment of it. *It is good that they know how important this is, that everything is at stake.* "Operations commence in one hour. Most of you have been given your assignments. Are there any issues or concerns before we begin?"

"*Neg,*" replied Galaxy Commander Elise Ward. "My forces are fully reequipped with replacement BattleMechs from our reserves, though we have had little time to fully master them. But we will overcome. We stand ready to fight."

Alaric glanced at Vickers, then back to his commanders. "The WarBear designed these new BattleMechs to counter Jade Falcon tactics." He enjoyed the idea that in some way, Ramiel Bekker would still be on the field of battle today. "Most have close-quarters fighting in mind. Our new *Dominator* is heavily armored but highly mobile. The *Amarok* is designed to resist death from above maneuvers. These should give us an edge against the Falcons.

"Remember, our enemy will come in hard and fast. They favor a quick fight over a prolonged campaign, and have embraced the use of physical combat with their BattleMechs. Our intent is to engage them, but prevent them from overwhelming us quickly. Flexibility will be critical to the coming fight. We have no intention of micromanaging our forces in the field. You are all great warriors, so prove that today by outthinking our enemies."

Spurlock Conners spoke next. "Our intelligence says that the Falcon *touman* has been battered and rebuilt with reserve equipment and whatever they have salvaged from defeated Republic troops. But do not discount Republic BattleMechs. Many of them, as you know from firsthand experience, are on par with our own."

There were nods from the gathered officers.

"We will move out with the Wolf Hussars along the shore of Lake Superior," Alaric said. "The Snarling Wolves will head north on a long hook to the west."

Vickers stepped in. "Malvina will anticipate some sort of flanking maneuver from us, and will likely place forces to blunt them. Delta and Gamma Galaxies will put up a good fight, then fall back to avoid a general engagement."

"Why execute flanking moves if she will expect them?" asked Galaxy Commander Billie Sender from the Snarling Wolves.

Alaric smiled. "The key to defeating Malvina is thinking the way she does. She knows I favor flanking maneuvers, and thus she will seek to counter them. Her defensive maneuvers will distract her from Zeta Galaxy's primary mission in the evening." He pointed to the holomap display on the central table. "Galaxy Commander Cooper, I will need two Clusters. I recommend volunteer troops, given the nature of this mission."

"And that is?" asked the blond-haired Galaxy Commander.

"You are to strike the Jade Falcons' primary munitions and repair facility," Alaric said.

For a moment, his words brought a silence to the room. Grins rose from the Wolves.

"Zeta will not fail you, my Khan," Cooper replied.

Alaric nodded. "Zeta never does. I will be sending a detachment from Beta Galaxy with you to hold the beachhead. Galaxy Commander Fetladral, you will commence the next operation first thing this morning, which will blind one of Malvina's eyes. For that, I need your Ninth Wolf Cavalry, specifically your VTOLs."

Lois Fetladral nodded. "We are ready, Khan Ward."

Alaric's gaze swept the room, and he made sure to lock eyes with each of his commanders in turn. "I want to be clear on this point: Malvina has told me she intends to eradicate Clan Wolf, either during this trial or after she wins. She means it. Her Mongol Doctrine has made her blind to true honor. We *cannot* lose this fight. If we do, we will all be slaughtered, and our Clan erased from memory. I will not stand for that.

"Malvina wants to rewrite history." Alaric Ward shook his head. "Today, I intend for Clan Wolf to *make* history."

0700 HOURS

Star Commander Manning banked his rebuilt *Jagatai* in a tight turn over a stunning array of *Rifleman IIC*s, LRM Carriers, and Aesir anti-aircraft vehicles, all concealed under camouflage netting or hidden by trees. He almost pitied any Jade Falcon daring enough to try attacking the Wolf Clan's command-and-control hub.

Almost.

The battles against the Republic had taken a toll. One of his pilots, Keelin, had been killed outright in a vicious dogfight against the Northwind Highlanders in Scotland. Another pilot, Delaney, had ejected after being shot down in Germany, and had broken her ankle upon landing. She had insisted on flying on this sortie, however, even with her ankle in a cast and painkillers in her system. Dirg, Keelin's replacement, was fresh out of *sibko*, with no battle experience at all.

"Ravager Star," Manning radioed. "We are extending our operational sphere by five kilometers. Keep in formation and follow my lead. Dirg, I want you to keep close." He eased out of his arc of flight.

"Ravager One," Vigdal replied. "Incoming targets—I see two, possibly three, Stars' worth. Bearing one-one-zero."

"Confirmed," signaled Guethler. "Targets consist of *Scytha*s and *Sabutai*s and *Lucifer III C*s, closing fast."

Manning signaled Buzzard Star on the command channel. "Buzzard One, this is Ravager One. We are facing three-to-one odds here. I could use a little help."

"Roger that, Ravager One," came the voice of Star Commander Melissa Carns. "Burning hot. You will need to hold your own for few minutes, however."

Manning studied the incoming bandits and his own Star's position. "All right then, Ravagers, help is on the way, but we drew the short stick and will be on our own for a while. Break on my orders. Paint your targets and bring them down. Watch for ground fire from our AA support. Break in three...two...one—break!"

His *Jagatai* banked as if it were a part of him, swinging into a tight turn. He locked on the lead *Scytha* and triggered his LRMs and ER PPCs. The enemy pilot executed a tight inverted weave, avoiding many of the missiles, but the Falcon could not outmaneuver the PPCs, which tore into their starboard wing. A stream of white smoke poured from the wounds.

"Tallyho on *Scytha* Alpha!" Manning called out as he climbed steeply to avoid the large lasers that stabbed out at him. Four of the beams slashed and seared his OmniFighter's fuselage, one just under his cockpit.

"Tallyho on *Sabutai* Bravo," Guethler called out. Manning watched Ravager Three barrel roll, barely avoiding the incoming Gauss rifle round. The *Sabutai*'s pulse lasers peppered Guethler's *Jagatai* with black burn marks.

"Tallyho on *Lucifer* Alpha," Dirg called out.

Suddenly the air filled with pulses of emerald-green lasers from the *Rifleman IIC*s on the ground, followed a moment later by waves of long-range missiles, twisting and snaking into the bright blue sky all around them. The Aesirs' autocannon rounds, tipped with proximity fuses, exploded into the mix as well. The air burst with countless explosions all around. Manning banked hard to keep the *Scytha* in his sights, though the Jade Falcon pilot was not making it easy.

"I have problems here," Delaney called out, her voice strained. Manning could not see her, but his sensors showed her OmniFighter in a steep dive. "I have lost controls."

"Punch out," Manning ordered, and seconds later he saw the tracking tag on her ejection seat launch out into the maelstrom.

Two Jade Falcon fighters dove on the mobile headquarters nestled in a small copse of pines, barely visible from the air. Dirg swung in behind them, breaking off from the pursuing *Lucifer III C* that banked high and hard into a cloud formation. One Falcon disintegrated in midair, devoured by Dirg's pulse lasers and ER PPCs. The other juked hard and broke off their strafing run.

Manning throttled up to the maximum, burning fast in a long arc as the *Scytha* slowed, clearly looking for its ground target in the hurricane of ground-support fire stabbing up at it. As he came around facing the *Scytha*, which had circled for a few moments, his quarry fired its Ultra autocannon at him. The shells devoured his portside fuselage, sending bits of armor raining down on the defenders below. He returned the gesture with his PPCs, hitting the fuselage and cockpit. The *Scytha* arced over into a steep dive, black smoke streaking behind it. Manning followed it tightly to ensure it did not pull up at the last moment.

It didn't. Instead, it angled down on one of the Aesirs and crashed straight into it, consuming both in a massive fireball that rose from the ground.

Instinctively, he kicked up his thrust back to full power and banked around for the next target. Missiles rose up from the ground, commingling with the missiles in the air. Manning shifted his focus to another *Scytha* that dove and released a bomb over the target area. He scored several hits of brilliant green laser pulses on the Falcon aerofighter, which tried to get away, only to find itself in Vigdal's sights. His Pointmate's autocannon blew apart one of the angled vertical stabilizers on the *Scytha*, and the fighter sideslipped through the air, avoiding the Gauss rifle round intended for it.

"Got mine!" Guethler called out. "It is a nest of hornets up here."

Manning checked his tactical display and was pleased to see Dirg still in the air, tightly tailing a damaged *Lucifer III C* as it dove. Maneuvering out from the battle area to give himself a chance to align on a new target, Manning spotted a dive-bombing Jade Falcon as it dropped its payload.

"Freebirth," he swore, powerless to stop it.

The bomb streaked into the rain of fire pouring up from the ground forces and went off some thirty meters from the mobile HQ, right next to one of the *Rifleman IIC*s.

Bloody near miss.

"Find another target," Manning said as his body strained under the G-forces of his turn, trying desperately to lock onto the departing Falcon fighter.

"*Aff,*" Guethler called out. "Choose your hills wisely..."

"...and be prepared to die on them," Manning finished as an impact from some unseen foe slammed hard into his *Jagatai*. He reeled about and glanced at his tactical display. *Come on, Buzzard Star! Hurry it up! There are still plenty of targets for all of us!*

WINNIPEG
0725 HOURS

The Jade Falcon Watch command post consisted of a mobile headquarters and trailer to carry numerous antenna and sensor domes. It was situated on a small knoll ringed with new-growth pine trees. A Star of Nacon armored scout vehicles were concealed in the trees, tasked with providing fire support should the command post need it. The sleek little armored cars, topped with advanced tactical missile racks and light machine guns, were also draped with camouflage netting. Three were covered in pine boughs their crews had placed for additional concealment.

Star Colonel Abzug Helmer huddled over the holodisplay map with his staff, studying every dot, every bit of new information that came his way. His new jaw twinged, and he unconsciously rubbed it, only to feel the synthskin and plastic of the prosthetic. *Phantom pain...the price of failing the Chingis Khan.* There was nothing cosmetic about the replacement. It seemed much larger than the original, his own flesh and bone, and he could not get used to how artificial it felt.

These thoughts distracted him as he tried to concentrate on the data. The air strike on Clan Wolf had not yielded immediate results. Seen in the combat footage, the Falcon fighters had dropped payloads near the Wolves' mobile headquarters,. Of the three Stars of fighters sent, only one Star had made it back. Though they had dropped bombs around the Wolf HQ, their battle damage assessment did not indicate that it had been destroyed. *Let them tell Malvina of their failure. I did my job; I pinpointed their target.*

Khan Ward was indeed formidable—even Malvina had admitted that during their planning sessions. But she claimed she understood him. She said he would use misdirection. Alaric favored flanking attacks, so Malvina had moved her own Galaxies into position to intercept such actions.

General Vickers, though, was an entirely different matter. She was a mystery to Helmer. *It is as if Alaric kept her hidden for years, only to release her in the campaign for Terra.* Unknown variables like Vickers made his job difficult.

"Star Colonel," called Star Commander Micks, his tactical plot officer. "Another sighting—Wolf VTOLs. They hit one of our forward supply caches."

"On the table please," Helmer said.

A red pulse of light flashed on, and he studied it for a moment. This was the third sighting of Wolf VTOLs this morning; he presumed they were the same group. He saw the other dots and realized they formed a flight path. "Connect those dots, Star Commander. I want a plot for possible targets." The line was not a straight path, but he followed it with his eyes. Then he felt the color drain from what was left of his cheeks. "Damnation—"

An air-raid alert light flickered red on the ceiling over him.

A low rumble rose from outside as the Nacons burst from cover and fired their ATMs at a swarm of VTOLs approaching from low altitude. Other nearby BattleMechs joined in, blazing away at the Wolf raiders as they opened fire on their position.

The mobile headquarters rocked with explosions, tossing Helmer against one of the interior bulkheads hard enough to dislocate his shoulder. Smoke poured from the forward driver's compartment, and the holodisplay flickered off.

"Get clear!" he commanded, struggling to his feet. "Signal our CAP that we need air support, now! Move!"

His staff bolted for the hatch and he followed them. As Helmer emerged from the hatch, he saw eight Balac VTOLs hovering and weaving just at treetop level, all facing him and his command staff. Each was adorned with a crimson wolf's head on a green five-pointed star.

The VTOLs looked like they were waiting for him.

One exploded instantly as waves of ATMs ravaged it. Two pieces of blasted rotor flew in the air and scythed into the trees at the far end of the knoll, cutting one in half, mangling another.

The Nacons scrambled on the hilltop, roaring out to lock onto other targets. Missiles and lasers from above filled the air, chopping the dirt as they walked toward Helmer's position. A nearby *Griffin IIC* fired its own LRMs, which plastered the side of a Balac and rained armor downward as it spun and broke off, bellowing smoke. Another VTOL peeled off, obviously hit by ground fire, but it blasted away at a Nacon that lay on its path of retreat. The other Balacs targeted the intelligence post.

Helmer leaped aside and tumbled in the dirt. His command staff scattered. The nearby blasts knocked the wind out of him, and he struggled to get air again. His ears ached and went silent, and his eyes blurred. As he gasped for breath, he tasted dirt in his mouth—his damned replacement mouth.

Desperate to see what was happening, he tried to look around, but could only open his left eye; dirt and blood—*his* blood—obscured the other. Panic tore at him as smoke stung his one good eye. The lack of air started to spin and tunnel the world around him. A wave of nausea gripped him as he fell face-first back into the dirt.

Curse you, Alaric Ward!

EAST OF WINNIPEG
0925 HOURS

Star Colonel Marv Roshak and his Falcon Guards charged at the Clan Wolf Cluster before them in the black waters of the swampy bog.

They were on the front line of the Jade Falcons' center advance, but thus far resistance had been only moderate. Roshak was not complaining. His Cluster, even with the fresh *sibko*-cadet replacements, was still down thirty percent due to their fight with the Republic Old Guard. There was no shortage of volunteers to join his Guards; their reputation was already the stuff of legends in the Jade Falcon ranks.

At the edge of the bog, a squat, boxy Wolf *Linebacker* blasted away at Ashford's *Atlas III, isorla* from their epic stand in Yucca Valley. Both PPCs crackled into the menacing *Atlas III*'s center torso and shattered massive pieces of hot metal that hissed and steamed as they hit the murky waters. Another 'Mech, one his *Night Gyr*'s battle computer could not identify, ran along the edge of the bog, blasting with its own PPC. *Where did Clan Wolf get all of these new BattleMechs?*

Roshak lined up a shot at the fast-moving flanker, but its speed was so great that he missed with both PPCs. One hit a nearby pine, superheating it, and exploding the trunk into kindling. Nearby, Ashford's rotary autocannon purred its deadly tune, raining hot brass into the water as it stitched up the *Linebacker*'s frontal armor.

There was a distant rumble that Roshak recognized as artillery explosions—a lot of artillery. The blasts came from the hilltop at the far end of the swamp, the end of the Wolf lines. The crescendo of explosions crept toward the swamp itself—toward the Falcon Guards. The moment he heard it, the Wolf 'Mechs turned and sprinted to the south and west, skirting the incoming wall of death and destruction as fast as they could back toward their lines.

"Redeploy!" Pharaoh said from his position behind him.

"Falcon Guards, fall back now!" Roshak ordered.

They did so as the wall of fiery blasts churned the swamp into a bog of death. Chunks of black soil rained down as the Falcon Guards pulled back. Checking his sensors. Roshak saw that the Wolves were not pursuing, not capitalizing on the artillery barrage as he would have expected.

Khan Hazen said they would pursue us...but they are not. Why?

WABAKIMI DISTRICT PARK
1725 HOURS

Stephanie Chistu moved Delta Galaxy off the winding road and into the forests of the large, wooded park. She marched her *Jade Hawk* up a rolling hill, her warriors following in column formation. The last bits of snow, hidden under low pine boughs, still defied the warming air of spring. She had fought on worse ground before. While this terrain had limited fields of fire due to the trees, the rolling hills offered areas where her Galaxy could maneuver out of sight.

She hated this assignment. Her Galaxy had been sent on a long sweep north—away from the action to the south, where Malvina suspected the Wolves would try to flank the Falcons' main body.

This is punishment, Chistu thought. *We are being marched out to the wilderness in hopes that we will either play no part in the battle with the Wolves or be wiped out.*

The Chingis Khan proved an insurmountable obstacle. *Malvina has always hated me for my failure to take Coventry, and throwing her own orders back in her face. She would have had me use nuclear weapons and kill many thousands in her name.* And with Alaric fostering even more animosity between her and her Khan, Chistu knew her life depended on this Trial. *If Malvina wins, she will kill me...I am sure of it. If Clan Wolf wins, chances are I will die in the battle.*

Malvina could have challenged her to a Trial of Grievance at any time and killed her, but Chistu knew she was only alive because Malvina did not want to ignite any more infighting within the Jade Falcon ranks. *She would rather see me utterly fail, be defeated, and die at the hands of our enemy. My death would prove to others that my ideals are the wrong ones.* Her current prospects were daunting, but not insurmountable. *I have always found a path to victory. I will this time, too.*

A flicker appeared on her sensors, a crimson triangle on her tactical display. The battle computer logged it as a *Wulfen* A, a light OmniMech. *What is it doing up here?* As soon as her sensors identified the target, the image disappeared.

She paused just before the crest of the hill and opened her Galaxy-wide comm channel. "Delta Galaxy, I have a possible enemy contact. Disperse, Extended Wing formation, centered on me."

"Deploying," came Star Colonel Lisa Hazen's voice. "But so far I have nothing on my screens."

Her sensors had been right, Chistu was sure of that. "Sharp eyes, everyone," she said, bracing herself. "Weapons free."

"Enemy contacts in sector four!" called Star Captain Kaor from the Fifth Battle Cluster.

Chistu saw the signals light up on her sensors. "Kaor, demonstration fire. Get them to close on you. The rest of you, prepare to execute Exalted Wings."

The fight broke out a half kilometer away as Kaor's Cluster opened fire. The rest of her force, mostly behind the rising hills, let the Fifth Battle Cluster get the Wolves' attention. Chistu watched on her sensors as the Wolf force, at least two Clusters' worth, surged forward.

"Exalted Wings is go!" she barked, and fired her jump jets to rise up and over the hill. She immediately spotted the *Wulfen* that had tipped her off. The other jump-capable Jade Falcons followed her into the air on hot plumes of blue and red thrust.

The *Wulfen*'s extended-range PPC hit her *Jade Hawk* as she landed, washing her canopy in azure energy. The blast melted armor just above her right leg as she unloaded a devastating retort of short-range missiles. The *Wulfen* took more than half of the volley, twisting and contorting under the impacts, then maneuvered into a dense clump of pine trees. Chistu followed and fired blindly into the trees, deliberately raising her heat level. Her 'Mech's triple-strength myomer gave her stunning speed as she charged into the trees and swung wide to the left to come up on the *Wulfen*. She fired her quartet of extended-range small lasers, searing hot holes in the side and arm of the enemy as she ran. The light 'Mech turned and fired again; its brilliant blue stream of charged particles missed, igniting several pines.

Chistu gave her enemy no quarter, rushing it on a collision course. A wave of her short-range missiles hit the *Wulfen*, throwing off entire plates of armor and sending it staggering. Its armor crumpled as the 'Mech tottered back from the sudden charge. It lowered its stance as if about to run, but a row of thick pines hemmed it in, making it pause.

That hesitation was all Chistu needed. Firing her jump jets again, she landed directly in its path. She punched it with both arms, stabbing titanium claws into the damaged armor. One blow shredded the right-side armor, while her left punch went deeper and tore into the *Wulfen*'s gyro housing, sending a shower of sparks up her forearm.

The *Wulfen* staggered and fell. She kicked the hole in its side, a devastating blow that plowed into the 'Mech's fusion reactor. The Wolf pilot popped the canopy and emerged with her assault rifle aimed at Chistu's cockpit. She emptied the magazine, but the bullets hit harmlessly, ricocheting off the ferroglass canopy with little more than the patter of a rainy downpour.

Brave—and foolish. Malvina created this, with her take-no-prisoners approach. It only inspires the enemy to fight on, even when they are already defeated. Chistu swung one of her small lasers in the direction of the warrior and fired. There was a beam of light—then no sign of the warrior but a blast of smoke.

The ground rumbled as the earthbound 'Mech in her force rushed toward her position and engaged the Wolves emerging from the forest. *This must be it...the major thrust Malvina expected.*

She spotted a tan-and-gray Wolf Epona tank drive through thick pine trees, blazing away at her and another Jade Falcon behind her. A pulse laser left a string of hot holes along the upper body of her *Jade Hawk* as Chistu turned toward it.

It is only a tank... Where is the rest of Alaric's flanking attack?

THUNDER BAY
1930 HOURS

Star Commander Parac Shaw took cover in the cold scrubland off the shore of Lake Superior. Darkness was setting in, necessitating the use of the night-vision system in his battle armor. A Jade Falcon *Gyrfalcon* was blasting at his Bane Star with its pair of LB-X autocannons. The explosive shells blew rocks and sand all over Parac's dark-gray Elemental armor as Stroud took a violent hit in the chest and went flailing backward behind a low sand dune.

Shaw fired his short-range missiles into the hulking *Gyrfalcon*, blasting a pair of pockmarks on the light-green armor. Jac did the same, and hit it in the left side of the cockpit, drawing the Jade Falcon's attention. *Jac is moving better with his new leg*, Shaw noted.

"Bane Star, fan out," he barked.

Shaw shifted to the right and fired his small laser into the leg of the enemy BattleMech. Stroud rose and fired his laser as well, which seared a diagonal burn mark on the *Gyrfalcon*'s upper body.

On paper, their mission was simple. They had moved along the shore of Like Superior and established a beachhead. At the same time, a contingent from Zeta Galaxy was moving underwater along the coast of the lake; they had a mission inland, behind enemy lines, one Parac knew little about. Kalidessa

Kerensky had simply told him, "We need someone to hold the beach for Zeta's attack and withdrawal. Your Star is to go in first, behind the Falcons' lines, and force that beachhead open. However, this will not be an easy assignment. If it were easy, you would not have gotten it." Such was life in the Howling Furies.

When Bane Star had emerged from the thick forest in the dark, they had stumbled into a Jade Falcon patrol.

The *Gyrfalcon* pilot fired their right-arm ER large laser. The brilliant red beam stabbed into Kobler's left leg, taking the limb off in a smoky wisp. Kobler howled in pain over the communications channel, and his status indicator on Shaw's tiny tactical display went offline, meaning he was gravely injured...or worse.

Shaw ignored it; he had to, or he would share his Pointmate's fate. "Alpha Point, swarm that *surat!*" he commanded, activating his jump jets with his thumb control. "The rest of you, take down that *Turkina*, and be quick about it."

The other three members of his Point leaped toward the *Gyrfalcon*, firing with short-range missiles, lasers, and flamers. The 'Mech tried to swat at Shaw, but missed. Instead, the Elemental collided hard with the partial wings assembly that fanned out on the *Gyrfalcon*'s back, jarring every joint in his body. In a flurry of jabs with his suit's battle claw, he found a handhold just behind the 'Mech's raptor-shaped head. Jabbing his laser right on the surface of the armor, he fired and melted a glowing-hot hole there.

Shaw saw Jac clinging like a tick on the 'Mech's right arm, just as it began to spin around in an attempt to throw off the Elementals. He felt the pull of centrifugal force as the whirling *Gyrfalcon* picked up speed. Jac held firm with his claw and clumsily fired his laser at the Falcon 'Mech, scoring a few hits. One member of Shaw's Star, Eris, came into view as she held onto the 'Mech below him, her legs flying around as she clung tight. *The Tutuola blood in her runs true!*

Then the *Gyrfalcon* fired its jump jets, taking the clinging Elementals into the air with it. Jac lost his grip, but managed to fire his suit's leg jets before landing. For a millisecond, Shaw's body came back down near the hole he had started. He jabbed his arm-mounted laser in and fired another sustained beam. Splatters of melted metal hit the exterior of his battle armor, but he ignored it.

He saw the faint outline of the *Turkina* in the darkness, framed by the dozen or more of his Elementals that were systematically ripping it apart. That 'Mech also twirled like a dervish, throwing off at least two warriors as the rest on the ground poured laser fire into it.

His own target, the *Gyrfalcon,* dropped down hard, and the jarring impact strained every muscle in Shaw's body. Warrior Eris lost her grip and fell onto her back at the feet of the BattleMech. The Jade Falcon MechWarrior lifted the big, taloned footpad into the air and drove it into Eris like a piledriver. The tactical-display indicator for Eris blinked crimson.

Shaw's ears roared as if filled with thunder. Crawling up across the upper torso, he turned and fired a snap-shot of crimson laser light into the BattleMech's shoulder, searing a black scar into the armor. Turning, Shaw jammed his laser again into the head of the *Gyrfalcon* and blasted. Heat rose, and sparks sprayed out. Rolling black smoke rose as he kept blazing away with everything he had.

The *Gyrfalcon* listed forward and toppled, careening into the dunes and scrub. Shaw went flying forward from the fall and skidded in the sand. He quickly rose to his feet and ran toward the fallen 'Mech while taking another precautionary shot at the head with his laser. Jac came to his side and did the same. The *Gyrfalcon* stilled, and there was no movement at all from the pilot within.

Shaw climbed up onto the cockpit canopy and looked in. He could see light coming in from the hole he had burned. His shot had hit the left shoulder of the warrior in the command console, burning down straight through her heart.

Off to his side, some 100 meters away, the *Turkina* collapsed.

"Jac, check on Kobler," he commanded.

"What about Eris?" Jac asked.

Shaw's hands shook from the rush of adrenaline still coursing in his veins. "She has passed with honor."

Before anyone could respond, the voice of Galaxy Commander Elise Ward came over the communication channel. "Howling Furies, this is Bane Actual. Execute Bloody Paw Retrograde. We form up at the beach."

"We are falling back?" Jac asked Shaw. "I thought we were winning."

A passing *Timber Wolf* unleashed a salvo of long-range missiles at a distant Jade Falcon Shaw could not see. "Our job was to open the beachhead, which we have done. We must trust our Khan."

EAST OF WINNIPEG
18 APRIL 3151, 0030 HOURS
(T+98, DAY 2 OF THE ILCLAN TRIAL)

The lead elements of Zeta Galaxy's Seventy-Ninth Wolf Battle Cluster fanned out in the tree line, linking up with the Ninth Wolf Assault Cluster, just as Star Colonel Skinner had ordered. The shimmer of Star Captain Benno's night-vision system bathed his cockpit interior in an eerie green as he maneuvered his *Hauptmann* through the darkness.

Benno paused to rub his arms. His 'Mech had been *isorla* claimed after combat in the Lyran Commonwealth, and its heater was malfunctioning. The Seventy-Ninth had spent long hours in the ice-cold waters of Lake Superior, moving undetected to the rear of the Jade Falcons lines. The water was so cold that small chunks of ice were floating along the shore when they had emerged. *I must get my tech to fix the cockpit heater before the next mission.* A Star of Beta Galaxy Elementals had opened up the beachhead for them, and now he and his force had their mission to perform.

And as if spending hours in ice-cold water is not enough, now we fight a night engagement. They had arrived late near their objectives, and dawn was more than six hours away. Benno had been operating with night vision in his cockpit, and the two Zeta Galaxy Clusters had managed to avoid contact with the enemy thus far. That would end in a matter of moments...he could feel it. *We did not come all of this way to creep through the dark. We came to wage war.*

"Warriors of the Seventy-Ninth," said Skinner over the comm, "our mission this morning is strategic in nature. One kilometer north is the Falcons' primary supply depot. That is our target. The Ninth Assault will go after their repair and munitions facilities. Between us and them are picket lines of battle armor and light tanks. We are going to hit them hard and fast, target the warehouses and dump sites, then fall back. The minute we open fire, the Jade Falcons will know where we are and descend on us. If we take out these facilities, we will hamstring the Jade Falcons' ability to repair and rearm. Khan Ward expects us to return once we have completed our mission—and that is my intent as well. On my order, we charge—Starving Wolf formation."

Benno nodded, gripping his joystick and throttle. *The waiting is the worst part of an ambush. Just say "go" already.*

"All right then... Seventy-Ninth, attack!"

Benno charged forward, along with his entire Cluster. In the darkness he could not see the trees he knocked down, but he heard them cracking at both sides as the 'Mechs rushed forward.

The moment his *Hauptmann* broke through the trees, a Bellona hovertank lit up on his night vision and quickly roared to life. He fired his LB-X autocannon, and the brilliant flashes of the exploding shells hit the right side of the vehicle as it started to move. Armor flew into the darkness as the hovertank locked onto a *Mad Dog* and fired; the autocannon rounds tore the Wolf OmniMech's leg apart. Benno could not see the missiles in flight, but he saw the detonations on the Jade Falcon tank, which erupted in a brilliant flash that momentarily overpowered his night vision. Somehow the Bellona made a dash across the field, flames lapping behind it as it moved, only to be taken out by a Wolf *Warhammer IIC*.

The two-story warehouse was Benno's objective now, barely outlined except for its heat signature. Once he was within range, he fired his large lasers at the structure. The twin beams shimmered as white lines in his night vision, stabbing into the side of the building. He had already started his Streak missiles' target-lock sequence, and he fired the four warheads the moment he heard missile tone.

Other Wolves from his unit poured fire into transports and other nearby vehicles, blowing them apart. Off to his left, a sandbagged ammo dump erupted, filling the night air with fireworks. Benno moved forward, and his medium pulse lasers easily penetrated the structure as well.

"This is far too easy," he muttered, suspicious of their progress.

As if to emphasize that, a distant explosion from another munitions bunker buffeted the air around his 'Mech. In the distance, he saw an orange ball of flame rising into the air—followed by another a few seconds later from farther away. Bits of the blown bunkers landed in several tall pine trees and set them on fire.

Without warning, a Gauss rifle slug slammed into his *Hauptmann's* right shoulder, and he felt his massive BattleMech reel. *I spoke too soon.* Benno turned and saw his tactical display light up with red triangles.

Dozens of them.

An explosion burst from inside the building Benno had been shooting, but he ignored it.

"It is an entire Jade Falcon Galaxy!" a voice cried over the comm.

"Incoming BattleMechs and tanks!" barked Star Colonel Skinner. "Seventy-Ninth, wheel right! We make our stand here. Bravo Star, provide suppression fire to the front. The rest of you, target those structures. We must take out as many as possible."

As Benno targeted the facility again, he realized he was finally feeling warm.

CHAPTER 28

JADE FALCON PRIMARY SUPPLY POST
EAST OF WINNIPEG, NORTH AMERICA
TERRA
18 APRIL 3151, 0615 HOURS
(T+98, DAY 2 OF THE ILCLAN TRIAL)

In the predawn darkness, Malvina could make out the smoke still rolling up from the rubble of the warehouses, illuminated by a few fires. Her nostrils stung from the smoke, a scent familiar from dozens of battles and dozens of worlds. She stood with one foot propped on the cornerstone of what had been a warehouse. Her warrior togs were just starting to dry in the cool air.

She surveyed the damage critically, bitterly. She was surprised at the amount of damage a lone Wolf Cluster had managed to do, despite being outnumbered. The Wolves had destroyed well over two-thirds of her ammunition reserves. The repair depots and bays had been hit, but not as badly. Still, everything lost could not be easily replaced. *As it is, we have already had to salvage a large number of Republic BattleMechs to replace our losses.*

Galaxy Commander Clarence Pryde of Rho Galaxy approached her, also still in his coolant vest. "Very few Wolves managed to extract themselves once we surrounded them, Chingis Khan," he said. "They clearly were not expecting us to have this large of a force here."

But Malvina had expected them to attack. She had studied Alaric Ward carefully, thanks to the Watch's intelligence reports. She knew he would strike her primary logistics hub. *What I did not count on was them using Lake Superior to mask their approach—or their near-suicidal defiance and last stand that allowed them to take out so many important structures here. If this Trial persists, I will need those supplies. But I have no intention of allowing that to happen.*

"I thought 'this large of a force here' could have taken the Wolves apart before they destroyed our warehouses," she said coolly, eyeing a building where a fire crew still was at work.

"We did not anticipate them coming from the lake," Pryde said nervously, rubbing the stubble of his black beard as he spoke. "We reacted swiftly and destroyed those that stood their ground. Star Colonel Skinner, who led them, was tenacious in his last stand."

"Did he live?"

"*Neg*," Pryde responded. "We followed your orders. No Wolf prisoners."

Malvina nodded. "Good. Still, we lost a great deal of equipment and munitions here."

Pryde squared his shoulders. "Chingis Khan, I have failed you. If you seek to strip me of my command, I understand. All I ask is that you allow me to die in this battle. Our future is at stake."

Fear rang in every word he spoke. Malvina was used to it, she appreciated it. *Fear is a form of respect.*

She looked away from the rubble to study Clarence Pryde. She appreciated that he showed her the respect she was due, and that he admitted his mistakes. Far too many Jade Falcons, especially from the Pryde bloodline, tended to be stubborn until their bitter end. *This one, however, has potential.* "*Neg*, Galaxy Commander. All I require is that you do not fail me again."

Pryde bowed his head and departed.

We have lost a great deal, she thought. Replacement parts could be salvaged, as could some ammunition—it would be enough to see them through, if it came to that. *But it will not come to that. I intend to finish this today, tomorrow at the latest.*

She had hoped to destroy the Wolves by now, but Alaric was not making it easy, as the Wolf Khan had failed to commit to an all-out assault. Her positioning of troops on the flanks had blunted his attempts to encircle her there. *I knew you would try that, Alaric.* She had thrown four Galaxies into the center of the line, rushing through the hills and thick forests, slamming into the Wolves. Three times her forces had hit and deliberately fallen back to lure in the Wolves, and three times they were denied.

The Wolves did not want to be drawn in en masse. If they had been, Malvina would have flanked them, cut them off, and killed them. It would have been a glorious victory, but Alaric was proving to be a cunning Wolf. He seemed to sense what she was trying to do, and had ordered his officers to hold back. *He did not come at me as I expected...despite all of my threats. I presumed he would want a quick victory. I will not underestimate him again.*

Her wrist communicator chirped, and she raised it to her lips. "Proceed."

"Chingis Khan, this is Star Captain Jakapan of the Watch. We are picking up indications that the Wolves are adjusting their lines. Beta Galaxy is moving to the south, and Tau is taking its place in line."

"Acknowledged," she replied. "What of these new BattleMechs we are getting reports of?"

"We have seen three thus far," Jakapan replied. "We have been relaying their configurations and known weapon loadouts into updates to our battle computers."

"Where did Alaric get them? We have operatives in the Wolf Empire. None spoke of new BattleMechs being built in their factories."

"*Aff*, Chingis Khan, so I have learned. But from what I have gleaned, we believe Clan Sea Fox may have manufactured these new 'Mechs for Clan Wolf."

Malvina's foot slipped off the cornerstone as fury rushed through her. *There will be a reckoning if the Sea Foxes have aided Alaric. Once I rule all of the Clans, their Khans will pay for their scheming.*

She took a breath to calm herself. "What was the damage assessment on Alaric's HQ?"

"The Wolves have maintained air superiority since the attack. The battle-damage assessments indicated near-misses. That does not mean they were utter failures, though."

"That is wishful thinking on your part, Star Captain," she snapped. "Not what I want or expect from a Watch Commander. Look to your predecessor and consider your reports carefully." She had lost Abzug Helmer and several of his subordinates, forcing her to promote Star Captain Jakapan, a junior officer, to her new Watch Commander. She loathed to admit that she missed Helmer, but Jakapan's work had only marginally pleased her so far. *Fear will motivate him.*

"I will correct that going forward, Chingis Khan," Jakapan replied.

Malvina cut him off by switching to her command channel on the communicator.

She headed back to her *Shrike*, stomping through the ashes, leaving a cloud in her wake. The embers and remaining fires warmed the cold morning air around her. *Today's fight will be critical and should be the end of this trial. I need to force Alaric to commit his Clan. He was wary yesterday, sensing a trap. When we fell back, our losses were not convincing enough to make him think the retreats were indeed genuine. I will change that.*

Alaric likes to believe he is the smartest person on the battlefield. He thinks he has outfoxed me. We will hit him hard, take losses, then fall back. If we can engage them hard enough, his field commanders may respond before he can rein them in. But to make this work, I have to bait a big enough trap to justify the losses. More importantly, to lure him in, I must make him believe that it is his *idea rather than mine.*

Malvina paused at the footpad of *Black Rose*, looking up at the replacement armor plates—which now outnumbered the original ones. *Sacrifices will need to be made so Alaric thinks he is winning. Real Jade Falcon warriors understand this. We cannot afford to engage in a sustained campaign. He knows that, or he never would have risked so much to attack our supplies and munitions.*

She climbed the ladder toward her cockpit. From up here, she could see the coming sunrise. A plan began to ferment in her mind, and at the top of her 'Mech she activated her command channel.

"Star Commander Heath, I need you to assemble our heavy transports and a Cluster of *solahma* troops. Have them gather up all of the petrocycline we have in storage and meet me in Sector Charlie."

"As you wish, Chingis Khan," Heath replied.

She grinned as she climbed into *Black Rose*. *I will draw the Wolves into a trap that will cost them dearly, one Alaric will never expect.*

CHAPTER 29

WEST OF OTTAWA, NORTH AMERICA
TERRA
18 APRIL 3151, 1140 HOURS
(T+98, DAY 2 OF THE ILCLAN TRIAL)

The battle had raged since the break of dawn, with the Jade Falcons throwing four Galaxies at the center of the Wolf battle line. Alaric had been mentally prepared for it, his warriors had been as ready as possible, but the ferocious assault had stunned even the most battle-hardened Wolves. Gaps had opened in the front, and the Jade Falcons exploited them, rushing forces into the rear areas.

So far Alaric had resisted the urge to be at the front directly, but he had been operating in the second line of battle, trying to catch those that broke through while still directing his entire Clan.

The few Falcons that penetrated the lines ignored other Wolves and drove at him directly. The first time it happened, he flashed back to the death of Ramiel Bekker and the assassination attempt. He doubted Malvina was sending warriors to headhunt him, for he was a prized target for any Jade Falcon.

A fast-moving green-and-gray *Eyrie* burst through a cluster of pines and angled toward him the moment he had been spotted. As the light 'Mech ran circles around his *Savage Wolf* and chipped at both his armor and patience with its micro lasers, Alaric fired a fusillade of eighteen advanced tactical missiles into it. Five of the ATMs slammed into the Jade Falcon's right leg and blasted it off. The *Eyrie* fell forward as its MechWarrior tried to fire their jump jets. Given the angle and timing of the fall, all it did was drag the 'Mech along the ground to slam headfirst into a nearby hillside.

Behind Alaric, twenty meters back, was Tara Wolf—in the cockpit of a *Sun Cobra*. Having her back there gave him a sense of comfort. *The only way she will learn how to be a Wolf warrior is to be a Wolf warrior.*

Tara brought her 'Mech's pair of Gauss rifles onto a green-and-tan Jade Falcon *Cougar* that was following the path the *Eyrie* had made. Both shots slammed into the *Cougar* and blasted apart its fusion reactor. There was a flash, and the 'Mech's gutted remains poured out onto the ground. As the metal carcass fell, it crushed a thick pine and rained bits of armor down on the lush spring grass.

"It seems every Jade Falcon wants the honor of taking you down," Tara said, moving up alongside of him.

"Indeed." The Wolf Khan swung his 'Mech around, looking for another target, but the Falcons had faded back out of range. The morning had seen a series of vicious Falcon assaults, each one repulsed, each one costly. For a moment, there seemed to be a lull around them.

Malvina is throwing her forces right at us, ripping small holes in the lines. I expected larger penetrations like this yesterday...not today. Why now?

1245 HOURS

General Chance Vickers hovered over the holomap at the latest aerial reconnaissance feeds. Initially she thought the Jade Falcon thrusts were uncoordinated, but a pattern was emerging. They kept driving into the Wolves' center with a certain degree of precision. Some units would continue on to the second line of defenses, but often the Falcons wheeled about, hit the Wolf front lines again, then rushed back toward their own lines.

The reaction of the field commanders was to advance in small pursuits, shifting the entire line in tiny thrusts. Bit by bit, the Wolves were moving westward without even realizing it. *Our system of honor compels warriors to complete their victories.*

As she looked at the holomap, one thing became clear. In the jumble of units from both sides, the Wolf forces were indeed advancing. *Our commanders at the front are responding to individual attacks, not quite seeing the big picture.* Slowly, almost methodically, the three Wolf Galaxies in the center were being drawn forward by the Falcons' rushed onslaughts, penetrations, and retreats.

She turned to Jathniel Kerensky, the communications officer. "Put me through to the Galaxy Commanders of Upsilon, Iota, and Theta."

The officer worked her keyboard, then cocked her head aside with a look of puzzlement.

"What is it?" Chance asked.

"We are getting a lot of ECM interference, General," Jathniel replied. "Heavy jamming of comm traffic. I am having difficulties reaching our forward forces."

Jamming? The Falcons would only be jamming if they did not want us to communicate...

An icy resolve washed over her in that moment. Her eyes darted down to the holomap. "Get me Kalidessa Kerensky...her Furies are between us and them."

Jathniel nodded. "The Star Colonel is up."

Above the holomap, the three-dimensional face of Kalidessa Kerensky appeared. Her black neurohelmet faceplate flickered red and orange from the light inside her cockpit. "General Vickers—we have a problem here, a *big* one..."

1255 HOURS

"Alaric," Chance said over the communications channel, "we have an emergency."

She rarely used his first name over the comm. *This is serious.* "Proceed," Alaric said.

"Look westward. Do you see smoke on the horizon?"

Alaric did, and his stomach immediately tightened. A black smear darkened the purple cloudy skies off to the west. Smoke—a great deal of smoke. It stretched across his whole field of vision north to south, toward the Jade Falcons. A low rumble in the distance, like thunder, grew in intensity. *What has Malvina done?*

"The situation is as follows. Bombers dropped a carpet of inferno gel and incendiaries between your position and our forward three Galaxies, on a north-south axis, and they have ignited a wall of fire over two kilometers thick all around our forwardmost elements by seeding the ground with flammable materials. Most of Upsilon, Theta, and Iota Galaxies are completely cut off and taking artillery fire. I have a recon flight over them now...and it does not look good."

"Call them out of there now," he commanded.

"The Falcons have blanketed the area with an intense ECM field. I am sure our warriors are trying to fall back, but the Falcon bombers keep making new passes, lighting up more of the forest between them and us."

"Get our fighters in there."

"Inbound," she replied crisply. "Our CAP got pulled to the south to intercept a series of strafing attacks there. We should have local air superiority over our forces in a few minutes."

"*Stravag!*" Alaric spat. He moved his *Savage Wolf* toward the wall of white and gray smoke that seemed to rise even higher as he advanced. "Chance, get the construction and forestry 'Mechs from Ottawa ASAP. We are going to need them."

His jaw clenched as he heard the distant rumble of artillery. *Malvina is a worthy enemy indeed.*

THE CAULDRON
1325 HOURS

The Jade Falcon fighters had made their latest firebombing run minutes earlier, this time directly over the trapped Wolf forces, all the easier since they had doused the trees and the bed of pine needles with accelerant. Now the region within the thick wall of raging forest fire, which Star Commander Noran Kerensky had dubbed "the Cauldron," was a scene from hell itself. The Wolf CAP showed up and chased the Falcon bombers off, but the damage was already done.

Fire now surrounded the three Wolf Galaxies. But the flames were only part of the trap the Falcons had set. Their artillery had massed behind a curtain of burning pines kilometers to their rear and were executing fire missions on the trapped Wolves, turning the interior pocket of the Cauldron into a literal hell of hot shrapnel, smoke, and death. Each passing minute, the ring of fire grew smaller, tighter, and the artillery was unceasing. The wall of flames between the trapped Wolves' position and the rest of their Clan was so thick that the few 'Mechs that tried running through the fire reported shutting down in the furnace-like conditions, never reaching safety. The flames were so hot that moisture in the ground rose up like mist, mixing with the smoke and filling the area with a dense haze.

Noran Kerensky felt the deep vibrations of an artillery round go off near him. Bits of blasted trees and shrapnel littered his *Executioner*'s cockpit canopy, the charred debris still smoking. A thick, gray haze of smoke hung around him, with bits of ash whipping by. The distant artillery, too far away to neutralize, was killing the Wolves with each salvo. *This is no fight—this is a slaughter.*

He saw a *Linebacker* B suddenly explode as its long-range missiles cooked off. Even with CASE, the explosion inflicted damage the internal structure could not withstand. The 'Mech fell over, collapsing in the middle of a burning cluster of pines. An artillery shell slammed into a Wolf Carnivore tank, hitting its turret dead center. The turret caved inward, and the tank burst into flames, the crew never getting a chance to evacuate. *If the flames do not kill us, the artillery will.*

"Wolf Fang Actual," Noran said on the command channel, hoping to reach Star Colonel Hope of the Twenty-Ninth Wolf Garrison Cluster. "This is Lockjaw Leader." Another nearby explosion rained more dirt on his BattleMech.

"Wolf Fang Actual is down, so is Wolf Fang Two," said a woman's voice—deep and commanding. "This is Star Captain Dukes."

Another nearby explosion rattled Noran's 'Mech with shrapnel. "Any word on that relief column?"

"*Neg*," Dukes said grimly. "With all of the jamming, I only received every other word. I assume we are on our own."

Another thunderous blast of artillery fire fell farther down the line, shaking Noran in his own cockpit. "We cannot stay here, Star Captain."

"Do you have a plan, Lockjaw Leader, or are you just complaining?"

"Their artillery is situated to the west, behind the fire wall."

"*Aff.* And the Falcons have massed on the flanks. Iota tried to punch through, but the enemy is entrenched outside the wall of fire and were ready for them. Iota was so hot from the flames they could not bring enough firepower to bear to make a dent in the Falcon formation."

They are waiting. Once they have whittled us down, once the flames start to subside, they will come and finish us off.

"We cannot stay here," Noran insisted. "We have no idea how many kilometers of forest are burning between us and the Jade Falcon artillery, but remaining here is certain death. I suggest taking a force through the fire to our front. If we can get to that artillery, we can buy ourselves some time."

"Go into that oven and you will be cooking off your ammo before you get a half kilometer in. Even if you dump your ammo, you risk overheating and shutdown."

"If we stay here, we will die. This is not how I planned on going out, roasted and blasted. Let me take a Trinary of 'Mechs. We can try weathering the heat, and with those flames, the Falcons will never see us coming. We take out that artillery and wait for the Khan to come for us."

There was a pause before Dukes replied. "All right, Lockjaw—take three Stars. Find that artillery and take it out."

"We will not fail," he promised.

Noran barked out commands, and his forces assembled despite the barrage.

Without orders, three Elementals from the Wolf Rangers Star started climbing up his *Executioner*, grabbing onto handholds.

"Tapscott," Noran commed, "what are you doing?"

"We are going with you," the Elemental said as he grabbed onto the skull-like cockpit of the OmniMech.

"But I am going *into* the fire," Noran replied.

"I am well aware. We have lost two *sibmates* to the artillery so far, and we would rather take our chances with the fire," he said. "I have no intention of dying here. Our suits are fire-resistant, we will live."

"Very well," said Noran. "Then we will walk through hell together. Wolves, follow me, single file. When we hit open ground, we have to take out that artillery. Every piece we destroy saves lives in this hellish Cauldron."

WEST OF OTTAWA
1400 HOURS

General Vickers watched the fire brigade fight their own war against the inferno. The plan was not to completely extinguish the forest fire, but to cut a pathway to the trapped Wolves so they could get out. The ring of flames was over two kilometers thick and growing each time the wind blew.

Frustration tore at her. *This is taking too long. We warned our forces to not overextend—that Malvina favored traps. One of this scale speaks volumes to her tactical prowess.* Chance did not respect Malvina Hazen, but even she had to acknowledge the planning and execution of such a plan.

ConstructionMechs and bulldozers moved earth out of the way while ForestryMechs cleared trees and FireMechs poured on flame retardant that consumed the blaze in 1,000-square-meter swaths. Several of the fire brigade's IndustrialMechs had gotten stuck in the wet soil, which added to the delays. Also, a number of Jade Falcons on the Wolf side of the fire had emerged at one point, destroying one of the heavy CargoMech haulers before the Wolves eradicated the raiding force.

Progress was slow, and she could feel the heat even from inside the cockpit of her *Savage Wolf*. Even if a pocket of fire was contained, it was likely to flare up again because the dense pine forests and thick beds of winter needles on the ground were dry tinder just waiting to catch.

"Push forward!" she commanded.

"General," came a transmission from a *solahma* warrior at the front line. "We are about to burst into flames ourselves up here."

"I do not care," she growled back. "Good warriors are fighting and dying up there. Keep going!"

Wolf aerospace fighters had been making bombing runs on the Jade Falcons hovering at the edge of the fire zone, in case they opted to rush into the flames to finish off the trapped Wolves. The Falcon CAP over their artillery park had prevented the Wolves from stopping the endless barrage, though they had hit the Falcons' ground forces hard. And the artillery continued whittling away at three Galaxies of Wolves; those who avoided the Falcon artillery were roasting alive.

For the first time in the campaign, Vickers felt helpless. She watched water trucks, including some commandeered from Ottawa, pull up and their crews start uncoiling hoses. *This will be difficult for us to recover from.*

White smoke rolled past her cockpit canopy, momentarily blocking her field of vision. Against the raging wall of fire, all of this effort simply did not seem enough.

JADE FALCON FORWARD FIRE BATTERY ALPHA
1415 HOURS

Despite the heat sinks and environmental controls, walking through such a long stretch of raging fire made Noran Kerensky's *Executioner* feel like the inside of a blast furnace. Two of the BattleMechs in his task force had fallen during the trek so far; the ammunition in one had cooked off, and another had suffered heat-sink failure. Neither of those MechWarriors ejected. They simply succumbed to the flames.

The Elementals were faring better. Their suits were well insulated and resistant to the flames for short periods of time. But even now, he was sure they were near dehydration from the oven-like conditions. *None of our equipment is built to withstand fires like this.*

When he and his Stars came to a fresh earthwork berm, a firebreak half as tall as his BattleMech, he saw that the flames had burned out in this place, though the ground was still searing hot. A sound caught his ear: the rumble of Jade Falcon artillery launching on the other side of the berm.

"All right, you charred Wolves, nothing fancy," Noran said as he angled his 'Mech up the steep incline. "Rush in and take out the artillery. Every one of these launchers we take down saves lives."

Weary "*affs*" came back, but the task force's 'Mechs followed him.

As Noran crested the berm, he saw it the artillery park: a dozen Thumper artillery launchers, their tubes angled skyward. On the flanks were four Gurzil fire-support tanks, armed with missiles and 'Mech mortars. They roared as they fired round after round, rocking backward from the recoil.

Raising his left arm, Noran heard the capacitors in his Gauss rifle start to hum. With keen precision, he shot a round at the lead Gurzil; the slug plowed a deep crater into the turret. Then he rushed forward, stabbing a pair of laser beams into the tank.

He ignored the heat—in fact, his cockpit no longer seemed hot, given that he had waded through a forest fire. Licking his cracked lips, he rushed to the lead Gurzil and kicked it hard, crushing its right-front tread assembly in the process. Machine guns sprayed his 'Mech, but he ignored them.

The Elementals fired their jump jets and landed on the adjacent tank, firing their machine guns and ripping at hatches. Noran watched as Tapscott, the paint on his armor blackened and peeling from the flames, ripped off a hatch and poured laser fire into the bowels of the vehicle. *No quarter—not after what they have done to us.*

As the rest of the charred Wolves arrived at the fight, a raging howl filled the communications channel. The battle raged for several minutes as the few surviving Thumper launchers attempted to break off, then signaled for support.

As Jade Falcon infantry and battle armor arrived, Noran Kerensky faced a difficult prospect. Stand, fight, and die—or face the flames again. He gave the order, and his attack force fell back into hot, glowing hell of the Cauldron.

THE CAULDRON
1420 HOURS

Star Commander Manning looked down at the orange circle of flames and was in awe at the scale of destruction Clan Jade Falcon had unleashed. At this altitude, the smoke dissipated enough for him realize how desperate the situation on the ground was.

Between the dark purple clouds rolling in, he saw huge fire breaks cut into the forests and behind them, masses of Jade Falcon BattleMechs and tanks poised to rush in. Off to the west, he saw the Wolves cutting a pathway into the flames, but they were still far from breaking through to the other side of the fire.

In the middle of the inferno, he could see a staggering number of downed and destroyed Wolf tanks and BattleMechs amid the craters and pockets of fire that still burned. The fire and artillery had destroyed a massive amount of the three Galaxies caught in the Jade Falcons' trap. They had died without honor.

He felt worse for the tankers: BattleMechs and Elementals could endure some fire, but tanks became little more than semi-mobile crematoriums for their crews. The heat alone had taken out a lot of the Wolf equipment there, and what the fires did not get, the artillery did. It made Manning's stomach knot to see the carnage.

"Ravagers, keep alert," he said, diving his *Jagatai* down. "I have to get down there and see if I can penetrate the ECM." He switched to an open Wolf channel and began to transmit. "This is Ravager One, to any Wolf unit in the fire zone. Ravager One, to any Wolf unit—

His voice was cut off through the hiss of ECM with a snap and crackle of an open comms link: "Ravager One, this is Wolf Fang Actual, Dukes speaking. We could use some help down here..."

Manning stabbed his fingers at the transmit button. "Help is on the way, but you have to get to it. I am transmitting coordinates of a relief corridor for your evac. Also, be warned, the Falcons have massed at the edges of the fire zone. When the flames start to die down, you are going to have company—a lot of it."

"Roger that, Ravager One," Dukes replied, her voice weary. "We appreciate the assist."

Manning banked his fighter in a tight spin over the fire zone, through the haze of smoke. "Wolf Fang, we will try to narrow the odds for you. Head for those coordinates and get out of there." He switched to his tactical channel. "Ravager Star, commence strafing runs on the Falcons at the edge of the zone. It might not be much, but maybe we can buy our ground troops a few minutes."

1440 HOURS

Star Commander Caldwell swung his *Firestorm* around on the Jade Falcon *Mad Dog* and took off its right leg at the knee with his plasma rifle. The Falcon toppled over into a crater and crumpled its missile rack on impact. A fast-moving *Loki Mk II* immediately replaced the *Mad Dog* and shot Caldwell in the chest with a Gauss rifle slug. The *Firestorm* reeled backward from the hit, nearly stumbling over a blown-up Wolf *Ice Ferret*.

The artillery barrages had ceased for several long minutes—giving the forces in the Cauldron some momentary relief—only to be replaced with a surge of Jade Falcons pouring in from the north and southwest. Caldwell had volunteered to be the rear guard, to help evacuate the last few Wolves from the charred hellscape, then the Jade Falcons had stormed in for the final kill.

The heat in the Cauldron was still unbearable, but the flame were subsiding, replaced with beds of glowing white-and-orange coals as far as the eye could see. Flames still lapped at the sky in some areas, and the air rippled with heat all around, but Caldwell chose to ignore all of it. His cockpit had never been this hot for this long, and he struggled with a throbbing headache.

He fired his plasma rifle at the *Loki Mk II,* and the yellow plume of superheated plasma washed across it, some splattering on the cockpit canopy. *Let us see how* you *like a taste of the heat...*

The Falcon MechWarrior returned fire with their large lasers, both searing away Caldwell's armor plating. Caldwell recovered and sprinted his *Firestorm* to the right, then juked the left, triggering his plasma rifle and ER medium laser into the light-green *Loki Mk II*. The plasma blast seared the Falcon's armor just as Caldwell was hit by a spray of long-range missiles from the *Mad Dog* that had managed to right itself.

Something else also pelted his cockpit canopy. Not shrapnel or debris, but—raindrops. They sizzled as they landed. There was a rumble—dull and long, and a crack of lightning split the sky. Rain poured down, and his charred *Firestorm* began steaming.

There may yet be hope for us.

His medium lasers took off the *Mad Dog*'s one remaining leg at the hip and sent the 'Mech furrowing face-first into the ash and dirt. Then the *Loki Mk II*, now coping with the heat the pilot had been struggling with for what seemed like an eternity, lined up its arms, tracking him for another shot.

Then suddenly, from the shimmering wall of heat, a charred-black *Executioner* emerged, with Elementals clinging to it, their paint blackened. Caldwell's IFF tagged the OmniMech as Lockjaw Leader, and it came up behind the *Loki Mk II*.

The Elementals fired their jets and leaped toward Caldwell's target as the *Executioner* placed a Gauss rifle slug through the Falcon's thin rear armor. The *Loki Mk II* lurched forward under the surprise assault just as the *Executioner* fired its pair of large lasers. The crimson beams stabbed deep. The *Loki Mk II* took a wobbly step forward, then fell over into the hot coals, sending sparks and ashes into the air when it landed.

Caldwell transmitted on the tight-beam to his comrade. "Thank you for the assistance."

"*Aff*, you are welcome," Star Commander Noran Kerensky said, his voice weary and exhausted. "Please tell me someone has a way out of this hell."

Caldwell managed a smile in his neurohelmet. "We are falling back. Follow me and I will get you out of here."

WEST OF OTTAWA
1515 HOURS

The spring thunderstorm was a gift, and Chance Vickers was thankful for it.

Her teams had evacuated nearly all of the trapped Wolf forces via the thin roadway they had cut into the Cauldron. The survivors from the fiery hell had rushed through the smoldering flames to the south to follow their narrow path out to safety. Few of the Wolves that began in the Cauldron had emerged.

Even with the steady sheets of rain, the ground was still hot from the fires. An ethereal fog-like smoke hung heavy in the air, smothering the dead and dying. Chance sat in her *Savage Wolf*, prepared to provide cover should the Jade Falcons opt to use her rescue roadway as an avenue of attack. Slowly she realized the Falcons were not coming. *They do not have to. They have inflicted massive losses already.*

The last of the Wolves to emerge from the Cauldron were the worst she had seen, their 'Mechs so black from the fires that it looked as if they had been painted a dull, flat black on purpose. Gray ash clung to every crevice on the surface of the *Executioner* that emerged. Riding high atop its shoulders were two Elementals, so covered with black soot that not even the rain could wash it away. She angled her *Savage Wolf* to get a view through the haze obscuring the burned area, but could see nothing.

"Sitrep," she asked the *Executioner*'s MechWarrior, whose IFF transponder read simply as "Lockjaw Leader."

"Star Commander Noran Kerensky reporting in, General," the pilot said, weary. "We are the last, all that remains of the rear guard. I have three warriors in my cockpit, and we all need medical attention."

"Your BattleMech is badly damaged," Chance said.

"The price of taking out the Jade Falcon artillery. We destroyed their artillery reserve, at great loss. I have been through the flames four times today."

"You took out the artillery, *quiaff*?"

"*Aff*," Noran said.

Vickers was impressed. "You will be remembered for your actions this day."

"Thank you, General. If it is all the same to you, I would like some cold water. Then I want revenge."

1915 HOURS

The rain subsided outside the Clan Wolf mobile headquarters as twilight set in. With the thick cloud cover, it was dark earlier that the previous night. The smell of burned wood permeated the air.

Alaric Ward paced around the holotable, studying the map. Chance stood at one end, saying nothing. Along the far interior wall, Tara Wolf watched as well. The former Northwind Highlander usually simply observed him, but this evening he saw she was studying the map as well. *A lifetime of service has become instinct for her. I must use that in the fight to come.*

Another officer stood with the Wolves—Star Admiral Haake Sukhanov. He had taken a shuttle down from the *McKenna's Pride* three days ago, insisting that Alaric allow him to pilot a BattleMech or an aerospace fighter in the trial. His presence gave everyone some degree of comfort. Haake always brought an energy to a room that had been missed with the passing of Ramiel Bekker.

"Give me the battle damage assessment, General."

"Upsilon, Theta, and Iota suffered seventy-two percent losses in the Cauldron," Chance said. "We have shattered command structures as a result. I am reorganizing them as best I can so that we retain some form of command and control."

"How did the forest catch fire so fast?"

"It appears Malvina planted barrels of flammables in the area just ahead of her initial advance, so when the bombs started dropping, they ignited the trap. The Jade Falcons pressed us hard, but we held the line at the Cauldron." Vickers squared her shoulders. "I have failed you, sir, at the cost of three Galaxies."

Alaric offered her a very thin smile. "This was not your fault, Chance. We are dealing with a cunning strategist. Malvina planned her trap well. Rather than try to take on our whole Clan at once, she opted to weaken us. She used penetrating attacks to lure us into small advances without even realizing it. Frankly, *I* should have seen it coming. These losses are not on your head. I am the Khan; the responsibility falls to me." *If not for that rainstorm, our losses might have been worse. Perhaps destiny has decreed that we live to fight another day.*

"Some good did come from this," Chance said. "I met with Star Commander Noran, who led the assault on the Jade Falcon artillery. They took out all of the Falcons' artillery reserve—two large battery parks."

Alaric nodded. "And we took out a great deal of her expendables, based on the report from Star Captain Benno of the Seventy-Ninth Wolf Battle Cluster, so the raid last night was a success. Costly, but a success. Not to mention the damage done to her technician caste."

Benno had reported that a Jade Falcon Galaxy had defended the supply base, so Alaric had lost nearly two Clusters to hit those facilities. He did not like phrases like "acceptable losses," but he knew that raid had dealt Malvina a major blow.

He looked at the map again. "Let us not dwell on what happened today, but instead look to the future."

"Can we recover from this?" Tara asked. "You have lost three Galaxies."

"*We* have," Chance said, a less-than-subtle reminder that Tara was a bondsman of the Wolves. "And we can and will recover from this."

She moved around the holomap, stalking the image. "We fought longer than Malvina expected, which likely disrupted her timeline. Our lines are confused and broken after the battle of the Cauldron, so she will likely redeploy her Galaxies during the night. Tomorrow she will come with everything she has. She no longer has an artillery reserve, and by now, their ammunition should be running low due to Zeta's raid." She looked up from the map and smiled. "Malvina thinks she has the upper hand because we have lost more forces than she has. She will smell blood and think us a wounded animal, ripe for the kill."

Alaric's smile broadened. "A mistake, to be sure. A wounded Wolf is more dangerous than any other. Send out the order: all worthy bondsmen are to be made *abtakha* of the Clan this night." He glanced at Tara, then waved her closer. She said nothing, but her eyes were wide.

Alaric continued, "Equip them with whatever we have in the reserve or repair pool. Assigned them where needed. I will not let them die without a chance to save the Inner Sphere from the Jade Falcons."

Tara gave him a single nod as she toyed with the bondcord around her wrist. "You saw me on the field today, Khan Ward. You know I will fight against the Falcons. If you deny me this, I will pick up a rifle and fight from the field. I want a piece of Malvina Hazen."

"You will have to wait in a long and illustrious line," Alaric said. "But you shall get your chance tomorrow." He turned to Chance. "That reminds me. 'Athena' says she demands an audience with me. Suffice it to say that she chafes at sitting on the sidelines."

Chance smiled. "I will handle it."

"Good. Get them ready. She will get her opportunity tomorrow."

"Who is Athena?" Tara asked.

"Our last reserves," Alaric answered, without answering. He turned back to Vickers. "Tomorrow will be the most vicious fighting of this trial. We need to be prepared to fight—and to adapt if the situation changes. But if all goes according to plan, tomorrow may be the end."

CHAPTER 30

LA VERENDRYE WILDLIFE RESERVE
NORTH OF OTTAWA, NORTH AMERICA
TERRA
18 APRIL 3151, 2215 HOURS
(T+98, DAY 2 OF THE ILCLAN TRIAL)

Chance Vickers arrived at the row of unmarked DropShips in the darkness. Even their external lights had been shut off. She could make the ships out only against the brilliant stars in the sky that night. The security perimeter troops wore plain gray uniforms, devoid of insignia. They escorted her up the gangway to one of the *Overlord-C* ships and into a stateroom, and the door was swung open for her.

The cold, gray stateroom was packed with faces that for the most part, she did not know. Some uniforms were red and black, and others were gray trimmed in white. As she entered the room, everyone rose to their feet. Her eyes fell on Star Captain Marotta Kerensky, and she felt like smiling, but maintained her emotionless demeanor. He had been sent to bring Wolf's Dragoons to Terra to fight alongside Clan Wolf. His presence only confirmed the success of his mission.

Then Chance spied Anastasia Kerensky's red hair and emerald eyes, a look of great frustration on her face. Chance opted to keep her grin to herself. Anastasia had been sent to bring the Wolves-in-Exile and return them to their rightful place in Clan Wolf. *The last pieces of this great war game are here, waiting to be deployed on the map.*

The door closed behind her, and she spied a short, muscular, bald, ebony-skinned man wearing almost the same expression as Anastasia. She recognized him from Spurlock's intelligence briefings. "General Brubaker, I presume." Chance extended her hand, and he took it in a tight grip.

"And you are?" he asked.

"That," Anastasia said smoothly, "is General Chance Vickers. Alaric's right hand."

Brubaker gave her a penetrating gaze, nodded once, and moved to his seat.

"Please, let us sit," Chance said, pulling up a stool.

Anastasia remained standing to do the introductions, starting at the general's position and going around the packed table. "This is Colonel Aaron Krull, head of their Spec Ops forces, the Seventh Kommando. That is Colonel Nicholas Crews of Gamma Regiment," she said pointing to a bright-faced man who nodded at her. "The big man next to him is Major Andrew Krull of Gamma, his aide."

The Krull brothers exchanged quick grins, with Aaron Krull looking downright excited, as if in awe of the people seating around the table, where the others were far cooler and more reserved. Andrew only stroked his black beard and mustache anxiously.

"Over here you have Colonel Lyons of Alpha Regiment, and Colonel Cameron of Beta," she said as both officers dipped their heads respectfully. "You know Marotta already. Next to me here is Captain Deborah Sheridan of the Black Wolves Company, and Galaxy Commander Miriam Shaw, former Khan of the Wolves-in-Exile and commander of Omega Provisional Galaxy."

Miriam had the sternest face out of the gathering, as if it was carved in granite. She had a streak of white in her auburn hair like a thick stripe, right down the middle of her head."

"It is pleasure to meet all of you," Chance said as Anastasia took her seat. "Khan Ward would have come himself, but as you can imagine, he has many things to attend to. He does send his regards and most sincere thanks. Clan Wolf welcomes you all. I could go into a long speech about why stopping the Jade Falcons is so important, but I will not waste words with such an experienced audience. Suffice it to say, we are glad you are with us."

Brubaker shifted in his seat and spoke first. "We have been monitoring the Trial. With all due respect, when in the *hell* are you going to put us in?" There were murmurs and nods around the table, and the tension level elevated. "I risked *everything* to bring my Dragoons here, and you keep us sidelined, hidden. I didn't come to be an emergency reserve; I came here to end the Jade Falcon threat. And from what I saw on the live feeds, you need us *now*. Cut us loose, and we will pulverize the Falcons for you."

Chance leaned her elbows on the table. "I will pay you the compliment of being candid. We took a beating today. Aside from the fighting we anticipated, we have little left of the three Galaxies that were trapped in the Cauldron; less than one reconstituted Galaxy came through. We knocked out the Falcons' artillery, which helps us, but surely that was not worth the cost of two Galaxies worth of casualties.

"What you may not know is that earlier today, Alaric staged a strike on the Falcons' munitions and repair depot. We believe the Falcons may be low on munitions and spare parts. We also took out their Watch HQ, which leaves them somewhat blind."

Brubaker nodded, crossing his thick arms. "So you won day one, lost day two. That still means you need us to wrap this up."

"*Aff*, we do. But, General Brubaker, you know timing is everything in a fight such as this. Alaric wants to hold you for the right moment, one where you will have the most effect."

"And when is that?" Miriam Shaw asked. While she was middle-aged, her voice sounded much older. "We have been cooped up on these DropShips as spectators far too long. My Wolves are also ready for action. We came back to rejoin Clan Wolf, but we are being denied the honor of fighting with our *trothkin* thus far."

Chance nodded. "I do not know. What I *do* know is this. He has missions for all of you. When the time comes, he will deploy you to one of the flanks. We will bring in your DropShips, and when the word is given, you will pursue your designated objectives."

There were nods around the table, though Chance still felt some tension in the room. *Ages of distrust are hard to shake.*

"What is the Dragoons' target?" Brubaker asked.

"General, in respect for your history with Clan Wolf, you will be given the task of driving into the Falcons' flank. Marotta claims you desire to be the 'tip of the spear,' I believe is the phrase." With a wry smile, Marotta Kerensky nodded from his seat. "Well, Alaric wants you to take that spear and drive it right into the middle of the Jade Falcon forces while he comes in with the rest of Clan Wolf from the south and east.

"In addition, the Seventh Kommando is to undertake an operation in the Jade Falcon rear, to neutralize their aerospace bases near Lappe. The Falcons established temporary airfields there. Taking them out would hamstring their air operations."

Colonel Krull grinned at those words.

For the first time since Chance had seen him, General Brubaker released a slow but broad smile. "It will be our pleasure."

"Miriam Shaw," Chance said. "Khan Ward desires your forces to swing around and hit the Jade Falcons in their rear area."

Shaw's tough face let out the faintest of smiles. "We are home with the pack again, and live to serve Clan Wolf once more. Our payback for Malvina Hazen is long overdue."

Chance at last turned to Anastasia, locking gaze with her green eyes. "Anastasia Kerensky, you have only one mission. Hunt down Malvina Hazen. Alaric promised her to you, and now you must deliver. If she goes down and stays down, the Falcons may stop fighting."

Anastasia's jaw flexed as she nodded once. "She is mine." Her eyes swept the room. "Anyone sees her, tag her and send me the feed."

"I am not a person given to public speaking or flowery speeches," Chance said to everyone present. "The Inner Sphere hangs in the balance. Malvina is no fool, she showed us that today. We do not just have to outfight her, we have to outthink her as well. I can think of no better group to deliver the killing blow to the Falcons than you."

Chance paused, and all around the table, small side conversations started. "I will transmit details to you upon my return to HQ," she said, rising.

Anastasia and Marotta Kerensky rose and moved to escort her out. In the hallway, behind the closed door, Anastasia stopped, planting her firsts on her hips, staring at her.

"I have been following all of the fighting," she said, "from the initial landings with the Republic to now. I reviewed a lot of footage and data while waiting for this moment." She paused, as if searching for the right words. "I know I come across as arrogant sometimes. Sometimes I say things to goad people. When we first met, I tried to get under your skin, to get you to react. I regret that now. I have seen what you can do, how your plan unfolded. You have exceeded my expectations. Alaric chose his people well."

"You included," Chance said. "At first I did not understand the trust he gave you, especially after what you did to him. If I recall, when we first met, I threatened to kill you if you betrayed him. I am pleased I did not have to do that. Tomorrow, you must do what Devlin Stone tried to do and failed. You *must* kill Malvina. If you do that, we stand a good chance at victory. If not..."

Anastasia Kerensky stared back at her with a grim nod. Then she did something Chance never expected—she saluted.

General Vickers slowly responded with her own salute.

"I will see you on the field of battle tomorrow, General," Anastasia said, and walked away.

Chance turned to Marotta Kerensky. She saw he wore both Clan Wolf and Wolf's Dragoons' regalia on his uniform. *Clearly there is a story to tell here.* "Star Captain, I trust you will accompany me back? You fulfilled your mission, brilliantly I might add. We will get you a BattleMech and assign you to Alaric's command Star in the Silver Keshik. He recognizes what you accomplished in bringing Wolf's Dragoons to this fight."

Marotta shook his bald head. "*Neg*, General. With all due respect, General Brubaker and I, we share something—a, shall I say, *unique* bond. With that comes a commitment. While I appreciate the offer, until this matter with the Jade Falcons is settled, I believe I should fight alongside the Dragoons. It is only fitting. Many things had to be done to get them here, and those things come with a price. This is a matter of honor—not just for me, but for our Clan. I hope you understand."

Chance nodded. "Alaric will be disappointed, but where honor is involved, he will overcome that. Tomorrow will be a battle like no other. Certainly the stakes have never been higher."

"Please extend my thanks to him. Honor demands that I fight with the Dragoons tomorrow.

"Watch yourself, Marotta. I will see you when this is over."

Marotta Kerensky saluted, and Chance returned it. *I doubt anyone will sleep tonight...knowing what the dawn is likely to bring.*

JADE FALCON COMMAND POST GAMMA
THUNDER BAY, NORTH AMERICA
19 APRIL 3151, 0530 HOURS
(T+99, DAY 3 OF THE ILCLAN TRIAL)

Star Colonel Khalus Pryde stared at his *Jupiter* in the dimly lit repair bay as the techs finished working on it. It did not look like the same BattleMech he had been piloting. Only four pieces of armor were original from when he had first landed on Terra. Everything else was a replacement. Some was salvage—the armor was splotched shades of brown where his had been green. Some of the armor had to be forced to fit; he could see where the cutting had been done.

None of that matters. That was what he tried to tell himself, but only half-believed it. *I cannot afford for something to fail tomorrow.* The Chingis Khan had said that tomorrow would be the end of it, the destruction of Clan Wolf. The orders he had received were simple: "Destroy them all." He knew it would not be that easy. *Malvina believes she can make things happen solely by her force of will, but if she becomes ilKhan of the ilClan, that may be the case.*

The armorer tech came to his side. "We have half-loaded you with autocannon rounds and missiles, Star Colonel."

"Well then, finish the job."

"We can't," the tech replied. "We have no more reserves. The Chingis Khan has ordered half-loads where practical."

"Where practical." No doubt this is deliberate. Being an opponent of the Mongol Doctrine, my name must be on a list of warriors to be denied full ammo loads. He had heard stories of a Wolf raid on their munitions depot yesterday, but rumors abounded in such battles. *Perhaps this was not a slight. If we are short ammo, our ability to fight is greatly diminished.* His *Jupiter* had paired ER PPCs, but he did not want to rely on them alone.

"Understood," he muttered, and the armorer went back to his duties.

A mustached Star Captain approached. His jumpsuit was remarkably clean, which struck Khalus as strange. Every other warrior he had seen showed signs of sweat, grime, and wear on their uniforms. The Star Captain stood in front of him and saluted. "Star Colonel, I am Archer Pryde. I was ordered here as a replacement."

Khalus returned the salute and lifted his gaze. His Cluster was down nearly 50 percent, yet replacements had come in at a trickle. Those that did come all seemed to have one characteristic in common. "Star Captain, you are the seventh replacement assigned to me. I am going to venture a guess. You do not support the Mongol Doctrine, *quiaff*?"

The question caught Archer visibly off guard, and he cleared his throat. "I am a loyal Jade Falcon" was all he said.

"Of course you are," Khalus replied. "As am I. Yet I have noticed that anyone who is not an *ardent* supporter of the Chingis Khan's beliefs tends to get shuffled to my command or to Delta Galaxy. There is a reason for that."

Archer relaxed at those words, shifting to parade rest. "What is that reason, Star Colonel?"

"My command, the First Falcon Jaegers, has drawn assignments that should have destroyed us. It is clear the Chingis Khan is trying to send us to our deaths. If you are here at her bidding, I can assume you are also a marked officer, on her list of nonbelievers."

Archer's right eyebrow cocked at his words. "How do you know I am not a member of the Watch, sent to test your loyalty?"

Khalus grinned. "Malvina is determined to end this trial tomorrow. We will be in the vanguard, thrusting right into the heart of the Wolf lines, and that is where the fighting will be the thickest. She intends for me and my Cluster to die. If you are from the Watch, you will be there to die as well. Besides, I am the blood of Aidan Pryde. My loyalty to Clan Jade Falcon is above reproach." *It is my loyalty to Malvina Hazen that is in question.*

Archer nodded. "I am not from the Watch."

He still refuses to admit he loathes the Mongol Doctrine. I respect that. Khalus could not suppress his grin.

"My previous Star Colonel seemed quite elated to have me reassigned," Archer said. "We were in the last DropShips to land, so we missed most of the fighting with the Republic, and we were held in reserve during the first day of the trial. I feared I might miss out on any real action."

"You will not miss the fight, Archer," Khalus said. "Come the dawn, the Jaegers will be in the thickest of it. Our Khan has seen to that. For warriors like us, there are two things we can do. Fight and survive. Malvina is counting on our deaths. I say we take our lesson from Aidan Pryde himself, and create our own path out of this situation. Malvina may have robbed our Clan of its honor with this madness of Mongolism, but she cannot take away our personal honor. As long as warriors like you and I live, we pose a danger to her way of thinking. I, for one, refuse to give my life in her name."

Archer nodded and smiled. "Now I understand why I was sent here. I look forward to the dawn."

CHAPTER 31

Warriors Hawkins and DuJordan performed a final inspection of *Fratricide* as they shivered in the predawn darkness. Even with the space heaters they had brought out, the cold Canadian air bit at them.

Hawkins' nostrils stung with the scent of lubricants, paint fumes, and diesel fuel from the depot. The touched-up maroon-and-yellow paint job was sloppy, and the name on the right side of the hull was barely readable, still smudged with the filth of battle. When the techs said painting vehicles was a low priority, Hawkins and DuJordan had undertaken the task themselves. In the blackness before the dawn, with the help of the dim lights of the repair depot, Hawkins could make out every line of the 'Mech-busting tank. *You have served us well, old friend. Now you must do it once more.*

"I heard the Falcons did a reconnaissance-in-force earlier," Hawkins said. "Word is we sent them running away."

DuJordan shrugged. "You hear a lot of gossip I do not. It does not matter what they did a few hours ago, only what they do at the break of dawn."

"They say that today we will face the full fury of the Jade Falcons." Hawkins caressed *Fratricide*'s hull—or started to. Maroon paint smeared his hand.

"I do not know about this 'full fury' you speak of." DuJordan sneered. "We nearly got killed yesterday morning against the Turkey Beak Galaxy."

"*Turkina's* Beak," Hawkins corrected. "And *neg*, we did not almost get killed. I had the situation well under control."

The fighting the day before had been vicious along the southern front, and a Jade Falcon *Night Gyr* from the Turkina's Beak Galaxy had engaged them in a deadly slugfest. Colonel Kerensky had deployed the Furies along a hillside when the Jade Falcons had tried to overrun their position. Hawkins had driven the tank on a hair-raising ride through the dense pine forest while DuJordan scored consecutive hits on the Falcon's head, eventually turning its MechWarrior into superheated paste with a precision shot to the cockpit.

Another Jade Falcon *Mad Dog* had shredded the tank's right-side armor before it fell victim to DuJordan's deadly aim with his paired Gauss rifles, which tore the 'Mech's left leg off at the hip.

"We need to get one more fight out of *Fratricide*," Hawkins said, patting a spot where the paint was old and dry. *I just need you to hold together for another day.*

"It should not be difficult," the wry gunner replied. "Most of this tank is replacement parts. Terra has taken a toll."

Just then, Hawkins heard the tramp of boots on ferrocrete. Entering the refit facility around their tank were the warriors of the Howling Furies, led by the iron lady herself, Kalidessa Kerensky. She had been taken down by a death from above attack during yesterday's fighting, yet true to form, she had come through quite alive and remarkably uninjured.

Hawkins saw the hulking form of Parac Shaw, his arm bandaged, his face covered with a shadow of gray stubble. A dozen Elementals were with him, all that was left of Bane Star. The aerofighter pilots were there too; Star Commander Manning of Ravager Star led them in and around *Fratricide*. The three new members of the Cluster, the *abtakha* pilots of the repaired *Ares*, lingered at the rear of the gathering.

The various members of the Howling Furies milled around the tank, talking with each other, some smiling, some not, some pointing to areas where *Fratricide* had been patched up and hastily repainted. Every warrior present showed signs of weariness, but none could sleep.

"To what do we owe the honor, Star Colonel?" Hawkins asked.

As she stepped forward, the gathering of Furies quieted. "You two have earned quite a reputation. You defeated two of the Republic's esteemed Paladins, the highest rank in the Knights of the Republic. Visril," she said, nodding to a tall, fair-skinned Elemental who grinned broadly, "is a bit of an artist. We all thought we should give you something—for this last time out. Special kill markers."

She held out two pieces of polished brass, both in the shape of a chessboard knight, symbols of the two Paladins they had taken out.

Hawkins held them in his hand. "I will mount them on the turret myself." Smiles broke out with the Furies as he climbed up and held up the markers for everyone to see. He started to scrape off a spot where they could mount them when Star Colonel Kerensky climbed up on one of the front treads, standing over what was left of her command. Hawkins stopped, as did everyone in the unit. The voices went silent one more time as all eyes fell on the commander who had led them on so many operations.

"In a few hours, we will enter the final fight against the Jade Falcons, one last time. You all have performed brilliantly during the many weeks of this campaign, but the time has come for us to put this behind us and move forward. We *will* be the ilClan. Alaric Ward brought us here, and I know he will lead us to victory. All I need from you is to go all-in. Hold nothing back. We are all that stands between a madwoman and the rest of the Inner Sphere...no pressure, *quiaff*?"

A chuckle rose from the Furies. "I will not kid you about the odds... We are outnumbered. But we are Clan Wolf, which means that the odds do not matter. What we lack in numbers, we make up for in spirit. Follow your honor, and I will see you once more when this battle is over."

With that, she jumped down. Hawkins put down the brush for a few minutes and took the time to see his comrades. A part of him, a nagging thought in the back of his mind, worried it might be for the last time.

0600 HOURS

Star Colonel Kalidessa Kerensky stood in line at the depot with only one warrior ahead of her, wishing she did not have to get a replacement BattleMech. She had left the last gathering of her Howling Furies twenty minutes ago, confident they were as ready as anyone could be for what would be coming at them.

Her *Dire Wolf*, crushed by a death from above attack in the fighting, was deemed beyond repair and stripped for parts. Parac Shaw's Elementals had torn apart the *Jade Hawk* that had taken her down, which gave her some small degree of satisfaction. *It was a lucky 'Mech for me. It brought me victory over the Republic and made many Jade Falcons little more than memories.* Her shoulders still ached from the ejection earlier in the day.

The warrior ahead of her left the line, and Kalidessa stepped forward.

"Callsign?" asked the clerk behind the collapsible table.

"Howling Fury Actual," she said.

"Star Colonel Kalidessa Kerensky, *quiaff*?"

"*Aff.*"

The clerk's fingers flew on the noteputer. "Here you are. You are being assigned a brand- new BattleMech—an *Amarok*, the last one in the yard. Most warriors must undergo a Trial of Possession to pilot one, but this one came through after being refit." He pointed out into the yard. "Row four, sixth in line. The security protocols have been wiped."

"I have never piloted an *Amarok*," Kalidessa said. "Any chance at a *Dire Wolf?*" She had heard positive things about the *Amarok*, but there was something to be said about familiarity. *Every BattleMech has nuances about it. I will be learning to pilot it, mastering those idiosyncrasies, while fighting the most important battle of our history.*

"*Neg*, Star Colonel. If you do not want the *Amarok*, I can put you into the reserve pool, and you can wait."

"*Neg*," Kalidessa said firmly. "I will take the *Amarok* and make it my own." *My people expect me on the field. I will do what a good Wolf warrior does. I will adapt, overcome, and lead my Furies to victory.*

"Excellent," the clerk said. "Next."

A few minutes later she stood before the 100-ton BattleMech. Its large pulse laser, PPC, and rotary autocannon gave her some confidence. What she had heard about its speed made her happier. The armor plates were strange geometric shapes, giving the illusion of being streamlined, a rarity among her Clan's original 'Mech designs. The configuration of the arms—strangely reinforced at the shoulders—was odd to her, then she remembered some of the unique features it offered.

Kalidessa climbed up into the cockpit and configured the security system with her voiceprint and code phrase. The fusion reactor throbbed to life, and she surveyed the streamlined cockpit, memorizing where every control was, pleased it was not too different than her *Dire Wolf*.

One new control was a red button marked DFA. The *Amarok* was supposedly designed to nullify a death from above attack. She hit the button, and the 'Mech's massive arms of snapped upright into a preprogrammed position: they reached over her cockpit, and the hand actuators interlocked with each other. Looking up through the canopy, she saw the reinforced arms formed a sturdy pyramid over her. Any jumping 'Mech that attempted to land on her would find themselves deflected by the configuration.

She reached out and patted the control station. *I could have used this yesterday! Such is fate.* This Amarok *may yet serve me well.*

OPASATIKA
0655 HOURS

The tiny town of Opasatika was a small town nestled along the Trans-Canada Highway, one of the few east-to-west highways in the battle zone. There were a dozen or so antiquated buildings where hearty people had formed a community. The locals had left prior to the trial, warned by Alaric of what was to come.

Opasatika itself was unremarkable. Chance had chosen it as one of the forward assembly areas for Clan Wolf, and Alaric had approved. In the park in the center of town, he stood atop his mobile HQ and surveyed the sea of BattleMechs, combat vehicles, and gathered warriors.

He was tired, having been able to only sleep for a few hours since the Trial began, but he did not long for rest. *There will be time for that after we defeat the Jade Falcons.* His thoughts were a maelstrom. *I was created for this purpose, to become the ilKhan of the Clans, to unify our people.* He knew the blood pulsing in his veins was a mix of Victor and Katherine Steiner-Davion, along with a hint of Vlad Ward. It was the right combination, he was sure of that. A part of him wished his genemother could have seen this moment, but that was checked with how much she would have ruined it for him. *This was never about her. It is about* me *fulfilling destiny.*

All that remained was Malvina Hazen and the Jade Falcons.

Clan Wolf's plan was simple. They would advance in a long, bowed arc, bending to the west. The majority of the Wolf force would be to the south. When the foremost Galaxies made contact, they would reverse the bow and execute an oblique order, re-fusing the line to the east and opening up the northern flank. Malvina would be rushing the center in hopes of splitting their lines. The larger Wolf force to the south would then go on the offensive, driving northwest into the Falcons' flank. *If we are fortunate, we will not need our last reserves.*

Pausing, he swept the crowd with his piercing blue eyes, feeling their gazes all locked on him. It hit him in that moment: *This is not about* me. *It is about* them.

He lifted the handheld microphone before his mouth and spoke loudly, crisply:

"Warriors of Clan Wolf. This is a day you will remember for the rest of your lives. You will look back at it fondly, proudly, gloriously. The other Clans will ask to be told of your deeds on this day, and you will tell them of the honor you brought your Clan during the defeat of the Jade Falcons. You will tell them what it was like in that moment of ultimate victory, when we became the ilClan. They will hang on your words longingly, knowing they can never achieve what you will do today.

"Our enemies have stripped themselves of honor to be here. They have shed their decency to stand in these forests and hills to fight you. The Jade Falcons will come at us today with everything they have, and they will take no bondsmen, leave no survivors. Malvina Hazen seeks to remake the universe in her own black, twisted image, and in that universe, we do not exist. She seeks to make us Not-Named. If she is triumphant today, she will erase all records of Clan Wolf's existence."

He paused for a moment of dramatic effect. Use of the word "Not-Named" would conjure images of the Annihilation of Clan Wolverine. *None want to share that fate, to be expunged from history.*

"We do not fight for just our Clan, or the heritage of Nicholas Kerensky and the Great Father—we fight for the entire Inner Sphere. They may not know it, but we are their best and only defense against extinction at the Jade Falcons' hands. We alone can prevent atrocities at the hands of the Mongols. We can win the greatest victory ever, and become the ilClan.

"We are the last line of defense. Trillions of lives count on each and every one of you, on hundreds of worlds from here to the Homeworlds. While they may not know of your actions right now, in the weeks and months to come, they will learn and be grateful for your efforts and sacrifices on this day.

"Today is about history. In only a few hours, your names will be added to histories that will be studied in *sibkos* for generations to come. Your genes will be the most prized, and your progeny will be proud to carry your Bloodnames for what you are about to do. They will marvel at what you accomplished against such an overwhelming evil. Warriors to come will only ever hope to be as great as you.

"Your Galaxy Commanders have their orders—follow them, and we will prevail. In the name of Nicholas Kerensky and the generations that came before us, we will be victorious. *Seyla!*"

The whole of Clan Wolf responded in unison, in a cry that echoed for kilometers: "*SEYLA!*"

Alaric climbed down from the HQ roof, where Chance greeted him. "General Vickers, I trust that you are ready?"

"I have been ready for this for a lifetime, my Khan." Her reassuring voice centered him.

"Very well. Prepare Reunion and Amalgamation for Athena Rising."

LONGLAC
0655 HOURS

Malvina Hazen moved *Black Rose* out in front of the Raptor Keshik's BattleMechs. The battle plan was laid, so simple she considered it elegant. Her technician caste had salvaged as much equipment and ammunition as possible for the fight. She knew she did not have enough for a prolonged engagement, but that would not matter. *The ilClan will be decided today, and quickly.*

The Jade Falcons would form a massive Ripping Beak formation, the largest ever executed. It was a diamond shape, with the flank points of the diamond flattened, like a giant arrowhead. She would lead her Falcons into the center of the Wolf line; once they penetrated, she would swing her force to the north, wipe out the Wolves there, then drive to the south. Divide and conquer...a strategy as old as warfare. *We will move on Alaric so quickly he will not know what hit him. He will have no time for any of his usual trickery.*

Her broadcast was going out to her whole Clan, and she relished the power she felt in those moments, knowing that her warriors would hang on every word. "Jade Falcons, today I lead you to victory and the ilClanship. The Wolves have been bled. We crushed three of their Galaxies yesterday, burning them to a crisp—which is better than they deserve. The day before, we blunted their flanking maneuvers. They have fought well, but they are bleeding...dying. All that remains is for us to put them out of their misery.

"The Wolves represent complete failure. They represent the failed approach of the former ilKhan, a Wolf, to complete the Grand Crusade. They have blindly followed the ways of Nicholas Kerensky, never bothering to consider how flawed his vision of the future is. They pivoted between the Warden and Crusader philosophies, never settling on a firm vision for themselves, and suffering a split of their own people, who left the Clan and were allowed to live. They are weak, foolish, and look only to the past, where the Clans have failed time and again to seize their destiny.

"I brought you here to Terra to seize control of all of the Clans. United under our divine guidance, the Inner Sphere will burn and be born anew from the ashes.

"Any Jade Falcon that gives up a meter of ground, that falls back, I will kill you myself. Today there is only way one to win, and that is to go forward—through our enemies and beyond.

"Follow me to victory! Follow me to the final defeat of Clan Wolf!"

Her Jade Falcons cheered over the communications channel. In that moment, Malvina knew they were all with her—focused on their singular objective: the eradication of Clan Wolf.

SOUTH OF HEARST
0815 HOURS

As Star Colonel Kalidessa Kerensky led her Howling Furies westward, she passed areas where the fighting had taken place in the previous two days. They stumbled across several battlefields, one still smoking from yesterday's fires. Bits of blasted armor plating, the occasional burned-out tank, and severed BattleMech limbs littered the ground.

She had volunteered her Cluster for Beta Galaxy's vanguard duty as they advanced on the approaching Jade Falcons. Her new *Amarok* handled remarkably well, and she was impressed with the model. The center of gravity was lower than on her *Dire Wolf*, which took some getting used to, forcing her to adjust her neurohelmet settings, but otherwise it piloted well. *So, the Sea Foxes built this? Let us see how well it holds up in battle...*

She hated going in without Ravager Star, but Manning's aerofighters had been tasked to provide air support to the north of her position. They were invaluable assets in such an area. Aerospace units could often spell the difference between victory and crushing defeat.

She advanced through the pine forest and came to an area where a timber company had logged off half a square kilometer of forest. The ground was littered with stumps, bits of wood, pulled up roots—unsteady terrain at best. At her sides, the rest of her Furies broke through the tree line and awaited her order.

Across the clearing, the trees moved, wavering. Then they emerged: a line of emerald BattleMechs and tanks. Upon seeing the Wolves across the open ground between them, the Falcons stopped right outside of the pines as well.

For an agonizingly long moment, the two forces, roughly the same size, faced each other—looking into the eyes of their enemies.

Kalidessa Kerensky walked forward alone toward the Jade Falcons. A moment later, her Furies advanced at the same pace.

Across the battlefield, a lone *Jade Hawk* stepped out at the front, walking, leading the Falcon force in an eerie mirror of what she was doing.

She stopped her slow gait for a moment and focused on the Jade Falcons. "All right Furies, enough of this. Follow me!" She broke her *Amarok* into a run.

The *Jade Hawk* lit its jump jets and soared into the air as the Falcon line rushed forward.

CHAPTER 32

Jack Traver saw the charging *Onager* and tagged it as his target. The rebuilt *Ares* he and his crew had brought back to life maneuvered slowly, but Cheetah did not wait for the *Onager* to get closer. She rained down long-range missiles on the rushing, dark green Falcon 'Mech.

The *Onager* fired its hyper-assault Gauss rifle, and a flurry of small, silvery projectiles punched deep divots across the *Ares'* upper-torso armor. The combined force of the slugs struck hard, making the 'Mech fight Jack's piloting, but he shrugged it off.

This was the fight they had come to wage. They had been in the first two days' worth of battles, but only on the periphery. Two Points of Elementals had tried to take them out the day before, only to be slaughtered when the anti-battle-armor pods on the hulking *Ares'* legs had detonated. While they had fought in Star Colonel Kerensky's Cluster, today felt markedly different. Maybe it was Khan Ward's speech, or the solemn behavior of the Wolf warriors, but Jack could feel that today was not like the others.

We are all in, that's why. Today it is win or lose.

"They're coming in range of the MRMs," Cheetah called out.

"Tear 'em a new asshole," Jack replied angrily.

"On it." There was a massive *whoosh* as the *Ares* launched forty medium-range missiles. Jack felt the 'Mech lurch when the Ultra autocannon blasted a stream of shells downrange.

The *Onager* rushed into the wall of incoming fire and was enveloped in explosions, disappearing from Jack's view. Some missiles plowed into the ground and blew up a stump and the dirt and grass around it. Smoke swirled around the Jade Falcon 'Mech as it emerged from the explosions, its armor blasted and cratered along its right side and upper body. It fired its massive hyper-assault Gauss Rifle again; some of the slugs missed, but others plowed into the thick belts of armor on the *Ares'* upper body and rained armor fragments onto the ground below.

"Mia..." Jack called.

"On it," the engineer called back.

"Cheetah, they're moving into optimum range for everything. Let's show 'em not to mess with the big boys."

"Oh, it's *on*," she replied. Jack could imagine her fierce grin from the seat forward and below his own.

He heard the whine of the TSEMP discharge, followed by the hum of the ER medium lasers. More missiles fired, both long- and short-range. The temperature in the cockpit rose appreciably, but he didn't care.

The *Onager* lost its footing and stumbled slightly under the barrage, possibly fighting the effects of the tight-stream EMP pulse. It fired a dozen short-range missiles, but the salvo missed by a good five meters, the exhaust flares briefly lighting up his cockpit as they shot past.

It was a desperate shot as the Jade Falcon MechWarrior lost control of their 'Mech and fell. The *Onager* skidded forward upon impact, plowing up the ground.

"Nice shooting, Cheetah," Jack called down to her. "Traversing to the right."

Star Colonel Kalidessa Kerensky closed on the *Jade Hawk* and fired her *Amarok*'s rotary autocannon as the Falcon 'Mech began another jump. Shells tore at its legs as it rose, raining down chunks of blasted armor.

All across the massive clearing, the air came alive with lasers, PPCs, and smoke trails. Explosions tore at the forest in every direction as she checked the deployment of her Furies. *So far, so good.*

The *Amarok* handled incredibly well under the initial exchange with the *Jade Hawk*. Ramiel Bekker, the WarBear, had designed it to be a close-range brawler with just enough speed to throw off an enemy, given its size. Bekker's reputation was already nearly legend, especially given how he had died saving Khan Ward's life. *Now I am living with the results of his efforts.*

The *Jade Hawk* she fought was already running hot, meaning it was enhanced with triple-strength myomer. As it soared over her, it sprayed her *Amarok* with a fusillade of short-range missiles, which she shook off as merely lost armor.

Kalidessa saw where the *Jade Hawk* was going to land and moved to intercept it. She fired her rotary autocannon, PPC, and large pulse laser in unison as the enemy 'Mech landed, its big legs flexing upon impact. The Star Colonel's purring autocannon tore into the partial-wing assembly sprouting from the back, destroying three of its feather-like sections. The brilliant burst of whitish-blue energy of her PPC tore off the Falcon's remaining right-arm armor and scattered it onto a squat *Adder* that was firing at Parac Shaw's Elementals.

The Jade Falcon warrior sprinted away with a speed almost inconceivable for a 'Mech that size, using a combination of a supercharger and the heat-activated triple-strength myomer. The *Jade Hawk* darted for the northern edge of the clearing as Kalidessa pursued, hitting it squarely in the back with a pulse-laser burst. Twisting, the *Jade Hawk* shot small-laser fire that did little but burn short scars on the *Amarok*'s armor.

The Jade Falcon warrior skidded to change the path of their run, and sprinted back toward her, passing through a wave of LRMs Jack's *Ares* had fired at another Jade Falcon target. She braced for the impact and danced her targeting reticle over the enemy. Without looking, she switched all of her weapons to a single target-interlock trigger and made sure she was at close range.

Kalidessa fired her weapons all at once. The heat in her cockpit soared, but she did not care: all that mattered was her part of the battle in that moment. The right side of the *Jade Hawk* caved in, melting and erupting as Kalidessa's weapons burned deep. The rotary autocannon shredded the Falcon's right arm at the elbow and blew it off entirely. The missile ammunition inside the 'Mech cooked off, and the blast ripped through the internal structure.

Despite what should have been crippling damage, the Falcon MechWarrior fired their jump jets again, bringing the *Jade Hawk* right over her. Memories of the previous day's death from above against her *Dire Wolf* surged into memory. *Not this time.*

She hit the red button marked *DFA*, and the *Amarok*'s arms rose and snapped into place to form a triangle over her cockpit. The *Jade Hawk* came down, hit the interlocked arms, and slid off to the side.

The WarBear designed this one right!

The Falcon fell onto its ride side less than five meters away, and Kalidessa wasted no time capitalizing on her moment of surprise. Despite the heat, she disengaged the DFA function and fired another PPC shot, which burned a manhole-cover-sized opening in her target's weak rear armor, then her rotary autocannon roared again and tore into the smoldering back. The shots shredded the fusion reactor housing and assembly, and there was a flash as the reactor was breached. Kalidessa felt the temperature spike in her cockpit, and inside her neurohelmet, sweat trickled down her face as she tried to vent the excess heat.

There was no time to celebrate the demise of her foe. Moments later, a wave of long-range missiles raked her left side.

"Howling Furies, form up on my position," she said over the tactical channel. A Star of Jade Falcons near the center of the clearing angled toward her. "Reave them!"

The fighting ended in a matter of a few minutes, though to Kalidessa, it felt like much longer. As the last Jade Falcon in the clearing dropped, she surveyed the damage done to her Second Wolf Assault Cluster. A full third of her force was out of the fight. Wolf *solahma* infantry moved out to recover ejected or downed MechWarriors and get them to the rear areas. Reports from the previous two days of fighting told stories of Jade Falcon infantry slaughtering any ejected warriors they found.

She was pleased to see Jack's *Ares* still operational, though a bit battered, with several black scars from PPCs that had melted furrows in the armor plating. *He and his crew are Wolves now.*

Kalidessa activated the command channel. "Raptor Actual, this is Howling Fury Actual, report," she said as she advanced to the line of trees where the Jade Falcons had emerged.

"We are a bit busy up here, Star Colonel," Raptor replied. "Looks like you are at the side door. The real action is to the north at the front door."

Kalidessa checked her tactical display and turned her *Amarok* to the right, facing the north edge of the clearing. "All right, Furies, follow me."

NORTHEAST OF HEARST
0845 HOURS

The main thrust of the Jade Falcons' offensive collided with Clan Wolf in a thickly forested area northeast of the crossroads at Hearst. Alaric's Beta Galaxy had been to the south of that push, but Kappa Galaxy, the Werewolves, caught the brunt of the enemy's initial contact.

The Falcons had been moving fast, and when the two forces slammed into each other, they immediately intermixed. Malvina's other forces pushed forward, and Alaric saw what would happen if he did not act—the Falcons might cut the Wolf lines entirely. While Kappa slugged it out for every meter of ground, Alaric brought several Clusters of Beta northward to relieve some of the pressure, to try grinding the Falcon offensive down.

The moment his *Savage Wolf* was recognized, the Falcons shifted in his direction. The area was dotted with clearings, some only a few hundred square meters wide, but enough for some deadly fields of fire. All around him, Beta Galaxy and Kappa Galaxy elements were using the open spaces to unleash volleys at deadly ranges. Small fires broke out in trees that were superheated by laser or PPC fire. Many clumps of forest disappeared under enemy barrages when BattleMechs tried to use them for cover.

Alaric aimed at a *Turkina* as he ran along its flank and fired his pair of large lasers at its damaged left side. Both shots hit the mangled left arm, blasting it off at the shoulder and twisting part of the boxy LRM rack. The glow from the hit still shimmered as Alaric moved toward its rear; Tara followed him closely, as if her *Sun Cobra* was his own shadow.

The *Turkina* ignored him for a moment, still focused on a bright-red and yellow Wolf *Orion IIC.* It fired its remaining particle projection cannon and long-range missiles. The *Orion's* MechWarrior twisted at the last moment, blocking the hit with its right-torso Gauss rifle—which exploded when the PPC hit it, peeling back the barrel and part of the torso armor like a metal banana. Gray smoke rolled from the damaged 'Mech, and the *Turkina* sprayed it with LB-X autocannon shells. The barrage hit what remained of the damaged arm and furrowed deep into the gaping hole on the right side. The Wolf 'Mech toppled backward and fell hard.

Alaric fired his ATMs, and eighteen of them slammed into the *Turkina*'s rear. Bits of armor flew into the air. The squat assault 'Mech fired its jump jets, turned to face Alaric, and launched a flight of LRMs—but only five missiles exploded against his left side. He fired his large lasers and hit the *Turkina*'s damaged flank as it landed again. Glowing orange holes marked where the lasers had melted through the armor.

A brilliant lance of PPC energy arced out toward Alaric but missed, sending excess static sparks dancing across his 'Mech. The *Turkina*'s LB-X autocannons followed, sending a stream of shells in his direction, but only a few hit his legs.

He saw Tara moving in closer to his target, and continued to move so she would be in position.

As the *Turkina* twisted to track him, it exposed its damaged back to Tara's *Sun Cobra*. Without hesitation, she fired both of her Gauss rifles. The *Turkina* had no armor left to resist. One Gauss round shattered the gyro, propelling shrapnel out its front side. The other slammed into its engine and sent a ripple of heat into the air. The Jade Falcon fell, throwing bits of armor into the air as it spun and dropped.

"Tara," Alaric panted. "That target was mine. You acted without honor—"

"*Neg*, Khan Ward. General Vickers told me to protect you, and I am doing just that. A shot at you is a shot at me and my honor. My kill was legitimate." The defiance in her voice was oddly reassuring.

I made the right choice taking her as a bondsman. She is a true Wolf at heart.

"Regardless, I will kill my own Jade Falcons today," he chided.

"Duly noted," Tara replied.

Alaric was not certain she was being entirely honest.

NORTH OF HEARST
0905 HOURS

Galaxy Commander Stephanie Chistu whirled her *Jade Hawk* around on the black-and-gray *Skinwalker* and bathed it in a salvo of short-range missiles. The Wolf BattleMech emerged from a cloud of smoke, sprinting off to her right, small craters marking its upper body. *Running will not help you.*

She broke into a sprint of her own, this one enhanced by triple-strength myomer bundles and a supercharger. The *Skinwalker* accelerated as she tried to close, telling her she faced an enhanced BattleMech like hers. *So much the better.*

Delta Galaxy was on the northern edge of the Jade Falcon assault, slamming into the Wolves' Tau Galaxy. This was the kind of battle she preferred—fast moving and honorable. She had spent the previous day fighting a number of units along the northern flank, then had been deployed to mop up what remained in the fiery trap Malvina had laid.

As Chistu had walked through the charred hell of the burned-out fires, seeing the melted and blown-up remains of the Wolves who had died there, it tore at her. A few Wolves had tried to escape to the north instead of fleeing to the south. They were blackened, battered by artillery fire, and they fought viciously, refusing to yield, no doubt fueled by the knowledge that the Jade Falcons would not take them prisoner.

Since then, her Delta Galaxy had fought a dozen or so skirmishes with the smoldering Wolves before finishing them off. As she surveyed the cratered and charred fire zone during the thunderstorm that had extinguished much of the flames, she could not help but imagine she was seeing a glimpse of what Malvina had in mind for her reign as ilKhan. *That woman would burn all of humanity and tell them it was progress.*

The *Skinwalker* twisted its torso and fired its two extended-range pulse lasers at her; one hit her squarely in the chest. She triggered her short-range lasers as she closed to optimum range. The lasers were not devastating, but they melted four scars on the sprinting Wolf's legs. Beyond her target, she saw a pair of her *Mad Dogs* launching a devastating barrage of long-range missiles at some target in the distance. Explosions off to her right told her the battle was raging all around her, but her focus remained on the *Skinwalker.*

Chistu fired her jump jets again and took to the air over the enemy, firing her short-range missiles downward. Two slammed into the *Skinwalker*'s head, while the rest riddled its body. As she came down, she saw it stagger slightly; if nothing else, she had rattled the warrior piloting it.

Then she saw it—the low ammo warning. *Stravag!*

The depot had rationed munitions in the morning, as they had every day of the trial. Chistu had four more salvos for each of her short-range missile launchers, then she was out.

The *Skinwalker* throttled down to a trot, and she closed in on it, running full tilt. Emerald pulses of laser light from her foe danced along her 'Mech's upper body while the bright scarlet beams missed her completely. The Wolf pilot fired their short-range missiles next, most of which hit, but she ignored them.

As she drew even with the *Skinwalker,* she coiled back her right arm, then thrust it into the enemy's side. The sharpened metallic claws punched a devastating hole through the armor. She threw another punch to its other side; this one carved deep into the 'Mech's internal structure. As she extracted the fist, a wiring harness clung to it, sparking.

Whatever she damaged, it must have been severe. Explosive bolts opened the cockpit canopy, and the ejection seat rocketed the MechWarrior into the air. The pilotless *Skinwalker* toppled over. The parachute deployed above, and the Wolf warrior's command couch floated down gently. Beyond it she saw one of her BattleMechs, a birdlike *Fire Falcon*, fall under a wave of Arrow IV missiles, collapsing in a heap. Still, for reasons she could not explain, the ejected warrior captivated her attention.

A blaze of Ultra-autocannon fire suddenly spat upward, and the warrior's ejection seat exploded into metal debris, red mist, and a haze of smoke. Furious, Chistu turned to see Lamm—a member of her Galaxy—lowering the autocannons on her gray-green *Jupiter.*

"Lamm!" Chistu snapped. "What have you done?"

"The Chingis Khan ordered it, Galaxy Commander," she replied.

I do not care what Malvina ordered. Killing a defenseless warrior is without honor. "You wasted precious ammunition killing a warrior we already defeated," Chistu said through her teeth. "Do not do that again. We have a long day ahead of us. Pray that you do not need that ammo when it counts."

If our ammunition levels are indicative of the rest of our Clan, things may be more precarious than Malvina is willing to admit. "Signal the technicians," she commanded. "They should be able to salvage munitions from the Wolves we have destroyed."

She scoured the landscape for her next possible target.

CHAPTER 33

Tara Wolf hated to admit that the Clan Wolf MechWarrior jumpsuit she wore was comfortable—or that the 55-ton BattleMech she piloted, a *Sun Cobra*, was an incredible machine to handle. But it literally danced at the twitch of her fingers, and the jumpsuit *was* comfortable. The Wolf Clan technician caste worked miracles.

Her jaw ached from clenching her teeth as she angled her *Sun Cobra* alongside Alaric. In the distance she saw a Jade Falcon *Flamberge* savagely punch a Wolf *Gargoyle*, sinking its clawed first deep into the shoulder armor. The 80-ton OmniMech twisted under the kinetic impact of the punch, but it propped its left-arm LB-X autocannon against the Falcon's cockpit canopy and fired. A roar of shells slammed through the ferroglass, through the pilot, and out the back of the *Flamberge*'s head. The brilliant-green BattleMech collapsed, falling into a heap at the *Gargoyle*'s feet.

Tara winced at the sight. She was battle-hardened, but such images knotted her stomach. *These are not drones we are killing, these are human beings. Misguided by Malvina, but they are people nevertheless.*

Alaric paused his stride, possibly communicating to a Wolf unit, and she moved next to him. They had deployed in a line east of the Jade Falcons' thrust. Stubbornly, Alaric's forces were giving ground. Rather than allow them to retreat pell-mell, he formed new lines of defense farther to the east. Alaric liked to lead from the front, and she respected that. The problem was the front was constantly changing, methodically retrograding.

She was not protecting him because of Chance Vickers' command; she was doing so for personal reasons. Alaric represented the only hope of stopping Malvina Hazen. If he were killed, the Wolves might be triumphant, but what followed might just as well be chaos. Keeping Alaric alive had become her mission, her reason for being on the battlefield...the whole point of her existence. Being a Wolf warrior was not easy, but it was the price she had paid to save the Northwind Highlanders, and that gave her some degree of inner peace.

She thought she had understood the Clans before becoming a bondsman, but she had been wrong. The complexities of their customs, their use of language, and their regard for bondsmen as lesser people had humbled her. It had been years since someone last dressed her down like a cadet, but as a Wolf warrior, that had happened to her several times for simply using contractions or failing to perform her assigned tasks fast enough. The Clans were a binary people—things were either A or B. There was no middle ground in their society. While she intellectually had known that, living it had been something else entirely.

Now things were different. Alaric had cut her bondcord, which elevated her to full warrior status within the Clan. Almost instantly she was treated as an equal by people who, hours before, had treated her with disdain, as an inferior. It struck her as strange, but she had become used to strange during her time with the Wolves.

In the past few days, she had come to know Alaric as much as she suspected anyone ever did. The Wolf Khan did not reveal much except for his talent for war; Tara saw it in the way he directed his forces, in his ability to adapt to an ever-changing situation. She felt he was holding back, that he had something planned for the Falcons, but she had not seen it yet. There had been talk of "Athena," and she assumed it was code for the Wolves' reserves.

The only person who got close to Alaric was Chance Vickers, and even then, there was still a distance. *She is utterly devoted to him, yet a force all on her own. The Wolves treat her with almost the same respect they do Alaric.* Chance had told Tara to protect Alaric, and she had so far. *If he falls and I survive, she will come for me, regardless of whether I am to blame.*

Alaric reacted to explosions off to his left, swinging in the direction of the rumbles. Tara pushed her *Sun Cobra* after him through a line of trees, and saw him and another Wolf 'Mech engaged with two Jade Falcons in the distance. Suddenly an *Eyrie*—above her on its jump jets—landed at Alaric's back, and angled its two ATM launchers at his thinner rear armor. Alaric did not seem to realize the threat.

Tara hesitated, if only for a millisecond. Do nothing, and Alaric might be taken down. Attack the Jade Falcon and save him, and she would continue her descent into the world of the Clans. It was tempting—incredibly tempting—to do nothing. But the Khan's words from this morning still rang in her ears: *"We fight for the entire Inner Sphere...we are their best and only defense against extinction at the Jade Falcons' hands..."*

Damn! Damn it all! She raised her *Sun Cobra*'s arm-mounted Gauss rifles and locked onto the rear of the *Eyrie* as it prepared to blast the Wolf Khan. She fired. One of the shots punched deep into the *Eyrie*'s thin rear armor and knocked it face-first into the ground, hard enough that she felt the *thud* of the impact.

The Gauss rifles reloaded, and she heard the whine of their capacitors recharging. The Jade Falcon 'Mech struggled to rise, getting up on one knee just as Tara heard the tone indicating her weapons' readiness. She hit the target-interlock trigger and blasted two more massive holes into the enemy's rear hide.

Its reactor breached, and it went up in a brilliant flash, raining bits of *Eyrie* on her and Alaric's 'Mechs. The pilot punched out—*probably an automatic system*, she thought—but the ejection seat shot away at an angle. The ejecting MechWarrior slammed into the back of Alaric's *Savage Wolf*, pulverizing them. The corpse of the Falcon warrior left a wet, crimson smear on the light-gray armor plating as it slid to the ground.

Alaric turned toward her and took notice of the crumpled *Eyrie*. "Well done, Tara Wolf."

Tara grimaced. "*Seyla*," she said with deliberate intent.

"*Aff*," Alaric said. "Move in and cover me. I need to redeploy our front lines once more."

She stood at his side, her weapons sweeping the trees in the distance where she heard the staccato of battle raging.

"Beta Galaxy, form up on Phase Line Natasha," he said, and the line appeared on Tara's tactical display, just to the north of their position, running east to west. "The Jade Falcons are pushing through Kappa Galaxy, and we need to take the pressure off of them. Beta, deploy."

His *Savage Wolf* broke off in a trot, and Tara Wolf moved in alongside him.

PHASE LINE NATASHA
1000 HOURS

Star Commander Parac Shaw saw the charging *Onager* racing through the smoke and chaos of the battle. It was rushing straight for Kalidessa Kerensky, who was in a deadly duel with a squat *Shadow Cat II*. He wanted to call out to her, but saw how she was maneuvering around her target in an arc, which exposed her back to the raging *Onager*.

In his mind, the math of the fight played out: if he distracted her to the new threat, the *Shadow Cat II* would get the advantage. The solution was clear to him. "Bane Star—protect the Star Colonel!" Using his eye controls, he lit his jump jets and roared into the air, angling for the rushing green BattleMech.

The *Onager* MechWarrior saw Parac's dozen Elementals, all that remained of his Star, fill the air before him. It unleashed its hyper-assault Gauss rifle, which spat out a stream of slugs that cut Stroud in half. His leg jets continued to fire, sending his lower torso wheeling in the air, while what was left of his upper body dropped unceremoniously to the grassy ground.

Parac blazed away with his laser as he angled his flight right at *Onager*'s cockpit, which jutted outward. His laser melted a mark on the canopy as his body slammed hard into the ferroglass. A crunching sound filled his ears as ribs shattered. He stabbed his arms hard, and his battle claw ripped a small hole in the armored glass, just enough to hold onto.

"*Blitzking* ribs..." he cursed as he flailed for a moment. He suppressed the stabbing pain from his chest as he saw Kobler grapple with the shoulder opposite him.

The *Onager* pilot stopped running and twisted the 'Mech's waist hard, right to left, as the Elementals held firm, firing at point-blank range. Parac's arm ached as he turned enough to fire his short-range missiles right into the side of the cockpit. He was so close that bits of hot shrapnel and metal debris riddled his own armor.

Pain wracked his body, but he pushed through it. Kobler and Trenton, another of his Elementals, fired away at the left shoulder joint, and melted armor rained down. The *Onager* MechWarrior, who he could see through the side of the cockpit canopy, fired their jump jets. The 'Mech leaped straight upward, and used its one hand actuator to try swatting the Elementals off. It grasped Jac with its dagger-like fingers. Jac fired his leg jets and squirmed, but the MechWarrior merely squeezed harder. The jets shut off, and Jac's limp armor fell to the ground.

The *Onager* and its Howling Furies riders suddenly dropped as the Falcon warrior cut off the roaring jump jets. Parac's center of gravity shifted, and his legs went over his head, but he held on. He stabbed his laser barrel against the armored cockpit glass, where he had hit with his SRMs, and seared the hole deeper, deeper, and burst through in one spot. The metal around the hole glowed with heat. A grin rose to his face just as the BattleMech landed.

The momentum tore at him and broke his grip. He fell, and his back struck the bent knee of the 'Mech. The wave of pain continued when he hit a knocked-over pine and rolled to a stop on the forest floor.

Warning indicators flared on the small displays before his eyes. Looming over him, casting a huge shadow, the *Onager* swatted at the Elementals still crawling over it.

Parac tried to stand, but his legs did not move, and his damage display indicated nothing that would prevent it. He tried to move his right foot, but felt nothing. *Paralyzed!* His spine must have shattered during the fall.

When he tried moving his arm-mounted laser barrel, he was happy to see that the arm still worked. He raised it toward the 'Mech towering over him and fired over and over. Kobler and two other Elementals continued their work on the 'Mech's arm, and seared at the shoulder actuator until the limb went limp.

The Jade Falcon warrior turned and stepped forward, its footpad landing six meters from Parac. He ignored the proximity—he had no choice. He fired upward, cutting hot scars into the legs, one slash at a time. He strained, trying in vain to move his legs even a little as he kept firing. Another Bane Star Elemental, Jessie, roared over him, firing away at the cockpit as she rose on orange and crimson flames.

The *Onager* lifted its foot to move. Parac tried to roll aside, but his body refused to comply. The footpad came down. He heard the crunch of armor and bones—followed by an overwhelming wave of pain. Looking down, he saw the footpad's edge resting at his waist. Beyond that, his body was utterly crushed.

The *Onager* dropped to its knee, thudding into the loam nearby. Parac's vision tunneled, and a continuous roar like the sound of waves crashing filled his ears. Bane Star swarmed over the BattleMech, ripping it apart. A moment later it fell over.

Pain wracked his body, pain and heat. Still, he clung to consciousness for another few seconds, savoring the defeat of the Jade Falcon next to him.

Parac Shaw smiled as the hot darkness took him, strangely comforted that he had died fighting on Terra.

EAST OF HEARST
1100 HOURS

"Falcon Guards—charge!" Star Colonel Marv Roshak commanded as his *Night Gyr* burst through a barrage of incoming artillery fire. The explosions rained down on his OmniMech's large, arched shoulders and arms. The shells that hit the ground in front of him blew apart pine trees and threw up black clods of soil, splattering and hissing against his 'Mech's armor as he ran. On both sides of him, the other fifteen BattleMechs of the elite unit tore through the trees, seeking out targets.

As he entered the clearing, he saw one of the new Wolf BattleMechs, one streamlined and built for speed. It darted toward the onslaught of his Falcon Guards, firing its particle projection cannon at Mathews. The shot melted off a substantial bit of the *Black Lanner*'s right arm as the pilot struggled to keep track of the lightning-fast Wolf, but Roshak knew Mathews was up to the task.

His Falcon Guards consisted of the handful that had repulsed the Old Guard's assault on Malvina Hazen, and a number of new recruits. The Falcon Guards had been high on the list to get replacements, thanks to the Chingis Khan. He got the best recruits, fresh from the Falcons' *sibkos*, and the last two days of fighting the Wolves had given them much needed experience.

This day had gone well for the Jade Falcons so far, and the Guards were in the forefront of the assault. The Wolves refused to make it easy. They kept throwing in more forces in front of the main body of Jade Falcons, sometimes blunting each drive. The Falcon Guards refused to stop or even slow their advance. *The Chingis Khan demands we push through the Wolves, and that is what we will do.* Determination kept Roshak's grip tight on the targeting joystick.

As Mathews fired a wave of missiles at the sprinting foe, Roshak locked onto a four-legged Wolf 'Mech his battle computer tagged as a *Goliath*. It looked like a *Goliath*, but modified, due to its armor-reinforced knees and a dorsal turret bristling with weapons. The Star Colonel coolly brought his targeting reticle onto the *Goliath* and triggered his two ER PPCs the moment he had weapons lock. The pair of flashes filled the air and tore into one of the front legs and the raised body. Excess electrical arcs danced around the Wolf 'Mech's torso, searing the paint.

The strange *Goliath* aimed its turret and fired a Gauss rifle round, followed by an ATM salvo. The impact on his left leg staggered him, nearly toppling his *Night Gyr* as he ran forward. The missiles savaged his 'Mech's upper torso, gouging out holes in his armor. Roshak stumbled back several steps, fighting gravity and his gyro, struggling to keep upright. The moment he felt balance return, he swung to the right, maintaining his target lock.

His Ultra autocannon roared, spitting shells into the legs of the Wolf, and his medium pulse lasers sent emerald bursts into them as well. Armor bits, hot and glowing, rained into the brush under the *Goliath* as it slowly turned to keep tracking Roshak.

The Wolf MechWarrior shot another Gauss round at him, which tore into his left leg, destroying what armor remained there. He slowed his pace and focused on his target. He knew his heat was high, but the *Goliath* was an obstacle he could not simply bypass.

Roshak fired his pair of PPCs once more, turning his cockpit into a sauna as their capacitors discharged with a hum. The flashes lashed into the *Goliath* and blew the right foreleg off at the knee. The second shot slammed into the cockpit canopy. That blast lit up the interior of the cockpit in a flash, followed with a secondary explosion. The *Goliath* fell on its side and plowed into a trio of pines, snapping them off under its mass.

Roshak turned and saw Mathews still struggling with the fast-moving BattleMech. The Wolf warrior darted madly between Mathews and Loris, another Falcon Guardsman, and opened fire with a PPC and large laser, burning and blasting off the left arm of Mathews' *Black Lanner*.

Mathews pivoted tightly, breaking off his charge, then firing his lasers, he managed to riddle the legs of the fast-moving Wolf 'Mech and send it tumbling into a copse of trees, breaking them off as it fell. In the distance, he saw Pharaoh putting the finishing shots into a *Loki Mk II*, dropping his foe into a burning pine tree.

On the tight-beam channel, Roshak contacted Mathews. "You should have fired your missiles," he chided.

"I am out of SRMs, Star Colonel," Mathews' fast, breathy voice replied. "And I have only three salvos' worth of LRMs left."

"We are Jade Falcon! We are more than our munitions!" he said, switching to the tactical channel. "Falcon Guards, continue east!"

Roshak faced the enemy and returned to his advance.

STAUNTON CREEK
EAST OF HEARST
1305 HOURS

The wave of missiles hit the front of *Fratricide* one right after another, pitting the heavy frontal armor. Hawkins flinched as he banked the tank to the edge of Staunton Creek, but tried to ignore the missiles and concentrate on keeping the *Pinion* in DuJordan's sights. As he swerved, the tank dived down the embankment near the fast-moving creek and slid a few meters away from entering the icy waters.

A damage indicator light flickered on the right side armor. "What the hell...? Did we get hit in the right flank?"

"*Neg*," DuJordan called back. "Our right-front glacis plate *fell* off!"

"*Blitzking* techs!" spat Hawkins. "They must have just tack-welded it on."

"Let us hope they were not as sloppy with the rest of the repairs," DuJordan said. "Bring us right and tight, up the embankment. I have heat lock."

The Carnivore lurched up the embankment at Hawkins' firm guidance, his eyes torn between what he saw on the enhanced screen and the tactical display. The tank roared up over the embankment, and the *Pinion* came into perfect view, in the open, framed by the forest in the distance. Sensors indicated that a *Thresher Mk II* from a Gamma Galaxy Cluster was coming through the wood line in a matter of minutes, closing on the same target they were pursuing.

Our forces are getting commingled. The Jade Falcons are pushing us back, and hard.

"DuJordan, lock and fire!"

"Stop telling me how to do my job," DuJordan grumbled, but Hawkins heard the whine of the capacitors then felt the lurch of *Fratricide*'s Gauss rifles firing.

The slugs struck the *Pinion*'s left arm, destroying the heavy large laser there, leaving the barrel of an arm severed and sparking. The other slug gouged a smooth furrow across the frontal armor.

"Good shot!"

"I am well aware," DuJordan replied.

The *Pinion* fired back with its medium pulse lasers, which hit the side of the hulking Carnivore tank. The bright green bursts did not penetrate, but they warned Hawkins that he and DuJordan were far from safe. As if to emphasize that point, the *Pinion* broke into a run straight at them.

"I think you got his attention," Hawkins said, angling the tank around and throttling it.

"Do not blame me for this." DuJordan rotated the turret. "*You* told me to fire."

"Hit them again."

"Widen your turn," the gunner snapped back.

DuJordan fired the extended-range medium lasers, and the scarlet beams stabbed into the *Pinion*'s torso. He fired their Gauss rifles next. The tank lurched around them, and the nickel-ferrous slugs slammed hard into the *Pinion*'s center mass. The Jade Falcon fell into a pair of pine trees, splintering them into kindling on the way down.

"There. That is good enough for you, *quiaff*?"

"*Aff*," Hawkins said. "One down, two hundred more to go."

A badly battered Wolf *Thresher Mk II* emerged from behind the *Pinion*, smeared with mud, clumps of sod, and pine boughs. The Jade Falcon BattleMech started to rise, but the *Thresher* loosed an alpha strike of its laser, PPC, and missiles. The *Pinion* quaked under the hits—signs of explosions from within. Plumes of flames roared up from the holes the *Thresher* had carved, sending black smoke into the air.

"Hey! That was our kill!" DuJordan snapped on the proximity channel.

"*Neg*," replied the MechWarrior, whose IFF read as Burger. "I engaged them first. I am *not* having someone else claim another kill shot from me." With those words, the *Thresher Mk II* left them behind.

"I think we can argue that was ours," DuJordan said.

"I am picking up three Jade Falcons rushing our quadrant," said Hawkins. "I think there are more than enough enemies left for us to bathe ourselves in honor." He turned *Fratricide* around to brace for the coming onslaught, hoping that nothing else fell off of their precious tank.

EAST OF STAUNTON CREEK
1345 HOURS

Khalus Pryde's *Jupiter* roared as its four Ultra autocannons tore into the hide of a rushing Wolf *Gargoyle* that charged at him over the long, rugged hilltop where the center of the Jade Falcon line had formed.

The First Falcon Jaegers had been near the tip of the Falcon thrust. They had pursued the lead elements of the Wolves' Alpha Galaxy, splashing across the churning waters of Staunton Creek in devastating pursuit. The Jaegers did not hesitate, but clung tight to their targets.

The right arm of the *Gargoyle* dangled from a few myomer strands, sparking as the 'Mech ran, and Khalus' shots tore off the other arm. The Wolf did not break off and flee for their lines, which would have been the smart move. Instead the armless *Gargoyle* turned around in a tight circle and rushed forward, charging straight at him.

An amber warning light for his autocannon ammo level flickered, but Khalus ignored it. He leaned his *Jupiter* forward and broke into his own rush, straight at the *Gargoyle*. The *Jupiter* ran with massive, thudding steps and long stride in a full sprint. As the battle raged around them, the Jaegers struggled with the Wolves' elite Golden Keshik. For a few seconds, the fighting raging on around him meant nothing—all that mattered was this enemy.

The two 'Mechs hit with a staggering force, the sound of crunching and grinding armor plates filling Khalus' world. Damage indicators flickered as he lost balance, and he staggered forward an awkward step, then dropped to his right knee. He had blown past the Wolf 'Mech, sending it spinning just before he fell. Behind him the *Gargoyle* whirled, its frontal armor gone, crushed and mangled under the impact. It fell over hard, not moving.

Khalus Pryde grinned.

As the sweat stung his eyes, he slowly brought his *Jupiter* to a standing position. Moving in front of him was Archer Pryde's *Shrike*, only a few meters away, giving him cover.

"Star Colonel, are you functional?"

"I suspect I look worse than I feel," Khalus said. "I am still in this fight."

A wave of long-range missiles arced in the brilliant blue sky and rained down on Archer Pryde's 'Mech. The blown off armor clattered harmlessly off Khalus' *Jupiter*. He surveyed the battlefield, both the broken ground on the hilltop and his tactical display. The crimson and green dots from IFF transponders showed a confusing array of units and formations. *We are losing our momentum. Our units are getting mixed together. We need to regroup, but the Chingis Khan will not stand for it.*

"Your orders Star Colonel?" Archer asked.

"Standing on a hilltop will just draw unwanted fire. We need to consolidate our lines...regardless of what the Khan wants."

He switched to the tactical channel. "First Falcon Jaegers, this is Jaeger Actual. All units, move to the bottom of the hill and re-form down there, out of the enemy's line of sight. Finish off your targets and home in on my signal."

I cannot fight my battles out of fear of the Chingis Khan. What I must worry about more is this Golden Keshik. Whatever is left of me after them, Malvina is welcome to.

1410 HOURS

Khan Ward angled his *Savage Wolf* to a wooded hilltop to afford him a view of the approaching Jade Falcon line. From his perch, he saw the emerald green 'Mechs as they pushed back the Golden Keshik. Zooming out his tactical display, he saw the broader picture.

Most of his forces were to the south, where Beta Galaxy had been an anchor. Everything in front of the Jade Falcon assault was crumbling. Explosions and smoke rolled off dozens of individual battles as they raged. Occasionally a laser or PPC fired wildly into the air, deadly fireworks gone awry. The Jade Falcons were slowly eroding his center and northern line. To a casual observer, all things being equal, it seemed that the Jade Falcons were going to drive his Wolves from the field.

But all things are not equal...

In that instant, with Tara at his side, as Alaric looked at the display, he saw what a Jade Falcon victory would look like. They would drive eastward, churning up what remained of Clan Wolf, then wheel to the south and finish their bloody work.

He crunched the inescapable mathematics of the battle; the odds were almost even, but the Jade Falcons held the advantage. If he did nothing, the Jade Falcons would be ilClan and his Wolves would be erased from history. Immense power and responsibility surged in him at that moment.

He hit the command channel. "General Vickers, how does it look to you?"

"I believe it is time," Chance replied from her position some four kilometers east at the mobile HQ.

"As do I," he said with remarkable calm. He opened a channel to all of Clan Wolf. "This is Wolf Prime. Oblique the lines. Northern and center forces, wheel right and swing like a door."

The Wolves did not respond verbally, they acted. He saw the lines move in the distance, slowly at first, then with rapidity. He switched over to the command channel again.

"General Vickers, execute Athena Rising. Bring them in on the northern flank of the field, and have them await my order."

"Confirmed—executing Athena Rising," Vickers replied with a hint of relief in her voice.

1424 HOURS

Malvina's *Black Rose* delivered a devastating punch to the *Timber Wolf*, hitting it in the side near the reactor housing. The Wolf 'Mech stumbled away from her, sidestepping. She fired both of her medium lasers at point-blank range, further melting the hole her clawed fist had made.

The black-and-gray-streaked *Timber Wolf* staggered in clumsy, swaying steps and crashed onto its side. Malvina fired her jump jets and rose over the fallen foe as the pilot rocked the big 'Mech to try righting it. She cut the jets and dropped ten meters to land directly on top of the *Timber Wolf*. She ignored the metallic grinding and crushing noise as she shifted her center of balance to keep *Black Rose* upright. Her damage displays showed the enemy 'Mech's fusion engine was offline. *Your Bloodline ends here.*

Movement caught her eye. A row of spheroid DropShips were flying in, forming a long line to the north of her offensive, some six kilometers distant.

SaKhan Ryan Pryde's stressed voice came over the command channel. "Chingis Khan, the enemy is deploying numerous DropShips along the northern edge of the zone of combat."

"I am not blind, Ryan," she said calmly. "They are of no concern."

"No concern, *quineg?*"

"*Aff,*" Malvina said as she studied the tactical display. "This is the kind of misdirection Alaric Ward is known for. All of the Galaxies he has left are engaged and accounted for. He is distracting you with empty DropShips." *I refuse to play your game, Alaric.*

Malvina switched her channel to communicate to all of her Jade Falcons. "This is the Chingis Khan. Ignore those DropShips and concentrate on punching through the Wolves' center. They seek to distract us. Omega Galaxy, shift to the south and concentrate your efforts in a thrust to the southeast."

She stepped into a muddy bog of black sod and pushed toward the last fragments of the Wolves that were starting to fade back to the south. *Alaric Ward will now watch his Clan die at my hands. This is the final hour of the Wolf.*

1427 HOURS

Alaric watched the long line of DropShips flying low and ready over his position, all with their names and designations painted over. The air around him rumbled with explosions and the crackle of PPC fire. A quick check verified that the

Wolves still held the north, and below them to the south was the vanguard of the Jade Falcons.

"General Vickers—cut them loose!"

1432 HOURS

The Chingis Khan was leading her Command Star up a hill for a better view when she heard the sudden explosion in comm chatter. She stepped *Black Rose* up the hillside, avoiding the mangled arm of a fallen Wolf *Wulfen*, and looked to the north, where the sounds were resonating from.

On the hilltop, she could see the DropShips' doors were opened, the ramps extended. Pouring out of the ships and right into her flank were hundreds of BattleMechs and tanks...there seemed to be no end to them. They fanned out all along the northern edge of the Jade Falcon flank.

Impossible!

Activating her zoom feature, she concentrated on the first wave of forces that had debarked. She saw rust-red BattleMechs trimmed in black and other large units in a shade of green that mimicked her own Jade Falcons. Then she saw the insignia: a red circle with a black snarling wolf, with a teardrop under the eye.

Wolf's Dragoons. Impossible! They are mercenaries...bellycrawlers! They would never *fight for Clan Wolf.* Her eyes, however, told a different story as they hit the northern Falcon flank.

Then she remembered their history. Many of the original Wolf's Dragoons had been freeborn Clan Wolf warriors. *Alaric could never have brought them back to fight here...now.*

Looking to the west of the long line of DropShips, she saw maroon-and-orange BattleMechs and tanks plowing south, right into her lines. Brown-and-gray BattleMechs mingled with a long line of black ones. These bore the insignia of Clan Wolf...but she knew the paint schemes all too well.

The Wolves-in-Exile? Stravag! *Alaric has united with the wayward Wolves!*

She immediately realized the threat and reacted. "Jade Falcons, form a defensive arc to the north and east!" she barked over the chatter on the channel. "Vau and Gamma, hold the center with Alpha. Raptor Keshik, pull forward to my position."

A voice came over one of the open channels—a voice Malvina had heard before, and one that set her blood ablaze:

"Malvina Hazen, this is Anastasia Kerensky. I am coming for you."

CHAPTER 34

EAST OF STAUNTON CREEK
NORTH AMERICA
19 APRIL 3151, 1422 HOURS
(T+99, DAY 3 OF THE ILCLAN TRIAL)

Anastasia Kerensky charged her *Savage Wolf* out of the DropShip and saw the battle raging in almost every direction. Most of the fighting had been to the west. A few fires smoldered, some raged. Dozens of BattleMech footpads and tank treads had torn up the ground. Trees were knocked over, crushed, snapped off at various heights, and in some cases blown apart by errant rounds.

Combat vehicles and BattleMechs of every conceivable mass and combat role were shooting, fighting 'Mech-to-'Mech, running, or lying blasted apart on the battlefield. Clusters on both sides were intermixed, and it was chaos, the likes of which she had never before witnessed. Then there was the sound, a continuous, erratic rumble of explosions, the occasional moan of protesting metal, the *snap-crack* of PPC fire—like an opera written in the bowels of hell.

Anastasia grinned like the Wolf she was. *This is where I belong.*

She, the former Wolves-in-Exile, and Wolf's Dragoons had been sitting in DropShips since February, watching events unfold across Terra. It had been frustrating, and when alone, she often cursed Alaric for not bringing her into the fight earlier. That was part of her problem. *When you know you are the best at something and are not allowed to do it, it generates rage.*

Anastasia had been sent to bring back the Wolves-in-Exile. The negotiations had proven challenging. *I have never been a diplomat... I am a warrior, a leader. He may have been better served sending someone else. Alaric gave me leeway in negotiating with them, so I hope he approves of my method.*

Several times she thought she might be denied the honor of killing Malvina, but true to form, the Falcon Khan had survived. *She is as hard to kill as a cockroach and as easy to deal with as a cornered rat. So much the better, because it means I get to do what I was brought here to do.*

The time aboard the DropShips had given her the opportunity to observe Alaric and Chance wage their war against the Republic and the Jade Falcons. It had been brilliant. Alaric luring of the Northwind Highlanders out of their redoubt and into the open was something Anastasia admired. She could not fault the Republic for trying to take out the Clan leaders...after all, that was what she was going to do with Malvina.

Anastasia begrudgingly admitted that Malvina had shown herself to be every bit a great strategist. Her siege of Geneva followed the classic Clan military doctrine of taking the capital, but Anastasia would not have done it that way. *I would have saved Geneva for the end, let them starve for a while, enjoy some long-range artillery.* Still, Malvina's Falcons had managed to battle in Africa, the Americas, and Europe with a high degree of skill. Only in Japan had she suffered a devastating loss to the Republic, allegedly losing an entire Galaxy, with no reported survivors.

As much as she admired Malvina's military prowess, Anastasia saw her for what she was. *She is a cancer, one that must be excised and utterly destroyed.*

Her heart pounded in her chest like a war drum, urging her into the fight. Every sense accelerated as she soaked in the massive field of battle and switched to the command channel. "General, this is Athena. Paint me a picture. Where is my objective?"

"One moment, Athena." Chance kept her on the line as she barked out commands. "Wolf aerospace forces. I need the location of the Raptor Keshik, and I need it now."

There was a wave of "*Roger thats*" and "*Affs*" then a few moments of silence.

Anastasia moved her *Savage Wolf* forward, watching as Wolf's Dragoons slammed into a large formation of Jade Falcons that had wheeled around to face them. *Come on...* She broke into a trot, heading south, toward the fighting.

Then a male voice came on, "General, this is Ravager One. Tallyho on Raptor Keshik. General. Gray, black, and light green...in Quadrant Lima. Tagging them now."

"Did you copy that, Athena?" Chance asked.

"*Aff.* I am heading there now!" Anastasia broke her gray and red-striped *Savage Wolf* into a full run toward the coordinates Ravager Star was feeding her.

A brilliant green *Fire Moth* fired at her flank as she ran past a fallen *Dire Wolf*. The light 'Mech's pair of medium lasers hit her right side, and she torso-twisted, sending a wave of advanced tactical missiles streaking into the already-damaged Jade Falcon. The *Fire Moth* twisted in place, its run suddenly halted. A quick shot with her right-arm ER PPC hit it square in the cockpit. There was a brilliant explosion within, and the *Fire Moth* toppled over.

Without breaking stride, Anastasia continued her sprint to Quadrant Lima.

1445 HOURS

Star Captain Marotta Kerensky piloted his red-trimmed black *Dominator* right into the path of a damaged *Ryoken II*. Having spent months away from his Clan and missing out on the battles to take Terra from the Republic, he wanted to prove himself, and the larger, 75-ton Falcon 'Mech would prove a more than suitable opponent.

Khan Ward had sent Marotta to the Wolf's Dragoons to broker an agreement where the Dragoons would return to Clan Wolf on their own accord, and the Dragoons deploying to the battlefield on this day meant he had fulfilled his mission and brought them back to their ancestral home.

In this battle, Brubaker's command was to be the tip of the spear against the Jade Falcons. They had spent the past several weeks spent cooped up on their DropShips, to ensure the Jade Falcon Watch had no hint of what awaited them. Now, the Dragoons sprinted forward, plowing right into the heart of the Jade Falcon formations. In a matter of minutes, they had driven deep, wreaking havoc in every direction.

Marotta had not only studied the mercenaries, read everything he could find on them, he had already had the honor of fighting with them during the brief internal insurrection back on Parma. They were elite...he knew that. But to fight with them as they performed their craft was like watching a master sculptor or painter working. The only difference was that the Dragoons' art was the art of war, and their BattleMechs and tanks were their brush.

Marotta had used the time aboard the DropShip to custom paint his *Dominator*. Just below the cockpit, he had a perfect representation of the Jade Falcon insignia, surrounded by a circle of red with a slash painted diagonally through it.

Marotta had fought on many battlefields, but none on the scale and scope of this one. It looked like a continuous fireworks display around him. The ground was churned by explosions, old and new. Dirt splattered on his cockpit canopy, as did a rattle of shrapnel from a nearby blast. Flashes in the smoke cast eerie shadows everywhere, and the roar and thunder were continuous and without pattern. His eyes fell on a severed *Timber Wolf* leg that stood alone, upright, like a grave marker.

He smoothly brought his targeting reticle onto the battered *Ryoken II* and slashed its right side with his large laser. Molten armor sprayed into the air as he followed up with his ER PPC, which speared deep into the remaining protection there.

The *Ryoken II* turned on him like a wounded animal and fired one rack of long-range missiles and a salvo from one of its LB 2-X autocannons. The cluster rounds hit Marotta's *Dominator* like buckshot from a massive shotgun, shredding some of his armor.

Juking to the right, Marotta blazed away with his particle projection cannon again and seared a white-hot hole in the left leg. Smoke swirled out as the *Ryoken II* spun in place to keep him in its sights. Another barrage with the same autocannon riddled Marotta's right side with cluster rounds.

Normally the *Ryoken II* had the firepower to be a deadly foe, but this one was holding back for some reason. *Why is it not firing its LRMs?* His targeting-and-tracking system told him the enemy's LRM launchers were undamaged. *Is the weapon malfunctioning?*

Marotta's Streak missiles squealed a high-pitched target-lock tone, and he let them fly. Four hit the long cockpit canopy of the *Ryoken II* while the others exploded lower. A spider web of cracks appeared in the ferroglass as the MechWarrior swung around to protect their 'Mech's head. Doing so exposed their rear armor for a shot.

Marotta tuned out the other battles raging only a half kilometer away, and focused as only a Clan Trueborn could. His PPC capacitors whined, and an azure bolt of charged particles filled the space between the two BattleMechs, connecting them for a moment.

The shot seared through the enemy's weaker rear armor, lancing deep into the body of the Jade Falcon 'Mech. It seemed to have a seizure of some sort, quaking in place—unable to move. It looked as if it were preparing to sprint, but could not. One leg rose slightly, which made it tip to the side, then collapse. The boxy right-side missile rack crumpled under the force of the fall.

The launch tubes were empty, and no missiles tumbled out of the destroyed launcher. Neg, *they were just out of ammunition.*

The Jade Falcon MechWarrior jabbed the 'Mech's massive hands into the ground and started to rise. Marotta moved around it, to try for another strike to the rear while charging his PPC. The enemy 'Mech got on its knees, perfectly exposing the huge, blackened hole his earlier shot had left.

Marotta lined up the shot, and another brilliant, blue-white blast hit just above the hole, lighting up the interior of the *Ryoken II* and sending arcs of excess discharge flailing around the 'Mech.

There was a blinding flash as the fusion reactor was breached and exploded, the light auto-darkening Marotta's cockpit canopy. The 'Mech's right hand spun in the air and hit Marotta's left side. It did no damage but clattered down to the ground.

A black *Blood Reaper* approached the destroyed *Ryoken II*, now a shallow crater filled with bits of smoking BattleMech. "Excellent work, Star Captain," said Captain Deborah Sheridan. "I need you to form up on me. The Black Wolves have been assigned the Falcons' Zeta Galaxy as our objective."

Marotta followed the Dragoons officer as Andrew Roy's *Ice Storm* and Silva Schröder's *Goliath C* fell in behind her. The rest of the Black Wolves Company swung in line behind Marotta as they rushed to the south, with the battle still raging on both sides of them as far as the eye could see.

1505 HOURS

Stephanie Chistu chased after a Dragoons Plainsman hovertank and caught it at the outermost range of her *Jade Hawk*'s short-range lasers. The scarlet beams stabbed at the tan hovertank, hitting it in the vertical stabilizer, blasting it to pieces—but the hovertank didn't stop. It poured on the speed, raced out of range, and shouldered through a dense copse of pines. The Plainsman disappeared in the smoky haze.

Chistu's body ached as she turned her 'Mech around. Everything was going wrong.

An hour ago, the Jade Falcons were poised to win everything. But then Wolf's Dragoons and the former Wolves-in-Exile arrived. The Dragoons were like a storm unleashed on the Jade Falcons, multiple regiments of fresh troops and equipment commanded by skilled warriors. Expectations of victory had disintegrated into thoughts of mere survival. *How did we not see them coming?*

Her Delta Galaxy had formed the northern edge of the Jade Falcon formation, and the Dragoons had cut straight through it, splitting her forces in half. At first she feared they would swing right or left and finish them off, but the Dragoons just kept going, heading farther south. *Their losses do not stop them...the mark of elite warriors.*

Chistu assessed the battle zone. A Dragoons *Annihilator* toppled about a half kilometer away after being struck by multiple lasers. The 'Mech's black color with red pinstriping told her it was from the infamous Spider's Web Battalion. While she should have been overjoyed at the sight of the *Annihilator*'s defeat, it only made her feel weary. *The Wolf Spiders... Can it get any worse for us today,* quineg?

As if to answer her question, the downed 'Mech fired a deadly salvo into a Jade Falcon *Gargoyle* and nearly cut it in half. Its fusion reactor flared in a brilliant flash as the OmniMech died from the inside out.

Chistu's weapons loadout discouraged her. Aside from her quartet of small lasers, she had one flight of short-range missiles left. She had done everything possible to conserve her expendables, but it still wasn't enough. *I can count on one hand the number of times I have run out of ammunition in a battle.*

That realization stirred fury in her mind. Chistu was angry—at Malvina Hazen for getting her beloved Jade Falcons into this plight. At Alaric Ward for delivering such a devastating blow. *We were so close to victory an hour ago, and now we are being overrun. For all of Malvina's successes thus far, Alaric's strategy has tipped the scales of victory to his favor.*

She broke into a run to keep her heat level high enough to maintain the effectiveness of her triple-strength myomer. *I am still in this fight, and as long as I live, Clan Jade Falcon lives.*

She turned around to look for a target to the north, and spotted an undamaged midnight-blue *Marauder IIC* breaking through the pines, its weapons sweeping in her direction. The Galaxy Commander clenched her jaw and broke into a blazing sprint across the fresh 'Mech's field of fire.

CHAPTER 35

Colonel Aaron Krull of Wolf's Dragoons Seventh Kommando had the driver of his Bandit stop just short of the hilltop. He climbed out and peered in the distance. The rumble of the main fighting was to his rear, and he wanted it to stay there, at least until his team fulfilled their mission. Somewhere in that chaos, his brother was fighting, and he hoped Andrew was still in the mix. *Hopefully he knows not to do anything foolhardy...*

Then he saw it, a large airstrip, with technicians and pilots running around. A few combat vehicles—captured RAF gear, no doubt—were positioned on the perimeter: A Ranger VV1, a pair of Scapha hovertanks, and two Fox armored cars that still bore the Triarii Protectors markings on their forward hulls. There was infantry too, a lot of them, no doubt *solahma* assigned to garrison a rear area. Most non-Clan people thought of *solahma* as washed-up old warriors, but Colonel Krull knew differently. *They* want *to die in battle, which makes them much more dangerous.*

He returned to his hovertank, his mind racing through targets, objectives, and the firepower they faced. Climbing aboard the Bandit, he grabbed the comm system mike.

"All right, Kommandos, here's the plan. Alpha Company, you will target the vehicles and make their crews un-alive. Move south of here, target the big boys, and catch them before than get up to speed.

"Bravo Company, there is a lot of infantry out there... Come in from the north and draw them to you. Watch for human-wave attacks, since they know the stakes by now.

"Charlie Company, we will go in for the prize after Alpha and Bravo get the defenders' attention. Our APCs will drop us on the tarmac, and we will plant charges on the fighters and blow them quickly. Then we will drag them and whatever other equipment we can out to block the runways."

As he spoke, a pair of Jade Falcon fighters warmed up their burners, preparing to take off. "All right, move on my command."

The Kommando companies moved to their staging positions in a matter of minutes, and signaled Aaron when they were ready. He took off his helmet and rubbed his spiked blond hair. It was so sweaty and itchy—just like before every battle. Putting the helmet back on, he drew a long deep breath, lowered himself into the hovertank, and closed the hatch.

"All right, Seventh Kommando, you know the drill. Hit them!"

The *purr* and *pop* of small-arms fire came from the north and south as the Dragoons Special Forces hit the airfield from two different directions. "Charlie—let's roll!"

Five hovercraft—the two Bandits and three zoomers—roared over the low hill. To their credit, one Point of *solahma*—twenty-five Falcon infantrymen— had not taken the bait, and stood ready to face Aaron's troops. Small-arms fire pinged and dinged the Bandit's front armor, along with a portable SRM launcher that shook the vehicle hard. Looking out the main viewport, he saw the infantry rise up and rush straight at them, guns blazing.

Fools.

His Bandit launched its short-range missiles into the *solahma* ranks, leaving huge holes where warriors had once been. The other Bandit let go with LRMs that tossed Falcon infantry into the air upon detonation.

Aaron's hovercraft closed the gap in two more heartbeats as infantry bullets ricocheted off the armor harmlessly, but the Bandit did not slow down. It collided with three of the Jade Falcons, and the dull *thuds* that rang throughout the fighting compartment spoke to the fate of those warriors. *What a waste of fine infantry.*

As the vehicles fanned out on the tarmac, Colonel Krull popped his hatch and stood. Off to the left, Alpha Company blew up a Fox and Scapha almost simultaneously. Semi-portable PPCs flashed into the Ranger as it tried to wheel around, turning two of its right tires into worthless slag and sending the vehicle into a roll. A Jade Falcon SM1 fired its massive autocannon and blew up a black Kommando Bandit, consuming the hovercraft in a ball of flames.

The pair of warmed-up aerospace fighters gunned their engines and taxied toward the runway, but a Dragoons Savannah Master from Alpha darted and weaved through the small-arms fire and rammed the fighter's front landing gear. The nose of the fighter came down on top of the tiny hovercraft and crushed it flat, blocking the runway.

Small-arms fire from Charlie Company poured into the second fighter as its pilot attempted to turn and bring its weapons to bear. Sergeant Gideon sprinted over to the fighter's flank, slapped a shaped charge on the side of the cockpit, and hit the detonator. The charge blasted a plume of superheated energy into the fuselage, filling the cockpit with fire and smoke. The engines winked out and stopped.

Aaron rose out of his hatch. "All right, Charlie, set charges on the rest of them! Move, move, move!"

The infantry on the zoomers jumped out, and everyone slapped their shaped charges on the wings and fuselage of the aircraft. Krull hoisted himself out of his hovertank with a pair of charges in hand. He came up on a battered Jade Falcon *Chippewa IIC* parked over the rearming pit. Aaron climbed up to the cockpit, pried open the canopy, and slapped the charge on the controls. *Let's see you fly after this.* He slid off and darted back to his Bandit.

Off to his right, he saw a flight-suited pilot rush out from one of the tents and spray automatic fire at his troops. Three of Aaron's Dragoons were hit and went down. Eight others returned fire, cutting the warrior in half with semiautomatic rifles and crimson laser beams. *He should have stuck to piloting.* One of his downed troopers rose to his feet, his body armor having shrugged off the bullets.

On Aaron's far left, a trio of Falcon technicians with pistols made the mistake of firing at his Kommandos as well. They were just as efficiently cut down by returned small-arms fire from the Dragoons.

"Charges set, Colonel," Captain Matthew "Bloodbath" Behrens called out.

"Clear the area," Aaron barked.

The infantry loaded back onto their zoomers, which whisked away from the airfield alongside Aaron's Bandit. Once they were all seventy or so meters away, he made the call.

"Pop 'em, Bloodbath!"

The shaped charges devastated the aerospace fighters in a roar of explosions, blasting massive holes in wings and stabilizers, destroying engines—anything to disable the fighters. Parts of aircraft rained down on the tarmac. Aaron smiled. *That should make the Old Man happy. Unity!*

The fighting still raged to the north of the airfield, though by now the remaining Jade Falcon *solahma* must have known the Seventh Kommando had drawn them off. Random shots, some laser, some ballistic, peppered his Bandit. It was enough to make him duck. The Jade Falcon warriors were determined—he had to give them that.

"Charlie Company, swing over and provide suppression fire for Alpha," he ordered as the Bandit turned.

A Jade Falcon Sokar sprayed one of his squads with its flamer. In horror, he saw his Kommandos on fire, dropping and rolling, and in one case, running in panic. The Bandit to his right fired its PPC into the Sokar's side armor, and hot-metal splattered into the air as the excess electrical energy danced across the Jade Falcon's hull.

"Michael, take that bastard out!" Aaron barked to his gunner.

The Jade Falcon SM1 was sputtering away, dragging its rear right-side hover skirt as his infantry raked it with small-arms fire. It made a slow arc, not to flee, but to turn and fire again. *Damned Falcons!*

As the Sokar exploded, Colonel Krull's trained eyes surveyed the remainder of the Falcon infantry making their last stand as his troops rained mortars down on them. *Now that we have taken the airfield, we have to* hold *it. One thing is for sure: the Jade Falcons won't be launching these fighters anytime soon.*

Then he heard the roar in the distance. Jade Falcon fighters—no doubt returning from a strike mission and looking to land. *Double damn...*

"Heads up, Kommandos! We have incoming!"

CHAPTER 36

EAST OF STAUNTON CREEK
19 APRIL 3151, 1522 HOURS
(T+99, DAY 3 OF THE ILCLAN TRIAL)

Malvina's *Black Rose* slammed a fist into a gray-and-white *Pack Hunter*, driving into the cockpit. The *Pack Hunter* went limp and hung on the end of her 'Mech's arm, lifeless. Malvina withdrew the limb, and the Wolf-in-Exile 'Mech collapsed into a heap.

This should not be possible. The Wolves and the Exiles have never *seen eye to eye, and Alaric's last attempt at negotiation with them had failed. Yet here they are.* She would have killed Abzug Helmer for this intelligence failure, but he had denied her that privilege by getting himself killed on the first day of the trial.

Then there had been the transmission from Anastasia Kerensky. That infuriated Malvina even more. *She is said to be the best Clan Wolf warrior, and I will have the satisfaction of killing her for her Steel Wolves' involvement in Aleks' death on Skye.* She had all but forgotten about the missing Kerensky, and now here Anastasia was, at the head of an advancing Galaxy, *I will kill her and then show her corpse to Alaric so he knows the price of his failure.*

Malvina ignited her jump jets and rose up as three battered Points of Callisto Clan Wolf battle armor bore in on her. They had just finished off a Jade Falcon *Fire Moth*, reducing it to little more than a smoking, gutted shell. She licked her lips at the sight of them. *I am the Chingis Khan, and I will not be taken down by mere battle armor.*

The moment she landed in a churned-up spot in a clearing, Malvina sprinted her *Shrike* straight at them, unloading her ER PPCs as she charged.

1530 HOURS

The burly Major Andrew Krull of Wolf's Dragoons Gamma Regiment angled his *Marauder IIC* backward, away from the incoming *Jade Hawk*. He had never seen a faster and nimbler BattleMech of that size; it dodged back and forth as it closed the distance with him. After weeks of being cooped up on a DropShip, he had wanted nothing more than to engage in battle. Now that he was in it, he remembered just how dangerous it could be.

This was unlike any battle he had ever experienced. The size was staggering, and it raged everywhere around him, as far as the eye could see. Hundreds of warriors were battling as the lines became blurred, with the Dragoons and Jade Falcons caught in a hurricane of running and shooting 'Mechs. Somewhere in rear of all of this chaos, his brother Aaron was undertaking his own mission, though Andrew tried to not think of him as missiles flew past.

The battlefield was littered with bits and pieces of vehicles and 'Mechs. Random fires filled the air with a strange, fog-like smoke. The air was alive with missiles and autocannon tracer rounds. Laser and PPC beams pierced the chaos in every direction. The ground and air vibrated around him, and there was an erratic rumble of explosions, some far away, some dangerously close. Random death rained down and blasted the air around him. It was exciting and deadly, far beyond his previous experience. *This isn't like fighting the Federated Suns at all. This is controlled chaos.*

The *Jade Hawk* chasing him had already dispatched two Dragoons 'Mechs in a matter of heartbeats. It had moved like a green blur, firing and shooting with a speed and accuracy that shocked Krull. The last one to fall, a rotund *Imp* piloted by Captain Johnny Watson, had been struck three times in the rear while Krull had battled with a *Jupiter*. The *Imp* had fallen hard into a clump of trees and mud, sizzling with heat as it fought to stand up.

Come on Johnny...push it! Krull tuned out the *Imp*'s struggle, focusing on the *Jade Hawk* instead. Blazing away with his three ER PPCs and pair of medium lasers, his entire universe became that *Jade Hawk*. His lasers missed, the beams of green energy leaving wisps of smoke on the black soil around the wily Falcon 'Mech. The PPC blasts slammed into the *Jade Hawk*'s right leg, peeling back a massive armor plate that ground against the other leg.

The *Jade Hawk* was a close-combat brawler—and with its triple-strength myomer, Krull knew it would want to get into melee range. He broke into his own run, away from the Jade Falcon, to give himself some distance and time. For those moments, it felt as if his *Marauder II C* was an extension of his body, like a deadly layer of skin.

The Falcon warrior was dogging him, closing distance but not firing yet. Krull twisted his 'Mech at the waist and fired two of his three PPCs at his pursuer, hoping to make the pilot keep their distance. One grazed the cockpit, and the second shot slammed into the torso. Krull followed up with his medium lasers. One missed; the other gouged the damaged leg. The bits of melted armor trailed smoke and small fires in the charging 'Mech's wake.

When the enemy got into missile range, Krull braced himself for a flight of short-range missiles, and was not disappointed. Some hit his right side and leg, doing little more than marring his paint scheme. Small lasers stabbed at him and hit his right side and arm, but also did little damage.

The capacitors for his PPCs reached a high pitch, indicating they were ready. Steadying his targeting reticle, Krull squeezed the triggers. The air between him and his target flashed brilliant white, dazzling his eyes for a moment. The beams of charged particles slammed into the *Jade Hawk*'s right side and arm. The arm, already hammered from the day's fighting, tore off and bounced on the ground behind the oncoming 'Mech.

Krull allowed himself a moment to grin, bristling his black beard and mustache inside his neurohelmet. *If you want it up close and personal now, you've got it.* He fired both lasers again, and the brilliant crimson beams seared into the *Jade Hawk*, hitting the cockpit and body. *How is that MechWarrior still standing?* Slowly, it hit him that he was fighting someone who might be a better pilot than him.

The *Jade Hawk*'s damaged leg struggled to move, and the run became a slow limp as the warrior dragged it, flopping the leg forward only enough to keep moving. It fired again—lasers only, this time—slashing Krull's *Marauder IIC*, but doing no serious damage.

He moved in closer, narrowing, keeping the target in his sights, and he suddenly had complete control of the engagement. His medium lasers flashed scarlet as a surge of heat rose around him. The Jade Falcon MechWarrior, knowing their frontal armor was little more than random fragments, had twisted at the last moment, letting the shots strike their relatively intact but thinner rear armor.

Krull's eyes widened; it had been a gutsy move; he gave his enemy that much.

He continued circling the *Jade Hawk*, waiting as his PPCs built up the energy for another shot. He fired the right-arm one, and the searing energy smashed into the *Jade Hawk*'s damaged leg, which spun away into the burning forest. His thoughts raced ahead to the moment when he would see the Jade Falcon BattleMech collapse once and for all.

To Krull's amazement, the *Jade Hawk* fired its jump jets rather than falling from the limb loss. It rose and blazed away with small lasers, most of which Krull simply ignored. The enemy came toward him in their flight arc, clearly trying for a Death From Above. *This MechWarrior is nothing if not persistent.* Krull quickly ran out of its jump range.

When the *Jade Hawk* landed, it bent its remaining leg hard, struggling like hell to stay upright—but did so. *Unity! Am I fighting Natasha Kerensky herself?* The MechWarrior even managed to hop a few steps toward him, trying to angle for a shot.

This ends now. Krull fired his left-arm PPC and pair of medium pulse lasers, turning his cockpit into a sauna. The PPC took off the *Jade Hawk*'s left arm, sending it spinning away, and one of the medium pulse lasers riddled the cockpit while the other blasting apart an innocent pine tree into wooden shrapnel.

Krull watched the 'Mech drop like a puppet whose strings had been cut. Wasting no time, he checked his tactical display and found a *Loki Mk II* a quarter kilometer away. He took off toward it, leaving the *Jade Hawk* pilot to their fate.

Stephanie Chistu now fought in a brand-new battle—this one between consciousness and death.

The dark blue Dragoon *Marauder IIC* had torn her *Jade Hawk* apart one limb at a time. The last hit had filled her cockpit with the smell of ozone and left a coppery taste in her mouth. A wet, red sheen blurred the faceplate of her neurohelmet, and she realized it was a mist of her own blood. *Taken down by a mercenary!*

She cursed the Chingis Khan for putting her in this position. *I will not die, not on her altar of madness!* Her determination, however, was fading with each beat of her heart. She began to hyperventilate, and panic threatened to consume her for the first time in years.

Chistu tried to raise her arms, but her left one felt as if it were on fire and did not respond. She popped her faceplate and smelled smoke and the stink of charred flesh. Dizziness from blood loss swept over her, but she managed to activate her rescue beacon on the console before succumbing to the darkness.

1550 HOURS

Star Commander Manning tried to juke his battered *Jagatai* clear of the approaching Jade Falcon *Scytha*, but the Falcon pilot was too good and too intent on colliding with him. It barely clipped his wing, but it was enough to tear into the control surfaces. The Jade Falcon careened off in a death spiral, nosing down for the battlefield below.

Vigdal and Guethler had already been taken down. The Jade Falcons fighters had massed against his Star. He hoped they had managed to eject, but it was impossible to keep track of them in the continuous dogfighting that thundered over the Canadian skies. *I am all that remains of Ravager Star, and my fighter is dying.*

His controls now wanted to fight him as the OmniFighter began a shallow dive. He wanted to accelerate, hopefully pull up and build enough energy to flatten out the dive—but it was clear that was not going to happen. Ejection was possible, but by the time he considered it, the window of opportunity had passed. Punching out low was not the same as ejecting from a BattleMech. *I need to ride this one down.* Crimson warning lights flickered on his neurohelmet visor as he interlocked his fingers on the control stick and hauled it back with all of his might.

Cutting his engines would have turned the OmniFighter into a flying brick, so he kept the power up; at least he could use them to control his decent somewhat. Glancing down, he saw an almost endless field of battle: blackened ground, destroyed BattleMechs and vehicles, and brilliant laser shots being fired in every direction. *As long as I do not land in Jade Falcon territory, I should be all right.*

The *Jagatai* leveled off slightly as Manning closed on the ground far too quickly. He hit the flap levers, alternating them to provide some degree of steering, and the OmniFighter again tried to buck what little control he had. He plowed through the haze and plumes of smoke rising from the battlefield, and spotted a small pond and a swampy area in the distance. Manning's shoulders ached as he pulled to the right, aiming for it. *Come on...hold together for just another second...*

He landed hard, and his body was tossed against his safety harness as the fighter skidded for fifty meters before hitting the edge of the pond. Water washed over his canopy and splattered down on him when he hit the emergency release. As he removed his harness, he felt a pain in his lower chest. *My ribs—bruised or broken.* Stravag!

The *Jagatai* settled into the shallow pond, steam rising off it as he stepped out onto the shrapnel-riddled wing. He made sure his sidearm was loaded before wading into the muddy, waist-deep waters away from his fallen craft. The exterior of his flight suit was soaked, but it was of little consequence. *I am thankful to be alive. I will be more thankful once I am back at the airfield.* He was not looking forward to telling Kalidessa Kerensky he had been shot down.

Only a few hundred meters way, he saw a dusty-gray *War Dog* topple, riddled by a brilliant green *Onager*'s hyper-assault Gauss rifle. The *War Dog* bore the snarling wolf's head of Wolf's Dragoons.

Manning was stunned. *Wolf's Dragoons...? Khan Ward must have brought them into this fight somehow!* He allowed himself to smile for the first time in many days.

As a PPC beam from afar struck the *Onager*, sending molten armor spraying into the air, Manning realized just how vulnerable he was. He pushed through the water, scrambling for the bank.

Suddenly, a hand gripped his shoulder. He turned and saw a Wolf warrior—old, bald, with a long scar running up his neck to his gleaming, sweaty scalp. The old man's rank insignia marked him as a Star Captain. "That was an incredible landing, Star Commander. Are you okay?" he asked in a voice that sounded years younger.

Still stunned, Manning gave him a thumbs-up.

"Stick with us," the *solahma* Star Captain said. "With just your laser pistol, you are exposed in this battle zone. The Falcons have infantry squads out hunting downed MechWarriors and pilots. You are my charge now." The old man turned to his squad. "Juanita, Jade Falcons are approaching from the northeast."

The female warrior, her skin wrinkled like leather, grinned. "We still have a dozen mortar rounds left, Star Captain."

He nodded. "Do not wait for me—target and fire for effect."

A mortar team of four began setting up while two more of the *solahma* infantry climbed into a crater, and using the edge for cover, swept the area with enhanced binoculars to locate targets. Suddenly gunfire burst from where they were looking. One of the pair was tugged backward as a bullet pierced his shoulder and exited the other side in a spray of blood. The other pulled back as the bullets hit the edge of the crater. Manning ducked low, as did the Star Captain.

"Elevation two-one-seven," Juanita called.

The mortar team dropped a single round into the tube, and it launched with a *whoomp*. A few moments later one more explosion mixed with the other sounds of pitched battle.

"Adjust three right, fire for effect!"

The crew dropped in mortar rounds so fast it was as if they were a machine. Machine-gun fire raked the edge of the crater, which provided scant cover. Hunched over, the infantry Star Captain pushed Manning flat and lay between him and the incoming rounds.

"Splash three," Juanita called back as the gunfire abruptly stopped. "Hold fire."

They all rise, slowly, still hunched. The old warrior rolled off Manning and got up, oblivious to the mud and grime. If anything, he looked happy.

"Thank you," Manning said, extending his hand. "What is your name?"

The Star Captain grinned and shook. "I am Rowland. Stay close to me, and we will get you back to our rear area. Until then, you fight with us."

1603 HOURS

Colonel Nicholas Crews of Wolf's Dragoons angled his *Tundra Wolf* around a small clump of dense pine trees. He had already engaged in battle individually against three battered Jade Falcons, taking each one down. They all had managed to land a shot or two though, and his midnight-blue *Tundra Wolf* had lost armor along the way, spread out between here and the DropShips, some fifteen kilometers away.

Crews had sacrificed everything to be here. When Alaric had offered the Dragoons a chance to stand with Clan Wolf against the Falcons on Terra, General Brubaker hesitated. The general had been willing to let Clan Wolf face the Jade Falcons alone, putting the rest of the Inner Sphere at risk of Malvina Hazen becoming the ilKhan.

In Crews' mind, the Jade Falcons were the greatest threat humanity had ever faced, so he had done the unthinkable: he led a mutiny against General Brubaker, even firing on fellow Dragoons. Crews and his regiment had defeated the general's forces, but to prevent the Dragoons from fracturing and protect its reputation, Brubaker had agreed to go to Terra with him. Ultimately, Nicholas did not care. All that mattered was that he was here, now.

A Jade Falcon *Shrike* rose up in the distance, some 200 meters away, angling on his position, riding a plume of orange and blue flames—outlined by an explosion in the distance. The 'Mech was a dull green, but its partial wings were a bright, florescent green. It had taken a lot of damage, but was clearly targeting him with its pair of ER large lasers as it reached the apex of its trajectory.

Both lasers hit him hard, destroying what was left of his right-side armor, rocking his 'Mech to the side from the sudden loss of weight. He turned back to the *Shrike* that was about to land a mere twenty meters in front of him, and launched his LRMs and ATMs. A rattling string of explosions consumed the *Shrike*. Bits of armor rained everywhere as the 'Mech landed on flexed knees.

For a moment, both warriors paused, looking at each other, sizing up their foe. Crews instantly knew what was going to happen—*they are going to charge.*

Instinct and years of training in the most elite mercenary unit in the Inner Sphere kicked in. Nicholas leaned at his enemy and charged forward at the same moment the *Shrike* lined him up and started to sprint. He fired his Streak missiles as he ran; they tore into the *Shrike*'s torso and legs, but did not slow it.

The two 'Mechs collided with such force that it threw Crews hard against his safety harness. The restraining straps dug deep into his flesh. Metal groaned all around him, stressing, bending.

Both BattleMechs fell, Crews on his back, the Jade Falcon landing on his left arm, further damaging it with the fall. His shoulder ached, no doubt dislocated, but he focused, suppressing the ripple of agony. Rocking his *Tundra Wolf*, he hoped to get up before his foe could.

To his dismay, he wasn't fast enough. The mangled *Shrike* pushed off him, getting to its knees with remarkable speed. Crews swung his right arm into action—hoping the medium lasers there still worked.

At the same instant, the *Shrike*'s MechWarrior pulled back its right arm to punch. The sharp, clawed hand would definitely drive through his armor, but in that instant he saw it was not going for his torso—it was aimed over his cockpit like a pile driver.

The fist came down faster than he could get his arm into play. At the last moment he rocked to the left, hoping to throw off the impact. It helped, but not much. The claw crashed through his armored ferroglass and hit his leg with a sickening crunch of bones shattering. A roaring filled his ears, and warmth washed over him. *Can't pass out, Crews! Not now!*

He fought the nausea coming over him, the pain, the dizziness, and brought his 'Mech's arm to the side of the *Shrike*'s head. He doubted the Jade Falcon even saw it as it leaned over him, pulling the fist back for another deadly jab.

Nicholas squeezed the thumb trigger for the lasers. They fired, searing through one side of the *Shrike*'s head and out the other. A red smear splattered on the ferroglass as the 'Mech locked up, still looming over him.

Nicholas Crews looked down and saw his leg was missing just above the knee. Grabbing his coolant-vest hose, he struggled to tie it off as a tourniquet, his breath ragged in his ears.

As he finished, he slumped back in his seat just in time to see the *Shrike* topple off to the side. His eyes fell on the stenciled name of the MechWarrior piloting it: sakhan ryan pryde.

He chuckled weakly as the *Shrike* collapsed on his *Tundra Wolf*'s left arm and side. The darkness came for him fast. *My regiment... What about Gamma?*

Crews tried to reach for the comm controls, but blackness consumed him first.

1618 HOURS

At the southern flank of the battlefield, not far from Staunton Creek, Star Colonel Kalidessa Kerensky waded into the firestorm of battle with a calm that came from pure self-confidence. *My entire lifetime of training is for these minutes, here, on Terra.*

A wave of missiles slammed into her from a crumpled Jade Falcon *Cougar* that was dragging its left leg along, myomers dangling. Her *Amarok* shrugged off the rumble of the explosions. Turning back to it, she fired a flight of Streak short-range missiles and a brilliant azure flash from her ER PPC. The crippled *Cougar* never stood a chance. The PPC shot savaged its right arm and side, and the missiles exploited that hole, piercing deep into the 'Mech's internal structure. It quaked as the MechWarrior attempted to keep it upright, but its gyro was melted to slag. It fell over hard.

That is three.

Her tactical display showed Jack's *Ares* slowly coming up off to her right. The superheavy had been blasted and lazed so many times it hardly looked like itself anymore. Its huge right arm had hung limp for the last hour; its potent MRM racks were twisted and gnarled. But Jack and his crew kept fighting well. *Truly, they are Wolves to the core.*

The rest of her Cluster was nearby but spread out, as the furious onslaught of the Jade Falcons had fractured any semblance of order on the battlefield. The arrival of Wolf's Dragoons and the former Exiles had surprised everyone, including Kalidessa. For the Jade Falcons, it made them only more desperate—more dangerous.

She had moved her unit into a large, cleared area that was relatively flat, with only a few scrub pines showing. Now she swung about, looking for more targets.

Almost as if it had read her thoughts, a Jade Falcon *Dire Wolf* emerged from the north and headed toward her, its four large lasers stabbing at her *Amarok* like the lance of some medieval knight. One missed, scarring the soil next to her. The others lashed at her legs, slicing the armor deeply.

Staggered under the assault, Khalidessa locked her rotary autocannon on the hulking green-gray OmniMech, then squeezed the fire button. The autocannon *whirred*, spitting out a stream of shells that tore into the center of the charging 'Mech. Torn-off armor went flying. She fired her large pulse laser as the autocannon roared, adding the green flashes of death to her ballistic firepower—but the *Dire Wolf* continued running right at her.

Jack Traver saw the rushing *Dire Wolf* and realized it was heading for the Star Colonel. His *Ares* was nearly spent. Its only remaining armament was four lasers, one medium and three small. A Jade Falcon tank had rammed one of the legs, damaging the knee actuator so much that Jack could barely lumber the 'Mech along.

Nevertheless, he moved in behind Kalidessa's flank. "I'm going to take it out," he announced.

Cheetah, from her seat below him, craned her head back. "With what?"

"With us," he said, moving alongside the Star Colonel. "Mia, you might want to strap in!" Fowler was somewhere deep in the hull of the *Ares*, attempting to keep the battered superheavy going.

"This is insane," Cheetah said as Jack pushed what was left of the 'Mech forward.

Perhaps it is...

Kalidessa braced herself, knowing the impact would devastate both BattleMechs. Suddenly a large shadow appeared next to her, and Jack's *Ares* appeared. As the emerald Falcon 'Mech came within seconds of hitting her, Jack threw the superheavy into the charging *Dire Wolf*'s side.

Both monstrous 'Mechs hit hard. The *Dire Wolf* went down under the *Ares'* 135 tons with a metallic grinding that shook her *Amarok*. Smoke rolled from rents in the side of the *Ares*, and one of the tripod legs, mangled in earlier fighting, hung by only a few thick strands of myomer fibers.

In all the commotion, Kalidessa had not been watching where the *Ares* was. "Jack," she called on the tactical channel.

"We had lost most of our weapons anyway, Star Colonel," Jack's voice coughed through the smoke.

Kalidessa was about to thank him for the sacrifice when she saw a bright green and black *Jade Phoenix* D rushing past, heading for an all-too-familiar maroon-and-gold Carnivore tank. The 85-ton Falcon assault 'Mech was coming in on *Fratricide*'s left rear flank, and its crew clearly had not seen the threat.

She pursued as fast as the *Amarok* could, locking her ER PPC and rotary-autocannon on the charging *Jade Phoenix*. It was at long range, but her aim was true, and she blasted and riddled the 'Mech's rear armor. The Jade Falcon stopped its charge on the tank, skidded in the grass, and slowly pivoted in place to face her.

That is right, she thought. *Here I am. Come to me and die.*

It was already missing its Gauss rifle, but its two ER PPCs flashed in unison as she juked her *Amarok* hard to the left. Both shots hit her right arm and side, shattering and melting what little armor remained there into a hot, glowing-red spray that sizzled on her ferroglass cockpit.

The heat made her skin tingle, and the sweat made her blink fast to keep her aim true. Kalidessa fired everything she had. Her Streak missiles slammed into the upper body of the wounded *Jade Phoenix*, and her large pulse laser stitched its left arm. The arm detached at the shoulder joint and went flying, landing not far from *Fratricide*, which was firing at an unseen target downrange. Kalidessa's rotary autocannon riddled the damaged side of her target, pounding deep into freshly melted slashes already there. One of her Streak missiles hit the Falcon's cockpit canopy, forcing the 'Mech to jerk around hard at the waist.

The loss of the arm and armor was too much for the MechWarrior to maintain balance. The *Jade Phoenix* staggered two steps before falling over. It landed on a dead Wolf Elemental, crushing what was left of it on impact.

Kalidessa closed on her prey as the heat rose in her cockpit. The *Jade Phoenix* managed to contort enough to stand just as she fired her ER PPC once more. Her heat spiked higher as the shot lanced into the Jade Falcon, cutting it open like a roasted turkey. The charged-particle blast smashed away huge pieces of armor, and oily black smoke rolled from the scar that furrowed deep. The *Jade Phoenix* toppled backward, landing hard—its reactor offline.

And that is four... Sweat stung the corners of her eyes, and she licked her lips. *One more Jade Falcon that will not kill any more of my Clan today.*

Fratricide drove up behind the fallen *Jade Phoenix*, the tank's deadly Gauss rifle turrets leveled at the fallen 'Mech.

"Are you all right, Star Colonel?" asked one of its crew—Hawkins.

"We appreciate you covering us," added DuJordan.

The temperature in Kalidessa's cockpit had started to diminish, and she sighed in relief. "Well, I could not let that *Jade Phoenix* take out the most famous tank crew in the history of Clan Wolf." Just saying the words made her smile.

"Begging your pardon, Star Colonel, but you never struck me as the caring type," Hawkins replied. "Appreciate it all the same."

"I am your CO, and we are Wolves—we protect the pack." She eyed her tactical display, trying to sort out the many transponders and targets intermixed around them. "I show three Falcon *UrbanMech IIC*s closing in on us from the southwest, Quadrant Epsilon. Let us destroy them together."

"*Aff,*" agreed the other man in the tank, DuJordan. "Only a true madwoman would outfit a Star with so many *UrbanMech*s."

Kalidessa glanced back at the fallen, smoking *Ares* atop the crushed *Dire Wolf*. "Jack, you and your crew have fought valiantly. Now get them out of here."

Jack could not agree with his CO's words more. "Time to evac," he said. "Cheetah—Mia, we need to leave now."

He hit the release on his straps and stumbled out of the sideways cockpit. Off to his side, Mia emerged, a huge knot on her forehead that was already bruising. Jack was relieved to see her, and helped her to the forward portion of the cockpit.

Glancing down, he saw a massive slab of *Dire Wolf* armor had punched through the lower cockpit where his gunner sat. Tina "Cheetah" Charms had never had a chance. He only saw a bit of her hair and blood on the Jade Falcon armor that had completely crushed her body. His jaw hung open in shock. *I did that... I got her killed.*

Mia saw what he was staring at and began to cry, huddling close to him. Jack just stared down, knowing there was no way to get Cheetah's remains free. His whole frame sagged—he was unable to move, his eyes fixed on the crushed cockpit. *A meter either way, and she would have lived...*

Mia pulled away from him and hit the emergency escape control on the side of the cockpit, which was now overhead, and the explosive bolts fired. "Sir, we have to go," she said between sobs.

Jack nodded and helped her out. Slowly, painfully, he started his own climb through the hatch, his anguished thoughts hammering his psyche. *I brought us here... We could have been POWs, but at least we all would have survived... What have I done?*

CHAPTER 37

EAST OF STAUNTON CREEK
19 APRIL 3151, 1628 HOURS
(T+99, DAY 3 OF THE ILCLAN TRIAL)

"Wolf Spider Keshik, form up on near that boggy area to the east," commanded Galaxy Commander Miriam Shaw of the former Wolves-in-Exile.

Alaric had ordered her Omega Provisional Galaxy into the rear of the Jade Falcon lines to wreak havoc. It had proven far from easy. Several lead units of the Jade Falcons anticipated that threat when the DropShips arrived, and had moved back to protect their rear. Now she faced the First Falcon Jaegers, a unit Spurlock Connors' reports claimed was full of misfits and rejects who refused to follow Malvina's Mongol Doctrine. *Their beliefs do not matter to me today... All that matters is stopping them.*

A *Night Gyr* rose from behind a low, tree-lined ridge and shot its extended-range PPCs at her. Miriam reeled her reddish-orange *Timber Wolf* to the right, but both beams still tore into her right side and arm so hard that her 'Mech almost fell over.

The last time she had fought the Jade Falcons was on Arc-Royal. The memories of standing in the Wolves' destroyed *sibko* and decanting facility, the children slaughtered in their iron wombs...they still woke her from sleep with sweat-filled nightmares. *The Jade Falcons have much to answer for.* Today, finally, they would pay.

Rumors abounded that Khan Ward would not use her provisional Galaxy in the fight—that Anastasia's offer was merely a cruel ploy to bring them to Terra and deny them the honor of battle the Exiled Wolves' greatest foe. Miriam had told her people to ignore the rumors and resist their fears. Anastasia Kerensky, who had come from the Exiles herself, was with them—and Alaric would not deny *her* a chance to fight. When she went into battle, Miriam's warriors were destined to follow.

Destined. Destiny! That was what this was about for her and many others. For almost a century the Wolves had been a divided people, split by differing ideologies. *That is over now, history.* Anastasia had provided them a means to return to the fold. Clan Wolf was strengthened by the Exiles' return, and the Falcons would pay the price for that new strength.

Miriam's sensors told her the *Night Gyr* had already suffered damage. All around her, the former Wolves-in-Exile engaged their targets, their shots blazing in every direction. She swung her own targeting reticle onto the *Night Gyr* and fired her ER large lasers, then followed up with a salvo of long-range missiles. One laser hit, and the melted scar it left trailed up the rounded right shoulder of the hulking 'Mech. The missiles arrowed in on its blackened and scarred torso. Each explosion tossed away more bits of armor plating. The Falcon should have fallen, but merely stopped its movement and fought gravity and the loss of armor to remain upright.

Miriam ran across the *Night Gyr*'s field of fire, firing her medium pulse laser as she went. The *Night Gyr* fired its Ultra autocannon in response. Some of the barrage missed, but the bulk of it tore into her *Timber Wolf*'s right thigh, tossing away armor. Then the autocannon stopped mid-barrage, which was odd. *Perhaps it jammed.*

She closed the distance between them and unloaded everything she had in one devastating alpha strike. Her machine guns spat, her lasers hummed and throbbed, and her missile racks roared on both sides of her cockpit. For a moment, the heat rose around her, but she disregarded it...all that mattered was destroying the Jade Falcon 'Mech.

The devastating assault engulfed her battered foe in a lethal cloud of explosions, smoke, and jabbing green and red lasers. Two pulse lasers scored burning holes on the canopy—followed by a stream of machine-gun rounds that tore into the cockpit. The *Night Gyr* slumped forward into the exploding missiles, and fell flat and unmoving on the side of a short knoll, pushing up the black soil as it landed.

"That is for Arc-Royal," Miriam spat.

Khalus Pryde's *Jupiter* was mangled. The four Ultra autocannon barrels were twisted, the result of an unfortunate PPC hit. His missile racks were out of ammunition. In the distance, he saw Mathews' *Night Gyr* go down on a small hillside, blasted by a *Timber Wolf* from the Wolves-in-Exile.

In the distance, off to the south, he saw a Clan Wolf aerospace fighter strafing some target out of his line of sight. *Where are our fighters?* The moment he thought of that question, he wished he hadn't. *They are either destroyed or unable to join the battle.* Neither scenario appealed to him.

He saw Archer Pryde's battered *Shrike* emerge through a dense cloud of rolling black smoke off to his right. The *Shrike* had its left arm attached, but little else. One leg dragged behind the 'Mech as it limped toward him. Its right arm and weapons were no doubt lost somewhere else on the battlefield. The holes in its upper torso were so numerous, Khalus could actually see the fusion-reactor housing, which was sending out ripples of hot air as Archer staggered in his direction.

Khalus looked at his tactical display and winced. His Cluster had thrown itself to the rear to stop the Wolves-in-Exile forces and had paid the price. All that remained of his First Falcon Jaegers was his and Archer's 'Mechs, and they were worthless. *Nothing lies between us and our rear area now.* The Wolves seemed to sense that and were heading that way, away from him and Archer. *We are not even worthy enough for them to finish off.*

Malvina Hazen said victory was assured...that she had the situation under control. As he looked over at the fallen *Night Gyr*, then back to Archer's *Shrike*, Khalus shook his head. *She never expected Wolf's Dragoons or these former Exiles, and we are playing the price for her arrogance in blood.*

"Your orders, Star Colonel?" Archer asked as he stopped a few meters away.

Khalus shook his head again. "What can we do? Both of us are of no use in the fight."

"We could rush the enemy, charge into them," Archer offered.

"*Neg,*" Khalus replied. "I have ordered enough good warriors to their death today. In this moment, the lives of two Jade Falcons will not make a difference, not against what had been thrown at us. When the dust settles though, we may yet prove our worth." He dropped what was left of his *Jupiter* to its knees, then turned, sitting the BattleMech in an upright position. Exhaustion swept his body.

Archer moved next to him and rested his crippled *Shrike* next to Khalus', back-to-back. "So, we just sit here and wait?"

"*Aff.*" Khalus sighed. "If Malvina somehow claws out a victory, we are dead anyway. If the Wolves win, we will not have squandered our lives for her idiotic cause." Leaning back in his command couch, he watched as the battle drifted away from his field of vision.

1630 HOURS

Major Andrew Krull of Gamma Regiment fired his *Marauder IIC*'s PPCs into the *Flamberge* before him. One of the searing bolts scored a direct hit on the cockpit, and the Jade Falcon 'Mech collapsed from the hit. Krull lined up another shot on a different target as he moved his 'Mech along, but a barrage of mortar shells landed on his position, almost hitting him directly. The explosions sprayed his legs with shrapnel and threw chunks of black sod onto his canopy. *They do not have to hit me directly to kill me.*

He looked out over the blasted grass plains, now filled with craters and destroyed 'Mechs and vehicles. What trees had been there were gone, blasted, broken, or burned at this point—only a few jagged stumps jutted skyward. Mud and torn-up sod made the ground look barren and inhospitable.

So far, the Dragoons had driven nearly a dozen kilometers south of their DropShips, fighting for every meter of ground. Cluster after Cluster had been thrown at them, each one pummeled into retreat or destroyed outright. Now the Falcon Guards had been thrown into the Dragoons' path and tore into them with a savagery he had rarely experienced. Dragoons units and their commanders were separated by the ferocity of the assault.

Colonel Nicholas Crews, Krull's CO, was down, and Krull had been left in command of Gamma Regiment—or rather, what was left of it. Keeping his MechWarriors organized had been nearly impossible. The Falcon Guards had plowed through their lines, operating in Star-sized units, forcing Krull to pull to the south and try re-forming his surviving troops.

As his field of vision cleared, Krull saw General Brubaker's *Tundra Wolf* blast another Jade Falcon BattleMech with laser fire and a wave of advanced tactical missiles. Brubaker was a good 250 meters away, standing out in a white 'Mech on the charred landscape. The *Cygnus* he targeted, no doubt *isorla* the Falcons had taken from Clan Hell's Horses, responded by shredding the general's frontal armor with Ultra autocannon fire followed with emerald blasts of pulse lasers.

The white *Tundra Wolf* was bathed in fire, and hot melted armor sprayed into the air and into the green-brown sod around it. For the first time since he had begun serving under Brubaker, Krull saw the general's BattleMech stumble, then slowly regain its footing. He started to run back, to aid the general, but artillery dropped indiscriminately everywhere in a sixty-meter radius around his position. The dance of hot shrapnel rattling against Krull's canopy slowed his advance.

Two Dragoons 'Mechs caught the *Cygnus* in a crossfire of Gauss-rifle rounds and lasers. Krull let loose too, slamming the 'Mech's right arm with a PPC blast and severing it at the elbow. The *Cygnus* toppled under the combined firepower, allowing Krull to turn his attention to General Brubaker.

"Dragoons Actual is down!" he called over the proximity channel. "Medevac now. Say again, Dragoons Actual is down!" He hovered over the fallen BattleMech, shielding it with his own. "Dragoons, rally to your gener—"

His voice was cut off as another artillery barrage screamed down all around his *Marauder II C*. None of the shots were direct hits, but they were close enough to rattle his usual calm.

"General," Krull said in horror at the thought that Brubaker may be dead, "can you stand?"

There was a moan, painful and excruciating. "Oh, God..." Brubaker rasped, followed with a gurgle. "I need to pass on command—damn it! I can't get anyone on the command channel. Colonels Lyons and Cameron are both down. The Seventh is running silent."

The mention of the Seventh Kommando made Krull think of his brother Aaron for a moment, and he hoped he was okay. "So is Colonel Crews, sir. I've got command of Gamma," Krull said, swinging around to provide the general's fallen 'Mech more cover. For a moment, the artillery barrage ceased, but that did not remove the danger.

"All right, then," Brubaker croaked, gathering his resolve. "Major, I am passing on command to you. *You* are in command of the Dragoons until a superior relieves you. Straighten out our lines of battle and drive south, toward Clan Wolf. Pinch those Falcon bastards up against the Wolves to the south and shake them hard—" He paused, and his breathing quickened. "Damn it!" he said to the pain. "You can do this, Andrew. For Unity's sake, you have to. Wipe out the Jade Falcons...all of them. Tip of the spear..." His voice faded away.

The medevac team arrived as Krull turned away from Brubaker's fallen 'Mech. *Unity! I am in command of the Dragoons.* A lifetime of training and experience had led to this moment, and it helped him gather himself and reach down deep into his resolve. *I will not fail you, General.*

"Wolf's Dragoons, this is Major Krull. I am now designated Dragoon Actual. I want all Dragoons forces to rendezvous at the coordinates I am transmitting. The Falcons have wounded General Brubaker and our other COs, and we are going to make them pay!"

Howls of "*Unity!*" filled the channel as the Dragoons shifted to the new line of fighting.

1645 HOURS

Anastasia Kerensky moved through the dense pines in pursuit of her prey. Malvina had been shifting her position, drifting north toward the row of DropShips, with Anastasia always closing in on her. The small clearings she crossed were littered with parts of BattleMechs or bits of random armor from destroyed vehicles. Several flaming tanks were nearby, but Anastasia only noted them for possible uses in the coming battle. The haze in the air from all the smoke was like a toxic fog.

Then she saw her target across a wide clearing—the distinctive black *Shrike* with green accents. Malvina was firing at a Wolf Elemental that rushed at her, and cut the warrior it diagonally in half.

Anastasia's tactical senses came alive. She felt as if she was no longer in an OmniMech; instead she was facing Malvina while wearing a suit of armor in the shape of a *Savage Wolf*.

"Malvina Hazen," said Anastasia Kerensky, "your part in this Grand Crusade is about to come to an end." She steered her *Savage Wolf* around a burning lumber truck, and at last came face to face with the Chingis Khan's 95-ton *Shrike*.

"Anastasia Kerensky," came back the haughty voice of the Jade Falcon Khan. "I owe you so much. You have been a thorn in my side ever since Skye. Let us end this now. Come and get me, if you dare."

As tempted as she was to rush right in, Anastasia took a moment to plan her assault. She had taken some damage during her search for Malvina, thanks to a *Loki Mk II* foolish enough to challenge her. Malvina's *Shrike* could land a deadly punch Anastasia could not afford to take. This fight was about targeting, here in this clearing. There would be nothing to block line of sight, no cover to hide behind. This was a duel between two artisans of war.

I will go for her left arm. It holds her PPCs. Take that off and she loses much of her firepower. She will want to use that claw of hers, make it personal and painful. I need to keep her at range and avoid that as for long as possible. I want her to think she has the advantage, get her close, and then take her down once and for all.

She brought her PPCs onto her target and aimed high, at Malvina's left side. Malvina fired first, the battering ram of paired PPC fire rattling Anastasia's gunmetal-gray BattleMech as she accelerated into a sprint and fired her own shots. The hum of the PPCs firing filled her ears, the precise shots pulverizing and melting what armor remained on the *Shrike*'s left arm. A bundle of green myomer dangled from the hole, smoking as Malvina fired her jump jets to pursue.

The pent-up energy of being holed up in a DropShip for weeks erupted from Anastasia in a flurry of movements—dodging and weaving. Malvina fired her medium lasers, which hit Anastasia's right leg and left a hot furrow in the armor.

Anastasia triggered both of her PPCs again the moment she heard the whine of the capacitors topping off. Brilliant blue-white energy beams slashed into the *Shrike* and left two smoking gashes in their wake as Malvina turned to protect her damaged left arm.

The Falcon Khan spun and sprinted the 95-ton BattleMech directly at Anastasia, no doubt hoping to use her claw to rip the Wolf apart. Wanting nothing to do with that, Anastasia used her *Savage Wolf*'s speed to keep the distance between them.

Her PPCs charged far too slowly for her liking, but at extreme range, she spun and fired them again. One missed, blazing past the *Shrike*. The other slammed into the upper torso. Hot melted armor sprayed into the air as the *Shrike* careened backward, nearly toppling over. *That shot went deep.*

"You will pay for your constant annoyance to my Clan," snarled Malvina, firing her medium lasers. One beam missed; the other hit Anastasia's damaged right leg and seared a new black scar there.

"You will join Aleks soon enough," Anastasia taunted, smiling. "Make sure you give him a kiss from me." She moved again, now with a slight limp on her right side from jerking the throttle bar between maximum and full stop between strides, to simulate an injury. *Let her think I am damaged...that I am slowed.*

Malvina closed the distance, and Anastasia continued to feign her limp, luring the heavier BattleMech in for the kill. Anastasia activated the targeting sequence for her twelve Streak short-range missiles as she fired off both PPCs again. One slammed into Malvina's left leg, burning a deep, black hole as she ran.

Just a little closer... The moment Anastasia reached optimum range, she skidded her 'Mech to a halt. Malvina, sensing blood, fired her PPCs, and both struck home in Anastasia's torso. Her 'Mech rocked under the scintillating battering rams, and her damage indicator went from green to amber. She ignored it.

Anastasia heard the tone of missile lock, followed a second later by the high-pitched whine of her PPC capacitors. She kept the targeting reticle on the center of the oncoming *Shrike*, and squeezed the triggers.

The PPCs hit first, bathing the *Shrike* in charged particles and brilliant white light. The Streak missiles followed, snaking and twisting through the air, and blasted all along Malvina's front and side. The mangled left arm exploded, blowing the limb off entirely, shooting it into the air as Malvina surged forward. The other missiles sank deep into the *Shrike*'s armored hide, exploding and leaving holes billowing smoke.

The loss of so much armor made Malvina's BattleMech unwieldy, and it started to sway. Anastasia then broke into a wild sprint as she saw the Jade Falcon Khan lose balance entirely and fall hard on the ground.

But the Falcon Khan was clearly still in this fight. Anastasia watched her push the *Shrike* off the ground with its one good arm, then to its knees, then rise to its feet. Mud spilled from the holes in the 'Mech's armor as Malvina fired her jump jets to reposition herself. While the *Shrike* was airborne, Anastasia vented her excess heat for a moment, then broke into a tight circular sprint.

Malvina touched back down and fired her long-range missiles and medium lasers. Only a third of the missiles slammed into Anastasia, spraying all over the front of her *Savage Wolf* as she continued her run. One of the crimson beams hit her right leg and burned away the red Alpha symbol painted there.

"Is that all you have, Malvina Hazen?" Anastasia broadcast on an open channel. "I expected so much more." Her short-range missile racks made a metallic *rattle* and *click* as the missiles reloaded. She fired her left-arm particle projection cannon, lancing a bolt of charged particles into Malvina's left side. The hit seared away the last of the 'Mech's green highlights, making the *Shrike* look almost completely black.

"Come here and fight me up close," Malvina snapped. "I will give you a better death than you deserve."

Anastasia laughed. "You take me for a fool." The missile-lock tone hummed in her ears, and she launched another wave of SRMs downrange. All of the Streak missiles found their mark and hit Malvina's right arm and side, exacerbating damage done by other engagements. A muffled rumble went off—an ammunition explosion from within the torso, blowing out the rear armor with a brilliant yellow-orange flash, spraying out structural fragments like a shotgun going off. The cool, wet soil around the *Shrike* misted from the heat, engulfing Malvina in a low fog.

Anastasia fired again the millisecond her missiles reloaded. Two of the twelve Streak warheads slammed into Malvina's cockpit, mangling the head assembly so much that Anastasia doubted she could eject. *She would not anyway... She means to kill me even if it kills her.*

Heat plumed out of the Falcon 'Mech's torso in a billow of rippling air as Malvina ran, trying to put some distance between her and the *Savage Wolf*. Anastasia's PPC capacitors hummed their readiness, and she squeezed the trigger again.

Both charged-particle beams struck home. The *Shrike* fell again to the right, and as it landed, its right arm bent backward like a broken human appendage and crushed the cockpit canopy upon impact. Myomer dangled, sparking on the hot armor from the stub, hissing on the grass.

The *Shrike* did not move. Anastasia saw from her tactical indicator that Malvina's reactor was offline.

A trick? Just to be sure, she fired another PPC shot into the *Shrike*'s mangled legs and blew the left one off at the knee. It stayed down.

Malvina was never going to kill anyone again.

"Wolf Prime, this is Steel Wolf Actual," Anastasia said. "Mission accomplished."

"This is Wolf Prime," Alaric replied. "Excellent work. Now swing to the north—the Falcons have thrown in their last infantry reserves."

Anastasia looked at the fallen *Shrike* one last time with a sneer on her face. "Give your *sibkin* my regards, Malvina Hazen."

1650 HOURS

Alaric angled his *Savage Wolf* alongside Chance Vickers on a ridge that had been wooded days before but was now barren, thanks to the raging tide of battle.

Tara Wolf was still at his side, her *Sun Cobra* blackened and battered from the savage combat they had waded through. This ridge had been the Jade Falcons' high-water mark, the farthest they had gotten in their drive east. From the low ridge, he had a good view of the battlefield to the west.

"Alaric, to the north," Chance signaled. She had gotten into her OmniMech to be in the field rather than continue to direct the battle from the mobile HQ. Alaric appreciated that feeling; it was why he too was here.

He wheeled his 'Mech around and moved past Tara's battered 'Mech. The former Wolves-in-Exile were driving west, into the Falcons' rear, but the Dragoons were advancing into the enemy forces fighting with Beta and Alpha Galaxies from the south. Already the Jade Falcons were starting to fall back, turning to face the Dragoons and former Exiles. Alaric's tactical display tagged the enemy warriors as belonging to the Falcon Guards.

This final honor—the utter defeat of our enemy—belongs to true Wolves. From what Alaric saw, the Dragoons had already seen horrific devastation. Word had reached him that General Brubaker was either badly wounded or dead. Their ranks were thinned, but their zeal was still evident.

Chance sensed it, too. "Alaric, the Dragoons are going to finish the Falcons off."

Not today. Alaric opened the channel reserved for him and the Dragoons leadership. "This is Wolf Prime to the commander of Wolf's Dragoons."

"This is Major Krull," came a strained voice. "Command has fallen to me."

"I order you to break off your attack. Withdraw to the northwest and engage any remaining Falcons in Quadrant Foxtrot."

"General Brubaker ordered me—"

"I am the Khan of Clan Wolf, whom you serve," Alaric said firmly. "You will obey me. Disengage, and move north. The final destruction of the Jade Falcons falls to Trueborn warriors of Clan Wolf."

BLAINE LEE PARDOE   327

"My people will get mangled trying to break off our assault!" Major Krull fired back.

"You have your orders, Major," Alaric replied, and reached out to close the channel.

"Unity—!" Krull spat back before he cut the transmission.

Almost immediately the Dragoons began to fall back, withering in the process by the Falcon Guards' stubbornness. Alaric watched it and smiled. *Malvina is down, but we still need to cull what remains of the Falcons. They can never come back from this, at least not as they were. Malvina's defeat is not enough. The entire Clan's defeat must be utter and complete.*

He switched to a channel for all of his Clan to hear. "Clan Wolf, now is the time to finish off our foes. Alpha and Zeta Galaxies, drive through to connect with Anastasia's forces. Beta, Delta, and Gamma, we will head north. We will then converge on this line of hills." He transmitted the map image from his tactical display. "This ends now."

He began to move down the ridge, heading into the nearest group of Falcons, and broadcast on an unsecured channel that all Jade Falcons could hear: "Clan Jade Falcon, your Khan has fallen. End this now, and you may yet live. Continue to resist, and my Wolves will destroy you."

Then he ordered his Wolves to attack.

Star Colonel Marv Roshak's *Night Gyr* was in shambles, its armor blasted through in several areas. His right PPC was useless slag, melted by a laser strike. All the armor on his left footpad was peeled back, the result of a Wolf artillery round. All of his right-leg armor was gone, exposing bare myomer. Heat from his damaged reactor housing rippled the air around him, but he still managed to fire his remaining PPC at a Dragoons Zhukov tank and blast through the turret, setting off the ammunition inside. The crew popped the hatches and tried to scramble free, but it was too late for them to escape the explosion and fire within.

A black-and-red *Goliath C* seemed to see him, but it turned and moved away. Pharaoh's *Mad Dog* was barely standing as well, but his target, a Dragoons *Imp*, also turned and started to fall back.

"They are retreating!" Pharaoh called out.

Roshak's remaining medium pulse laser hit the *Goliath C*'s rear legs, but it did not return the salvo. "We have driven them off!"

We have done it. We have beaten Wolf's Dragoons! He glanced off to his right at the long, barren ridgeline to the west. There were a handful of Clan Wolf 'Mechs there, and they advanced down toward him. For a moment he did not cringe. *There are only a few...*

Then came more. From the far side of the ridge, they spilled down like a tsunami of death and destruction. His tactical screen showed a crimson wave washing in from the south, more Clan Wolf forces. *Neg...we have* won*!*

A wave of sixty long-range missiles soared up and over the charging 'Mechs, all aimed at him. He twisted his *Night Gyr* under the first few explosions. Then his legs were swept out from under him, consumed in the seemingly endless detonations. His 'Mech fell, and he was thrown hard against his harness. Damage indicators flashed nothing but crimson in the faceplate of his neurohelmet. Roshak strained to get his 'Mech to move, but the explosions had cored his fusion reactor, and the *Night Gyr* lost power.

The battery backup brought a voice to his ears via the comm system: "Clan Jade Falcon, your Khan has fallen..."

Unconsciousness took Marv Roshak away from the rest of the message, away from the turning tide of battle.

1655 HOURS

Galaxy Commander Stephanie Chistu used Tickler, her hand-forged knife, to cut her restraining strap. Her body dropped to the side of her cockpit, and she felt the aches that almost matched the one inside her head. *How long have I been unconscious? What is the state of this battle?*

As she got on all fours, a voice she knew—Alaric Ward's—came through crisp and clear through her neurohelmet's earpiece: "Clan Jade Falcon, your Khan has fallen. End this now, and you may yet live."

For a moment, Chistu was unsure what to think. Part of her rejoiced. Malvina had threatened her so many times and tried to maneuver her into her own death that the thought of th Jade Falcon Khan being dead gave Stephanie a wash of relief.

But the thought that the Jade Falcons had lost the ilClanship also filled her with despair. *To have come so far, gotten so close, and lost... Can that be right?* Her concussion throbbed even harder as she tried to cope with the mix of emotions and confusion that was now her enemy.

She waited a minute or two, hoping to hear the voice of saKhan Ryan Pryde or any of the other Galaxy Commanders, but none came. Her tactical display still worked, and on it were only a few green dots signifying the remaining Jade Falcons. The crimson Wolf dots—dozens of them—were moving in, encircling them.

They are so tied to Malvina's Mongol Doctrine that they are forced to fight to the end. Many have committed atrocities in her name, so defeat means they would face justice at the hands of the victor. She understood that. At the same time, she could not see the Jade Falcons wiped off the stage entirely, not when she could prevent it.

I alone will accept responsibility for what follows. I have to save my people.

She toggled to the open channel. "This is Galaxy Commander Stephanie Chistu of Clan Jade Falcon. This Trial is over. All Jade Falcons stand down."

She paused, the ache in her temple still there, and let the moment of dizziness pass. "Khan Ward, I proclaim Clan Wolf the victor of this Trial. The ilClanship is yours."

1810 HOURS

Alaric had returned his *Savage Wolf* to the long ridge line that had marked the pinnacle of the Falcons' eastward advance. Gray and white smoke hung in the air everywhere, obscuring the carnage as he climbed higher on the hill. The scene all around was not lost on him. *This ridge is a place warriors from all of the Clans will come to. It is the place where the Grand Crusade ended. It is here that Clan Wolf earned the right to be called ilClan.*

The final mop-up was still continuing. Despite his broadcast and Stephanie Chistu's radioed surrender, some of the Jade Falcons had fought on. Some had not gotten the message. Others refused Chistu's orders to stand down. The *solahma* warriors preferred death to defeat. Others maintained the hopeless illusion that one final push might somehow turn the tide. Alaric had sent out Anastasia Kerensky to deal with those still clinging to the belief that it was possible to defy the odds. *Some have no choice. Their actions have so tainted them that they continue on regardless of the forces against them, hoping for an honorable death.*

A Wolf recovery team had reached Malvina's *Shrike* at the order of General Vickers. Surprisingly, the Falcon Khan was alive. They took her to a Wolf field hospital, where she refused to order her Clan to stand down. *Defiant to the end.* Sedatives had ended her dispute.

"I have run out of Jade Falcons to kill," Anastasia had proclaimed when she returned from securing the area. Her *Savage Wolf* was badly battered; covered in bullet holes and laser burns, only one Streak pod recognizable, and with smoke pouring from a smashed heat sink.

She had flown into a rage at the thought that Malvina was still alive. "Damn it, Alaric! Let me go finish her off. I will make it quick and honorable. You will thank me for it later."

It had been tempting for Alaric, if only for a minute. *Summarily executing Malvina, while solving several of my problems, would send the wrong impression to the other Clans.*

Ultimately, he had refused. "It is not the Way of the Clans." He had no doubt Malvina would have never given him such a lease on life, were their fortunes reversed, but honor still bound him. He half wondered if Anastasia might defy him and storm off to the hospital in her OmniMech to finish the job she had started. Somehow, Anastasia had managed to curb her rage, although he knew it would simmer until the Jade Falcon Khan was well and truly dead.

Chance Vickers stood her *Savage Wolf* at his side; apparently she too was soaking in every detail. The smoking battlefield stretched as far as he could see. Fires still burned in every direction. Bits of vehicles and BattleMechs littered the ground to the point where Alaric doubted anyone could cross the field without stepping on a broken part of some destroyed war machine. Hulks of fallen 'Mechs, torn apart, burned, and gutted, lay everywhere. An unusual one caught his attention, as it was charred black from top to bottom—disabled, but standing like a statue overlooking the death all around it. The sight struck him as odd.

"I have a summary from our field commanders if you would like it," Vickers stated.

"*Aff.*"

"The enemy has been completely crushed. When we told them Malvina was defeated, it only infuriated some of them more. They just kept coming. Some tried a breakout to the west, but Omega Provisional Galaxy caught them. A few Falcon commanders succeeded in getting their warriors to stand down. In one case, a Trinary turned on their commander and killed her, then continued fighting, and were destroyed. Our aerial recon has found no operational Jade Falcon BattleMechs or vehicles outside the battle area, and the Dragoons neutralized their aerospace capabilities. We have reached the Falcons' rear areas, but there are no reserves, just wounded and dying warriors and very nervous technicians."

More Clan Wolf units began to form up around the hilltop. Their BattleMechs were battered, but they still stood, weary but operational. Infantry converged on the hillside, as did tanks and hovercraft. Wolf's Dragoons appeared there as well, their ranks having been badly mauled by the Falcons.

I have risen above the mistakes our Khans made in the past. I have crushed the memories of Tukayyid. Alaric pictured the holoimages of ilKhan Ulric Kerensky he had seen in his youth. For a fleeting moment, he thought of Victor Steiner-Davion, and even his mother Katherine. *None have achieved what I have. All have fallen short. Terra is ours, and ours alone. My name will be mentioned next to Aleksandr Kerensky as one of the greatest leaders in history.*

Vickers broke the silence. "We are the ilClan. You have fulfilled Nicholas Kerensky's dream. Our people have taken Terra, and there are no challengers. None are our equals."

The words hit him strangely. "Our work is just beginning," he replied.

Then the chant began, low and over the open channel, until it grew and roared into the approaching night:

"*AL-AR-IC! AL-AR-IC!*"

INTERLUDE

For the first time in more than seventy years, Devlin Stone was nothing more than a civilian in a realm he had no role in.

He sat in his wheelchair at the small kitchen table. A tube ran from his nose to the oxygen pack that hung on the chair, another reminder of his declining health. A colostomy bag was at his side, a constant reminder of how weak he was becoming. He had lost so much weight that his skin hung on his body. *Just a few weeks ago, I could at least stand. Now I am shackled to this breathing unit and my chair.*

The doctors had told him that despite the cocktail of drugs he was taking, his body was failing quickly. They blamed the freezing process, but Stone felt other factors were feeding his decline. *What the Word did to me...it's finally catching up. Their final bit of vengeance.*

The house had once been a refuge for his Ghost Knights and other agents during the Republic's existence, and it had been furnished to be unremarkable, so the residents would blend in. It was an older house, English Tudor-style, with matching décor. Now it was merely a house where he and his dwindling entourage stayed.

I was once the ruler of a great realm. Now I sit here, in suburbia, slowly withering away. His legacy worried him. *I built the Republic, but some would paint me as the man that lost it.* Glancing out the windows, he saw a bird in a tree, but his eyesight had faded so badly in the last few weeks that he couldn't tell what kind.

Janella Lakewood joined him at the small wooden table, carrying a steaming tea cup she set down in front of him. Whenever she visited, Tucker excused himself to the small living room. *He knows we will talk about politics, and wants nothing more to do with it.*

Khan Ward had refused to take Janella as a bondsman, and from what Stone saw, her fire for battle was gone. She was broken, crushed by the loss of the Republic and her role in its fall. Like him, she was now Dispossessed, cast adrift. Khan Ward had forbidden her from leaving Terra. Stone understood the command; Alaric did not want former Paladins stirring up trouble in what had been the Republic of the Sphere. That order only added to her gloom. *She is no longer my fierce soldier. The people failed her as well.*

Stone pulled a folded piece of paper from his pants pocket, wincing when he saw how yellow his fingernails had become. His fumbling hands shook as he unfolded it. It was the reply from Julian Davion, telling him he and the Federated Suns would be unable to help the Republic.

Stone peered at the letters, and realized they were harder to read today. He lifted it closer to his eyes, staring at the words that had extinguished his last vestige of hope. Slowly, he refolded it and slid it in his pocket. *All of our so-called allies and friends either feasted on our body or left us to fend for themselves. I sent tens of thousands of good soldiers to their deaths to help the Federated Suns. In the end, Julian hung us out to dry... just like all the others.*

Janella had been on the communicator for a long time. Stone had been trying to keep tabs on the clash between the Wolves and Jade Falcons, but there had been only scant media coverage. Alaric had chosen a location away from prying eyes, and few reporters were willing to risk traveling into a raging battle zone—especially one where the Jade Falcons might be the victors.

The media had not been kind to Stone after the fall of the Republic. Some "experts" claimed he had employed a failed strategy from the beginning. One or two claimed he was senile, and should have abdicated leadership to someone younger. Few stood in his corner now that he had been deposed.

Traitors...all of them. They trumpeted my return, and now they blame me for the failings of others. The few that did support him pointed out that he had faced the might of two entire Clans at once. Mostly, the press fretted over what life would be like under Clan rule. Would they have caste assignments imposed on them? What about their freedoms? Stone heard their concerns on the news holovids, but ignored them for the most part. *Where were all of these pundits when the shooting started? How many of them picked up a rifle to defend my Republic?*

"Any word on the battle?" he asked Janella. *The Inner Sphere hangs in the balance not far from here.*

Lakewood nodded, setting her communicator aside. "Shimmer is in the area. The Jade Falcons are no more. Clan Wolf holds the field."

Stone wanted to rejoice, but couldn't. *Terra is still lost to the Clans, thankfully to the lesser of two evils.* "The best of bad news, I suppose."

"What will become of us?" Tucker Harwell said as he joined them.

"I always have a plan or two in play, even now," Stone said. "Conquering is the strength of the Clans. Ruling...well, that requires something else entirely."

I only hope my health holds out long enough...

THARKAD CITY SPACEPORT
THARKAD CITY, THARKAD
DONEGAL MILITARY PROVINCE
LYRAN COMMONWEALTH
20 APRIL 3151

Archon Trillian Steiner watched the last BattleMech back into the DropShip. At her side was General of the Armies Roderick Steiner, her cousin and confidant. The smells of the spaceport and heat there were no strangers to Trillian, but she rarely came there. This mission was important though, as it entailed the future of the Lyran Commonwealth. Her security detail milled about, uncomfortable about her being in the open like this.

"The operatives know they are not to engage the Jade Falcons," she said. "We want them to contact our people on-planet and deliver the equipment." Caution rang in her every word.

Of course." Roderick turned to her and smiled. "It was *my* plan, remember?"

Operation Black Ice had been Roderick's brainchild. When they had learned that the Jade Falcons and the Wolves were on Terra, he had eagerly proposed it. The worlds in the Jade Falcon Occupation Zone were almost entirely stripped of their garrisons; at least that's what the Lyran Intelligence Corps reports claimed. On almost every world there were Lyran veterans who had been trapped behind enemy lines when the planet fell. Black Ice was meant to provide some of those veterans combat equipment to give them a chance to retake valuable and strategically important worlds.

Trillian knew she was playing a dangerous game. One option on the table had been to launch an all-out offensive against the worlds the Jade Falcons had seized. Roderick had actually been the one to veto that, a strange stance for the military leader of the Commonwealth. "The last thing we want to do is trigger open war," he had said. "There is a chance the Jade Falcons may be the victor on Terra. It is far better to allow a dozen or so insurrections by the locals than to start another war." Trillian had agreed. Black Ice might give her back some planets without painting her as the overt aggressor.

Clan Wolf held Commonwealth worlds as well, but Trillian did not want provoke the Wolves in any way. Melissa, her cousin and predecessor, had done that, against Trillian's counsel. It had cost Melissa her life, and brought the Clans to Tharkad itself. Trillian was not going to make the same mistake.

Compounding matters, Alaric had proclaimed himself a Steiner heir while on Tharkad, in a broadcast to the masses. The DNA sample he had left confirmed that he possessed the genetic traits of Katherine and Victor Steiner-Davion. *Even after all of these years, she is still meddling in the affairs of state.*

Alaric had made the claim to the people of Commonwealth, then left Tharkad. Her own propaganda machine had written off the announcement as the ravings of an unstable, delusional man. The problem was that some people believed his claim. Worse, some questioned whether he might be a better Archon than she. If he spoke the truth, he had the appropriate lineage in his blood. *People latch onto conspiracy theories, and the more you try to squash them, the more legitimate they appear.* While Alaric didn't have a lot of followers, his proclamation had laid the foundation for something she couldn't control—and that worried her.

Roderick seemed to be studying her face, then spoke again. "Stop worrying, Trill. We must do something. Black Ice will work. You know that. If we sit here while those planets lay nearly undefended, people will be up in arms against us both. This is the least provocative way to take back those planets."

"I know," she replied as the loading ramp retracted and the door to the *Union*-class DropShip began to close. "We cannot withstand a major war right now. That is why the priority for Black Ice is the worlds around Hesperus. You said it yourself, if the Falcons park a WarShip there, this is all over." Trillian looked around to make sure no one was in earshot, then lowered her voice slightly. "The people do not realize how thinly stretched we are. We lost Jasek—"

"But we saved Coventry," Roderick countered. "And that factory is producing for us again. You don't have to remind your General of the Armies how battered we are. Black Ice will give us back some key worlds, it will build a buffer around Hesperus, and more importantly, it will give our people a much-needed morale boost."

Trillian nodded as the door to the DropShip *thudded* into place and sealed. *The Wolves-in-Exile have disappeared...and the Kell Hounds are missing in action. We have no allies. Melissa waged war against the Free Worlds League, and the only other friendly House Lord is Julian Davion, and his own realm is hanging by a thread.*

The nobles no doubt already smell blood, and a few have already conspired against me. Melissa certainly tainted many of those relationships. To rule the Lyran Commonwealth, Trillian knew it was not just a matter of the title: it meant keeping the nobility on your side as well. *They will be the death of me as quickly as any invader.*

Add in the very real chance that the Clans might unite under one ruler, and our situation is truly dire. If Malvina is ilKhan, we will no doubt be the first realm she comes for. If it is Alaric—well, we share some genes, so I may be able to reason with him. Then again, he may come back to Tharkad, reassert his claim on my realm, and attempt to take it by force.

There were few scenarios in which the Lyran Commonwealth could prevail. *One thing is for sure, we will not go down without a fight.* She turned and walked back to her limousine. *But how long can I hold my realm together if the Clans truly unite?*

CAMERON-CLASS BATTLECRUISER CSR *ICE STORM*
NADIR JUMP POINT RECHARGING STATION
PROSERPINA
PROSERPINA PREFECTURE
THE DRACONIS COMBINE
21 APRIL 3151

Snow Raven Khan Sterling McKenna looked out at the recharging station as the last of the Ice Storm Naval Star materialized at the jump point. On the

Ice Storm's bridge, she floated in front of the display screen that showed the station operator, a Draconis Combine *sho-sa*. Beads of sweat ran down the man's face.

"We demand recharging for our vessels at this station," she said calmly. "I will not repeat myself again."

The *sho-sa* nervously nodded, clearly shaken by the arrival of a task force of Clan WarShips in the system. "As I said, I am not authorized to provide such services to a foreign invasion fleet."

Despite his nervousness, Sterling respected that he was willing to take a stand when so clearly outmatched. As much as she admired his fortitude, she did not have time for this.

"Then allow me state it in a different way, *Sho-sa*," she said calmly. "We are not invading your precious Combine. We are merely passing through. However, if you do not provide us with access to your facilities, then you will need to inform me what forces you intend to commit to the defense of this recharge station."

"I...I—we do not have defenses here."

"Then you need to decide if dying here and now is the best way to fulfill your service to the Combine. One way or another, we will get our recharges."

He gulped and nodded again. "Please accept my invitation on behalf of your friendly neighbors, the Draconis Combine, to dock and commence recharging operations." Despite his apprehension, the *sho-sa* dipped his head in respect.

Sterling smiled. "Bargained well and done." She shut off the screen. "Commence recharging ops, Star Captain."

Amanda McKenna, captain of the *Ice Storm*, fired off a string of orders, and the Khan felt the mighty WarShip begin its maneuvers.

"Awfully brave man, that *sho-sa*, facing a fleet like ours," saKhan Iqbal Lankenau said, flashing a broad grin as he drifted into Sterling's view.

"Even with the recharging stations we plotted, I worry that we are still going to be late to the show," Khan McKenna said.

Lankenau nodded grimly. "It is no one's fault. The Raven Alliance is in the Periphery. With the lack of HPG communications, it took our Watch operatives weeks to get us news of the Wolves and Falcons landing on Terra."

Sterling gritted her teeth in frustration. "The reason for the delay does not matter. I feel that we may have missed out on our role in history."

Anger and a sense of guilt tore at her. *We knew the Jade Falcons and Wolves were close to Terra. I should have moved earlier and secured a staging world in the Republic. If we had taken action a year or two earlier, we might have been a contender for being the ilClan.*

"We could challenge the results," Iqbal prodded. "As a Clan, it is our right to do so."

"Is it? I think not. The words of Nicholas Kerensky are clear: the Clan that conquers Terra becomes the ilClan. There is no challenge to that. To even consider it would go against our *rede*. While the reference to the ilClan is obscure, it is Clan law. Our people are many things, but they are not without structure and order."

"So, we are lost," Iqbal said slowly, dejected.

Sterling floated away from her station to the nearby viewport, and stared off into space for a moment, then turning back to her saKhan. "One of these Clans is likely the ilClan by now. Our role in Clan matters will change. We will have one Clan elevated over us, a true ilKhan, a new order. As loyal children of Kerensky, we will conform to that. It was the will of Nicholas Kerensky, and I will not break with that out of petty ego or desire for power. We are above that. We are Snow Raven."

"If Malvina Hazen is ilKhan, we may be facing dramatic changes," Iqbal replied.

A vast understatement, Sterling thought. "Khan Hazen is destructive, arrogant, and vicious," she said. "If she has become ilKhan, we must acknowledge that her way...this Mongol Doctrine...is the right way. If she has defeated the Republic of the Sphere and Clan Wolf, then that is the path we must walk. We are warriors, you and I, the bravest of the Clans because we favor the most dangerous battlefield: the void of space. If Malvina has won, then her way is to be our way as well."

"What of Alaric Ward?"

"What of him?" she countered.

"What if he is ilKhan?" Iqbal asked. "He won a *ristar* from our Clan at Victor Steiner-Davion's funeral, and it embarrassed us. We should not forget such a slight."

Sterling narrowed her eyes at the saKhan. *This is not the first time we have had this discussion...but it needs to be the last.* "To be candid, Iqbal, you have always disliked Haake Sukhanov. You gave him assignments that were beneath his skill, all over some slight that, frankly, I do not understand. You treated him poorly when you should have embraced him. At the time, you felt no loss with Haake's departure. I think it would be best to never mention this matter again. If Alaric is ilKhan, you should hope that Haake has not filled his ears with stories of your perceived slights."

Her words hit the SaKhan like a Killer Whale missile. Lankenau's face reddened, and he slumped slightly in his chair.

"To your original question," Sterling continued, "if Alaric is indeed victorious, we will align with him and his thinking. That does not change who we are."

"So, you would have us bend the knee to the victor, *quiaff*?"

"*Aff*, in a matter of speaking," McKenna replied. "However, I do not offer blind obedience to the new ilKhan. We have the most potent WarShip fleet in the Inner Sphere. We will open a dialogue with the victor and discuss what they desire of us, and we will assure our position and the sovereignty of our realm. Our Clan has a great deal to offer the victor, and I have no intention of giving away a thing of such value for nothing in return."

She paused for a moment and stared out of ship's viewport into the vast darkness. *For now, we go and pay our respects. Beyond that, it is the beginning of a new era, with new opportunities for all.*

CHAPTER 38

Alaric entered Malvina's residence, a luxurious apartment she had taken as her own. It was larger than the room he had claimed for himself near the Court of the Star League. Despite calls to have her imprisoned, Alaric had insisted she be treated as any defeated Clan warrior. By the same token, he was not ignorant. Spurlock monitored her communications and had insisted on posting guards on the building, but so far she had remained in self-imposed isolation without incident.

Her injuries had been treated with the finest of Clan medical technology, though he made sure that Stephanie Chistu's field-hospital bed had been nowhere near Malvina's. While Alaric felt confident Malvina would honor her defeat to Clan Wolf, he could not be sure she would extend the same honor to Chistu. *There is still a Clan Jade Falcon, and it needs leadership. Malvina must accept this defeat and bend to my will.*

Tara had suggested accompanying him, but he had politely refused her offer. This was not a discussion he looked forward to. *Things would have been easier if she had had the good graces to simply die during the fighting.*

Cynthy opened Malvina's door and gestured for Alaric to enter. Malvina keeping a human as a pet was just one more thing that made him uncomfortable. *Why would anyone torment another person in this manner?* The answer was only in the dark recesses of Malvina's twisted mind, a place he preferred not to go. *Perhaps I should have listened to Anastasia and had her kill Malvina.*

The Jade Falcon Khan greeted him with a drink in hand—neat bourbon, by the smell of it. Her facial bruises had faded to dull purple and brown on her pale skin. Her new bionic arm was glossy black and reflected the lights. Her casual uniform was black, her Mongol Doctrine still on parade for him to see. A small holoprojector showing a map of Terra had replaced the coffee table.

"Please enter, *ilKhan*," she said gesturing to the couch. "Would you like a drink? Cynthy will make you whatever you wish."

"That is not necessary," Alaric said, taking a seat.

Malvina coiled herself in an easy chair across from him, crossing her legs and almost smirking at him. "I take it you have come to gloat, *quiaff*?"

"*Neg*," he replied. It *was* tempting, but now was not the time. "I have sent word of my Wolves' victory to the other Khans via JumpShip couriers, and have invited them to join me here on Terra. Some will arrive shortly."

She took a sip of her bourbon and set down the glass. "How nice for you. Why tell me?"

"You are still Khan of the Jade Falcons," Alaric said, watching Cynthy out of the corner of his eye as she took a seat behind Malvina. He saw the bruise on her forehead, at her hairline. *That poor, sad girl.*

"What is left of the Jade Falcons...that is what you mean, *quiaff*? What *is* left of my *touman*? Just over a hundred warriors—all wounded; no fully operational equipment. You killed the Republic, then killed my Clan. Your little puppet Chistu was even the one to order my warriors to stand down. You did what generations of Wolves could not even conceive of accomplishing. All of your little plans came together. I imagine you are quite proud of yourself."

"The Jade Falcons will rise from the ashes, Malvina," he said. "If I wanted them completely dead, they would be. Your Mongol Doctrine, however, has no place in the new order of things. That does not diminish what remains. The Falcons can serve a higher purpose."

"As what?" Malvina fired back. "A symbol of failure? Proof of what happens when you cross Clan Wolf? They failed me, all of them. I would rather all of them were exterminated instead of living as a constant reminder of your victory."

"You have not tended to your people," Alaric said, ignoring her anger. "They need you now more than ever."

"I have been recovering," she said, her drink back in hand. "Cynthy has been helping me recuperate from the injuries your lapdog Anastasia inflicted. But you did not come here to remind me of my duty. Why *are* you here?"

Alaric looked into her eyes and saw nothing but burning hatred. "You are the only surviving Khan of your Clan. I am telling you what I will tell the others: Nicholas Kerensky laid the path for us to return here, and I intend to lead us into the future."

"And how do you intend to do that?" she snarled.

She does not realize the gravity of this conversation. "Our future is the Star League reborn, and I will be the First Lord. I won that right on the field of battle."

Malvina glanced down at the holomap of Terra. "I have been thinking about that, Alaric. I started studying the map, looking over some of the after-action reports. You say you won that right on the field of battle. In reality, however, you could never have taken Terra without my help. Our arrival forced the Republic to fight a two-front war. They redeployed many of their best units against my Falcons, which let you and your Wolves achieve victories and take ground. You did not take Terra alone, Alaric, regardless of what you want others to believe. If not for the Jade Falcons, you could not have been victorious."

Alaric felt the verbal dagger hit, and immediately sought to mitigate the injury to his pride. He grinned as he took a moment to gather his thoughts. "Your Jade Falcons were a tool, a tool that I used to my advantage. I manipulated you into coming to Terra, Malvina. I used you to help crush the Republic, then defeated you in a legitimate combat trial. This victory is mine because I controlled every aspect of your being here."

She eyed him silently for a few moments before replying. "If that is what allows you to sleep at night, so be it. Now then, what of my Jade Falcons? What future do you see for them?"

"Your people will serve in the new SLDF, as they were intended to do."

"To do your bidding, no doubt?"

"*Aff*, Malvina. Again, Clan Wolf won that right fairly."

"Fairly? *Neg*. You used Wolf's Dragoons—mercenaries. Your victory is tainted in my eyes."

Alaric's lips quirked in a slight grin. "The Dragoons originally came from Clan Wolf. They came to Terra of their own accord, not at my command. There is no loss of honor."

"So, you expect me to bow to you?"

"Physically, *neg*. But you *will* follow my orders, or I will have you removed from your post," he warned. "I want to respect the sovereignty of your Clan, but do not underestimate what I am willing to do if I must."

She offered him an empty laugh. "You are smug, Alaric. Overconfident. Know this: your position is precarious. You are one Trial of Refusal away from death. Until you name a successor, your ilClan is vulnerable. Remember how Nicholas Kerensky died?"

She dares to threaten me? "I am unafraid of the future, because I shall forge it myself."

Malvina shook her head. "You speak of the future, yet still cling to the past. Another Star League?"

"The Star League has always been a symbol of hope for humankind, and under my rule, it will be again. We will build a new Star League, as the Great Father would have wanted, without the weaknesses of the old. We will maintain our traditions, but the days of 'occupation zones' and fighting over the House Lords' scraps is over. We will truly unify the Inner Sphere. That is our new goal, our new ambition as Clan."

Malvina took another long sip of her drink, emptying the glass. "Very well... 'First Lord,'" she said, rising to her feet. "You defeated my Clan. I will submit...for the time being. I think we can agree that my choices are limited."

Alaric shifted in his seat, getting ready to leave, but Malvina held up her hand. "Before you go, Alaric, I have one last question. Sitting here, going over everything that has taken place, something continues to nag at me..." She took a breath and fixed her ice-blue gaze on him. "How did you learn to penetrate the Fortress barrier? My scientist caste struggled with that problem for years, but you seemed to divine the solution at a most opportune time."

Alaric stared calmly back at her, refusing to let his face reveal anything. "My scientist caste arrived at a solution through much trial and error." In reality, the solution had mysteriously appeared among his scientist caste, its source unknown. *It does not matter where it came from, only that we had it.*

He rose to his feet, glancing at Cynthy and then back to Malvina. "Visit your people, Malvina. They need you." He walked to the door. "And I want you to free this girl," he said, nodding at Cynthy. "What you are doing with her is below your stature."

"She is *mine*!" Malvina snapped, slamming her empty glass down so hard it shattered.

"Not anymore," Alaric said firmly. "Fight me on this, and you will lose. You will either hand her over to authorities that can care for her by the end of today, or I will send a squad here to take her by force."

He opened the door, then glanced back at her. "That is the will of your First Lord."

1412 HOURS

Galaxy Commander Stephanie Chistu, her arm in a sling and her face bruised and cut, arrived at the apartment door where Malvina Hazen had taken up residence. She drew a long, deep breath before knocking. SaKhan Ryan Pryde was dead, as were the other Galaxy Commanders, which meant she was the only one left who could deal with Malvina.

Khan—neg, *the ilKhan*—Ward had asked her to visit the Jade Falcon Khan. He had said he needed Chistu to salvage what could be saved of the Jade Falcons. It was a great favor he asked for, given her and Malvina's tempest relationship, but Chistu understood. She knew how bitter and vindictive Malvina was. *If only she had died, all of these changes would have been much easier.*

She knocked on the door, but heard nothing. After knocking again, she heard a raspy, desperate voice call out, "Get in here!"

She opened the door and was stunned into silence. Malvina lay on the white tile floor in a pool of dark blood. Crimson gore soaked her uniform and matted her platinum-blond hair. At the far end of the room was Cynthy, near a shattered mirror, holding a laser pistol that she shifted between Malvina and Chistu.

Stephanie's heart pounded in her chest. *Is this an assassination attempt?* Her combat instincts told her to fight—but whom?

On the floor between the two of them lay a knife, covered in blood. Chistu recognized it instantly. *I forged that knife and gave it to Cynthy years ago, after the invasion of Coventry.* She could barely make out the words honor is not bestowed, but taken etched on the blade.

"Call for help," Malvina commanded from the floor in a low, rasping voice.

Chistu's eyes fell on the girl with the laser pistol. *I cannot call for help without risking being shot.* Ignoring her Khan, she focused on Cynthy. She closed the door behind her and cautiously took a few slow steps toward Cynthy. For years, Malvina had tortured the young girl. Cynthy looked afraid of the world, and had every right to be.

In that moment, Stephanie made a choice to go to Cynthy, not her tormenter. "Are you okay?"

Cynthy's eyes were huge, and she looked terrified. *She has been cut, probably from the broken mirror.* Tears ran down the girl's cheeks.

"Forget her," Malvina said from the floor. "Get the medtechs here *now*! That is an order from your Khan!"

"Shut up," Chistu said firmly. *Bringing in more people could result in more casualties at this point.* She took another step forward, avoiding Malvina's blood, and extended her hand. "It is going to be okay, Cynthy. She cannot hurt you now. Give me the gun. You know me. You know I will not harm you."

For a moment, Cynthy seemed to relax. Her arms retracted slightly as she trembled, holding the gun still.

Chistu took another step forward. "She will never hurt you again, Cynthy, you have my word."

"She *stabbed* me," Malvina spat. She shifted on the floor, using her bionic arm to turn herself to watch Chistu better. "Alaric said she could leave, but I told her she could not. That brat stabbed me from behind, like the cowardly freebirth she is." Malvina choked out a wet, thick cough behind her.

Stephanie ignored Malvina's raving and kept her focus on the girl. "Ignore her, Cynthy. She is not going to hurt you or anyone ever again."

Cynthy broke down crying as Chistu wrapped her hands around the laser pistol. The safety was still on. Chistu stuffed it into her jumpsuit pocket, then stroked the young girl's hair, brushing it out of her face.

"Come, let us sit down." She led Cynthy to an armchair, and the frightened girl clung to her. "Everything is going to be fine. I will handle this." She had to gently pry the girl's arms from her.

With Cynthy settled, Chistu grabbed a dining-room chair and placed it between the door and where Malvina lay, still oozing blood. Then she bent to pick up the bloody knife. The blood had dried slightly and was sticky. For a moment, she admired her own craftsmanship. *A part of me always knew it would find its way to Malvina. I am thankful I was here to see it.* She returned to the chair and sat, looking down at her Khan.

Malvina twisted on the floor, smearing her blood on the white tiles. "What are you doing? I ordered you to call for the medtechs!" Blood dripped from a corner of her mouth onto the floor.

"I do not think so," Chistu replied.

"I am your *Chingis Khan*! This is murder! You *must* help me."

"It is not murder. You abused this girl, and she fought back in self-defense. You caused this, not me."

"*I command you*!" Malvina growled, struggling for breath as she labored to rise, then fell back, wheezing.

"Not any longer. I am a true Jade Falcon." In that moment, those words she had embraced had new meaning to her, new strength.

Malvina made a guttural noise low filled with rage and hate. "I should have had you killed long ago.... Yaroslav squandered his chance."

You tried several times, and failed. "When you die, everything you have wrought will die with you, starting with your Mongol Doctrine. You will be remembered only for your failures, and the ultimate failure: losing the ilClanship to Clan Wolf. There will be no line in *The Remembrance* for you."

"No..." Malvina closed her eyes, fighting for consciousness. "Not like this..." Her voice was weak, almost a whimper.

Stephanie Chistu looked down at the knife in her hand for a moment. "Know this: it was Alaric who sent me here."

She looked up at the grounded Jade Falcon Khan. "The First Lord sends his regards."

She rose from her seat.

1620 HOURS

The open door was guarded by one of Spurlock Conners' men. Alaric brushed past him to enter the apartment. Chistu was there, her arm in a sling, her injured face expressionless. She moved with a slight limp as she walked to the doorway to meet him.

Farther into the room, Spurlock Conners squatted down to study the crime scene. When he saw Alaric, he rose, shaking his head. The head of the Watch dismissed everyone else from the room.

Blood was everywhere, indicative of the savagery that had taken place. *This is not suicide...this is murder.* Malvina lay face down on the floor, dead, surrounded by a pool of blood. A part of him was horrified. *This is not how warriors are to die. They should meet their fate in combat.* That thought was tempered by the knowledge that the victim was Malvina Hazen. *She is no longer a threat to me or anyone.*

"What happened?" Alaric asked.

Conners looked over at Chistu, then back at Alaric. "IlKhan, the Galaxy Commander found Khan Hazen like this when she came to call, as you had requested. From what we can piece together, it seems the girl, Cynthy, stabbed Malvina from behind and fled the scene before the Galaxy Commander arrived."

"Malvina bled to death," Chistu said with a remarkable lack of emotion, given the circumstances.

"We have kept this quiet so far," Conners said. "Only a handful of people know about it."

"Was she dead when you arrived?" Alaric asked Chistu.

"Mostly," Chistu replied. "She was beyond help." There was something in her choice of words that struck a chord with Alaric. *Yes, she was...*

Alaric looked at her for a moment, and she met his gaze squarely. *She is every bit the Jade Falcon I thought her to be.*

"Where did the girl get a knife?" he asked.

"Only she knows the answer to that question," Chistu said. "We are warriors, so knives are not uncommon. But to be perfectly honest, I am not surprised that this happened..." She nodded at the Khan's bloody corpse. "Malvina abused that poor girl for years. Some people can only be bent so far before they finally snap."

Alaric studied her for a long moment. "The girl had been abused," he said. "I saw the evidence firsthand when I was here earlier today, and I told Malvina to release her immediately. No doubt my words triggered what happened here."

"I do not think that fact needs to be made public," Chistu replied.

"Agreed," Alaric said. "Spurlock...as far as anyone needs to know, Malvina died from unforeseen complications from the wounds she received from fighting Anastasia in the battle. Her death was...unfortunate. But Anastasia will be delighted by the news, since she can claim she killed Malvina in combat."

Conners understood. "*Quite* unforeseeable, ilKhan. One might even say *tragic*. Khan Hazen's remains will be cremated quickly, of course." He looked at Alaric. "Unless you wish her *giftake* extracted."

Alaric glanced at Chistu, then back at Spurlock and shook his head. "I think we can proceed quickly. Continuing her genetic line would be...unproductive."

"Very well. My agents will deal with the medtechs to ensure her demise, per official record, is plausible."

"As for the girl," said Alaric, "have your most trusted agents track her down and bring her to me unharmed. It is important that no one ever learns Malvina died under these circumstances."

Connors nodded. "I will see to it personally."

Alaric dismissed him, then returned his gaze to Malvina's body. *In many respects, Cynthy, you have done me a great favor.*

He turned to Chistu. "You are the ranking survivor of Clan Jade Falcon now."

She nodded. "I stand to serve you, ilKhan."

"The Jade Falcons need leadership. I can think of none better to lead them in this time of great change. You will need to organize votes for the role of Khan and saKhan."

"It will be done," she replied.

"And one more thing," Alaric said. "I am counting on you winning the vote for Khan."

Chistu gave him a thin grin. "I am a true Jade Falcon. I live to serve."

CHAPTER 39

The cobblestone courtyard of the Court of the Star League had been cleared of all of the tourist trappings. The sun shone brilliantly over the large space, warming the wet chill in the morning air. It was a fitting place for the rebirth of a Clan.

On New Earth, Alaric had met the Custos of the Fidelis and learned their true nature, that their ancestors had come from Clan Smoke Jaguar. The bargain he had struck with Paul Moon agreed that, should he become ilKhan, he would make the Fidelis a provisional Clan. They were, as a people, his bondsmen, until such a time as he saw fit to give them a vote on his new Star League council.

Now, having won the victory against the Falcons, he wanted the Smoke Jaguars at his official coronation—not as the Fidelis, but as a true Clan. He had summoned them from their DropShips at the jump point, where they had remained for days while awaiting word of Alaric's official invitation to the most solemn of ceremonies.

The final Trials of Bloodright for Smoke Jaguar Bloodnames were taking place here, in the Court of the Star League, and Alaric presided over them with a sense of hope. *For far too long the Jaguars have hidden in plain sight, kept in check by their service to the Republic. Today is the first day of Clan Smoke Jaguar's rebirth.*

Each day, Alaric moved the game pieces on his mental chessboard. Even Malvina Hazen's death served a purpose to him. But with each meeting and ceremony, every step he took was deeper into uncharted waters. *History can only help me so much. If I am to reestablish the Star League, I need to find my own course.* Discovering that the Fidelis were the descendants of Clan Smoke Jaguar was a pleasant surprise. *Now the time has come to legitimize them.*

The first step was the Trials of Bloodright, limited to those Bloodnames the Jaguars had brought with them from Huntress. Second, the newly

Bloodnamed warriors would elect a Khan and saKhan. Clan Smoke Jaguar was to be a provisional entity...a non-voting Clan, bonded by the ilKhan himself. *At the right time, I will fully restore them.* When that time would be, Alaric did not yet know.

Chance Vickers stood at his side as part of the Circle of Equals, her arms crossed, watching the Trial of Bloodright. "I am curious, Alaric," she said. She was one of the few people he allowed to refer to him by his first name rather than ilKhan or First Lord. "The Jaguars...you are willing to reconstitute them. Why?"

The new Smoke Jaguar Loremaster Josh Wirth initiated the Trial of Bloodright. Both Wolves watched as Alaric replied. "The Star League is a symbol—not just for us, but for the whole Inner Sphere. The second Star League had but one goal: the elimination of the Smoke Jaguars to invalidate the Clans' claim to supremacy. By bringing this Clan back to its rightful place among us, I show that that League's efforts were all a lie, a deception, a failure." *One perpetrated by one of my genefathers, Victor Steiner-Davion.*

Vickers nodded. *She understands the power of symbols in the right hands.*

The Circle of Equals was just over 150 warriors, spread out almost shoulder to shoulder. The trial seemed like a blur as the two female contenders for the last Bloodname, Moon, tore into each other with punches and kicks. Prohaska, half-Elemental and all warrior, delivered a staggering uppercut to the jaw of the much larger Elemental Colby, lifting her several centimeters off her feet, then sending her unconscious body down hard. Colby moaned as Prohaska moved in, fully prepared to continue her brutal assault. Colby raised her head slightly, then dropped it back hard on the stonework with a *thump* that made several in the Circle cringe.

Prohaska turned slowly, basking in the audience's attention, and stopped when she saw Alaric. She looked upon him with reverence, as if he had given her a great gift. With one hand she wiped the sweat from her short reddish-brown crewcut and bowed shallowly to him, a demonstration of respect.

Loremaster Wirth stepped forward and raised his hands as Prohaska panted hard, her sweat dripping onto the cobblestone. "By the *rede* of the Unopened Work, our *Remembrance*, I proclaim this warrior to be henceforth known as Prohaska Moon, a Bloodnamed warrior of Clan Smoke Jaguar."

The warriors in the Circle of Equals cheered, and Prohaska held up her arms to encourage them. Then she turned to Alaric, who stepped forward. "You honor me with your presence, ilKhan," she said, still panting.

"*Seyla*, Prohaska Moon. It is you who honor your Clan. You would have made your genefather, the Custos, proud."

"I believe I would."

Another freshly Bloodnamed warrior, Richmond Howell, stepped forward. He said, "Let us now vote for the warrior who will be our Khan!" A cheer rose from the gathered Smoke Jaguars. "The ilKhan himself came to witness Prohaska Moon's Trial of Bloodright. Her genefather was the Custos of the Fidelis. We should honor our past as well as our future. I nominate Prohaska Moon as Khan."

Another cheer rose from the ranks. Loremaster Wirth then called off the handful of Bloodnamed warriors one by one. All voted for Prohaska.

The Loremaster stepped forward. "Once more, the Smoke Jaguars stalk our enemies. We are not what we were; we are much more. Our long journey on the Road of Pain is near its end, and it will be completed by our new Khan, Prohaska Moon. Let this vote stand until a stronger leader emerges."

Prohaska, still standing next to Alaric, bowed her head deeply. "I will not fail you, *trothkin*. I will honor who we were, what we have become, and where we are going. We will show this new Star League what the Smoke Jaguars are capable of."

Alaric nodded to her and raised his voice to the gathered Clan. "Prohaska Moon is the first Smoke Jaguar Khan in over nine decades. While you will be a nonvoting Clan on my Star League Council, your journey to restore your people has taken a giant leap forward on this day. Khan Moon, the time has come for your people to emerge from the shadows, set down the burden your people have borne for so long, and take your place at my side."

A deafening cheer rose from the ranks of the Smoke Jaguar warriors—now a Clan once more.

Four hours later, Alaric observed a similar trial, one he had even an greater interest in.

The election of the new Jade Falcon Khans was a smaller event than the Smoke Jaguars'. Almost all Falcons left were still recovering and in no kind of fighting shape; such was the damage they had incurred during the fight against his Wolves. Malvina had ordered no quarter be given, and some of the Wolves had returned the gesture. Those Falcons who could attend still bore the fresh scars and fading bruises from the battle. Few did not still wear bandages of some sort.

They had assembled in a circle of chairs arranged on the flat grounds of the Court of the Star League. Alaric had no illusions as to the importance of these talks. They would determine the fate of the Jade Falcons going forward.

Seventy-two Jade Falcon warriors attended the assembly. Alaric sat between Chance Vickers and the newly anointed Khan Moon of the Smoke Jaguars. Next to Moon was Tara. A third of the way around the circle sat Stephanie Chistu. She made eye contact with him as he took his seat, dipping her head slightly as he crossed his arms to listen.

Chistu, as the ranking Jade Falcon, rose to her feet, cleared her throat, and spoke, "*Seyla*, warriors of Clan Jade Falcon. We have no Loremaster to lead us, no Khan or saKhan. These positions must be filled so that we can begin the work of rebuilding."

A burly Elemental shook his ebony head then spoke, his voice was penetrating and strong. "Are we even a Clan? How many of us are left?"

"There are one hundred and twenty-eight Jade Falcon warriors alive here on Terra," Chistu replied. "We left some minor garrisons in the occupation zone—*sibko* cadets and *solahma*, mostly—but I do not have accurate figures for them."

"We are still a people," said another warrior. His head was bandaged, and he sported a patch on his jumpsuit from the Falcon Guards. "*Aff*, we have suffered losses, some grave, but we are still Jade Falcon."

"Khalus Pryde is right," the mustached MechWarrior at his side added. "We may have lost our leaders, but that does not mean we are lost as a people."

A muscular female Elemental spoke. "We followed Malvina Hazen here. She gave us victory after victory. She taught us that victory comes through strength. We *should* continue as a Clan, if only to validate her thinking."

Murmurs rippled around the circle.

Chistu, still standing, shook her head. Alaric saw this and winced internally, though his expression remained calm *Even in death, the specter of Malvina still haunts us.*

"There are two things we must address. First, whether we should continue as Clan. Second, if we are still a Clan, we should determine the path we will continue to fly along. I, for one, want nothing to do with the Mongol Doctrine. While it gave us victories, it did so at a terrible price...our honor and integrity. As is the way with our Clan, whoever leads us will set our direction."

Tomaszewski Mattlov, a thick-necked Elemental, spoke up. "Why would we change our beliefs? If not for the Mongol Doctrine, none of us would be here. If not for Malvina Hazen, we would not even be on Terra."

Stephanie looked over at him. "You have so little faith in our Clan, *quineg*? I look around and see great warriors who fought harder and farther than all but one Clan. I believe in all my heart that we would still be on Terra today, even if Malvina had never been conceived. The difference is we would have arrived here with our honor and dignity intact."

"You never supported the Khan," a female aerospace pilot spoke up. "It is because of faithless warriors like you that we lost this battle."

Chistu's eyes narrowed at the woman. "Watch your words, Karen Roshak. How dare you insinuate that I did not fight every bit as hard as those of you that followed Malvina's twisted dream? I conquered South America in the name of our Clan. I fought longer and harder than most, otherwise I would not be here now. I bear no shame in standing against the Chingis Khan's ways."

Stephanie paused, gathered her composure, and spoke again in a calmer tone, turning to Alaric. "Khan Ward, you are the victor of our trial. You have ascended to be the ilKhan. What do *you* see as the role for our Clan?"

Alaric rose and felt the stares from the assembled Falcons. "You have lost much. Your *touman* will not be what it was, not for some time. That does not mean you are any lesser of a Clan—simply not as numerous.

"The origins of your Clan lie in the Royal Black Watch. They were the personal bodyguard regiment of the First Lord, drawn from the best of the Star League,. Because of this noble history, I see you fulfilling two roles. First, I wish you to be the best fighting force among the Clans. The Jade Falcons should be the whetstone every other Clan sharpens itself against. My Wolves have borne testament to the tenacity and fierceness of the Jade Falcon Guards." Alaric glanced at Star Colonel Marv Roshak, who grinned at his words and nodded in respect. "I see that tenacity and fierceness as the benchmark for all Jade Falcon warriors."

Alaric continued. "In your second role, I would see your warriors restored as the honor guard of the First Lord." Those words brought puzzled expressions and murmurs from the assembled Falcons. "Do not be surprised. As I said, your origins stem from the Black Watch. My role as ilKhan will inevitably draw those who seek to harm me, and I can think of few better than the Jade Falcons to protect me."

Alaric returned to his seat, noticing several warriors' faces redden with pride at his mention of the famed Black Watch Regiment. *They are already seeing a return to honor and glory, even higher than what they achieved under Malvina. Now, Chistu must do her part...*

"Thank you, Khan Ward," Chistu said. "My fellow Jade Falcons, let us deal with the first issue: Should our Clan continue? Those in favor, raise your hands."

All but five of the Falcons raised their hands—and those that did not, from what Alaric could see, were the diehard Malvina supporters. Tomaszewski Mattlov crossed his thick arms and glared at Chistu. Alaric could feel the venom in his body language.

"Then it is settled," Stephanie said. "We are Jade Falcon, now and forever. Next, we must elect a Khan. Who among us is worthy of this honor?"

Karen Roshak spoke up. "I nominate Star Captain Tomaszewski Mattlov. He is a true believer in the philosophy of our lost leader, Chingis Khan Malvina Hazen. In the battle against Clan Wolf, he gave no quarter and stayed true to the ways of our Khan." Tomaszewski beamed at the praise heaped on him.

Several eyes had fallen to Alaric at Karen Roshak's mention of the Wolves, but he said nothing and made sure his face betrayed no feelings. *I know what Malvina ordered, but I will not hold these warriors accountable for following her orders.*

Khalus Pryde then spoke, "I nominate the one leader who remained true to the way of the Jade Falcon, Galaxy Commander Stephanie Chistu. We were not always the creatures Malvina Hazen turned us into. Think back to *The Remembrance*. Out first Khan, Elizabeth Hazen, was the heart and soul of the Black Watch. We were not brutal killers; we were simply the best warriors— the standard for all others to aspire to. Galaxy Commander Chistu has long stood against Malvina Hazen's policies. Speaking as one who has suffered under the Khan's wrath, I understand the plight she faced. Every day she risked death—not just from our enemies, but from our own leader. Our Clan's future needs new vision, a new direction. That will not be found in the failed paths that brought us to defeat on Terra. It comes from a leader willing to plot a new course for the Falcons. That leader is Stephanie Chistu."

Chistu turned to Alaric amid the murmurs. "We need someone to call the vote. Khan Ward, you are a Khan—will you help determine the winner?"

Alaric rose. "It would be an honor. A show of hands for Tomaszewski Mattlov."

A dozen hands shot up.

"For Stephanie Chistu?"

Sixty hands rose. Tomaszewski's face reddened with anger.

"Stephanie Chistu has obtained the greater margin of votes to be Khan of the Jade Falcons."

Tomaszewski Mattlov shot to his feet. "Stephanie Chistu, I challenge you for the leadership of our Clan."

There were no cheers at his declaration, only a few low murmurs of agreement. The Falcons all rose, grabbed their chairs, and spread out to give the two combatants room to maneuver.

Chistu did not shirk from the challenge. The trial was to be fought with weapons, on the same ground where the Smoke Jaguars had waged their Trials of Bloodright. Chistu demanded to fight with blades, and the brutish Elemental agreed. She removed her sling and tossed it on the ground. Tomaszewski chose a curved saber, while Chistu brandished two knives, one in each hand, despite her cast. Alaric's eyes fell to the weapon in her right hand and noticed an inscription on the shimmering blade, one he could not read from this distance.

The pair stalked each other around the circle for nearly a minute before moving in. Mattlov slashed through the air, the blade whizzing close to Chistu as she artfully dodged back. She blocked another vicious swing with the cast on her arm. After several more sweeping blows, Mattlov changed his approach, lunging straight at her. Chistu parried it with her left-hand knife and managed a quick slice on his thick forearm in the process.

The brutish Elemental ignored the spray of blood and kept on lunging. Chistu caught one thrust with her crossed blades but struggled to hold back the furious assault. Alaric noted how skilled she was as she once more cut Mattlov's sword arm.

The Elemental tossed the saber over to his other hand. "You will find I am ambidextrous, Galaxy Commander," he taunted, pacing near the edge of the Circle of Equals.

Chistu flashed a predatory smile. "You will find I have other skills as well."

Lightning-quick, she hurled a knife at Mattlov—and the blade struck near the base of his throat. Blood jetted into the air, and he dropped the sword, grabbing the knife to pull it out.

The Elemental fell to his knees onto the cobblestone, gurgling air and blood, then toppled the rest of the way over onto his side. As the medics attended him, Chistu walked over and recovered her blade, paying no attention to his plight. Those around the Circle were not shocked by the violence, for such was the Way of the Clans.

"We have no Loremaster," Chistu said. "IlKhan, will you declare a winner for our Clan?"

Alaric nodded, and his smile broadened. "By the *rede* of our people, Stephanie Chistu has defeated all challengers. She is the true Khan of Clan Jade Falcon."

There were cheers and smiles, though the diehard Mongols did little more than dip their heads in her direction to acknowledge her victory.

Chistu bowed to Alaric, and he stepped into the Circle of Equals so that all of the Falcons could hear him. "Khan Chistu, your Clan bravely fought against my Wolves, and did much to honor your traditions and your codexes. You embody the honor and strength your warriors so revere. You will need both in the wars to come."

"Clan Jade Falcon will rebuild, ilKhan," she promised, wiping her knife on her pant leg as Mattlov was carried off, still spitting blood. "My Jade Falcons will not fail you." She wiped the sweat from her brow and turned to the Jade Falcons. "We shall adjourn for a short time, then discuss the selection of a saKhan and a Loremaster."

Slowly the gathering of warriors spread out, and Alaric motioned for Tara to join him and Chistu. "Tara Wolf, have you met Stephanie Chistu?"

"I have not." Tara extended her hand, and Chistu shook it. "I read the Republic's account of the affair on Coventry though, so her reputations precedes her."

"Tara was my bondsman," Alaric said. "She is the Countess of Northwind, and led the Highlanders. Only a few people have ever bested me in battle, and Tara is one of them."

"The deeds of Tara Campbell and the Northwind Highlanders are well known in our ranks," Chistu replied.

Alaric nodded. "During the ilClan trial, she fought against the Jade Falcons as an *abtakha* and saved my life more than once." He paused for a moment, letting the words sink in. "Tara—tell us, what does the Inner Sphere think of the Jade Falcons?"

Tara paused, glancing at both Khans, then spoke in a measured tone. "The people of the Inner Sphere fear the Falcons—not because they are skilled, but because they are brutal. From our youth we are taught what alien monsters the Clans are. It was mostly propaganda...but in recent years, the Jade Falcons made all of those fears real."

"I intend to change that," Stephanie said proudly.

Alaric nodded. "As you should. Tell me Tara. The Black Watch—during the Star League they recruited only the best of your Northwind Highlanders into their ranks, *quiaff*?"

"*Aff*," she replied. "And during the Second Star League, the Highlanders fulfilled the Black Watch role again."

"Few units in the Inner Sphere have a higher reputation for honor and skill in battle than your Highlanders, correct?"

Tara nodded eagerly. "We take pride in our heritage and ties to the Star League Defense Force. The birthright of the Highlanders is steeped in tradition. We fight hard, but we fight fair."

"If I may be so bold," Alaric said, turning to Stephanie Chistu, "what you need, Khan Chistu, is someone fresh and new—a proven field commander and a leader who knows the true ways of honor. Someone who can help you build a new direction for your Clan."

The two women looked at each other for a moment, then back to Alaric.

"My Khan," Tara said, "are you suggesting—"

"I am," he replied. "None of us wish to see the Jade Falcons drift back into the Mongol Doctrine. Having someone with the same historical ties as the Black Watch there, but steeped in honor as well—that might be just what the Falcons need. I could order you to join the Falcons, Tara, but I do not wish to.

You have been a great Wolf warrior, but the Inner Sphere needs you to take on a greater role. Be a great Jade Falcon. Help make them into something respected and only feared for their fighting abilities, not a capacity for terror or brutality. They need a conscience, a voice to support Khan Chistu...someone to show them the right path."

Chistu nodded. "Tara, you would be a welcome addition to our Clan. We are a proud people, but some have lost their way. Clearly we have much to learn from you, and you from us."

Hesitantly, Tara stood next to the new Khan. "I don't...do not know what kind of Jade Falcon I would be, but I do know I will not stand for the Falcons to be the monsters they became under Malvina."

"Good," Chistu replied. "Neither will I."

"I never anticipated this," Tara said under her breath.

"Nor did I," Chistu said in the same low tone. "But together, Tara Jade Falcon, you and I can create a force capable of defeating any enemy who stands before us."

CHAPTER 40

ILCLAN TEMPORARY COMMAND POST
UNITY CITY, PUGET SOUND
NORTH AMERICA
TERRA
27 APRIL 3151

Alaric sat at a table in his makeshift command post, a commandeered hotel not far from the Court of the Star League. The room was a dull green with dark-blue curtains—the original flowered ones having been replaced at his request. The table was a dark wood, with none of the technology he was accustomed to having.

It does not matter. This is a day where we are not mapping battles, but planning for the future. Gathered around the table were the people who enabled him to fulfill his destiny.

Chance Vickers, almost fully healed from the wounds that had nearly taken her life, had been elected saKhan, something even Anastasia Kerensky admitted she had more than earned. Spurlock Conners, his faithful Watch commander who had given him the keys to Malvina's mind, sat next to Chance. Haake Sukhanov, his former bondsman who had orchestrated the magnificent space battle that had brought them to Terra, was across the table. Anastasia Kerensky, who had brought the Wolves-in-Exile back to his Clan, sat at his left. Her new role, according to Alaric, was to be the Commanding General of the Star League Defense Forces, like her distant ancestor, Aleksandr Kerensky. *She has faced countless enemies in her time roaming the Inner Sphere. It will be useful as the Star League grows.*

Almost everyone looked subtly different after the weariness and strain of such a prolonged and important conflict had finally drained away. Their faces were now fuller, their energy returned in the way they talked and moved, and the bags under their eyes were gone. All seemed happy for the first time in months.

There were empty chairs as well, reserved for those they had lost. Damon Ward, who had handled the monumental task of coordinating the technician caste, had died in the last few minutes of the Trial with the Jade Falcons.

Agustin Tutuola lay in a hospital with a crushed spine; his recovery would take several agonizing months. Garner Kerensky's chair sat empty as well. The last empty seat was for Ramiel Bekker, the loss that pained Alaric the most.

"It is good to see all of you again," he said as he took his seat. "Let us get started. Where do we stand in terms of strength?"

Chance looked at her noteputer and spoke. "The influx of the personnel and equipment from the former Wolves-in-Exile somewhat skews our numbers, but as it stands, our *touman* is at forty-two percent of its full strength. We have *sibkos* in the Empire that will graduate in the coming months, but it will take us some time, years, before we reach full strength again."

"What of Wolf's Dragoons?" Alaric asked.

"Devastated," Chance replied. "Eighty-one percent losses. They have mounted their own salvage operations to recover equipment, but they are not the units they were when they arrived on Terra."

Alaric nodded. *As anticipated.* "I take it we still have the Fortress Republic protocols operating?"

"*Aff,*" said Conners. "Though from what we have learned, the system cannot be sustained indefinitely. Our estimates are that without further support, it will fail in the next twelve to eighteen months."

"Most likely we will turn it off before that, but for now it serves its purpose." Alaric turned to Star Admiral Sukhanov. "Did our courier ships go out as planned?"

"*Aff,* ilKhan," Sukhanov said with a grin. "The courier JumpShips to the Sea Foxes, Snow Ravens, and Hell's Horses left days ago. They should be receiving their invitations soon, and we will coordinate with the technicians to escort them through the Fortress Wall. The Ghost Bears have already responded. Their Khans are on their way and should be here in a week or so. Two couriers found that the Hell's Horses and Snow Raven Khans were already en route and will be arriving in the Terran system shortly."

The invitations were important. Alaric knew some of the Clans would respond positively to a Clan Wolf victory on Terra, while others—especially the Hell's Horses—would be offended. That did not bother him. *None have grounds to challenge Clan Wolf for what we have rightfully won.*

"Where do we stand on repairing the damage here on Terra?"

"Stone had the foresight to evacuate most of the major urban targets," Anastasia said. "Still, Geneva is almost a total loss. It will take years to rebuild. I have been working with the Khans of the Smoke Jaguars and Jade Falcons to ensure that we connect displaced families and secure housing for those who lost their homes. It is logistically challenging, but work is progressing."

"Excellent," Alaric said. "You have all done a remarkable job." His eyes swept the room. "This leaves us to discuss the pending ceremonies."

Vickers spoke up. "We have the BloodRibbons, and the Court of the Star League has been prepared for the ceremony. The workers completed the vault yesterday, and it is ready for the interment. We are set for tomorrow's ceremony. As for the ascension ceremony—that is still a month away, but preparations are on schedule."

"Thank you, Chance," Alaric said. "These events are important, especially the one tomorrow. We need to begin to heal. I do not want a rivalry to linger between Wolf and Falcon. That time has passed."

Two events were scheduled for his ascension to ilKhan of the Clans. One was for those who fought on Terra—acknowledging their sacrifices and their role in deciding the ilClan. The other ceremony, to be attended by the other Clans, was to formally institute him as ilKhan of the Clans and First Lord of the Star League. Most of his warriors had already started to call him First Lord, and he did nothing to discourage it. *I have earned that title with blood and battle. The old Cameron First Lords saw themselves as firsts among equals. I have shown that I have no equals. I have fulfilled the worlds of Nicholas Kerensky, despite the thousands who failed in the past.* Together, the two ceremonies would cement Clan Wolf as the ilClan, and allow Alaric to lay a path into the future for his people.

Anastasia grimaced at his words. "IlKhan, that rivalry is not likely to evaporate overnight. The Jade Falcons' casualties accounted for ninety-eight percent of their forces on Terra. There are roughly a hundred and twenty Falcon warriors left here on Terra, and most are injured, some severely. They threatened to eradicate us if they won. That is not something our warriors are likely to forget any time soon."

Alaric nodded. "I understand their feelings, but the trial has been settled according to our *rede*. The Jade Falcons will never come back as they once were. They will remain a small Clan, but they will be elite. Their role in the new order is critical. As my personal bodyguards, the new Jade Falcons will be bathed in honor, but they must always remember that in the trial that mattered most, they lost to Clan Wolf."

"It will take time before we come to terms...our two Clans," Chance said. "Many lives were lost on both sides. Our *rede* is one thing. Memories of fallen comrades is another."

Alaric nodded. "We have all lost things we cherished during this campaign. Now we must heal, renew, and start making things better for all. That process begins tomorrow." He looked around the room, "If there is nothing else to discuss, we all have a role in the ceremony to come. I will see you all at the Court of the Star League."

COURT OF THE STAR LEAGUE
28 APRIL 3151, 0900 HOURS

A new tomb of white marble had been erected in the Court of the Star League. It was plain, spartan, but with the crest of the Star League etched on it. Alaric had ordered the tomb placed over the antechamber where the murdered members of the Cameron family had been buried after Aleksandr Kerensky liberated Terra. The next occupant of that space, however, would be interred with the highest of honors. It was a fitting place.

Windblown Clan Wolf banners surrounded the white chairs placed at the center of the courtyard. On the stage, flanking Alaric at the podium, stood his command staff in dress uniforms. Five film crews were positioned around the perimeter to capture the moments that were to come.

Seated in front of Alaric were the several hundred surviving warriors of Clan Wolf. Behind them sat Clan Jade Falcon's walking wounded, and then Wolf's Dragoons at the rear, a mere few dozen. The Khans of Clan Smoke Jaguar sat to the side, replete in their gray dress uniforms.

The day was cloudy, but the sun broke through for just a moment, warming his face as he looked over the gathered warriors. He gripped the podium tightly and surveyed his people. *They are all mine now...I am the ilKhan of the Clans.*

"*Seyla,* warriors!" he said into the microphone.

"*SEYLA!*" they responded in unison, their voices echoing off the ruins and rubble of the old courtyard.

"We are here today to start a new journey together, a long road to the future. To do that, we must honor our past. When we began this journey to Terra, we brought with us centuries of our culture. Two people forged that culture. General Aleksandr Kerensky led our ancestors into the depths of space so that we could not be used to plunge the Inner Sphere into deeper chaos. The other was his son, Nicolas Kerensky, who created the Clans so that we could one day return to Terra and assume our rightful place.

"The Great General knew he would never see Terra again, but he also knew his offspring would. This was his Hidden Hope, and we begin today by fulfilling that destiny."

Chance Vickers rose to her feet. "Attention!"

The mass of warriors rose as one, even the badly wounded, and snapped to attention. A half dozen Elementals in the full regalia of Clan Wolf entered from the rear of the courtyard. Between them they carried the sealed, glass-topped coffin of Aleksandr Kerensky on their shoulders into the Court of the Star League. Their footfalls echoed over the silence of the gathering.

"Honors, hut!" Vickers called out, saluting the coffin.

The silent crowd stared as the honor guard carried the Great Father through their ranks and into the new tomb, where they laid him to rest on his beloved Terra. When the Elementals emerged, they walked in unison to their seats of honor.

From his podium, Alaric could see tears streaming down the cheeks of many warriors. The symbolism of this was extremely important to him. *This tells them that an era has come to an end, and a new age is beginning. We are not the marauding barbarians we have been made out to be, but instead we are respectful of our shared past.* Soon, images of the Great Father's interment would be broadcast to all of Terra, and eventually the whole Inner Sphere.

"As you were," Vickers said, and the warriors returned to their seats as one.

Alaric eyed the rows of warriors and smiled. "Every one of you came to Terra with the dream to fight for the title of ilClan. You fought well, and in the ways of our people, a victor has emerged from that monumental trial. But the time of trials has passed. Clan Wolf fulfilled the immortal directive of Nicholas

Kerensky and emerged as the ultimate victor. Clan Wolf is the ilClan, for now and all time."

A cheer rose from the Wolves, and Alaric did nothing to suppress it. *We earned that right.*

"Today we acknowledge everyone who fought—not just the Wolves, but the Jade Falcons as well. Those of you gathered here made history by completing the Grand Crusade our predecessors started a century ago. We are not a people given to medals or commendations, but that changes now."

He held up a small red ribbon for all to see. "This is a BloodRibbon. It is only worn by those who fought for their Clan during those three days here on Terra. Red ribbons are for the Wolves. Green for the Jade Falcons. Gray is for the others that came here to fight as well. Those who wear it are above other Clan warriors, for they fought here, spilled blood here, lost *sibkin* and *trothkin* here... on Terran soil. They brought about our destiny.

"It is only fitting that the first of these be awarded to the general who helped make this victory a reality—Chance Vickers."

Chance rose to her feet, surprised at the honor, as evidenced by her wide eyes. *She knew about the ceremony, but not this part.* She stepped forward and snapped to perfect attention. Alaric pinned the ribbon on her uniform, and with his right hand, he touched his heart with two fingers. Chance returned the gesture.

"Two fingers on the heart is the way warriors will greet you when you appear with this ribbon," Alaric told the crowd. "It signifies the two Clans that fought here, Wolf and Jade Falcon. Now then, rise when called to receive your honor."

The roll call began, starting with the Wolves. Even the most stolid of Jade Falcons clearly respected the gesture, nodding respectfully at Alaric he presented their ribbons. The last called were the survivors of Wolf's Dragoons, led by General Brubaker, who moved on crutches and was still heavily bandaged. He frowned at the gray BloodRibbons his troops were given, but said nothing as he hobbled back to his seat.

The whole ceremony took more than an hour to complete. Alaric saw warriors in the crowd face each other and put two fingers over their hearts in their unique salute for the first time. Some mingled with a few Jade Falcons as well.

Today, the healing begins.

1105 HOURS

Jack and Mia stepped in front of Kalidessa Kerensky as she walked away from Aleksandr Kerensky's tomb. A steady progression of Clan warriors had filed past the tomb, silently paying respects to the great general. Jack and Mia had been waiting for a chance to speak with their commander off to the side.

When Kalidessa saw Jack approach, she smiled and pressed two fingers to her heart. Jack and Mia did the same. He felt his BloodRibbon on his Wolf dress uniform in the process.

"Jack, Mia—this is a great day for the Inner Sphere," Kalidessa said. Since Jack had known her, she had showed brief signs of happiness, but nothing like the expression she now wore.

"Star Colonel," Jack said, "Mia and I hoped for a few moments of your time."

"Of course. What is on your mind?"

"We are leaving," Jack said bluntly. "As soon as the ilKhan allows travel off-world, we are leaving Terra."

Confusion washed Kalidessa's face. "You are leaving, *quineg*? You are part of Clan Wolf now."

Jack nodded. "We appreciate what you did for us. Because of you, we were able to have a part in the Jade Falcons defeat. That was why I signed up for the RAF in the first place. But we cannot stay."

"No...you are part of Clan Wolf," she said solemnly.

"Yes," Jack said. "But this concept of being a bondsman and then a warrior, it is not who we are."

"You would walk away from Clan Wolf, the ilClan?" Amazement hung in her question.

"We did our part," Mia said. "We saw the Jade Falcon threat end. This is not our Terra, though. We were raised in the Republic. I don't want to see it under Clan rule, even a Clan we are a part of."

"Where will you go?"

Jack shook his head. "I do not know. Perhaps the Federated Suns...I hear they are hiring almost anyone to fight for them. Maybe to Galatea. I just know we can't stay here."

"I could order you to remain," Kalidessa said in a low tone.

Jack looked her deeply in the eye. "I have found no provision in Clan law that prevents a warrior from leaving the Clan voluntarily. We saved your life, Star Colonel...and it cost us Cheetah to do it. Let's not make this messy between us."

Kerensky regarded him for a long moment, then slowly nodded. "You have been honorable in our dealings, and fought like any one of my Trueborn warriors. Know this, Jack and Mia—you are, and always will be, Clan Wolf warriors. Wherever you go, whatever you do, your place here will be waiting."

Jack extended his hand, which Kalidessa took and firmly squeezed. "Well bargained and done, Star Colonel."

OFFICE OF THE FIRST LORD, TEMPORARY COMMAND POST
UNITY CITY, PUGET SOUND
NORTH AMERICA
TERRA
28 APRIL 3151, 1510 HOURS

Alaric sat in his office, feeling more confident and secure than ever before. The big mahogany desk was inlaid with a holoprojector. The bookshelves were empty; he had little use for souvenirs or reading material. As he looked around the room, he could not resist the thought that this red-leather chair and wooden desk were now the seat of power in the Inner Sphere.

"General Brubaker and several of his officers are here to see you," his adjutant said from outside his office.

They have come. Alaric smiled. "Send them in." He had been expecting this meeting since the end of the Trial, and was more than prepared for it.

He rose from his thick leather seat as the general entered, moving carefully on his crutches, followed by his entourage. Colonel Lyons' face was half-bandaged. Colonel Crews had one heavily bandaged leg truncated above the knee, and maneuvered on his own crutches, his face gaunt and pale, his eyes sunken. Only Major Andrew Krull and Star Captain Marotta Kerensky, who had brokered the Dragoons' arrival on Terra, seemed relatively unhurt.

The general's ebony face was flushed with rage. Deep wrinkles on his forehead told a story of fury and frustration.

"What can I do for you, General?" Alaric asked.

"Why the hell did you pull my people out of the fight?" Brubaker demanded. "We were on the verge of destroying the Falcons when you ordered us to break off." He paused and closed his eyes to curb his anger. It did not seem to work. "Our agreement was that we would be the tip of the spear, at the forefront of the fighting. We were about to crush the Jade Falcons once and for all, and you pulled us away at the last moment. A lot of my people died to earn the right to that final kill. Why did you do that?"

Alaric kept his face expressionless as he spoke. "The honor of defeating the Jade Falcons belonged to Trueborn warriors of Clan Wolf."

Brubaker looked thunderstruck. "We-We came to fight alongside you...at *your* request."

"And you chose to grant my request of your own free will," Alaric countered. "I thought you would be honored that we acknowledged your contribution at all."

"I lost over eighty percent of the Dragoons—"

"For which you have my sympathies." *And my thanks.* "If, however, you thought your participation would entitle you to claim the kill ahead of my own warriors, you are gravely mistaken."

Marotta Kerensky stepped forward, emotionally and physically, between Alaric and Brubaker. "IlKhan, surely we can arrive at a suitable accommodation. If there is a mistake, it is mine. I thought the intent was to bring the Dragoons back to Clan Wolf all along."

"Which you did," Alaric said. "And for that, Marotta Kerensky, you have my deepest thanks."

"You *used* us!" Colonel Crews said. "We thought we were coming to fight *with* Clan Wolf, not *for* Clan Wolf. Surely our efforts qualified as a Trial of Position in the Clan Wolf *touman.*"

Alaric chuckled. "You made assumptions, Colonel, and they were incorrect. But you do have my gratitude for your service. And knowing Wolf's Dragoons are mercenaries—mercenaries who turned your back on Ulric Kerensky during the Clan invasion—I thought this would be an appropriate payment for services rendered." He opened his desk drawer, pulled out a small, purple velvet bag, and handed it to Brubaker.

The general dumped the bag's clinking contents into his large hand and stared at it, dumbfounded.

"What is it?" Colonel Lyons asked.

"Thirty goddamn pieces of silver," Brubaker fumed, and hurled the bag and the coins across the room. The coins rattled and *ting*ed, rolling on the inlaid-wood flooring.

Brubaker threw his BloodRibbon on the floor at Alaric's feet. "You manipulated us to come here and bleed for Clan Wolf," he spat. "We are leaving. Know this, Alaric Ward, you have made an enemy of Wolf's Dragoons, and you will regret what you have done to us this day."

The other officers tore their ribbons off and threw them down on the hardwood floor as well. Marotta tried to stop the general, but Brubaker dropped a crutch and slugged him with a devastating punch to the jaw that dropped him to the floor.

As the Dragoons left, Marotta rubbed his reddening jaw and rose to his feet. "IlKhan...I beseech you. We do not want the Dragoons as our enemies. I went to them in good faith, faith they feel we have broken. My honor..."

Alaric smiled. *Poor Marotta... Even now he does not understand my true goal.* "You have performed admirably, Marotta. I never intended to bring the Dragoons back as equals, merely as a weapon to be used as I saw fit. They turned their back on all of the Clans generations ago, and even fought against the Clans during the Grand Crusade. It would be folly for me to bring traitors into our midst—to say nothing of welcoming them back as our own—at our moment of triumph.

"As for them being our enemies, that is of no concern to me. I have done what few can claim—I have hamstrung Wolf's Dragoons for years to come. I devastated their best warriors without firing a single shot. Gamma Regiment exists only on paper at this point, as does Alpha. From your own report, Brubaker's position in the Dragoons is now compromised because he covered up a mutiny in his own ranks. This could not be better for us. In the short term, they may very well tear themselves apart for their role here. They have become a shadow of their former selves, a mere tattered regiment at best. They do not pose a threat to Clan Wolf now, nor to the Star League in the near future. By the time they recover, we will be ready for them. Everything that has happened—including this meeting—has gone according to my plans."

Marotta Kerensky's cheeks sagged, and his mouth hung agape. He looked at the closed door the Dragoons had walked through moments before, then back to Alaric, speechless.

"Marotta," said Alaric, "your service has been exemplary, and your mission with the Dragoons is complete. As such, I wish to appoint you Loremaster of the Star League during our ceremony next month. "

The Star Captain's face twitched with confusion and rage. "*N-Neg*," he sputtered. "My place is with them now. I fought alongside them to get here, and again during the Trial with the Jade Falcons. By doing your bidding, my own honor is tainted. I can only set that straight with them, not with you."

"As you wish," Alaric said. "But know that you will always have a place of honor here in the ilClan." He gave Marotta the two-finger salute over his BloodRibbon, which the other warrior returned hesitantly, fury and pain warring on his face, before rushing out the door.

KERENSKY SPACEPORT
UNITY CITY, PUGET SOUND
NORTH AMERICA
TERRA
25 MAY 3151, 0905 HOURS

Alaric and Chance stood at the gangway leading to the DropShip that had landed. Delegations from the Clans had been arriving for days, most offering him modest congratulations. The Ghost Bears had been aloof until he had told them about the deeds and death of Ramiel Bekker. "This victory was one you shared—your Clan's blood fought and died valiantly on Terra as part of Clan Wolf." Saying those words warmed the Ghost Bear Khans to him. It had not been easy. Speaking about Ramiel Bekker still stung Alaric's emotions.

The Snow Ravens had been deeply respectful, as had the Sea Foxes. The leaders of both Clans had complimented Clan Wolf and him personally for his great victory on Terra, but he had put off having in-depth meetings with them until after the upcoming ceremony. *I want them to see me in my new role first, then we will meet to work through our new order.* Still, as the conqueror of Terra, he felt it only appropriate to greet the arriving dignitaries.

Only one such greeting remained, with Clan Hell's Horses. They had arrived at a pirate point and burned in-system quickly, and had insisted on meeting with him immediately upon planetfall. Alaric knew what to expect. He had heard that they had already begun to seize Jade Falcon planets, creeping toward Terra. *They will have their blood up at not having been included in the trial to be ilClan. Eventually they will see the truth in affairs as they unfold.*

General Vickers stood at his side, as always. "I have never met members of the Hell's Horses," she said. "I only know them by reputation."

"They have always seen themselves as equals, but they migrated here instead of taking part in the Grand Crusade." Alaric said the word *migrated* as if it left a bad taste in his mouth. "For some time they were aligned with the Jade Falcons, so I anticipate some resistance."

Khan Gottfried Amirault strode briskly across the open gangway, with a bearing that screamed of overconfident egotism. The long ponytail draped over his shoulder flopped with each heavy footfall. SaKhan Fulk Lassenerra followed a step behind.

Where other Khans had bowed when they had greeted Alaric, there was no sense of similar decorum from the leaders of Clan Hell's Horses.

Alaric eyed both of them coolly. "Welcome to Terra, Khans Amirault and Lassenerra."

"Alaric Ward," Khan Amirault replied.

"I appreciate you coming in time for the ceremony later today."

"Khan Ward," Amirault began, "there is much we—"

"*IlKhan* Ward," Alaric corrected. "And later today, your First Lord."

"I refuse to acknowledge that title," Amirault said grimly.

As expected. "Truly?" Alaric said, staring into the Khan's deep brown eyes.

"I demand—"

Alaric cut him off again. "You are in a position to demand nothing. Perhaps this discussion is best served by waiting until after the ceremony."

His words only stoked the rage boiling up in Khan Amirault. "Our Clan was blatantly and deliberately denied the honor of fighting for Terra," he snapped. "We should have been invited along with the Jade Falcons!"

Alaric ignored the anger; it meant nothing to him. "I am puzzled by your words," he said. "'Invited'? A true follower of Nicholas Kerensky would not sit in their paddock and await an invitation to fulfill their destiny. A true Clan warrior fights for what they want. You sat in your occupation zone, content with the handful of planets you claimed from the Wolves and Falcons, the morsels from our table scraps. Your Clan was not part of Operation Revival, and you did nothing to drive on Terra once you gained a foothold in the Inner Sphere. Your people did not earn the right to fight here. You are unworthy of any such consideration."

"The Jade Falcons—"

"The Jade Falcons, despite the twisted combat doctrine they took from you, fought right up to the Fortress Wall. They would have eventually found a means to Terra. They acted like a true Clan...just as Nicholas Kerensky envisioned. They earned their right to be a participant to take Terra. Hell's Horses did not. Now you show up here, fuming like some Lyran merchant who claims they were cheated, demanding what? A right to contest for the ilClanship? *Neg.* That right has already been won by Clan Wolf on the field of battle. That contest is well bargained and done for all time."

"By not including us, you have insulted our Clan and denied us a chance at destiny."

"I denied you *nothing*," Alaric snapped, his tone ice-cold. "Did Nicholas Kerensky say that any Clans wishing to be the ilClan would be 'invited' to Terra? *Neg.* He said that the Clan that *conquered* Terra would be ilClan. *You* denied yourself and your people their opportunity to fight on Terra. As a result, I imagine you will not be their Khan for much longer."

Alaric had meant it mostly as a dig, but Khan Amirault saw the truth in it. His jaw clenched in fury as he spat, "I challenge you to a Circle of Equals...right here, right now!"

Alaric's answering smile was stiletto-thin. "I am ilKhan of the Clans...First Lord of the Star League. There will be no Circle of Equals because I *have* no equals, nor do my Wolves. Such is the will of Nicholas Kerensky, or have you forgotten our ways? We have evolved beyond your feeble demands or your perceived slights of honor. You do not have the *right* to challenge me, nor am I obligated to accept, or even acknowledge it."

"Our people will not stand for this," Amirault said.

"Perhaps. But know this: The Star League will happen, with or without you. If you come at us, think carefully about what that means. You will be turning your back on our shared history. You will open yourself to utter defeat."

Both Khans spun and stormed back up the gangway to their DropShip.

Chance remained at his side. "You knew they would react this way."

"You know me all too well."

"They will want blood and war."

Alaric nodded. "That is what we were bred to give them. They believe they will face only Clan Wolf. They will face something else: the Star League Defense Force."

CHAPTER 41

Alaric and Chance sat in the back of the limousine as it pulled up the hospital. While Chance wore her Clan Wolf dress uniform, Alaric wore a Star League uniform—patterned after the original. Olive drab in color, it was perfectly tailored for him. His red BloodRibbon was pinned on the jacket. The collar had a Clan Wolf insignia and the Cameron Star.

Image and symbols are important—on this day more than any other. This is the day the Star League returns to Terra. Not some faux alliance, but the true *League.*

"You had him transferred here, *quiaff*?" Chance asked.

"*Aff.* He is dying, or so he claims," Alaric said as the driver stopped and opened the door for them. The armed Jade Falcon security detachment preceded him, scanning the area for threats.

"But why do we care?"

As Alaric exited the vehicle, he turned back to her. "I want him to see the Star League, to realize that the Republic of the Sphere has been replaced with a superior institution. I want to savor our victory just a little more." *I deserve it…I have earned it.*

Chance raised an eyebrow as they walked inside the building. "There has to be more than that."

Alaric tipped his head side to side. "Perhaps. Stone still has a lot of secrets in his head. I am hoping to cajole one or two of them out of him before he passes."

They took the elevator up and were directed to his room. Chance opened the door for Alaric, and he stepped inside.

His eyes closed, Devlin Stone lay on the bed, wired to monitors and with several IV bags hung next to him. A mechanical device covered his chest, clearly helping him breathe. His face was sunken, his skin sagging almost to the point where he looked skeletal. The harsh stench of antiseptic in the room battled with the odor of a dying man.

Seated next to him was his aide, Tucker Harwell, who gave them a sorrowful glance before bending over the old man. "They're here," he said into Stone's ear.

The old man jerked slightly, startled by the announcement. His eyes flickered open. "R-Raise the bed, son. I want to see them."

Tucker complied, and the mechanical whine of the bed sat up what was left of Devlin Stone. Alaric saw his quivering hands. The dark purple veins made his skin seem reddish, hot.

Stone's gleaming eyes squinted as he looked at Chance first, then over to Alaric. "Nice uniform, Khan Ward," he said in a hoarse voice.

"*IlKhan*—and after today, First Lord."

Stone nodded, but just a little. "Tucker, why don't you and this lady step out into the hall? I would like a few minutes alone with the First Lord, you know, leader-to-leader."

Tucker rose, but Alaric held his hand up. *How dare he think he can command us. We are the victors here.* "*Neg*. General Vickers will remain here with me."

Tucker glanced at Stone, who barely inclined his head, the small movement seeming to take all his strength. With a last look at Alaric and Chance, Harwell left the room.

"I'm glad you came," Stone said to Alaric. "There are so few people in the universe I can confide in...people on the same level as me."

Alaric ignored the remark. "Your message said you were dying."

"Damned cryogenics," Stone groaned. "The Inner Sphere will be rid of me soon enough. According to the doctors, I have another few weeks at best. But I wanted to see you first. I have something to tell you, Alaric...something I have wanted to say ever since we met face-to-face on Belle Isle. I might not get another chance."

"What is that?"

The old man's wizened mouth split in a sudden, wolfish smile. "You're welcome!" Stone said with glee.

"I am welcome? Welcome for what?" Alaric's first thought was that Stone's mind was failing faster than his body.

"Why, your conquest of Terra, of course. If it wasn't for me, you wouldn't be in that spiffy uniform right now, off to your little celebration. Enjoy it, Alaric, but remember that it was *all because of me*."

Alaric scoffed at the idea. "You need to increase your oxygen levels, old man. You did *nothing* for me. I came to Terra and crushed you, then I defeated the Jade Falcons. *You* tried to kill me, not help me, remember?"

Stone chuckled. "You truly have no idea, do you? You really believe you were behind all of this? Well then, it is time for some hard truth.

"*Everything* here—everything you think *you* accomplished, *I* set in motion. Granted, I was building off some events that occurred while I was in stasis—like the HPG Blackout, for example."

Alaric decided to humor the old man. "Exactly—you were not even awake when that happened. What could you possibly have had to do with it?"

"Well, I found out who was behind it, for starters. Despite what certain people thought, and although we did have the technology and means to do it, activating Clarion Call was *never* my idea. Plunge the worlds of the Inner Sphere into crippling isolation for who knows how long?" Stone shook his head. "Not even *I* am that ruthless.

"No, the Blackout was caused by a deep-cover Word of Blake sleeper cell. I suppose it was some kind of last fail-safe, apparently planned to go off once I was out of the picture. I guess if they couldn't bring the Inner Sphere together, they would make damn sure it would tear itself apart."

"But," Chance interrupted. "If you knew this, why didn't you share the information with the Inner Sphere?"

Stone turned his watery gaze on her. "Believe me, I thought about it...but what would be the point. Honestly, it almost sounds like something someone would make up, a convenient long-gone enemy to blame everything on. I have the reports from my intelligence division—*I* know it's the truth. But even if I did release it, some would believe it, others wouldn't. Hell. there'd still be those who'd think *I* had something to do with it." He leaned back on his pillow. "But you're nitpicking at history—ultimately, it's not truly important who was behind the Blackout, just that it happened.

"Anyway, imagine my surprise when I was woken up decades early and came back to this mess. But I've always been adept at turning a bad situation to my advantage. I'd already given the Inner Sphere a free sample of peace, hoping they'd get hooked on it. But as long as the House Lords were in place, that peace would always be fragile—and then, with the Blackout, all bets were off."

Stone coughed and sucked in a wheezy breath, then fixed his gaze back on Alaric. "Sure enough, the Great Houses were back to tearing each other up again before you could say go. And they were looking to loot the Republic as well. I knew the House Lords would consume a lot of it—we couldn't fend all of them off, so those worlds had to be considered acceptable losses. You understand, you're a military leader. Besides, if things got really bad, we had the Fortress Republic protocols.

"And once the House Lords and you Clanners were done beating the shit out of each other, the Republic would re-emerge. We'd come out from behind the Fortress with our big army, mop up what was left, and rebuild the whole thing. No more Houses, no antiquated feudal systems, no Clans at all. The Republic would rule everything. I would have brought in a new golden age."

"You mean *you* would rule it all," Chance said, her gaze narrowed.

"Well, to the victor go the spoils, isn't that right?" Stone flicked a glance at her, then turned back to Alaric again. "But I didn't plan on you and Hazen and your damn fool crusade for Terra. I thought the people of the Inner Sphere would crave peace after they'd had some. But they opted for war instead!"

He shook his head wearily. "We couldn't keep the Fortress up forever... the damned system eats up K-F drives, and there's a limit on how many we had. Eventually, the Wall would collapse, and everyone would rush to Terra. The planet would be laid to waste, again...I'd seen it before, during the Jihad..."

"And?" Alaric, said, crossing his arms. "I am still waiting for your so-called direction of *my* plan to conquer Terra."

"Patience, son, patience." Stone's steel-gray eyes glittered in the harsh hospital light. "I didn't want everyone rushing in at once, so I decided to control the fight from the start. How else do you think you got the means to penetrate the Fortress Wall, hm? That was *me*. I sent one of my Ghost Knights, Shimmer, to infiltrate your scientist caste, and she left it there for your people to find."

In that instant, Alaric was struck speechless. He remembered the night Malvina died, and her words came back at him like a salvo of incoming missiles: *"How exactly did you manage to penetrate the Fortress barrier?"*

Neg, this cannot be! Blinking in confusion, he took a step back from Stone's bed as the old man continued, "You're figuring it out, aren't you? I can see it in your eyes. Good. I *wanted* your Wolves here, at my Republic's side to fight the Jade Falcons...but I *never* anticipated that you'd actually invite that witch and her Clan here, too. Got to admit, I was impressed...and that's not an easy thing to do, Alaric. You are good...damned good. You're going to need that sort of unconventional thinking in the years ahead, 'First Lord.'" He smirked.

"*Neg*," Alaric said. "You were *not* manipulating me—"

Stone interrupted him, his formerly weak voice gaining strength as he spoke. "Oh, but I was. Think about it. I was sure we could beat one Clan—even you and your vaunted Wolves—but our victory would have to be definitive, a true demonstration of strength. When you landed in Australia, my plan was to let you beat yourself senseless on my redoubts. I only allowed Damien's Redburn Guards to pummel you there, when I could have sent in countless other regiments. But you brought in Hazen and her damned Falcons, so I had to rethink my strategy. When you were battling across Asia, don't tell me you didn't notice that some of my best units were withdrawn from your front and shifted to fight the Jade Falcons? That wasn't just done because she was slaughtering her way across Europe, but once you brought her in, I had to control who was going win against us.

"In North America, I pulled the Roughriders and Gray Gunny Lancers away from you and deployed them against the Falcons. My best units, my Lament, the Old Guard—I threw them at Hazen while you played Alexander the Great and gobbled up territory. Don't get me wrong—I still wanted to defeat the Jade Falcons—hell, I wanted to defeat both of you somehow, right up to the end. I kept hoping someone would get lucky and take one or both of you out, but even my best troops couldn't do the job. Damien, the damned Old Guard—all of them let me down."

"You are wrong..." Alaric said slowly, his hands clenching into fists at his sides.

"No, I'm right...and you *know* I am. You're just now realizing how much I played you. You were dancing to my tune the whole time, and never even heard the music. Everything that transpired since I woke up, I was pulling the strings on. What was it you said at the surrender, 'Terra's under new leadership'?" Stone shook his head again. "You wouldn't even be *standing* here today if it wasn't for me. *I* made all of this possible."

Alaric felt as if he had been punched in the stomach. He stepped back and lowered himself into one of the guest chairs. *This was* my *victory—not his.* I *did this—not him.* Worse was the realization that Malvina might have suspected Stone had given him the key to Fortress Republic. He could not form a coherent response as his entire world crumbled around him. His breath became ragged, almost panicked with each word Stone spoke.

But Chance Vickers didn't hesitate. "This is a lie—it is all lies. If it were true, it would mean that you signed the death sentence of millions of lives in your own Republic. What kind of a man does something like that? Who would do such a thing to the people he claims to cherish?"

Stone turned the full force of his storm-gray gaze on her. "You ever hear of the phrase 'peace through strength', girl? If I hadn't done this, Terra would have been torn to pieces by every Great House and Clan swooping in once the Wall fell. But if we beat the biggest foe among them first, the rest would back down. Hell, that's how I formed the Republic, by crushing those Word of Blake bastards and carving out a chunk from each House as payment—except for those damned Capellans!

"So *I* brought the Wolves in, planning to beat you soundly as a message to the rest of the Inner Sphere—*don't mess with the Republic.*" He took another ragged, wheezing breath. "Didn't exactly go as I planned, but I did what I had to do to save the Republic...my Republic..."

"*Neg,*" Chance shot back. "If you already knew your forces were going to lose, yet you kept fighting with no chance of victory, that does not make you a hero. It just makes you a monster."

"I'm no monster," Stone replied. "I'm a fighter, a great leader. I am a *creator.* I beat the biggest army the Inner Sphere had seen in centuries, and forged an empire out of the ruins." He chuckled. "Those damned Blakists never saw *that* coming..."

"Never saw what coming?" Even in her anger, Chance raised an eyebrow. "What are you talking about?"

Stone cocked his head, his keen vision unfocusing for a moment, as if he was somewhere else. "I used to get the question all the time, you know. 'Who are you?' So much speculation, and none of it quite right.

"The truth is, near as I can recall, that I was a *nobody,* some ignorant grunt captured by the Word of Blake. They tortured me, used me for experiments, and purged most of my memories. There were three of us they tried this on, and I'm the only one that made it out with half his brain intact. Who am I?" Stone shrugged weakly. "I honestly don't know, and the records are long gone. I kind of remember serving with the Federated Suns, but even now, those memories are fuzzy. Doesn't matter anymore anyway.

"The Wobbies remade me. They created a new persona, one they called Devlin Stone. They planned to make me their ideal weapon of war, a perfect general to lead them to victory. Their wonderful technology imprinted my brain with everything I'd need to know about military and political strategy and tactics. I was given a body of knowledge it would normally take lifetimes to achieve, squeezed into every nook and cranny in my brain. The process was agonizing—it almost drove me insane—but they didn't care. They just thought

I would be a great leader for their cause, a valuable tool, another weapon against the corrupt powers of the Inner Sphere.

"But I broke free of their control. Deception is a time-honored military strategy—and I used it on my so-called masters. I used everything they shoved into my brain against them. At first, I took them down solely out of revenge. They hurt me, stole my life out of my own head, and I made them *pay* for it. Then afterward, everyone was looking to me, the hero of the Jihad, to lead them...so I did."

Stone blinked, and seemed to return to the present. "You might say the Republic is the only thing I created that was truly mine...although, since I made Alaric here a First Lord, I guess that's two things I created, isn't it?" He grinned triumphantly at both of them.

Alaric stared at him, still processing what Stone had said. *Were there... other instances where he had... helped me?* Suddenly, he began questioning every decision he had made. His face was flushed, his palms sweaty. *It cannot be...this cannot be happening.*

Knowing he somehow had to regain the upper hand in this conversation, Alaric cleared his throat. "Even if I were to believe that these...ravings were anything more than a product of your failing mind, that you were somehow able to reach across the Inner Sphere to manipulate me as you claim, what does it matter now? You have lost *everything* you built, everything you ever cared about, Devlin Stone."

"Oh, I've already taken that lesson to heart, First Lord." The old man turned his steely gaze back to Alaric. "But you have yet to learn it, son, and school's going to be in session sooner than you think.

"Alaric, my boy, you are about to learn the cold, hard truth: Conquering is much easier than ruling. You may think you've founded your new Star League— but now you have to keep it. You will think you have friends and allies, but all you really have is rivals, all around you. If you manage to live long enough, you'll realize that you are all alone in this universe. Then again, some rulers don't even get that chance. Ask Simon Cameron..." Stone's attempt to laugh devolved into a coughing fit that went on for long seconds. Neither Chance nor Alaric made any move to help him.

"You've kept Fortress Republic running, which is smart," he continued once the fit had passed. "But the Wall around Terra won't last forever—not unless you want to sacrifice your fleet to keep it going. And when it comes down, House Liao is poised and waiting out there, ready to take away your precious prize. They're not the only ones, either. What do you think the Clan Homeworlds have been up to in your absence? Or maybe you should ask the Ghost Bears whether they got an invite to the party you and Malvina were throwing ay our expense. Their answer might just surprise you. My reach is still long and far, boy."

Stone paused for a moment, licking his dried lips. "Last but not least, good luck getting the HPG network back up. Even my boy Tucker couldn't figure out how to undo all of the damage those Wobbie bastards did to it."

Alaric could not process everything Stone was saying—it was all washing over him in a jumbled buzz. Confusion and anger tore at him. *It is not possible. Chance is right—he must be lying.*

"If even half of what you said is true, you are still an honorless war criminal," Chance spat back with a look of complete disgust. "The blood of millions is on your hands."

"'War criminal'? Victors get to toss around titles like that. I'm no worse than any House Lord—or Khan, for that matter. Look at the horrors Malvina perpetrated in the name of her Clan. I'm no different than you will be, Alaric." Stone looked past Chance to where Alaric sat slumped in his chair. "But history will be kind to me. Enough people believe in me to ensure that. You think you're the hero of this story? *I* am the valiant leader of the doomed Republic—and the history books will support that."

"You are nothing but pure evil," Chance growled.

Stone rolled his eyes. "Ha! Cheap insults won't hurt me, girl. And in case you think you're going to rewrite the story, Alaric, remember this: We already poisoned the well you have to drink from. A century of propaganda—plenty of it justified, by the way—has made Inner Sphere people fear and hate you. They won't accept Clan rule, you'll see. You'll constantly be looking over your shoulder for the next stab in the back.

"The First Star League lasted only 210 years, and *only* because the House Lords were willing to bend the knee. You won't have *any* of that going for you. Every one of them will be gunning for you from the start. Hell, I'm willing to bet some of your fellow Clans are plotting your downfall right now. Maybe even warriors in your own Clan—after all, 'might makes right' with your kind, doesn't it? How long do you think you can hold your little Star League together when everyone already wants you deposed?" Stone's laugh again broke into another long coughing fit.

Chance looked at Alaric, but he could not meet her eyes. She turned to the coughing man in the bed. Pulling one of his pillows out from behind his head, she put it over his face and pushed down hard.

Stone struggled. His feeble arms flailed, the tubes from his IVs whipping around as he tried to shove the pillow away.

Alaric rose to his feet, unsure of what to say or do for the first time in his life.

Stone's body quaked for a moment or two, then went limp. His heart monitor sounded a warning, but Chance held the pillow in place for another minute, just to be sure. Once satisfied, she replaced it behind his head.

"No one will *ever* know of this," she said. "Old men die in hospitals all the time. His schemes and lies will die with him." She turned to Alaric. "Go—get to the ceremony. I will wrap things up here and join you shortly."

Alaric mutely walked to the door and opened it. He expected to see Tucker Harwell waiting there, but the hallway was empty except for a nurse rushing toward the room, crash cart in front of her. "Clear the door!" she called out.

Still numb from Stone's revelations, Alaric headed to the limousine, not remembering how he got there. As he sat in the vehicle and it departed for the

Court of the Star League, for the first time in his life, Alaric felt alone...alone and lost.

ABOUT THE AUTHOR

Blaine Lee Pardoe has been writing *BattleTech* fiction for decades, starting with the first *Technical Readout* in 1986. Blaine has been involved in the gaming industry for decades, writing for a number of companies and universes. His true crime books earned him a spot on the *New York Times* Bestsellers List, and the US Naval Academy and the US National Archives have lectured from his military history books.

When he is not writing or solving real-world crimes, he is a fan of *BattleTech*. He can be reached at bpardoe870@aol.com or via Facebook.

BATTLETECH GLOSSARY

Clan military unit designations are used throughout this book:

Point: 1 'Mech or 5 infantry
Star: 5 'Mechs or 25 infantry
Binary: 2 Stars
Trinary: 3 Stars
Cluster: 4—5 Binaries/Trinaries
Galaxy: 3-5 Clusters
Nova: 1 'Mech Star and 1 infantry Star
Supernova: 1 'Mech Binary and 2 infantry Stars

ABTAKHA

An *abtakha* is a captured warrior who is adopted into his new Clan as a warrior.

AUTOCANNON

This is a rapid-fire, auto-loading weapon. Light autocannons range from 30 to 90 millimeter (mm), and heavy autocannons may be from 80 to 120mm or more. They fire high-speed streams of high-explosive, armor-piercing shells.

BATCHALL

The *batchall* is the ritual by which Clan warriors issue combat challenges. Though the type of challenge varies, most begin with the challenger identifying themself, stating the prize of the contest, and requesting that the defender identify the forces at their disposal. The defender also has the right to name the location of the trial. The two sides then bid for what forces will participate in the contest. The subcommander who bids to fight with the number of forces wins the right and responsibility to make the attack. The defender may increase the stakes by demanding a prize of equal or lesser value if they wish.

BATTLEMECH

BattleMechs are the most powerful war machines ever built. First developed by Terran scientists and engineers, these huge vehicles are faster, more mobile, better-armored and more heavily armed than any twentieth-century tank. Ten to twelve meters tall and equipped with particle projection cannons, lasers, rapid-fire autocannon and missiles, they pack enough firepower to flatten anything but another BattleMech. A small fusion reactor provides virtually unlimited power, and BattleMechs can be adapted to fight in environments ranging from sun-baked deserts to subzero arctic icefields.

BLOODNAME

A Bloodname is the surname associated with a Bloodright, descended from one of the 800 warriors who stood with Nicholas Kerensky to form the Clans. A warrior must win the use of a Bloodname in a Trial of Bloodright. Only Bloodnamed warriors may sit on Clan Councils or hold the post of Loremaster, Khan, or ilKhan, and only the genetic material from the Bloodnamed is used in the warrior caste eugenics program.

BONDCORD

A woven bracelet worn by bondsmen who has been captured and claimed by a Clan member. Warrior-caste bondsmen wear a three-strand bondcord on their right wrists, with the color and patterning of the cords signifying the Clan and unit responsible for the warrior's capture. The cords represent integrity, fidelity, and prowess. The bondholder may cut each strand as he or she feels the bondsman demonstrates the associated quality. According to tradition, when the final cord is severed, the bondsman is considered a free member of his or her new Clan and adopted into the Warrior caste. Each Clan follows this tradition to varying degrees. For example, Clan Wolf accepts nearly all worthy individuals regardless of their past, while Clan Smoke Jaguar generally chose to adopt only trueborn warriors.

BONDSMAN

A bondsman is a prisoner held in a form of indentured servitude until released or accepted into the Clan. Most often, bondsmen are captured warriors who fulfill roles in the laborer or technician castes. Their status is represented by a woven bondcord, and they are obliged by honor and tradition to work for their captors to the best of their abilities.

CASTE

The Clans are divided into five castes: warrior, scientist, merchant, technician, and laborer, in descending order of influence. Each has many subcastes based on specialized skills. The warrior caste is largely the product of the artificial breeding program; those candidates who fail their Trial of Position are assigned to the scientist or technician caste, giving those castes a significant concentration of trueborn members. Most of the civilian castes are made up of the results of scientist-decreed arranged marriages within the castes.

The children of all castes undergo intensive scrutiny during their schooling to determine the caste for which they are best suited, though most end up in the same caste as their parents. This process allows children born to members of civilian castes to enter training to become warriors, though they belong to the less-prestigious ranks of the freeborn.

CIRCLE OF EQUALS

The area in which a trial takes place is known as the Circle of Equals. It ranges in size from a few dozen feet for personal combat to tens of miles for large-scale trials. Though traditionally a circle, the area can be any shape.

CRUSADER

A Crusader is a Clansman who espouses the invasion of the Inner Sphere and the re-establishment of the Star League by military force. Most Crusaders are contemptuous of the people of the Inner Sphere, whom they view as barbarians, and of freeborns within their own Clans.

DEZGRA

Any disgraced individual or unit is known as *dezgra*. Disgrace may come through refusing orders, failing in an assigned task, acting dishonorably, or demonstrating cowardice.

DROPSHIPS

Because interstellar JumpShips must avoid entering the heart of a solar system, they must "dock" in space at a considerable distance from a system's inhabited worlds. DropShips were developed for interplanetary travel. As the name implies, a DropShip is attached to hardpoints on the JumpShip's drive core, later to be dropped from the parent vessel after in-system entry. Though incapable of FTL travel, DropShips are highly maneuverable, well-armed and sufficiently aerodynamic to take off from and land on a planetary surface. The journey from the jump point to the inhabited worlds of a system usually requires a normal-space journey of several days or weeks, depending on the type of star.

FREEBIRTH

Freebirth is a Clan epithet used by trueborn members of the warrior caste to express disgust or frustration. For one trueborn to use this curse to refer to another trueborn is considered a mortal insult.

FREEBORN

An individual conceived and born by natural means is referred to as freeborn. Its emphasis on the artificial breeding program allows Clan society to view such individuals as second-class citizens.

HEGIRA

Hegira is the rite by which a defeated foe may withdraw from the field of battle without further combat and with no further loss of honor.

ISORLA

The spoils of battle, including bondsmen, claimed by the victorious warriors is called *isorla*.

JUMPSHIPS

Interstellar travel is accomplished via JumpShips, first developed in the twenty-second century. These somewhat ungainly vessels consist of a long, thin drive core and a sail resembling an enormous parasol, which can extend up to a kilometer in width. The ship is named for its ability to "jump" instantaneously across vast distances of space. After making its jump, the ship cannot travel until it has recharged by gathering up more solar energy.

The JumpShip's enormous sail is constructed from a special metal that absorbs vast quantities of electromagnetic energy from the nearest star. When it has soaked up enough energy, the sail transfers it to the drive core, which converts it into a space-twisting field. An instant later, the ship arrives at the next jump point, a distance of up to thirty light-years. This field is known as hyperspace, and its discovery opened to mankind the gateway to the stars.

JumpShips never land on planets. Interplanetary travel is carried out by DropShips, vessels that are attached to the JumpShip until arrival at the jump point.

KHAN (kaKhan, saKhan)

Each Clan Council elects two of its number as Khans, who serve as rulers of the Clan and its representatives on the Grand Council. Traditionally, these individuals are the best warriors in the Clan, but in practice many Clans instead elect their most skilled politicians. The senior Khan, sometimes referred to as the kaKhan, acts as the head of the Clan, overseeing relationships between castes and Clans. The junior Khan, known as the saKhan, acts as the Clan's warlord. The senior Khan decides the exact distribution of tasks, and may assign the saKhan additional or different duties.

The term "kaKhan" is considered archaic, and is rarely used.

LASER

An acronym for "Light Amplification through Stimulated Emission of Radiation." When used as a weapon, the laser damages the target by concentrating extreme heat onto a small area. BattleMech lasers are designated as small, medium or large. Lasers are also available as shoulder-fired weapons operating from a portable backpack power unit. Certain range-finders and targeting equipment also employ low-level lasers.

LRM

This is an abbreviation for "Long-Range Missile," an indirect-fire missile with a high-explosive warhead.

POSSESSION, TRIAL OF

A Trial of Possession resolves disputes between two parties over ownership or control. This can include equipment, territory, or even genetic material. The traditional *batchall* forms the core of the trial in order to encourage the participants to resolve the dispute with minimal use of force.

REMEMBRANCE, THE

The Remembrance is an ongoing heroic saga that describes Clan history from the time of the Exodus to the present day. Each Clan maintains its own version, reflecting its opinions and perceptions of events. Inclusion in The Remembrance is one of the highest honors possible for a member of the Clans. All Clan warriors can recite passages from The Remembrance from memory, and written copies of the book are among the few nontechnical books allowed in Clan society. These books are usually lavishly illustrated in a fashion similar to the illuminated manuscripts and Bibles of the medieval period. Warriors frequently paint passages of The Remembrance on the sides of their OmniMechs, fighters, and battle armor.

SEYLA

Seyla is a ritual response in Clan ceremonies. The origin of this phrase is unknown, though it may come from the Biblical notation "selah," thought to be a musical notation or a reference to contemplation.

SRM

This is the abbreviation for "Short-Range Missile," a direct-trajectory missile with high-explosive or armor-piercing explosive warheads. They have a range of less than one kilometer and are only reliably accurate at ranges of less than 300 meters. They are more powerful, however, than LRMs.

SUCCESSOR LORDS

After the fall of the first Star League, the remaining members of the High Council each asserted his or her right to become First Lord. Their star empires became known as the Successor States and the rulers as Successor Lords. The Clan Invasion temporarily interrupted centuries of warfare known as the Succession Wars, which first began in 2786.

SURAT

A Clan epithet, alluding to the rodent of the same name, which disparages an individual's genetic heritage. As such, it is one of the most vulgar and offensive epithets among the Clans.

TOUMAN

The fighting arm of a Clan is known as the touman.

TROTHKIN

Used formally, *trothkin* refers to members of an extended sibko. It is more commonly used to denote members of a gathering, and warriors also frequently use it when addressing someone they consider a peer.

TRUEBORN/TRUEBIRTH

A warrior born of the Clan's artificial breeding program is known as a trueborn. In less formal situations, the Clans use the term truebirth.

WARDEN

A Warden is a Clansman who believes that the Clans were established to guard the Inner Sphere from outside threats rather than to conquer it and re-establish the Star League by force. Most Wardens were opposed to the recent invasion of the Inner Sphere.

ZELLBRIGEN

Zellbrigen is the body of rules governing duels. These rules dictate that such actions are one-on-one engagements, and that any warriors not immediately challenged should stay out of the battle until an opponent is free.

Once a Clan warrior engages a foe, no other warriors on his or her side may target that foe, even if it means allowing the death of the Clan warrior. Interfering in a duel by attacking a foe that is already engaged constitutes a major breach of honor, and usually results in loss of rank. Such action also opens the battle to a melee.

BATTLETECH ERAS

The *BattleTech* universe is a living, vibrant entity that grows each year as more sourcebooks and fiction are published. A dynamic universe, its setting and characters evolve over time within a highly detailed continuity framework, bringing everything to life in a way a static game universe cannot match.

To help quickly and easily convey the timeline of the universe—and to allow a player to easily "plug in" a given novel or sourcebook—we've divided *BattleTech* into six major eras.

STAR LEAGUE
(Present–2780)

Ian Cameron, ruler of the Terran Hegemony, concludes decades of tireless effort with the creation of the Star League, a political and military alliance between all Great Houses and the Hegemony. Star League armed forces immediately launch the Reunification War, forcing the Periphery realms to join. For the next two centuries, humanity experiences a golden age across the thousand light-years of human-occupied space known as the Inner Sphere. It also sees the creation of the most powerful military in human history.

(This era also covers the centuries before the founding of the Star League in 2571, most notably the Age of War.)

SUCCESSION WARS
(2781–3049)

Every last member of First Lord Richard Cameron's family is killed during a coup launched by Stefan Amaris. Following the thirteen-year war to unseat him, the rulers of each of the five Great Houses disband the Star League. General Aleksandr Kerensky departs with eighty percent of the Star League Defense Force beyond known space and the Inner Sphere collapses into centuries of warfare known as the Succession Wars that will eventually result in a massive loss of technology across most worlds.

CLAN INVASION
(3050–3061)

A mysterious invading force strikes the coreward region of the Inner Sphere. The invaders, called the Clans, are descendants of Kerensky's SLDF troops, forged into a society dedicated to becoming the greatest fighting force in history. With vastly superior technology and warriors, the Clans conquer world after world. Eventually this outside threat will forge a new Star League, something hundreds of years of warfare failed to accomplish. In addition, the Clans will act as a catalyst for a technological renaissance.

CIVIL WAR
(3062–3067)

The Clan threat is eventually lessened with the complete destruction of a Clan. With that massive external threat apparently neutralized, internal conflicts explode around the Inner Sphere. House Liao conquers its former Commonality, the St. Ives Compact; a rebellion of military units belonging to House Kurita sparks a war with their powerful border enemy, Clan Ghost Bear; the fabulously powerful Federated Commonwealth of House Steiner and House Davion collapses into five long years of bitter civil war.

JIHAD
(3067–3080)

Following the Federated Commonwealth Civil War, the leaders of the Great Houses meet and disband the new Star League, declaring it a sham. The pseudo-religious Word of Blake—a splinter group of ComStar, the protectors and controllers of interstellar communication—launch the Jihad: an interstellar war that pits every faction against each other and even against themselves, as weapons of mass destruction are used for the first time in centuries while new and frightening technologies are also unleashed.

DARK AGE
(3081-3150)

Under the guidance of Devlin Stone, the Republic of the Sphere is born at the heart of the Inner Sphere following the Jihad. One of the more extensive periods of peace begins to break out as the 32nd century dawns. The factions, to one degree or another, embrace disarmament, and the massive armies of the Succession Wars begin to fade. However, in 3132 eighty percent of interstellar communications collapses, throwing the universe into chaos. Wars erupt almost immediately, and the factions begin rebuilding their armies.

ILCLAN
(3151-present)

The once-invulnerable Republic of the Sphere lies in ruins, torn apart by the Great Houses and the Clans as they wage war against each other on a scale not seen in nearly a century. Mercenaries flourish once more, selling their might to the highest bidder. As Fortress Republic collapses, the Clans race toward Terra to claim their long-denied birthright and create a supreme authority that will fulfill the dream of Aleksandr Kerensky and rule the Inner Sphere by any means necessary: The ilClan.

LOOKING FOR MORE HARD HITTING BATTLETECH FICTION?

WE'LL GET YOU RIGHT BACK INTO THE BATTLE!

Catalyst Game Labs brings you the very best in *BattleTech* fiction, available at most ebook retailers, including Amazon, Apple Books, Kobo, Barnes & Noble, and more!

NOVELS

1. *Decision at Thunder Rift* by William H. Keith Jr.
2. *Mercenary's Star* by William H. Keith Jr.
3. *The Price of Glory* by William H. Keith, Jr.
4. *Warrior: En Garde* by Michael A. Stackpole
5. *Warrior: Riposte* by Michael A. Stackpole
6. *Warrior: Coupé* by Michael A. Stackpole
7. Wolves on the Border by Robert N. Charrette
8. *Heir to the Dragon* by Robert N. Charrette
9. *Lethal Heritage* (The Blood of Kerensky, Volume 1) by Michael A. Stackpole
10. *Blood Legacy* (The Blood of Kerensky, Volume 2) by Michael A. Stackpole
11. *Lost Destiny* (The Blood of Kerensky, Volume 3) by Michael A. Stackpole
12. *Way of the Clans* (Legend of the Jade Phoenix, Volume 1) by Robert Thurston
13. *Bloodname* (Legend of the Jade Phoenix, Volume 2) by Robert Thurston
14. *Falcon Guard* (Legend of the Jade Phoenix, Volume 3) by Robert Thurston
15. *Wolf Pack* by Robert N. Charrette
16. *Main Event* by James D. Long
17. *Natural Selection* by Michael A. Stackpole
18. *Assumption of Risk* by Michael A. Stackpole
19. *Blood of Heroes* by Andrew Keith
20. *Close Quarters* by Victor Milán
21. *Far Country* by Peter L. Rice
22. *D.R.T.* by James D. Long
23. *Tactics of Duty* by William H. Keith
24. *Bred for War* by Michael A. Stackpole
25. *I Am Jade Falcon* by Robert Thurston
26. *Highlander Gambit* by Blaine Lee Pardoe
27. *Hearts of Chaos* by Victor Milán
28. *Operation Excalibur* by William H. Keith
29. *Malicious Intent* by Michael A. Stackpole
30. *Black Dragon* by Victor Milán
31. *Impetus of War* by Blaine Lee Pardoe
32. *Double-Blind* by Loren L. Coleman
33. *Binding Force* by Loren L. Coleman
34. *Exodus Road* (Twilight of the Clans, Volume 1) by Blaine Lee Pardoe
35. *Grave Covenant* ((Twilight of the Clans, Volume 2) by Michael A. Stackpole
36. *The Hunters* (Twilight of the Clans, Volume 3) by Thomas S. Gressman

NOVELLAS/SHORT STORIES

1. *Lion's Roar* by Steven Mohan, Jr.
2. *Sniper* by Jason Schmetzer
3. *Eclipse* by Jason Schmetzer
4. *Hector* by Jason Schmetzer
5. *The Frost Advances (Operation Ice Storm, Part 1)* by Jason Schmetzer
6. *The Winds of Spring (Operation Ice Storm, Part 2)* by Jason Schmetzer
7. *Instrument of Destruction (Ghost Bear's Lament, Part 1)* by Steven Mohan, Jr.
8. *The Fading Call of Glory (Ghost Bear's Lament, Part 2)* by Steven Mohan, Jr.
9. *Vengeance* by Jason Schmetzer
10. *A Splinter of Hope* by Philip A. Lee
11. *The Anvil* by Blaine Lee Pardoe
12. *A Splinter of Hope/The Anvil* (omnibus)
13. *Not the Way the Smart Money Bets (Kell Hounds Ascendant #1)* by Michael A. Stackpole
14. *A Tiny Spot of Rebellion (Kell Hounds Ascendant #2)* by Michael A. Stackpole
15. *A Clever Bit of Fiction (Kell Hounds Ascendant #3)* by Michael A. Stackpole
16. *Break-Away (Proliferation Cycle #1)* by Ilsa J. Bick
17. *Prometheus Unbound (Proliferation Cycle #2)* by Herbert A. Beas II
18. *Nothing Ventured (Proliferation Cycle #3)* by Christoffer Trossen
19. *Fall Down Seven Times, Get Up Eight (Proliferation Cycle #4)* by Randall N. Bills
20. *A Dish Served Cold (Proliferation Cycle #5)* by Chris Hartford and Jason M. Hardy
21. *The Spider Dances (Proliferation Cycle #6)* by Jason Schmetzer
22. *Shell Games* by Jason Schmetzer
23. *Divided We Fall* by Blaine Lee Pardoe
24. *The Hunt for Jardine (Forgotten Worlds, Part One)* by Herbert A. Beas II
25. *Rock of the Republic* by Blaine Lee Pardoe
26. *Finding Jardine (Forgotten Worlds, Part Two)* by Herbert A. Beas II

ANTHOLOGIES

1. *The Corps (BattleCorps Anthology, Volume 1)* edited by Loren. L. Coleman
2. *First Strike (BattleCorps Anthology, Volume 2)* edited by Loren L. Coleman
3. *Weapons Free (BattleCorps Anthology, Volume 3)* edited by Jason Schmetzer
4. *Onslaught: Tales from the Clan Invasion* edited by Jason Schmetzer
5. *Edge of the Storm* by Jason Schmetzer
6. *Fire for Effect (BattleCorps Anthology, Volume 4)* edited by Jason Schmetzer
7. *Chaos Born (Chaos Irregulars, Book 1)* by Kevin Killiany
8. *Chaos Formed (Chaos Irregulars, Book 2)* by Kevin Killiany
9. *Counterattack (BattleCorps Anthology, Volume 5)* edited by Jason Schmetzer
10. *Front Lines (BattleCorps Anthology Volume 6)* edited by Jason Schmetzer and Philip A. Lee
11. *Legacy* edited by John Helfers and Philip A. Lee
12. *Kill Zone (BattleCorps Anthology Volume 7)* edited by Philip A. Lee
13. *Gray Markets (A BattleCorps Anthology)*, edited by Jason Schmetzer and Philip A. Lee
14. *Slack Tide (A BattleCorps Anthology)*, edited by Jason Schmetzer and Philip A. Lee

MAGAZINES

1. *Shrapnel Issue #1*
2. *Shrapnel Issue #2*
3. *Shrapnel Issue #3*

Made in the USA
Monee, IL
09 February 2021

59999212R00213